THE
BARTERED
Bride
ROMANCE COLLECTION

9 Historical Stories of Arranged Marriages

THE
BARTERED
Bride
ROMANCE COLLECTION

Cathy Marie Hake, Kelly Eileen Hake,
JoAnn A. Grote, Amy Rognlie, Janelle Burnham Schneider,
Lynette Sowell, Pamela Kaye Tracy

BARBOUR BOOKS
An Imprint of Barbour Publishing, Inc.

Joie De Vivre © 2006 by Lynette Sowell
Button String Bride © 2001 by Cathy Marie Hake
The Wedding Wagon © 2002 by Cathy Marie Hake
From Halter to Altar © 2003 by Cathy Marie Hake
From Carriage to Marriage © 2003 by Janelle Burnham Schneider
From Pride to Bride © 2003 by JoAnn A. Grote
From Alarming to Charming © 2003 by Pamela Kaye Tracy
A Vow Unbroken © 2000 by Amy Rognlie
Finishing Touches © 2007 by Kelly Eileen Hake

Print ISBN 978-1-68322-643-7

eBook Editions:
Adobe Digital Edition (.epub) 978-1-68322-645-1
Kindle and MobiPocket Edition (.prc) 978-1-68322-644-4

Scripture quotations marked KJV are taken from the King James Version of the Bible.

This book is a work of fiction. Names, characters, places, and incidents are either products of the author's imagination or used fictitiously. Any similarity to actual people, organizations, and/or events is purely coincidental.

Published by Barbour Books, an imprint of Barbour Publishing, Inc., 1810 Barbour Drive, Uhrichsville, Ohio 44683, www.barbourbooks.com

Our mission is to inspire the world with the life-changing message of the Bible.

 Member of the
Evangelical Christian
Publishers Association

Printed in the United States of America.

Contents

JOIE DE VIVRE

by Lynette Sowell

Dedication

To Kathleen Miller Y'Barbo.
You have truly blessed me with your friendship
and mentoring moments over the past few years.
It's been a joy to see this brainstorm of ours come to life. *Merci!*

To Lisa Harris.
Thanks for your critique,
and for all the critiques we exchanged during those early days
when I was in my first critique group ever.
I'm glad our paths have crossed again in "Writing World."

As always, to Zach and Hannah.
You add to my *joie de vivre*.
Thank you for letting me take the time to follow a dream.
Follow the dream God gives you.

And to CJ.
I love our life together.
Thanks for always believing in me
and encouraging me to never give up.

Chapter 1

La Manque, Louisiana—July 1819

Hurry!" Jacques LeBlanc shouted over his shoulder. "We'll be late!"
"If Papa LeBlanc is angry, it'll be your fault." Josée Broussard held her skirt high enough with one hand to keep from tripping on the hem. "You're the one. . .who let Philippe. . .fall into the bayou."

She gasped for breath. Little Philippe bounced on her hip while she trotted along the path through the tall grass. The boy was too small to keep up with their hurried pace yet heavier than a sack of flour. Josée tried not to think he might not settle down to sleep tonight after Jacques telling him the legend of the great snake of Bayou Teche.

Jacques paused and faced her. He grabbed her hand, and the touch made her stomach turn like the curving dark waters behind them. *Jacques has been my friend for so long, why should his hand make me feel. . . ?* Josée's skirt swirled down around her ankles.

He smiled, and his black eyes sparkled with a secret. "Ma'amselle Josée, it's your birthday, and Papa will be in a good mood. *Bon temps* tonight!"

She tried to smile but bit her lip instead. Couldn't Jacques carry his younger brother?

Prickly heat surrounded them like a heavy blanket. Josée longed for the cool bayou, thick with moist air but cooler than where the larger LeBlanc house stood, farther away from the banks of Bayou Teche. Papa had turned from the bayou to farming.

Philippe wriggled from her hip and ran. *Not through the garden!* Jeanne and Marie scolded him where they stood by the house, their arms reminding Josée of flapping hens' wings. She waved at them.

"Happy birthday, Josée!" they called.

"Merci. I'm sorry Philippe ran through your garden."

Jeanne, six months older than Josée, ruffled her littlest brother's hair. "Why so wet, then?"

"He thought he was a fish," Jacques said. The sisters both laughed then fell silent and stared at Josée's and Jacques's hands clasped together.

9

Josée pulled free and wiped her palm on her skirt. "It's hot today."

"*Oui*, and you're brown already, just from being down by the water." Jeanne linked arms with Josée. "We must get you ready for the party tonight. I think Mama has a surprise for you."

"Wait for me." Marie followed behind.

"How does it feel, being eighteen?" Jeanne leaned closer. "Now you've caught up with me."

"Eighteen's not much differen' from seventeen."

"Ah, t'is different. When you're eighteen, you're a woman. As soon as I turned eighteen, Josef Landry asked Papa for permission to marry me." Jeanne sighed. "He already has a small farm next to his papa's. Then once his house is built. . ." She sighed again.

Josée laughed. "I can guarantee you that no one will be asking your papa's permission to marry me."

They entered the LeBlanc farmhouse, and the three girls climbed the ladder to the loft where they shared half of the space with the boys. A curtain divided the long loft in two.

Mama LeBlanc, the only mother Josée had ever known, had hung a new dress where they could see it. Mama turned as the girls entered the loft. "Beautiful, *n'est-ce pas?*"

"Yes, it's very beautiful." Josée wanted to cry. She held scant memories of her own parents. The fact that the LeBlancs accepted her as one of their own comforted her, yet the same fact reminded her that they had taken her in when she had no one.

"Merci, Mama." She hugged the short, stout woman who stood beside the dress.

Mama LeBlanc returned the hug then held Josée at arm's length. "Your papa LeBlanc has another su'prise for you tonight."

"I wonder if he's found a man for you, Josée!" Jeanne started brushing her own black tresses. Marie, sixteen, giggled and flopped onto the mattress so hard that a tuft of Spanish moss stuck out the side.

Josée touched the soft cotton frock and almost shuddered. Marriage? A man? Yet if she were to marry anyone, it would probably be Jacques. At least he would make her laugh and listen to the songs she made up. But she, Josée Broussard, orphan, had nothing to offer a man. "I couldn't imagine."

※

All afternoon, Edouard LeBlanc had endured the squeals and laughter that disrupted the tranquillity of his secluded LeBlanc bayou cabin. If he hadn't caught enough fish for the day already, he'd have sent the brood back to the big house. To him, violating the quiet of the bayou was sacrilege.

Edouard stared up at the canopy of cypress trees that blocked most of the late afternoon heat. He had time to shave before the party. No sense in hurrying. If it wasn't that Papa had requested—no, demanded—his presence, Edouard would be content to lie in his hammock and watch the fish jump from the bayou tonight. Or maybe not. A wayward mosquito found Edouard's arm, and the sting spurred him to leave the hammock and enter the cabin.

Today Josée Broussard turned eighteen years old. All grown up and always with a song on her lips and spring in her step, Josée's ways needled him like pesky mosquitoes. Not that he'd been close enough to feel any bites. Listening and watching her from a distance was enough.

Edouard prepared his shaving mixture and propped up the chunk of mirror, a remnant from an old looking glass. Careful of the long scar running from under his ear to the end of his chin, he used the long shaving blade to remove his scruff of beard.

The scar made its appearance on his face. He would dare anyone to stare at him tonight, like Celine had done on his return from the war. Believing in a cause and following its course had made him follow Jean Lafitte to New Orleans five years before. If he had known his actions would cost him his only true love, he would have planted himself along the Bayou Teche and never have departed from La Manque.

Satisfied he'd removed enough of the beard, Edouard put the glass away. After sunset, maybe the light of the bonfire and lanterns would give enough shadows to cover most of the scar. He found his comb and pulled it through his wet hair then secured the length in the back with a leather thong.

Edouard limped to the bureau at the other end of the cabin and took out a clean but rumpled shirt. He could endure the fiddle music and the songs as long as he didn't have to dance. Storms approached. His bad leg told him so.

Out of respect for Papa and because of Josée's birthday, Edouard resolved to go to the party and stay no longer than necessary. Then he could retreat to the cabin and try to forget the life that swirled around him persistently and tried to draw him in.

⁂

Josée's sides ached from laughter. She smoothed the skirt of her new dress and gave Mama LeBlanc another smile of gratitude. Jeanne had helped her put her hair up on her head, and she felt as fancy as any lady over in Lafayette. Merry fiddle music matched the bonfire's roar, and Josée tapped her bare feet to the beat of the drum played by one of the village boys.

Then she saw *him* at the edges of the crowd. A tall man with eyes as black as the murky bayou water at midnight. Jacques's brother, Edouard, the eldest of the LeBlanc clan.

"Looks like my brother made it to the party," Jacques murmured into her ear.

"I. . .I'm glad." Although, Josée wasn't sure how she felt. Dark. Brooding. His eyes spoke of a soul deeper than the waters that flowed through La Manque. She wondered if he ever laughed. The only time she ever saw him was when she and the other LeBlanc children would go to the bayou to fish and play by the water. If the children grew loud, Edouard would hop into his pirogue and drift away.

Whenever Josée would ask Jeanne or Marie if they should be quieter, one of them might say, "Ah, pah. It's just Edouard sticking his head from his shell like a *tortue.*"

Tonight she could feel his gaze on her when Jacques gave her a bottle of ink as a gift and when Jeanne and Marie gave her their present, a writing pen. Where had they found such treasures?

Josée was, as they called her, "the smart one" and could read and write. Perhaps the LeBlanc children admired her, even if they did not grasp the use of such activities. Tonight when she met Edouard's gaze, she couldn't tell how he regarded her. *A'bien*, she wouldn't let his opinion bother her. She stuck her chin out and tried to stand like a lady.

⁂

"My son, my eldest." Papa clapped him on the back. His voice boomed loud enough to be heard over the crowd's chatter. "You honored your papa and your family by comin' tonight."

"I could do no less." Edouard knew he should have left after the dances began. Yet the sight of Josée, her hair up, and flitting like a bird around the bonfire, her arms linked with his sisters', had made him stay. Several times he caught her stare at him. Did she see the scar, or was she watching his limp? He dared her to say something.

Here she was now, arm and arm with Mama LeBlanc, so close he could see the skin peeling from her sunburned nose. Her hair glowed almost blue black in the firelight. He wondered if she looked like her *mère* who had borne her. She gave him an uncertain smile.

Then Papa bellowed again, "*Mes amis* de La Manque, tonight we celebrate! Josée Broussard, raised as my daughter since she was but six, is now eighteen years old!" He gave a great laugh. His belly shook and the buttons on his vest threatened to pop. A few whoops and hollers and cheers rose up from the merry group.

Josée's already bronze skin glowed with a deeper blush that crept to her neck, which curved gracefully to her shoulders. Edouard's throat felt like he'd put on a tie tonight, except he had not.

After the cheers gave way to silence, Papa continued. "Tonight, I have a special su'prise for Josée an' another member of my family."

Edouard saw Josée dart a glance at Jacques, who jerked his head in their direction. Then he watched Josée's gaze shift to him, and he saw her eyes dawn with a sudden, horrible recognition.

"As is the custom of our people," Papa shouted gleefully, "I announce the betrothal of Josée Monique Broussard to my eldest son—Edouard Philippe LeBlanc!"

Chapter 2

Like the tears coming from Josée's eyes, rain fell on the LeBlanc's farmhouse roof. The crowd had celebrated until late, but Josée found it hard to sleep after the family settled to bed for the night. Snores from various areas of the attic told her the LeBlanc siblings rested with as much vigor as they'd rejoiced at her betrothal to Edouard.

In two weeks, the priest would meet them at the village common house. He would marry and bury, then move on and leave them until his next passage through.

Mon Père, I do not understand Your plan. Josée rolled onto her back and looked up into the darkness, as if to see through the ceiling above her and up to heaven. *My mama—my real mère—always said You work Your will in our lives. How can this be Your will if I'm not happy? Edouard is moody and dark. Jacques is—*

Everything Edouard was not. Josée sighed. She should accept what Mama and Papa LeBlanc had decided for her—for *them*, she corrected herself. After all, her world wasn't the only world that had been disrupted. Edouard looked as if he'd been sentenced to hang.

She couldn't picture any other unmarried man in the village being happy at the prospect of marrying an orphan without a dowry. She had nothing except herself to bring to the marriage. Josée shivered and pictured lonely years ahead.

Forgive me, mon Père. I should be thankful You are providing for me for the rest of my life. Yet like a snake from the dark waters not far away, fear slithered around her heart. What if Edouard was a cruel man?

Josée flung back the quilt and tried not to disturb Jeanne who slept next to her. *She* was destined to marry someone she cared for, and he for her. Tonight the soft mattress that smelled of moss did not comfort Josée. Her feet found the cool plank floor. Perhaps a cup of coffee, reheated on the coals, might do her good. She descended the loft's ladder and entered the kitchen.

Mama LeBlanc stood at the table in the warm glow of lamplight.

"Mama?"

A wooden trunk lay open before Mama LeBlanc. "I thought you might be down, *chere*."

"I couldn't sleep." She hoped Mama did not see the traces of tears on her face. "What's this?"

"Some things from your family. Look." Mama patted a yellowed paper wrapper.

Josée pulled the paper away to find an old dress that pricked at the edges of her memory and hurt a little. Her real mère's dress. A lump swelled in her throat. "Oh. It's beautiful. I'd almost forgotten."

"We'll have jus' enough time for you to try it on and see if I need to sew the hem." Mama's rough fingers smoothed the lace. "Your mère would be proud to see you wear her dress. There's more in here for you. You may take this trunk when you move to your new home."

Josée's heart beat faster, and she nodded. A new home. With Edouard.

"The coffee should be ready. Would you like a cup?" Though her surroundings remained the same, for the first time Josée felt as if she'd changed merely by reaching her eighteenth birthday.

"Of course." Josée settled onto one of the wooden benches as if she were one of the local village women visiting Mama for a cup of coffee and a talk.

Mama LeBlanc placed two mugs of coffee between them and rested her ample form on the bench across from Josée. "Marriage brings lots of changes."

One sip of the dark brew made Josée sit up straighter. "Oui, I am sure." She clutched the mug with both hands.

"Edouard is a good man. A hurt man, a disappointed man, but a good man." The older woman exhaled deeply, as if unburdening herself. "I know, deep down in his heart, Edouard understands *le bon Dieu* carries his troubles and cares for him. But—"

"Then why couldn't I marry. . ." Josée made herself stop. She had no right to question the LeBlancs' choice of husband for her. She had grown up with the knowledge that one day she'd likely marry one of the older LeBlanc brothers.

"Why not Jacques?" Mama patted Josée's hand. "Jacques is too young. He is impulsive. He would keep you laughing, oui. However, he cares more for himself than anyone else. He is a *pourri*, a spoiled young man. I am to blame, and his papa."

"I care for Jacques, and I think he cares for me, too." Josée's dismay at the words she spoke aloud caused her to touch her hot cheek.

"Ah, but is his affection the kind of carin' that would last? *Chéri*, I love my son, but Jacques is too young to marry and shoulder such responsibility. For when marriage comes, then come *bébés*."

Bébés. Josée's mind spun like a top. She could scarcely breathe. If only she could have stayed seventeen forever.

❧

Edouard let the July sun soak into his bare shoulders. He spread more pitch on the cabin's roof. In spite of his anger at his father's decision, he wouldn't dream of causing his family—or the innocent Josée—any dishonor. So he must prepare the cabin and make it fit for a young bride. A woman around would be like having a hen loose in the cabin all the time.

"You don't want to marry her, do you?" Jacques scuttled across the roof like a crab and squatted next to him. "Wish I was older."

"Not her, not anyone." Edouard spoke the words truthfully enough. Heat

14

radiated from the tar paper and roofing. Jacques was delaying their job by his talk. Edouard wanted nothing more than to be done.

"Not even Celine Hebert?"

"Celine Hebert forgot me and married another four years ago." Edouard clenched his jaw. Jacques's words irritated him more than the sweat trickling a path down his back.

The anguish over his lost love that had once torn his heart had dulled to a dismal memory, but Edouard still hadn't the inclination to seek anyone else as a wife.

"You haven't forgotten her."

"I don't love Celine, if that's what you mean. What's done is done." Marrying Josée without any thoughts of love would be best.

"Yet you'll marry someone you don't care for to please Papa." Jacques shook his head and picked up a hammer.

"For honor's sake I marry Josée Broussard. She has no feelings for me, so we begin the marriage even." Edouard recalled her dark-eyed expression the other evening at the party, as if she were trying to see inside him. He wasn't sure he welcomed her curiosity. But at least she didn't flinch from the sight of his scar. Aloud, he continued, "And perhaps over time she will forget what feelings she *thinks* she has for you."

Jacques shrugged. "I should have never told you what I heard her say the other night, the night of Papa's announcement and the big storm. Like I said, if I were older—"

Edouard's gut twisted, and he glared at Jacques. "Once Josée and I are wed, you'll not come around and cause trouble. I'm marryin' her. You are not. And I noticed you speakin' with several young ladies at the party. I will be faithful to Josée—mon Dieu requires no less."

"As you try to forget your lost love Celine!"

Enough! Edouard shoved Jacques and sent him hurtling over the edge of the cabin's roof. The young man whimpered like a pup on the ground. Edouard sprang from the roof. He managed to land on his feet, his hands curled into fists. How dare Jacques accuse him of harboring love for Celine?

Jacques leaped to his feet and doubled over. He used his shoulder to ram into Edouard's midsection. Edouard let the motion carry him backward and onto the grass. He flipped Jacques over his head then whirled to pin his brother down.

"I. . .don't. . .love her. Now you see why I wish to be left alone!" Edouard ground out the words. He held Jacques by the shoulders.

A sudden shadow blocked the light. Edouard glanced up to see Josée standing over them. The summer wind teased her hair, and she clutched a basket over one hip. A tendril of blue black hair, glossy as ink, wafted across her full lips.

Josée's capable hand moved the offending wisp out of the way. "I. . .Mama sent me with lunch. You both must be hungry and thirsty." A blush swept down her neck. She averted her gaze from their shirtless figures and looked at the cabin instead.

Edouard remembered where he was and released Jacques. He grabbed his nearby shirt and gestured for Jacques to do the same. "Jacques and I are done workin' on the roof for today. I can finish the rest on my own. Thank you—and thank Mama—for lunch."

Jacques, who took longer putting on his shirt than usual, busied himself with the contents of the basket. Josée ambled around to the entrance of the cabin that faced the bayou. Edouard wanted to stop her. He hadn't finished making the place habitable for a lady.

Which is exactly how Josée carried herself. He tucked his shirt into his trousers and caught up with Josée. "The cabin ain't very big. Two rooms. I have a good fireplace that is easy to cook over and makes good fires. I keep some things cool in the bayou water." He found himself in a struggle for words. He did not understand the effect this young woman had on his speech. She could see this for herself.

Yet she paused on the tiny porch and turned to face him and the bayou. "I—I wanted to see the view. If it's not ready, I won't go inside. Not yet." Then came another blush.

Edouard felt unspeakable relief. "Mornings are best here. Early, you can see the sun risin' up over the cypress trees and hear the birds calling. The pelicans feed, and you fight 'em for a catch of fish."

"It's very peaceful here," Josée said. She looked as though she was being fitted for the hangman's noose.

He knew she could read and write. Maybe Josée would be better off in a place like Lafayette, where she could be a nanny or a governess or work for a rich Creole family. If the prospect of marriage seemed as undesirable to her as to him, now would be a good time for them to talk. Maybe it would be better if they didn't marry after all.

"Josée, I didn't know my papa had planned this for us."

"I know. You looked as surprised as I imagine I did." Josée leaned on the porch railing. "Remember, like Papa said, it's the custom of our people."

"We don't have to follow the custom, not if both of us don't wish to." Edouard felt a pang at the clouded expression that crossed Josée's face at his words. "It wouldn't be the first time I went agin'st my papa's wishes."

"What about the plans of our bon Dieu? Could He be plannin' this for us?" Josée faced him again, her arms crossed across her body. "And when you went to war, it cost you greatly to go against Papa LeBlanc's wishes."

"Our bon Dieu." Edouard ground out the words. "He let me be scarred. He let my one love marry another. He left me with a bad leg. What is good about such things?"

Before Edouard could undo his hasty speech, another voice intruded. "*Bonjour*, young Edouard! We bring a gift from the Landrys, a new bed for you and your bride!"

Jean Landry and two of his sons came around the edge of the cabin. They carried a bed frame wrought from cypress wood, sturdy enough to last generations.

Edouard saw Josée glance at the bed before she fled toward the main house. First the fight with Jacques, then his words with Josée, and now a marriage bed, paraded down the path to his cabin.

Chapter 3

For the next week, Josée purposed in her heart not to speak of the conversation she had shared with Edouard on the cabin's porch. He didn't want her. Worse, he seemed angry at God, his anger like a festering wound that would not heal.

The families of La Manque had sent gifts along with gentle teasing, and others teased not so gently about the upcoming union. Josée tried to smile and give her thanks. Already she had several bolts of cloth as well as pots and pans. Edouard had already cleared a small patch of land by the cabin so she could plant a late-summer garden. The tilled land waited for her after it had lain dormant for years.

Now, Josée perched on a footstool in the center of the kitchen while Mama altered the hem of her mother's old dress.

"You will soon call the LeBlanc family cabin home, chere." Mama LeBlanc took up another section of the hem. "The first LeBlanc settler, Michel, came here after Le Grand Dérangement and built the cabin for his young bride, Capucine. Oui, the LeBlancs have much more now than then. But my Nicolas keeps the cabin to remind us of how good our God has been to us. And now our joy spills over, knowing that you and Edouard will start your lives together there."

The heat was unbearable, the prickly kind that made Josée want to run for the cool bayou, shed her garments to her pantaloons, and dive in. Marriage. In seven days, the priest would pass through La Manque and change their lives forever.

Anger that rivaled the summer heat rose within Josée. "Mama, I do not think Edouard wants to marry me. He. . ." She struggled to find the words. On that day when the Landrys brought the bed, at first Edouard seemed proud of his cabin, as if he wanted her to like it. Then he changed, as if he believed she didn't belong there and wanted to convince her of that, too.

"Edouard has spoken to his papa." Mama seemed to consider her words carefully. "He somehow thinks that you are too good for this place, and for him."

"Why? La Manque has always been my home." Josée sighed.

"You can read. You can write. You speak like one who has been to school."

"I know that my mère would want me to study. So I have, borrowing books and helping Jeanne, Marie and the others. Books aren't much use to them, though."

"Edouard is searching for reasons which do not exist. His papa has persuaded him that marriage is for the best." Mama LeBlanc patted Josée's shoulder. "There. You can put your other dress on. This one will be fine for the wedding. Perhaps you can find Edouard and bring him a piece of that pie you made for supper last night."

Josée's pulse thudded in her ears. "I don't think pie will convince Edouard."

"Go. Speak to him. I have been married many years, and I know this: Good conversation and a slice of pie cure many things."

Minutes later, Josée headed toward the bayou cabin. She clutched a plate of pie covered with a cloth napkin. She felt as if the *teche* waited, coiled and ready to strike, as she approached the cabin. When she rounded the corner, she saw Edouard stretched out in his hammock, his eyes closed. *So the teche sleeps.*

Josée cleared her throat. "*Pardon*, I brought you some pie."

Edouard opened his eyes and sat bolt upright, as if embarrassed to be caught lounging. "Merci."

She could not gauge his expression. He took the plate from her hands, and Josée watched him taste the pie. She tried not to grip the edges of her apron. She wanted him to say something. Why wouldn't he? Should she speak first? An inner nudge suggested she sit on the porch step. And so she did, though keeping silent about the pie and the more urgent matter of the wedding nearly smothered her.

"The pie's good. You made it?" came Edouard's voice. He settled onto the step next to her and took another bite.

"Oui. Mama said I should share it with you, and she said that you talked to your papa." Josée watched the bayou drift silently by. She took a deep breath and let the dark green canopy of trees calm her.

Mon Père, help me. I want whatever You have for us, Edouard and me. Help him see it, too. She heard a bird's call far away through the trees.

He finished the pie, acted as if he were going to lick the plate, and then stopped. Josée would have chuckled if Edouard's silence hadn't made her want to drag conversation out of the man.

"I. . .my papa says I am much like his papa, who built this cabin." Edouard gazed out at the dark water. "He lost many things. His home in Acadia. My papa's mama, Capucine—she, too, knew loss."

Josée watched his hands. He placed the plate on the top step behind them then rested his chin on folded fingers.

"Jacques, he is like Papa, so full of *joie de vivre*." Edouard turned to face Josée, and she could scarcely breathe. She had never been within arm's length of the man, and now he seemed to loom over her, although he was sitting on the top step. "I think more than I speak. But you would not miss such liveliness here? My life is simple."

"It's—it's peaceful here." Josée realized she was studying the scar on Edouard's face, dulled by stubble. "And I would not miss Jacques's liveliness so much. When we marry, I will not think of him again." She shifted her gaze to his eyes. Their brown depths almost begged her to explore the secrets inside.

⌘

I haven't wanted to kiss anyone since—

Edouard wished that he no longer thought of Celine but of the young woman who had willingly come and offered him part of herself with a simple piece of pie.

He had sensed Josée's urgency to speak and gave her credit for her silence. Her mouth opened and closed like a fish several times while he ate the pie.

Now while she waited, her mouth, well, it practically begged for a kiss. Thoughts of fish left his mind.

He stood and tried to keep his wits about him. This was Josée Broussard, who tutored his younger siblings and had somehow grown up when he wasn't looking. And soon she would become his wife.

"Josée." Edouard bent, took one of her hands in his, and pulled her to her feet. "My papa has arranged for us to marry. I doubted his choice at first, but then I do not trust easily. I cannot promise you much. I have little. But"—he gestured to the cabin behind them—"the cabin is snug and the bayou is good to me. I will provide for you, and you will lack nothing."

Her fingers tightened around his hand. "Edouard, I know you will. While you may not, as you say, have the joie de vivre of your papa, you work hard. And I promise you I shall be true to the vows we make before *notre* Dieu. I can do no less. I will be a good wife to you."

At that, Edouard raised the hand he held to his lips and sealed their agreement with a kiss.

※

Josée carried the memory of Edouard's chaste kiss for the next several days. Sometimes she found herself rubbing the spot his lips had touched with the thumb of the other hand. No longer did she want to cry when considering the idea of the upcoming marriage. It was also too late for her to make plans to escape to Lafayette or another large town.

Jacques even kept away, which was also a relief to her. She didn't understand how the dizzying sensations Jacques used to cause inside her by his very presence instead occurred at the mere thought of Edouard. She wanted to find a reason to visit the bayou cabin yet didn't want to overstay her welcome. And perhaps Edouard was only making the best of the situation he'd found himself in. She reminded herself he didn't promise to love her.

She did cry, though, when she slipped her mère's dress over her head and Mama LeBlanc fastened the buttons at the back. The afternoon sun made long shadows through the windows.

"No, no tears today! This is a day of joy for our families." Mama dabbed at Josée's full eyes with a handkerchief. "Plus, your Edouard would be worried to see you with red eyes."

My Edouard. Evidently Mama LeBlanc carried the notion that love would grow between them. Josée tried not to think of love.

Mon Dieu, I submit to Papa and Mama LeBlanc. For the rest of our lives, Edouard and I will be together.

"I wish it was my turn." Jeanne's wistful voice summoned Josée from her thoughts. "Papa and Josef have agreed to wait until spring. And Mama and I have yet to sew my new dress."

"You'll be happy to move into a new home, too." Josée resisted the urge to suggest to Jeanne that she and Josef take her and Edouard's place in front of the priest.

All too soon, the LeBlancs set out by wagon and across Breaux's Bridge to the common house where the villagers gathered. Josée did not see Edouard; perhaps he had traveled alone. Her throat hurt. She wondered if she would find her voice once it was time to say her vows.

Two other young couples of La Manque also waited to be married, and Josée didn't mind sharing the day with them.

She saw Edouard standing by himself outside the common house as they approached. She felt herself smile. He stood tall and broad in his suit coat, his ink-dark hair pulled back from his face and shoulders, his face clean shaven. He hadn't seen them yet, and Josée's throat constricted when she saw what had caught his attention.

Celine Hebert—no, Celine *Dupuis*—had arrived, her features evident even from a distance. Her husband's back was to them as he helped Celine from their farm wagon.

And the closer Josée got to the common house, she wondered if she saw regret in Edouard's eyes.

Chapter 4

The pounding drums matched the beat of Edouard's heart. He and Josée led the *promenade* of newly married couples as the entire party performed the traditional wedding march around the edge of the grounds. The well-wishers' cheering grew louder than the blare of horns and the wail of fiddles.

Edouard clutched Josée's hand, whether to hold himself up or keep her from toppling over, he didn't know. One thing he did know was they were now officially married.

He did not look at Celine, though he knew her to be there with her husband. He had glimpsed signs of a life growing inside her, and tonight as he whirled Josée into his arms at the dance, whatever he felt for Celine died inside him.

Surprise entered his wife's eyes. Maybe he held her too tightly. *His wife.* Perhaps they would learn to love each other.

At that, he found himself stepping on her feet. "I'm sorry."

Josée drew in a sharp breath but stayed in the circle of his arms. "I don't dance so well, either."

"Oh yes, you do. I've seen you." He should have kept his mouth closed. Now she would know he sometimes used to watch her play with the others on the banks of the bayou. "Here. We'll sit down to give your feet and my bad leg a rest."

Edouard kept an arm around her as they headed to the edge of the crowd where the LeBlancs had spread blankets on the ground along with the other families of La Manque. The other two married couples continued to dance, and the villagers rejoiced with them.

He looked at Josée's slippered feet. Where she'd found dancing slippers was a mystery to him. "Do your toes hurt?"

She smiled a slow smile at him and blushed. "The cow has done worse to them on milkin' days." Looking as delicate as a blossom as she took a place on the blanket, Josée had opened a door inside him he thought had been shut forever. With one smile. But he could ask nothing of her that a husband had a right to demand, not without having her heart first. He would not crush the sun-kissed flower that sat at his feet.

Edouard's throat felt like the time he'd been out fishing for two days and his water jug ran dry. "I—I'll get us somethin' to drink." He stalked off toward the family's wagon to find the water cask and a cup.

Someone clapped him on the back along the way, and Edouard tried to make out the face in the shadows cast by firelight. Josef Landry.

"Edouard, mon ami, you are undone. No more eating what you will, no more sleeping and working when you want. *Quel dommage!*" Josef's grin took the bite out of his words.

"Oui, it's a pity." Edouard shook his head.

"So where do you go with the long face?"

"To get water for us."

"Ah, the hen is already pecking at the rooster!" Josef let out a whoop and slapped his knee. His gaze darted over to Jeanne. "Dance, ma'amselle?" With that, Edouard's sister gave a toss of her black hair and entered the crowd with Josef.

Edouard reached the family wagon, found the cask, and fumbled for a tin cup. Papa waved at him from where he sat with Mama. They should have chosen a better husband for Josée. He did agree that Jacques was unsuitable—the boy would probably have broken her heart—but marry *him*? In truth, Edouard had not thought much beyond the actual idea of being married—past the ceremony—and on to life with a woman underfoot.

A pecking hen. Someone to tell him not to track dirt in the cabin, to work, to not sleep when he wanted. He had not shared a bed since he was a child and piled in with Jacques. Marriage was a different matter altogether. The hangman's noose settled around Edouard's neck once again. *Mon Dieu, why are You doing this to me?*

The contents of the cup nearly sloshed over the sides. Edouard looked down to steady his hand and nearly collided with a figure in his path. Celine, with her husband looming beside her.

"Bon temps *ce soir*, non?" Jean-Luc Dupuis shook hands with Edouard.

Edouard shrugged. *"Je ne sais pas."* He did not know if tonight was a good time, nor if the days to follow would be either. Celine looked like a startled *grosbek* about to flap its long wings and soar away over the bayou, instead of ending up as someone's supper. Edouard hoped his expression read that she had nothing to fear from him.

"A'bien, Edouard, I wish you and your bride long life, happy years, and many children together." With a nod, Jean-Luc whisked his wife away from Edouard and toward their wagon.

Many of La Manque stopped to speak with Edouard on his way back to Josée. He did not regret so much his decision to keep to himself and stay at the bayou.

He wondered if any of them whispered, "That's the one who left our village to join with Lafitte. He should have left well enough alone." Did they laugh at the hermit saddled with a lively wife? Or was she the object of their pity?

No matter how many well-wishers greeted him, cheered him, punched him good-naturedly in the arm, Edouard knew that their sincere efforts could not ensure him and Josée much of anything.

❧

Josée let her feet tap to the sound of the merry dance. She longed to have someone whisk her out into the happy group of villagers. But she remained seated on the blanket and clapped along with a few of the others. Where was Edouard?

"He's left you alone, has he?" Jacques's lanky form blocked her view of the firelight.

"Edouard is getting us a drink." Josée would not rise to her feet. Jacques, she knew, wanted to pull her to the dance. The band now played a mournful ballad of a lost love.

Jacques reached down for her hand.

"Non. I'm waiting for Edouard."

"One dance?" Jacques's voice took on a wheedling tone.

Josée shook her head. "I promised. . . ." She did not think it would be difficult to refuse Jacques's request.

"Find someone else to dance with." Edouard stood next to Jacques. Josée had never seen such a look on her husband's face. Like a gator prepared to attack, Edouard's expression should have been enough to make Jacques leave them alone.

"Josée looked like she was not havin' fun."

"She is my responsibility, not yours." Edouard used his free hand to point a finger at himself, then at Jacques's chest.

Josée stood and took the cup from Edouard. She had to tug a little to get him to release it. Perhaps a distraction would soothe his irritation.

"I was resting, Jacques. Good night!" She sipped from the cup and returned it to Edouard. "Merci."

"Yes, good night," Edouard echoed. He slung the cup to the ground. It scudded across the grass. He grabbed Josée's hand so hard that tears pricked her eyes. "Josée, we'll go home."

"But—"

He swung away from the party. Josée's shoulder jolted, and she gasped.

"Edouard—" She flung a glance back at Jacques, who stood staring after them.

"I have had enough of people for one night, perhaps for a good many nights." Even in the moonlight, Josée could see the pulsation of Edouard's jaw. She trotted to keep up with him. Words seldom failed her except for now. Crickets clamored in the summer evening.

Edouard slowed his pace and grimaced. "I'm sorry I pulled your arm like that. I wasn't tryin' to hurt you. I did not think. Mon Dieu reminds me of my bad leg."

"I do not think your pain was God's doing. I think if you had remembered and walked more slowly—" Josée stopped and bit her lip. "Anyway, my arm is fine, no worse than a cow pulling on its rope, trying to get away. Jacques—"

"Jacques is an *idiote*. He does not listen, and it was not your fault."

"Thank you. I did not speak to him first." Josée squeezed his hand, but he did not return the gesture, and she blinked back tears. "Do you mean for us to walk all the way home?"

"Oui. Last I knew, I had no grosbek wings."

Humor on the heels of his outburst spun in Josée's head. "True." The trees shadowed them along the road, and Josée shivered. She let go of Edouard's hand and rubbed her gooseflesh-covered arms.

They approached Breaux's Bridge, a recent boon to La Manque and the surrounding farms. A half-moon showed them the way to cross. One of Josée's slippers skidded on the new planks.

Edouard took her hand. "Careful. I don't want you to slip." Josée wondered what had happened to his earlier tones, when they had danced. The only depth of feeling his touch held was protection. Bayou Teche drifted below them.

Once back on hard ground, Josée's feet began to throb. She never should have accepted Jeanne's loan of slippers a size too small. "You'll wear them only for a few hours," Jeanne had assured her.

Edouard stopped and looked at her slippers. "You can take those silly shoes off." He shook his head. "Women!"

Josée straightened her shoulders after she found she could not wiggle her toes inside the slippers. "I'll be fine."

He fell silent the rest of the walk home. Josée never wanted to walk that far again. Between her feet and the thick silence, Josée was ready to explode. The bayou cabin waited in sight. Josée wished she had listened to Edouard and taken off the slippers, but she did not want to bend.

They moved around the side of the cabin and saw the bayou. A lump the size of an apple lodged in Josée's throat. Her new home. A breeze tugged on the moss draped on the cypress trees, and their branches moved as if to wave her inside.

Edouard climbed the steps and flung open the door. "Er. . . I will rebuild the fire."

Josée followed him. "No, I can." At least she hoped she could. Around the LeBlanc family, most of them took turns. And most of the other females would end up helping Josée coax the smoldering embers to life.

Feeling Edouard's gaze on her, Josée kicked off the slippers by the door and crossed the room. She fell to her knees and glanced at Edouard, who lit the lantern.

"Do you have moss?"

"There's a box by the hearth." Edouard sat on one of two stools at the table and took up a knife and a piece of wood.

Josée found the moss and placed it on the glowing embers. She wanted to beg the moss to catch fire but did not dare ask aloud.

"Burning a hole in the moss with your eyes won't start the fire."

Her face flamed. "I always had help with the fire. I thought I could do it."

Edouard swung around and set his whittling down. "I'll take care of it. You, you, just. . ."

Josée realized he did not know what to do with her. She was not a new cow or a chicken that could be fenced in or cooped up.

Her throat hurt. "Are you hungry?"

"No, no." While she watched, Edouard soon had the moss aglow and piled some kindling on top of the flames. "I am fine."

She stood back, feeling useless as a leaky cup. They were not the first couple wed because of a family's wishes. No one was guaranteed love.

I want to be happy again.

"There." Edouard stood and brushed dirt from his trousers. "A fire. In case it rains, we will not be cold tonight."

The distance between them might have been miles, but Edouard made no move to get closer. He tossed his hat onto the table and gestured to the doorway leading to the back room.

"If you are tired, you can. . ."

A'bien, so that was it. Josée's gaze glimpsed her quilt, spread over the bed tucked in the corner of the back room. The bed, handcrafted for them. New, never used. The remembrance of the Landrys' pride when they toted the bed to the cabin as a gift flickered in her mind.

"Thank you." Josée rubbed her arms. The gooseflesh would not go away, and she dared not draw closer to the fire. . .and Edouard.

"I. . .I. . ." Edouard shifted from one foot to the other, and he looked at the door as he spoke. "I'm going to check the pirogue. I must go fishin' soon." With that, he clomped to the door and left the cabin.

Josée burst into tears. Her feet felt like she had walked on glass for three miles, her head pounded, and she realized she was hungry because she failed to eat any of the lavish dishes brought by the villagers to celebrate the weddings. She satisfied her hunger pangs with generous gulps from the water bucket.

She found the trunk Mama LeBlanc had sent down to the cabin earlier that day and took out a soft chemise for sleeping in. She washed her dusty feet before climbing onto the soft mattress.

Josée said her prayers, missing the whispers of Jeanne, Marie, and the other girls alongside her as they prayed. *Notre Père*—

Our Father. She had never felt so alone in her life. Josée finished praying and tasted more tears before sleep overcame her.

Chapter 5

Edouard jerked awake on the hammock and nearly rolled over and hit the ground. Shouts rang in the air, and his gun remained inside the cabin. Was a group of bandits descending on them? No, it was Papa, Mama, and the rest of the clan racing toward the cabin. Edouard squinted at the morning light shining through the trees.

"Bonjour, my son! And where is our daughter-in-law?" Papa reached him first, clasping Edouard to his chest and then planting a kiss on both cheeks.

"Ah, she still sleeps." Edouard could not bring himself to say he had slept on the steps the night before. He could face a gator on the bayou but not a woman alone in a cabin.

"No matter. We are here for breakfast!" Papa's voice thundered across the water.

"Edouard, we are hungry. Ask your bride to feed us!" one of the family shouted.

"Oui!" They called to him like a flock of gulls. Did he ever act so when he was a child?

Edouard retreated to the cabin and headed for the bedroom. Josée lay sleeping, her breaths even. A blistered foot peeked out from under the blanket. Hair dark as midnight streamed across the pillow and begged for him to touch it.

"Josée, wake up."

She stirred, a flush blooming on her cheeks. "Edouard?" She propped herself up on an elbow and snatched the blanket to her chin with her free hand.

"Don't worry, nothing's wrong. The family is here for breakfast."

"Breakfast?" A furrow appeared between her brows.

Edouard licked his lips. "Oui, you know the tradition. The new, uh, bride always makes breakfast the morning after the weddin'." It was his turn to feel color blazing into his neck. Worse, he realized if he remained in the cabin too long. . .

"I'll be up and dressed." Josée reached for a simple dressing gown on her small trunk. She held the garment in her hand and stared at him.

"Oh, yes. Pardon." Edouard turned and faced the fireplace and the table. "You will find cornmeal on the shelf. I have salted fish. Mama left dried herbs for you to use as well. She knew I did not have much to make a suitable meal."

"Ed—dee! Why take you so long waking your wife?"

"I had to tell her where the food was!" he shouted toward the door.

"Then tell her faster!"

Mon Dieu, I prayed to be left alone. I prayed for peace, and this is how You answer me? Edouard didn't dare turn around until he knew Josée was finished dressing. He couldn't let himself see her, although he knew he had the right by marriage.

"I'm ready." Josée had also made the bed and stored her clothes in the trunk. Edouard reminded himself to take his shirts down from the rope he had stretched across the cabin.

"*Bien*, 'cause I'm hungry, too." He tried to smile, but at his words her eyes grew round as a fish's. "I'll draw us more fresh water from the cistern." He grabbed the bucket on his way out the door before the family really started to tease them.

❧

Josée's head ached as if someone had danced a jig on her forehead all night. Cook? Breakfast? She wanted to climb through a window and run up the familiar path, back to Mama's table and the warm, snug, happy kitchen. This place? It held nothing to comfort her.

She ducked under two hanging shirts she'd missed the night before in her struggle to light a fire. They had plates, cups, and bowls, thanks to Mama and Papa LeBlanc. But food? For everyone?

Nestled in a nook in the fireplace, Josée found her new pots and pans. She did not have the heart to tell Edouard all she could make without burning it was pie.

"Mama, if only I could have written the recipes down." Josée shook her head. She couldn't remember how much lard to add to the cornmeal to start biscuits. Worse, no biscuit cutter. She fingered the edge of a cup. A'bien, that would have to do.

Where to make the dough? Josée took one of the two bowls and placed it on the table. She guessed at how much cornmeal and lard to use, and started mushing them together. Biscuits weren't much different than piecrust. Ah, wait. She needed leaven for the biscuits to rise like Mama's.

Josée slapped her forehead before she remembered her hands were covered with cornmeal. Oh, she was failing miserably in the kitchen. Or cabin, rather. She did not know if she wanted to be outside, hearing the family tease them both.

Tease them? Josée shook her head. For all she knew, Edouard had slept outside on his trusty hammock. Poor man. He had gained a wife but lost his bed and privacy.

A soft rap on the door made Josée look up. "Who is it?"

"Bonjour, may I come in?"

"Oui, Mama." The door opened, and Mama entered. She placed a round covered pan on the table. The sight of her brown rotund figure made Josée wipe her hands on her skirt and embrace her.

"So, how goes it?" Mama asked.

Josée shrugged. "I have no breakfast cooking. I have no coffee to offer my guests." She gestured to the table.

Mama made a soft hissing noise. " 'Tis my fault. I did not pay attention enough when you helped in the kitchen."

"Truthfully I was wanting to read, so it's partly my fault as well." Josée wanted to toss the lump of meal and lard into a refuse bucket.

Mama gave her a pointed look. "Yet when I asked, 'how goes it,' I was not asking about your cooking this morning."

"I. . ." She could not tell Mama she did not want to be there.

Mama smiled. "Ah, *l'amour*. There is more to love than an embrace, a touch. Much more. Just as there is more to joy than feelin' happy."

Josée found a rolling pin and tumbled the dough onto the wooden table. "I don't know what to do."

"Do?" Mama patted the hand that rolled out the dough. "Make corn bread. Learn to make gumbo. Know Edouard. And speak to notre Père. He will show you the way and bring you the joie de vivre you seek."

Josée nodded. For now, making biscuits was enough for her.

"I'll leave you be, unless—"

"Breakfast?"

Mama patted the pot she had placed on the table when she came in. "See to the biscuits, and place this pot to warm until the biscuits are done."

"Oh, Mama, merci—"

"*D'rien*. You can tell Edouard about my help with the meal after we have gone." After a kiss on the cheek, Mama left the cabin.

Josée placed the pan of dough in the oven. They would bake and not rise but would be better than nothing. While crouched down, Josée saw a thin spine of a book nestled between the fireplace bricks and the wood box.

A book? As best Josée knew, Edouard could not read.

Josée pulled out the volume, parchment bound in leather. A book handmade with much care, left in a hiding place. The pages crackled when she opened the cover and read the first page.

In the year of our Lord, 1769

I, Capucine LeBlanc, write this with my own hand. These are my thoughts in this new land. After much sorrow, much joy. My dear Michel has built me a home. My long-lost mère is nearby. Comforte sleeps on my shoulder as I hold the pen. Life is full.

She closed the book and ran her hands over the cover. Capucine, the mère of Edouard's papa. This treasure was different than the usual stories passed down through the family. Why had this been placed in the nook? The books in the LeBlanc home had been Josée's, secured away in the trunk that rested next to the bed, and were only taken out by her.

"You will no longer be hidden, little book." Josée's face grew warm. What if one of the others heard her? She stood, crossed the cabin, and placed the book in her trunk. As she went to check on the biscuits, she cast a glance over her shoulder.

Did Capucine burn her food, or was she a fine cook? Did she have songs springing forth, unbidden, from her heart? Perhaps instead of songs, she wrote from her heart. Josée would have to find out. It warmed her to think that another woman cooked at this hearth and bounced bébés on her knee in this very room.

"Josée! We're hungry!" chorused the voices outside.

"*Un momente!*" she called back. *Mon Père, merci for the book.* But she would appreciate help in learning to make gumbo. As for Mama's suggestion to know Edouard, that would wait. . . for another time.

Chapter 6

As if in answer to Edouard's prayers for help, rain poured from the heavens upon La Manque. He stood on the tiny porch he had built overlooking the bayou, which swelled with freshwater. After three days of rain, the tiny garden which Josée had lovingly tilled now looked like stripes of mud and water. He did not understand le bon Dieu's joke. Since the wedding two weeks ago, he had spoken to God more than he had in a long time. And he did not remember asking Him for rain.

This morning the melody that Josée sang lilted above the drumming on the roof. Edouard's stomach growled. He had thought *his* cooking was bad. After two bites of her gumbo last night—the first to be polite and the second out of hunger—breakfast arrived after a long night. He had not meant to cause her tears. He ended up listening to her sniffle as they fell asleep. The rain would not allow him to sleep in his hammock or on the porch, so he had claimed one side of the bed. An invisible line seemed carved between them. Edouard did not mind that so much. He did mind waking up cold in the hours before first light with no quilt. Josée slept, wrapped like a moth in its cocoon.

"Edouard, this journal, it's so beautiful. Her words, after going through so much. . ." Josée's voice rang out inside the cabin. He heard her feet grow louder on the wooden floor.

Ever since Josée had found that journal, she trotted behind Edouard, reading parts of it. He did not mind stories so much, but the fact that Josée understood the writing—he shook his head. After three days of rain and her chatter about the journal, he didn't know which noise grated more to his ears.

"What is that?" Edouard turned to face her where she stood in the doorway. She looked like a spot of brightness in the gray day. Of course, she had slept well the night before. In other circumstances, he might want to steal a kiss. That is, if she would keep quiet long enough. What had happened to her demure attitude on that hot day she brought him a slice of pie?

"Listen. Capucine writes, 'As I look back upon the years of sadness in my darkest days, I see how my heavenly Father watched and worked on my behalf. Even though I did not believe for a time, my questioning did not banish the truth, that my God is still there. I wish I knew then that joy is not based on people, places, and things. Those change. My God does not.'"

In spite of his growling stomach, Edouard almost believed the words. Then his bad knee twinged. "But my knee, my heart." He touched his chest.

Josée placed her warm hand over his, and his heartbeat kept pace with a woodpecker. "I am sorry, so sorry, that these things happened to you. Will you let your heart heal?"

"I don't know how." Edouard moved from her touch and looked out at the bayou. Where had his quiet life gone? "I was fine here by myself. I did not have you askin' me questions and reading from that—that book!"

Edouard glanced back to see Josée whirl on grubby feet and enter the cabin. He turned again to face the water. Joie de vivre—oui, Josée had plenty of that. He had not intended his words to hurt, but there it was. So he was not used to having someone around all the time. He had himself and the water's inhabitants for company.

Her approaching footsteps made him turn yet another time. Josée blazed through the open doorway and came so close he could see dark flames in her eyes.

"You are not the only one who has suffered loss." Josée's face reminded him of a storm on the gulf with its clouds rolling in before the full fury broke.

"You are not the center of the world! That family"—Josée pointed toward the LeBlanc home—"loves you. They wept and prayed and begged for God to return you to them. But *nooo*! No one has suffered like the great Edouard Philippe LeBlanc. You act as if you have had no one to help you. You act as if no one's love is enough. Not your family's, not God's, not—" Josée clamped her hand over her mouth and hiccupped. Tears streamed down her face. She ran inside the cabin.

Edouard curled his fists. His eyes stung and his breath came in short gasps. This was a new pain, to be sure. Josée had no right to come at him with the vengeance of a mama gator. She did not know him or his pain at all.

☙

Josée paced the floor. *That man* was right outside, and if she wanted to race to Mama LeBlanc's home, she would have to pass by him on the way. She had never thought one person could cause her so much fury. And she had almost admitted that she loved him. A one-sided love that would surely crush her heart. That man had to have been one of the most selfish creatures le bon Dieu had ever created. *"My knee, my heart,"* indeed. Yet here she was the one crying like a bébé.

She dashed the tears from her cheeks then stoked the fire. After tossing more moss on the embers, she coaxed the flames back to life and added a fresh log. A cold spell with the rains brought a damp chill into the cabin, unexpected in this summer season.

A smile tugged at her mouth. Poor, poor Edouard. He had eaten two bites of supper and no doubt had a long hungry night. She had also stolen the blanket, and by the time she realized it, Edouard had already risen and built the fire and made coffee. She did not admit she was as hungry as he after she tasted her gumbo. The burnt roux did not a savory gumbo base make. Edouard had pitched the mess into the rubbish pile outside then fished to no avail.

"No rules here," he'd assured her in their first few days together. "I get up when

I want, eat when I want, sleep when I want."

Life must be very different than when there was only one person under the roof. *Très différent* for both of them. At the large LeBlanc house, Josée knew her place. Here she did not know when to cook, or try to. She did not know when it was time to sleep, other than Edouard turning off the lamp on the table. He did not wake her most mornings. How could she learn her place when Edouard treated her as if she were not there?

Enough! Josée snatched her shawl, wrapped it around her shoulders, and pulled a corner over her head. She *would* pass him and go up to the house, whether Edouard liked it or not.

She moved for the doorway and was relieved to see Edouard leaning on the porch railing. He faced away from her.

"I'm goin' to see your mère." Josée did not ask permission to go. Nor was he a child who could not be left alone. He could fend for himself quite well without her. She pushed past him and pounded down the wooden steps. She did not look his way but trotted through the rain and along the muddy path to the big house.

By the time she reached the kitchen, her feet and ankles were covered with mud, her shawl soaked, the hem of her dress soiled. She knocked on the door.

Mama LeBlanc answered. "*Ma chéri*, what brings you here?"

"I needed to see you. May I come in?"

"Of course. Let me bring you some water to cleanse your feet."

After Josée washed the dirt from her feet, she entered the warm home. By then her hands had stopped trembling and she no longer felt as angry. She'd also just made extra work for herself come wash day.

Mama placed a steaming cup of coffee on the table. "I have not seen you for days."

"It's the rain. I tried to start the garden, and now that is flooded and I am stuck indoors. Edouard can't fish right at the moment either, so. . ."

"I see. Well, Papa LeBlanc has remained inside, as well. I send him out to tend the animals, and he's welcome to stay out there a while, also." Mama stirred a bubbling pot over the fire.

"I know Edouard is your son, and you love him, but now he's worse than a mosquito bite on my back that I can't scratch." Josée frowned. "I do not know what he expects of me. I burned the gumbo last night. The roux smelled strange, and I should have known. And did you know? Edouard does what he pleases when he pleases."

The thoughts tumbled out. Josée did not know how to tell Mama about the extent of Edouard's bitterness. She did not know how to admit that she loved the man, as well. How could you love someone you'd like to throw in the bayou?

"You two have been like a hen and rooster cooped up with nowhere to go. The cabin is Edouard's. But it is yours to run." Mama pointed at Josée. "You decide when breakfast is served. You clean the floor. You tell him to clean his boots and not track mud, although, after twenty-five years Papa LeBlanc will leave a trail on the floor."

"Papa LeBlanc, still?"

"Oui, even after I made him scrub his tracks."

Josée grinned at the thought and blinked back the rest of her tears. "I thought—"

"You thought we never argued?" Mama shook her head. "I must forgive Nicolas daily, and he must forgive me. Would you like a bowl of gumbo?"

"I *am* hungry," Josée admitted. "Is Papa LeBlanc in the barn?"

Mama simply nodded, a twinkle in her eye. "And I have good news. The Landrys sent word that they are having a *fai do do* tomorrow night at the common house. We will dine together, play music, and dance if there is room enough. You must ask Edouard to bring you."

Oh, a fai do do! Time to spend with the LeBlancs, the Landrys, and other families who decided to venture out. Josée's heart leaped in anticipation.

"Mama, please help me make a roux. Then I shall go home and try again." Home. She realized she'd called the cabin *home*.

"That I can do. You must feed well the man you love."

Josée touched her hot cheeks. "You can see that?"

"I saw the moment I opened the door."

"I'm afraid he does not love me." It hurt to speak the words.

"Time, chéri. It will take time. Pray to le bon Dieu, and He will answer you and show you what to do."

Josée hoped so. Both her heart and her stomach were hungry.

❧

Edouard took the path up to the big house, passed it, and went to the barn instead. He saw the trail of Josée's footprints to the kitchen door. Better he not go there. Instead, he sought out Papa, who had probably gone to check the animals.

He entered the barn, and the scent of straw and horse pricked his nostrils. "Papa?"

"Up here." Papa's voice came from above.

Edouard looked to the hayloft and climbed the ladder. His Papa was lying on his side, whittling a lump of cypress wood.

"Ah, so she drives you from your home, eh?" Papa chuckled.

"She does not. I. . .I needed to get out. After three days of rain, I needed. . ." Edouard shrugged then found a comfortable spot to stretch out.

"Remember, son, Josée is very young. She does not know how to run a house. My sweet Clothilde was a good mère to her after Josée's parents died, but I'm afraid with all these children, she did not see to Josée's trainin' as well as she should." Papa shook his head. "That, and Josée always wanted to read the books left by her own mère."

"Oui, I know. Josée found a journal written by your grand-mère, Capucine. She is always reading to me." Edouard waved his arms. "It's 'Edouard, listen to this,' and 'Edouard, listen to that.' The only time she ceases talking is when she sleeps."

Papa leaned back and laughed, his belly heaving up and down, his face red. "*Bienvenue* to marriage, Edouard. Women must talk. It's their nature. Let her."

Edouard did not find this advice helpful or humorous. No one seemed to understand the quiet he craved had been denied him and would never come again.

"And you, you treat her well. Teach her what you know of cooking, if you must. And let her do her job." Papa shook his head. "I should have dragged you back to the house years ago instead of letting you take the cabin by yourself. It was not good for you—"

"Papa, I was injured and broken—"

"Listen to me. You have built strong walls that you no longer need. I see what Celine Dupuis did to you. I was sorry for your pain, but a faithless young woman was not fit for my son. You must go on, with Josée. She is full of faith and joie de vivre. She will share with you, willingly, I believe."

Edouard nodded. He had to agree with Papa. Wasn't that what Josée had been trying to do? "I have not been so smart."

Papa chuckled again—Edouard had forgotten how much Papa loved to laugh. "My son, that is the first thing you've said in years that makes sense."

An hour or so later, Edouard left the barn and headed back to the cabin. It had felt good to talk to Papa, man-to-man. No longer was he an unmarried man but had to consider someone else in his home. He had no doubts that he and Josée would clash heads again, except he knew he must learn to build bridges between them.

The rain had slowed to a gentle patter on the trees. As Edouard rounded the corner of the cabin, he heard a voice praying. *"Notre Père qui est aux cieux! Que ton nom soit sanctifié. . ."*

He paused and whispered the words. "Our Father in heaven, holy is Your name. . ." Oui, he wanted to do God's will, provide for Josée, and he needed to learn to forgive. One step at a time, he would.

Chapter 7

The fai do do, Edouard, it's tomorrow night." Josée served up steaming gumbo and freshly baked corn bread (a bit flat) for supper. Thanks to Mama LeBlanc, Josée had realized she needed to count to three hundred when stirring the roux. Stop stirring too soon, and the roux would not thicken. Stir too long, and the mess would burn. The thick soup smelled heavenly tonight. Josée determined she would write down how to make roux so she would not forget. She watched Edouard inhale the aroma.

"My mama helped you."

"She did. I am going to try to do better."

He surprised her by clasping her hand. "I know." His thumb rubbed her palm. "Me, too."

Josée's head swam, and she pulled her hand away to cut the corn bread. "Like I was saying, your mère told me the Landrys are having a fai do do, and we must go. Oh, I mean, I would really like to. I think it would be good to get out of the cabin." She sat down across from him.

Edouard nodded. He said the blessing, and Josée waited for him to continue talking about the fai do do. She ate, although she was not too hungry after two bowls of Mama's gumbo.

"I suppose we can ride in the wagon with Papa and Mama and the others." Edouard sounded reluctant.

"It's been so long since we've spent time with anyone besides your family, and—" Josée heard herself starting to talk up a stream and fell silent. She took another bite. Edouard had managed to net enough fine sweet shrimp that blended with the broth.

"You should wear the dress from when we married." Was that a smile she saw tugging at the corners of his mouth?

"I think I will." She didn't mention she would change dresses because what she wore had mud caked at the hem. Even if she washed the dress tonight, it might not dry come tomorrow. Worse, what if the stains were permanent?

Edouard apparently did not see the need for further conversation, so Josée figured now was as good a time as any to follow Mama's suggestions.

"I will be sure to make breakfast in the morning." Her voice sounded unnaturally high to her ears. "I'm your wife, and I have responsibilities, too. I will cook for you. Mama's been helping me, and I will keep improving, I'm sure."

Josée did not miss the expression on his face.

She continued in spite of it. "If you are going to fish and will be away, I will send something with you to eat. I don't know what you have that you can trade, but I want to buy more seed and replant the garden. I will sew and hang curtains, too. Also, I will be moving the line where you hang the wash to another place where the shirts don't get in my way. Wash day will be Mondays." She hoped he would remember everything. The clunk of a spoon in a bowl surprised her.

"You're goin' to make me scrape my boots before I come in, too, I suppose?"

"It will save scrubbing the floor so much." She smiled at him, thinking of the way he'd touched her hand earlier. He did look handsome by firelight, now that her anger had burned off. She prayed his heart would soften.

Edouard tugged at his suspenders and pushed back from the table. "I left one mère to gain yet *un autre*." He had spoken as if she were a thorn in his foot. A mosquito on his neck. Josée kept eating and did not break his gaze.

Josée thought her anger had burned off, but a few embers reignited. "I am not your mère. I am your *wife*."

"And I am finished." Edouard stood up and left the table and tromped to the porch. She heard nothing except the dripping trees and the crickets singing their nightly songs. Josée did not touch the rest of her gumbo. She poured it back in the pot over the fire. Her appetite had left her. She scrubbed their bowls and spoons and heard the sound of Edouard whittling outside.

❧

The rain had stopped, though clouds hung in the sky. Edouard looked westward down the bayou. The sun was trying to peek at them on its descent into night. Josée hummed again inside the cabin. After their words the night before, Edouard had apologized. He had not acted as if he were trying to build a bridge. Change did not happen quickly, either, and he asked if Josée could make one change at a time. She responded with a breakfast of *couche-couche* that almost rivaled his mama's. But then a body couldn't easily ruin fried cornmeal drizzled with cane syrup. She must have gotten the milk from Mama, besides the recipe.

Now Josée bustled from pantry to table as she packed a basket to take to the fai do do tonight. Her capable hands folded a cloth to cover the bread. Her hands. Edouard wanted to touch them again, as he had when he woke up that morning to find one of them clasped to his chest in both of his. They were small yet very strong, and one finger of the right hand had a spot of ink from writing in the book she had found. He remembered touching the ink stain. She had a burn on another finger, which he also caressed. It must have hurt, for she murmured in her sleep. He had not known what it felt like to protect someone, to have someone so close. . .

He swallowed hard and called out, "Are you almost ready?" His neck hurt from the freshly pressed shirt buttoned to the top.

"Here I am." Josée emerged from the cabin, her shoulders wrapped with a shawl and the basket hung over one arm. She had somehow braided her hair and wrapped it around her head like a black crown. Her cheeks flushed, she smiled at him.

"You look très *jolie*," he whispered. Where had his voice gone?

36

"Merci." It sounded as if she had lost her voice, as well.

Edouard tucked her free hand over his arm, and they set out together for Mama and Papa's house, where they would ride with the family on the wagon. He would have preferred to walk with her so they could be alone, but he knew she would not want to soil her dress on the muddy roads. Even with hard scrubbing, Josée had not been able to remove the mud from the dress she had worn yesterday.

"Don't worry, we will get you another dress," he assured her.

"Edouard! Josée! We are ready to go!" someone called from the wagon. He waved to them and walked faster. Already he could smell the good foods wafting from Mama's baskets.

The wagon seemed more crowded than usual, and Edouard ended up pulling Josée onto his lap for the ride. Nearly cheek to cheek with her the entire trip, Edouard could scarcely breathe. He sensed Josée's heart galloping away with her, and a pretty blush colored her neck.

Jacques stared at them from across the wagon until someone asked about a girl he planned to see at the fai do do. *Patience, little brother,* Edouard wanted to tell him. He would not wed his first love, but le bon Dieu would take care of him. It felt as if salve had been rubbed on the painful spots of Edouard's own heart. He wanted to hold Josée closer, if that were possible. *Merci, mon Père.*

When they reached the common house, Edouard regretted having to release Josée. He did not notice his knee hurting so badly, either. Perhaps he would work enough to buy or trade for a wagon and an animal to pull it.

Josée hopped from the wagon and received the basket Edouard gave her. "I'll put this with the rest of the food and meet you inside." Her eyes twinkled at him. Mama gave him a knowing smile.

The fiddles called them indoors, where the benches had been cleared away for the dance floor and a table for the food had been set up at one end of the room. Edouard found Josée right away.

"Edouard, I'm glad we came." She clutched his arm, and his stomach turned over. "Merci."

"I'm glad we did, too." Although he wanted to whisk her away from the crowd, he would not because of the others' teasing. The two couples who had also been married at the same time were present, and soon it seemed like all of La Manque and those who lived on outlying farms had come. Night fell, and still the music played on.

Edouard managed two fast dances with Josée, who was extremely light on her feet. A familiar face flashed by him. *Celine.* He was surprised to find he felt the barest twinge instead of feeling like a scab had been opened on his heart.

The dance ended, and Josée stepped back. "I'm going to speak with a few of the other ladies. They are in a sewing group and meet together sometimes, and I should like to go and learn how to sew better."

"Of course, go on. Are you hungry?"

She shook her head. "Not yet." Then off she went, Edouard following with his gaze. He wanted to have her at his side, but he would definitely be teased if he tried to enter the circle of women.

He tugged at his collar. The room swelled with people, and Edouard wanted air. He decided to go outside, where some of the men gathered, talking about the farms and feed and the bayou. And the rain.

Once Edouard left the crowded building, he inhaled the night air as he stood on the steps. Laughter filtered outside. He went out toward the wagons and the side of the building.

"Edouard LeBlanc, so how goes marriage?" Josef Landry tugged on his sleeve as Edouard passed a trio of men who stood and talked by torchlight.

He stopped. "It has been. . .très different. I'm not used to having someone around."

Josef sighed. "I count the days until your sister and I marry. I expect to have the house finished by spring and a new pirogue. Lucky for you, you had your family's old home."

"I was glad they let me keep it." Edouard shifted his weight from one foot to the other. "You have a good night."

Josef nodded, and Edouard went on his way to the outhouse. A figure stood under a cypress tree, shadowed by a canopy of moss. He could hear sniffles from where he stood.

"*Qu'est-ce que c'est?*" Edouard walked in the direction of the tree. What was it? Were they hurt? The hazy moon slid out from behind a cloud, though thunder rolled in the distance and humidity hung in the air. Another storm was brewing. His knee could feel it. Edouard stopped short when the figure looked up at him.

Celine. She wiped her eyes.

"It's you," she said. "Please, I don't know what to do."

"Is there something wrong? Shall I fetch one of the women?"

She flung herself at him and clamped her arms around his waist. "I was so *stupide*! I was so blind. I should have waited for you."

Edouard tried to get himself out of her gator's grasp before someone saw them. "I think you should speak with someone else, my mère perhaps?"

Her arms tightened. "Jean-Luc, he does not understand me. You always did."

He pushed harder but did not want to hurt someone in her condition. "Celine, this is wrong. You should not be doing this."

"*Je t'aime*, Edouard." Her big eyes, dark as the bayou water, pleaded with him. "I need your comfort."

He managed to get free and held her by the shoulders. "I don't love you. Not anymore. We can never go back. Our lives are different. And I love Josée." The whispered words rang through his mind at the realization.

"Edouard—" She came at him again, her lips parted. Light footsteps on the grass sounded behind them.

"Edouard, are you there?" an all-too-familiar voice called.

Josée. Edouard whirled to face her, knowing he had done nothing wrong. The look she gave him spoke more than any words she could say.

She ran off toward the front of the building.

"Josée..." Edouard left Celine without worrying about her troubles. He needed to explain to Josée. Quickly.

He started to run, not caring about the pain in his leg. "Josée!"

She stopped and turned to face him. "How could you?" They stood in a triangle of lamplight shining through the window.

"Let me explain."

"I saw nothing that needed explainin'." Josée's words felt like darts. "I saw clearly."

"Things are not like they seem."

"What am I supposed to think, my husband hidden under a tree with a woman?" Lamplight reflected from her flashing eyes. "I am young, but I am not stupid."

"Josée—" He reached for her.

"Don't touch me." Josée waved his arms from her shoulders. "And to think I looked forward to having you hold me in your arms tonight, thinking that *I* was the one you wanted to be with."

She *wanted* him to hold her close? Edouard rubbed his forehead. "I did not break my vows to you, even in thought." Celine marched past them and around the corner of the building. Another clap of thunder rolled.

"I'm goin' inside." Josée shrugged him off again, though he walked by her side. "We will talk when we get home. Do not think I will forget this."

At that, Edouard dropped the matter for the time being. Later tonight, he would try to explain. *Mon Père, please, do not disappoint me again.*

Chapter 8

Josée cut her loaves of bread at the serving table and felt like her heart had been cut into slices as well. She closed her eyes, trying to forget the sight of Edouard with Celine under the tree. Josée was the one who had hoped to find her husband outside for a moment.

If Mama LeBlanc or Jeanne had noticed her expression, she could not tell. She managed her brightest smile while the women served the meal. She could not bear to look at Edouard. Nor could she stop glancing at Celine. Josée wanted to cross the distance between them and rip the woman's hair out. However, such an act would displease le bon Dieu. Celine would pay the price in her own way, and Josée would not pay with her own bitterness.

She had not known loving someone would cause her to want to behave in such a way. Her heart swelled as she at last let herself look at Edouard, already seated between Josef and Simon Landry. One of them said something, and Edouard appeared to chuckle.

Josée clamped her lips together. He was having fun, and she was here only taking up space. Her stomach complained, but she did not think she could eat. Neither could she breathe after the room had filled with villagers. The air felt thick after the many dances throughout the evening.

She leaned over and whispered to Jeanne. "I'm going outside."

"Why? The rain comes."

Josée reached for her shawl and put it around her shoulders. "I do not feel well, and the fresh air should help me." She reached for a nearby lantern.

"I'll get Edouard if you want."

"No!" Josée touched Jeanne's arm with her free hand. "I do not want to speak with him right now." She did not want to continue the conversation they'd had earlier. Not until they were back in the cabin, anyway.

"Are you sure?" Jeanne's forehead wrinkled.

Josée nodded. "I. . .I'm not very happy with him tonight." She slipped through the crowd and paused at the doorway. Edouard looked toward the serving tables. When he turned back to face Josef, he wore a frown. Josée stepped into the night. If anyone saw her, maybe they would think she was headed for the outhouse. She covered her hair with the shawl and inhaled, the air thick with the promise of rain. The falling rain would mask her tears très bien.

When Josée crossed the yard where the animals stood hitched, a clap of thunder made her jump, but she continued walking. The teams of horses and mules pulled on their leads and one nearly trampled Josée's foot.

"Whoa." She patted the mule's neck and quickened her steps.

Raindrops hit the muddy road that wound to the edge of La Manque and eventually crossed Breaux's Bridge. Josée pictured the LeBlanc cabin, waiting for her. When she made it to the cabin, she would build a fire and start the coffee and wrap herself up in their big blanket. She would have her cry, write down more recipes in Capucine's journal, and wait for Edouard.

Another boom shook the ground, and Josée started to run. The lantern in her hand made wild arcs of light in the darkness. Yet she was not going back to the common house. She could not. She would make it home, even though the rain would soak her through.

Breaux's Bridge lay ahead of her, outside the circle of lantern light. The cold wet surface, slick with mud from the crossing wagons, would be hard to tread. Josée leaned into a fresh gust of wind and winced at the stinging rain. She took a few hesitant steps onto the bridge, her feet slipping on the mud. The overflowing bayou roared below her.

A rumble from behind made Josée stop and grab the thin railing. Hoofbeats on mud and the rattle of a wagon. Josée skittered like one of the LeBlanc's young foals trying to stand. She hit her knees, and the lantern rolled away from her reach.

Josée squinted back in the dark. "*Arret*—wait, I'm on the bridge!"

The wagon did not slow. It hugged the bridge's rail. Josée knew she could not make it to the other side of the bridge without being struck. She scrambled to the edge and squatted near the railing. Rain soaked her hair and ran down her neck. Somehow her shawl had slipped from her shoulders.

Lightning flashed. The team of horses barreled onto the bridge. Their reins dangled, without a driver on the wagon seat. Josée reached up to grip the railing. The wooden planks shook as if a giant hand jerked the bridge. Her feet slid out from under her. Her fingers lost their hold.

She fell into empty space, and the roaring water rushed up at her.

❧

A crack of thunder shook the common house. Edouard glanced to the serving table where the women were packing up the food. Where was Josée?

He should have turned and left the moment he had seen Celine under that tree. Now he was faced with waiting until his wife's anger cooled enough to listen to him. He knew a tirade would come, one that he did not deserve completely.

Like a thunderclap, the realization that she loved him jolted him to the core.

"Ed–dee, we are leaving." Papa put on his hat. "The storm is going to be bad—Simon Breaux's team already ran out of here like their tails were on fire."

"Oui, I must find Josée." Edouard began to search the room. No one had seen her.

Then Jeanne offered, "She told me she was goin' outside. She was unwell."

Edouard moved through the crowd leaving the building. He didn't ask why she did not come to him. He would have taken her home had she not felt well. Women, as mysterious as the dark bayou. And he knew the bayou much better.

Wind yanked at his shirt, and the pelting rain stung his freshly shaven cheeks. He borrowed a lantern and searched the grounds. After most of the families of La Manque had left the common house, he could see Josée was not among any of the wagons nor under any of the cypress. He also found the outhouse empty. Papa, Jacques, and Josef Landry joined the search.

Simon Breaux returned with his team. "I caught these rascals on the other side of the Teche and found this on the bridge. Whose are these?"

He held up a lantern and a muddy shawl.

Edouard felt his stomach drop into his feet.

❧

Josée surfaced, flailing her arms in the darkness. The cold of the bayou water, fed by fresh rain, sucked the breath from her lungs. As the current dragged her along, Josée felt as if an unseen force had her in its grip. She could not see the banks, the trees, or worse, anything in the water with her. Closing her eyes made no difference. The darkness remained unchanged. She tried to find the bottom with her feet, but her skirt twisted around her legs like a funeral shroud. Her efforts at kicking were futile. She fought down panic yet screamed.

A flicker of light from the bridge gave her hope. "Help me! Please!"

The light grew smaller as the bayou pulled on her, along with the shrinking hope that she might be heard as she fought against the current. The beating rain numbed her head and shoulders above the water. Her teeth chattered.

Wind howled through the trees and carried a hint of an old song. *"Watch*, petite enfants, *for the teche of the bayou. He will come to find you if you don't watch out."*

The stories told around the fire when she was a child hissed in Josée's ears. *Please let the gators stay in their warm hideaways deep underwater, and let the teche sleep through the rains.* The natives considered the teche sacred, but Josée shuddered at the slithering way they moved and their narrow eyes.

Something hard bumped against her, and Josée screamed again. She reached out, unsure if it was friend or foe. The something turned out to be a chunk of wood not much larger than the top of her footstool. She clung to it and leaned her cheek on its solid surface and floated to give her legs and arms a rest.

The glow from a cabin's window pierced the inky night. Josée let go of the wood so she could kick through the water toward the light. An undercurrent tugged at her dress again, and she ended up farther away from the light, probably back in the center of the bayou. She shouted for help again. No one came to the window. If she could get close enough to grab one of the knobby knees of the cypress or a hanging frond of moss, she might be able to pull herself out.

After she passed the lighted cabin, the darkness swallowed her up once more.

Mon Père, please help me!

With the twists and turns of the bayou, she hoped to find a place to get her footing, but in the shallows, she did not know if she would disturb a sleeping gator. If she were attacked, no one would know where she was.

Just like no one knew where she was now.

Then Josée slammed into something so large and solid it rattled the teeth in her head. She screamed.

❧

Edouard hugged the shawl to his chest, and a deep moan came from his throat. He thought he was beyond such pain, but this was worse than coming home and learning of Celine's betrayal and of feeling like an outcast for leaving the seclusion of their bayou world.

"We must find her." He looked at Papa, who was helping Mama into the wagon. "She should not have left on her own."

After a thorough search of the grounds, he guessed that Josée had begun to walk home. He helped Papa get the family loaded onto the wagon.

Jeanne shed many tears. "I should have come to find you when she did not come back."

Edouard hugged his sister. "You did not know. Do not worry yourself."

Papa urged the horses as fast as they could safely move on such muddy roads. Edouard wanted to beg him to drive faster. Papa slowed the horses to a halt on the bridge and lifted the lantern to show where Simon had found the shawl.

Edouard inhaled so fast his chest hurt. "It looks like—"

"Someone might have slipped from the bridge." Papa shook his head.

He could hear Mama praying, "Notre Père qui est aux cieux! Be with our Josée. Deliver her from evil."

Papa turned to face him. "Your Josée is a smart girl and strong. We will go home and start searching for her by foot along the bayou. We will stop at every cabin and tell them to listen for someone and search for her."

"Or," Jeanne spoke up, "maybe she made it home."

Edouard did not tell his sister he knew she was wrong. The one time he had walked Josée home after the wedding, she had not liked it, and it would have been worse for her in the dark. He would not rest until he found her and spent the rest of his life telling her how much she meant to him.

They reached the LeBlanc house at last, and Edouard leaped from the wagon before it stopped moving. Yet even from here, he could see no light in the cabin window.

"My son." Mama touched his shoulder. "We will find her. We must believe."

"I do not know why I should. Le bon Dieu has taken from me once again my joy."

"You cannot make Josée your joy. Ah, she is joyful, but she is just a woman." Mama ran her hand on his hair, a gesture which used to comfort him when he was a bébé. "Even if you have her safely in your home, you know she will disappoint you at times, and you her."

Edouard nodded at that. Mama had probably been talking to Papa. Fresh memories of Edouard and Josée's silly fight from the day before swam through his head.

"Trying to make her your joy is like trying to catch a fish with your hands. The harder you grasp, the more it struggles to get away."

"I must find her." Edouard grabbed a lantern. He did not have time to stand talking. Why did women try to talk everything into the grave when a man could be *doing* something?

"You will." Mama nodded. "And I will wait up with warm blankets and hot coffee."

Edouard set out with Papa and Jacques to the bayou's edge. *Oh, my sweet Josée, I am so sorry to have caused you pain. Please, bon Dieu, do not take her away from me.*

Chapter 9

A pirogue. The boat smelled of fish, but at the moment Josée could not think of a better thing to find. She did not know whose boat it was or how it had come to be in her path in the water. She tore the encumbering skirt from the bodice and leaned onto the side of the pirogue. With a heave, she swung her legs in their waterlogged pantaloons onto the floor of the boat.

She was out of the water, no longer feeling at its mercy as the rain drummed down. In the dark, she reached around to see if she could find an oar or even a pole she could use to maneuver to the shore. Nothing.

Battered by rain, Josée hunkered in the bottom of the pirogue and cried.

A wild thought struck her. *You could float away to the next town. Start over. . . .* She could go far away and teach in a school. *Stop it.*

Acadians, with their language, were not welcome everywhere. If she stayed among her people, Edouard would find her. Did she want to be found? *Oui, except. . .*

Le bon Dieu had let her marry Edouard. If He was all-wise and all-knowing, He knew this would happen, this fiasco with Celine. Josée found no joy in that knowledge. Despite their troubles and childish disagreements, she had begun to look forward to her future with Edouard. Until now.

What had happened with Edouard and Celine? She could remember seeing Celine about to kiss him. She closed her eyes and turned on her side to keep the pelting rain from hitting her eyelids. *Think harder.* Edouard. He'd had his hands on Celine's shoulders, his arms straight out in front of him.

He'd been trying to hold her away.

Josée sat up straight at the realization then screamed when a drape of Spanish moss touched her neck. She slapped at the air around her head and yanked the end of some moss from whatever tree she had passed under. The coarse, fuzzy moss made a shawl to block out the chill. Wind moaned in the trees as the storm roared on. She did not know how long she lay there in the dark, begging le bon Dieu to let the storm end.

Bone-jarring shivers set in as Josée recalled her anger at Edouard. Tonight she had not let him explain himself, but when had she ever let him speak? She always wanted him to listen. She realized she needed to apologize. She huddled down in the pirogue to find relief from the storm's chill.

The wind and rain lessened, and Josée sat up again and squinted through the darkness. She would never tell a scary tale to the younger LeBlancs again, should she ever get the chance to tell them another story.

A rustling, close at the edge of the bayou made her freeze, yet her pulse hammered in her throat.

※

Edouard held the lantern aloft and his rifle over his shoulder. Papa and even Jacques tromped along farther down the bayou and called out for Josée. But the rushing water and occasional clap of thunder covered up the sound of their voices.

He would find her. Not Papa, and especially not Jacques.

Josée was probably frightened, cold, and unsure of where she was. Edouard refused to think of the water claiming her like it had claimed a child one spring. He would not imagine a gator dragging her under in the dark. That had happened to him before, and even with daylight shining into the muddy waters, Edouard had felt like he was dying. He had been strong enough to fight the animal off and get away. Josée was not.

Le bon Dieu would take care of her. Edouard refused to believe that God would turn his life upside down with a wife only to rip her away from him when he learned to love her. The darkness did not scare him, because he knew this bayou well.

Then Edouard stopped a dozen paces or so from the bayou's edge. Shallow water from the brimming bayou swirled over his boot tops. He thought he heard a scream.

"Josée!" He ran, spraying up water that sparkled in the lantern's light.

Edouard saw her inside a pirogue tilted against the stump of a cypress. A gator growled, mere footsteps away from her, likely disturbed by the water and a pirogue drifting into his shallows.

"Edouard!" She squinted at him where she hunched in the pirogue, just beyond the circle of the yellow light. Then she glanced into the shadows. He saw her reaching for a broken-off cypress branch, thick as a man's leg and just as long.

"Don't move!"

She grasped the branch with both hands, not taking her gaze off the gator. The animal's tail started to curl. Edouard took a step toward them.

"*Ooo-eee!* Brother Gator!" He moved the lantern in an arc, hoping the gator would turn this way. "I am here! Come, fight me! It will be more to your liking."

"No, Edouard!" Josée crept from the pirogue as the gator turned to face him. The gator's head cocked to one side, as if it were unsure of whom to approach first.

Edouard set the lantern down on the nearest patch of grass that peeked over the water. "Josée, don't move." He readied his rifle. When he moved his foot, he kicked something solid. He glanced down. The lantern had fallen onto its side.

In a flash, the gator came for him. Josée screamed like a wild woman. Edouard fell onto the mud. The gator whipped its tail around and clubbed him with it. Gasping for breath, Edouard reached for his gun. He glimpsed Josée, hitting the gator with her cypress branch as if she were beating a rug.

The gator whipped its tail again, knocking Josée to the ground, before the beast fled to the water and disappeared.

Edouard crawled to Josée, who had rolled onto her side. "We were more than he wanted to fight with tonight."

She nodded, her normally sun-browned skin pale by lantern light. She sat up and wrapped her arms around her waist. Tears streamed down her cheeks along with the rain.

"*Mon amour*, I am so sorry." He reached for Josée, pulled her onto his lap, and held her while she cried. Even with her matted hair and torn clothing, he thought her beautiful.

"I'm sorry, too." She leaned back and caressed his face. "I didn't mean to fall in and worry everyone. I was going home, and then this wagon came, and—"

"*Shh.*" He placed his hand over her mouth, a mouth he very much wanted to kiss. But he would wait until they were back inside the cabin and warm once again. "Let us thank le bon Dieu for saving us and go home." After signaling to Papa and Jacques with a shot from his rifle, Edouard picked up the lantern, and they started on their way.

❦

Josée never wanted to let him go. She did not know how far they walked through the night to get to the cabin. She waved at Papa LeBlanc and Jacques, who headed to the big house. Edouard told them to tell Mama LeBlanc that *he* would take care of Josée.

He whisked her into the cabin and lit the fire while Josée slipped out of her wet clothes and into her chemise. Her breath caught in her throat. When they had left for the fai do do, she knew they had grown closer, in spite of their bickering like rooster and hen. Tonight, safe at home, her stomach quivered at the thought.

"Warmer?" Edouard approached with a blanket.

"I'm better now." She tried not to let him see her shiver.

Edouard took her hand. "I am sorry about what happened earlier. I did not realize it was Celine under that tree. . . ." He glanced at the fire, and Josée made herself wait for him to continue.

"Then she kept comin' towards me. I had to hold her off like a gator. I was trying to get Mama or someone else to help her, and then you appeared." He pulled the blanket around her shoulders.

"I am sorry that I did not let you explain. I only knew how bitter it must taste for one's heart to break—"

He fairly crushed her in an embrace and gave her a kiss that she never wanted to end. *This* was what she had longed for while out in the darkened waters. The shelter of her husband's arms and knowing he loved her with his whole heart. Edouard kissed her again, something she knew she'd never tire of now that she knew what a kiss was like.

They sat before the fire and shared the blanket. Edouard poured coffee for them, and Josée sipped hers at first. Then she hurried and burnt her tongue, so she waited until the brew cooled.

"Edouard, I must ask you something. What did you mean earlier, when you said le bon Dieu saved you?"

"When you were missing, I was angry at the thought of losing you. I do not always understand you, but you are my world now." His eyes glittered in the firelight. "Then I realized I had been wrong ag'in, as I had been about Celine. When I lost her, I thought I had lost my world and had no reason for joie de vivre. Not that I love you less than I once loved her, but I hope to love you better, my sweet Josée, and love our bon Dieu most of all."

"He is good to us, isn't He?" Josée ventured another sip. "Even with the bad that has happened, we can trust Him to watch over us."

"That is true."

Josée set the cup on the hearth. She stroked the scar on Edouard's cheek with one finger and shook her head. "I also meant to say, when I had time to think on that bayou, I realized you were doing nothing except trying to keep her away from you. I grew so angry because I knew how you had loved her a long time ago. I should have known how you truly felt now, though, because of how you held me on your lap on the way to the fai do do."

Then she stopped talking, because Edouard covered her lips with his. After the kiss, which ended too soon, she sat there, saying nothing.

"Well, that's one way to quiet you." His dark eyes twinkled.

She smiled at him. "In that case, mon amour, I'll make sure I always have something to say."

Epilogue

Josée sat back on her heels after pulling a handful of weeds from her garden and watched her *enfants* playing in the sun. Francois and Mathilde giggled and clapped. Francois, happy and singing; Mathilde, quieter like her papa. They kept their mama busy.

Edouard had been gone for three days on a gator hunt. Josée touched her growing stomach. Another bébé to feed soon, but le bon Dieu would take care of everything. That, and help Edouard get a good gator to trade for more lumber. The bayou cabin seemed to be shrinking.

She hoisted herself to her feet, not as easily as a few weeks ago. "Children, let's eat dinner, and then I will tell you stories."

They clapped again then grabbed each other's hands and ran ahead of her to the cabin.

Josée made them wash their hands before they ate. A familiar journal lay on the table. She would teach her children to read and write and love the language of their people. For now, her time of writing in this book was over. Josée no longer needed the recipes to help her remember. Edouard was starting to get a bit round like Papa from her cooking.

She touched the book's cover. One day, another LeBlanc might read these pages and learn from her as well as Capucine.

"Bon soir, *journale*," she whispered. Josée rose and placed the journal with the other books in the trunk to keep until her children were old enough.

The sound of a pirogue moving over the waters made Josée look toward the doorway. The children scrambled to their feet and ran.

"Papa, it's Papa! He's home!"

Josée moved as quickly as her feet would let her. The familiar face and form she knew and loved so well came into view. "Oui, he's home."

Lynette Sowell has had a love affair with words since childhood. The author of more than 23 fiction titles, she's also the managing editor of her local newspaper. Lynette was born in Massachusetts, raised on the Eastern Shore of Maryland, but makes her home on the doorstep of the Texas hill country with her husband, their Texas heeler, and a duo of cats. She loves traveling, reading, cooking, watching movies, spoiling her three granddaughters, and is always up for a Texas road trip.

BUTTON STRING
BRIDE

by Cathy Marie Hake

Dedication

Dedicated to two of my greatest joys,
Kelly Eileen and Colin James.
May you each wait on the Lord
and seek His choice for you—in life and in love.
Whatever joys or trials lie ahead on the path,
walk with the Lord and let Him light the way.

Love,
Mom

Chapter 1

M iss Davis, the trail master ordered us to combine wagons if we want to continue on to Oregon. Otherwise, they'll leave us behind when we reach Fort Laramie." Ethan Cole shifted his weight more firmly into the heels of his scuffed cowhide boots as he broke the news. "We'll try to make the best of it. A single lady like you shouldn't be stranded among all of the soldiers, and to be perfectly frank, I need help with my young'uns."

Miss Davis wet her lips and whispered, "I'm willing to watch your children, sir. I just don't see how you can do more..."

From the way her voice trailed off, Ethan knew she didn't understand exactly what the order entailed. He cast a quick look to the side. Banner Laswell had come along to lend the soothing support of her presence. She stayed silent, so he softened his voice and strove to break the news gently. "The plan is for you to put your essentials in my wagon. We're to leave your rig behind." Every speck of color seeped out of Miss Davis's cheeks, and he feared she might keel over from the revelation. Ethan cupped her elbow and coaxed her to sit on a nearby log.

Other than knowing her ma was the first to die on their trek due to a snakebite and her pa's heart gave out a few nights ago, Ethan knew virtually nothing about Charity Davis. He'd been too busy with his own troubles to mind anyone else's business. For a few moments, he silently studied her and tried to take her measure. Most of the women set out on the trip in simple, full gowns made from calico feed sacks; but quality bolt goods draped artistically over Miss Davis's hoops, and her outfit boasted more frills and doodads than any gown he'd ever seen. Small and fine-boned, she looked hopelessly out of place in this wilderness. All it took was a bit of bad news, and she was nigh unto swooning. Ethan barely disguised his grimace. He feared he'd been saddled with a temperamental, helpless female.

"I'll mind your children." She wrapped a fancy shawl about herself more tightly. "If you hunt for us, I'll do all of the cooking and still keep my own wagon. Wouldn't that suffice?"

Something in her voice tugged at him. *Poor gal. She's lost her folks, and now she's losing everything else.* Sympathy replaced his concerns. It felt wrong to hover over a vulnerable woman, so Ethan hunkered down to stay at eye level. "Miss Davis, we set out knowing each wagon had to be self-sufficient. Betwixt the two of us, we can't drive both wagons, care for all of our beasts, do our fair share of guard duty, and mind the kids. By leaving behind one wagon, we'd halve several obligations. We're both in a fix, and the council ruled we either join up or fall out. I can't go on without your help."

Though he paused to allow her an opportunity to speak, she said nothing. Ethan cleared his throat and added, "I know it's an awkward situation, but I'll bedroll beneath the wagon, and you can sleep inside with the kids."

Tears glossed her wide blue eyes, but she didn't shed a single one. He had to hand it to her. Though both shocked and embarrassed, she didn't indulge in an emotional show. Instead, she looked at Banner and quavered, "I can't pack tonight. It's my turn to stand guard."

Banner quietly offered, "One of the other men is covering for you tonight. I know you're heartsore, but Mr. Cole is a fine man. The council felt it was for the best. For what it's worth, I agree."

"I see." Charity smoothed back a strand of fiery hair with an unsteady hand. "Please let me know who took my guard shift. I don't want to be beholden to anyone."

Ethan grabbed her wrist and turned her palm toward the flickering campfire. No calluses dared mar her dainty hand, but a prime crop of new blisters showed she'd done hard work—man's work—in the past few days. "Do you have salve for these?"

"Yes, sir." She slowly pulled her hand free and rose. "Please pardon me. I have a lot to do before morning."

"Best thing you could do right now is turn in for the night, Miss Davis. The train is staying put tomorrow so some of the men can go hunting. We'll have a full day to do what needs doing." He paused then softly added, "Come morning, you'll see the wisdom of this."

She gave him a woeful smile and shrugged. Tired, aghast, and heartbroken as she was, he figured he ought to be glad Miss Davis wasn't sobbing or pitching a fit. *Poor thing's so shaken, she probably can't react,* he thought. He offered her his arm. "I'll walk you to your wagon."

"I thank you for the offer, but I need to be alone." After whispering those timid words, she fleetingly squeezed Banner's hand then walked toward the edge of the campfire's light to reach her wagon. This would be the last night she'd spend in it.

Ethan watched her go. Banner Laswell filled a chipped enamel cup with scorched coffee and handed it to him. "Don't fret. She's got a lot of polish, but that gal is pure hickory straight through."

"No one told me her age," he said grimly. "She looks young."

"Small but not young," Banner corrected. "Charity's nineteen. Don't be fooled by appearances. She's shouldering heavy grief, but she still managed to keep up with us all. Give her the night to let this news settle. Come mornin', things will be better."

Banner's words echoed in his ears the next morning. *Things will be better. . . .* It was going to be a rough day. Wagons measured all of forty inches across and ten to fourteen feet long at the base. The sides flared upward to permit ease of movement and make them float boat-style if fording a river became necessary. He'd built his to the maximum specifications, so he had a bit of room in his for Miss Davis's things. Still, he reckoned she might be unreasonable about wanting to haul too much. He whispered a prayer for wisdom then rapped on the side of her wagon.

She peered down at him. The moisture in her eyes didn't bode well at all, but he acted like he didn't notice. "Good morning, Miss Davis."

"I've started sorting through things." She gingerly handed him a brand-spanking-new Colt patent rifle. "Careful. It's loaded. Banner said you're a crack shot, so I presume you'll want all of the ammunition and arms."

"I'll bag you some fine meals with this, miss. Before you start handing more down to me, it might be best if you come look at my wagon. It'll help us decide what to take and what to leave." He added on, "Gracie Adams said she'd watch the kids for us today, but they're hoping to meet you first."

A timid smile lit her face. "I'd like that. Thank you."

Ethan set aside the rifle and reached up to help her out. The tentative way she set her hands on his shoulders told him this gal wasn't accustomed to a man's touch. He braced her tiny waist and swept her earthward. Yards of petticoats whispered—a sound he'd just about forgotten after three years of being widowed. She'd left off her hoops and donned an apron today. Did that indicate she possessed a streak of practicality? He sure hoped so. A hint of flowers swirled in the air, and since she barely came to his chin, he realized the fragrance came from her hair. In daylight, the red and gold strands blended together like a fine piece of carved cedar. Half a dozen faint freckles sprinkled across her finely chiseled nose. A fetching pink suffused her cheeks, and she shyly dropped her lashes. "Thank you kindly, sir."

He picked up the rifle and fought the urge to caress the sleek walnut stock. He'd seen fine Colts like this in a mercantile, but they were far too costly for a simple carpenter to own. "I'll pull my wagon alongside yours in a while. It'll make transferring things easier."

She gave him a perplexed look. "I thought I was just to bring essentials. Food, clothing, my Bible, and a quilt."

Ethan settled his free hand on a wheel spoke and looked into eyes bluer than the sky. Her unwavering acceptance of the necessary sacrifices came as a complete surprise. "Miss Davis, I'll do my best to help you take as much as possible. You're going to need more than that to set up a home once we reach Oregon. We'll work on it."

Charity thanked him, but she tried to quell her hope. She hadn't yet seen his wagon and didn't know if he had any space at all. She walked beside him to his rig. Two bedraggled children sat on the seat. Both had their daddy's deep brown hair and eyes. From the way the little girl wiggled, Charity knew she was excited. Charity opened her arms, and the tike leaped at once. After all of her grief, an armful of love felt heaven-sent. She cuddled the waif and looked up at the boy. "Hello."

"This is Tad." Mr. Cole set the rifle under the wagon seat and lifted down his son. "He's eight. This is Catherine, but we call her Cricket. She's three. Kids, this is Miss Davis. You are to obey her at all times."

"Yes, Pa," they said in unison.

"We'll get along just fine," Charity declared. She shifted Cricket onto one hip and touched the button string around the girl's neck. "You sure have a pretty collection of charmglass started. My gracious, what a big girl you are!"

Mr. Cole took his daughter and unlooped the string over her head. "She has thirty-one buttons already. Cricket, I told you you're not to wear this 'cept for Sunday worship. If you lose the buttons, you'll never collect enough to be a married lady when you grow up!"

"Gotta have a thousand buttons to marry a beau," Tad said. "How big is your button string, Miss Davis?"

"If you'd like, I'll show it to you later, Tad. It has 982 buttons." Like so many of her friends back home, Charity's parents started her collection on the very day she was born. An exquisite assortment of buttons, all carefully corded on her string, lay nestled in her trunk. She'd earned buttons for spelling bees and gotten them as gifts. She'd traded with friends, too. . .all with the understanding that someday a very special man would follow the custom and give her the last button—the thousandth—then ask for her hand in marriage.

"Son," Mr. Cole said, "we've got plenty to do. You take Cricket and go off to Gracie Adams. Take the milk with you."

Charity turned her attention to the wagon. She knew Mr. Cole was a carpenter. He'd made his own wagon, and folks said it was the finest in the train. The tar seams promised it would be watertight. He patted the side and said, "I'm hoping to fasten one of your water barrels here and balance it with a flour barrel on the other side. We'll try to work in a fair share of your goods. Let me lift you in so we can get to work."

Charity suspected he tried hard to be gentle. The breadth of his shoulders and the strength in his hands made it clear he was a powerful man. Brawn like his would mean protection—something she appreciated after the last few days of feeling terribly vulnerable and alone. The fact that he kept a sheathed jackknife on his belt instead of wearing a holstered pistol reinforced the fact that this man, though reputed to be a marksman, preferred preparation to violence. He followed her into the wagon and winced.

"I didn't pay much mind. I fear it's a mess."

"We've both had more important things to tend." Clothes cluttered the floor. A trunk and wooden crates lined the walls. Food storage looked haphazard, at best. A lumpy straw mattress rested atop a square of wood. When he shoved the ticking out of the way and flipped up a hinged lid, Charity's nose twitched.

"Cricket is too tiny to sleep outside. The kids sleep safely on this makeshift bed, and I built storage boxes below it. The other side has my tools. Over here, there's a section for each kid." Two sections each held a few things, but the third lay conspicuously empty. "That space was my nephew, Sam's. My sister-in-law, Lydia, wanted to make a new life for her and little Sam, but she didn't bargain on travel being so hard. They turned back with the Wilsons and Chroners when we reached Chimney Rock. Things fell apart when she left."

"I'm not managing any better on my own," Charity confessed. "I've had to have men see to my oxen and do guard duty for me."

"We need each other, Miss Davis. I give you my word, I'll provide as best I can and do all it takes to keep you and the kids safe. I know you must feel uneasy, but I'll continue to observe the same proprieties I did when Lydia was with me."

At least he was sensitive to the more delicate aspects of combining their wagons. His words gave the reassurance she'd prayed for. Charity promised, "I'll tend the children diligently and do my best for you. Would you mind if I worked in here a bit so I can determine what essentials to bring along and how to combine our food?"

"Not at all."

Charity knelt and surveyed the contents of the children's boxes. She rocked back on her heels and thought for a moment. She needed to say some things, but they weren't easy subjects to bring up. The last thing she wanted to do was offend him.

"I can see you're struggling to be polite. We may as well speak plainly between ourselves, Miss Davis. Tiptoeing around is liable to cause us more problems than being outright."

"Your daughter is still young. She's not gotten up enough at night." She didn't want to dwell on the problem and chagrin him, so she hastened to solve the difficulty. "We need to dispose of the mattress and bring one of mine over. The quilts are in need of attention as well. I have a length of waterproof gutta-percha we can put under her in the future."

He nodded curtly. "My sister-in-law took the length we kept under Sam and Cricket. I should have thought about that." Relief mingled with embarrassment. This gal was already seeing to the housekeeping and food supplies. Could it be that God had blessed him with a truly remarkable travel partner?

"With everything else we need to do, I'm not sure salvaging the quilts is a good use of time. Do you object to leaving some of them behind and bringing more of yours along?"

"I have plenty. As long as you don't care. . ."

"The only one I'm particular about is the wedding ring quilt. My Justine made it our first year, and I hold it dear."

"I'll see to it."

Ethan waited at the end of the wagon while she separated the quilts. He'd posed the question tentatively, but after it was out, Ethan was glad he'd asked. She actually almost smiled. He should have realized how hard it was for her to give up most of her possessions. Women were, as a rule, quite proud of the quilts they spent hundreds of hours making.

He looked at her ruffled day gown and glanced at the elegant way she'd styled her hair. It stretched his imagination to picture her cleaning, cooking, and minding the kids for more than a day or two. "Miss Davis, the trail is only going to get harder. It's best you know from the get-go that I'm a man who isn't fancy in the least. I reckon things are going to be difficult betwixt us because you're a lady, and I'm a common man who lives by the sweat of his brow and the swing of a hammer."

She gave him the sweetest smile. "I cannot imagine better company. Jesus was a carpenter, too."

Chapter 2

E than Cole grinned. "You mentioned your Bible earlier. Am I to take it you're a sister in the Lord, Miss Davis?"

"Yes." The way he phrased that let her know he was a believer, too. "Undoubtedly, our faith will ease things between us." She drew a breath to bolster her gumption. "Mr. Cole, my father was about your size. You should go through his things and have first call. I don't mean you any offense; but you've been without a wife, and my father had two women to care for him. His breeches and shirts were all newly made for the trip and should last you a long while. Whatever fits, you're free to claim."

"That's very generous of you, Miss Davis." His compassionate brown gaze didn't waver. Between his neatly trimmed mustache and beard, a warm smile tilted his lips. "In truth, I could use a few things."

"While I see to combining our sugar and cornmeal supplies, maybe you could go through Daddy's things. There's a crate holding his ammunition and pistols, too. I'm sure you'll want those."

He stepped over a box and went to the front of the wagon. "If you stay put, I'll roll this rig next to yours so we can set to work."

As he got the oxen from the rope-fence enclosure and hitched them, Charity cast out the mattress and three spoiled quilts. Once done with that, she untied the edges of the double-layered, homespun wagon cover and rolled up the sides. Air wafted through as she carefully examined each article of clothing. If space permitted, Charity quickly determined to bring along more of Mama's clothing. The fabric in one of the wool skirts would yield a couple pairs of britches for Tad, and Cricket needed flannel nightgowns and another frock or two. *Poor motherless children!*

Charity's father bought whatever he felt necessary. A restless man, he'd come just for the sake of adventure. After Mama died, they discussed going back, but Charity declined. He had wanderlust, and she knew he would never be happy being tied down. Luckily, his inheritance had been enough to support them in whatever his whim happened to be. He'd spared no expense in outfitting them well with clothing, food, and trade goods.

Ethan Cole, on the other hand, was a hardworking man of meager means. He'd laid by modest food supplies but obviously counted more on hunting than Daddy had. His clothing had seen far better days, but he'd gotten a new set for both of his children. The way he prized the quilt meant he cherished his wife's memory, so beneath that rugged exterior, he had a tender heart.

Charity began to tidy the chaos and assess his goods. Clearly, his sister-in-law had taken food and supplies without regard to how it robbed him of essentials. *More soap, a washboard...* Charity mentally listed basic things to bring along.

He drove his wagon so close to hers, they nearly touched. She let out a small sigh of relief. It would make her job far easier if she could simply shove things across.

While they'd been gone, Banner and her oldest daughter pulled the heavy cotton bonnet off Charity's wagon and folded it. "You'll need this to make a tent to live in once we reach Oregon," Banner said as she pulled a strip of twine tightly to make the bundle smaller. "You two take a bit of time to work out some details, then I'll be over with breakfast."

"Much obliged, ma'am," Ethan said as he set the brake. "We'll certainly work up an appetite today." Banner left, and he climbed into her wagon and stood by Miss Davis. In the short time he'd been gone, she'd worked wonders in his wagon. "I'll take the oxen back. Is there anything you want me to do before I go?"

She bit her lip and surveyed things. In an uncertain tone, she asked, "Is there any chance we could take along my highboy? I'm using it as a pantry, and I could add your supplies to it."

Ethan studied the walnut piece. *A master craftsman must have spent weeks making this.* He reverently ran his hand across the satiny finished surface, clearly appreciating the fine fit of each drawer and the exquisite carving of a ribbon. He thought for a moment then nodded. "It'll actually free up some floor space if we empty a few bags and crates into it. I'll need to counterbalance the weight by putting another water barrel out on the other side."

A few men came over to help, and the job was done in a flash. They also moved Charity's trunk across and set it in the corner. One of the men said something under his breath to Ethan, cast a quick look at her, and then left.

Charity started tucking food tins and bags of beans into the highboy. Ethan came alongside her. "Miss Davis, we need to discuss a few matters before we go on. I could see by their mark the Studebaker brothers made your schooner. They're fine wainwrights, and it's a well-built rig."

She stopped working and faced him. "Mr. Cole, even to my uneducated eye, your wagon reflects remarkable workmanship. Due to your talent, it has several extras my wagon can't match."

He felt a surge of pleasure at her words. "It's mighty nice of you to notice. Jed Turvey's getting by with his old farm wagon, but I doubt it'll last the trip. He asked how much you want for your rig."

Her eyes widened. "Of course I'd much rather see one of our fellow families get it than leave it behind. Please tell him he's more than welcome to have it."

"We'll get back to that in a minute." Conducting business with a woman made him feel awkward. Ethan took a deep breath and broached the next subject. "Between us, we have ten oxen. Providing water for all of them will become impossible. Folks are asking about them. I'm of a mind to sell the extra."

She knelt and started to sort through other bags to see what they contained.

"Daddy knew nothing about livestock, so I know full well yours are superior. Why don't you choose my best pair to keep and give the other four away?"

"Miss Davis, you can't afford such a generosity. You're going to need every last cent when you reach Oregon. I helped bury your pa. The two hundred dollars from his pocket won't last you very long once you have to set yourself up again."

She dipped her head and tried to blink back tears. "I thank you for your concern, but Daddy didn't leave me destitute."

He made a wordless sound of comfort and squeezed her hand. Neither of them moved for a few moments. She finally took a deep breath to gather her composure. When she looked at him, he tenderly wiped away her tears from her soft cheek with a brush of his thumb. "Mind you, I'm not asking for any specific number, but did your pa really leave you so you aren't too strapped?"

She swallowed hard and whispered, "That was his carrying money. I have more." She ignored his sigh of relief. "Please make the oxen a thank-you gift to the Washingtons for helping me these last days. Rick already lost an ox to the rogue log in the river and didn't replace it at Fort Kearny, so I know money is tight for them. My conscience would trouble me if I took his money—especially since I'm in his debt. As for Mr. Turvey—he's using that old wagon because a new prairie schooner was too expensive. They floated across the river instead of paying the five dollars for the ferry, and I overheard Leticia mention most of their things got soaked. I can't think of anything more shameful or selfish than to deny them a sound schooner."

Ethan shook his head. "I won't argue about the wagon. If the Turveys don't take it, it'll be left behind. Oxen are a different story. An ox costs twenty-five dollars back at Independence. By the time we get to Fort Hall, one will be worth forty, maybe even fifty. Men can't accept something that valuable as a gift."

She lifted her hands in a helpless gesture. "I'd be delighted if the Washingtons took a pair. If pride is at stake, maybe you could charge them five dollars. Certainly no more. Since your oxen will be carrying me and my belongings, it's only fair that you determine the terms of what happens to the other pair. You must promise one thing though: you'll keep that money to help pay for river crossings and such. I fully expect to cover those expenses since you're kind enough to take me on."

His voice went harsh. "I don't accept charity!"

She arched her brow. "Oh, yes, you have. Charity's my name, and you've taken me on." Sensing she'd dented his pride, she then curled her hand around one of the prairie schooner's riblike bows. "Please, Mr. Cole, let's not quibble. I'm stranded without your help, so I'm thankful you're willing to let me ride with your family. If I cannot contribute, I'll feel as if *I'm* accepting charity. I'd feel so very wrong. There is so little I have to offer. You must accept what I am able to give toward our eventual success."

"We'll see about that."

Charity pursed her lips. "We have work to do, Mr. Cole."

He rubbed his beard. "We're going to be shoulder to shoulder for the next few months. This formal business strikes me as being ridiculous. I'd rather have you call me by name. I'm Ethan."

"And you'll address me as Charity?"

"Only by your leave." She nodded, and he looked from wagon to wagon then jumped down. "Fine, then. I won't be gone long. Don't go lifting anything heavy."

During the night, Charity had already repacked her trunk. Dear friend that she was, Banner sacrificed her sleep and had come to help. They'd gone through Charity's belongings and even winnowed through her mama's things. Charity held up fairly well until they came across a muslin-wrapped length of pure white satin in the bottom of Mama's trunk. Carefully included in the folds was Mama's wedding veil. As Charity began to weep, Banner made a soft hushing sound. She simply placed the bolt at the very bottom of Charity's trunk and started layering in clothes. "Some dreams you don't give up on. Your mama left you that. It goes along."

Charity felt relieved she'd already seen to the intimate details of choosing clothing and packing her personal belongings. She'd have been mortified to have Ethan watch her do so. When he came back, he pitched right in, helping her make decisions; but to his credit, he didn't get nosy. He cleverly determined their washtubs were just an inch different in diameter, so he nestled them together. "We'll both have tubs when we reach Oregon!"

At one point, he caught Charity tracing her finger over the dainty flowered edge of a teacup. "Charity, we're going to have to leave some duplicate things behind. Space is limited. It would gall me if you thought I'd arranged to take you on so I'd have your high-class wares, but since you'll be doing the cooking, it's only fair you keep your better household goods."

She gave him a shaky smile. "You've been most generous. I sensed your reticence last night when you told me the news, and I know you're not a grasping man. Naturally, we both worry about having to replace things once we reach Willamette, so I'll do my best to fit as much in as I can without weighing down the wagon."

He helped her out and watched for a moment as she opened the cook boxes hanging from the tail ends of both wagons. Skillets, dishes, and towels filled them. She whispered, "Please go look through Daddy's trunk while I keep busy here."

When she'd finished with the dishes, Charity climbed back into the wagon. "Can you make use of Daddy's things?"

Ethan looked at her for a minute before answering. "First, sit down."

"What's wrong?" She hesitantly sat on a barrel.

"I need to know: Will it bother you to see me in your pa's clothes or using his things?"

"I've saved many of Mama's clothes to wear myself."

"That didn't answer the question, Charity. They are two entirely different situations. Life has been hard enough on you lately," he said softly. "I wouldn't want to add to your grief."

She looked at him. *He has such kind eyes. A kind heart, too, if he's willing to forgo having clothes he really needs just to spare my feelings.* She felt compelled to return that consideration, and in realizing it, no longer felt the misgivings that flitted through her mind earlier when she'd originally made the offer. "Daddy would want you to have them. I'll try to think of it as him passing his mantle of protection on to you."

The smile on his face made her decision worthwhile.

"Gal, I think we're going to make this work."

Chapter 3

Smoke, food, and coffee. Every morning, Ethan awakened to those same scents; but for a solid week they had come from other wagons, not his own. He'd farmed the children off for breakfast and satisfied himself with reheated mush. The aroma of coffee wafted over and teased him. Ethan burrowed in for a second more before he opened his eyes and realized Charity was up already. He hiked off to the shrubs then ran his comb through his hair and beard. By the time he returned, Charity was ready to dish up his breakfast. Lydia hadn't been half as attentive. He'd needed to awaken her each morning.

"Do you take anything in your coffee?" Charity asked as she handed him a steaming mug.

"I like it black. Thanks. It smells wonderful."

She flipped three flapjacks onto a plate, added bacon, and passed it over. "When do the children wake up?"

"Anytime now." He wolfed down the food and grinned broadly. "Mmmm!" Folks had been kind enough to provide meals for them yesterday so they could finish combining their wagons. This was his first sample of her cooking, and it more than pleased him. "Someone did a fine job of teaching you to cook."

She flipped a flapjack and caught it midair in the heavy cast iron skillet. "Miss Amanda's had a French chef."

"A fancy finishing school?" When she nodded, his heart sank. She didn't just have some of the expensive doodads and trappings of money. She'd been reared in privilege. That would put even greater barriers between them. He muttered wryly, "Imagine that. Finishing schools hold a course on flapjacks."

Charity arched a brow. "Not precisely. I liked the chef. Much to Miss Amanda's dismay, I'd slip off to the kitchen in my spare time. I learned how to make crepes first then several other dishes. I've had to adjust a few recipes for the trail."

Most of the day, her words played over and over in Ethan's mind. Charity was a lady, born and bred. She'd been trained in all of the finer things. Gals like her were social butterflies. Pretty, bright, and spoiled. Right now she was playing at a new game. Would she soon tire of minding the kids and cooking? He didn't want to judge her wrongly, but he needed to evaluate the matter carefully. His kids' welfare was at stake.

Her name certainly fit. She'd virtually given away four oxen and a wagon yesterday, and her pa's clothing—everything from shirt to boots—fit Ethan perfectly. She had a bit over two hundred dollars; he, on the other hand, had forty measly dollars to his name. Ethan worried about the finances, but there was no way around it. A man did his best and trusted in the Lord. His family had always been blessed with their daily bread, and the move to more fertile ground would ensure that it would continue. It also meant that there would be some mighty lean years ahead until things were established.

At midday he pried Cricket away from Charity's side and tucked her in atop the new feather bed Charity brought along. Every last thing Charity owned was grand. To her credit, she'd never once turned up her nose at his things.

Goodness only knew, Charity was blessed with more than anyone he'd ever known. Still, it tugged at his pride a bit when he took off Cricket's sunbonnet and spied a rose-embossed pink satin ribbon in her hair. She smelled dainty, and her skin didn't have any of the little red, rough patches it usually did since Charity used her own violet-scented glycerin soap to bathe his daughter last night then shared her skin cream, much to Cricket's delight. He'd never had money to buy such fripperies.

❧

It took no time at all before Tad and Charity were thick as thieves. They sat by the fire together and looked at her button string. She'd praised Tad for his new skill at multiplication and let him make marks in the dirt to practice ciphering. *Nine hundred eighty-two. Eighteen to go. Who is the lucky man who will give her the thousandth button and become her husband?*

Charity walked most of the day, but she'd driven the wagon for a short while this morning as he rode out with a few of the men to hunt. Ethan had taken along the new Colt rifle with her blessing and even lent her mare to Steven Adams since his gelding had gone lame. Charity congratulated them warmly on their successful hunt, but she'd turned three shades of green and disappeared when he unsheathed his knife and started to dress and butcher the pair of pronghorns he'd bagged.

A few days later, Tad caught a fine pair of trout. Ethan happened upon Charity as she valiantly tried to gut them. At first, he thought she was simply inept, but then he noted how pale she'd grown, so he simply took them from her and finished the chore. "I'm sorry," she said thickly.

"Gal, no one can do everything. If it makes you queasy to dress out meat, I'll handle it. All you had to do was say so."

She kept her hands clasped in front of her and stared out at the horizon. "I'm so gutless, we ought to serve me for supper."

"You're too hard on yourself." He handed back the fish. As she walked away, Ethan marveled at her. It was the only time he'd seen the fancy lady balk at anything.

❧

The rhythm of trail life continued on—rising before dawn, hitching up the oxen, eating, and traveling until midday. Nooning break for man and beast, then dusty travel until they reached the spot their scout designated for evening. Wagons circled, supper eaten, and men holding watch over the camp and livestock by night. Charity stepped in beat to that rhythm, but she sang in a different range. They tried to be mindful and adjust so harmony reigned. Still, for the first time in his life, Ethan felt discontented. He simply didn't measure up, and the glaring disparity between her polished ways and fine goods and his common holdings made it clear he was second-rate.

※

Charity knelt in the creek bed as she rinsed out the laundry. The cold water felt delicious after the heat and dust of the last several days. Farther down the creek, men watered the livestock. The captain of the wagon train strictly enforced the rules governing water usage. Whenever they reached a stream, water for drinking was taken from upstream. Once the drinking water was dipped out, folks could fish from upstream, too. Bathing and laundry was at midstream, and livestock drank from downstream. So far, no one had gotten cholera, so the rules seemed beneficial.

"Kids sure do get filthy, don't they?" Banner asked in a cheerful voice as she scrubbed the knees on her sons' britches.

"Yes," Charity agreed. She twisted Cricket's little nightgown to wring out a bit more water. It wouldn't be dry by nightfall, but the little girl could sleep in one of Mama's camisoles. Charity carefully rinsed the rest of the lye soap from each garment. "I'm not much cleaner than the children, though. I'm looking forward to finally washing my hair."

Leticia Turvey squinted at the horizon. "I reckon we'd better hang these things out to dry. I'm aching to take a swim myself, and the boys are so eager to hit the water, the menfolk will be hollering at us to hurry up."

All of the women laughed at the truth in that statement. The routine was practical enough: As the women did laundry, men repaired wagons, saw to the livestock, started fires, and strung temporary clotheslines. Once the women hung up the clothes, they'd take the small children back to the water, scrub them, and send them back to their daddies. The women bathed wearing their chemises for the sake of modesty. If the water was shallow, they helped each other rinse the soap from their hair. The men and boys swam last while the women fixed supper.

Charity hastened back to the fire so Tad and Ethan could have their turn. To her surprise, Ethan squatted on his heels by the fire. He had catfish sizzling in the pan. He glanced over his shoulder. "Go on ahead and comb out your hair. See if you can't dry it a bit with your towel. It's going to be cold tonight, and you don't want to catch a chill."

"Why, thank you." She did as he bade. The whole while she coaxed the tangles from her hair, Charity marveled at how thoughtful and capable Ethan was. Considering all of her misgivings and fears, things had turned out quite well so far.

Ethan bathed quickly after supper then warmed up with a cup of coffee before he took his turn at guard duty. As he came by on one of his passes, he spied Charity huddled by a lantern. He thought to come closer to see what was wrong but then saw her Bible. She faithfully read the Word each day—most often first thing upon rising. If circumstances prevented that, she made sure to find a time later. The Good Book said it was easier for a camel to fit through the eye of a needle than for a rich man to enter the kingdom of heaven. Ethan smiled to himself. The verse didn't say anything about a rich woman.

Later Ethan came around again. To his surprise, Charity was still up. She sat huddled in her shawl, close to the fire. Instead of banking it, she'd added a few more buffalo chips. Just as he turned toward her, she got up, went to the wagon, and lifted her arms. Cricket climbed down, and Charity carried her off a short ways. Ethan met them. "Here. I'll take her." He took Cricket and headed back to the wagon.

Rick Washington ambled toward him. "Your shift is over. Sleep well."

Cricket snuggled closely and lazily combed her fingers through his beard. "Daddy—pretty."

"Yes, princess, you are." He kissed her cheek.

"No, Daddy. See? Pretty." She patted the garment she wore. "Smells pretty, too."

Now that they were closer to the fire, he could see she was wearing a woman's beribboned chemise. It smelled of violets. Men tried their best to turn a blind eye to the small clothes women hung to dry on the laundry lines. As a decent, God-fearing man, he'd tried his hardest to ignore Charity's personal garments. He cleared his throat and made no comment.

Embarrassment colored Charity's voice as she murmured, "I washed Cricket's nightwear, so it was too wet for her tonight. I'll sew her a second gown soon."

"Fine. Night-night, Cricket." He gave his daughter a swift kiss and lifted her back into the wagon. Charity started to climb up the wheel spokes. "Hold it there." He cupped his hands around her tiny waist. "How many times am I going to have to tell you not to scramble up these things when I'm around to help you, gal? You're likely to catch your hem and fall. I'd hate to see you get hurt on account of foolish independence. You have to take back a bit of help for all the help that you give others. You aren't alone out here." He yanked her backward and set her on the ground in front of him. "Do you hear me?"

Tears glittered in her eyes, making him catch his breath. "Yes, I am. I am alone, and—" She clapped a hand over her mouth to capture a sob, spun away, and started to scramble into the wagon.

"Oh, Charity," he groaned. Ethan quickly grasped her waist and pulled her back to earth. He twisted her and clasped one arm around her back while using the other hand to cup her head to his chest.

Charity struggled for all of a few seconds then gave way to her tears. She flooded his shirt with her grief and clung to him like a drowning victim would. He murmured soft, comforting words. The cradle of his arms supported her when she sagged, then he scooped her up and still held her tightly.

Ethan remembered the soul-deep anguish of fresh grief and couldn't fathom the fragile woman in his arms had to shoulder two recent losses. Her sobs tore at him, made him long to lend her his consolation. Holding her made him feel both strong and tender. He gently swayed side to side until she calmed and almost fell asleep. As her damp lashes fluttered shut, he urged, "Go to sleep, honey-gal. Leave your sorrows behind. You'll never be alone again. I promise."

She whispered tearfully, "I'm s–sorry."

"You don't have a thing in the world to apologize for. Now go on to bed." He lifted her into the wagon and listened as she eased down beside Cricket. Satisfied she'd settled in, he went over to the fire and poured himself some coffee. A hand on his shoulder made him turn around. "Yeah, Jason?"

The captain of the wagon train tilted his head toward the Cole schooner. "She's been spoiling for that cry for a good long while. My missus saw her brooding by the fire and said she was due to fall apart. You did right by her."

"Can't do much of anything for her but pray. That poor gal has been through far too much, and you'd never guess it by watching her. She's. . ." He shrugged in want of words.

"She's quite a little woman," Jason said softly. He stayed silent for a time. Finally he pushed, "I'm going to ask, because I am responsible for her, too. Are you starting to have feelings for her?"

"What man in his right mind wouldn't? She's gentle as a spring rain and sweet as honey. My kids have taken to her instantly, and she changed us from a haphazard willy-nilly group back into a family."

"I'm asking about feelings that run deeper than gratitude."

"The way things are is more than enough for the present." Ethan tossed back the last of his coffee. "Charity is a fancy lady; I'm a rough man. Whatever I might feel isn't the issue. She deserves far better."

"Voices do carry. I heard you tell her she's not alone anymore."

Ethan winced. He'd revealed far too much when he'd uttered that pledge. "I was a fool to say so. I'll hope by the morning she takes that as a pledge of friendship. Peasants don't marry princesses."

Chapter 4

Everyone was road weary by the time they pulled into Fort Laramie. To their dismay, the scout announced they'd only stay overnight. "There's another train on our heels. If they get ahead of us, we'll have fouled water and lousy hunting. The council has voted to take Sublette's Cutoff to spare us more than a week of travel. That means we'll bypass Fort Bridger. This is your last stop to get supplies until we're through most of the mountains, so load up and be ready to go by first light."

Charity climbed into the wagon and reappeared a few minutes later. Ethan noted she'd changed her dress, combed her hair, and put on gloves. A reticule dangled from her wrist. "I'm ready."

"Not yet, you aren't," he said firmly. He needed to set matters straight first. "When we joined wagons, you had a bounty of supplies. Lydia took the lion's portion of my foodstuffs, but you brought a complete pantry, furnished plenty of extras. Expensive extras," he stressed. "Like those Edwards's preserved potatoes and all of the dried fruits and vegetables. There's not another wagon on our whole train that enjoys a fraction of our treats. I'll not have you spend one red cent on a thing."

Charity looked at him and raised her brows. "I seriously doubt you have much idea as to what we do or do not need, Ethan. Furthermore, I saw how you salvaged the main portion of the headboard to my bedstead and situated it beneath the mattress. If I had to have one made to match the highboy, it would cost a minor fortune. Whatever I spend is a pittance in comparison."

"Reasoning with you is hopeless," he snapped. Instead of escorting her to the post store, he turned and hastened ahead. Once he beat her there and placed his order, she'd be sensible enough to defer.

Ethan arrived before the crowd and grimly noted they'd posted a sign that placed limits on nearly everything. He'd assessed their supplies and decided on some basic items. As soon as he started ordering, Charity arrived. She walked directly up to him. "Mr. Cole, your partner asked that you buy the limits of everything and sent this." She held out four twenty-dollar gold double eagles. When he refused to accept them, she placed them on the counter and sashayed off. She'd given him almost half of her money! Ethan planned to serve her a healthy slice of his mind once they were in private.

An assistant came in and asked, "Who's next?"

Charity smiled and handed over a lengthy list. "What are you doing?" Ethan demanded hotly as soon as the storekeeper went into the back room.

She pulled her fan from her reticule and whispered from behind it, "Ethan, the limits are too low. The others won't be able to stock up enough. The limit is per family, and so our wagon qualifies for twice as much. We'll buy everything we're allowed, then our friends can get the excess from us tonight at the campfire."

"I'm eavesdropping, and I'll admit to it. I want to buy some of your extra flour and sugar," Stu Green murmured, brushing past. He went over and whispered to Banner. Banner came over and pled for first call on excess cornmeal, and Mary Pitts put in for the salt.

"You sure can skin a cat nine ways, Charity." Ethan lifted his hands in defeat. "I'll admit when I'm beat."

"Goodness, I forgot baking powder!" Charity cried. She twirled around and headed back to the counter. By the time she was done, she added on another two-pound tin of Ely's fine gun powder, four spools of thread, one pound of gum drops, a paper of sewing pins and needles, and several buttons.

Gracie teased her, "You can't buy buttons for your own string, Charity. That's breaking the rule!"

Charity laughed. "Oh, I know. I got some for a frock for Cricket, and these others will be special treats for her. There are two end-of-day glass buttons on this card. Since no two buttons can be alike on her string, would you like the other for your Priscilla's string?"

"I'll buy it from you."

"No, you won't!" Charity sidled closer and murmured, "Gracie, I feel so beholden to you. How many times have you gently shared your wisdom and advice so I'd be able to care better for Tad and Cricket? A button is nothing—it's a tiny thank-you, and I'd be offended if you didn't accept it."

After Gracie consented to accepting the button, Charity went back to the counter to get a final tally. "Lady, yer order comes to a hundert an' three dollars an' ten cents," the exasperated storekeeper warned. The other pioneers in the store didn't even bother to muffle their gasps.

"Well, then, here we go." She opened her reticule and produced five more double eagles and a five-dollar piece.

The man behind the counter gaped at her.

"Before you make change, how much is that container of marbles?"

"A buck even."

"I'll take it and ninety cents' worth of lemon drops, then."

"Whatever you want, lady." He shook his head in disbelief.

"Ninety cents of just lemon drops!" one of the women in the background gasped.

"With the prices they've got posted, 'tain't gonna be no bushel of 'em," Jed Turvey grumbled. "Flour's a buck a pint!"

The storekeeper snapped, "It'll be a good gallon, an' then some. She'll be takin' half of my stock of 'em with her, and you won't find sweets again till you reach the Willamette Valley. Iff'n you don't like my prices, you can go without the goods!"

"I do apologize for setting this off." Charity blushed becomingly. "I just felt I'd taken a fair bit of your time and hoped it would simplify things if you didn't have to make change."

"Aw, forget it, lady. Do ya mind just takin' a gallon jar and callin' it even 'stead of havin' me measure it up?"

"But of course. Would you care if I opened it and offered everyone a few in the interest of peace?"

"They're yers. Do whatever ya want with 'em. Maybe ya ought to. I'd druther not sell any more to yer train so I have some for the next one. Never thought I'd have to set limits on lemon drops!"

A while later, Charity fanned herself and murmured, "I'm sorry if I embarrassed you, Ethan. I didn't mean to."

"I'll live through the embarrassment, but I'm worried. You have no idea who was in that store. It's dangerous for anyone to advertise they're holding money like that. Stu and Rick are both smart enough to pass the word that you just went a bit trail crazy and spent the last of your money. Hopefully, it'll keep you from being robbed when folks on our train pay you back."

Charity sucked in a deep, shocked breath. "I'm sorry! It never occurred to me. . . ."

"Yeah, well, remember that in the future. The other thing is, you can't go tossing your gold away with both hands, Charity. If you do, you won't manage at all once we reach the trail's end. To my reckoning, even if everyone pays you back for what you bought, you'll only have eighty bucks to your name. Gal, that's about four months' wages for a man—and you won't be able to last long on that!"

Charity cast a glance all about her then leaned close. "Ethan, please don't worry about that anymore. I've not quite spent all of Daddy's carrying money. That was only a small fraction of what he had. The highboy has a false bottom. I have funds" —she looked down then back at him—"*considerable* funds left in it."

Ethan stared at her in shock. He'd almost convinced himself that they might consider matrimony. Even with her fancy upbringing and fine goods, she never acted superior or haughty. Now he knew better. There was more than just a class barrier between them. No self-respecting man married a woman whose wealth eclipsed his to the point of humiliation.

Oblivious to the fact that she'd poleaxed him, Charity said, "Daddy told me to keep it a secret. I owe you peace of mind to not fret about me. I'm sorry I let you worry. I understand now that I acted far less circumspectly than I should have back at the store, but I was appalled at how stingy he was with his limits." She paused a moment longer then added, "I promise to exercise reserve so there won't be any more awkward moments."

Until now, Ethan hadn't realized he'd let his heart get ahead of his mind. He forced himself to sound conversational when he really wanted to walk off and kick a stump. "I can't believe you bought all of that stuff," he shuffled uncomfortably, "and I can't figure out for the life of me where you put it all."

Charity smiled. "I had it all planned out. Aren't you glad we can give the others our surplus?"

He shook his head. "I'm not sure it's wise for you to give stuff away. Even if you trust them and figure they won't rob you, you need to concern yourself with the fact that folks will feel beholden."

"Nonsense! I owe so many of those people more than I can ever repay." In an instant, her cheerful countenance melted. Tears welled up, and she choked out, "Banner helped me prepare Mama for her burial. Rick took my guard duty. Jed minded my oxen. You helped bury Daddy and took me on. . . ."

"Hush," he crooned softly as he squeezed her hand. "We all help one another, Charity. It's the Christian thing to do."

She turned soulful eyes to him. "Then please don't be upset with me when I use the money the Lord blessed me with to help others. It's all I have to give. The Bible says, 'To him whom much is given, much is required.'"

A short while later, as Ethan sat whittling a button for Cricket, Tad asked, "Pa, was Miss Davis crying?"

"Yes, son. She lost both of her folks since we've been on the trail. That is a powerful lot of sorrow to bear."

"Pa, that makes me wonder," Tad asked as he scratched his knee, "why doesn't she cry all the livelong day like Aunt Lydia did?"

"Because people are different. Miss Davis is a very strong young woman, and she seems to be able to bear a big burden without complaining. She mostly does it by leaning on the Lord. Those are qualities to admire, Tad."

"There are lots of good things about her."

"I kind of feel that way myself." Ethan admitted that much, but he said nothing more. As the days passed, his feelings for Charity deepened. All along, he'd known it was unfair for him to reveal the attraction. Tenderhearted and sensitive as she was, she'd probably feel indebted and accept his suit, but he didn't want a wife who married him out of gratitude or pity. Now, staggered by the fact that she could spend such a sum and still possess "considerable funds," Ethan pushed aside any hope of marriage. He knew they'd have to part at the trail's end in the Willamette Valley.

❧

They continued along the north fork of the Platte River. The water supply grew less and less tasty as they traveled on, but the oxen were happy with it. Previous parties had been displeased with the river water taste and tried to dig water holes. The guide warned them not to—much of the water was too salty or plain bad. They made do the best they could.

Their scout seemed satisfied with the distance they'd managed each day. On average they covered a bit over fifteen miles, but he'd warned once they hit the Continental Divide and traveled through the mountainous terrain, they'd slow down considerably. Fear of not making it through the mountains before winter storms hit motivated them to push onward.

Delays happened—a broken wheel needing to be repaired or replaced, an axle that cracked after the wagon ran over a big stone. Several wagons benefited from Ethan's skills. Never once did he ask to be paid for his expertise. Most of the travelers were lean on cash, so when Ethan fixed a yoke or repaired a wagon, the recipient usually offered to pull his guard duty in return.

Working together and learning to give and take kept the train moving along. On occasion, they encountered an abandoned wagon. If there was anything to be salvaged, the men did so quickly and efficiently. The Laswells had just used their only spare wheel when an abandoned rig was found with two good ones still available.

Everyone gave praise to the Lord for His providence, but their guide heaved a sigh. "Folks, I'm just as grateful to the Almighty, but I may as well use this time when you're all together to give you warning. The going will be getting much rougher. In another month, things will be downright miserable a fair part of the time. Tempers will get mighty short, and if things get bad, I'll suggest that the troublemakers take back a portion of their fee and join up with another train or go on to the California Territory instead of heading to the Willamette Valley with us. I don't cotton to backbiting or gossip, but if there's a problem, you aren't to keep it quiet. Come to me or Jason at once. I've seen men get riled up enough to come to blows on several trips, and on two crossings there were even shootings. I'll not abide anything of the sort. Far more men die from fighting with their trail mates than fighting with Indians. First wind I get of discord, I want a full account."

Solemn faces stared back, and heads nodded in slow assent. This was the ugly side of humanity. The crucible of hardship and grief had drawn them together. It sobered them to hear their unity was tenuous.

❦

The evening they reached the Sweetwater River crossing, Jason walked through the train and collected a string of women. He specifically chose them and left others out. Charity felt a twinge of worry when he nodded his head at her and said, "You, too, Miss Davis."

Jason pulled the knot of women off to the side and set his weathered hands on his hips. He gave them a stern look. "I'm not putting up with no nonsense."

Nonsense? What have I done? Charity shot a worried glance at her friends then focused back on their leader.

"Trail's getting harder. Hotter, too. Them hoops have gotta go. Shuck 'em and leave 'em here." He swung his arm in an arc. "The womenfolk who went ahead of you already did, so I don't want no fuss." Without another word, he paced away.

Abby Legacy started to twitter, and her cousin, Hyacinth, gasped, "Dear mercy! They've hung their hoops from the trees!"

Charity had been busy with Cricket, so she hadn't noticed the strange sight. Months ago, when they set out, she would have blushed at anything half as indelicate. Now she smiled. "I'll bet the birds here make odd nests." Everyone laughed.

Myrtle looked down at her gown. "I'd best do some hemming. I can't stand to leave a stitch of clothing behind. Guess I'll cut the hoops from my crinoline and shorten all of my things."

"Add some buckshot to your hem," someone said. "It'll keep your skirts weighted down so the wind won't cause you grief."

Daddy read women did that, and he'd instructed the seamstress to stitch gold coins into the hems of their skirts and gowns. It worked well. Charity determined she'd simply move them. As she walked back to the wagon, she decided to use the fabric she cut off to make Cricket a gown. She turned to Myrtle. "You're right. Wasting fabric would be foolish. Had Jason waited until morning to make his announcement, we wouldn't have time to salvage the fabric. Scraping the ground all day would ruin it."

"I'll save my extra for quilt blocks," Hyacinth decided. "Maybe we could all trade a square and make memory quilts."

"You're forever trading things," Abby said. "I'd venture to say your button string doesn't have a single button on it that hasn't been swapped!"

Hyacinth laughed as she reached up and touched the piece. "They're called memory strings, too. I remember everyone I ever traded with to have these. Each one means something to me!"

Myrtle said, "Back home we always called them charmstrings because most of the gals had charmstring glass buttons on them. Charity has more kinds of buttons than I ever imagined existed on hers—but it's the charmingest thing I ever did see!"

"Thank you," Charity said. Somehow, the single women and girls on their train had come to the habit of wearing their button strings on Sundays. Life and work was too hard to subject their treasured pieces to daily wear, but it was sweet to bring them out once a week. Leaving friends and family behind was hard; being able to finger a button and remember those loved ones still helped them feel in touch.

Charity smiled. "Ethan is carving beautiful little buttons for Cricket's string. He's so clever with his hands. He uses all kinds of wood. He brought a few corozo nuts to carve so she'll have vegetable ivory, and he has horn he saved to do the same. Her string will surely become a family heirloom. He helped Tad make a leather bag for his marbles last night, too."

Myrtle held her back as the others went ahead. "Charity, are you losing your heart to him?"

"Ethan? Myrtle, I deeply admire him. He's a godly man. He cherishes his children and has been kindness itself to me, but we've both done our utmost to remain cordial and circumspect, so I'd be mortified if anyone thought there was anything improper between us."

"Oh, now, I didn't mean to imply you were chasing after him," Myrtle said as they started to walk again. "He's a fine young man. I've wondered if perhaps he's taken a shine to you."

Ethan remained kneeling by the Jasons' wagon. He'd needed to replace a cracked doubletree. He hadn't meant to eavesdrop, but Charity's words warmed his heart. It was good to know she held him in high regard. Their relationship didn't fit into any of the usual molds, and he tried to make things easier for her when he could. Keeping things balanced strained his mind at times. Because he could never wed her, he didn't want to do anything to give the appearance that they might be courting, but she deserved special treatment for the countless ways she eased life for him and his kids.

He agreed with Myrtle. Even to a common man's undiscriminating eye, Charity's string held rare and wondrous buttons. Sometimes she'd tell Cricket a nap-time story about how she'd been given a particular button. In those moments, Ethan learned little things about Charity she'd otherwise never have revealed.

The touch button—her first—was a big, gold military button from her great-great-grandfather's Revolutionary War uniform. Her birthday was in July, which accounted for the buttons that held genuine rubies. A small cluster of buttons commemorated her first formal tea when she turned ten: a pearl, a cameo, two china portraits from Austria, a thumbnail-sized gold teapot from Silesia, and a coral flower. She cherished a simple crocheted button from a church widow every bit as much as she enjoyed the jet button her grandmother had worn when she met Queen Victoria.

He knew she kept track of each button in a tiny red leather book that had dainty, gold vines embossed down the cover. Her joy wasn't merely in having a collection of beautiful baubles; she used it as a means to remember important events and cherished people in her past. Memory by memory, charm by charm, she'd recorded each addition to her button string.

Tad took a liking to the buttons because Charity made doing his sums and multiplication tables fun by concocting problems for him using her string. The kaleidoscopes, swirlbacks, paperweights, and charmglass buttons kept his attention long enough to cipher. When he was especially clever, Charity sometimes gave him another marble from the supply she bought back at Fort Laramie.

❧

"Charity, I don't hold with paying my son to do essentials," Ethan said quietly after the kids were in bed one evening. He shook his head. "Kids must learn to do things just because they need to be done."

Charity's eyes darkened. "I'm sorry, Ethan. I mean no harm."

"You don't need to apologize, gal. I just figured we'd best talk this over since Tad's marble bag seems to have developed a notable bulge."

"The only reason I have so many kaleidoscopes on my button string is because my teacher loved them and gave them to us as awards." She dipped her head. "I treasured them, and I simply wanted Tad to have good memories about learning."

He winced. "I didn't mean to hurt your feelings."

"He's your son, Ethan. As a father, it's your duty to step in when I've done something wrong."

He stayed silent for a moment. "You didn't do anything wrong, Charity. As a matter of fact, I recollect earning a few prizes for spelling bees and the like. I reckon it won't hurt to have the boy develop a fondness for studying. I want him to learn and to help others because it is good and right—not so he can be rewarded."

"Your goal is noble, Ethan. I know God loves cheerful givers—and the giving isn't supposed to just be money in an offering plate. Tad sees how often you lend a hand to others. I hold no doubt he'll grow up to emulate the servant's heart you demonstrate. If you'll excuse me, I need to fetch my shawl."

She slipped away, and Ethan shook his head in disbelief. She thought *he* had a servant's heart? Those first days, he'd worried she was too dainty, frail—even prissy—to tend to matters. She'd proven him wrong. Little Charity Davis pitched right in. Just yesterday he'd told Banner, "The word *idle* isn't in Charity's vocabulary."

As a matter of fact, Charity's attitude made their wagon a pleasant place. She was a cheerful riser and always saw to it that everyone had a good, hot breakfast to start off the day. She corrected the children with a fair balance of firmness and humor. No task was too dirty, too small, or too tough. She was never too tired to help with one more thing or to see if someone else could use a bit of assistance. Who would ever guess this fine lady would walk long, dry, dusty miles each day and collect buffalo chips to fuel her cook fire?

With her acceptance of the hardships, those around her realized they had no more call to complain than did she. . .yet she sat there, complimenting him simply for doing a man's work to provide for his own and assure the wagon train kept moving.

Lord, what am I to do with this longing in my heart? Your Word teaches we set our affections. I'm doing my dead-level best not to set my heart on that gal, but I'm failing at it. We're both believers, but other than that, we'd be unequally yoked. I'd never be the fancy kind of man she deserves, and I'd never be able to provide the kind of life she's accustomed to. Give me strength, I pray. . . .

Chapter 5

T he sun beat down unmercifully, and Charity wished for nothing more than a sip of cool lemonade and a chance to soak her feet. She'd already walked nine miles today, and from the looks of it, they'd cover another five or six before Jason called a halt. Cricket didn't want to ride in the bumpy wagon, but her legs were too tired for her to walk any longer. She lifted her arms high and pled, "Up."

"All right, sweet pea." All of the muscles in Charity's shoulders and back protested this new load, and she finally admitted to herself she couldn't manage this much longer. *Just a few more days,* she told herself, *but how can I last in this terrible heat without water?*

Patterson pushed them hard for the next three days. Now, as they used Sublette's Cutoff, they had no source of water whatsoever. Banner convinced Charity to stop wearing all three petticoats.

She wore two.

Instead of having one wet cloth to comfort them through the day, Charity started making two. She even caved in and started leaving the uppermost button of her dresses and shirtwaists unfastened. Patterson was firm about everyone keeping on a hat or sunbonnet. The storekeeper at Fort Kearny had flavoring bottles, and she'd bought a few. She took to placing a dab of spearmint or vanilla on the stones they sucked on to keep their mouths moist.

Even with it as hot as it was, Tad seemed almost immune to the heat. Cricket seemed more affected, and Charity finally took to dressing her in just her frock and drawers, leaving off the slip entirely. When Myrtle confessed she was doing the same with little Emily, Charity let out a small sigh of relief. Minding children demanded making hundreds of tiny decisions on a daily basis.

At noon Cricket scooted into the wagon for a nap. Ethan silently saddled Charity's mare. "Charity, the oxen are straining in the heat. We'll reach water in two days, but you'll never survive the heat if you don't ride."

"But Queenie must be feeling the heat," she protested.

"Your mare's a fine animal," he said quietly. "But if it comes down to you or her, there's no choice to be made."

She blushed vividly. "Still, I cannot ride."

"Why not?"

Charity stared at the horse. "We don't have a lady's saddle."

He cupped his hands around her waist and squeezed in gentle reassurance. "Your gown's full, Charity. You can ride quite modestly. It's actually far more stable, and I'd not have you ride sidesaddle. Simply put, your safety is too important. Other women are riding western style, so you needn't fret."

Western style. He'd chosen his words carefully in order to avoid crassly mentioning she'd be astride. Before she could agree or disagree, he murmured, "Here you go, gal," and lifted her into Queenie's saddle. Silently, he tugged her hem down to cover her, handed her the reins, and walked off.

She carried Cricket in front of herself for the next day and a half. Small as she was, the little girl still radiated heat like an oven. The hours in the saddle caused pains to shoot through Charity's lower limbs and back, but she knew it was the only way she'd manage to assure little Cricket and she would both survive until they reached water.

❧

"Happy birthday, Charity!" Banner called over in the morning.

"Thank you! How did you know it was my birthday?"

Banner grinned. "Your ma mentioned you'd be having your birthday on the trail. I remembered because it's my anniversary."

"Felicitations, Banner! God surely blessed you with a fine man." Charity lifted the lid on the Dutch oven to check on her biscuits. "I brought along a bit of cocoa. I could bake a cake for us to share at supper."

"I thought you said you were just about out of eggs."

Charity shrugged. "I am, but my recipe only uses one." Folks stored eggs in the flour barrels to keep them from breaking. Several families had a few chickens in cages strapped to the sides of their wagons, but jostled around as they were, the hens didn't lay well.

It took a bit of ingenuity, but Charity's cake turned out fairly well. One corner got a bit crisp, but they'd all learned to eat singed food while on the trail. Food couldn't be wasted. They gathered about the campfire that night, and Banner slipped something to Charity in a knotted hanky.

Charity gave her a questioning look.

"Go ahead. Open it."

Charity carefully unknotted the cloth and found three buttons inside. "The pewter one, that's from me. The other two, I swiped them from your mama's chest. She had them tied together with that there pretty little bow, so I reckoned she planned on giving them to you today."

Charity fingered them all. Her eyes filled with tears until she couldn't even see the buttons clearly anymore. "Thank you, Banner. You don't know how precious these are to me."

"Let's string them on now. You don't know how much I've worried about losing them!"

Within minutes, Hyacinth, Myrtle, Abby, Gracie, and Leticia all gathered about. Soon, more of the ladies from the train joined the circle around Charity. Each gave

Charity a button as a birthday gift. While Charity visited, Banner carefully added each of the birthday buttons to the collection. The strand of thick thread was almost filled.

"Not many more, and you'll have that string done," Harriet decided. "We'll all keep an eye out for that thousandth button. When you get it from your beau, we'll all know your heart's taken."

After all of the women left, Charity banked the fire and turned toward the wagon. Ethan blocked her way. He pressed something into her hand. "I didn't want you to go to sleep without this. Happy birthday."

Charity turned so the moon would cast a beam on the button. Though just an inch across, the wood had been whittled into a bow with flowing ties. A tiny heart nestled in the center point. "Oh, Ethan, it's exquisite! Did you do this yourself?"

"It's nothing," he said modestly.

"I disagree! You astound me. Why, it even matches the ribbon carved on my highboy and headboard! Thank you. Thank you so very much. You're such a talented man. I'll treasure this."

"You can slip it on your string tomorrow. It's been a long day. You'd best turn in." He lifted her into the wagon and softly said, "Good night and pleasant dreams."

The next morning, Charity added Ethan's bow button to her string. Tad started playing with the opposite end and singsong counted along the strand. At one point, he frowned. "Miss Davis, I never noticed this wasn't just one button. Look."

She leaned over. "Yes. Those were from the Shay twins. See? One bell is silver; the other is gold." Charity secured Ethan's lovely bow to her string and tied the end.

"Can I ride in the wagon and look at your buttons this morning?"

"It'll be bumpy."

Tad hitched a shoulder. "I don't care."

A long while later, Tad jumped out of the wagon and ran to her. He grabbed her hand and paid no attention to the fact that several women and children were within earshot. "Miss Davis!"

"What is it?"

"Your button string. I counted it three times to be sure. You finished it. You don't need any more. . .and the button Pa gave you is the thousandth!"

Chapter 6

"Mr. Cole, I need a moment of your time." Charity clutched the button in her hand. She cast a quick look at the others. They milled about within hearing distance instead of tending to their nooning chores, so she tacked on shakily, "In private."

Never, in all of her years, had she felt so self-conscious or nervous. Not once in all of her lessons regarding etiquette and comportment had she been taught how to handle such an embarrassing catastrophe. Everything inside her quivered. She knew from the virulent heat of her cheeks that she had to be utterly, completely, unmistakable scarlet.

How could I have let this happen?

Ethan's forehead furrowed, and he studied her for a moment. "If you can wait just a jiffy, I'll see to the kids."

"I–I've already asked Banner to keep them for nooning."

His brow rose in surprise. "Very well, *Miss Davis*. What can I do for you?"

She hastily looked around and knew every eye was on her. On *them*. She pulled in a choppy breath and couldn't seem to find her voice. *Why can't I just keep it? Why can't he love me? I'd be a good wife to him. I already love his children, too. Too? Oh, mercy in heaven—I love him! What should I do?*

"Perhaps you'd like to sit down," Ethan said. His hand cupped her elbow.

He's such a gentleman. So polite, so concerned. This is dreadful. He'll probably do the honorable thing and ask me to marry him just to spare me the embarrassment.

"It's not like you to be this rattled. Are you feeling poorly? You're flushed." He seated her on a rock and pressed the back of his fingers to her cheek. "Perhaps I should get Banner or Myrtle for you."

"No!" The concern in his eyes shifted to surprise when she blurted out that one word. She heaved a very unladylike sigh and cast away every hope or dream she might have entertained about having a happy future. She wanted this man. No other. No other man could ever make her as happy. *Then why am I going to let go of this opportunity? Because it's honorable. I never knew being honorable could hurt so badly. Dear Jesus, give me strength.*

Charity turned her hand over and very slowly uncurled her fingers. The lovely button lay cradled in her hand. She wet her lips and whispered, "I've inadvertently placed you in an untenable position. I'm so sorry, Mr. Cole."

"I'm afraid I don't understand. I thought you liked it." What could very well pass for hurt flickered in his eyes.

"Oh, I do!" Charity paused then said somberly, "But I cannot accept it. Banner— she was helping me pack. I didn't realize. . . That is, I don't mean to hold her to blame, because I alone am responsible. . . ."

"Charity, what are you trying to tell me?"

"I lost count. She saved a few buttons off of Mama's clothes the night we were packing, and when I slipped them on the string, I lost count." Every word ached with the misery she felt as she whispered, "I take full responsibility, Mr. Cole. I wanted to give this back to you privately. Please understand, it was a lovely gift. I've never seen anything so wonderful, and no one ever troubled himself to make something by his own hands just for me; but I cannot keep it under these circumstances, and I hope you forgive me."

"What are you saying, Charity?"

She carefully transferred the button from her hand to his. His hand was large, rough, and calloused. In his palm, the button looked minuscule. How had he managed to create anything so dainty? Charity stayed silent for a moment then realized he still didn't comprehend what she was doing. "Mr. Cole, I was mistaken about how many buttons decorated my string. This," she swallowed and whispered thickly, "would be the thousandth."

"The thousandth." He repeated the word in a husky tone.

She wanted to run away. She wanted to hide from all of the prying eyes turned their way. She wanted to burst into tears. Most of all, she wanted him to slip that marvelous button back into her hand and ask her to be his beloved wife.

Instead, she tried to give him a smile. From the reflection in his eyes, Charity knew she'd failed miserably. "Certainly, I have no expectations. Had I been more careful, you'd not be in this awkward position. If you'd like, I'll be happy to sew it on the yoke of Cricket's new frock."

❧

"I see." He stared down at the dinky ribbon. He'd spent the last week making it. Twice he'd broken it and had to start afresh. Charity deserved something wonderful, but this was all he had to give. The whole time he'd carved it, he'd thought of the elegant, fancy, and expensive gifts she'd undoubtedly received all of her life. This cost nothing but spare time, yet she acted like she appreciated it. That was another mark of her fine manners. She could make a pauper feel like a prince. Nonetheless, he was a pauper. He had no right to hope this princess would ever set her heart on him.

She blinked back the tears in her eyes. "I'm afraid Tad counted them and wasn't discreet in breaking the news to me. Though I know you might have wished otherwise, others already know. Truly, Mr. Cole, I never meant for this to happen. Please forgive me for my carelessness. I'll take responsibility. I'll be sure folks understand."

The temptation to take advantage of the situation nearly overpowered him. It would be so easy to simply insist she wed him. She'd accepted the button and added it to her string. He'd have her for his wife, and he'd cherish her every last day of their marriage; but would she resent him for taking advantage of this mistake, and could he maintain his self-respect for trapping her when she'd agreed to the union only to avoid social embarrassment?

Ethan cleared his throat. The words stuck. He wanted to drop onto his knee right there and pledge his heart, but the last thing he needed to do was humiliate them both by making a public spectacle of this mess so she'd feel even more obligated. It took every shred of self-discipline for him to tamp down his own wants and needs and put hers first. Finally, he rubbed his thumb across the loop of the bow. "What do you want to do about this, Charity?"

She pressed her fingers to her mouth to hold back a sob. Her shoulders shrugged in silent turmoil as a few tears slipped down her cheeks.

He tilted her face up to his. "Some things in life you don't rush. The decision to marry is definitely one of them. For the weeks we've been traveling together, we've prayed with the children. That was wise. I think it would be wise if we prayed separately and together about this. If we seek God's will, He'll honor our hearts and show us the way."

Charity nodded.

"Tell you what: Why don't you sew this button to the bonnet of our wagon? When we see it, it'll serve as a reminder to us to truly consider our paths and seek the Lord's intent."

"That would be best," she agreed in a strained voice.

"At any point in time—even now, if you know your heart and mine won't be a comfortable match, I want you to take it down and. . ." He searched his mind for what she could do with it. He'd never again want to set eyes on the piece. "Set it beneath a wheel so it is crushed and left behind in the dust so there will be no doubt and no keepsake to act as a thorn to our memories."

She simply looked at him. He knew she'd heard him, but she gave no response. "Charity, if you are mortified by even the possibility of being my wife, you can say so now. I'll still carry you and your things to Oregon. You know that, don't you?"

"We'll continue on and pray. I'll stitch it securely so it won't accidentally get jostled loose."

"Fine." He wanted to let out a shout. At least she hadn't rejected him outright. "I'm not letting you shoulder the explanation for this alone. Best we make a general announcement than let tongues wag."

He reached out his other hand. She took it, and he helped her rise. Their hands clasped for the first time as he bowed his head. "Father, Your Word instructs us to come to You for wisdom. Charity and I believe in You and want to live to please You. The union of two hearts is not a light matter. Please grant us strength to take time in considering this, and make Your plan for our lives clear. I want to thank You for the way You've allowed us to work together well thus far and ask that You would continue to bless us as we continue on, on the trail and in our lives. In Jesus' name, amen."

"Amen," she whispered.

Ethan didn't let go of her hand. He walked her to a small knot of folks who suddenly tried to appear occupied in anything other than observing them. Cricket skipped up. She wound her arms around his legs and looked up at him. "Pa, are you and Miz Davis gonna get married?"

"Sweet pea, we haven't decided yet. It's in God's hands."

Chapter 7

A woman could hope. Charity threaded her strongest thread through the needle. With great care, she stitched the button to the wagon bonnet. Seven. Eight. Nine stitches to secure the shank to the fabric. No, ten. She couldn't resist putting that one last extra stitch in for good measure. She'd carefully chosen the place to sew the button so she'd see it first thing upon waking and last thing at night.

"Delight thyself in the Lord, and He will grant thee the desires of thy heart." She whispered that verse as she knotted the thread and cut it. *Heavenly Father, You know the desire of my heart. If it is not in accordance with Your wishes, please let me know right away.*

She gently, almost reverently, touched the piece then turned to put away her sewing supplies. As much to avoid others as to get supper, Ethan suggested she drive the wagon in the afternoon while he went hunting. The time they had allowed others to gossip or speculate, so she and Ethan both hoped folks would be circumspect in the days and weeks ahead. Ethan had come back with a bighorn sheep, so as she sewed, he went to the edge of the campsite and dressed the meat.

Fresh meat was meant to be shared. When someone made a good-sized kill, he divided it up as he saw fit. Banner hadn't exaggerated that first night when she praised Ethan's prowess with a rifle. Most of the folks in the train had benefited from his hunting skills.

They'd seen another wagon train where folks strung strings across the wagon bows and hung thin strips of buffalo meat on them. Their guide, Mr. Patterson, spat in disgust over that practice. "Smells of blood. It invites wolves to close in. Indians, too. They depend on the buffalo for everything; white man wastes a good part of the beast. I know most of the other trains slaughter 'em, but I don't want anyone bothering buffalo unless there's no other meat to be shot."

By now they were in the mountains. Obtaining water wasn't a problem any longer, but the terrain became much more difficult to cover, and the nights grew cold. Buffalo and their chips were mere memories. Other kinds of game abounded, but men still didn't hunt to their hearts' content because of the sheer work it took to get the wagons up and down the steep mountain grades.

"Charity?" Ethan's voice came through the wagon cover clearly. She closed her eyes for a moment and savored the sound of his voice. Like his velvety brown eyes, his voice held a depth that soothed and comforted.

"Yes?"

"I thought perhaps you'd like to decide how to divvy up the meat. I've already spitted half of this, so we'll eat freshly roasted meat tonight. If you don't mind my asking, I have a hankering for meat pie. I'll set off some of the smaller slivers and hunks of meat in the stew pot. Pies would make nooning easier tomorrow since it looks like it's going to be a grueling day."

"That does sound good." Thankful he'd given her a mundane conversation topic to ease their time together, she went to the end of the wagon and allowed him to lift her out. Was it her imagination, or did his hands give her a tiny squeeze a split second before he let go?

"Clara needs to build up her blood after the birthing. Do you mind if we give them the liver?"

He smiled. "No. I'll take it over."

"Oh, I'll fix it for her! She shouldn't be getting up yet."

"I'd like to give the Legacy wagons a hind quarter to share if that's all right with you. Abigail and her mama are both feeling poorly. I'm sure Hyacinth can cook for all of their family, and they can use the excess for tomorrow's meals, too."

Charity nodded. She nervously pleated her skirt and asked, "Would you mind if we asked the Laswells to join us for a roast? I want to be sure Banner knows I hold no hard feelings and don't feel she's to blame. Besides, the meat will spoil before we use it all ourselves, and they've got eight mouths to feed."

"You may as well ask Myrtle and her brood, too. She's looking fretful as a ready-to-foal mare. Best we calm everyone else down right away. We'll have enough meat for that, and all of you women can make meat pies with the leftovers afterward."

Lard buckets hung from the wagons. While the women cooked, Tad and Banner's two sons went from wagon to wagon and painted the axles to keep the wheels spinning easily and reduce the chance of the axles splitting. The boys saw to the milking and several other chores each day. After eating, they went off to the side and shot marbles. Charity mopped Cricket's grimy hands and face and tucked her into bed. After a prayer and a kiss, Charity touched the button and whispered a quick prayer before going back to her tasks.

❦

A man could hope. Ethan rose earlier than usual the next morning. He'd stayed up late praying. Just as he finished his devotional time, he'd seen Mrs. Jason scurrying toward the Legacy wagon. She carried her small box filled with glass bottles of medicinals. That fact let him know things had worsened.

Rob Laswell had quietly roused him this morning. He rose with a heart heavy. The task ahead was not an easy one. Jed Turvey joined them, and they headed off to a place beside the path. Silently, they dug three graves.

All yesterday Ethan had hoped a miracle would happen and Charity would consent to be his bride. Today his thoughts traveled a different path. He hoped they'd all survive. So far he'd tried to ignore the deaths. Last night their guide, Patterson, grimly stated the toll thus far: five women, three men, four children, and two babes...

but Abby, her mother, and Hyacinth's father all succumbed to a wretched fever. Seven, four, four, and two. . .seventeen dead. That kind of ciphering put the fear of God into a man. *God, I beg of You, wrap Your mantle of health and protection around Cricket and Tad and Charity.*

Travel that day was quiet out of respect for the grieving family. Men chopped down small pine trees and leashed them to the rear axles of wagons to help slow their descent down a steep road. Even with that precaution, the Adamses' wagon careened out of control and crashed.

A burst flour barrel left an explosion of white, and splinters of wood affirmed that the wagon and what little furniture in it were beyond repair. A trunk, shattered bits of china, and a dented washtub bore testimony to the devastation. Gracie sagged to the ground and melted into a puddle of tears. Steven knelt beside her, gathered her in his arms, and Charity heard him say in a hoarse voice, "Darlin', we're all fine. You and the kids—you're what matters."

A small group took sticks and beat about the rocks and shrubs to scare away any snakes then set about trying to salvage what they could for the Adamses. Ethan took one of the shattered wheels and walked off a few paces. Soon thereafter, he took out some of his tools and started to tinker around. Charity and Leticia kept all of the children off to the side.

Soon other women made nooning meals for their families. The day had already proved disastrous. Funerals and a decimated wagon left them all apprehensive, and sticking to a routine helped keep a sense of purpose. Though the train was full of believers, the midday prayers grew more ardent than usual.

Charity gave Ethan one of the meat pies. He mumbled a hasty thank-you, gobbled it down, and barely paused from his work. She handed him a second, and he twitched her a grateful smile. Even after he'd finished eating, she watched a few more minutes as he fastened the altered hub between a few square pieces of wood with a big bolt. He nodded to himself then paced off toward Jason with the odd-looking device in his hands.

As block and tackles went, it was crude as could be. Still, Ethan felt certain it would be of assistance if they'd secure it around a tree and the men would thread the rope through it and lower the wagons in a more controlled fashion. "I grant you, it's not much to look at; but I'm certain it'll serve its purpose, and it could spare us another disaster."

Jason grimaced. "Are you willing to try it out on your own rig?"

"Yes."

It took more time than using the tree-drag method, but Ethan's contrivance worked. They lowered four more wagons, but six still remained at the top of the incline as dusk approached. Tonight there'd be two camps and two sets of guards.

Charity tucked the kids into bed; then Ethan drew her off to the side. "Before we pray, I'd like you to see if you could spare a bit of lye soap. The two Legacy wagons are going to combine as we did. They've offered their other to the Adamses, but we're worried since the folks in that wagon perished from fever. Mrs. Jason thinks if they empty it out, air it overnight, and scrub it with lye soap, it'll be all right to use."

"Lye soap?"

"She read something by Dr. Semmelweis about hand-washing and soap stopping childbed fever. She vows washing seems to stop many fevers from spreading. I'm not sure I put any store by it, but Gracie is already so upset, if it makes her feel better. . ." He shrugged.

Charity opened the dish box hanging from the rear of their wagon and pulled out a cake of soap. Since Ethan used lye soap for everything and she'd brought along glycerin soap for bathing, they had a bit extra. "I'll take it to them."

Ethan curled his hand around her wrist. "No, Charity. I don't want you to be exposed. I'll take care of delivering the soap. Since we have two camps, I'll pull duty the first half of the night. Could I trouble you to put on some more coffee?"

"It's no trouble."

Ethan paced away with the soap.

When he returned, he sat on a felled log and patted the spot next to himself. "Prayer time."

Charity sat down, leaving discreet space between them. Unsure of what to do, she busied her hands by pulling her shawl more closely about her shoulders.

Ethan frowned. "Are you cold?"

"Not particularly. It will get much colder tonight. You'll need another quilt for your bedroll when you turn in."

"I'll be fine, Charity. Keep the quilt and share it with the kids."

His protective ways and concern for her warmed Charity's heart. *Lord, I know I'm supposed to be taking this time to seek Your will. It's so hard, Father, because my heart is already set. Please, give us Your blessing. I've already lost Mama and Daddy. I couldn't bear to be parted from Ethan and his children.*

Ethan reached out. "While we speak to the Father about our future, I'd like us to join hands." As soon as she placed her hand is his large, calloused palm, his long fingers curled around to engulf hers. His strength and warmth made her heart beat faster. He gently squeezed and asked, "Are you ready to pray?"

"I already was," she blurted out. Charity felt her face go warm.

A rich chuckle rumbled out of him. "Oh, gal, you weren't alone. Heaven's gate must be atilt from all of the supplications I've been stacking up against it!"

❦

Since Gracie needed to scrub and pack the wagon they'd been given and the Legacys needed to combine, the wagon council decided to take the next morning as a "rest and catch-up time." By afternoon the men would lower the last wagons down the incline. The scout reported there was a good spot less than two miles ahead for stopping.

The sky hadn't even gotten a touch of gold to it when Charity rose. She made triple portions for breakfast and went over to the spot where the Adamses spent the night. "Gracie, bring your family to eat. I'll watch the children while you tend to matters." Gracie's eyes filled with tears, and Charity felt her own well up. She gave her friend a quick hug and a wobbly smile. "I know what a help that was when you minded the children the morning Ethan and I packed our wagon."

Ethan used the morning hours to inspect the Adamses' broken items. Without a blacksmith to forge new bands or straighten out bent hoops, it made no sense to try to repair barrels. He salvaged parts of two chairs and said he'd be able to construct one from them. A bit of clever patching fixed one trunk, and new leather "hinges" and a strap closed another. A few nails, and two crates came up to snuff.

By late afternoon, they'd gotten all of the wagons down and traveled to their evening campsite. A meandering creek outlined one side of the place. The scout insisted the water be used only for livestock and washing. "It's too slow-moving. Folks get sick when the water isn't white or tumbling over rocks."

"I'm afraid Cricket will take a sip if I bathe her."

Rob Washington rested his hands on his hips. "What say we string laundry lines betwixt trees and a wagon to make up a bathhouse? The water's chilly, so we could collect enough dead wood to make a fire and heat it a bit."

"Women ought to go first," Rick proposed. "I figgur they'll want to wash their hair, and if they wait till later, they'll catch a chill."

Myrtle giggled. "Are the menfolk offering to bathe the children?"

"Sure are," Ethan said as he hoisted Cricket into his arms.

Cricket squirmed and shook her head. "Wanna be with Miss Davis. She gots pretty flower soap, Pa. Makes me smell good."

"Don't be stubborn, Cricket. We're trying to do something nice and spoil the womenfolk."

"I'm a womenfolk, Pa. I even gots ninety-'leven buttons on my string!"

Charity laughed. "I'll take her, Ethan. It's no trouble."

"You deserve to be spoiled," he said under his breath. The look in his eye and the tone of his voice warmed her more than the hot water in the bath she took a short while later.

❦

Breakfast, nooning, and supper, they said grace before their meals. Now Ethan and Charity snatched a bit of time out each evening to set their future before God. She noticed he'd sometimes touch the spot on the bonnet where the button was sewn when he passed it outside. Once he gave her a scampish wink when he knew she'd seen him do it.

Nothing momentous happened to give them a sense of direction. "Waiting on the Lord isn't an easy task for me," Ethan confessed one night.

"I'm not a very patient person, either."

Ethan looked at her and shook his head. "Gal, I can't believe you said that. You're more long-suffering than a saint. I can't imagine for the life of me how you've listened to Tad's endless soliloquies about wanting a jackknife, carried Cricket when her little legs got too tired to walk, and settled their squabbles. You've put up with me when I've been grumpy after a long day, too."

Charity looked at him at length. "Ethan, I grew up as an only child. You simply cannot know how much I relish spending time with the children. To my way of thinking, a man who misses half a night's sleep and drives a team of oxen all day is entitled to being a shade moody. I tried to drive for just a few days, and I was a weeping mess."

"You'd just lost your pa and ma, Charity. You've gone through terrible hardships on this trip."

"I won't pretend it's been easy." She averted her face. "But my trust lies in the Lord."

Ethan cupped her cheek and gently coaxed her to look at him. "Do you think you could learn to trust me, too?"

"I already do." Her lashes lowered. The intensity of his gaze made her heart beat far too fast.

"You must know you have my complete trust. I've put my children in your care. A man cannot show his confidence in a woman more plainly. I believe it's my turn to pray tonight.

"Our praised heavenly Father, we give You our gratitude for seeing us through another day safely. Each night, Lord, we've come to ask for wisdom in the matter of our hearts. You abide in each of us, but we still wait for the assurance of Your blessing or the clear sign that You do not will the union of marriage betwixt us. Grant us courage and composure as we endure. Prepare our hearts so we can carry on Your will. We pray in Jesus' precious name. Amen."

He lifted her into the wagon for the night. Charity curled around Cricket with his prayer still threading through her mind. As far as she was concerned, marriage to Ethan was the only way God could make her happy. How was Ethan able to lay the matter before the Lord day after day so impartially? Though he spoke well of her and to her, could it be he fostered no deep, heartfelt affection for her? She buried her face in the pillow and wept over that notion.

Chapter 8

In the middle of the night, Charity knew something was amiss. She lay still and tried to decide what woke her. Tad mumbled something and thrashed. She smiled. He was a restless sleeper. Ethan had made a bundling board to divide the bed to protect Cricket since Tad never stayed stationary. Charity started to caress Cricket's hair but stilled at once. She was burning hot!

Charity whisked on her wrapper. She felt for a lamp and hastily lit it as she called out, "Ethan! Ethan! Wake up! Cricket's sick." Her voice broke. "It's a fever."

They quickly established Tad was well, so Ethan moved him under the wagon. Charity hastily stripped Cricket out of her nightgown and sponged her off. She glanced up at Ethan. "She's so hot! Oh, Ethan, she's so hot."

"Willow bark," he decided. "Willow bark tea works fine on her. We'll give that a try. I brought a bit." He brewed the tea, but Cricket barely roused enough to take a few scant sips.

By morning, Mrs. Jason paid them a brief visit. "She doesn't have a rash, and she doesn't have dysentery. There's nothing to be done but to give her plenty to drink, sponge her off, and try to knock that fever down."

Charity and Ethan exchanged anguished looks. They'd spent the whole night doing precisely that—to no avail.

Mr. Jason wore an apologetic look. "The whole train can't afford to stay put here when only one child is ailing. If we don't push ahead, we'll be stranded in the mountains in the winter instead of reaching Oregon. At least with two hale adults, one of you can tend the lass while the other keeps the wagon in formation."

Charity spent the whole day sponging Cricket and drizzling little bits of broth and willow bark tea into her. Wagons had no springs—something she'd learned her very first day on the trail. Instead of the buffered ride of a springed carriage, wagons jolted and bumped dreadfully. Every yard they covered felt like a mile.

By midday, Cricket started coughing. Charity held her upright so she'd breathe a bit easier. Ethan took a turn while Charity took an essential moment at that stop, and Mary Pitts brought over bacon and fry bread for their noon meal. "How's the little one?"

Ethan gave no reply. He looked down at his daughter. Every shred of his love and concern showed on his grim face.

Charity dunked the washrag in a water bucket and sponged Cricket as she whispered, "She needs prayer." After Mary left, Charity fretted, "Her cough is worsening. I have an elixir in the bottom drawer."

Ethan somberly handed his daughter over and moved his heavy toolbox so the drawer could slip open a bit of the way. "I don't see any medicinals in here."

"I'm sure they're there." She pressed the damp cloth to Cricket's fever-cracked lips. "Oh. You're looking for glass bottles. Daddy said the glass would likely break. He had the apothecary pack all of the tinctures, concoctions, and elixirs into metal containers. There's a small book with them that holds the labels and notes from the doctor."

Ethan tilted the kit and yanked it free. As he did, the false bottom of the drawer slid aside, revealing a wealth of twenty-dollar gold coins. He ignored them and reached for the half-inch-thick book wedged alongside another box. He pulled the book free and set it on the bed. A small velvet bag enveloped each container. Frustration flooded him. He needed to access the medication quickly. Charity had opened the book and told him, "We need flask number eight."

Desperate, Ethan dumped the whole kit and started to rifle through the bags.

"Oh! They were in order in the satchel!"

Her cry came too late. At least each bottle was etched with a number. Together, they exposed each flask until his fingers closed around the right one. "Number Eight! How much do we give her?"

"The book says half a teaspoon, accompanied by a mustard and onion poultice."

His worry for his daughter erupted into unreasonable anger. "Mustard and onion? Just how am I supposed to get those out here?" He waved at the flasks with disgust. "Silver and gold don't take care of all of life's problems."

Charity gave no reply. Ethan stared at her and saw the hurt in her eyes. She dipped her head, and her lashes lowered. Her cheek pressed lightly against Cricket's. In a thick, hushed voice, she directed, "My measuring spoons are in the top drawer."

His anger fled, only to be replaced with remorse. *A soft answer turneth away wrath.* The verse ran through his mind as he poured the cherry elixir into the spoon and gave it to his daughter. "Charity—"

"If you hold her," Charity interrupted, "I'll make the poultice." She didn't look at him. Instead, she shifted Cricket.

Ethan accepted his daughter's limp form and wondered afresh how dainty little Charity had managed to prop her up these past hours. "Charity—"

She shook her head. "I need to think. Please don't distract me." Her voice was thick with tears. She said nothing more. Neither did he. The drawer holding spices had a tin of mustard. The drawer with dehydrated fruits and vegetables scraped open. Most folk hadn't been able to afford much of them, but the Davis family brought along a wide variety. To keep the flavors from mingling, they were stored in decorated tins.

Less than ten minutes later, Charity pressed the compress to Cricket's chest. She'd torn her own flannel nightgown to use for the fabric, and since no fire had been struck for nooning, she'd melted the lard in a pie tin over the kerosene lantern, then added in the onions and mustard. With the plaster made and in place, Charity said in a tight voice, "The wagons are starting to pull out. Do you want to hold her while I drive?"

"The terrain is rough. I'd better drive." Charity sat on the edge of the feather bed, and Ethan carefully transferred his daughter's weight into her arms. "Get better," he murmured to Cricket then gave her a kiss on her cheek. His head lifted a bit. He cradled Charity's jaw. "Gal, now's not the time, but we need to talk. I'm sorry—"

"Now isn't the time," she cut in. She pulled away, but not before he saw tears sparkling in her eyes.

Ethan let out a groan of remorse and climbed onto the seat. He let out the brake, took up the reins, and set them into motion. "Holler if you need my help," he called to her. It was a useless thing to say. He couldn't make a difference. Almost as bad, he'd just crushed Charity's tender heart, so turning to him was probably the last thing she'd want to do.

By nightfall, Cricket's cough was still bad, but Charity managed to care for her as well as could be expected with the plaster and elixir. Sucking on the lemon drops seemed to help Cricket's throat feel better. The fever concerned them most. Cricket stayed hot as a pistol. Common sense dictated they each take a shift during the night with her so they'd both be able to function the next day. Neither slept much at all—worry interfered. Mrs. Jason warned them against using the quinine for the fever because her medical book said it wasn't to be given to young children.

By the third evening, Ethan knew his little daughter couldn't weather another night of the fever. Out of desperation, he looked at Charity and said, "We have to give her the quinine. Look it up in that book. Whatever the lowest dose is, we'll give her half of what they recommend."

Charity fumbled with the book and found the correct pages. The label stripped from the original glass bottle warned not to administer quinine to small children. In a neat hand, the pharmacist had added several comments and admonishments.

Ethan put a few drops of the bitter medicine in a small cup and added a bit of water. He stared at it. "God, I'm fresh out of prayers. My little girl's in Your hands. Please"—he let out a mix between a sigh and a groan—"please. . . ."

"Amen," Charity breathed. She gently stroked Cricket's throat to make her swallow.

Ethan watched tears pencil down Charity's wan cheeks. She was hollow-eyed and pasty. *Oh, not you, too.* He touched her forehead, but she drew back. "You're exhausted. Go lie down."

She shook her head. "I can't leave my little girl." She dipped the cloth and wiped Cricket's tiny body by rote, yet every move was done with loving tenderness.

Ethan stilled her hand. "Just curl up on Tad's side of the bed, Charity. I'll see to her awhile, then you can take the rest of the night."

Charity barely laid her head down before she fell asleep. Ethan leaned his head against a wagon bow as he rolled up his sleeves. It took a long while until he was sure: Cricket's fever was waning. He coaxed a bit of cider and more cough elixir into her, and she fell into a peaceful slumber.

Ethan looked at the button on the canvas and knew he had one last thing to do.

Chapter 9

How could a woman go from the heights of elation to the depths of despair in a single heartbeat? Charity was thrilled beyond words to wake and find that Cricket felt better. Then she saw the bare spot where the button belonged. She scrambled out of the wagon with more haste than manners, but she didn't care. She sat at the edge of camp, out of sight, her spine pressed to the trunk of a tree. All she wanted was to be alone.

Alone.

Yes, she was by herself. She folded her knees up, wound her arms around them, and buried her face in her skirt. She wept half an ocean. From how he'd acted, she'd suspected Ethan had made his decision. After his comment about silver and gold, she'd cut him off before he could tell her then. She'd hoped maybe, after the strain of Cricket's illness waned, he'd reconsider. He hadn't. The missing button said it all. Though she'd suspected it, it still crushed her to know the man she loved chose to reject her.

❧

"Pa?"

"Yes, Tad?" Ethan looked over the tailgate of the wagon and smiled at his son.

"Sissy didn't die and go to the Hereafter?"

"No." He grinned. "God was good. Sissy's much better."

"Great!" Tad's features twisted into confusion. "Then why did Miss Davis go tearing through camp, weeping?"

❧

Charity heard the crunch of boots and tried to stop crying. "Aww, honey-gal," a velvety voice crooned before she had a chance to wipe away the tears.

Ethan! I can't bear to have him see me like this. She needed time to regain a semblance of composure. How could she do it? She was committed to helping him with the children for the rest of the trip, but knowing he didn't want her or love her was too painful. Another sob welled up.

He knelt beside her and made a soft hushing sound as he pulled her into his arms. For an instant, everything within her rebelled. Charity tried to push him back and scramble away, but he held her fast. "I'm not letting go of you, honey-gal. Not now. Not ever."

She couldn't believe he'd said that. Charity rested her forehead on his shoulder and still cried. He pressed his lips to her hair and stroked her arm and back.

"I've been a fool, Charity. I've let my pride and your possessions come between us instead of seeking the truth. The truth is, you are one of the sweetest gifts God ever gave me. I got to thinking last night. If God sees the sparrow fall and can count the hairs on my head, He certainly counted the buttons on your string. He knew I was carving that button. He knew the desire of my heart, too. I'd been fighting it for weeks—wanting you as my wife, but I kept telling myself and anyone else who asked that I wasn't worthy of you. You're a wealthy woman—"

She looked up at him with aching eyes. "You're the rich one, Ethan. All of the silver and gold in the world wouldn't ever buy me a f–family." Her voice cracked. "I—I have nothing."

"Sweetheart, that's where you're wrong. Last night you called Cricket your little girl." She gave him a blank look, so he nodded to punctuate his words. "Yes, you did. You said, 'I can't leave my little girl.' That said it all, Charity. In our hearts, we've blended until we're already a family. The only thing missing is a ring on your finger to make it official."

He'd brought her shawl. He reached to the side and unfolded it to reveal her button string. "I'm no good at stitching." He chuckled. "You knew that, seeing the sorry way I'd tried to mend my own clothes before you came along. I couldn't wait, though. Last night I took that button off of the wagon bonnet and secured it to your string. It's the thousandth, Charity Davis. I know it full well, and I'm staking my claim. I'd best warn you I knotted this button on so tight it would take a twenty-mule team to pull it off. I'm giving you my heart with that button, and you'd better know it's given with all the love God put in my heart for you."

He pressed his lips to her temple.

"I love you, honey. I need your sweetness and comfort. I want to be your strength and protection. Maybe things haven't started out like a storybook, but that doesn't mean they haven't been arranged for us by the hand of the Almighty. I love you. Don't you love me?"

"Oh, Ethan, I was so scared. I never wanted to give the button back in the first place! That night I realized I'd lost my heart to you."

He slipped her button string around her neck. "Then, Miss Charity Davis, will you do me the honor of becoming my wife?"

"Ethan Cole, I love you. Nothing would make me happier."

He dipped his head. "Let's seal it with a kiss and a prayer."

❧

With the resiliency of youth, Cricket recovered quickly. After Charity was sure all was well, she dug to the very bottom of her trunk and brought out the white satin Mama had brought along. Ethan would have been satisfied for the wagon train captain to wed them straight away, but he said she deserved the wedding of her dreams. According to their scout, they had ten days until they made it through The Dalles and reached the Willamette Valley. There was a church at the end of the trail, and

Charity was determined to have a bridal gown done by then.

"Ethan, you may as well go on over and share the fire with Rob," Banner said. "We ladies are fixin' to help Charity with her finery. Everyone knows a man's not allowed to see it till the wedding day, so you can just resign yourself to being kicked out of the way for the next week or so."

Charity giggled as he winked and paced off. Soon Banner, Myrtle, Mary, and Gracie helped her spread the bonnet she'd saved from her wagon on the ground to protect her satin. When they unrolled the bolt, Charity gasped. Mama hadn't just packed the satin—she'd included elegant lace and packets of seed pearls and minute, crystal beads.

Myrtle oohed and aahed. Banner's brows knit for a moment. "I can't imagine why she didn't just bring her gown for you. Certainly you were both of a size that would have made it possible."

Charity smiled. "Mama was the middle of three daughters. Though she wore the gown, according to family tradition, it belonged to the firstborn daughter."

Gracie said, "Then it's time to start a gown for a new family. Ladies, it's time to gild our lily. Let's get busy." They measured, talked, snipped, and pinned. True friends that they were, they worked afternoon and evening with her until the last stitch was done.

The gown featured a tightly fitted bodice that ended in a downward point. Fabric swagged from side seam to side seam in order to form horizontal scallops down to the floor, and the back draped over a bustle. Closely fitted sleeves hugged her arms and came to a traditional medieval point to call attention to her slender finger where Ethan would place the wedding ring. Lace and seed pearls adorned the entire bodice then edged the hem and sleeves.

"Your mama's veil is your something old, and this gown is your something new," Banner said as she and Charity hid the completed gown away from Ethan's sight. "I made a garter for your something blue. Have you borrowed anything yet?"

Charity smiled. "I'm borrowing Ethan's children, but I'm not giving them back. I'm keeping them as my own forever."

❦

At the end of the trail, everyone camped for the night. The next day, after folks had a chance to do laundry and visit the bathhouse, they all met at the church. Cricket, dressed in a pretty little sky-blue frock Charity made for her, skipped down the aisle, carrying Charity's beloved Bible. She took her place beside her daddy.

Ethan forgot to breathe when he saw Tad escort Charity down the aisle. Her gown sparkled, shimmered, and flowed like a dream. Through her mama's veil, he could see her smile. As she drew closer, his smile broadened. Instead of ribbons, her beloved button string draped around and hung from the bouquet.

Epilogue

M a, you'd best better get in here," Tad hollered. "Cricket's getting into your fancy talcum powder and making a mess!"

"Cricket!" Charity's feet pattered on the hardwood floor of the beautiful home Ethan had built for them. "Mama didn't want you to get messy! We're supposed to surprise your papa with the anniversary cake as soon as he gets home!"

Ethan stood behind his children. He rested a hand on each of them. Tad hadn't lied one bit. Cricket had gotten into the violet talcum he'd gotten Charity for Christmas. The whole bedroom smelled like a flower garden. Hopefully, his wife would be so taken with this next gift, she'd ignore that misbehavior.

The crystal doorknob turned, and they all held their breath. Charity entered the room and stopped cold. "Ethan! When did you get home?"

"While Tad had you out in the garden."

"Can we say it now?" Cricket whispered loudly.

"Yes."

"Surprise!" Ethan, Tad, and Cricket exclaimed in unison. They moved to the side, revealing the wedding chest he'd been making in secret. The look on Charity's face made all of his work worthwhile.

"Oh, Ethan! It's lovely! Oh, it matches!"

He rocked back on his heels and proudly gazed down at the front panel of the piece. He'd sent back East just to get walnut for it. He'd used the last of his own money to do it, too. "Yup. I traced the highboy and headboard to be sure the ribbon was just right."

She wound her arms around him. "I was thinking this matched the button you gave me. It's beautiful, Ethan. Thank you."

She kissed him, and Tad groaned. "Can we please have the cake now?"

"Go ahead and cut it." Charity held Ethan back while the kids dashed to the kitchen.

"You can keep your wedding gown inside, honey-gal. I lined it all with cedar. Look." He opened the lid. Charity's laughter pleased him. Inside the lid, he'd wood-burned a design of a string of buttons. "It took me a while, but this is my groom's gift to you."

"I have a surprise for you, too." She took his hand and placed it on her tummy. "How about if the chest becomes a family heirloom?"

A Letter from the Bride

To my dear daughters, granddaughters, and all future brides,
I thought it would be a wonderful tradition for each bride to write a little note and leave a legacy for those who come after her. How I wish my own mother had lived to see my wedding day and been present to share her wisdom!

I make no pretense at being wise, but God is. The Bible says we can ask for wisdom, and God will honor our request. As you consider marriage, first seek God's will and ask Him to direct your heart. Do not hasten to take your vows. Pause and reflect before you take such a momentous step, and be sure your mate honors God. A marriage is not just between a man and a woman—it is a holy union which must include the Lord to flourish.

Ethan was God's gift to me. His patience, strength, and companionship were like a balm to my grief. We learned to work together and rely on one another until respect and affection sparked. Love came softly and grew in our hearts. How I thank God for bringing us together and blessing our union!

Though hardships test us and extraordinary things thrill us, life is made up of mundane days. Love each other in the little, commonplace matters of life to strengthen your marriage, or it will wither from neglect. Appreciate what you have, and forgive as freely as you laugh.

My darlings, my prayer is for you to make wise decisions of the heart—first in devoting your spirit to the Lord, then in giving your hand to a man. May each of you be blessed with a godly mate and know the joy of growing close together and growing old with him.

With love, hope, and prayers,
Charity Davis Cole

THE WEDDING
WAGON

by Cathy Marie Hake

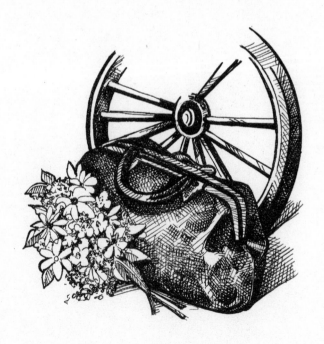

Prologue

Baltimore, 1860

"Miss Handley." Bethany startled from her daydream and accepted the letter. Most of the other girls in the airy parlor were sharing snippets from their missives, and one girl got yet another box from her mama, but Bethany expected nothing. The bold script on this envelope made her heart flutter. "Thank you, Mrs. Throckmorton. Please excuse me."

Ignoring the other girls' pleas to stay and read the post aloud, Bethany hastened to her bedroom with less decorum than might be seemly. She rounded her four-posted bed with the candlewicked spread and sat in the window seat. Carefully, she opened the envelope and withdrew the letter. Joshua used plain white stationery for his other three letters—each two pages long. This envelope was ivory vellum and contained but a single sheet.

My dear Miss Handley,

Over the past five years, I feel I've had an opportunity to get to know you by way of my sister's letters. In no way did Penny's tales of the escapades, wit, and friendship you shared prepare me for the vibrant young lady I met when you joined our family for Christmas. The missives we've exchanged since then have deepened my regard for you and assured me of your Christian commitment.

If there is no man who claims your heart or hand, I would be delighted and honored for you to consent to become my bride. I will endeavor to be a steady provider and thoughtful husband. The life of a physician's wife is not an easy one. Above that, instead of offering an elegant bridal trip, we would set out to traverse the Oregon Trail. I know I ask much of you. Nonetheless, I am a man of faith, and I hope you will find it in your heart to accept my proposal.

Should you be willing to be my helpmeet, join me in Independence on April 8th. We can wed at once, then spend the first days of our union settling the last-minute details for our adventure. In the event you hold other dreams and plans for your future, I wish you every happiness.

Very truly yours,
Joshua Rogers

Tears filled her eyes. Ever since Penny became her roommate and shared all of her stories and letters from home, Bethany had desperately wanted to belong to such a family. During the Christmas season, she'd been their guest and met Joshua for the first time. The cheerful holiday season and the warmth the Rogerses—especially Joshua—extended to her counted as the happiest days of Bethany's life.

"Oh, Lord, You're giving me everything I could ever want. I'll have a husband and finally be part of a wonderful family. Thank You for this."

Bethany kept Joshua's letter beside her as she sat at her writing desk. She dipped her pen in the crystal ink well and began,

Dear Dr. Rogers,
  Thank you for your lovely proposal. I'd be honored to become your wife. I cannot think of a sweeter home than a wagon or a finer roof than a canopy of stars. . . .

Chapter 1

O uch!" Bethany cringed as Penny shoved another hairpin into her light brown curls. "The Indians won't have a chance to scalp me—you're getting the job done before we even leave civilization!"

Penny giggled and shoved one last pin in place. "There. Independence will never see a lovelier scalp."

Bethany looked up at her friend's beautiful blond upsweep and refuted, "Your hair always looks wonderful."

"Spoken like a true friend. Let's get you into your gown. I don't doubt Mrs. Throckmorton measured the seams within a half breath."

"She did, but Letty was a dear. She added on a tiny bit so I wouldn't have to be laced so miserably tight." Bethany slipped into the white satin gown with Penny's help and let her fasten the seemingly endless row of satin-covered buttons from hips to neck. She glanced at her reflection in the oak cheval mirror and fussed. "We cut the skirts much narrower so it wouldn't take up so much space in my trunk."

"You're so wasp-waisted, we could have had you wear a pillow slip for a skirt, and you'd turn every man's head." Penny's light blue taffeta gown rustled as she stood back and bobbed her head in approval. "We only have a few minutes. Where are your mama's pearls?"

"Here. Uncle Bartholomew sent them."

As Penny draped the luminous strand around Bethany's neck and fastened it, she muttered, "You'd think the old goat could have delivered them himself."

"I'm glad Uncle sent them. Had he come, he might well have given them to some other woman. I doubt he would have recognized me."

Bethany didn't even feel a pang at that fact. Orphaned at six, she'd spent the next five years trying, and failing, to be invisible and silent under the strict eye of Uncle Bartholomew's housekeeper and a stern governess. While they both went out to a Temperance League meeting one afternoon, Bethany took it upon herself to sled down the stairs on a silver tray. Skirts flouncing, stockings drooping, and one braid unraveled, she ran straight into her uncle. The very next day, she'd been shipped to Mrs. Throckmorton's Ladies' Academy. Fortunately, the headmistress valued loving-kindness as much as decorum and education.

"Well, your mama's pearls are your *something old*, and the dress Mrs. Throckmorton and the girls made you is your *something new*." Penny pulled a gold and crystal hat pin from her own sash. "I brought this to help keep your veil in place. It'll be your *something borrowed*."

"Oh, Penny! It's the one your papa gave to your mama—"

"On their first anniversary," Penny completed with a smile. "She would have wanted you to borrow it, I'm sure."

As they settled the sheer veil in place, Bethany confessed, "It feels scandalous, wearing a blue garter."

Penny laughed. "For all of our escapades, that makes you feel disreputable? What about the time we—"

A knock on the door interrupted them. "Ladies, it's time to go."

❧

Joshua stood at the altar and could hardly believe the vision beside him was real. Bethany handed his sister the bridal bouquet of Star of Bethlehem, phlox, flax, and violets he'd had delivered to her hotel, then knelt beside him so they could share Communion. The back of her gloved hand slid beneath her gossamer veil so she could partake of the elements. *Lord, bless our union. . . .*

He spoke his vows with assurance that no other woman could please him more. From the moment he'd met her, he'd lost his heart. Two weeks at Christmas and a few letters since were scarcely the courtship she deserved. Joshua thought about proposing and sending for her once he'd gotten settled in Oregon, but he was too smitten to wait. Then, too, he feared someone else would capture her affections if he delayed.

So here Bethany stood by his side. She turned to allow him to slip his mother's wedding ring onto her finger. In accordance with tradition, she'd split the glove along the fourth finger to make it possible, and he noted with pleasure that his bride's hand was both warm and steady. The flower-etched band fit perfectly. "With this ring, I thee wed and pledge thee my troth."

She looked up at him through the veil so he could see her tremulous smile and wide green eyes. *This beautiful woman is my wife.*

"You may greet your bride."

Joshua carefully lifted the veil and tucked it back over her glossy curls. She blinked; but since her cheeks turned a fetching pink, he suspected it was more from nervousness than the light. Settling one hand at her tiny waist, he cupped her cheek with the other and kissed her for the very first time.

Before he even drew back, Penny intruded and gushed, "Now we're really sisters!"

His father embraced Bethany. "Welcome to the family, dear. You're to call me 'Papa' from now on."

Josh watched his bride's smile warm. In that instant, he felt an odd twinge. He wanted the warmth of her smile to belong to him. *What if she just married me to be with them? She has no family, and Penny always said—*

Bethany turned back to him. "Thank you for the flowers, Joshua. They're lovely."

"As are you." He stepped into the space beside her that his father had vacated and barely touched the delicate lace on her sleeve. "Your gown does you justice."

"Mrs. Throckmorton and all of my friends helped me."

He chuckled softly. "You had three weeks. From what I've heard, the redoubtable headmistress could have marshaled an army and led it to victory in that time."

Her gloved hand covered her lips as merry laughter bubbled out of her, and her eyes sparkled. "In half that time!"

With a few loud, bright flashes, the photographer took their portraits, and the wedding party moved to the hotel's dining room. Josh wondered if Bethany regretted not having a huge wedding with pews full of guests, but her easy conversation and cheerful attitude convinced him she didn't find their special day a disappointment.

Penny could take the credit for that. He'd never paid much attention to the fripperies and silly details of these affairs. The pricey ladies' academy obviously taught those essentials, because Penny had swept into Independence and arranged for the church, music, the bridal suite at the hotel, and a special wedding supper. She'd even selected a new suit for him in honor of the occasion. In the end, Josh tended but one detail: Penny insisted Bethany wouldn't want fancy hothouse roses. Though Josh had seen brides carry lilies, he associated them with his mother's funeral, so he went out and gathered a bouquet of fresh wildflowers that very morning. When he'd seen them in Bethany's hands, Josh knew he had chosen ones that suited her—bright, pure, and fresh.

Josh rose from the table and extended his hand. "May I have a bridal waltz?"

"Why, I'm honored to accept. Thank you." Bethany beamed as she took his hand and let him lead her to the floor. Others noticed her attire and veil and left the floor as the chamber orchestra struck up a waltz.

"Doct—I mean, Joshua, this day has been perfect," she said as she gracefully followed his lead.

He spun her and relished her graceful moves and the way they made her satin gown whisper. "I worried it would be a disappointment to you."

"A disappointment? Oh, never!" She swayed to the music in his arms and flashed him an impish smile. "If anything, I'm relieved. I'd be embarrassed to make a big fuss when I've no family to fill my half of a church or reception. If you feel we're missing out on any important customs, I'll be sure to tie flowers and strings of old shoes to our wagon when we depart."

Josh drew her closer and chuckled along with her. Her lightheartedness and ready laughter captivated him at their first meeting; and each time they were together, he grew to appreciate her sense of humor. He gave her hand a little squeeze and teased, "I hear shoe leather is too precious on the trail to waste like that."

"Far be it from me to be a wasteful wife."

"Or a barefoot one," he added.

Bethany turned a beguiling shade of rose. "Oh, Penny didn't tell you about that, did she?"

"About you being barefoot?" He had no notion what she referred to, but she'd sparked his curiosity.

"Truly, Joshua, I normally wouldn't be so bold as to be caught in public in such a state, but it was the price of vanity."

He chuckled and repeated, "Vanity?"

Her eyes glittered with humor, and her beguiling smile demonstrated the ability to laugh at herself as she confessed, "I'll never again waste money on shoes that are too big."

"Even if they're beautiful?"

"I assure you"—she winked at Penny and Papa as he swept her by their table—"those slippers weren't worth it. Penny and I spent over an hour scrubbing the mud off the hem of my dress after that debacle."

"Where are those shoes now?"

She let out a small gasp. "You're naughty. You didn't know the story, after all."

"You can't leave me wondering."

"Very well. I doubt those lovely Italian leather slippers are still stuck in the mud. Most likely, someone happened by and declared they were an answer to prayer."

He smiled down at her. "Bethany, my dear, I'm sure you're right. I firmly believe in answered prayers."

Chapter 2

O h dear. I didn't think Uncle Bartholomew's wedding gift would be a problem." Bethany emerged from behind the dressing screen wearing her new
bottle-green-and-gold-striped dress and hastily slipped her snowy nightgown into the top bureau drawer. "Are we having our first fight?"

"It's hard for me to tell. You hid behind the screen until you were buttoned up
suitable for church, and now you won't look me in the eye." When she summoned
the courage to glance at Josh in the mirror, he patted the mattress in a silent invitation to come sit beside him.

Too embarrassed to share that perch since it was the site of last night's intima-
cies, Bethany sashayed to the raspberry velvet settee and tilted her head in a counter-
offer for him to join her. To her relief, he was mindful of her sensibilities and didn't
even comment about the fact that her heated cheeks must match the furniture.

Josh padded across the floor in his stocking feet and sat beside her. "I confess,
you surprised me."

Bethany couldn't hold back her laughter. "No doubt, I'll do plenty of that over
the next fifty years or so. Seriously, though, Joshua—Uncle Bartholomew insisted."

"We were going to share the wagon with Papa and Penny."

"The wainwrights already made and delivered the wagon. I even chose a beautiful shade of emerald and had them paint it."

"Pretty or not, it'll still need a team of oxen."

"Of course it will. They're in the stable with the wagon."

Josh's brow knit, and his eyes sparked with an emotion she'd not seen yet as he
said, "You've taken to arranging a lot on your own."

Bethany laid her hand on his muscular arm. "Don't you see? This way we'll start
out with a little home of our own, and we can take more essentials."

Looking less than convinced, he cast a glance at the trunk in the corner of the
bridal suite. "Just what essentials are we supposedly missing?"

"Oh, I started with 'Ware's Guide to Emigrants' as a foundation and composed
a list of necessities. Some things are already packed in the wagon."

He pulled a folded list from his shirt pocket. "I think we'd better compare lists.
Mine is from Marcy's *The Prairie Traveler*."

Bethany twisted to the side, opened the reticule she'd set on the table, and pulled
out a list at least five times as long. "Yes, well, that list was written by a military man.

He simply didn't expect to have to set up a decent home at the end of his trip. I've pared this down to the barest essentials."

"Let's have a look." He took the slip and began to read. His very stillness amazed her. The men she'd seen at church or the fathers who came to visit their daughters at the academy often rattled coins in their pockets, drummed their fingers, or jiggled the foot they crossed over the opposite knee—but Josh had a way of settling onto a seat and looking completely at ease and in command. At Christmastime that instilled a sense of calm in her. Now it made her nervous. She'd never sat alone with a man, yet she was married to this one!

At first he nodded in agreement with the items she'd listed. As the seconds ticked by, his expression became guarded. Finally, he turned and gave her a look of disbelief. "Calling cards!"

"They weigh nothing and take almost no space. I know every inch has to count, so I selected dishes and pots that all nest together. What did you think of the furniture?"

"Two chairs, not four. The bench and table are fine. Papa and I already lost the battle with Penny about the quilts." He winked. "I'm not going to waste my breath and go down to defeat again."

She eased back a bit on the settee. "I'm so glad you've agreed to the wagon. Since Uncle had his man procure it, it never occurred to me to ask you."

The corners of Josh's mouth pulled tight for a moment. "We're a team now, Beth. I'll always expect you to consult with me."

They went down the list, and Bethany tried to compromise. She would have anyway, but after unsettling Josh with the wagon, she wanted to ease his concerns. She sacrificed her barrel of straw-packed china and crystal. Wishing to show her cooperative spirit, she even agreed they'd bedroll beneath the wagon instead of using military camp cots.

"I'm not sure why you're taking a cookbook. You'll be making beans, biscuits, side meat, and mush."

Bethany shook her head. "Oh, no. Mrs. Collins's *The Great Western Cook Book* was a wedding gift from the girls at the school. They've been helping me research what will store and pack. We made jerked beef, dehydrated vegetables and fruit, and found other things to take so we'll have nice meals. You might have noticed I don't list salterus because I'm taking something new called Rumford baking powder. I bought some foods already, but we'll need to buy others at the mercantile here in Independence."

"Penny bought some supplies, but she was waiting until you arrived to get most of the provisions."

Sliding her hand over his, Bethany tried to choose her words carefully. "I know it's a delicate subject, but I'd rather discuss it with you." Encouraged by his approving nod, she continued. "Since. . .funds. . .have become a temporary issue for Papa and Penny due to your father's reversal of fortunes, I thought perhaps you and I could beg their indulgence because it's our honeymoon and shop for the supplies ourselves."

He smiled. "That would suit. Papa's pride has him spurning my assistance, but

I doubt he could refuse you anything."

"Perfect!" Bethany drew another item from the reticule. "Here you are."

"What's this?" Josh took the folded envelope and about choked when he looked at the letter of credit inside.

"My inheritance. The family attorney wired the funds to Mrs. Throckmorton once I received your proposal. I'm so relieved to give it to you. Carrying it made me nervous."

"It's a very substantial legacy. We'll endeavor to be good stewards. Did you have any hopes or plans for this?"

"I thought we'd use it to buy our supplies."

"Sweetheart, I can more than afford to provide for us. God's been very gracious to me. After our tithes and offerings on this, why don't we save the remainder and use it to build a nice house in Oregon or fund our children's educations?"

His reference to children made her cheeks grow warm. Eager to change the subject, she insisted upon Joshua showing her everything in his trunk so she could determine whether he had all he'd need, then was mortified that he insisted on inspecting the contents of her trunk. To her relief, he simply dipped his head when she held her hand against one drawer and choked out, "Small clothes."

"I'm pleased at how practical you've been," he praised, studying her dress. "Pretty, but not too many frills."

"Hopefully, the green and gold won't show dust or grass stains too badly." She looked down and pretended to brush away a speck of lint. "Everyone at the academy was so excited. They sewed clothes for me, and we figured out just how to use every last inch in the trunk. I don't think I could wedge in another thing."

"Not even another pair of Italian leather slippers?"

She buried her face in her hands as laughter bubbled up.

Josh took her wrists, kissed the backs of her hands very tenderly, then winked. "I'm teasing, but I'm not. I really do think you need another pair of shoes. Since I don't know how many pairs of stockings you have, we're going to get you a few more pair."

"Me? Oh, I don't think I'll need any. Quite the opposite; I was trying to find a diplomatic way of telling you I think we still need to stock up on essentials for you."

"I followed the list." He patted his pocket.

"That list was designed for an army man, not a doctor or family man. I'll make a deal with you: I'll get another pair of shoes and see to completing your necessities, and you can obtain more medical items to pack. One of the advantages of taking our own wagon will be that you can have a better supply of implements and pharmaceuticals."

After room service delivered their breakfast, they dined over by the window and watched the streets bustle with folks all preparing for their westward treks. Bethany added cream to her tea and asked, "Do you think we ought to buy a milk cow to take with us?"

"Have you ever milked a cow?"

"No." She waited a beat and added, "Just a goat."

He chortled softly then leaned forward. "Papa already bought one and named her Lady Macbeth because she's almost all white and has reddish brown spots on her forelegs."

A school bell clanged nearby. Josh consulted his pocket watch. "We're supposed to be at the meeting in fifteen minutes."

"I'm eager to meet all of our traveling mates. Aren't you?"

He rose and pulled out her chair so she could rise then bent down so his breath brushed her cheek. "Not especially. The most charming one is already in my wagon."

❧

Josh sat next to his bride and looked at folks in their square of benches. For the past twenty minutes, their guide, James "Rawhide" Rawson, had outlined their route and set out the rules for their train. He'd then divided everyone into three groups of twelve wagons apiece. Each group was to get acquainted.

Though Bethany sat with her knees pressed together primly, she folded and unfolded her hands in her lap. Just about everyone else seemed to be in motion, too. They crossed and uncrossed legs, fiddled with clothing, and gawked around, but Josh sat motionless. He could focus better when he stayed still, and he'd learned while sitting at his mother's bedside as her health faltered that tranquillity tended to be contagious. Whenever he sensed others needed calming, he purposefully acted restful. As far as he could tell, half of these folks were far too eager and needed to settle down; the other half were nervous enough that they needed to calm down. He shot Bethany a quick look and decided she fit into the latter category, so he slipped his hand over hers and gave her a reassuring squeeze as he suggested, "Why don't we get going on the introductions?"

A spry, fiftyish woman stood and bobbed her head at everyone. "I'm Willodene Haywood. Y'all just call me Granny Willodene." She cast a glance at the collection of children all wiggling in the middle of their square. "I reckon we'll never keep straight whose young'uns are whose today. May as well let 'em go out and frolic. You biggers mind the littlers. We're all gonna be together, so best you all learn to play nice." The children obediently traipsed outside.

Following Granny Willodene's example, folks introduced themselves. The Greens, Schmitts, and Barneses were all farming families, looking for a brighter future. Clearly, Orson and Eulalie Millberg counted themselves a cut above the rest of the travelers—they brought a little Irish maid along and hired a sturdy, taciturn man named Dillon Trier to haul their prissy daughter's piano in a second wagon. Rawboned Mr. Sawyer announced he'd be happy to use his carpentry skills to help folks out with their wagons if problems came up. The three Cole brothers looked brawny as oxen, and Josh thought the pharmacist, Mr. Harris, might be a nice companion for his own father and a professional ally for himself. He'd not paid attention to the man's daughter, but Bethany whispered, "Emma has such a shy, sweet smile." Young Parson Brewster, who performed their wedding, came over and took a seat. Bethany perked up a bit, and Josh suspected she subtly nudged Penny. He quelled a smile. Penny had played matchmaker for them; it would serve her right if Bethany returned the favor. Mr. Crawford, a book and Bible salesman, looked to have his hands busy with a wife, sister, and kids in tow. With Papa and Penny's wagon and theirs, the full dozen were accounted for.

Josh thought everyone in their circle looked hale. Both of the other circles belonging to their train had folks who hacked with consumptive coughs. He made a mental note to stock up on more eucalyptus and cherry bark.

Once their group finished the round of introductions, the menfolk seemed antsy to get out and see to matters. On the other hand, Josh noted how the women kept chattering and working at getting to know one another. The division seemed pretty clear: Most of the men were eager; most of the women worried about what lay ahead. He didn't want Bethany to fret, so he shot her a bolstering smile.

"Rawhide" banged on a post and gained everyone's attention. "Enough of the palavering. Weather's looking good, the prairie grass is four inches high so the oxen will have plenty to eat, and the mud on the trail's hardening. Since everyone has already mustered, we'll leave Thursday at daybreak."

"At least give us one more day—make it Friday," Mr. Millberg demanded in an officious tone.

"Nope." Rawhide turned his head to the side and spat a stream of tobacco into a brass spittoon. Without missing a beat, he added, "Friday's the thirteenth. Call me a superstitious heathen, but I ain't gonna set out on a day like that, and if we wait till Saturday, another train will set out ahead of us. Their livestock will eat the grass and foul the water."

"That part I agree with," said Parson Brewster diplomatically.

Rawhide smacked his gloves on his thigh in acknowledgment. "All of you are to bring your wagons and beasts to the edge of the west pasture by noon tomorrow at the latest. The Coles and I will guard them for you. Remember—pack for survival, not sentiment."

Bethany hopped up and tugged on Josh's arm. "We'd better hurry! He just cut our time in half."

Chapter 3

"Careful!" Josh drew Bethany closer as they walked down the rowdy streets of Independence, back toward the hotel. They'd just finished wedging the last of their supplies into the wagon. "I have to hand it to you, Bethy-mine. You jammed more into that prairie schooner than I could have believed possible."

She smiled up at him. "I think we work well together. It felt right, making those difficult choices as a team."

Accompanied by his big yellow mutt, Parson Brewster came toward them. He hefted a small crate of supplies and said, "We'll move out at dawn tomorrow. I'm inviting everyone to meet by my wagon for a quick word of prayer before we start."

Josh gave Bethany's hand a squeeze. "My wife and I will be there."

The next morning, he held her hand again as folks gathered together to ask God's blessing on their journey. The feel of his strong hand clasping hers and the first golden rays of sunlight made Bethany feel this adventure was blessed. Afterward, she scampered to their wagon while the men listened to a few last-minute details from the guide. She quickly attached the ribbon streamers and bunches of wildflowers she'd gathered to the back and sides of the wagon.

Penny brought over a sign that sent them both into giggles. Josh came over, took one look, and chuckled as he tacked it over the dish box. *TIED THE KNOT AND UN-AFRAY-ED.*

It temporarily covered the golden caduceus Bethany had painted on the wagon. "A traveling shingle of sorts," she'd told Josh with a shy smile. His pleasure at that tiny gesture warmed her heart.

The second Penny had seen their pretty-colored wagon, she'd dashed off to the mercantile and returned with a bucket of paint. That wagon now sported a coat of blue paint, and several spatters dotted the wheel spokes, giving them an odd likeness to robins' eggs.

Penny glanced ahead at her wagon then back at the other wagons. She moaned as she read the crudely lettered OREGON OR BUST the Cole brothers had painted on their wagon's canopy.

"Sis, don't you dare say a thing to them," Josh teased. "They just might start admiring the blue paint job you did and hire you to—"

"Bethany," she interrupted, "let's walk together."

"No, my bride's going to ride with me this morning." Josh slipped his hand about

Bethany's waist and snuggled her to his side. "We've been racing about for the past few days. It's time to take a breather."

"I'd like that," Bethany whispered.

The road away from Independence was so wide, the wagons lined up twelve abreast to leave. Folks shouted out with glee as Rawhide gave the order to set in motion.

"This is going to take some getting used to." Josh braced Bethany as she nearly slid off the seat after another jolt. They'd been riding almost half an hour, and every yard brought another bump.

"I read the ride would be jarring."

"You like to read a lot?"

"Oh, yes. Do you?"

He smiled at her. "When I have the time." Josh looked at the oxen again and said, "Papa grieved at selling off the library, but the books were too heavy to bring. All I have are Marcy's *The Prairie Traveler*, my Bible, and a half dozen medical books."

"Your father has a whole library memorized. I've never known anyone who could recite so many pieces. It's enthralling."

"I suppose it's not uncommon for an English professor to know so much, but he and Penny both have the gift of oration."

He shot her a quick glance. "I saw a few books in your trunk. What were they?"

She waved her hand dismissively. "Nothing much. Whoops!" She jounced into him. "You're going to need to doctor yourself for all the bruises I'm causing, crashing into you!"

Josh didn't press her about her choice of reading material, though he felt a stab of curiosity. The fact of the matter was, he and his bride needed to get to know one another. He moved on to a new topic. "When did you milk a goat?"

"When I was twelve, Mrs. Throckmorton arranged for me to spend Christmas with some of her relatives. I learned all sorts of wondrous things about animals. Other than last December with Penny and Papa and you, it was the best Christmas I remember."

Penny and Papa and you. She stuck me last on the list.

"I thought Lady Macbeth was easier to milk this morning."

Josh squinted to look past the oxen to the rear of his father's wagon. Papa had roped Lady Macbeth to it. "She's ambling along nicely. With all of this dust, she won't be white by noon."

"Neither will the milk." Bethany twisted backward and pulled a jar from a small bucket she'd hung behind their seat. As she let him peep beneath the wet dishcloth, Bethany chirped, "All of this jostling will turn it into buttermilk!"

"I've never had much of a liking for buttermilk, but I relish buttermilk flapjacks."

"Do you mind if I give one of the families with lots of children the extra buttermilk then make flapjacks later in the week? I have a menu all worked out for the next two days."

"Fine." He braced her as she turned to put the jar away. "Hold tight. Bump ahead."

Bethany pivoted and slipped her arms around him. The sweet scent of her honeysuckle perfume made him hold her even closer. Charmed by her self-conscious giggle, Josh brushed a kiss on her cheek and patted her before he let go. "Best put on your sunbonnet, Sweet Beth. The sun's starting to sneak over the top of our wagon."

As she tied the ribbons in a jaunty bow beneath her chin, his bride said, "I didn't know you disliked buttermilk. I recall from Christmas that you have a hearty appetite and prefer apples to cranberries. Tell me more about what you do and don't fancy."

"Everything you put in the food supplies looked good to me. You brought stuff I've never seen before."

"Oh, when I came back from Christmas without Penny because she was going on the trail, Mrs. Throckmorton used her upcoming adventure as a school project. We researched food, weather, and geography. Once you wrote and proposed, the cook went to the shipyard and train station to select the freshest fruits and vegetables from Florida, the islands, and South America. Everyone helped me preserve them. Mrs. Throckmorton and the girls have been like my family." She gestured ahead. "But now Penny and Papa and you are my real family."

Josh nodded. He didn't say a word.

❧

Bethany almost wished she'd walked with Penny, after all. Conversing with Joshua wasn't very easy. For the past four days, they'd had plenty to talk about and do. Now that they were all set and traveling, she came to a disquieting realization: she'd married a man she barely knew. She drew her cocoa-colored kerseymere shawl about her shoulders—as much to hide her shudder as to fight the April chill.

"Cold?"

"A little." She forced a smile. "I'm interested in hearing about what you've planned to do once we reach the Willamette."

"Each family is allowed to claim 120 acres. Papa and I will each claim land. We thought to build cabins close to the shared property line so you and Penny can help each other and visit."

"Wonderful!" She paused, then wrinkled her nose. "What about your medical practice? You'll be away from town."

"Not necessarily. We'll not be in a big city, but townships are springing up everywhere. Choosing a good location shouldn't be overly difficult. I anticipate I'll be called away at times, so I wanted our cabin close to others so you'd have help."

"You're most thoughtful, Josh, but you needn't fret. I'm quite independent."

"Are you, now?"

She heard the challenge and amusement in his voice. "Yes. Why don't you teach me how to drive this thing?"

"There'll be time for that later. The wainwrights designed a clever seat here, but we can ride my horse or walk alongside to spare the oxen."

"Did you get new shoes for your pony, as you did for me?"

His chuckle lightened her mood. "Yes, but I won't expect you to eat grass. I had a friend go to Chicago and do some horse trading for me." As Bethany looked at the two black-splotched white horses, Josh continued, "The one on the left is Tincture. He's Papa's. Ours is named Tonic."

"With names like that, they ought to stay in the pink of health."

"I hope so. That Tennessee walker of Orson Millberg's is a beautiful beast, but he'll end up in bad shape because he's accustomed to eating hay and oats. My friend got Papa and me these Indian paints because they're content to graze on the grasses."

"I hope you'll be content with grasses, too." She darted a look from beneath the brim of her sunbonnet. "I brought oatmeal, rice, barley, corn, and wheat."

"All that's fine—but I do like my flapjacks."

They spoke in fits and starts all morning. The awkwardness waxed and waned. Realizing her groom had sharp wit, Bethany tried to use humor to draw him out. By the time the wagons stopped for lunch, she was relieved to have Penny and Papa to help carry the conversation.

Papa threw a rust-red blanket on the ground near a patch of violet and yellow wood sorrel, and Penny brought buttermilk. While Josh delivered their buttermilk to the Sawyers, Bethany set out the fried chicken, cheese, and apple tarts they'd gotten as a boxed lunch from the hotel.

Up ahead a small ruckus drew their attention. Rawhide stayed mounted, glared down at the Millbergs, and waved at their maid. "Miz Katie, you put that chair right back in that wagon. You folks can sit on the ground just like everyone else. Noontime stops are necessities. Eat simple, rest up."

Mrs. Millberg huffed, and her daughter fussed about her frilly pink dress while Mr. Millberg scowled and rumbled, "Now see here. These are ladies—"

Rawhide interrupted, "Are you implying the other women in my train aren't ladies, Millberg?"

Papa leaned forward and helped himself to a chicken leg as he quoted under his breath, " 'Twas yet some comfort, when misery could beguile the tyrant's rage, and frustrate his proud will.' *King Lear*, act IV, scene 6."

Penny whispered, "Oh, I thought that was from *Taming of the Shrew*!"

Bethany dropped her chicken wing as her composure slid toward mirth.

Josh snatched it from the blanket. "Fly, little bird!" He tossed it toward the parson's big yellow hound that lay in the grass.

"Josh!" His name came out in a shocked interruption to her laughter. "You wasted food!"

"No," he said as he handed her another piece of chicken. "I paid a pittance for your priceless laughter."

Rawhide gave them only a short rest before he spat out a wad of chewing tobacco then rumbled, "Oregon ain't coming to you. Best get a move on. Want to gain as much distance as we can while folks and beasts are fresh."

By nightfall they'd traveled to the Methodist Shawnee Mission. For the first time, Bethany saw Indians. The men bought feed for their livestock, and a few of the women started to cook supper.

Josh insisted, "I'll arrange for supper for us. It's been a long day. I want you to rest."

Penny limped up. "Rest? Oh, that sounds heavenly. My feet are beyond sore. I'm inviting Papa and myself along. The honeymoon is over for you two."

"You're welcome to join us." Josh tugged Bethany away from the wagon wheel she leaned against. "But the honeymoon isn't ever going to end."

The honeymoon isn't ever going to end. . . . Josh's words echoed in Bethany's mind as he held her arm and led her back to their wagon after they'd enjoyed a delicious roast beef supper at the mission. All around them, folks unfurled bedrolls beneath their wagons. She smiled at him. "I guess this is our first night to have a canopy of stars."

Penny soaked her blistered feet in a bucket while they listened to some of the other travelers sing and fiddle.

Bethany continued to stand by the campfire. She longed to rub her aching hips, but that simply wouldn't do. Papa stood and swept his hand toward the chair in a gallant motion. "Thank you for the offer, but I prefer to stand."

Josh refilled his blue-speckled graniteware coffee mug and shot her a look. He sidled closer. "Wagon jounce you a bit too much?"

She felt her cheeks go hot and confessed under her breath, "I'm liable to lose either my molars or manners if I sit down."

"Feel like a naughty girl who got a spankin'?"

Straightening her shoulders, Bethany declared, "I have no idea what one of those would feel like."

Josh nodded his head knowingly, but his eyes sparkled with the impish humor she'd learned he exercised with endearing frequency. "I suspected as much. You must have been a very spoiled child."

Bethany made a show of looking about the wagon train as she declared, "I see all of the children have been tucked in. I suppose since I already have cinnamon rolls for our breakfast tomorrow, I'll turn in now, too."

Papa chuckled. "You napped along with the children while we crossed the Blue River, too. Fast as it was moving, I expected the roaring water to wake you up, but you slumbered on. Josh promised you'd already bought enough flour, but we stopped at Fitzhugh Mill and bought one hundred pounds more of flour and fifty of grist corn."

Bethany stumbled, and Josh steadied her. She laughed as if she'd been clumsy. . . but fear welled up in her throat.

Papa's so he and Penny could view this, too."

y rode back toward their green wagon, Bethany rested her head on his
He relished the feeling of her leaning against him, as if she fully entrusted
o his care. Still, he needed to say something. "About supper last night—we
osed to dine alone, and you invited a guest."

so sorry! Penny's terrified of Rawhide, and she insisted you wouldn't mind
g her from him. I didn't know what else to do."

stayed silent. If he complained about helping out his family, he'd certainly
off. Besides, she'd almost paid him a compliment by saying he was capable of
g them. Seeing as she'd apologized, he let the matter drop.

sh? I hate to ask, but how did you know which Cole brother is which? I can't
m apart!"

here's a space between Bert's front teeth. With Beau and Buck being identical
, I'm as lost as you are."

You're good at noticing little details."

It's part of being a doctor." He dipped his head and whispered, "It's part of
g a husband, too. This honeysuckle perfume of yours sure appeals to me."

"I confess, I dabbed it on to disguise the scent of those biscuits I incinerated."

"And here I thought you were being biblical."

She gave him a baffled look.

"I saw you reading Leviticus last night." He couldn't hide the chuckle in his voice
he teased, "So I figured you were inspired this morning to give a burnt offering."

For an instant, she winced, then her expression changed to carry a playful air.
I was just practicing for tomorrow. Since it'll be Sunday, I want to be sure to char
them to perfection."

"I suppose we'll be healthy, then. One of my medical texts recommends charcoal
for digestive complaints."

"Only thing is, you're complaining and won't digest," she muttered. "Mrs.
Throckmorton always gave me peppermint for such maladies. I like her medicine
better."

"I like this medicine the most." He dipped his head and kissed her sweetly.

❧

Sunday, after they spent part of the morning listening to a fine sermon on persever-
ance and had a quick noon meal, the wagon train set out. Penny started to plan a
supper menu aloud.

"Actually"—Bethany felt her cheeks go hot—"since our plans got scuttled
because you were afraid of our guide, I'm going to insist that you're on your own
tonight. Josh and I are going to celebrate our one-week anniversary."

That evening Bethany lit a candle, stood back, and smiled. She'd covered the
table with a white linen cloth and put a fistful of Johnny-jump-ups and poppy mal-
low in a tin cup. Her corn bread turned out perfectly. When Josh came around the
wagon, she singsonged, "Happy anniversary!"

He'd just seated her and taken his place when Megan Crawford ran up with her

Chapter 4

All too early the next morning, the crack of a gunshot sounded as the train's
wake-up call. Bethany crept from their quilts beneath the wagon so she
could start breakfast. Chilly air had her making coffee and oatmeal to go
with the cinnamon rolls.

"Delicious oatmeal, sweetheart," Josh said as she refilled his mug. He smiled and
leaned closer. "Do we have any hot water?"

"A bit to do the dishes."

"Good. Dip your hanky into it then sneak it to me." When she started to ask
why, he silenced her with a quick kiss before whispering, "Tell you later."

Josh wandered off as soon as she handed him her mug. Inside, the soaking
hanky steamed in the morning air. A few minutes later, he sauntered back, tossed
back another mug of coffee, and hitched up their oxen.

As he handed back her handkerchief, he murmured, "I needed it to draw a
splinter out of Dillon Trier's hand. It's not a big deal, but his boss, Millberg, is so
disagreeable, we want to keep quiet about it."

She whispered, "You trust me to keep a secret?"

"Trier doesn't mind you knowing as long as his boss is kept in the dark. I owe
my patients their privacy, Beth. Many's the time you won't understand what's happening. I'll expect your blind trust on those occasions."

Bethany nested the dishes in the dish box mounted on the rear of the wagon
then tucked her hands into the pockets of her apron. "If it's all the same to you, I
think I'll walk today."

Josh studied her for a long moment then said, "Fine, but we get to eat supper
alone then." He tapped her nose playfully. "And don't leave your shoes in a mud
puddle along the way."

As she walked along, Bethany thought of Josh each time she saw wet patches of
earth. This was the first day since their wedding that they'd been apart, and though
she'd felt awkward with him yesterday, she missed him now. Plans for a nice, private
supper filled her mind. What would make him happy?

Happy. He'd bent over backward to make her feel cherished. Guilt speared
through her as she wondered how he'd react when he discovered her fear of water.
Would he be understanding, or would he be mad? Deep in her heart, she knew she
ought to have told him about this weakness of hers, but Bethany had feared he'd not

wed her if she confessed how she dreaded water, and she couldn't let him leave her behind.

Penny chattered about the other folks on the trail, and she caught Bethany's attention when she dropped her voice and said, "Mr. Millberg has the looks and temperament of a troll!"

Bethany choked on her laughter then said, "Our guide surely took care of him yesterday. Why, the way Mr. Rawson championed all of us ladies—I think he's quite clever."

Penny shuddered.

"You needn't fear him. Josh told me he researched the guides, and I trust his judgment implicitly. Rawhide's capabilities and character truly impressed him. I'm going to think of our guide as a tattered knight."

"Knight? He's as superstitious as a Saracen! If you want to talk about knights, I'm positively surrounded by them. Will you think me too bold if I invite any of the men over for supper?"

Bethany shook her head. "Not tonight. Josh and I want to have a supper for two. Maybe tomorrow night. Mrs. Throckmorton would suggest Josh or Papa extend the invitation, though."

"Invites for what?"

Bethany and Penny both spun around at the sound of that deep voice. Penny stumbled and landed in a flurry of skirts and petticoats with a shriek.

"We're discussing supper, Mr. Rawson," Bethany stammered.

He crossed one wrist over the other on his pommel and leaned forward. "Call me Rawhide. And call me for supper, too. I'm obliged for the invite. See you just after sunset."

After he rode off, Bethany helped Penny up. "You'll have to handle him tonight."

Penny clung to her. "You can't expect me to entertain that heathen alone tonight!"

"Papa will be with you—"

"Papa will wander off and start reciting Shakespeare. Josh is the one who's vouching for Mr. Rawhide. The least you two can do is help me. You'll have plenty of other nights to share a private meal. After all, we're family—you have to stick by me!"

Penny was right. . .but Bethany felt her heart hitch. Would Josh be disappointed? Maybe not. He'd sent her off quite easily this morning. She spied a stem and white flowers and yanked a wild onion from the ground next to where Penny had fallen.

"See? That is a sign." Penny folded her arms resolutely. "I'm sure of it."

Bethany looked at the onion pensively. Surely Josh would agree that his sister needed their support. "With this as a start, what kind of menu do we serve to a Saracen?"

The next morning, Bethany moaned when she lifted the lid to the dutch oven. Last night's stew and fry bread turned out quite creditably. Josh hadn't said a word about them dining with his family and Rawhide, but she'd sensed tension in his shoulders, and he'd jiggled his leg instead of sitting still. Nonetheless, he'd said a kind word

about the food. Unfortunately, her luck hadn't held biscuits still looked gummy, but the bottoms. . .

"Ma'am," the bass voice of one of the Cole brothers "them biscuits of yourn are burnin'."

The lid clattered and dropped onto the ground. "Oh.

"Ain't no need to fret." The big, black-haired man stoop unbuttoned brown shirt to lift the lid, and shook off a few le swiped her favorite crimson potholder, took the dutch oven, a onto the inside of the lid, then neatly slipped them back into th "Iffen you settle coals atop the lid, they even up the heat so's the

Bethany stared at the charred biscuit bottoms and chewed h from crying. She knew her face must match the hot pan holder. Su lip on the dutch oven's lid made sense.

"Betcha ain't cooked none on an open fire."

"Just supper last night," she confessed thickly.

The black-haired giant leaned forward and rested his hands on hi be at eye level with her. His voice rumbled softly. "You'll learn. My m me. I reckon a smart lady like you'll pick it up right fast."

"Thank you, Mr. Cole." *Whichever one you are. . .*

"Ain't nothing. I was fixin' to start our vittles. Just need to reheat cornmeal mush and coffee. Iffen you don't mind me sharin' your fire, I'd obliged."

Five minutes later, Bethany watched as Josh tucked bacon into a singed and gamely ate it. Papa and Penny exchanged a look, said nothing, and unburned portions of their biscuits. Bethany intentionally served herself the of the batch. Bad enough she'd burned them—the least she could do was suffe consequences. Both of them looked like lumps of charcoal. The first bite taste dreadful, she sneaked the bacon out of them, then secretly dumped both into the as she reached for the coffeepot.

Mr. Cole turned out a neat breakfast and deftly slipped a wedge of fry bread int her apron pocket. Looking innocent as could be, he offered, "Doc, iffen you wanna take yore missus up to see Blue Mound today, I'll drive your rig awhile."

"I'd like that. Thanks."

Later Joshua cradled Bethany across his lap as Tonic crested the peak of Blue Mound. She gasped, and his arms tightened as they stared out at the expanse of prairie ahead of them. "Land! Hundreds of miles of land." *And not a river in sight. . .*

"Ready to cross that?"

"The books said the trip takes six months, but it looks like we'll take an eternity to traverse that."

"We'll make our way across together." He turned her face to his and brushed a kiss across her lips.

Bethany whispered against his cheek, "The adventure of a lifetime."

"Rawhide groused about folks coming up here for a peek. I wish we had longer to gaze out, but if we hurry back, Bert Cole said he'd jump from driving our wagon

to driving
As the
shoulder.
herself in
were sup
"I'm
protectin
He
set her
protect
tell th

twin

bei

arm about her nephew, Jeremiah. "Doc, I'm sorry, but this can't wait."

Later, while Josh carried Jeremiah back to the Crawford wagon, Bethany took a deep breath and picked her beautiful Irish linen tablecloth out of the dirt. Josh had swept supper clean off the table so he could lay the twelve year old there to set his badly broken arm. By the time Josh came back, she was prying cold corn bread from the pan to serve with the rest of the stew. Two hounds had slunk over and feasted out of the bowls that got knocked off the table. Yesterday's burned biscuits, now a ruined anniversary supper. . . She tried to tamp down her disappointment. Either her dreams were going up in smoke or to the dogs.

Chapter 5

J osh watched his wife and sister walking in the distance. They'd joined the other
women and children, keeping free from the dust the wagons kicked up. Penny
and Bethany chattered like two magpies on a clothesline. He didn't want to
begrudge his wife and sister their friendship, but it irritated him to feel as if he had
to keep walking a tightrope between being a newly wedded man and an amiable son
and brother. Everyone else seemed more than satisfied with how things were going.
Everyone but him.

Indeed, most of the folks had settled into traveling quite nicely. Farmers sat at
the campfire at night, remarking on how they'd normally be plowing and planting,
so this felt like a pleasant holiday. Little girls plucked fistfuls of wildflowers; and the
women had taken to harvesting handfuls of watercress, wild parsley, and wild onions.
Boys threw rocks and played with slingshots. Because the wagons jounced so badly,
most of the men walked alongside the wagons and occasionally cracked whips in the
air to direct the oxen instead of riding on the hard, wooden seats.

Why doesn't Bethany walk with me?

The temperature dropped to freezing last night. They'd awakened to frost on
everything. Instead of complaining, Bethany cheerfully whipped the cream she'd
skimmed from the milk she'd gotten from Lady Macbeth last night, added in a bit of
sugar, and whisked it with a few drops of cherry extract. They all ate their ice cream
atop buttermilk flapjacks for breakfast. Remembering how she'd recalled aloud how
he held a particular fondness for those flapjacks made him feel guilty for being surly
about her skipping along with his sister.

He wondered what Bethany planned for supper. The first few days she'd cooked
over the fire, she'd incinerated most of their food; but after a week and a half, she'd
grown quite adept at making delicious meals.

They'd decided after the first few days that a morning prayer together would
have to suffice, rather than lengthy devotions. With him needing to hitch the oxen
and her seeing to breakfast, matters were too hurried for much more. In the evenings, they'd sit side by side and have their Bible reading time. He'd thought she
might enjoy starting with the story of Noah—it struck him as fitting. As a matched
pair, they were on a journey to a new life. It was the only time he'd noticed she didn't
seem to enjoy their spiritual time together. Every once in awhile, he thought he
caught a flicker of discontent on her face; but just as he got ready to ask, she always

managed to say something perky that proved he'd simply misread her.

Marriage wasn't quite as easy as he'd expected it to be.

⁂

"So much for honeysuckle perfume," Bethany sighed as the sun set the next day.

Josh took one good look at his wife and sister and burst out laughing. "Gloves?"

Penny peeled off her elbow-length, once-white glove. "This is never going to wash clean!"

Bethany pulled off the other filthy glove from the pair of once-elegant ballroom gloves they'd obviously shared and nudged the basket of buffalo chips down at her feet. She cast a wry look at Penny. "If Mrs. Throckmorton could see us now!"

"She'd have a fit of vapors!"

Josh looked at the dried plate-sized chips, then at the gloves, and chuckled. "Would she be more upset about your gloves or about what you've collected?"

Bethany waggled her finger at him. "If you make fun of us, Joshua Rogers, you just might have to cook supper over those stinky things yourself!"

He twitched his nose. "Beth, the honeysuckle still wins as my favorite—but one of your suppers will, no doubt, smell terrific."

Penny spun her glove around like a slingshot and launched it at him. He caught it as she declared, "Mrs. Throckmorton always said the way to a man's heart is through his stomach!"

"I researched her academy carefully before I recommended Papa send you there. I knew she was a wise woman."

"That does it." Bethany went up on tiptoe and gave him a hug. "You're forgiven for teasing us. I didn't know you're the one responsible for Penny being my roommate!"

He hugged her back. "Do I get a kiss for making her your sister?"

Bethany pulled away and sashayed toward the wagon. Her words floated back to him. "No, but you'll get apple crisp for dessert!"

⁂

The evening after they traversed a hilly limestone region and crossed the toll bridge over the Wakarusa, Penny kept hovering. Some of the time, having family here was a blessing, not a burden. For now, Josh wished Penny would realize he and Bethany were entitled to some private time. More than a bit irritated, Josh finally groused, "Sis, we want to have devotions."

"Perhaps we could all join the others for a while," Papa suggested. "It's early yet."

Josh shoved his hands in his pockets and balled them into fists. He'd just about run out of tolerance.

"I don't think I could sleep quite yet," Bethany confessed, ruining his plan to take a stand.

Soon they all joined the others. Folks loved to hear Papa do recitations. He'd just finished Hamlet's soliloquy and beckoned, "Penny, come do Ophelia."

"Oh, great," Penny muttered. "I get to go die again."

Bethany whispered, "Want me to send that handsome Dillon Trier to rescue you?"

"I could only wish!" Penny sighed and took her place at the campfire. As she began, Rawhide tapped Josh's shoulder. Bethany grabbed his hand. "Do you need my help?"

Hours later, Bethany held Mrs. Wentworth's head as she got violently ill. Afterward, she blotted the poor woman's blue-tinged face and looked at Josh. He knelt quietly between two little boys who were curled double from stomach pain. None of the three of them stood a chance of surviving until morning. Mr. Harris was dosing two other children with some paregoric. With a miracle, that pair might pull through.

"Doc, we brought some tonic," one of the Wentworth men said. "Dr. C. V. Girard's ginger brandy. Says right here, 'A certain cure for cholera, colic, cramps, dysentery, chills, and fever.'"

"Fine. Give her a tablespoon."

"Here. I'll hold her head; you spoon it in," Bethany said. "It sounds like just what she needs. You're a very loving son, Mr. Wentworth."

Josh marveled at his wife's reaction. He'd plainly told her the woman wouldn't last another two hours. Instead of running from the face of death, Bethany wanted to comfort both the patient and her distraught family. In the midst of this travesty, he held on to the solace that she'd left the evening entertainment and willingly joined him here. Indeed, he'd truly married a helpmeet.

The next morning, after the assemblage listened to the pastor's brief prayer and sang a hymn, Rawhide stood between two of the graves. "Folks," he let out a belea-guered sigh, "Mrs. Wentworth and them boys drank tainted water. Let this be a lesson—no drinking, fishing, or washing downstream from where the animals water. Indians go by that dictum, and they fare middlin' well. I said it back in Independence, and I didn't want to have to repeat myself. Now let's move out."

Too weary to walk, Bethany rode next to Josh. She rested her head on his shoul-der and sleepily murmured, "Deuteronomy 1:21 says, 'Behold, the Lord thy God hath set the land before thee: go up and possess it, as the Lord God of thy fathers hath said unto thee; fear not, neither be discouraged.'"

He kissed her temple. "Thanks, sweetheart. I needed to hear that." As she drowsed, he pondered on the verse and wondered what discouragements and fears they'd need to overcome before they reached their promised land in Oregon.

❧

The mighty Kansas River's current churned by. The Pappan Ferry consisted of two very flimsy-looking canoes lashed with poles. One at a time, the wagons were taken across the two-hundred-yard expanse for four dollars apiece. The animals swam, and for the last trip, the ferryman put a set of boards across so the "raft" could carry the last group of folks across. He collected a dime from each passenger as he allowed them aboard.

"I've got hold of you, my Beth." Josh cupped her waist and swung her onto the raft. Excitement filled his voice as he said, "Come stand here. You can watch the last of the oxen swim across the river."

Bethany could scarcely make her feet move. When the raft bobbled, Josh balanced her and tugged her to the spot he'd indicated. The river rushed by; yet in contrast, her mouth was so dry, she could scarcely swallow.

Josh slid his arm about her waist and nestled her closer. She huddled there, desperate to draw strength and courage from him. He looked down and grinned. "Such bright, shiny eyes, sweetheart. I'm glad you're as excited as I am."

If only you knew the truth, Josh. . . .

All day long, their party's wagons had crossed the mighty Kansas River. When it was almost time for their wagon's turn, Josh answered an urgent call for medical help at the Crawford wagon. To Bethany's relief, several men volunteered to get her wagon to the other side. She'd spent the remainder of the afternoon trying to tamp down her fears. Now they all welled up, and Josh mistook her panic for thrill.

"Away!" the burly ferryman shouted.

The raft left shore, and Bethany's breath caught. Suddenly, the raft seemed horribly precarious. If a rogue tree snagged them, if boards slipped, if the current shifted. . .

Josh grabbed a pole and pushed a small keg away from the raft. Bethany watched in horror as it floated by. It fell off someone's wagon. What if Josh tumbled into the river? She grabbed at his shirt.

"Miss me?" he chuckled.

Bethany couldn't answer. She stared up at him as the sound of rushing water filled her ears and the sky dimmed and swirled.

Chapter 6

S he all right?" The ferryman gave Bethany a puzzled look. Josh cradled his limp wife in his arms and stepped ashore. Pale and clammy as could be, she'd not yet roused from her swoon. He strode toward their bright green wagon. It was easy enough to find.

Josh carefully laid Bethany in the late afternoon shade between two wagons. She'd started to stir a bit, but he was about ready to use this makeshift privacy to loosen her clothing. Surely, she couldn't be with child this soon. He didn't think she was laced too tight, and she hadn't struck him as the fainting type, but this swoon was lasting far too long.

"Here." His sister shoved a wet cloth at him then proceeded to wring her hands. "I feared this."

"Feared what?" He swiped at Bethany's wan cheeks and limp wrists.

"The river. It just—"

Bethany let out a small moan as her eyes fluttered open. Her brows knit as she blinked in confusion. "Where. . .what—ohh." A scant touch of color filled her cheeks as she struggled to sit up.

Josh heard his sister beat a hasty retreat. He kept his eyes trained on his bride and slipped an arm behind her shoulders to support her. "You want to tell me what this is all about?"

Her gaze dropped to her lap as she mumbled, "I'd rather not."

"I don't believe in husbands and wives keeping secrets." He tilted her face back up to his, and his heart skipped a beat when he saw how her eyes swam with tears. She tumbled into his chest, and he wrapped his arms about her.

"Bridge washed out," she said thickly into his shirt. "Mama and Daddy's carriage. . .they drowned."

"Awww, Bethy-mine." He kissed her temple and squeezed her. "Why didn't you just tell me you're scared of water?" A few minutes later, she pushed away from him, stood, and fussed with her hands. From the way she avoided eye contact, murmured something unintelligible, and hastened away, Josh knew she was still embarrassed.

"Psssst." Penny crooked a finger and beckoned him over to her wagon. Once he reached her side, she whispered, "Josh, I feel so stupid! I should have told you, but in all of the excitement, I forgot. Beth was in that carriage. The driver managed to save her, but she almost drowned, too."

He stared at his sister in shock. "Why didn't she tell me?"

"She's ashamed." Penny wrung her hands. "My guess is, she worried you wouldn't bring her along if you knew."

And she desperately wanted to be with you and Papa. . . . The instant after he thought that, Josh felt a surge of excitement. *This is how I can teach her to depend on me, to finally accept me as her protector and man. Each time we come to water, I'll be right at her side and see her through. She won't be thinking of Papa's stories or Penny's chatter at times like that—she'll need me to lean on.*

He strode off to find Bethany. The last thing she needed was to be alone right after reliving her worst nightmare. He wandered around the entire encampment and failed to find her. Frustrated as well as concerned, he glanced at their wagon and noticed how it jostled a bit.

"Bethany?" he called as he climbed inside.

She knelt atop a trunk and dusted her fingertips off on the skirt of her brown paisley dress. He'd noted she fussed with her skirts whenever she was embarrassed or uncomfortable. If ever a woman needed comforting, he was looking at her now.

Josh sat beside her and had to draw his left knee up to his chest because there wasn't enough room for both feet to hang down. He slipped his hand over hers and laced fingers. For a few moments, he sat motionless and let silence swirl around them. Finally, he said in his quietest tone, "It's not much of a home, but we've made every inch of it ours. It'll carry our goods to Oregon, and I'm going to be by your side every bit of the way—especially when we have to make crossings."

The Osnaburg canopy captured her soft gasp. She looked up at him, her eyes glistening. He wasn't sure whether it was with tears or determination. "I'm not well versed like Penny, but I have one quote by Shakespeare that I've claimed for our trip: 'Our doubts are traitors, and make us lose the good we oft might win by fearing to attempt.' I won't let my silliness hold us back."

"So my wife isn't just beautiful, she's also brave."

She bowed her head, but he still spied the single tear that slipped down her cheek. "No, Joshua. You married a coward."

"Nonsense." He tilted up her face, flashed her a rakish smile, and winked. "Clearly, you're a stalwart soul—you married me!"

"You're being too kind."

"Bethy-mine, I'm your husband. The day we took our vows, God made us partners. I'm here for you to lean on. Turn to me when you need help. I think it's about time for you to decide to do just that."

She gave him a wobbly smile. "I did determine one thing today."

"Oh?" He looked at her intently, hoping she'd show him a glimmer of trust.

"I decided how I want to spend my inheritance. I want us to drill a well and have our own pump so I won't ever have to see another stream or river once we reach Oregon."

❧

"I really do like wells," Bethany declared as she filled yet another bucket. It sloshed over and soaked her dress.

"Looks to me like wells don't like you," Emma Harris teased.

The women took turns while the men unhitched the oxen and fought to keep them from Vermillion Creek. Rawhide warned that the water wasn't good, so they were herding the huge beasts to troughs. The good grass helped keep the oxen in the roped corral after they'd been watered. It was only noon, but Rawhide declared they'd take the rest of the day and the next as "lay-bys" so the men could hunt and the women could catch up on chores.

"After I've had a drink, I've got laundry to do," Daisy Sawyer moaned as she rubbed her back with one hand and her very protuberant belly with the other.

Granny Willodene waggled a gnarled finger at her. "Time's a-comin' close for you to have that babe. You're gonna lay down in the shade and nap with the young'uns. I'll do your laundry, and your man can go look at my son's wagon. A wheel's getting the wiggle-waggles, so it's a fair trade."

"I'll never see the end of laundry," the Millberg's little maid, Katie, murmured.

Penny and Bethany exchanged a look. The Millberg women didn't do a thing. Poor Katie cooked, gathered firewood and chips, did the dishes, tended the laundry, and still had to attend to the silly and constant demands made of her. At mealtimes, after she served the Millbergs, she and Dillon Trier sat apart at a small crate because they were lowly hired help.

"Why don't we do the laundry together?" Penny suggested.

"Yes. . .and why not have a sewing circle tomorrow?" Bethany handed the bucket to Megan. "I have mending to do."

Buck Cole lumbered up and shifted his weight from one large foot to the other. "I overheard. I've got a heap of laundry to do, too. Fact is, I didn't bring enough soap, and I plum forgot Prussian blue powder. If you ladies are willing to share, I'll draw river water into your boiling pots."

No one said a word about a backwoods giant knowing about using the powder as laundry bluing. Later he grumbled, "Ain't fittin', them asking you to do this." He reached over and stole Orson Millberg's underclothes from Katie and scrubbed them himself.

Later, all of the river-rinsed clothes hung on ropes around the campground. The Sawyer's laundry was done, and the Barneses' wagon boasted a repaired wheel. Josh rode up on Tonic and swept Bethany right off her feet. She gave a surprised little yelp, and his laughter filled the air as they galloped off.

"What are you doing?"

He chuckled. "I'm kidnapping you. It's time we got away on our own."

❧

The next morning, the men got ready to go hunting. Josh had done guard duty all night and, though he would have enjoyed hunting, decided to nap awhile first. When he awoke, he scowled at the sound of Bert Cole talking to Bethany. After his romantic abduction yesterday, Josh felt sure Bethany understood he loved her. He'd even begun to hope she loved him back. She served him flapjacks every other morning, and at least once a week, she arranged for them to share a private supper.

So what was she doing, entertaining another man?

Josh hustled out of the wagon, ready to glower at his wife and blister Bert's ears, but he stopped in his tracks. Several of the women sat in a circle. Bert Cole had managed to wedge himself between Megan Crawford and Penny on a bench. A big giant of a man, he looked ridiculous with his elbows winged out and crowding the girls, stitching a button on an old shirt. "Done," he declared then bit the threaded needle loose from the shirt.

A second later, he glanced up. "Hey, Doc! I'm done with my chores. What say you and me take a hike over yonder? I set some snares, and I'm thinking we might get lucky."

Feeling guilty for harboring unwarranted jealousy and mean feelings for the poor man, Josh rasped, "I'd like that." He reached into the wagon and got his rifle, and off they went.

"Ya know, Doc, you and me, we're the only menfolk who know how to sew."

Josh let out a crack of a laugh. "I never thought of it that way. Now that I think of it, I do a fair amount of stitching."

"Well, I never woulda thunk it myself. I'm good at it, but it's 'cuz Ma made me learn to handle a needle and thread. With the three of us boys, we was goin' through the elbows and knees of everything we wore. Your bride—she's one dandy gal. She said you're a right fine doc—and from the way she glowed, I 'spect she's a mite biased in her opinion; but I seen how you set that busted arm and pulled two of them kids through the cholera, and I know she's not just boasting 'bout her man. Anyhow, in an emergency, your wife said she'd recommend my stitching to you iffen you needed help with suturing a body."

Well, well. Maybe I am making progress with my wife.

Unaware of Josh's musings, Bert rambled on, "I almost had to sew on all my shirt buttons, 'cuz they was in danger of all poppin' off. Right there in front of all them wimmin—and that pretty little Katie Rose—your missus said she figgers a man who can sew could stitch the gal of his choosin' right into his pocket." He patted the pocket over his heart.

"So you're carrying a torch for the Millbergs' Irish maid?"

"She shore is a beauty, but my brother helped her with some of the wash yesterday, and we might could come to blows over her, so we figured we'd best resist temptation. Besides, I seen her and Trier eating together all the time. 'Cuz I'm not a man to chase another's gal, I resolved to put her clean outta my mind."

Josh remembered those words late that night as he and Bethany snuggled under quilts beneath their wagon. They'd eaten a fine rabbit stew, thanks to the snares Bert set and Bethany's cookbook. Bethany whispered, "Penny is mad at me. When I got off the bench, Bert sat next to her. She's ordered me to protect her from his interest."

Josh snorted with laughter.

Bethany poked him in the ribs. "Shh!" She muffled a giggle and whispered, "But the funny part is, not five minutes later, Megan yanked me aside and begged me not to let Bert near her, either. She was positive he's sweet on her. The next time Papa wants someone to recite, I think Bert ought to do a selection as Romeo!"

"Bethany," Penny grumbled from the wagon next to them, "if we were at school, Mrs. Throckmorton would make you do dishes for a week for talking after lights out."

Bethany scooted closer to Josh and whispered against his lips, "Don't ask what Mrs. Throckmorton would do if she caught us kissing."

It was the first time his wife had alluded to their closeness. Josh gathered her tight. Finally, could she be falling in love?

R awhide ranks as the cagiest old coot I've ever met," Bethany groused. Josh stared at her. "You've been around Penny too much. You're starting to sound like her."

"Can you deny my assessment? He gave us all a day off, and now he's marching us twenty-two miles and over the Vermillion and the Black Vermillion, clear to the Big Blue all in one day."

She looked down and brushed a smudge off of her skirt and hoped he hadn't heard the way her voice cracked when she mentioned all three rivers.

Josh transferred the whip into his left hand and laced his right hand with hers. "You made it across the first with a verse."

"Judges 6:23," she quoted. " 'And the Lord said unto him, Peace be unto thee; fear not: thou shalt not die.' "

"So let's have a verse for the next river. How about Psalm 46:2? 'Therefore will not we fear, though the earth be removed, and though the mountains be carried into the midst of the sea—' "

Bethany squawked, "That's a dreadful choice!"

"Oops. Sorry."

"So am I. I shouldn't have snapped. It's horribly embarrassing to be such a baby."

"You're not a baby; you're a sensitive woman for very understandable reasons. I'll be by your side at each crossing. I'll take care of you, sweetheart." He paused then asked, "What about any other fears? Thunder? Lightning?"

She glanced off at a band of rapidly gathering clouds. "I'd better not have. That looks like a nasty storm brewing."

Rawhide kept the overlanders going, even when it started to rain a bit. Finally, he called a grudging halt.

Granny Willodene toddled by. She grinned from beneath her umbrella. "Saw me a gopher divin' into his hole, and two beetles follered right a-hind him. We're in for a three-day gullywasher. Best you think to make extry fry bread right quick-like."

Bethany and Penny took the old woman's advice to heart. They quickly mixed the batter and huddled under umbrellas as they struggled to light a fire. Bethany finally used four of her beautifully embossed calling cards as kindling. Once the flames started, they worked constantly to keep a fire going long enough to brew coffee, make the bread, fry some side meat, and prepare corn mush.

Josh got into their wagon and rearranged things. He slid a sheet of waterproof gutta-percha between the ribs of the wagon and the canvas to try to keep the worst of the water from dripping on their heads. Bethany lifted the food in to him. "Josh, some of the families are pitching tents."

"Rawhide suggested it for those who can't spend a couple of days in a wagon. The families have no choice." His voice dropped several notes. "And I'm not about to spend all of that time sharing you with Papa and Penny in a stinking tent."

The possessive quality of his voice pleased her, but she didn't have time at the moment to analyze just why.

"Rawhide said we'll be stuck here due to mud for a day or two after the storm. I'm just as glad the Sawyers have a good tent. Babies have a habit of picking stormy nights to make an appearance, and Daisy is close to term."

Bethany steeled herself with a deep breath. "I don't know precisely what to do, but if you need my help with her. . ."

"Granny Willodene and Nettie Harris already offered to assist with the delivery. I have no doubt that I'll need your help one of these days, but this birthing is covered."

Bethany let out a relieved sigh.

"Hey, you just told me you're not afraid of anything but water. Did the notion of tending a birth scare you?"

She bit her lip and shrugged. "I don't know what is involved, Josh. I'm trying my best to learn how to cook out here and be a wife. I'll do my best to fill in—you know that by now. You can't ask more than that." She fought tears as she turned away and tightened one of the ties holding the bonnet over the wagon's hooped ribs.

Long arms came around either side of her and retied the bow. In a carefully modulated voice, Josh said, "I know there have been a lot of adjustments. I'm proud of how well you're doing."

"I'm not doing well at all," she confessed in a choked tone. "The mush is lumpy and I singed my sleeve when I took the coffee off the fire."

He turned her around. "Did you burn yourself?"

"No, but I've ruined this dress."

"Dresses mend." He calmly unbuttoned what was left of her cuff and turned back the sleeve. "Your arm looks a bit tender. A little salve will help. You sit tight while I finish tying everything down, then I'll get some for you."

The wind howled and rain came down in sheets. After eating the lumpy mush and sipping tepid coffee, they decided to bed down for the night. Josh had grouped the trunks and crates together; then Bethany put towels in the dips to even it out as best as she could. Together they spread their feather bed across the not-quite-level heap and exchanged a wry grin.

"It's no worse than the rocky spot we slept on last night," Bethany said.

Josh slipped his arm around her waist, brushed a stray lock from her cheek, and kissed her. "I'd offer to pitch a tent, but we'd have company as soon as the last stake went in the ground. I relish the notion of being crowded in here with you for a few days."

A short while later, Bethany wiggled to find a less uncomfortable position, and Josh grunted. "Sorry. I can't sleep."

"Neither can I."

Bethany sat up, curled one leg beneath herself, and yanked his black leather bag onto her lap. Embarrassed by her emotional outburst earlier, she tried to sound composed. "Instead of moaning, why don't we make good use of our time?"

By the flickering light of a single candle, Bethany watched as he deftly pulled out each instrument, held it in his strong, capable hands, and identified it. She repeated the names of each item after him: scalpel, clamp, probe, retractor, lancet, tourniquet, burr, bone saw. . . .

A long while later, as the rain turned to sleet, he opened her trunk and helped her put on a second dress. He donned another shirt. Then they huddled beneath a quilt and talked between the ear-splitting rumbles of thunder.

During that time, something deep inside Bethany shifted. Josh had fallen asleep with his chest pressed against her back, his arm wrapped about her, and his breath ruffling her hair. Even in his sleep, he managed to settle into one position and stay put, solid as an oak. For the first time ever, she felt like she truly belonged. Ever since Mama and Daddy died, she'd been so very alone. Here, beneath a linseed-coated, double-thick canopy that leaked, in the middle of a sleet storm, she felt safe and secure in her husband's unyielding arms.

She'd started out with stars in her eyes and big hopes and plans for a perfect life as a good wife. *I was in love with the idea of being in love.* She nestled a tiny bit closer to Josh and felt an odd mixture of elation and serenity as she realized, *But now I'm in love with you, my dearest Joshua. Whatever battles lie ahead of us, I'll march by your side and depend on God's leading so we can make any obstacle crumble just as Joshua in the Bible did to Jericho.*

"Doc! Doc!"

"What is it?"

It took a moment for Bethany to realize that the light was a lantern, not lightning. Josh had already turned loose of her and was tucking a quilt back about her.

"Daisy—she's needin' you!" Zach Sawyer shouted at him. "It's time for the babe to come."

Groggily, Bethany sat up.

"I'll be right there, Zach," Josh said as he gently pushed her back down.

As the lantern light disappeared, Bethany shoved the quilts off and groped in the dark for his bag. "Can I get you anything?"

Josh yanked on his boots and muttered under his breath.

"What's wrong?"

"My lace broke."

"Pull on the other." She hastily lit a candle and fumbled to tie the ragged ends of the leather thong together. "There."

A streak of lightning illuminated his smile. "I'm set. You bundle up and go back to sleep, sweetheart. I don't want you to catch a chill."

"I'll be fine. Do you want some bread? I can heat up more coffee—"

He gave her a quick kiss. "I've got all I need. Pleasant dreams."

After Josh scrambled out into the rain, Bethany scooted under the covers, yawned, and smiled sleepily. They'd worked well together tonight. She hadn't really done much, but he knew she was willing to do whatever would help.

The first days of their marriage, she'd let herself get swept up in her husband's romantic ways and their fairy-tale adventure. In truth, that reflected honeymoon thinking. Really, this was a foretaste of what their marriage would be like—burned biscuits, blisters, and bad days all were part and parcel of a normal life. As a doctor, he'd get calls at all hours. She wanted to support him in every way possible—not just because that was what a good wife did, but because she loved him.

Chapter 8

Josh looked at Bethany and felt a surge of pride. She was an absolute wreck. Her hair hung in damp straggles and her skirts drooped in soggy clumps around her ankles. Dark circles shadowed her eyes, but she wore an angel's smile as she cooed and bathed the babe.

He turned back and spooned into Daisy the small dose of ergot he'd calculated. "You folks have cause to praise the Lord. Zach, your strapping son is as healthy as they come. Mrs. Sawyer, you stay abed and do nothing but feed him."

Bethany brought the baby over and tucked him in next to his mama. "He's got his daddy's husky build, but he favors you with his blond fuzz. I'll bring supper as soon as it's ready. I have some meat biscuits that turn into a rich stew when I boil them."

"That's right kind of you," Zach beamed, "but the Crawfords already offered tonight's viands. You folks did more than enough."

Josh pulled on his jacket and wrapped Bethany's cloak about her shoulders. "I'll check in on you tomorrow. Call if you need anything." He slipped out of the tent, hurried Bethany back to their wagon, and lifted her inside.

The birthing hadn't gone according to plan. Nettie Harris tried to help out, but she sheepishly admitted to suffering from *la grippe* and scuttled back to her own bed. Spry as Granny Willodene was, by midday, the rains proved too much for her old bones. Bethany had already slipped over to provide some of the savory stew she'd made from those odd meat biscuits, countless pots of coffee, and her own special brand of encouragement. When Granny hobbled away, Bethany volunteered to help. "I can ask Mrs. Green or Idabelle Barnes if you're uncomfortable."

To Josh's surprise, Bethany turned her head to the side and rasped something about Jericho that a rumble of thunder drowned out. By the time he could hear again, she'd pushed past him and knelt by Daisy's side. Bethany ended up doing far more than hold Daisy's hand and brew squaw vine tea to ease the pains; she'd actually assisted him with the difficult delivery. She'd done a fine job, too.

Partners. Yes, they'd been a true team, working together. He thought to praise her, but the words died on his lips. She'd taken off her cloak and promptly fallen asleep. He pulled off her wet boots and frowned at the way her damp skirts and petticoats stuck to her ankles. Still, it would be a shame to awaken her; and with a few more days of rain and mud ahead, every last garment they owned was bound to get wet. He took off his jacket and outer shirt. His warmth clung to the fabric. He swaddled her feet and calves in it then curled around her and drew up the quilts. Before he fell asleep, his last thought was that God had blessed him far beyond his dreams by giving him such a dear wife.

꙳

"It's a disaster!" Penny sat on a bench just a few yards from the clothesline Josh had strung between their wagons. Even the sound of the wind luffing the rain-soaked quilts couldn't muffle her wail.

The storm had taken a toll on everyone's nerves and possessions. Though inclined to agree, Bethany pasted on a bright smile. "You said the same thing last week when your hem caught fire while we made the beans, but that handsome Dillon Trier patted it out before you got burned. Looked to me like it was a pretty clever way of you asking him to join us for supper."

Penny blushed prettily, but she wasn't to be dissuaded. "This is a trouble too great to be borne!"

"Mrs. Throckmorton warned us to be careful about what we prayed for. You always fretted about how dismal your section of the garden grew, but now. . ." She let her words trail off as she tipped her head toward the soggy sack of flour at Penny's feet. Scores of tiny green sprouts poked out of it.

"It's all my fault. I bought middlings instead of finely milled flour."

"You were trying to be a good steward and economize. That's admirable. It's not really a disaster. Josh and I have plenty, and we can always stock up on everything once we reach Fort Kearney."

"But I can't accept charity—"

Bethany jolted and stared at Penny in utter dismay. "How could you possibly say such a terrible thing? You're my sister. That's not charity; families are supposed to work together."

Penny brushed a wisp of her golden hair back under her sunbonnet. "Thomas Jefferson said, 'It is in the love of one's family only that heartfelt happiness is known.' "

Leaning closer, Bethany said, "You know what's truly astonishing? I'm starting to feel like many of the folks on this train are family. The Cole brothers are like big, bumbling brothers, and Anna Schmitt is the sour-faced aunt who never has a kind word to say. Megan and Emma tend to be watching the children, but they are dear as can be."

Just then, Lavinia stepped in a mud puddle. "Daddy, *do* something! This is horrid! These boots were from *Paris!*"

"They've got mud in Paris, girl," Granny Willodene barked. "Stop havin' such a hissy fit. I swan, you're useless as antlers on a duck. Shake off the mud and help little Katie hang out the bedding."

"I may be muddy, but I'm not a lowly maid!" Lavinia huffed off.

Bethany turned away and grimaced. "I'm going to have to pray to have a charitable spirit, because I certainly don't want to claim Lavinia as family!"

"Good." Penny tapped her foot with emphasis. "If the Millbergs were part of your family and we're sisters, that would mean they'd be my relatives, too. I couldn't bear such a disaster."

"See? It put everything in perspective. Now the silly flour doesn't seem like such a catastrophe."

Josh returned from checking on Daisy Sawyer. He set his black leather bag on the wagon seat and playfully nudged Bethany. "I agree. Her Paris boots were no loss. I could have told her my discriminating wife suffered a far greater tragedy when she lost her Italian slippers."

Bethany tugged a long strip of leather from her pocket. "Speaking of shoes, Zach Sawyer made this replacement for your boot lace."

"Thanks, sweetheart."

"Oh, it's all part of being one big family on the trail," Penny chirped. "As if we aren't enough, Bethany is adopting nearly everyone."

Josh scowled. "Being friendly is fine, but you're going to have to draw some lines. There isn't enough time and energy to spend on everyone."

Chapter 9

Two days after the storm, Rawhide decided the mud wasn't enough to greatly hamper their progress, so he pushed the train ahead. The Vermillion loomed ahead. Josh watched as Bethany's face grew pinched and pale. By the time they reached the banks of the twenty-foot-wide river, he knew he had to do something to give her comfort. He stood behind her, commandingly turned her around, and wrapped her in a tight hold. "I'm here with you."

"Did Rawhide make it across?" Her voice shook almost as much as she did.

Josh stared intently at their guide as he dismounted midstream and held on to the saddle horn. He and his mount swam the rest of the way across. Rawhide had told the men that if he stayed mounted, they'd ford the river; if he had to swim, the storm swelled the river deeper than four feet, and they'd have to raft across.

"He made it, sweetheart. With God's help, we will, too."

Previous trains used the nearby oaks to fashion rafts. Once Rawhide declared those rafts sound, the party started crossing. Each day, the front wagon dropped to the back of the line. Though their wagon sat midway in the train, Josh decided his wife couldn't withstand the strain of waiting. He gave her a swift kiss and strode ahead.

"Fellows, I know my wagon's not first, but—"

"Say no more, Doc." Zach Sawyer slapped him on the shoulder. "You and your missus just hustle right on up here."

"Much obliged." Josh went back to his wife. "I've got just the spot for you, my Beth." He cupped her waist and swung her up into their prairie schooner. "Scoot over."

Bethany shimmied over, and Josh took his place beside her. One of the Cole brothers soothed an ox that seemed a bit fractious then led the team until they were at the river's edge. Men unyoked the team and sent them across while others pushed the wagon aboard the raft. Part of Josh wanted to help the men, but Bethany needed him. He promised himself that once they made it across, he'd help all of the others.

"Joshua." Bethany buried her face in his shoulder.

He slipped an arm under her knees and pulled her onto his lap. "First Samuel 22:23 says, 'Abide thou with me, fear not: for he that seeketh my life seeketh thy life: but with me thou shalt be in safeguard.'" He kissed her brow. "Now you say it."

"I don't know it." She trembled.

"It's a fine one to learn. Come on, sweetheart. 'Abide thou with me. . .'"

They made it across with her stammering each phrase after him. Pale and shaken, she looked up at him once their wagon hit ground. "We did it."

"Yes, we did. You can always rely on God's help, and you can depend on me, too, Bethy-mine."

"Thank you," she whispered as she slipped her hand around his neck and grazed a kiss on his jaw. His heart sang. Instead of paying attention to everyone else or swooning from her fears, she'd depended on him and appreciated his strength. Though he wasn't glad of her fear, gratitude for the opportunity to earn her trust and love filled him.

As Josh pitched in to help all of the others across, a verse flitted through his mind. *"In our weakness is he made strong."* Suddenly, a new sense of God's love and willingness to support and protect His children overwhelmed Josh. Just as he didn't mind Bethany's weakness and wanted to do all he could to give her succor, God willed to do those same things for him.

Someday, if God blessed them, Josh would be that same way with their own children.

❧

Twelve feet of water fell in joyous abandon into a crystalline pool. Bethany sat at the edge and soaked her feet. Being barefoot felt decadent, but all of the women were doing it together after finishing laundry.

Rawhide ordered the men to top off all of their water barrels. Fresh and sweet as it tasted, most men completely emptied their barrels, rinsed, and refilled them at an adjacent pool. Chafed by having to wait for the train ahead of them to cross the Big Blue, Rawhide paced between the men and women, spitting tobacco and grumbling under his breath.

"Alcove Springs." Emma Harris read the eight-inch-high chiseled words aloud. "One of my books says the Donner party—"

"Hush!" Rawhide rasped. "No one mentions them. Bad luck. Bad luck." He shook his head, scowled, and stomped off.

Noticing her friend's crestfallen look, Bethany swept her left foot in the water and splashed her. "You're going to have to read different material. I have something new—a thing by Beadle called a dime novel. It's the very first one, written by Ann Stephens, *Malaeska*. I read it during the storm. Would you like to borrow it?"

"Oh, I'd love to!" Emma's eyes shone.

"It's a dashing story," Penny chimed in.

"Humph," Lavinia sniffed. "I've seen you reading *Arabian Nights*. That was bad enough. A novel? And it cost a measly dime? Why, I would never read such trash. It's obviously morally inferior."

Irritated by Lavinia's judgmental ways and airs, Bethany pursed her lips then perked up. "There's Parson Brewster. Perhaps we could ask his opinion on the matter."

The parson listened then rubbed his chin for a moment before saying, "I'm a firm believer in bettering the soul. If you've spent generous time in Bible reading and devotions, though, I trust the Lord wouldn't frown upon His children improving their minds or lightening their hearts with either educational or pleasure reading."

"Thank you, Parson Brewster," Bethany and Penny said in unison.

After he walked off, Lavinia pulled her feet out of the water, stood, and stuck her nose up in the air. "I don't care. I refuse to sully my mind."

"At least she's consistent," Penny muttered. "She didn't like sullying her boots, either."

Bethany flopped backward and dissolved into guilty laughter. "Oh, Penny! That was much nicer than what I was thinking. I wondered if she really has much of a mind at all!" After she stopped laughing, she shielded her eyes from the sun and moaned, "Lavinia might be right: I'd better spend more time reading my Bible. It's much too easy to be catty."

Granny Willodene wandered past with some laundry over her arm. She chuckled. "Never thought that honesty was a sin. Does a woman good to speak her mind sometimes. We're taught always to be nice. Turn the other cheek. Grin and bear it. Well, seems to me that Christ got mighty hot at the temple when folks were doing wrong. He didn't mince His words with them Pharisees neither. Choose your battles, and keep a kind heart; but don't let the sourpusses like Lavinia spoil your joys, because if you do, you'll turn into someone just like her. Find happiness in the ordinary—it makes for a pleasant life and a serene heart."

❧

Bethany clung to Josh as they took the Independence Crossing over the Big Blue River. "Where to next?" she groaned once the train started moving again.

"We'll travel along the east side of the Little Blue."

She gave him a disgruntled look. "Who named all of these places 'Blue'?"

"Someone with no creativity," Josh quipped. When his lighthearted attempt fell flat, he wrapped his arm around her shoulders. "Not to rub in the word, but are you feeling blue today?"

Suddenly, the spot on the hem of her apron demanded her full attention. Josh watched as she tried to smear away the smudge. He tilted his head forward to see past the brim of her sunbonnet and noticed her cheeks carried an unexpected flush. "Bethany? What is it?"

"You've mentioned children." She paused then blurted out, "Not this month."

He stayed silent for a few moments then stroked her upper arm. "We have plenty of years ahead of us. The next months are going to be difficult on everyone—speaking both as your husband and as a doctor, I'm just as happy for you not to be in the family way yet."

She gave him a stricken look. "I thought you wanted children!"

"I do. I'm looking forward to a houseful of them, and you'll be a wonderful mother. For now, it's nice for us to have time together, alone."

"Oh."

He couldn't interpret her reaction. Was she simply surprised, or was she disappointed? Before he could pursue the issue, Penny came over and started to tag along, just like she had when she was a five-year-old pest. She chattered about Anna Schmitt gossiping about Megan Crawford and how Megan was a really nice girl who promised to teach them a new crochet stitch that night. Within seconds, Bethany livened up.

Josh withdrew his arm. Bethany didn't even seem to notice.

Chapter 10

They traveled along the east side of the Little Blue and halted for a day at the Hanover Pony Express stop. "Can you imagine?" Rawhide switched his wad of tobacco to the opposite cheek and continued, "The day after we left, the first Pony Express reached Caly-forny. They're a-running slick as cain be."

Papa brightened. "Excellent. It'll be no time at all before we'll have dependable mail service back to Boston so I can correspond with other scholars."

Everyone took advantage of the mail delivery and wrote letters home. Most sent several letters to friends and relatives. Bethany sent a single missive to Mrs. Throckmorton. The next day, they traveled fifteen more miles to the Holenberg station. Again, folks sat around chewing on pencil stubs and scribbling notes to loved ones. Bethany used some of her Baker's chocolate powder and Rumford baking powder to make three cakes.

"Sweetheart, wouldn't you like to send a letter to your uncle?"

She wrinkled her nose. "Last I heard, he planned to tour Europe. I have no idea where he is."

"I'm sure he'd welcome a letter waiting for him when he gets back."

She shook her head. "I wrote him faithfully for years. He never responded."

"Never?"

"Well, I did get one letter." She scooped more coals onto the dutch oven so the cakes would bake evenly. "When I told him of your proposal, he sent the note that he'd instructed one of his workers to acquire the wagon and oxen for us. When that man delivered them, he mentioned Uncle would be out of the country."

He tipped her face up to his. Instead of saying a word, he gave her a soft-as-spring-rain kiss. Her whole life had been devoid of gentle love and affection. He was more than willing to shower her with all of the care and attention she needed.

When they reached Rock Creek Station, Josh didn't bother to ask Bethany if she had anything she wanted to mail home. Instead, he sat beside her as she sewed. He'd learned if she curled one leg up beneath herself, she was content. He'd come to share the bench with her and smiled to himself as he watched her absently slip into that catlike position. "What are you doing?"

She bit a length of white thread from a spool and spoke slowly as she concentrated on threading her needle, "Your shoulders are getting broader. I'm letting out your shirts."

"We can buy some supplies here if you need anything."

Her eyes sparkled as she whispered, "Rawhide warned us not to. Mr. McCanless watches who spends a lot or dresses well. Then he charges more as they cross his toll bridge."

Though he'd heard the same, Josh enjoyed her animation, so he asked, "How much more could he charge?"

"Anywhere from ten to fifty cents per wagon!"

"That's quite a range. Then again, the stage comes here."

"I heard. Eloise Bearnoo is going back East on it instead of heading on to California. She says she's sick of being dirty, thirsty, and tired."

"You're heartier than that." He gave her an approving grin. "Tell you what: You might not be able to get some of the items later on the trail that they sell here. Go on in and get whatever we need. We've been out of eggs for a while. Get as many as you can."

She perked up. "Putting them in the cornmeal kept them from breaking till I used them up. I can do that again."

"Sure enough. Buy as many as they'll sell. Maybe get a little something special for Papa since his birthday's next week. I'll go speak with Mr. McCanless."

That afternoon, Orson Millberg blustered as he paid a full dollar to get both of his wagons across the bridge. Bethany scooted so close, she was practically inside Josh's shirt as he drove their wagon across. McCanless waved them, Papa, the parson, and the Coles' wagons across without asking for a dime.

As they stopped for the night, Parson Brewster walked up and shook Josh's hand. "That was kind of you—unnecessary, but kind."

"Appreciate your fine sermons. Seems like the least we could do."

Moments later gunfire sounded. Everyone gawked as Bert and Buck Cole wandered over to the Rogerses' wagon carrying five writhing rattlesnakes. "We reckon we'd like to repay your generosity today. We brung supper."

Rattlesnake, Josh decided that night, was a fine meal. It didn't taste half bad. Better still, as Bert fried it in two big pans, Bethany refused to leave Josh's side. To her relief, she hadn't found a recipe for preparing snake in the *Great Western Cook Book*. Best of all, Penny couldn't even sit at the supper table; and after the meal was done and folks left, Josh got to spend the rest of the evening just how he wanted to: without Penny or Papa hovering, completely alone with his wife.

❧

Bethany shoved her bonnet back and wiped perspiration from her brow. Mrs. Throckmorton would be mortified to see any of her young ladies in such a deplorable state. When they'd learned about the trail, some of the more basic truths got left out—like the fact that the Platte River was so shallow and muddy, they hadn't had fresh drinking water in days. . .so bathing and laundry were impossible. Add to that, she'd eaten rattlesnake twice in the last week, and Josh seemed to be losing his wits because he raved over what a delicacy it was.

A good wife unquestioningly follows her husband. . .but why can't Josh lead me to a big bathtub and pork chops?

As if he'd read her thoughts, he said, "We ought to make Fort Kearney late tomorrow."

Bethany held out hope until she spied the fort. Instead of the orderly military installation she expected, the plot of land was dotted with the saddest collection of ramshackle buildings she'd ever seen. Most of the buildings were soddies, and the soldiers lounging around them needed haircuts, razors, and baths even more than the pioneers. Almost a dozen men in patched uniforms went from wagon to wagon, offering, "I'll pay ya a dollar fer a half pint of whiskey."

The wagon train before them bought out most of the supplies at the store, so the stop barely seemed worthwhile. Upset that she'd find no respite here, Bethany tried not to reveal her feelings. Josh sat beside her and gave her a searching look. "Don't be so upset, sweetheart. We're doing fine—especially since you stocked up back at Rock Creek."

She bit the inside of her cheek to keep from crying and bobbed her head in agreement. Later, as she tried to hide her tears, the biscuits burned again.

※

"Wait a second. I need that bucket." Bethany ran up to Josh before he watered the oxen. She leaned over the bucket and carefully slid two eggs into the water and held her breath. Both bobbed beneath the surface, and she let out a sigh.

"Fresh or spoiled?"

She plucked them out of the water and didn't even mind getting her cuffs wet. It helped cool her off a bit. "Neither. They'll do for baking, though."

"We can't spare much water," he warned.

"I know. I'll use a can of Borden's condensed milk and fix custard."

Josh started to water the oxen. "I'm not keen on you using that canned milk. The Millbergs got sick on their canned lobster and East India sweetmeats."

"I already promised Papa I'd make it."

Josh slammed the empty bucket onto the sandy soil. "Does it ever occur to you to consult with me?"

Hurt, Bethany stepped backward and stared at him. He continued to glower at her, so she figured he expected an answer. "You took guard duty last night, and this morning you paid a call on Jeremiah to take off his cast."

His jaw jutted out as he shifted his gaze toward the rolling sandy hills. "Fine. Keep your word."

The rest of the day played out in silence. Papa and Penny raved about the custard. Josh and Bethany barely swallowed a bite. The rest remained in their bowls, and she finally scraped it out for the dogs.

"Let not the sun go down upon your wrath." The verse played through Bethany's mind. She couldn't very well go to bed and sleep next to Josh with this dreadful tension between them. She summoned her nerve and went to speak to him.

"Josh?"

"What?" he snapped as he smeared grease on the axles.

"I thought maybe we ought to talk—"

"Hey, Doc?" Rawhide strode toward them. "Some of the kids in the Caly-forny

142

group are getting croupy. Can you go see to 'em?"

"Sure." He climbed into the wagon, grabbed his bag, and stomped off.

Bethany scrambled into the wagon and whispered tearfully to herself, "He didn't even kiss me good-bye."

Josh was gone all night. The next morning, the party prepared to cross the Platte. Less than a foot deep, its sandy bottom could give way and cause a wagon to tip. Men carefully took poles and staked out a passage across the mile-wide river. Bethany kept watching her husband, but he never once looked back at her.

Weary beyond belief, Josh could hardly wait to tumble into the quilts. Two nights without sleep rated as a challenge back when he practiced medicine in Boston. Here, with hard physical labor all day, it tested his mettle. He plopped down at the supper table and barely tasted whatever kind of meat Bethany and Penny cooked.

"Music tonight, don't you think, Josh?"

He lifted his head and blinked at Penny.

She waved her hand dismissively at him. "Never mind. I'll just take Bethany with me. Mr. Green plays the fiddle divinely."

"I'd be pleased to escort you ladies," Papa said gallantly. "Penny and I will go get wraps and be back momentarily."

Josh waited until they left and shoved away from the table so forcefully, the bench he'd been sitting on fell backward. "So are you going?"

Bethany's eyes widened.

"Well?" he demanded.

"I—I guess so." She climbed into the wagon to get her shawl.

He followed her and found her hunched over her trunk, muttering. "What're you grousing about?"

"I don't know. I'm tired and dirty and can't even cook anything you like. You're mad at me, and I don't know why. I'm trying so hard to be a good wife."

"No." He bit out the word and shook his head emphatically. "You're not."

His harsh words nearly tumbled her into the trunk. She slammed down the lid and turned back to him. "I mend and wash your clothes. I make decent meals. I'm kind to your family. I've helped you with patients. I don't know what you want! Tell me what you want!"

"I want you!"

"I don't know what you mean."

"If you don't know, then this conversation is pointless."

She placed her hands on her hips. "Josh!"

He jammed his fingers through his hair in a single, vicious swipe. "Forget it. Just forget it. I'm too tired to deal with this."

"But—"

"Just go listen to the music. I need to sleep." He grabbed a quilt, climbed out of the wagon, and bedded down. As exhaustion claimed him, he could hear the plaintive notes of Homer Green's fiddle.

Chapter 11

“ranny?” Bethany drew her shawl closer and whispered in the old woman's ear, “Could you spare a moment?”

Granny passed the child on her lap to her daughter-in-law and stood. Neither of them spoke as they walked away from the campfire and music.

Barely a note of the music reached Bethany's ear. She'd been sitting there, pondering Joshua's words and the anger behind them. None of it made sense to her; but since she hadn't grown up in a family or around men, his behavior baffled her. *“Seek wise counsel.”* The words from Proverbs threaded through her mind, and she'd chosen the one older woman in the group she trusted.

Granny led her past the circle of wagons, waved off Homer Green as he strode his night watch, and settled into a sandy bank with a muffled grunt. Bethany joined her.

“You and your man havin' a set-to?”

Instead of feeling embarrassed, Bethany felt a surge of relief. “Yes. I don't know what to do.”

Granny stared up at the stars for a few minutes then asked, “So what do you think the trouble is?”

“I don't know what the problem is. Josh is mad, and he won't talk to me.”

“Men are a closed-mouth breed, child. Best you learn that straight off. He ain't said nothing a-tall?”

“He's weary, Granny. I've tried to make allowances for that, but he's gotten snappish over silly things like me promising to make custard for Papa without asking him. Tonight he told me”—she swallowed hard and whispered—“he told me he wants *me*. I've been his wife completely, so that can't be the problem. I just don't understand.”

Granny nodded and hummed sagely. “You sure you wanna listen to an old woman whose words have to cut so's the hurt will heal?”

“It can't hurt any more than knowing something is wrong.”

“Well then, put your hand in mine.” As soon as their hands joined, Granny prayed, “Lord, You're the Source of wisdom and love. We'd be grateful to You for an extry measure of both tonight. Amen.”

“Thank you, Granny. I don't have a mother or a mother-in-law to go to, and Penny—” She spread her hands in a gesture of helplessness.

“Good thing you didn't go to her. I'm 'bout to speak some truths, 'cuz you've asked.” She looked Bethany straight in the eye. “It's time you put being a wife first.”

Stunned, Bethany stared at her.

"Your man loves you. He protects you, provides for you, and treats you tenderly. Is it any wonder he wants the same commitment and consideration?"

"I do his laundry and keep the wagon neat and cook his favorite things. Mrs. Throckmorton always taught us the way to a man's heart was through his stomach, so I've tried hard to—"

"You're not getting the point." Granny leaned closer. " 'Member that sign on the rear of your wagon on the day we left Indy?"

"Tied the knot and un-afray-ed?"

"Well, darlin', he tied the knot, but you're at loose ends. He wants to hold fast to you, to be complete with you. The Good Book says a man shall leave, and the woman should cleave. Instead of cleaving to him and pulling the knot tight and secure, you keep snagging. You've lassoed his sis and pa into your lives, and the poor man is desperate for you to treat him like he's all you need to fill your heart. Instead of showing him your full loyalty and respect, you treat him like he's no more important than his kin. Betcha he's got it in his mind that you wed him to stick with his sister instead of because he captured your heart."

Granny's words triggered memories. *God made us partners. . . supposed to dine alone. . . I'm not about to spend all of that time sharing you with Papa and Penny.* Josh's words flooded back, and a terrible realization dawned. *He was telling me that all along!*

"Oh, Granny," she cried, "what have I done?"

"It ain't what you've done—it's what you're gonna do that matters. You love him, don't you?"

"With all my heart!"

"Figured as much. Time for you to talk turkey with your man. Time to tell him straight out that you love him. Then you're gonna have to show your devotion to him by putting everyone else a sad second. You got a big heart and wanna draw everybody in. When he tied the knot, he cut the strings to everyone else. What you need to do is put your man first. Let him know he's special, then all the rest'll fall into place."

Bethany nodded somberly.

"Best we get back and bed down. Tomorra's gonna come all too soon." They walked back to the wagons, and before they parted, Bethany gave Granny Willodene a hug. "I'll be prayin' for you, girl. Commit your marriage to the Lord, and it'll all come out right."

Bethany crept under the wagon, drew the quilts over herself, and snuggled close to Josh. Her chest ached with the sick feeling that she'd failed her husband so miserably. How he must have hurt to have finally spoken to her as he had tonight!

Even in his sleep, Josh rolled over and wrapped his arms around her. She pressed her ear to his chest and listened to the beat of his heart, all the while praying the Lord would reveal to her how to be the wife Josh needed.

❧

Josh crawled from beneath the wagon, yawned, and stretched. Somehow, he'd slept through the rifle shot to start the day.

"Good morning." Bethany brushed a kiss on his stubbly cheek and pressed a cup of hot coffee in his hands. "Breakfast is ready."

Papa plopped down in a chair and got an indignant look. "Where's my oatmeal? We had flapjacks yesterday."

"Josh likes flapjacks," Bethany stated as she put a small jug of molasses on the table.

Though everything else seemed the same, Josh sensed a difference in his wife. He couldn't put his finger on it. Last night he'd been sharp with her and stopped before he lost his temper. They needed to talk though. He'd let things get out of hand.

"Megan just finished reading *Malaeska*, so I thought we could walk with her and Emma today and discuss the book," Penny said as she cut her food.

"Go ahead. I'll be walking with Josh today."

Josh startled a bit at his wife's announcement.

"Marching alongside the oxen in this sand is no picnic," Papa announced. "You'll get gritty."

Bethany merely shrugged as if it didn't matter. Later, as she ambled at his side, she still ignored the unpleasantness of the terrain. "Josh, I need to apologize."

He glanced at her.

She slipped her hand into his and threaded their fingers into a weave she tightened with a squeeze. Then she turned her hand. "My wedding ring isn't shiny anymore."

"It can be polished."

"Our marriage isn't shiny anymore either, and it's my fault. I didn't grow up in a family."

"And you married me to be part of a family." Every word fell like lead bullets.

"Yes. No. Oh, Josh. I've done it all wrong." She let out a ragged sigh.

"Do you regret marrying me?"

"Never! I worry that you regret marrying me. Josh, we scarcely knew each other, and I've enjoyed getting to know you. You've grown in my heart until you've filled it completely."

He shook his head. "It doesn't come across that way at all. You've roped my family and half of this wagon train into our lives."

"Only because I felt so secure that my heart grew and I felt free to reach out. Now, though, I know I was wrong. My allegiance to you should have been the priority, and I ought to have made it clear that you rate above any other relationship."

"Even Penny and Papa?"

"Why do you even ask?"

He felt a pang at the confession, but it was time to settle the matter once and for all. "You're always asking what they want. You even list them before me." He kicked the sand with the toe of his boot and quoted the words he'd so often heard her say, "Papa and Penny and you."

"Josh, that wasn't what I meant. I was saving the best for last!"

The surprised hurt in her tone and the explanation acted as a salve to his wounded soul.

"It's not just your fault," he said. "I've been fostering the hurt instead of discussing it with you. I let my pride hold me back, and it's put distance between us."

She turned loose of his hand and wound her arm about his waist. He curled his arm around her shoulders and held her close. "I do love you," she said tearfully. "More than I ever thought possible."

"Those are the sweetest words I've ever heard. I love you, too, Bethy-mine."

"Granny Willodene once told me to find happiness in the ordinary because it makes for a pleasant life and a serene heart. I'm thinking that's true of a marriage, as well."

"You'll never be ordinary," he chuckled. "But I've already found considerable happiness in you. Ecclesiastes 9:9 says, 'Live joyfully with the wife whom thou lovest.' I think we've both been concentrating more on the future and our destination instead of enjoying each day as the Lord gives it to us."

"So we need to take pleasure wherever we are. . .even if it's a gritty, dry stretch."

"With the love God gives us, it's an oasis."

Rawhide rode up. "Keep a-goin', folks. We'll hit Ash Hollow tomorrow. Fresh water and trees."

Bethany stopped and wrapped her other arm around Josh and hugged him tight. "Our oasis!"

❦

Ash Hollow was the first steep grade they took. Men tied logs to the backs of the wagons to slow their descent. They camped for two days among the first trees they'd seen in over one hundred miles and relished the first fresh water they'd had in weeks.

Josh sat by his wife and smiled. She'd curled her foot up beneath her, and she hummed as she stirred something in a big bowl. "What do you have there?"

She held it up. "Have a taste."

He swiped his finger through the batter and licked the sweetness off. "Mmm. Apple something."

"Apple spice cake."

"Looks like enough batter to float a boat."

Bethany smiled. "Apple is your favorite, so I wanted enough for you, then I thought to make one for Granny Willodene as a thanks for her wisdom. Penny's going to sugar glaze all of them if she can have one to share while the girls discuss their books."

"Do we have that many pie pans?"

"No." She giggled. "So I'm baking one for the Cole brothers since they're lending me two pans."

❦

After a two-day rest in Ash Hollow, the train continued. A few men managed to bag some antelope. The women followed the recipe for roast saddle of venison in Bethany's cookbook. Penny made mashed potatoes with Edward's dried flakes, Bert made biscuits by the score, and nearly everyone else contributed dishes for a big feast. In the midst of all of the activity, Granny Willodene wandered toward a chair and swiped something from Lavinia's hands. "What is this?"

"None of your business!"

Granny turned the book over and read aloud, "*Malaeska*."

"I wondered to whom my book was passed," Bethany said.

"Well, I'm gonna hang on to this until Lavinia and her mama finish washin' the supper dishes," Granny announced. "Everyone else has worked for the meal. I'm sure they want to do their fair share."

Bethany thought the day had been surprising enough, but as the Millberg women washed the dishes, Buck and Bert Cole shuffled up. "Doc. Mrs. Rogers. Would you be willing to loan that dime novel to us?"

Josh raised his brow at Bethany, read her expression, and managed to sound completely unfazed. "Just as soon as Lavinia is done with it."

"Hope she reads faster than she does dishes," Bert grumbled.

"We have a long time on the trail. I promise you'll get to read it," Bethany said as she slipped her hand into Josh's.

Two days later during lunch, Lavinia returned the book, and Bethany passed it on to Buck as the wagon train started its afternoon travel. About an hour later, a huge mound of rock with a breathtaking spire came into view.

"Chimney Rock!" someone shouted.

"One-third of the way there," Papa declared.

"Well, what do you think?" Josh asked.

Bethany studied it. "It's certainly a magnificent thing. I can see why they call it Chimney Rock. It's aptly named."

"Are you longing for a chimney of your own?" Papa asked.

Bethany shook her head and smiled. "My hearth is an open fire. I'm content to walk toward the sunset and sleep beneath a canopy of stars, because God gave my heart a home in a green wedding wagon with the man I love."

FROM HALTER
TO ALTAR

by Cathy Marie Hake

Prologue

Littleton, Rhode Island—1868

B arney, anything interesting come in?"

"Ah-yuh. I posted them yonder." The young man jabbed his thumb at the wall.

Ellis Stack scratched his side and sauntered over to the collection of scraps of paper stuck on various nails lining the far wall. Squinting, he moved his thin lips as he sounded out each word. The middle post caught his attention.

> L. S. STOCKS
> BRIDLE ORDER: STURDY, DEPENDABLE, ABLE TO HANDLE THE
> STRESS OF HEAVY LABOR. PLAIN ONES ONLY. WILLING TO PAY FAIR PRICE.
> MANY NEEDED. CONTACT: JAMES COLLINGSWOOD, LICKWIND, DAKOTA
> TERRITORY

His pale face lit up with glee. "Send a reply straight off!" Ellis scrawled some words on a paper, crossed out as many as he could to save money, then shoved it at the telegraph operator. " 'Bout time things went my way. Let me know as soon as you get a response."

As he turned to leave, he heard Barney's twitchy index finger hitting the telegraph key. Every single dot and dash sounded like cash falling into his pocket.

> COLLINGSWOOD,
> REGARDING ORDER: FOUR READY TO SHIP. SUITED TO SPECIFICA-
> TIONS, WILL SERVE WELL. ONE FIFTY, PLUS SHIPPING, COD.
>   E. STACK

The next morning, Barney tracked Ellis down at the mercantile and handed him a folded slip. Ellis quickly opened the note.

MR. STACK,

AGREE TO PRICE. SEND WHAT YOU HAVE. AS MORE ARE FINISHED, SHIP AS WELL.

JAMES COLLINGSWOOD

Ellis smiled. The four headaches he'd been suffering were about to end.

Chapter 1

Matilda Craig stepped down from the Union Pacific train and sighed in relief. She'd had enough of the dust and smoke to last her a lifetime. Ellis hadn't told them they were coming to the western edge of the Dakota Territory. She'd listened to the man behind her call the place they were stopping by an Indian name. . .Wyoming. The name paired with the train's endless chug—*Why am I roaming? Why am I roaming?*

Small pebbles rolled beneath her black high-top boots, and she tried valiantly to keep her balance, but her effort was in vain. Both legs slid forward, and she made a very unladylike *oomph!* as she landed in a sea of ruffled cotton petticoats. The horse-hair bustle she'd hoped would make her appealing to her intended padded Matty's landing, but nothing would salvage her bruised pride.

"Here, miss." A mountain of a man plucked her from the ground and set her on her feet as if she weighed no more than a pail of milk. Concern lined his craggy, tan face as glinting hazel eyes scanned her. "Are you all right?"

"Nothing damaged but my pride," she confessed. "Thank you."

His large hand continued to cup her shoulder in a proprietary, protective manner. "The town hasn't put in a boardwalk yet. After the rocking of the train, you'll be a mite unsteady."

"I noticed." Matilda couldn't resist smiling at him. He'd been an utter gentleman—even if he wore fringed buckskin like a rough saddle tramp, and a thin veil of trail dust covered unruly waves of dark brown hair. She probably looked no better after five days on a train.

"Matty!"

Matilda turned at the sound of her twin's voice. Mountain Man kept hold of her, and she wasn't sure whether to shake him off or cling for dear life. The knucklehead who put this gravel at the train stop obviously never wore heels. The last thing Matty wanted to do was decorate the ground again. In the past two minutes, a full dozen men appeared and gaped at her. Bouncing on her bustle again simply wouldn't do.

"Is this it? Are we really here?"

Matty tilted her face up to the buckskinned behemoth. "This is Lickwind, isn't it?"

"Yes, ma'am." He shifted one hand to brace her elbow and reached out to help Corrine descend the slippery metal steps. "Careful."

"Thank you ever so much," Corrine murmured in her Sunday singing voice.

Though always sweet and painfully shy, she had a way of adding a lilt when she sang or found herself near a handsome man.

Matilda felt an unaccountable spurt of irritation. She'd found him first. Not that it meant anything. She wasn't going to get to choose her man, and neither would any of her sisters. Besides, Corrie hadn't done it on purpose; and she, more than any of them, needed folks to treat her gently.

With an air of expectation, Matty glanced at the rapidly growing collection of men who formed an arc around them. James Collingswood should step forward any minute now. He'd settle them in a boardinghouse until they courted a bit with their intended grooms. . .but if she could choose, Matty wouldn't mind a man like this one.

By the time pretty, dark-haired Bess descended, the men hurriedly started to preen. Hasty hands smoothed rowdy beards, hats came off, shirts were crammed into britches, and shoulders suddenly squared. By contrast, the mountain man calmly reached up to take four hatboxes, three valises, and a burlap bag and lugged two large steamer trunks from the disgruntled purser. Bess's beloved wooden hope chest came last, and her rescuer handled it with special care.

He set everything by Matty and her sisters then shot the cowboys and horsemen an amused look. A smile split his tanned face, and he murmured under his breath, "Ladies, I ought to apologize for them. It's been years since Lickwind boasted such a fine display of femininity. You must all feel like the only apple pie at a church picnic!"

His words broke their tension. They still stood in a close knot. Matty threaded her fingers with Corrine's to give her a bit of much-needed reassurance. "You've already been so kind. Could I trouble you to please introduce us to Mr. Collingswood?"

"I'm Jim Collingswood." He gave her a surprised look.

"Imagine that! Well, Mr. Collingswood." Matty tried to give him a composed look, even though she really felt like her insides were skipping rope. "We're the Craig sisters. I'm Matilda. This is my twin, Corrine, that's Bess, and Bertie is at the end. I have the papers for you in my valise."

"What papers?"

"To finalize the arrangements."

His brows knit. "What arrangements, Miss Craig?"

"Why, we're the brides you sent for."

❧

"Just how many brides do you think you get?" Jim's brother, Luke, asked as he nudged alongside him.

Completely thunderstruck, Jim stared at the women. "Brides? I didn't send for brides."

The gal who'd quite literally fallen at his feet pinched her lips together in a firm line. The one next to her, who had no more color than a mashed potato, huddled close. The last two exchanged horrified looks as the train started to puff off into the distance.

"We're just what you asked for on the bridal order. Sturdy, dependable, plain—"

It was too outrageous to believe. Jim shook his head. "Ladies, something has gone terribly wrong. I ordered plain, ordinary bridles for my horses—not brides!"

"I see," Matilda Craig said. She pivoted a bit, and Jim instinctively reached out to keep her from falling again. The way her shoulders started to shake made his heart lurch.

"No need to cr—" He jerked away as he realized she wasn't in need of consolation. Of all things, the woman started to laugh.

"We should have known Ellis would mess this up," she said, her voice bobbing up and down with mirth. Jim stared at her intently, hoping she wasn't sliding into hysteria.

"What do we do now?" the youngest one huffed.

"Told you this wouldn't work out," Bess said. "Matty, this isn't funny in the least."

"Oh, no!" The gal who was a very pale copy of Matty lost that pretty lilt from a minute ago. "What is to become of us?" She continued to clutch Matilda's hand and leaned into her, nearly causing both of them to lose balance.

Jim reached out to brace Matty before the two of them toppled over. In the middle of this whole confusing mess, he wondered how in the world Ellis Stack ever described Matilda as plain. Sunrise gold hair was plaited on top of her head like a crown. It framed wide, expressive blue eyes that would always let a man know precisely how she felt. The feel of soft fabric beneath his hand and the mind-boggling scent of flowery perfume made him all too aware he hadn't been around anyone half this appealing in ages.

But he wasn't about to marry her—or any of her sisters. What was he supposed to do with four females?

The youngest one scrunched up her freckled nose and repeated, "What do we do?"

"We'll just have to make do." Matilda pulled away from his touch, disengaged from her sister, grabbed two hatboxes, and handed them to the pale one.

Jim swiped them right back. "Your sister isn't up to this."

In a bizarre tug-of-war, Matilda grabbed hold of them. "Sir, I understand this was all an honest mistake, but you're not making it any better. Right about now, it would be best if you'd go mind your own business and leave us alone." One of the lids popped off, and gobs of thin-as-air, lacy stuff fluttered in the air.

Corrine sat down on one of the trunks and burst into tears.

As he helped Matilda cram the wedding veil back into the hatbox, she hissed under her breath, "Now look what you did!"

"Whatever it was, lady, I'm sorrier than you'll ever know."

Chapter 2

W e'd best come up with a plan." Bess gave the town a disparaging look. "Ellis already did that," Bertie grumbled as she flopped down on a trunk, "and look where it landed us."

"In the middle of nowhere, with no one to help us," Corrie whimpered.

Matty glanced at the odd collection of men and took their measure in a quick sweep. This lot rated more ragged than any group she'd ever seen. Most desperately needed to be reacquainted with scissors, a razor, and a tub. More than a few weren't refined sufficiently to keep from scratching like a hound with fleas. Even with all that counted against them, to the man, they'd all removed their hats and grinned. About half of them even boasted a full set of teeth. The minute one took a single step, the entire group trampled forward and formed a complete circle around them.

"Well." Matty injected a sunny tone to her voice and folded her hands in front of herself. "It's good to see so many strong, kind-looking men. My sisters and I seem to need to transfer our goods to the boardinghouse or hotel. Could I trouble a few of you—?"

"Back off." Jim Collingswood's low snarl made the men freeze. "Miss Craig, Lickwind doesn't have a boardinghouse or hotel."

Bertie banged her heels against the trunk and propped her fist on her hips in a most unladylike way. "Isn't this a fine kettle of fish? Not that I cotton much to the notion of getting hitched, but being stranded without a place to lay our heads or a decent meal—"

"Hush," Bess clipped as she lifted her chin. "We'll simply have to take the next train home."

All of the men bellowed in denial.

Matty opened her reticule and pulled out the last seventeen dollars she owned. "Here. Bertie, give us your money."

"I spent it."

"It's at least forty dollars apiece for the tickets." Corrie's voice shook as she stated the terrible fact.

Matty gave Bess a questioning look. Bess's thin-lipped expression made her heart fall.

"This isn't a normal train stop." Jim Collingswood's comment carried the flavor of a mortician's announcement. "Probably won't stop here for at least another week."

At wit's end and worried about the way Corrie blanched, Matty finally gave into temptation and turned around to invite Mr. Collingswood to keep his tidings to himself. . .but she forgot about the gravel on the ground. His lightning-fast reflexes saved her from another humiliating fall, but the result wasn't any more desirable. He'd grabbed and yanked, so she landed face-first into his buckskin shirt.

"For a man who don' wan' a bride, he shore seems to be stakin' a claim," one of the men said.

As several others hooted, Matty tried to summon a scrap of dignity and her balance. The minute she looked up into Jim's unblinking gaze, her tongue cleaved to the roof of her mouth.

"Easy now," he said in a strangely soothing tone.

"Whoa, there," another male voice said from a yard or so away. "Hey, Jim?"

Matty recovered her bearings enough to twist her head to the side and see who'd spoken. A man whose profile strongly resembled Mr. Collingswood's—good gracious; strong, handsome men were everywhere!—bent a bit. When he straightened, Matty realized he'd scooped up Corrie. Her twin drooped in his arms like a wilted daisy. He looked compassionate enough. . .until he curled his arms to hold her a bit closer. Then he looked as stricken as Matty felt.

"Hey, darlin', I'm right here to catch you," a straddle-legged man with a tobacco-stained moustache declared from behind Bess. "Always did favor the fillies with dark manes."

Bess served him a withering glare that made him back up a step.

While a handful of men all argued over who ought to get Bess and Bertie, Matty shook free from her captor and gave in to the very unfeminine urge to exercise a trick the hired hand back home had shown her. She stuck two fingers in her mouth, let out an ear-piercing whistle, then smoothed her skirts to recover her dignity while all of the men gawked at her in utter amazement.

"This has gotten out of hand. Where is the nearest patch of shade for my sister?"

"The rough seas," James Collingswood stated in a curt tone.

"There's no need to be mean." Matty glowered at him.

"It's my ranch." Jim Collingswood clamped hold of her elbow and started to drag her down the street as he ordered over his shoulder, "You men load the women's gear into my wagon. Luke, do you need to take that one into Doc's office?"

"Doc's gone again. May as well haul her home and get her rested up."

Jim stopped by a buckboard and cinched his hands around Matty's waist then hefted her up onto the seat without so much as a word of explanation. He boosted Bertie into the back as Luke laid Corrie in the wagon bed. Bess had managed to stop off at a pump somewhere and dampen her hanky. As she draped it over Corrie's forehead, Jim pawed through the possessions the townsmen hoisted aboard. The lacy parasol he pulled out looked ludicrous in his hands; and when he popped it open, Matty fought back the urge to giggle. None of this was funny in the least, but weariness and worry mingled to rob her of her manners. She started to laugh again.

As Jim turned to look at her, the rib from the parasol grazed through his hair and combed a furrow that stood at attention. His tawny eyes narrowed warily. "You're not going hysterical, are you?"

"No. Oh, not at all," Matty hastened to assure him. She smothered her levity and focused on Corrie out of concern for her as well as to keep from staring at his wild, parasol-framed hairstyle.

"Hold this over your sis," he ordered Bertie.

If Corrie hadn't been swooning so regularly in the past few months, Matty would have been far more alarmed. As it was, she fully expected her sister to rouse and feel mortified over all of the fuss, so she tried not to overreact. Clearly, what she needed to do was find someplace safe and cheap for them to stay until they could earn enough to catch a train back home.

Before she could pose any inquiries, Jim Collingswood swung up onto the seat beside her and put the buckboard in motion. "Sir, what are you doing?"

"I'm fixin' to clean up my mess." The angry glint in his eye made it clear just what—or who—that mess was.

※

"Kicked clean outta my own home," Jim muttered as he pitched hay into a pile that would become his bed.

"Yeah, and we helped Pa build every last inch of that place," Luke repeated once again from the adjoining stall.

Jim stared at the hay and forked over a few more hefty heaps then peevishly jabbed at a lump. "Propriety makes for an itchy bed. If Ma hadn't drummed respectability into us all those years, we could be sleeping in the study."

Luke let out a cross between a snort and a laugh. "Ma would skin your hide if she knew you'd sent for four brides."

"How many times do I have to tell you? I didn't send for brides; I sent for bridles."

Luke chortled as he flicked his wrists and the wool blanket fluffed out on the bed of hay. "If it weren't for that cute one feeling poorly, this would be a hoot and a half."

"She's feeling sickly? I thought only the one in the motherly way was under the weather."

Luke leaned across the stall and gave him an entertained look. "I was talking about the motherly one. Who are you so worked up about?"

"Not who. What. I made a close study of the ledger whilst you carried her up to a bedroom. A buck fifty for a bridle and shipping was fine—a hundred fifty apiece for four women is—"

Luke whistled. "More ready cash than we can scrape together. You know, maybe this was meant to be. That motherly one isn't in any shape to stick back on a train."

"Don't even think about it." Jim waggled his finger menacingly. "We lollygag around on this, and she'll be too far gone to travel. Spending the whole winter in the stable so's those gals can take over our house is just plain crazy. We have to come up with a plan."

"I'll concede that point."

"So I started thinking, maybe we can just send them back. You heard Matty: Tickets cost forty bucks. We'll do that and toss in an extra hundred so that brother-in-law won't have call to shove 'em outta their place this winter. It'll stretch our budget, but we can manage."

"Forty bucks is low-class accommodations. You couldn't possibly do that to those poor sisters, specially not the"—he patted his washboard belly—"one!"

"I suppose you have a better idea?"

"There's no rush. The next eastbound train won't stop here for nine days. Until then, you'd best cool your temper and figure on getting some tasty meals for a change."

Jim heaved a sigh as he flopped down on his itchy, makeshift bed. He stacked his hands behind his head and stared at the cobwebs adorning the barn's crossbeam ceiling. "I guess that's some consolation."

"Best meal we've eaten in years."

"Don't get used to it, Luke. No use compounding one mistake by making a bunch more."

Chapter 3

Matty sluiced water on her face and sighed with delight. Last night she and her sisters made good use of the tub. After that dreadful five-day train ride, she'd been sure she'd never come clean. They'd acquainted themselves with the kitchen and whipped up chicken and dumplings. While they shared the supper table with the Collingswood brothers, no one had concocted a solution to their quandary.

The Collingswood brothers revealed their father had died four years ago, and their mother and sister now lived in Chicago. Jim looked at Matty and waggled his fork to punctuate his words. "No woman was made to live out here. Our ma and sis got out alive—two others came and didn't make it through their first winter."

James didn't ask them any personal questions. That notable omission made it clear he was unwilling to entertain any notion of honoring the mail-order arrangement—mixed up as it was. He held no responsibility for the predicament, and Matty almost felt relieved. She hadn't been happy about being sent out here to husband hunt. . .so why did she still feel a twinge of regret that this cowboy didn't want her?

He'd answered enough questions for the sisters to learn the Rough Cs Ranch ran cattle; but during the spring and summer, the brothers also captured and tamed wild mustangs. Clearly, they were ambitious men; and from the looks of the buildings and grounds, they were also very hardworking.

Luke managed to coax a bit of information from Matty and her sisters; but for the most part, he'd avidly eaten every last bit of food on the table.

Corrie fell asleep over dessert, and Jim Collingswood shot her a worried look. "Doesn't appear as though that afternoon nap did her much good."

"Corrie's a widow," Matty said as she rose. She'd rehearsed how to impart the news as delicately as she could, but now that the time was at hand, the words nearly choked her. "She'll make aunts of us all just before Christmas."

Both men stood when Matty rose. The table manners and genteel customs they displayed came as a very pleasant surprise. So did the fact that Luke bent and carefully scooped Corrie into his arms. "I suspected she was in the family way when I caught her at the train stop. I'll take her back upstairs."

As his brother carried Corrie to her bed and Bess followed along to tend her, Jim held Matty back. "And she came out here as a bride?"

Matty sighed. "My sister Adele's husband took over our parents' dairy farm after they passed on two years ago and made life for us unbearable. Corrie came back to live with us a couple of months ago, the day she became a widow. Ellis knew she was in a delicate condition, but it didn't matter to him in the least."

Jim shook his head in disbelief. "I suppose bringing her here was more merciful than leaving her in his care."

❦

More merciful... His words echoed in Matty's mind this morning as she braided her hair. Quietly so she wouldn't wake Corrie, she slipped into the blue delft-patterned dress she'd made from feed sacks and tiptoed out of the room.

"How's Corrie?" Bess whispered in the hall.

"Still sleeping like a baby."

"Good. I just woke Bertie. She was upside-down in the bed and still won't turn lose of that hatbox of hers. She's never suffered wearing a bonnet gladly. Do you suppose we've finally started taming her into womanhood?"

"I dearly hope so. Perhaps all of our prayers are finally being answered."

Bess shook her head as they went down the stairs. "I'm afraid not. We prayed for godly men to be our husbands. Instead, we're going to have to make our way amidst the rabble and roughs until we earn enough money to get back home."

"Or we could settle here. Ellis will marry us off to whomever he can just to get rid of us. If we make Lickwind our home, at least we can stay together."

"I declare, Matty, you're always making the best of a situation. Problem is, I can't see how we'll ever manage here on our own for any longer than it'll take to earn train fare."

"We'll consider it as a challenge. I was thinking last night—"

Bess shot her an alarmed look. "Oh, no."

"Now listen. It's a good plan. Only one of us needs to get married. Ellis had no right at all to sell us off as if we were his property. He put us on that train, and he's keeping the dairy farm."

"Adele didn't look very sad, sending us off," Bess grumbled as they entered the kitchen. "She and Ellis deserve one another."

"I figure they owe us for taking our share of the birthright; and this whole trip was Ellis's idea, so I don't feel bad that they're out the money for our train fares. We need to put together whatever we have left. That'll be enough seed money to set up a solid business in town."

"Town didn't look any too industrious. It's no more than a spit in the wind."

"Bess!" Matty laughed. "Mama would have a conniption if she ever heard you talk like that." While Bess humphed, Matty continued. "We could do mending and baking. I'm sure we could make it work."

As her sister lit a kerosene lamp, Matty stirred the embers in the four-burner Monitor stove and added another log. "I'll go milk the cow if you gather the eggs."

"You can't go into the barn. The men are there!"

"Which is why the cow is tied up by the coop." Matty grabbed a pail and scooted out the door. She'd managed to cajole one of the hands to find her a heifer that was fresh last night. He'd looked at her as if she was crazy as a loon for making that request, but he'd also been more than eager to please. As it turned out, Western ranches only viewed the cattle as beef on the hoof and ignored the dairy possibilities. Matty resolved to discuss that matter with whichever rancher married her.

The lavender predawn light allowed her to pick her way across the yard. Matty patted the Rough Cs' brand on the heifer's hip. The three wavy, parallel lines with a tilted *C* riding them were both clever and would be hard to tamper with. It seemed the Collingswood brothers thought of almost everything except a milking stool. One would be nice; but since they didn't have one, she squatted down and set to work. Leaning into the warm side of the cow, she quickly hit a rhythm and filled the bucket.

"Forty-one eggs—half of them brown!" Bess declared as she exited the coop. "Can you imagine having such fine laying hens?"

"Beats frying lame hens," a man drawled as the sound of a shotgun being cocked clicked.

Both sisters jumped and yelped.

"Dear mercy!" Matty set down the milk before she spilled it.

"Sir, you have no business sneaking up on women." Bess clutched the egg basket closer and peered into the shadows.

The barn door crashed open. Jim and Luke Collingswood both bolted out with guns drawn. "What's wrong?"

"Found these two sneakin' round the henhouse," a gangly man said as he stepped from behind the privy. He bobbed his grizzled head. "Caught 'em red-handed. Cain't say I ivver seen prettier thieves."

"Thieves!" Bess stepped forward in outrage. "I'll have you know—"

"We were getting ready to make breakfast," Matty interrupted. "And we expect you'll be at the table in about fifteen minutes."

"Boss, is she givin' the invite to you or to all us hands?"

"Just us, Scotty," Jim growled as he cradled his rifle so it didn't endanger anyone. He looked as comfortable as a mother rocking a baby. The fact that his shirt hung wide open and he was standing barefoot on prickly straw and cold dirt didn't even seem to register.

"I heard tell you got yourself some brides from the train yesterday. Thought it was just Lanky's whiskey talkin'."

Luke shoved his revolver into his waistband and held his shirt closed. "I was wondering if I dreamed it myself."

Matty saw the impish sparkle in Luke's eyes, but the fire in Jim's made her decide to stick to the facts. "How many hands do you have, Mr. Collingswood?"

Jim closed the distance between himself and Matty. He scowled. "Don't you go getting any romantic notions about my men. I pay 'em fair, and they earn it; but not a one of 'em is marriage material, so you just stay away from them."

She nodded sagely. "I understand."

"Just what do you understand?" The muscles in his well-chiseled jaw twitched.

She turned away, dragging Bess along with her, and called over her shoulder,

"You're a man who needs his coffee before he's ready to face the day. See you in a quarter hour."

Fifteen minutes later, Jim figured his mind was playing tricks on him. He couldn't possibly be smelling coffee—not out here in the birthing shed when he needed to concentrate on the high-strung mare.

"Looks like you could use this," Matty whispered as she slipped up and pressed a steaming cup into his hands. She held a plate in her other hand—one with a mountain of fluffy scrambled eggs, biscuits, and gravy.

He hummed in appreciation as he took a bracing swig of the coffee then accepted the plate. "Miss, you don't belong out here."

Her soft-as-flannel blue eyes twinkled. "Mr. Collingswood, we had a dairy farm back home. Indelicate as it may be, I've tended to the business end of plenty of farm animals."

"Is that so?"

Her calm demeanor surprised him. "Your mare's taking a minute to gather up her strength. Why don't you have a quick bite while I wipe her down with some straw?"

"You?"

Instead of being insulted, she looked at the mare. Her voice took on an amused flavor. "Well, forget your breakfast, cowboy. This one's not going to wait."

A short while later, Jim stood by Matty's side and chuckled. "That foal's a hungry one."

Matty nudged him and giggled. "I'll bet you are, too. A dog ate your breakfast while we were busy."

He spun around and gave the empty plate a look of utter despair. "Dumb dog would try the patience of a saint. One of our hands went to town and, um—"

"Got lit?"

Jim could scarcely imagine this prim woman knew slang for a man making a fool of himself at the saloon. He cleared his throat. "Well, to make a long story short, he spent a whole month's wages on beer and what he thought was some fancy, purebred sheep."

"So now you're saddled with a poodle!" Matty's merry laughter filled the air for an instant, then she recovered her composure. "I apologize for making light of the situation. You're a good man to let him keep the dog, and at least he's one of the big ones so you don't have to worry about the horses trampling him."

Jim cocked one brow and drawled, "Are you trying to make me thankful to have that miserable beast?"

"It's not always easy to trust God when He puts odd circumstances in our lives, is it?"

"You talkin' about Ramon or about you and your sisters?"

"Maybe a bit of both."

The sparkle in her eyes warmed something deep inside of him. Instead of nagging or wailing, she acknowledged this wasn't a good situation.

"I'm sure you're still hungry. I'll be happy to fix you something."

Just as he opened his mouth to refuse, his stomach growled. Jim gave her a wry smile. "I'd be obliged."

They walked to the kitchen door. The whole way there, he kept getting a whiff of her flowery perfume. Nine days of this—then he'd have things back in order. He grabbed the doorknob, twisted, and pulled. . . .

And nearly got knocked over as the ugliest thing he'd ever seen cannoned out of the house. A second later, the poodle streaked past, making more racket than a stampede of wild mustangs.

"What was that?"

"Roberta Suzanne Craig!" Bess shouted from the kitchen as Jim turned to watch the dog tree a spitting ball of fur.

Matty sighed. "I guess Bertie didn't pack a bonnet in her hatbox, after all."

Chapter 4

Jim stared at the ledger and gulped the dregs of his coffee. A soft rustling at the study door made him look up. "I thought you might appreciate a draught so you'd sleep well." Matty approached his desk and set down a teacup that exuded a pungent aroma. "I've no doubt you're hurting."

"It's not necessary." The stuff smelled worse with each passing tick of the grandfather clock. Then again, his leg ached like crazy and so did his shoulders.

Once he'd snagged Bertie's very ugly, very pregnant cat, Rhubarb, from the cottonwood, both animals massacred him instead of each other. Bess dragged the dog away, Bertie claimed her hideous fur ball, and he'd stomped off toward the pump.

Matty got there first and had already filled a bucket. "Come into the kitchen. I'll take care of you."

She'd been more than true to her word. Matty did a remarkable job of cleaning and stitching up the dog bite on his calf, and she'd applied a soothing salve to the deep cat scratches on his shoulders, too. To his surprise, she never batted an eye at the blood or the fact that he had to remove his shirt. She'd been soothing as could be and skilled enough to earn his respect. Better still, she hadn't chattered or expected him to be sociable.

Corrine sat by the kitchen window to mend his shirt, Bess made him a gigantic ham omelet, and Bertie mumbled an apology for her wayward, hideous cat after locking it up in her room. She'd then gone to the barn and polished five saddles to make amends.

Jim hated each and every kindness because he didn't cotton to owing anyone anything. Now, instead of them owing him for bending over backward to keep them, they'd gone the extra mile to make atonement—and it was for nothing more than a pair of lamebrained animals acting true to form. All day long he'd thought of how those Craig gals pitched in to make things right.

Now Matty was at it again. She still had that serene, comforting air about her, too.

"You're not poisoning me, are you?"

Her smile could light up the ranch on a moonless night. "I'm afraid I didn't bring anything toxic in my medical supplies."

He motioned for her to take a seat. "I didn't ask this morning, but I wondered what a gal like you is doing with a doctoring bag."

165

On her way to the leather wingback chair, she straightened the portrait of his parents that hung a bit askew. Oddly enough, she didn't act all fussy about it; she calmly set it to rights and even smiled at his folks as if she held pleasant memories of them.

"Back home, Dr. Timmons was stretched too thin. I'm handy with a needle, and I'm not goosey about changing dressings. Papa finally arranged for me to tag along with Doc for part of a summer so I could learn a few handy skills. I'm glad to see Lickwind boasts a doctor."

Jim winced. "Don't put too much store in Doc Mitchel. He didn't get formal training—he picked up whatever he knows on the battlefield. Best you and your sisters stay fit until you're back where you can get decent care. . .especially Corrine. A woman in her motherly condition doesn't belong out here."

"Believe me, Mr. Collingswood—"

"Jim. Two brothers sharing the same last name and four sisters sharing theirs will make formal address confusing."

"Three sisters. Corrine's last name is Taylor. Though I acknowledge that we'll avoid considerable chaos if we follow your plan."

He picked up the tea, gave it a wary look, and took a quick gulp. He half lowered the cup, squinted at the remaining fluid, and shuddered.

"I can see you prefer my coffee over my curatives."

Just to prove he wasn't a coward, Jim glugged down the rest and shoved the cup across his desk, only to discover a butterscotch candy on the saucer. "What's this?"

"It'll take away the dreadful aftertaste."

"Something had better." He popped the nugget into his mouth and said around it, "I haven't tasted anything that pitiful since—"

"I burned the chili two nights ago." Luke chuckled from the doorway. "Neither of us can cook worth a hoot."

Matty tilted her head to the side and looked downright sympathetic. "You gentlemen must tell us what you enjoy. We'll be sure to make it for you."

"Since you asked," Luke dove in without taking a breath, "cinnamon buns. Pork chops. A nice, tender roast with mashed potatoes and gravy. I'd think my mouth died and went to heaven if you'd boil up a batch of some kind of jam. Yes, that would—"

"Be far more than is necessary," Jim cut in. With each thing his brother listed, he'd been able to imagine the taste until he practically drooled. He slammed the books shut and stood. "It's past time we parted company for the night."

A sweet pink suffused Matty's cheeks as she backed up and left the room in a swirl of blue-and-white skirts. Her voice drifted back to them. "Just wait one more minute!"

Jim glowered at Luke. "Don't let your belly take over your brain. We've gotta get these women shipped out of here."

Luke shoved his thumbs into his pockets and rocked back on his heels. "I wouldn't mind sleeping in the stable if we got fed as well as we have all day long."

"Come December, you'll sing a different tune. Let's go hit the hay—" He paused, stretched, and winced. "Literally."

Matty and Corrine stopped them as they headed out through the kitchen. Matty shoved plates that held huge wedges of pie onto a tray. Corrine hastily added two cups of steaming coffee as she said, "Black for you, Mr. James. One spoon of sugar in yours, Mr. Luke—just as you like it."

Jim tried not to scowl at Corrine. Though she and Matty looked similar, Corrine seemed so fragile. One false step, one harsh word, and he feared he'd send Matty's twin into another swoon. "Obliged, ma'am." He took the tray and lifted his chin. "Now you stop fretting and scamper off to bed. Best you take proper care of yourself."

Matty slipped up and curled an arm about her sister. The tenderness in her smile could bring a man to his knees. "Thank you for your concern, James. I'll be sure Corrie rests."

Jim lay in the barn with the sweet taste of Matty's canned-peach pie on his lips, the warmth of her coffee in his belly, and the smell of fresh hay for his pillow. A man could do worse. . . .

Luke cleared his throat in the dark and rumbled, "I was thinking—"

"That's always dangerous," Jim said wryly.

"If we married them, we could sleep in the house and eat like that all of the time."

"Luke, you whizzed right past dangerous and plum hit loco."

❧

"Tell me it isn't so!" Matty laughed as Bess and she held opposite ends of a sheet and wrung it out.

"Every last word is true."

"Will wonders never cease!" They pinned the last sheet to the clothesline then hastily hung all of their small clothes between the bedding so the men couldn't see the unmentionables.

Men had dropped by all morning. The Hatch cousins—Oscar and Linus—stopped by to "swap howdies." The blacksmith, Amos Freeling, came calling to see if someone could read his latest mail and write letters for him. A shipment from the feedstore was delivered. James scowled at the fact that it had taken Keith Squires and two other men to bring out that one buckboard. In fact, one-eyed Gideon, the saloon owner, managed to dig out some long-forgotten requisition for medicinal whiskey that suddenly ought to be delivered in case of emergencies. Jim had already shooed his own cowhands back to work when they'd been moseying around the barnyard.

"I'd best add this apron into the wash kettle," Bess mused as she pinned up one last petticoat.

"Better not. I already put the men's shirts in the pot. I won't be surprised if the dye on them runs."

"No telling what'll happen. I'm expecting them to fall to pieces. Dirt's probably all that's holding them together."

Matty looked at the ranch and nodded. "They're hardworking men."

"I grant you that. You'd be happy as a cow in clover, staying out here. Me? I've had enough hay and fences to last me a lifetime. I'd rather settle in town."

"I've been gathering information."

Bess pushed the shirts around in the laundry pot with the paddle as Matty added another log to the fire beneath it. "And here I thought you were just making friends with every cowboy on the spread."

"Well, that, too." Matty accepted the truth with a small ache in her heart. She'd always managed to befriend the men in their congregation and the dairy hands. Each one ended up treating her as his sister. That was part of the problem though—not a one ever actually looked at her as wife material. If she were dead-level honest, none of them seemed much like husband material to her either. Never once had she felt the spark she'd seen between her parents. Still, she longed to be a wife and mother.

"Are you going to daydream, or will you tell me what you found out?"

"Oh." Matty smoothed back a few stray tendrils. "The only place in town that's empty is the jail."

"The jail!"

"It's not as bad as it sounds. They don't have a sheriff here. The building is completely empty. It's between the barbershop and the, um. . ." She knew Bess would be unhappy with the other business.

"Not a house of ill repute!" Bess lurched backward.

"No. The saloon."

"Lord, have mercy on us," Bess muttered as she fished out a shirt. "It's not as bad as it sounds. It's worse!"

Matty watched as a sleeve fell off the garment and plopped back into the pot. She could see Jim walking toward them. Even from this distance, she heard his moan. She quietly echoed her sister's prayer, "Lord, have mercy on us."

"Matilda Craig," he thundered, "did you go into the bunkhouse?"

"Only after Chico assured me it was empty."

"Woman!"

She smiled at him. "Really, James, I was very circumspect."

He folded his arms across his chest. "Just what is circumspect about a woman in a bunkhouse?"

"Rhubarb went in there. I didn't think the men would be very happy if she decided to have her litter on one of their beds."

"Chico could have gone in and hauled her out. Chico should have."

"I'd normally agree, but Chico sneezes around cats."

"Buckwheat—"

"Your cook isn't to be trusted around animals. He threatened to dice Ramon and Rhubarb and put them in a stew!"

Bess said, "They need to boil awhile before they'll turn out right."

"Bess!" Matty wheeled around and stared in shock at her sister.

"I was talking about these filthy shirts," she said as she dunked a pair of them. "Bertie loves that cat. Our sister has been dragged halfway across the nation and doesn't have a place to call home. The way she clings to Papa's old felt hat nearly breaks my heart. The last thing I'd do is let anyone touch a hair on that cat's—" Bess's voice died out as she searched for an adequate description.

"What happened to that mangy-looking creature, anyway?" Jim asked.

Matty stuck her hands in her apron pockets and looked Jim in the eye. "Ellis tossed a garter snake at her. She leapt off the fence and landed in a bad patch of tares. Bertie couldn't pull them all out, so she snipped out the worst ones."

Jim didn't say a word. He shook his head in sympathetic disgust of her story then turned and strode off. When he got a few yards away, Matty heard him mutter, "Plumb loco."

Chapter 5

Matty sat out on the porch steps and savored a cup of coffee. The supper dishes were done, and she wanted to get away from her sisters for a few minutes. Though they got along well enough, five days on a train counted as enough togetherness. A little breather, and she'd be happy to go sit with them in the parlor.

"Ever seen such a sky?" asked a voice as velvety and rich as the star-studded, purple-black heavens.

Matty shook her head—partly because she hadn't ever seen anything as endless as the Western sky, but also because she felt unaccountably tongue-tied around Jim Collingswood.

He leaned against a post that held up part of the veranda and murmured, "Looks can be deceiving, Matty. It's so pretty and peaceful. Problem is, this land is wild as can be."

She took a sip of coffee and let silence swirl about them. "So you came from Chicago?"

He nodded. "Moved here in '62. Mama came because she loved Pa to distraction, but she rated the venture as pure folly. After one year, she sent my sister Annie back to a finishing school. Annie married within months. Pa, Luke, and I got the ranch started, but Pa fell off a hay wagon and got run over in '64."

"Oh, Jim, I'm so sorry."

"Accidents happen out here all of the time. It's why you don't belong. Women are too vulnerable." He stared at her.

"What about your mother?"

"Soon as Pa died, she went back to be with Annie. She couldn't wait to 'get back to civilization where a woman can be a lady.' Luke and I decided we had a good start on things, so we've been here on our own for the past four years."

Matty laughed briefly. "From what he said about your cooking, I suppose your survival is something akin to a miracle."

"If you're talking about marvels, explain to me why you're not married yet."

Matty gave him a weak smile. "Until I find a man who can hold me as dear as Papa held Mama, I don't want to marry. I didn't feel that special spark with any of the men in our church, but a handful of them turned out to be fine friends."

"Come on, Matty—there wasn't one special man?"

"No, but I played Cupid and matched a few of them up with my friends. I even introduced Corrie to her husband."

Jim squatted down and tilted her chin upward. "Matty, why didn't you marry one of those fellows? It was much safer than coming out here to a complete stranger."

The concern in his voice and eyes made her breath hitch. "Ellis made our lives miserable. Bess and he got along about as well as Rhubarb and Ramon, and Corrie needed to get away from all of her memories."

"Still, the man ought to be strung up for concocting the plan to send you here."

She sighed. "It's appalling. I'm not a husband-hunting kind of woman. I finally decided maybe it was a blessing in disguise—at least all four of us would still be together."

The muscle in his jaw twitched. He stood and pulled her to her feet. "I'll be sure you're all settled together, wherever I send you. Now go on inside."

Oomph! Jim landed in the dust and nearly got the wind knocked out of him. Any man with the brains of a trout would know to keep his mind and eyes on the mustang, but Jim had gotten distracted. Amos and Keith had come from town and sat up on the patio, sipping cool drinks with Matty. He'd chased both of them off just two days ago. What were they doing back here again?

He stood, drew in a few steadying breaths, and decided to stomp over and demand the men leave and the woman stop acting like someone had hung a courting swing from his eaves.

"She's about to do something foolish," Lanky called to him.

Jim was ready to agree, but then he realized Lanky was talking about the horse—not Matty. Refusing to make a fool of himself in front of his hands and townsmen, Jim focused on the skittish mare. She danced sideways, pawed, and tossed her head.

"There now, darlin', you got nothing to worry 'bout. I mean you no harm," he singsonged.

"She don't cotton much to being broke," Lanky said from his perch on the corral's split-rail fence.

Jim shot him a smile. "Not a female in the world who does."

"You shore got yerself a nice passel of gals in the house. And I'm a-tellin' you, the smells comin' outta that kitchen are nuff to make me pea-green jealous over that dumb poodle dog for getting the scraps."

"If I'm lucky, I'll get them to take that stupid beast back home with them." Jim murmured a few soft words to the mare and managed to stroke her.

"Pity you can't find it in your heart to handle 'em with the same skill and kindness you show these here mustangs." Lanky spat a wad of tobacco off to the side and sauntered away.

Jim concentrated on the mare, singing to her softly under his breath as he let her get accustomed to his touch again. He didn't need to respond to Lanky's comment, but it rankled.

He'd tried to be considerate of the women. Why, he'd worn his buckskins out here to break the mustangs so he wouldn't cause more laundry and mending. Each day for the past week, he made sure he washed up properlike and put on a fresh shirt before he went to the supper table. Not only had he given up his bed, he'd made every effort to make life easy on Matty and her sisters.

Having women around was a mix of heaven and hardship. Their soft voices, laughter, and good cooking surely did make for pleasant evenings. Though he'd never confess it, he looked forward to those last-thing-in-the-evening chats with Matty out on the porch. Fact was, little Matty managed to put her hand to work out in the stable without anyone mentioning what needed to be done. When something came up that she didn't know about, she was downright eager to learn. Jim hated to admit it to himself, but he'd actually started looking around for her.

Then, there were times he wished she and her sisters had never stepped off that train. He'd died about ten deaths when a stallion tried to kick down a corral fence, and a splintered board went sailing toward Matty. How in the world was he supposed to keep her and her sisters safe? He'd gotten a nasty telegram from Ellis Stack, demanding money for these women. On top of all of that, playing the role of guard dog and chasing away all of the randy bachelors of Lickwind wore thin on his nerves.

No, the women shouldn't stay. He needed to send them off. Regardless of how sweet Matty smelled or how interesting her conversations were, she didn't belong out here.

The whole time he reasoned through the need to send Matty away, Jim kept pampering the horse and shooting wary gazes at the guys on the porch with her. To his everlasting relief, she stood and the men took their leave. It wasn't until Jim headed toward the gate that he realized what he'd been singing. "Nobody knows the trouble I've seen. . . ."

⁂

Bertie stepped on the lowest rung of the fence. The toe of her scuffed boot caught in the hem, and she impatiently yanked the skirts to the side. Her battered brown felt hat tumbled into the dust, revealing that her strawberry blond bun sat askew on her head. As usual, she looked like she'd slept in her rumpled clothes. From the expression on her face, Jim expected her to shout out her thoughts. Instead, she extended her hand toward the horse and spoke in a low tone. "Mr. James, have you seen Rhubarb?"

To his amazement, the edgy mare walked over and nosed Bertie's hand. "Careful," he warned. "She's feral. I've been working to break her."

"You're a beauty, aren't you?" Bertie caressed her muzzle and forelock, and the mare stood still for it. The girl then flashed him a smile that faded just as quickly. "Looks like you're doing a fine job with her. Have you seen Rhubarb?"

"Can't say as I have. Better keep her away from Ramon."

Bertie nodded, got off the fence, and continued her search. As she left, he thought about what her sister had said. Poor kid—she truly loved that creature. He hoped it hadn't gone missing. He worked a bit more with the mare, but his heart wasn't in it. After a few more minutes, he turned her over to a hand so she would be groomed and watered, then he went in search of the cat.

A short while later, he stared in disbelief at the sight before him. Rhubarb lay in the corner of his stall with three mewling still-wet kittens. . .on top of his favorite wool bedroll.

❧

"Matilda, get Bertie."

Matty looked up from the shirt she'd been mending and gave Jim a startled look. "Is something wrong?"

Bertie peeked around the kitchen door. "Did I hear my name?"

"Yup. You two come along with me."

Matty exchanged a nervous look with her youngest sister and followed Jim out the door. He headed across the yard, straight toward the stable. Both of them had to pick up their skirts and half run to keep up with him.

"Where're you all headed to in such an all-fired hurry?" Buckwheat called.

"Leave the women be and go chop logs for the stove," Jim growled as he charged ahead.

Shafts of sunlight filtered into the stable. Silvery motes danced on them, and the smell of horses and hay filled the air. To one side, a mare nickered to her newborn foal. Matty jumped when Jim curled his hand around her arm and started leading her along the wide center aisle. He'd taken hold of Bertie's arm, too.

They went clear to the end, and he stopped. Pulling them both in front of himself, he settled a hand on Matty's shoulder and leaned forward so his breath brushed her cheek. "Look in the corner."

"Rhubarb!" Bertie cried with delight.

"Whoa now." Jim wouldn't let them go. "She's a new mama. She might not want anyone to bother her right now."

Matty spun around and tilted her head back to see his face. "Oh, Jim. On your blankets?"

He sighed and the left side of his mouth crooked upward in a rakish smile. "Never can predict the behavior of a female."

Unable to help herself, Matty started to laugh. He did as well, and the rich, deep sound of his chuckle warmed her as nothing ever had.

Bertie tiptoed over and knelt by the blanket. "Three, Matty—all gray-and-black striped like their mama."

"We'll be careful to keep the stall door shut so nothing can get in here to rile her—specially Ramon," Jim promised. "Anytime you want to come check on her during the daytime, you feel free. She's a fine mama—grooming them already, and they're feeding well. Not a runt among them."

Matty listened to the gentle way he spoke to her sister. He must have taken Bess's words to heart about how much Bertie loved her pet. Instead of kicking up a fuss over the way the mess spoiled his bed, he squatted there, praising Rhubarb as if she'd won a prize at the county fair. Who would have ever guessed that beneath his gruff exterior, Jim Collingswood was gifted with compassion and mercy?

"James, could you wait a minute, please?"

Jim stopped but didn't turn around. He didn't know why Matty whispered to him, but he figured he'd stay silent. She closed the door so quietly, he barely heard it latch.

"I have something for you." She pressed a bottle into his hand.

As he looked down, the muscles in his neck spasmed. He gritted his teeth against the pain. "What is it?"

"You're stiff. Bertie told me you were breaking an especially ornery mustang today, and when we went out to see the kittens, you grimaced when you knelt. I figured this might help out."

"I'm not a man to drown a few paltry aches in whiskey."

She covered her mouth, but he could still see her shoulders shake in silent laughter. Moonlight glowed on her fair hair and sparkled in her big blue eyes. When she lowered her hands, she whispered, "It's liniment."

Hmm. Later, when I hit the hay, I'll ponder on the fact that she's discussing my activities and watching me. For now, he lifted the bottle a bit higher. "It's red. It doesn't smell all flowery or girlie, does it?"

"No. Some of the hands back home tried it and claimed it worked well. Doc Timmons even said it's so good, he stopped mixing his own. If that's not enough, the company promises if you are dissatisfied with the results and only use it down to the 'Trial Mark,' you can return the bottle for a full refund."

"Who ever heard of a company promising to give you your money back?"

"I guess there's a first time for everything. The ingredients are sound—camphor, extract of capsicum, oil of spruce—"

Jim squinted and read, " 'J. R. Watkins Medical Company Red Liniment.' If they're as right about the effects as they are the color, it ought to do the trick just fine."

"You're a hardworking man, James Collingswood. I don't doubt your abilities for a minute, but I do hope you're being cautious."

Her concern warmed him, but he didn't want to feel that way. "Fretting doesn't get a job done."

"I suppose not."

His hand fisted around the bottle. "Don't think some good meals, cleaning, and a bit of doctoring are some kind of test like this try-it-for-a-bit cure-all, Matilda Craig. Sure as a coon has stripes, I'm not wife shopping. No matter what you do, you're not staying."

Chapter 6

The very next morning, Matty sat on the porch steps, humming and stitching. Jim thought about sauntering by to get a drink at the pump—maybe even tell her the liniment worked well—but before he could blink, Harvey and Mike ambled over to her. They stood there, jawing with her as if they had all day to talk and not a thing in the world to do. As a matter of fact, all of his hands were displaying the same bad habit. Every single time Jim turned around, one of them hovered over Matty.

It was her own fault, too. The woman was puppy-dog friendly. Why, she'd learn a man's name and greet him whenever he happened by. She could converse intelligently about important, interesting subjects—weather, livestock, repair work, and essential duties. She didn't fuss over fashions and simper silly things that left a man shuffling uncomfortably.

Luke nudged him out of his musings. "What are you scowling at?"

Jim nodded toward her. "That. The hands act like this is a Sunday picnic instead of a workday. That woman's setting out to find her a man, and I told her not to look for romance here. Bad enough I have to ride our own men, but half of Lickwind keeps roaming here to try to court, too."

Luke shoved his hat back on his head and absently rubbed his jaw—a shaven jaw, Jim noticed. He used to shave every third day or so when the itch started to bug him. Now he did it every day.

"Seems to me you said you're not interested. You don't have any right to keep others from courting her."

"I'm paying them to work—not woo women. And as long as she's under my roof, she can good and well follow my orders not to flirt!"

"She doesn't flirt. Matty doesn't have wiles like that. She's like a butterfly—she flits. She doesn't show any favoritism, and she's been good for morale."

Jim jabbed his forefinger into Luke's chest. "If you're all that sold, then go claim her."

"She's not for me."

"Then ride into town and make arrangements for them to be on the next train. Take the money out of the bank and buy the tickets now. I want this settled."

❧

"I'll be going into town tomorrow," Luke announced after saying grace over supper.

"I'm going with you." Bess passed the corn bread to Luke.

175

"No need," Jim said as he snagged a pair of thick slices of tender roast. "We'll buy your train tickets. It's the least we can do."

"No need," Bess echoed back. She squared her shoulders. "We're not leaving."

Matty watched Jim's eyes widen in surprise then narrow. Before he could speak, she shoved the butter at him and said, "We've decided to settle in town, but we've appreciated your hospitality."

He stuck the butter plate on the table with a thump. "There's no place in town."

"There's the jail," Bertie chimed in.

"The jail!"

"We can sew and do laundry. Maybe cook or bake a bit," Corrie said with resolve.

"There's a laundry in town—not that it gets used much," Jim growled. "And what makes you think men want you to sew? We all buy ready-made clothes."

"There's been plenty of mending," Bess cut in. "Furthermore, there isn't a decent place for anyone to get a nice meal."

"The jail isn't big enough for the four of you to turn around in. You can't live there, let alone live and run a business out of it."

"I can't bear to get on the train again," Corrie said quietly.

"None of us can," Matty whispered to her. She looked Jim straight in the eye. "We've discussed it. This is the way it's going to be. We'll settle here in Lickwind."

"Luke," Jim barked, "explain to these women so it'll make sense."

Luke swallowed a bite and grinned. "Good roast beef. What're we having for dessert?"

The next morning, Jim demanded his brother buy the train tickets; the women stubbornly asserted they were going to rent the jailhouse. The breakfast table crackled with tension.

Bess rose and ordered, "Bertie, no going out to the stable to see the kittens until you've helped Corrie with the dishes. Don't pester Scotty either. And for pity's sake, don't take advantage of our absence to go gallivanting off to who-knows-where again. We all have enough on our minds without worrying where you've disappeared to. Corrie, after dishes, you lie down and nap awhile. Matty, get your reticule. We're leaving."

"Lickwind is not a town for ladies. I don't know where you came up with this absurd notion, but I'll not be party to it." Jim stood and tossed his napkin onto the table. "Luke, ride on in. The ladies won't be going."

Luke casually spread freshly churned butter on a fluffy biscuit and didn't even bother to look up. "Matty and I already hitched the buckboard."

Jim gawked at Matty. "You did what?"

She shrugged. "We're not frail flowers, James. Just as your telegram ordered, we're sturdy, dependable, hardworking, and plain. My father had no sons. We all learned to do what was necessary."

Jim glowered at her. "Three of you are sturdy. Dependable? The only thing I can depend on is that you're stubborn and vexatious. Hardworking? You can work hard someplace where you won't have every man for miles around trailing after you like a moonstruck calf. As for plain—" He shook his finger at her. "You can just forget blinking those great big blue eyes at me and trying to tell that ridiculous tale. I know a pretty woman when I see one." He slapped his hat on his head and stomped out the door.

Matty stared at the door in disbelief. Back home, men said her dress was pretty or she'd done a fine job at something, but Jim stared her right in the eye and spoke with such unwavering conviction, it made her go weak in the knees.

"Hard to imagine he's the same man who was singing to a fractious mare yesterday," Bertie grumbled as she started stacking the dishes.

"It won't much matter in a few days." Bess lifted her chin and stabbed a hat pin through her bonnet to keep it in place. "We'll be in town, so we won't be here to plague him."

Matty walked to the hall tree to fetch her reticule. *I don't want to vex him. . .but I don't want to move to town either. He thinks I'm pretty!*

❦

"Trying to git yerself kilt?" Scotty stuck out his weathered right hand and yanked Jim to his feet. Instead of letting go, the old man tugged him close and said in a gravelly undertone, "Son, you gotta pay attention to the horse you're on—not the mares who went to town."

After taking his third bone-jarring, spine-crunching fall in less than an hour, Jim knew he couldn't deny the truth. He bent, picked up his hat, and smacked it against his thigh. Dust flew about him from that simple action—proof he'd spent more time out of the saddle than in it. He jutted his chin toward the mustang he'd been breaking. "He's about to see who's in charge."

Three hours later, when he'd broken the mustang and rewarded it with plenty of affection and soothing, Jim shot another look at the sun. They still weren't back from town.

Last night was sleepless and frustrating as could be. He should've been able to doze off in the stable—he'd slept on hard ground so much, it wasn't any skin off his nose. Though he'd never admit it to Luke, the sumptuous meals that the women served more than made up for sleeping out here. The fact was, Jim had come to the conclusion he liked having Matty around. In fact, he didn't even mind her sisters either.

He knew they wanted to stay. He wanted them to, too—but he couldn't let emotions lead him from the path wisdom and safety dictated. This was no place for them. Why, if Matty left the house to go to the stable during the winter, a blizzard could kick up and she'd die from exposure. And what with her around the horses and all, one was bound to kick her sometime. He'd taken to having her shadow him most of the day so he'd be sure she wouldn't meet with any harm. Her companionship was all any man could ever hope for—but his conscience wouldn't allow him to keep her. The minute something happened, he'd never forgive himself. He was morally bound to send them someplace where ladies were sheltered from the harsh realities of life.

Bertie ran out of the house and skidded to a halt in front of him. She held a drumstick in her hand and mumbled around the bite in her mouth, "Lunch is on the table for you. Corrie's lying down, so try not to slam the door. Bess said you need to oil the hinges—they squeak."

As she dashed off toward the stable to see Rhubarb and the kittens, Jim didn't know whether to chuckle or grumble. Ellis Stack had to be blind and stupid to think Bertie was either old or mature enough to be a bride. Then again, Jim didn't particularly cotton to the notion of a kid telling him to stay quiet in his own home—or her bossy oldest sister deciding what he needed to repair. He headed toward the house, consoling himself with the fact that Luke was buying the train tickets.

Jim choked down the miserable excuse for lunch Bertie left on the table for him, then finished oiling the hinges on the screen as Luke drove the buckboard up to the house. He nearly squirted oil onto his shirt as he caught sight of the sun glinting on Matty's hair. Teamed with her green dress, that golden hair made her look pretty as the yellow flowers Ma used to favor each spring. Seeing her sitting next to Luke made Jim grit his teeth.

"Get everything settled?" he asked his brother as he absently helped Bess from the buckboard.

"Not yet," Bess said as she stepped aside and lavishly petted Ramon's springy gray fur. The dumb dog somehow decided he belonged to her, and Jim immediately made a mental note to pay off his ranch hand and give the dog to Bess when she left.

Jim grabbed for Matty before Luke could. He settled his hands around her waist and drew her toward himself. The breeze blew that beguiling perfume she favored toward him, and he tried not to be obvious in sniffing to catch another whiff. He forced himself to listen to what she was saying.

"—but they'll need to vote on it."

"What?"

Matty squeezed his shoulders and looked downward to remind him to finish setting her on the ground instead of hanging on and letting her toes dangle. Still, she spoke to cover the awkward moment. "Mr. Potter, the attorney at the land office, said the town owns the jail, so they'll have to put an announcement in the paper and hold a vote."

Jim glared over her shoulder, straight at Luke. Luke shrugged. "Ma taught us it was rude to argue with women."

"You mean you wasted the entire morning—"

"Hey. You want 'em gone, you do your own dirty work."

Chapter 7

Yes, I know how to smile and nod. What kind of question is that?" Matty gave Jim a baffled look. He'd let her sisters walk ahead toward the buggy, but he'd held her back.

"All you do is smile and nod to all of the men in town. It's Sunday. You're there for worship—not courtship."

"I refuse to be rude!"

"Good," Jim cut in. He grabbed her arm and marched her to the buggy. "Just remember that. No talking in church."

She stopped in her tracks. "You missed breakfast and are surly as a coyote with crossed eyes. Do I need to get you a cup of coffee?"

"Matty, we're going to be late!" Corrie called.

The whole ride into town, Matty stewed over Jim's orders. Who was he to tell her how to conduct herself? He had no call to monitor her behavior. She'd done nothing to earn his orders.

By the time they reached town, all of the Craig sisters huddled a little closer to one another. An entire cadre of men surrounded the buggy. Men, each in his very best bib and tucker, had come to attend the monthly service the circuit rider gave; but from the way they greeted one another, most never darkened the door of the church.

Or, in this case, never bothered to gather in the jailhouse—which was where the circuit preacher normally held services.

"Josh, you old coot, what're you doing, all fancied up?"

"Why, goin' to the Sunday meetin'!"

"That's two miracles," Luke murmured for the sisters' benefit. "In the five years I've known him, Josh hasn't ever bathed or attended church."

Bertie burst out laughing.

When the sisters got out of the buggy, what looked to be the entire population of Lickwind stood in a bedraggled line, like soldiers awaiting inspection. A tall one with his fair hair parted in the middle and pomaded into two slick halves stepped forward with his bowler pressed over his heart and a fistful of wildflowers. "I'll be proud to claim any of you as my bride. I got me a purty little start-up ranch with a good, sound cabin—"

"Hold your horses!" Jim roared above the crowd. "No one's getting married today. You can all forget proposing to these women and start paying attention to the parson."

"I can do both," a grizzled man announced.

"Not today, you won't."

Matty stayed with her sisters as the men decided services could be held outside, on the other side of the railroad tracks. Chairs and benches got dragged from the saloon and mercantile, and the men all argued over who got to sit next to the women.

Parson Harris handled the situation by simply announcing the Craig sisters would be the choir and sit behind him. Bertie actually sat still through the service for the first time in her life. Bess made a point of keeping a parasol over Corrie to protect her from the sun's heat. Matty remembered Jim's advice to smile and nod. . . but why was he glaring back at her the whole time the parson preached on loving your neighbor as yourself?

❧

"Just what is the meaning of this?" Jim took the paper out of his vest pocket and flung it down on the table. He'd been fit to be tied ever since the moment he spied the paper tacked to the Jones's storefront. He'd hardly heard a word the pastor said after he'd grabbed a bench for church.

"It's one of the invitations," Bess said matter-of-factly as she checked on the rolls in the oven.

"You." Jim turned and waggled his forefinger at Matty. "You're behind this. You're so gregarious, you want every man in the territory to drop in and be your friend."

"Actually," Luke said, "it was my idea."

"What?"

"It's just a barbecue. These women shouldn't have to go back to where they're not wanted."

Angrily tapping the toe of his boot on the floor planks, Jim shook his head. "They don't have to go back there, but they need to go somewhere safe and decent."

"There's nothing wrong with them meeting men who could make them happy here in Lickwind."

Jim plopped into a chair and stared at his brother in disbelief. "You must've hit your head one too many times while breaking that last batch of horses." Suddenly, Bess's words fully registered. He shot forward. "What do you mean, 'One of the invitations'? Just how many got posted?"

Matty sashayed past him with a platter of meat loaf. Aromatic steam wafted off of it and made his mouth water, but Matty's words made his mouth suddenly go dry. "Bess posted about six of them in town. I only handed out a dozen or so."

Luke snitched a roll as Bess took them from the oven. He tossed it from hand to hand so it would cool as he tacked on, "But I gave a stack of them to Jones in the mercantile, Squires at the feedstore, and Gideon at the saloon. They've been passing them around. We ought to have a good turnout."

Jim, Matty thought, *looks and acts like a riled porcupine.* He'd barely spoken and not shaved at all since Sunday. It wasn't because he needed more of the Watkins Liniment, either. Each time someone said something about the barbecue, he'd bristled. Corrie sat on the edge of the bed and sighed. "After tomorrow, it'll all be over."

Matty heard the grief in her twin's voice. She set down her brush, sat beside Corrie, and squeezed her hand. "We'll manage better than you think. Bess has a good plan. Once the men all arrive, we'll get them to hold a vote to let us settle in the jailhouse until we can each have a chance to do some courting and decide on who suits each of us best. Don't worry—we won't send you off as someone's bride tomorrow."

Corrie gave her a watery smile. "Bess and her plans."

Matty nudged her shoulder. "Have you ever known Bossy Bess to come up with one that didn't work?"

"Turn around. I'll braid your hair." As soon as Matty spun around, Corrie started to finger-comb her twin's hair and plait it into a loose braid that matched her own. "You seem much happier here than back home."

"Getting away from Ellis is such a relief. There wasn't a day that went by that I wondered if God sent him as a test for my Christian patience."

"Papa willed that farm to all of us. He'd be so sad to see how greedy Ellis got."

Matty traced a sprig of daisies on her lawn nightgown. "Ellis is going to fly into a rage when he finds out he's not getting any money out of this."

"Bess is right though. We're not his legal charges, and it's illegal to sell people. He stuck us on that train, and we aren't even what the Collingswoods ordered. They don't owe him anything and neither do we."

"And our train fare is only a fraction of what he owes us for our shares of the dairy."

As she tied a narrow strip of ribbon on the tail of Matty's braid, Corrie quietly asked, "So if we're staying, are you interested in any of the men you've met yet?"

"They're all fine men. Some are a bit on the unpolished side, but they have good hearts." Matty hopped up, blew out the lamp, and crawled into bed. She snuggled under the covers. Matty waited as her sister wiggled to settle in next to her then whispered, "I know no one will ever be like Brian—but is there anyone you think you might get along with yourself?"

"I know I'm going to need someone to provide for me and the baby...." Corrie's voice hitched, then she blurted out, "But I can't imagine ever loving another man."

Matty scooted over and hugged her. "If any of the men want me as a wife, I'll see if I can't have him take you as part of the bargain."

"You would?"

The tremble in her sister's voice cut Matty to the core. "After getting here and seeing all that needs to be done, I think it's a very reasonable idea. Especially if he's a rancher, my husband would know that having an extra woman around to help with cooking, sewing, and cleaning would be a bonus."

"There's a world of difference between an extra pair of hands and a widow with a baby."

Matty propped herself up on one elbow and gave Corrie's braid a playful yank. "The only problem will be fighting back all of the men who come to call. Sis, you can't believe the way all of the hands keep sneaking into the stable to check on the kittens. Big, tough old cowboys—down on their knees, bringing treats so Rhubarb will let them pet her kittens. If they're that way with kittens, I know they'll go wild over your little baby."

"You're spinning a yarn."

"You just watch the stable and see if I'm not right. Lanky, Pete, and Scotty have all swiped eggs from the henhouse for her. Chico gave up one of his prized granite-ware bowls so she could have milk each day. Luke keeps taking over fresh hay to be sure the corner is soft and warm enough."

"Well, I'll be!"

"Yes." Matty flopped back down and stared at the ceiling. "Jim gave up that blanket, and I saw him hunkered down, singing under his breath while he hand-fed Rhubarb a rasher of bacon."

"Tilde?"

Matty started. Her twin rarely ever called her that pet name. "Huh?"

"Be careful of your heart. Jim's trying his best to get rid of us, but your voice softens when you say his name. You've never done that with anybody else."

"Nonsense. My heart's not in any danger."

"I'm not being silly. I sense a spark between the two of you, but he's every bit as stubborn as you are. You came here planning to be a bride, so your mind freed your heart to find love. The problem is—Jim's dead-set against marriage. I don't want you to get hurt."

"Corrie, when we set out, I told God I trusted Him to find me the right mate. I must have faith that He will direct my path." She tugged at the covers then muttered, "But so far, it's seemed like a rocky path on a moonless night."

Corrie giggled.

"Hey, you!" Bess called from the room next door. "Hush up and go to sleep!"

"It's Matty's fault!" Corrie sang out.

When Matty stopped laughing at that ridiculous fib, she whispered, "You told a lie. You have to say the bedtime prayer tonight."

Corrie fumbled and grabbed Matty's hand. She said a sweet prayer and asked the Lord to bless her baby's health and for Him to provide good men as grooms for each of her sisters. "And, Father, please give each of them a sense of assurance when You put that man in her path."

After Corrie was fast asleep, Matty still lay there and remembered thinking she wanted to marry a man like the one who rescued her at the train—even before she knew he was James Collingswood. He was a good, solid man, strong and honest. From all of the time she'd spent with him, she knew his gruffness hid a heart of gold. Other men here had become her pals—just like back home, but James Collingswood was different.

Lord, what Corrie said is starting to ring true. I never felt this way about a man before. If Jim's the man for me, You're going to have to change his heart, because he's all but shoved me out the door.

Clyde Kincaid rode up at the crack of dawn. Jim stood in the doorway of the stable and squinted at his neighbor as he dismounted. The wind carried the reek of his bay rum.

"Mornin'." Clyde swaggered over. "Gonna be some day, huh?"

"Not till noon. Men all have work to do before they socialize." Jim stuffed his hands into a worn pair of leather gloves. "I expect you'll be coming back after you've tended to chores at your spread."

"Naw. I can afford to take a day off. I'll marry up with one of the gals, and we can catch up on work tomorrow." Clyde tilted his head toward the house. "I seen them all at Sunday worship. Robust women. Able to pull their weight."

"They're women," Jim ground out, "not draft horses."

Clyde chuckled. "Soon as they're hitched, they'll be brood mares."

"Kincaid, you've got ten seconds to get clear of my property before I level you."

The dust hadn't settled from Clyde's hasty departure when Luke sauntered by. "I've seen friendlier-looking thunderclouds. What's gotten into you?"

"You and your idiotic barbecue, that's what."

"Come on, Jim. You don't want the women here. It's a good way to introduce them—"

"No." Jim glared at his brother. "If you think I'm happy about stuffing those sweet women back on a train, you can guess again. Fact is, it's the lesser of two evils. I'd never buy me a bride like I was bidding on livestock. This whole thing is a nightmare, but the best I can do is send them somewhere decent. There aren't a handful of men in the whole county who are fit to marry them."

"It's not up to us to judge that. You're gonna have a revolution on your hands if you interfere or send the Craig sisters away."

Jim took a step closer and gritted, "Clyde Kincaid was just here."

"He's about to lose his place." Luke roared in outrage, "What does he think he's doing, trying to get one of our gals?"

"Our gals?" Jim poked him in the chest. "Since when did you decide they were ours?"

"We can't let those kind of men around the Craig girls."

"That's the problem. Just you watch today. We're going to be overrun with every man in the county, and we'll be lucky if even one is able to provide decently. To take it a step farther, just how many of the leatherhands around here know how to treat a lady?"

Luke leaned back against the stable wall and banged his head on the boards as he moaned, "What have I done?"

"I started the whole mess, not ordering the bridles from the feedstore." Jim kicked at the earth and stared at Matty as the kitchen door banged behind her. Humming and swinging a bucket, she headed toward the milk cow. "Little brother, we're gonna have to bird-dog those women all day and scare off the undesirables."

"What a catastrophe."

"Here's the plan. . . ."

Chapter 8

Matty tried not to wiggle as Corrie used the curling iron to help her finish her coiffure. They'd studied the pictures in *Godey's Lady's Book* and decided this one would suit her.

"You look beautiful," Corrie proclaimed.

Matty laughed. "Somehow, it never seems quite right for us to say that to each other."

Bess finished pinning Mama's cameo to her bodice. "All we need is to convince the men to rent us the jail. Then we won't have to jump into any marriages."

"Jumping behind bars instead of over a broom." Bertie laughed as she swiped a finger around the base of a cake and licked off the icing.

The kitchen door opened. Jim stood at the threshold and scanned the room. He shook his head. "Bess, take off that jewelry. You don't want anyone thinking you're an heiress. Bertie, get your hair out of that—that—" He spiraled his forefinger in the air in a gesture of masculine hopelessness. "Put it in plaits."

"Plaits! I'm seventeen!"

Jim strode across the kitchen, his boots ringing on each plank. "Too young to get married, and that's exactly what we're telling the men."

Matty scooted free from her twin's fussing. "What about Corrie?"

Jim stared at her then glanced at Corrie. He looked back at her. "Try your best to make Corrie look drab—plainest widow's weeds, and be sure she's wearing that mourning brooch."

Bess leaned against the table. "James, I do believe I like the way you think."

Still, he continued to keep eye contact with Matty. She felt her cheeks growing hot under his scrutiny. He growled, "Do you remember what I told you before we went to church?"

"Smile and nod?" she said in a strangled tone.

"Well, I don't want you doing either today. For once in your life, try not to befriend everyone who talks to you."

"But how am I going to find a husband if—"

"Woman, when God's good and ready, He'll put a man in your life. Until then, use sense instead of smiles. It'll keep you outta trouble." He started to walk away but turned back around. "One more thing: wash off that flowery-smelling stuff you dab on. It's enough to drive a man daft."

The kitchen door closed behind him, and everyone stayed quiet for an embarrassing stretch of time. Matty drew in a breath then tried to sound breezy. "Well, how do you like that? The oil worked. The door doesn't squeak anymore."

Corrie shot her a knowing look. "It's not the hinges that matter—it's a secure latch."

A secure latch. . . Corrie's words echoed in Matty's mind as she wandered across the barnyard at noon. She'd never seen so many men in one place. Every last one of them tried to capture her attention.

"Miss, yore purdy enuff to make a man dizzy."

"Your collar's too tight, Nitwit," the man next to him said as he elbowed him out of the way. "Miss Matilda, I've got me a right fine piece of land and a good start-up herd."

"He's lucky if he's got a dozen head," Mr. Smit hooted. From what Matty gathered, he'd been an original settler and boasted a fair spread and a sizable herd.

Not five minutes later, Matty saw Mr. Start-Up over by Corrie. She hastened over to rescue her sister.

"A right fine place. Forty acres—"

"Excuse me," Matty interrupted. She got up on tiptoe and whispered, "My sister is newly widowed."

"Then I s'pose she's mighty lonesome."

To Matty's relief, Jim wrapped his arm around that persistent man's shoulders and led him off a ways. He murmured something, and the guy cast Corrie a terrified look then hastened toward Bess.

If a man ever kept busier than Jim did, Matty hadn't met him. She saw him stride toward the knot of men surrounding Bertie, elbow his way in, and playfully yank one of her plaits.

"Okay, baby girl, you've had a chance to talk with the grown-ups for a while. Scamper off to the stable now and go play with your kitties." He gave her a meaningful look. "Scotty's there. He'll keep an eye on you."

The men all complained. "She ain't no baby," one protested more loudly than the others.

"Why, Mr. Squires," Matty cooed as she hastened to Jim's side, "I'm certain you're not disagreeing with our host, are you?"

"She come out here as a bride," the feedstore owner groused.

"You're right," Matty agreed. "But that was before we understood what it would take to be a bride out here in a rugged man's world."

"You're not going to fight over me, are you?"

Matty wanted to pinch her sister for sounding thrilled over such an appalling prospect.

"You're worth a fight," the blacksmith, Amos Freeling, said as he twisted the end of his handlebar moustache.

Jim took Bertie by the shoulders, turned her toward the stable, and gave her a tiny push. "You run along now, squirt." He glowered at the men. "Stop scaring her. Poor thing. How'd you like it if a bunch of men chased after your kid sister?"

Baffled and shamefaced, the men muttered to themselves. Matty took pity on them. "I do hope you men are helping yourselves to the barbecue. It smells delicious."

"I'd be honored to escort you to the table." Hank proffered his arm.

Before she could reply, Jim grabbed her. "Sorry. Go on ahead, and Matilda will try to catch up with you. Her sister needs her."

Matty craned her neck to look for Bess. Jim didn't wait. He started hauling her toward the pump. "What—?"

"Trust me," Jim gritted. "This man is a scoundrel. Bess deserves better."

"Matty, this is Clyde Kincaid," Bess said as soon as they approached. "He owns the cattle ranch next door."

"Mr. Kincaid." Matty nodded to him coolly.

"Collingswood, it's about time you let us all have a chance at these women." Clyde waggled his brows. "I know I'm not alone, saying I'm ready to take 'em off your hands."

"Actually, there is an alternative—an excellent alternative." Bess squared her shoulders. "My sisters and I have decided to ask you kind gentlemen to take a community vote, since it seems the entire township is here today. We'd like to rent the jail and live in town. That way, we can have time to get to know all of you and—"

"Why bother?" Clyde slashed the air with his hand. "Only four of you. I say, those of us who speak up first get you."

"I agree." Jim gave a curt nod.

Matty almost fell over from the shock.

Jim reached over, snagged Bess by the waistband of her apron, and gave her a tug. At the same time, he clenched his arm around Matty and dragged her so close to his side, she couldn't have wedged a broom straw between them. "I spoke first. They're mine—all four of 'em. They're not going into town. Until I give my approval, they're not marrying up with anyone."

Clyde stomped off, and Bess turned on Jim. "Whatever got into you? How dare you foul up my plan?"

"Bess, look around. You're a capable woman, and I don't doubt for a minute that you'd be able to manage in town." As he spoke, Jim let go of Bess and absently stroked Matty's shoulder. She fought the urge to lean into him as he continued to speak. "But think of your sisters. Bertie's far too naive and will get into a peck of trouble, and Corrie needs to be sheltered."

"Matty and I can—"

"You will both stay here with your sisters until other arrangements—safe, wise arrangements—can be made. I—"

A commotion over on the porch made them all turn around. Luke smashed his fist into someone's face and knocked him clear over the railing. By the time Matty and Bess caught up with Jim, Luke already had Corrie in his arms and was carrying her to the door.

"What happened?" Bess breathlessly jerked open the door.

"Yahoos and idiots, the whole pack of them," Luke muttered.

"Corrie—" Matty rushed in and wet a cloth. She blotted her sister's wan face.

"Fainted again. I'll carry her upstairs."

"Bess, Lanky's right outside the door. Have him go alongside you to the stable and drag Bertie back in here," Jim ordered. "I don't want her out there with that pack of woman-hungry wolves."

Luke headed up the stairs, Bess scurried outside, and Jim stood with his arms akimbo as he glared at Matty. "I can't for the life of me figure out what I did that got God so all-fired mad at me that He dropped you in my lap, but He did. As long as He stuck you here, you're corralled here on the Rough Cs, and I expect you to keep your sisters reined in."

Matty shoved the damp towel in her hands at his chest. "If you're done listing your woes, I'll go see to my sister now." Without waiting for a response, she dashed from the room.

Jim tossed the wet rag onto the kitchen table, grimaced, and headed outside. He stood on the porch and looked over all of Lickwind's residents. The savory smell of barbecue hung in the air, but Jim knew good and well the dishes the men wanted weren't on the table. Lanky strutted along between Bess and Bertie, trying to skirt around the edge of the yard; but even then, they couldn't go two steps without someone trying to waylay the women.

Jim had hated to leave Matty's side for even one moment today, fearing all of the men would flock to her. The woman didn't understand just how beguiling men found her. Just looking at her could make a man's heart gallop, but the sound of her laughter—well, his heart just melted then. Jim wouldn't allow it. No, he wouldn't. She deserved far better than any man Lickwind had to offer.

At least for the moment, she was in the house and safe. He found a scrap of relief in that fact as he waited for Bess to plow ahead and propel Bertie into the kitchen. Josiah stopped Bess for a moment. Now there was a handsome man who had land and money enough to support her—but Bess gave him a look that would curdle milk and kept Bertie marching.

Males couldn't leave the Craig females alone. Why, even stupid Ramon had managed to get into Rhubarb's stall and dragged in scraps from the pig trough for the mama cat. The kitchen door banged shut, and Jim refocused his attention.

"Men." Then he whistled loudly and fleetingly recalled Matty had done the same thing back at the train station the day she'd arrived. "Listen up." He curled his hands around the porch railing, scanned the crowd, and waited for them to grow quiet.

"How's the little lady?" Chico asked. "Heard she swooned."

"Matilda is tucking the widow in for a nap." Jim narrowed his eyes at a man nursing a bloody bandana over his nose. "I suspect by now, you've all heard tell the Widow Taylor is in the family way. After just burying her husband and finding out she's got a little one on the way, she's in no condition to take on a new husband."

"That still leaves three!"

"Jones, you always were fast with your figurin' at the mercantile." Jim hoped to lighten the tone for a moment so they'd take his news better. "Since you're so good with numbers, let me give you another one: seventeen. Bertie isn't even out of the schoolroom, and I won't let her wed for a full year yet."

"Her kin sent her out here. That's consent enough," Mr. Smit shouted.

"That would be the same lazy, no-good brother-in-law who stole their dairy farm."

The men began to scuffle their boots in the dirt.

Amos let out a gust of a sigh. "I got a good look at the youngest, fellas. She's got a crop of freckles that make her look cute as a speckled pup. We'd be robbin' a cradle if we took her to wife."

Relief threaded through Jim. Men might well argue with him over the issue because he looked downright selfish over the whole matter, but few men were foolish enough to cross the hulking blacksmith. Matty's kid sister ought to be safe for a while. Now he could concentrate on sweet little Matty.

Luke stomped out of the house. He didn't even come to a stop before he thundered, "There are women, then there are ladies. The Rough Cs only has ladies. Do I make myself clear?"

"Well," Jones finally said, "that leaves two ladies. Now what're you gonna say, Jim?"

"I'm gonna say that since you're so good at sums and differences, I'll graduate to fractions." Jim widened his stance and lifted his chin. "Possession is nine-tenths of the law. The women are here. I sent for 'em, and they're mine."

Later that night, Jim slipped one last little bit of barbecued beef to Rhubarb and kicked hay into a pile for his bed. "Luke, you made quite a scene today."

"I was just protecting the gals."

"You went far past protective and hit possessive."

Luke folded his arms over the wall of the stall and gave him an amused look. "I did? You're not one to cast stones."

"Knock it off. I'm doing what Ma always taught us from the Bible—you know: taking care of the widows and orphans."

The stable rang with Luke's laughter. "If you're going to start quoting the Bible, I hope you don't hearken back to the Old Testament. Men back then had multiple wives, and I distinctly heard you announce the women were all yours."

❧

Matty looked at the neat rows of vegetables they'd planted and felt a twinge. Jim declared nothing would grow in the sandy soil, but for all of his grousing, he'd come out and plowed a nice patch for her. Soon the seeds Bess brought from home sprouted. If only love would flower so easily.

"Wonder if we'll be here for harvest," Bertie said as she leaned on her hoe.

"I don't know. Still, Jim and Luke have been so good to us; the least we can do is keep a garden."

Bertie snorted. "You pointed out how good they've been, so we're gardening and making cheese. Corrie felt thankful, so she had us making them shirts. Bess is glad, so we're going berrying and making jam. The only thing I'm grateful for is the fact that I don't have more sisters out here, or I'd have to do more work!"

"Cheer up. Jim said Rhubarb is ready to be moved back into the house. Ask Corrie for a feed sack. You can stuff it, put it in a box, and make a bed for the kittens."

Bertie started hoeing again. "Betcha she gives me that one with the purple zigzags on it. It's the only one of that pattern."

"Good thing, too. I've never seen an uglier pattern." Just last week, Jim had led Matty into the stable, opened the door on a huge wooden bin, and five years of empty feed sacks tumbled out. The memory of his generosity warmed her heart.

Bess and she had sneaked away with a few sweet little prints so they could sew baby clothes as a surprise and a few darker solids that would make much-needed maternity clothes for Corrie, who now wore her dresses unbuttoned beneath her loosely tied apron. Jim and Buckwheat carried the rest of the feed sacks over to the porch. It took a whole morning to wash them, but it felt like Christmas.

After all of the sacks were dry, Jim carried them into the house and watched for a while as the sisters matched up all of the patterns. He shook his head at what a production they made of it, but Matty laughed and said, "You started this!"

"Doesn't take much to make you happy," he said.

"After watching you eat almost half a jar of gooseberry jam this morning, I could say the same thing."

"Thanks for reminding me." He paced off to the kitchen and started banging around. Matty knew to expect the jar to be scraped clean. Jim's mother must have brought jars when they started up the ranch, and as fast as Matty could fill jars with jam, he'd empty them.

Each sister had selected fabric to make a shirt for each of the brothers; then she chose a pattern to make a new dress for herself. Word was, the town planned to throw a celebration for Wyoming being declared a territory, and the Craig sisters figured it would be a good excuse for new dresses. Several feed sacks remained, earmarked for dish towels, quilts, and more clothing. Still, that purple zigzag didn't have a match.

Bertie managed to strike a small stone with her hoe and made it flip into the air. It hit Matty's skirt and pulled her back to the present.

"For all of the feed sacks I've ever seen, I never saw one like that purple one," Bertie said.

"I haven't either."

God, am I like that feed sack—so peculiar that I'll never have a mate? Could it be that when You designed me, You had a specific pattern in mind so I'd suit only one special man? If that man were Jim Collingswood—

"So do we have a deal?" Bertie asked.

"Huh?" *I really need to stop daydreaming.* Matty stopped musing and gave her sister a questioning look.

"For true, Matty, you know how much I hate to sew. If I do the dishes for you for the next month, will you sew both of the shirts for me?"

"Laundry, not dishes."

Bertie glowered from beneath her brown felt hat.

"I'm being more than fair, and you know it."

"You? Fair?" a familiar nasal whine said from behind her.

Matty spun around. "Ellis! What are you doing here?"

His beady eyes scanned the ranch. "I'm here, dear sisters-in-law, to collect on a debt."

Chapter 9

Aaloon wasn't the most suitable location for a trial, but it was the biggest room in town. In honor of the auspicious occasion, Gideon Riker allowed all of the tables to be removed. Row upon row of benches and chairs filled the establishment.

Now that Wyoming had become a territory, no one was quite certain if the old circuit judge would be around next month. Then, too, Ellis Stack adamantly demanded money or the women at once. He had a return ticket on the next train. Due to his unyielding insistence, the town's only attorney, Donald Potter, now sat on a barstool behind the bar and acted as judge.

Jim winced. Whoever had draped a cloth over the oil painting didn't do a thorough job of it, so a delicate, bare foot peeped out from the right bottom corner. This was no place for a lady. . .and he had four of them sitting directly behind him. He didn't care what it took—he'd resolved before he got here that he'd do whatever it took to keep his sweet little Matty and her sisters.

A dozen men—all striving to look their best in hopes of catching the eye of one of the Craig sisters—sat off to the side. None of them wanted Stack to cart them off; then again, everyone knew those men weren't exactly pleased with the fact that Jim had claimed them as his own. He couldn't decide whether they might have a slight leaning for or against him.

The "judge" didn't have a gavel, so he settled for pounding on the bar with the handle of a Navy Colt. The gun promptly discharged, shattering a glass on the shelf just off to the judge's left.

"Oscar, I thought you told me this thing wasn't loaded."

"He was probably loaded when he tol' you that," someone drawled.

It took the judge a moment to regain order in the court. He then raised his brows at Ellis. "Mr. Stack, suppose you tell us why you've dragged us all away from our work today."

Ellis Stack was a contradiction—a large, rawboned man, he possessed a high-pitched, whining nasal voice. He dressed with great precision and style, yet his motions were singularly ungainly. Jim couldn't help wondering if that duplicity extended toward his version of the "truth."

"Your Honor, sir, I'm missing work myself. It took me five days to get here from my dairy farm in Rhode Island. I've been waiting four days for this trial. Even catching the train back tomorrow, I'll have missed two solid weeks. You know what a loss that represents to a businessman."

"Nobody dragged you out here," Luke said.

Stack turned toward them. "I had to come because I've been cheated out of more money than any man can afford to write off. I have a contract with James Collingswood for six hunnerd dollars. He ain't paid a cent."

"You have a copy of that contract?"

Stack pulled a sheet of paper from a leather satchel. "This is the telegram he sent. He agrees to my price and says to send them at once."

"Them?"

"The brides." Ellis jerked his thumb toward the ladies. "Just like he ordered: plain, sturdy, dependable ones who could do hard work."

The judge inspected the telegram then looked over the rim of his glasses at the jurors. "To my recollection, about four of you had schooling. I'll read this aloud so everyone in the jury and courtroom has the same information." He proceeded to do so and then passed the telegram down to the jurors.

Jim fought the urge to jump out of his seat and throttle Ellis Stack. The man twisted things about and slanted them something awful.

"Now, Collingswood, suppose you give us your version of the events," the judge finally invited.

Jim rose. "I'm calling Linus Hatch as my first witness."

Lickwind's telegraph operator came forward carrying a thick book. At Jim's urging, he produced the original telegraph message. "It says bridle here. B-R-I-D-L-E. The kind you use for a horse. A man who wants a mail-order woman spells it B-R-I-D-A-L. I looked it up in my dictionary before I sent it off, just to make sure I got it right."

Jim hummed approvingly. He wanted to be careful not to offend the jurors who were illiterate. Stack's mistakes were ones someone who couldn't read well would make.

Linus tilted his head to the side and studiously pointed toward the top of the page in his book. "I got it all right here. James Collingswood's telegram was addressed to L. S. Stocks in Rhode Island. A few of the ranchers hereabouts order gear from that company. Anybody can see right away that Mr. Stack blundered and botched things up on his end."

Bess testified that Ellis made the mail-order arrangements before consulting with any of the sisters. Jim thanked her then observed, "It's illegal in the United States of America to buy or sell human beings. By setting a price for each of these women and coming to claim the money, Stack is putting forth that he owned them and can treat them like chattel."

Unable to contain herself, Bertie stood up. "Yes, he treated us like chattel. And what about the cattle? Tell them about the dairy farm he said was his. It's ours, too, and he's sent us away so he can keep it for himself!"

"Your sister still lives there," Ellis snapped. "She agreed with me on this whole plan. None of the men in town would take any of you—Bess is bossy as a general, and Bertie is a tomboy. Corrine—well, no man wants to marry up with a widow who's on the nest, and then there's Matilda. She befriended every last man in town, so marrying her would be like kissin' his sister. We were doing them a favor, arranging for them to get married."

"Do you normally get paid for doing a 'favor' for a family member?" Jim shot back.

"Train fare was expensive!"

It didn't take long for the jury to huddle and come to a consensus. "Don—I mean, Mr. Potter—I mean, Your Judgeship, we done made up our minds."

Jim cast a look back at Matty. She held Corrie's hand and gave him a brave smile. Her courage impressed him. Openhearted, sympathetic, sweet Matty—worried more about her twin than about herself. There wasn't a woman on the face of the earth finer than Matilda Craig. He winked, hoping his reassurance wouldn't be false.

"Me and the boys figured Jim sent off for horses' bridles, and Mr. Stack made a mistake. Now, it's a mistake we can all understand."

Jim felt the air freeze in his chest.

"Them gals are right fine ladies—purty and nice, too—no matter what their brother-in-law said, and they deserve far better than they got. We don't care much that he paid their train fare—it's precious little compared to their share of the dairy when he booted them out."

The judge didn't risk using the handles of the Colt on the bar to quiet the noisy room. Instead, he smacked his palms on the countertop. "Order!"

"Me and the guys don't think Jim owes him anything since he didn't deliver what was originally ordered."

"Fine!" Ellis Stack jumped out of his chair and glowered at the sisters. "Bess, Matty, and Corrie can stay here and molder in this backwater place. Bertie, I've decided you're too young to stay here, and Adele needs your help. You're coming home with me."

"You can't have her!" Bess roared. She and Matty both leaped out of their seats and stood in front of their little sister like a pair of lionesses. The difference was, while Bess glowered at Ellis, Matty stared at Jim. Her eyes pleaded with him to do something—anything—to avert this disaster.

Jim turned to the judge. "Don, if I marry one of the sisters, wouldn't that give me as much say in whether Bertie stays in Lickwind or goes back to Rhode Island?"

The judge thought for a second then nodded. "Yes, it would."

Matty stared at Jim in amazement.

Ellis spluttered for a moment then crowed with glee, "Then he's accepting shipment of the brides, and he has to pay me! You can marry up with whichever one you want, but you're gonna pay me full price for all four of 'em—six hunnerd dollars!"

Though Matty didn't know the state of the Collingswood brothers' finances, she could tell by the way Jim went white beneath his tan that shelling out six hundred dollars would be a huge blow. She couldn't ask this of him; she couldn't not ask this of him—not loving him the way she did.

He straightened his black string tie and squared his shoulders. Ignoring everyone else in the crowded saloon turned courthouse, he faced Matty, took her hand in
his big, rough right hand, and went down on one knee. She stared into his earnest
hazel eyes and could barely breathe.

"Miss Matilda Craig, would you do me the honor of becoming my wife?"

Chapter 10

Yeeeehaw!" Lanky yelled. "The brides is stayin'!" Jim remained on bended knee, awaiting Matty's answer. The poor woman looked completely flabbergasted. She blinked and couldn't quite manage to keep from gaping. Still, she gave no answer. Something jabbing at his shoulder made him turn his attention to the side.

"You owe me six hunnerd bucks. Pay up."

A man could afford to kneel to propose, but Jim surely wasn't willing to be groveling at Stack's feet while settling this distasteful business. He slowly unfolded and towered over the weasel.

"Wait!" Jones called from the jurors' seats. "You all jest hang on to yer hats a second." He and the other jurors all huddled together.

Jim pulled Matty to his side and held her tightly as he waited.

"Your Judgeship, we're the jury, and we're thinkin' we oughtta have some say here."

Donald Potter leaned forward on the bar and pinched his lower lip between his thumb and forefinger while he deliberated. "Suppose you tell me what you have in mind."

Jones strutted over near the judge then turned to face Ellis. "Now it's true, if Jim Collingswood marries up with Miss Matilda, he's taking delivery on the brides."

Ellis let out a self-satisfied laugh.

"But—" Jones held up his hand to halt Ellis's celebration, "we looked at the telegram again. It don't say one-hundred-fifty dollars. It just says one-fifty. Me and the jury decided Collingswood's gotta pay Mr. Stack a buck-fifty for each of the Craig gals, and they're both settled fair and square."

"Done!" Potter banged both fists on the bar and stood.

Ellis turned purple with rage. "You can't do that!"

"I can, and I am." The judge pulled a silver dollar out of his pocket and tossed it to Jim. "Consider that part of my wedding gift."

Mr. Llewellyn stood and tossed a gleaming gold coin. "My bank is glad to see the community grow."

Doc did the same. "Me, too."

Soon coins rained all around—nickels, dimes, and a few quarters pinged as they hit the floor. Bertie laughed delightedly as she scurried to pick them up. Bess held out her hands to accept them then shoved a fistful at Jim. "Six dollars!"

Jim hefted the coins in his hand and listened to them jingle. "I haven't rightly counted them out, but I'd guess there are exactly thirty pieces in my hand. Seems fitting, somehow, Ellis, since you betrayed those you should have loved and protected. Take this and get out of town. We don't want your kind here."

"You haven't seen the end of this!"

Jim stared at Ellis and jutted out his chin. "This had best be the end, or I'll be filing a lawsuit so's my wife gets her share of that dairy farm."

Nervously yanking at his collar, Ellis spluttered and started to leave.

Jim grabbed him and thrust the coins into his shirt pocket. "You're all my witnesses. Stack is paid in full."

"Best deal you ever made," Luke declared.

"Come on, sweetheart," Jim said as he took hold of Matty's hand and gave her a gentle tug. "Let's take your sisters and go home."

More than half of the men in town accompanied them back to the Rough Cs. They said they wanted to help celebrate, but from the way they all jockeyed their horses to stay close to the buckboard, those men clearly hoped to get a chance to start doing a bit of courting with one of the other sisters. The rest of the men stayed in town—ostensibly to help put the tables back in the saloon. Bess muttered that they'd all be bending their elbows as soon as that task was done.

Matty and Jim didn't have a chance to say a thing to one another. They had no privacy, and everyone kept calling out to them. Amos Freeling shouted across the road, "Hey, Jones! I just had me a dandy thought!"

"Guess there's a first time for everything," Jones hollered back.

When the hoots died down, Amos shouted back, "Any of us who claims the other brides is only gonna have to pay Collingswood a buck and a half as a dowry."

Jim shook his head. "They're priceless women, not livestock. I never said they were up for bid."

"Never said they were forbidden, either," Luke piped up.

Jim groaned. He hoped he could ditch everyone and spend a little quiet time with Matty. Folks had jumped in so fast, she didn't even get a chance to answer his proposal. The half-hour ride home had never taken longer.

❧

The minute they reached the ranch, Matty mumbled an excuse and dashed to the outhouse. As a hiding place, it left lots to be desired, but she couldn't think of any-place else where she'd be left alone. She shut the door, latched it, and then buried her face in her hands.

This is all my fault. I gave Jim that pleading look in the courtroom. I asked him, just as plainly as if I said the words aloud. I've humiliated myself by forcing a man to propose to me so I could keep my sister. He's such a good man. He'll never say otherwise, but I've forced him into a marriage he doesn't want.

Tears blurred her vision.

Lord, what am I going to do? You gave me what I asked for, what I longed for—but now I don't want it. I don't want a husband who proposed just because he was being gallant. I don't want a man who marries me because of a mix-up. When I prayed for a husband, I figured You understood I wanted a man who would love me the way Papa loved Mama. Now Jim will have every reason to resent me instead of love me.

"Matty."

Jim's whisper stopped her prayer cold.

"Matty darlin', come on out here," he said in a quiet, gentle voice.

"Leave me alone."

"If I thought for a second you needed a private moment, I wouldn't bother you; but your skirt's caught in the door, and I can see the back of your pretty sunshine hair through the half-moon cutout on the door."

She moaned in acute embarrassment then felt him give the tail of her skirt a few jerks.

"We need to go for a walk. I'll make everyone leave us be."

I can't stay in here forever. I'll have to face him eventually.

It took every scrap of courage she could summon to open the door. Even then she didn't look Jim in the eye. He took her hand, steered her around toward the north pasture, and fished a bandanna from his vest pocket. As he offered it, he said, "You don't have to marry me."

Those words raked across her soul. Matty tried not to react, but she couldn't help herself. She stopped dead in her tracks and tried to muffle her wail in the bandanna.

"Aw, Matty." Jim leaned against the split-rail fence and pulled her into an embrace that only made her cry more.

She didn't know how long they stood there. The bandanna was a soggy mess, but Jim still held her. "I'm sorry," she mumbled.

He tucked a wisp of hair behind her ear and gave her a tender smile. "I learned long ago, sometimes I've gotta let a filly wear herself out before I can work with her."

She closed her eyes. "But you choose which fillies you catch and work with."

"I think I caught me a fine one." He snuggled her close and pressed a kiss on her hair.

Matty let out a sigh. "You're being noble. I don't want to marry you—a marriage shouldn't be an obligation or a rescue. It should be because a man and a woman love and respect each other. This whole mess—"

"Isn't a mess at all."

She sniffled. "The day we arrived, you called it a mess, and now I can see how right you were. Once Ellis leaves, we can tell everyone it was just an act. My sisters and I will move to town."

He tilted her face to his. Three deep furrows creased his brow. "Matty, is there someone else you want to marry?"

She choked back a nearly hysterical laugh and shook her head.

"Is there something about me that bothers you? I thought we got along."

"We do get along, but there's a world of difference between being acquaintances and being married."

"I thought we'd become much more than acquaintances." He cupped her jaw in his rough hand and brushed his thumb back and forth on her cheek. "We've shared a table for two months now."

"My sisters were there, too."

"You've worked by my side to deliver a colt, stitched my leg, and pulled out my splinters. They weren't around then."

She shrugged. "Those were just everyday things."

"Marriage is made up of days filled with 'everyday things.' I figure if we can find contentment in the commonplace together, we should be able to forge a happy union."

"A union—like our country after the Civil War?"

He chuckled. "I don't doubt we'll have some skirmishes now and then, but who wouldn't? Mild women won't survive out here. I didn't think any woman could until you came along. My sis was miserable, and once Pa died, Ma headed right back East. Only two other decent women have come out, and neither survived a year. Everything inside of me said I ought to send you back for your own welfare. Your gumption and fire changed my mind. If anyone could stand by her man and make a go of it out here, it's you."

"Hey, Jim!" Luke shouted. "Bring that gal back to the house. Everyone's waitin' to congratulate you!"

Matty wanted to sink under a fence post, but she just ducked her head and tried to hide her tear-streaked cheeks.

Jim cradled her close. "You're being a pest, Luke. Sweethearts deserve a bit of time alone."

"You're as bad as Pa was with Ma."

"It's the Collingswood way, and you know it. When we fall, we fall hard."

Matty leaned into his warmth and strength and wished his words were more than pretense to salvage their pride.

"Now that he's gone, I have a few things to say to you," Jim whispered against her temple.

Each word made her tremble.

"My parents had a solid marriage. No one could look at them for more than a heartbeat without knowing they loved each other. Luke wasn't teasing—he sees that same spark between us."

"Luke's a nice man, but his opinion doesn't count for much in this matter."

Jim chuckled. "Matty, my darlin', I fought tooth and nail against falling in love with you because you deserve better than living out here in the wilds with a bunch of rough men. Problem was, my heart didn't pay any attention to my mind.

"You can't begin to imagine how many sleepless nights I've spent in the stable, wrestling with God over this. The day of the barbecue, I made an utter fool of myself because I couldn't bear to think of you leaving here, let alone think of you leaving here with another man."

"You were simply being protective."

"I was protective—of your sisters. You? Oh, Matty, I was downright, unashamedly possessive of you. Haven't you noticed the way I've been assigning chores, just so we could be together?"

"I didn't know what to think. Corrie told me to guard my heart since you were trying to get rid of us."

He groaned. "I was an idiot. I went to that trial today ready to do whatever I had to, to make up for my foolishness and keep you here. I'd sell every last horse and cow to pay off Ellis, get down on my knees, and beg you to stay. And if all of that failed, I was going to bribe your sisters so they'd nudge you into my arms. If you don't have the sense to run from me, I'm going to lasso you and drag you to the altar."

"You don't have to."

He cupped her chin and growled. "I want to." Before she could reply, he branded her with a toe-curling kiss. When he lifted his head, he whispered, "Matty, God knows the desires of our hearts even better than we do. Why can't you trust Him to do a work in your heart so you can learn to love me back?"

His words made her heart sing. Matty nestled close and confessed, "I already do love you."

"It's about time!"

After they kissed again, Jim put his arm around her waist and started to lead her toward the house. "Jim?"

"Yes, darlin'?"

"You don't have to lasso me."

He threw back his head and started to chuckle. "I suppose not. I should have seen it from the start. I ordered a halter. Instead, God sent you to meet me at the altar. You can't escape His will any more than I could."

"I don't even want to. You're every wish and prayer I ever had for my husband."

Epilogue

Ten days later, it was the Sunday for Parson Harris to complete his circuit and preach in Lickwind. Instead of a standard service in the jailhouse or one out by the railroad tracks, he and the township all went out to the Rough Cs. Bess made it quite clear no sister of hers would ever get married in a saloon, and the porch would make a nice setting for a wedding.

Bertie didn't want to wear a fancy dress and carry flowers, so the Craig sisters managed to compromise as only they could. Bertie agreed to wear a new blue-and-green-striped dress and carried Rhubarb, who sported a ribbon to match. Next came Bess, looking somehow softer than usual in a violet dress with lavender trim. Ramon trotted by her side with great dignity in spite of the fact that his fur had been trimmed so it looked like a bunch of cotton bolls. Corrie was maid of honor in an appropriately sedate gray and mauve gown. Rhubarb's kittens filled the beribboned basket she carried, which managed to hide her tummy quite discreetly. The sisters lined up on the veranda and watched as Jim tried not to look impatient.

The open windows allowed the strains of "The Wedding March" to filter out. Harry, the barkeep, knew the tune and had volunteered to play it on the piano. Matty appeared on Luke's arm. She wore a wondrous white satin creation that sounded like the brush of a thousand angel wings as she walked toward Jim.

He could see her bright smile beneath the sheer veil. Over the past days, they'd not had to hide their feelings for one another, and she came to him now with her eyes sparkling with joy.

"Dearly beloved," Parson Harris began.

Matty and James exchanged a tender smile and mouthed the words to one another. Indeed, they were dearly beloved of one another and of the Lord.

Gooseberry Jam

3 pounds gooseberries, slightly underripe, stemmed and washed
1 pint water
3 pounds cane sugar
¼ ounce butter

Gently simmer gooseberries and water for about 30 minutes until soft and reduced. Pulp with wooden spoon or potato masher. Remove from heat and add sugar to fruit pulp. Stir until dissolved. Add butter. Bring to boil and boil rapidly for about 10 minutes. Stir to keep from scorching. When setting point is reached, take pan off heat and skim surface with slotted spoon. Pour into freshly boiled jars and seal.

Cathy Marie Hake is a Southern California native. She met her two loves at church: Jesus and her husband, Christopher. An RN, she loved working in oncology as well as teaching Lamaze. Health issues forced her to retire, but God opened new possibilities with writing. Since their children have moved out and are married, Cathy and Chris dote on dogs they rescue from a local shelter. A sentimental pack rat, Cathy enjoys scrapbooking and collecting antiques. "I'm easily distracted during prayer, so I devote certain tasks and chores to specific requests or persons so I can keep faithful in my prayer life." Since her first book in 2000, she's been on multiple best-seller and readers' favorite lists.

FROM CARRIAGE TO MARRIAGE

by Janelle Burnham Schneider

Chapter 1

Luke Collingswood dragged himself out of the bed that had proved no friendlier in the past six hours than it had in the past fifteen nights. He grunted as he pulled on long underwear and then a worn flannel shirt. Now that he had his own room in the ranch house, rather than sleeping in the barn with his brother, his sleep should be more restful. But warmth and comfort weren't enough to settle his mind.

Jim and Matty's marriage had sealed the destiny of the four sisters. The thought terrified Luke. He couldn't wish Matty gone. She'd brought too much light and joy to his solemn brother's life. And Bess would thrive no matter where she found herself. The woman wouldn't permit it any other way. Young Bertie had enough of the wild mustang in her that she'd likely do right well in Wyoming. But the little widow with the baby on the way caused Luke enough concern for all four of them. He just couldn't see how Corrie would survive in this harsh place.

He tried to push the thoughts aside as he poked kindling into the cookstove and waited for the banked embers to turn to flame. Once the fire caught, he added some larger chunks of wood to ensure the stove would be hot and the kitchen warm when the sisters came down to begin breakfast preparation. Quietly, he grabbed his coat and slipped out the back door toward the chicken coop. Gathering eggs was definitely women's work, and Jim would rib him severely if he caught him. But Luke knew gathering eggs was Corrie's chore. He also knew from the shadows under her eyes each morning that nights proved no more restful for her than they did for him. The least he could do was save her the trip out into the cold.

Such a wealth of sorrow lay in the widow's blue gaze.

Luke had always been drawn to the wounded creatures on their ranch. He'd even developed a knack for healing them—so much so that neighboring ranchers often asked for his assistance. However, it would take a lot more than warm mash or Matty's special liniment to set little Corrie to rights.

He'd seen what this country did to fragile women. He'd helped two neighbors bury their wives. His own mother, sturdy of both soul and body, had returned east as soon as possible after Pa's death. He'd pondered writing to see if Ma would take in the Widow Taylor but dismissed the idea instantly. One had only to spend a day around Corrie and Matty to see the bond between them. Corrie simply wouldn't survive separation.

As he left the henhouse with a full basket of eggs, he noticed a figure walking swiftly toward the barn. Jim? While Luke loved early morning hours, Jim was rarely at his best until he'd had his coffee and his breakfast. Something of importance must have enticed him out of his bed so early. Luke set the basket of eggs just outside the chicken yard then quietly followed his brother. He pulled the barn door open slowly so the hinge wouldn't squeak then almost let it bang shut in his delight at what he saw. His brother, who had strongly resisted the sisters' plea for a milk cow, now hunched on the milking stool, sending streams of milk into the tin bucket. Luke backed away from the barn, grinning. In the tradition of Collingswood men, Jim had obviously given his heart away in full. Only love would put Jim to work milking, rather than herding or butchering, a cow.

❧

Corrie turned over in her bed yet again, seeking an ever-elusive position of comfort. In recent weeks, her pregnancy had mounded her belly to the point that lying on her stomach was no longer comfortable. But it wasn't this physical change that disrupted her nights.

For the first time in her life, she slept alone.

From the day of her birth, a stronger person had shared her bed. First, it was her twin, Matty. Whereas Corrie felt intimidated by life, Matty embraced it with delight. Events of the day often penetrated Corrie's nights, waking her from troubling dreams. Matty had always been able to talk the troubles away with her cheerful common sense.

Then Brian entered their lives. The day he professed his love for her, Corrie felt as if the most impossible of dreams had come true. She'd always feared the day Matty would marry, leaving her to stumble through life alone. Instead, this handsome, smart, and personable young fisherman had chosen Corrie, ensuring she'd never be alone.

Corrie turned in her bed yet again, grabbing the coverlet, which seemed determined to slide onto the floor. Fall had come to Wyoming, bringing cold nights. She tugged the covering firmly over her shoulders and settled onto her side, hoping her memories would carry her back into sleep. The babe within gave a sharp kick, as if to tell Mama that her tossing and turning weren't helping. Corrie grinned to herself in the darkness. From the moment she'd begun to suspect her pregnancy, the thought of being a mama had delighted her. She just knew this little one would have Brian's charm and intelligence and her own depth of devotion. Perhaps being a mother would help her find her own place in life. As much as she loved being Brian's wife and Matty's sister, she secretly hoped to find an identity all her own.

But that dream belonged to happier days. Just two weeks after Doc Timmons confirmed her impending motherhood, a freak Atlantic storm turned Corrie into a widow. Matty immediately rushed to Corrie's side and stayed with her night and day. The bank repossessed the cheery little home Brian had worked so hard to provide for his bride, so Corrie moved back to the family farm, back to the bed she and Matty had always shared. Less than two months later, their brother-in-law, Ellis, had announced he was sending them and their other two unmarried sisters, Bess and Bertie, to the wilds of Wyoming to find husbands.

At least for her three sisters, the enforced adventure had worked out well. Bertie loved the freedom of the ranch, spending more time outdoors with the animals than indoors learning how to be the woman her sisters wanted her to be. Bess thrived on the constant work and activity.

And dear Matty. Corrie couldn't help but sigh over her twin's happiness. Jim Collingswood certainly wasn't the kind of husband Corrie would have chosen. Taciturn and sometimes downright grumpy—when Matty was around, the man turned to butter. One of her ever-present smiles softened him up for hours afterward.

But now Corrie was on her own for the first time ever. Yes, she had a roof over her head and good food to eat, but she couldn't depend on Jim and Matty's generosity forever. In a mere four months, the babe would be born, which would result in an endless list of needs to be met for many years to come. Corrie simply had to find a way to begin providing for herself and the little one. Marrying again might be the easy solution for some, but the mere thought gave Corrie shivers. She'd given her heart to Brian, and he'd taken it with him when he died. Some of the men hereabouts—that sleazy Clyde Kincaid for one—would quite happily accept a loveless marriage just to get a woman. The mere memory of his smell turned her stomach.

She shifted to her other side, untangling her flannel nightdress from around her legs. Ever since Matty's marriage two weeks ago, Corrie had spent night after night like this, unable to get comfortable, unable to come up with a solution for her own future. Useless as it was, she fervently wished she could set the calendar back six months and keep it there.

Slumber eventually claimed her, only to be nudged aside by faint daybreak. It took her a moment to realize she'd overslept again. She knew her sisters would be understanding, but she hated not pulling her own weight. If milking were her duty, the cow would be bellowing in discomfort by now. With a groan, she pulled herself from her bed. Her black dress lay draped across a nearby chair, frequent washings having dulled it to a muddy gray. She hated the thought of putting it on again. Though cut generously, it no longer fit properly. Besides, she'd been wearing it almost every day. Part of her longed for a more cheerful color, even while her conscience accused her of disloyalty. The love she and Brian had shared deserved at least a full year of mourning.

She firmly turned her thoughts away from the sadness. She'd never stop loving her husband, but one thing she'd learned in the past four months—if she let the grief dominate her thoughts upon waking, the entire day would be shrouded.

She pulled her fingers through the braid that she had plaited in her hair for sleep. Then she combed her hair smooth. With the speed of much practice, she rebraided it and wound the braid into a simple bun at the back of her head, not letting herself dwell on the memory of how Brian had loved to let her hair sift through his fingers. She carefully pinned her mourning brooch in place. The feel of its weight on her dress brought a fragment of comfort. Though she could no longer embrace Brian himself, this brooch made her feel as though he were still near. As she opened her bedroom door, the scent of coffee lured her downstairs.

As she expected, Matty stood at the stove, a steaming pail of milk on the counter beside her and a basket of eggs near the sink.

"You've been busy, Matty."

"Good morning." Matty's usual cheerful smile looked softer these days, even as her eyes narrowed with intense observation. "You look pale, Corrie. Are you okay?"

Corrie shrugged off her twin's concern. "I'm okay. Just slow waking up this morning, I guess."

Matty crossed the kitchen to put a hand on each of Corrie's arms as she continued her inspection, looking intently into Corrie's eyes. The twins had few secrets from one another; those that Corrie tried to keep, Matty could often discern with a mere look. But this time, Corrie refused to let her grief shadow Matty's fresh happiness.

Matty still saw more than Corrie wanted her to. "It's okay, little sister. I'm not going to pry. I just worry about you. You have more than yourself to take care of, remember?" She patted the as-yet-small bulge of Corrie's abdomen affectionately.

Though she wouldn't have appreciated anyone else touching her so intimately, Corrie cherished Matty's hands on her. They soothed, and she liked to think they pleased the baby, too. She wanted her little one to bask in Matty's abundant love even before birth. Matty moved her hands back to Corrie's shoulders. "Promise me you'll try to nap after lunch, okay?"

Corrie favored her with a small nod. "I'll try." She let herself relax in Matty's embrace for a moment, then she moved toward the counter. "Thanks for gathering the eggs."

Matty grinned. "That wasn't me. I think Luke must have done it while Jim was milking Betty."

Corrie exaggerated her gasp of surprise. "The grumpy cowboy actually did wimmen's work? Marriage must be making him soft."

Matty's face took on a pink tinge. "He'd be terribly embarrassed if he knew I told you. Please don't tell the other two."

"As long as you don't let on that I didn't do my chores, either," Corrie promised with a wink. "Perhaps I should stir up a batch of Mama's coffee cake as a thank-you."

"I've no doubt they'd leave nothing but crumbs," Matty assured her with a laugh. "How you do it, I don't know. I use the same recipes you use, but my baking turns out like bricks while yours is as light as anything Mama used to make."

This time Corrie's cheeks warmed. She would never say so out loud for fear of sounding boastful, but she knew she'd inherited her mama's touch with baked goods. Baking always made her feel connected to the mother she still missed, especially now that she was in a motherly way herself. She continued cleaning eggs in silence, wiping each shell carefully with a damp cloth then setting the cleaned eggs in a cloth-lined basket. The chickens Matty had talked Jim into buying were obviously settling in well. Every few days, egg production increased. Thankfully, with cooler weather coming on, they'd be able to keep the eggs for more than a day. Still, they'd need to think of ways to use the bounty. It would be a sin to have to feed the eggs to the pigs.

Then as she stirred ingredients together for the coffee cake, an idea began to form. Neighboring ranchers often dropped by, much to Jim's disgust. With the only three unmarried women for miles living at the Rough Cs, it wasn't hard to figure out what drew the male visitors. Corrie had noticed the way the men inhaled the home-baked goods. What if she made extra bread and cookies to sell to them? It seemed inhospitable to think about luring money out of guests at their table, but circumstances gave her some leeway, she felt sure. She wasn't at all interested in being courted, and neither was Bess, as near as she could tell. Bertie was just plain too young. So, if the men persisted in coming, why not turn the visits into something profitable? She'd have to start out using the supplies the Collingswood brothers had already purchased; but if her business did well, she'd be able to repay them.

Jim and Luke's response to her coffee cake provided the perfect opening for her to mention her thoughts. "I can't remember the last time I had a treat like this for breakfast," Jim pronounced, stabbing his third piece from the platter.

Luke snorted. "Perhaps the cinnamon rolls from two days ago? As I recall, you ate four for breakfast, two at coffee time, and stole the last one at lunch. Marriage is making your memory go."

Corrie loved to watch the men banter. They looked much alike, with their hazel eyes, broad shoulders, and tall frames. Yet, while Jim tended to be gruff, Luke had a gentle way about him. Solid affection lay beneath their frequently barbed comments to one another.

"And who was it that grabbed the last biscuit off my fork just last night?" Jim inquired. "I can't believe my younger brother would steal food from my very mouth."

"Sometimes it's the only way to get my fair share," Luke retorted.

As the laughter around the table faded, Corrie voiced her thoughts. "I had an idea while I was making the coffee cake this morning. I'm thinking I might turn the baking into a business, if you men don't object." She gave Luke and Jim each a glance but knew it was Matty she'd have to convince. "I could sell bread and cookies to the neighbors who come calling. Once I have a bit of profit, I'd pay you back for the supplies I've used."

Jim nodded. "Not a bad idea, Corrie. Might as well get some use out of these louts who seem to have nothing better to do than gawk at pretty women."

Bess also wore an encouraging expression. "That is a good idea. You have a real touch with baked goods. I'm sure the men hereabouts would pay well for whatever you could make. Just be sure you charge a fair price for what you do. You do tend to undervalue yourself."

Corrie warmed from the unexpected support, particularly in light of the matching expressions on the faces of Luke and Matty. She couldn't address Luke directly, so she made her appeal to Matty. "You know I love to bake, Matty. It wouldn't be hard. I'd feel good to be doing something practical. I'm going to need to be able to support the babe and myself eventually anyway."

The sound that came from Luke's throat sounded like a cross between a growl and the beginning of speech. But Matty beat him to it. "There's plenty of time to worry about supporting yourself after we get that little one safely here. In the meantime, you mustn't overdo. There's nothing more important than keeping yourself and that baby well."

"But I do feel well," Corrie protested. "I'd feel even better if I could do this. You have the cow and the chickens to look after. Bess has the garden."

She saw the softening in Luke's eyes before Matty's, but slowly Matty relented as well. "If Jim and Luke don't mind you using the supplies, I suppose it wouldn't hurt. But you have to promise me you'll spend at least an hour per day resting."

At that moment, Corrie would have promised anything. For the first time since Brian's death, she felt as if she were no longer just drifting on a tumultuous ocean of circumstances. Might the day come when she'd actually have dreams again?

Chapter 2

The first day of her venture, Corrie made four loaves of bread. She knew her plan would succeed only if she could show Matty it wouldn't require too much work. The next day, she found some dried apples in the pantry and, after cooking them, turned them into cookies, which filled the house with their spicy scent. She made sure a full dozen were available for Jim and Luke's afternoon coffee time, and both pronounced them better than the coffee cake.

Just as she expected, Clyde Kincaid, Josiah Temple, and Amos Freeling showed up in the late afternoon. None of them seemed to want to visit with any sister in particular, much to her relief, but all were willing to consume more than their fair share of the cookies. Rather than hide in her room as she often did during these visits, she forced herself to stay and make her business pitch. She waited for yet one more fulsome compliment on the goodies then took a deep breath. "As a matter of fact, Mr. Temple, if you'd like to take some home with you, I'm selling them for ten cents a dozen. I also have bread for sale if you like."

Clyde Kincaid let out a particularly nasty-sounding guffaw. "Now if that don't beat all. Not only is she purty, but she's got a business head about her. I'll take two dozen cookies and two loaves of bread, Miz Taylor. Looks like I'm gonna have to marry you after all, so I can get all these goodies for free."

Corrie didn't know how to respond. She wanted to flee, but she knew she had to learn how to handle situations like this on her own. But before she could think of a reply, a gruff comment from the back door surprised her. "Glad you appreciate our hospitality, Kincaid, but Miz Taylor doesn't have stock for more than one dozen cookies and one loaf of bread per customer. We'll try to have more for you next week at this time." With that, Luke scooped a loaf of bread and a handful of cookies into a square of muslin Corrie had set out on the counter. He wrapped the bundle then held out his hand. "I'll take your money, and you can take your goods and be on your way."

Clyde dug a grimy hand into his pocket and produced coins, which he dropped into Luke's palm. "I'll tell you, it's a good thing your mama ain't here to see how you boys have become downright inhospitable. She'd give you both a whuppin', I'm sure." He released that annoying hee-haw laugh of his that showed more gaps than teeth. "No need to rush me; I'm on my way." He tucked the cloth-wrapped parcel under his arm and tromped through the door, which Luke held ajar for him.

The two men remaining eyed the baked goods still on the counter. Mr. Temple stood and rummaged in his pocket, which looked a good deal cleaner than Kincaid's had. He looked from Luke to Corrie and back again, as though not sure whom he should address. "I'll take one of those loaves, if you don't mind, Collingswood, and here's an extra penny for the lady's trouble."

Amos Freeling also bought a loaf, as well as some of the cookies; and he, too, added a penny to the purchase price. With goods in hand, the two left together, as if the purpose of their visit had been business only.

Luke handed the money over to Corrie then left the house without comment. She couldn't decide whether she resented his actions or appreciated his intervention.

Word of Corrie's venture spread quickly. Two days later, four neighboring ranchers showed up to buy fresh bread. "It's been months since we've had anything this tasty, ma'am," one of them informed her as he cradled the muslin-wrapped loaf as gently as he might a sickly calf.

Corrie felt delight push her lips into a smile. "Thank you for the compliment. I'll have more for you next week."

He tipped his hat to her and rode back the way he'd come.

Corrie cradled the coins in her palm. Her venture was working! It wouldn't be easy to keep up with demand right after the baby came, but she'd find a way. She had to. No matter what the men around here thought, she wouldn't marry again. She'd have to work hard to provide for herself and her child, but any amount of hard work was preferable to marriage.

That thought kept Corrie going over the next days. It motivated her out of bed in the mornings and gave her energy for kneading batch after batch of bread. She made sure she always had plenty on hand for Jim and Luke so they'd never have cause to complain about her fledgling business. By working steadily, she found herself able to make up to eight loaves of bread every other day, with cookies and muffins on the alternating days. Some mysterious signal seemed to let her rough-edged customers know when new baked goods were available. A steady stream of buyers carried her products away almost as quickly as she made them. An equally steady stream of coins trickled into the old sock she used to store her earnings. Before long, she'd have to ask Jim or Luke to bring home more sugar and flour, and she'd be able to pay for them herself.

The other advantage of her work came each evening at bedtime. It took only moments after falling into bed before sleep claimed her. Most nights, she slept soundly until dawn. If she woke feeling less rested than she would have liked, no one else noticed.

As autumn progressed, the pace of life on the ranch increased. Bess and Bertie spent most of each day outside, gathering vegetables from the garden and preparing them for storage in the root cellar. They foraged for berries, which Corrie happily incorporated into her baked goods and Matty turned into jam. Corrie even found time to put together a gooseberry pie for the family's dinner. Not so much as a trickle of berry juice was left by the time Matty started clearing the table.

"That was a fine supper, ladies," Jim commented as he stood. Though his words addressed them all, his eyes remained fixed on Matty, whose cheeks blushed prettily.

In typical fashion, she turned the attention away from herself. "Corrie always has had the touch for baking," she said, laying a gentle hand on her twin's shoulder. "Our mama was that way, too."

"We're most grateful." Luke's gaze sought Corrie's across the table. "You're not working yourself too hard, are you? No dessert is worth making yourself sick over."

His concern warmed her through, and she smiled reassuringly, glad he couldn't feel the deep ache in her lower back from standing all day. "It feels good to be useful. Besides, Matty makes me take a rest every afternoon. I can't so much as sneeze without her fretting."

He didn't look convinced but said nothing more. As if his concern had infected the entire room, her sisters wouldn't let her help with the dishes. When she refused to retire to her room like an invalid, Bess waved her toward the parlor. "Then just sit with your feet up," she ordered, affectionate concern underlying her tone. "You have the baby to think of, remember?"

As if Corrie could forget. The little one seemed to move continuously. Most of the time, she relished the sense of companionship. But at times like this, when her entire body ached from weariness, the movements within increased her tiredness. She lowered herself onto the settee in the parlor then propped her feet on a nearby footstool. It felt good to get her legs up. She leaned her head against the back of the settee and let relaxation ooze through her. The chatter of her sisters in the kitchen and the rumble of the men's voices as they thumped around on the back porch provided soothing background noise. For the first time since Brian's death, she felt at home. She belonged here, on this ranch, with these people.

She awoke from a dreamless sleep to feel Matty tucking a quilt around her. Matty stroked her cheek with a gentle, though rough-skinned, hand. "You looked so peaceful here. I was hoping I wouldn't wake you."

"I don't mind, although if I'm going to sleep, I probably should go upstairs. I'd hate for the men to see me like this."

Matty's smile was tender. "I'm sure they wouldn't find a thing wrong with it. Luke seems quite concerned about you."

Corrie shrugged. "He's just protective. He can't help worrying about anything or anyone he thinks is hurting or fragile."

Matty raised her eyebrows as if preparing to argue with Corrie's conclusion, but instead she rested her hand on Corrie's abdomen. "How's the little one?" She rubbed in gentle circles, which eased the stretched, achy feeling.

"Busy as always." Corrie couldn't help but grin. "I think this one is going to have Bertie's energy."

"We can hope it's more easily channeled," Matty commented, then paused her rubbing to trace her fingers along the center of Corrie's apron where it covered the gap in her dress.

"It's not a problem," Corrie assured her. "My apron covers it, though the space seems to get wider by the day."

"For someone whose blessing was almost invisible for so many months, you're certainly advertising your condition now." Matty put a hand on either side of Corrie's stomach. She stretched her fingers wide, as though trying to encompass the entire width in her open hands. The babe squirmed. Matty's eyes widened. "Does the little one often kick on both sides at the same time?"

Corrie nodded. "Especially when I'm trying to rest."

A secretive smile came into Matty's eyes. "I wonder—"

Before she could say the words, Corrie comprehended. She felt her eyes widen with shock. "Two babies?" she whispered. "Twins?"

Matty caressed Corrie's stomach again. "Wouldn't that be wonderful? I've always loved being a twin."

Tears pooled in Corrie's eyes. For the first time since Matty's marriage, she felt as if the special bond she'd shared with this sister might not be broken after all. She hugged her twin fiercely. "It would be special for them, but how am I going to take care of two babies at once?"

Matty pulled back from the hug to look deeply into Corrie's eyes. "You won't have to do it alone, Corrie. We're all here for you, and nothing will change that, whether you have one baby or two." She must have seen the doubts that still swirled in Corrie's mind. "Sis, there's no way to know for sure until the baby is born. You fretting isn't good for the little one—or ones. Try not to worry, okay?"

Corrie tried to smile reassuringly, once again hoping her twin wouldn't read her thoughts. How could she tell Matty that being dependent on her sisters wasn't what she wanted?

Chapter 3

In the following weeks, Corrie found herself alone only at night. Bess and Matty took turns staying in the farmhouse while the other did outside chores. Even Luke seemed to always be nearby, ready to lift, reach, or bend for her. Rarely did she have to gather eggs anymore. No matter how early she awoke, when she came downstairs, the full basket sat on the counter, awaiting her attention.

Her girth continued to increase, and movement became more difficult. "If this baby gets any bigger, I'm going to explode," she complained to Matty one afternoon as she sat near the table with her feet up on a stool, as Matty had instructed. No longer were daily naps adequate. Matty now insisted Corrie stop her work every hour and put her feet up for at least ten minutes.

"I shouldn't tell you this, but you'll get a lot bigger, especially if there's—"

Corrie cut her off. "Don't say it. I don't want anyone else to know until we're certain." She couldn't confess that hearing the word *twins* out loud would make her intuition too strong to ignore. The mere thought of being responsible for two little lives, rather than just one, felt overwhelming. The bakery business expanded along with her waistline, and Corrie could see hope of supporting herself and her little one eventually. But she felt herself slowing down daily. By the beginning of December, she wouldn't be doing much baking at all and likely wouldn't be ready to resume until February. If she had twins, she knew it would be much longer before she'd be able to do anything but care for her little ones.

She rubbed her belly with one hand while using the other to hold a glass of water to her lips. That was another of Matty's edicts. Corrie had to drink one full glass of water during each of her breaks. "I declare, I feel as if I don't do anything but take breaks and go to the necessary," she often complained.

But Matty remained firm. "It wouldn't hurt you a bit if that's all you did do. Just be grateful I don't ban you from the kitchen entirely."

So Corrie sat and sipped her water. She already felt an indescribable bond with the little one—or ones—she sheltered within her body. Impatient though she felt with Matty's restrictions, she wouldn't, for a moment, do anything to harm this new life.

She saw the minute hand on the clock tick past the ten-minute mark and pushed herself to her feet again. A large bowl of dough awaited her attention. "Should I make buns or sweet rolls?" she wondered aloud.

"Sweet rolls are tempting," Matty admitted, ladling hot jam into jars. "But with Jim and Luke leaving in two days to herd cattle, buns would probably come in more handy."

Corrie agreed. "You're right. I'd forgotten about them leaving. If I have the energy tomorrow, I'll do up some sweet rolls to send with them."

"You spoil those men!" Matty declared with a laugh.

Corrie just shrugged and changed the subject. "How long will they be gone?"

Matty's expression turned sober. "Jim says maybe as long as a week. He says it takes awhile to round up all the strays and check the herd over for problems. This will be the first time we've been apart since we married."

The words brought a rush of memories. How well Corrie knew Matty's feelings! Just a month after Corrie and Brian's marriage, Brian left for a week on the fishing boat. The pattern for their marriage had been established then. Weeks away and days at home. Not once did Corrie find it easy to say good-bye to her husband, even though she knew his departure was necessary. She knew nothing she could say would make the separation any easier for Matty.

The morning the men left, she woke early to be with Matty. Silence hovered between them as Matty closed the door. It was a silence that went deeper than lack of conversation, the silence they'd shared at many other moments in their lives when words simply wouldn't express the emotions they felt. Corrie pulled her sister near in a tight embrace. With a firm prod, the baby protested being included.

"Goodness!" Matty laughed, even while wiping tears from her eyes.

"Tell me about it," Corrie groaned, moving slowly to the counter where the basket of eggs awaited her. Even on this morning, Luke had done his bit to ease her load. "His favorite time for exercise is just when I'm trying to fall asleep. Sometimes it actually hurts."

"Poor mama," Matty said in the tone that never failed to make Corrie feel utterly wrapped in love. She massaged Corrie's shoulders then worked her way down to Corrie's lower back. "Does that help?"

"Oh, yes!" Corrie hadn't realized how stiff those muscles were. "Too bad you can't just spend the day doing this."

As the days of the men's absence passed, Corrie voiced her discomforts more than she usually did. Pampering Corrie seemed to take Matty's mind off her husband's absence. For her part, Corrie enjoyed being alone with her sisters. Even the ranch hands, with the exception of Scotty, had gone herding with Jim and Luke. Other than a knock on the door and a quiet, twice-a-day, "You ladies okay up here?" Scotty kept to himself. The duties of autumn still demanded the sisters' attention, but the pace seemed slower. Meals didn't have to be as extensive, and thus cleanup happened more quickly.

Corrie's baking customers were also conspicuously absent. She hoped it meant because they, too, were gathering up their herds, not because they'd decided to do without baked goods.

A third possibility revealed itself the third day after the men left. Corrie decided to give the parlor a good dusting, and she happened to look out the window as she worked. A lone rider approached the ranch.

She called to her sister in the kitchen. "Matty!"

"What?" Matty hurried into the room, wiping her hands on her apron. "Are you okay?"

"Yes, I'm fine. But it looks like we have a visitor and not one I'm eager to see."

Matty peered out the window. "That Kincaid man. I know he's one of your best customers, but I don't think it's a good idea for him to be here when Luke and Jim are gone."

Corrie agreed. "What are we going to do?"

"Maybe we don't have to do anything." Matty pointed toward another rider approaching from the barn area—Scotty. Conversation seemed to pass between the two men. Clyde became visibly upset, and Scotty pointed back the direction from which Clyde had come. A bit more discussion followed, and then Clyde left the ranch.

"Well, I'll be!" Matty declared. "Looks like Scotty's doing guard duty. I don't know whether to be flattered or insulted."

Bess was less ambivalent. Hunched over a washtub on the back porch, she listened as Matty described what they'd seen. "I appreciate the thought, but I do wish those men would realize we can take care of ourselves! We're just as strong as those bridles they ordered!"

Matty and Corrie giggled at the reminder of Jim's blunder, and slowly a grin spread across Bess's face. "I wonder how Ellis feels about owning the entire dairy now that he doesn't have us around to keep things running."

Corrie didn't even want to think about it. Hard as it had been, getting sent to Lickwind and thus the Rough Cs had been the best thing to happen to her since Brian's death. At least here she had half a chance of making it on her own, regardless of how fragile everyone seemed to think she was.

The next day, Matty decided to clean and organize the pantry. "I guess it's my own now," she announced after breakfast, her diffident shrug very much out of character. "I might as well know what's in every nook and crack."

Corrie quietly slipped into the small room to assist. With her baking temporarily halted, she had to find something to do. Bess wouldn't think of allowing her to help pick the last of the vegetables from the garden, though she and Bertie were working tirelessly to bring the produce in before a hard frost damaged it. Matty had suggested Corrie try some needlework to keep herself busy, but Corrie found it too frustrating. While she sewed, her mind wandered into memories better left untouched. With each day of Luke's absence, she found herself recalling more vividly Brian's last day alive. Why Luke and Brian would share space in her thoughts, she didn't even want to consider. Far better to keep herself busy.

It took them two full days to finish, but Matty looked highly pleased with herself at the end of it. "Doesn't it look beautiful, Corrie? I can't believe I actually have my own pantry. I still have to pinch myself to be sure I'm not just dreaming I'm married."

Corrie advanced on her with a grin, fingers held as if to administer the pinch, but Matty quickly circled the table. "Now, now, Corrie dear. You mustn't get yourself all stirred up."

The baby kicked just then, strong enough to make Corrie gasp for a breath. Merriment vanished from Matty's face. "Are you okay?"

Corrie nodded. When she was able to draw a full breath, she explained, "Every once in awhile this little one kicks hard enough to hurt. With legs like this, it's got to be a boy."

"Or one of each?" Matty's words were teasing, but her eyes took in every detail of Corrie's condition.

"I'm not listening." Corrie stalked away with as much dignity as she could muster and set herself to washing the dozens of canning jars they'd found in a back corner of the pantry. Bess and Bertie's efforts in the garden had produced heaps of fresh peas, beans, and tomatoes. Corrie guessed they'd probably insist on her shelling the peas and snapping the beans, since both jobs could be done sitting down.

But the next morning that proved impossible. No matter which chair she sat in or how she arranged her work around her, she couldn't get comfortable. Her back ached unrelentingly. She did as much as she could while standing, but she finally asked Matty to let her peel the tomatoes or blanch the beans—anything to allow her some movement around the kitchen.

Matty's eyes narrowed. "You're not feeling contractions, are you?"

"No more than usual." Corrie dismissed the concern. She really didn't want to be fussed over today.

Her twin sensed her resistance and said nothing more. But throughout the morning, Corrie felt her sister studying her. Corrie watched the clock and sat down for her breaks before Matty could say anything. She sipped water faithfully. After lunch, she lay down on the settee in the parlor, unable to find the strength to climb the stairs. When a knock came at the door, she forced herself not to answer.

But Scotty's quiet tones carried clearly to where she lay. "Mrs. Collingswood, ma'am, would you mind coming out to the barn for a few minutes? One of the yearlings has cut hisself on the fence wire. Mr. Jim told me if any of the animals was sicklike, to let you tend them."

Corrie felt Matty's rush of pleasure at her husband's secondhand compliment. The delight in her voice made Corrie grin. "I'll be right there as soon as I grab my kit."

With her twin out of the way, Corrie returned to the kitchen. Reclining on the sofa hadn't helped. Bess looked at her sharply. "Are you sure you rested enough?"

Corrie silently gave thanks Bess wasn't as intuitive as Matty. "I'm fine. I feel better when I'm busy."

If the mountain of vegetables hadn't lay between them, Corrie knew Bess probably wouldn't have given in so easily. But the work had to be done. Their winter meals depended on it.

By the time dusk closed in, neat rows of cooling jars displayed their contents. Quarts of tomatoes, tomato sauce, and green beans stood ready to feed the four sisters and two brothers throughout the months until the garden would produce food again. Shelled peas lay on the drying racks above the stove. Matty still hadn't returned from the barn, so Corrie prepared a sandwich to take to her.

"No, you don't," Bess informed her. "You worked harder than you should have today, and Matty would have my scalp if I let you walk down to the barn. I'll go."

Corrie didn't argue. Now that the vegetables no longer occupied her attention, she felt every muscle in her back and abdomen protesting the three days of work she'd done. She lowered herself onto the settee again to rest for a bit before going upstairs to bed. But just as she felt sleep beginning to overtake her, a cramp around her middle jolted her to full alertness.

Chapter 4

uke's bay splashed across the stream, and Luke resisted the urge to nudge his stallion into a trot. It would take another half hour of steady riding before they reached the ranch yard. If he showed his impatience now, Jim would have plenty of time to tease him. He'd done a good job of concealing his concern over leaving the four women with only Scotty to turn to if things went wrong. If Jim had perceived his uneasiness, he would have known in an instant that it had nothing to do with the ever-practical Bess, the capable Matty, or even the irrepressible Bertie. All Luke's concern focused on just one of the sisters—the one most likely to succumb to the harshness of the frontier, the one with the most to lose, the one for whom he'd never be able to provide enough protection. She still grieved for her husband. Luke saw it in her eyes every time he thought about courting her. As much as he longed to have the right to love her, he refused to take advantage of her wounded spirit. Should he ever be blessed enough to become a permanent part of her life, it would be because she wanted the love as much as he did. Though he worried often about her physical safety, her emotional well-being concerned him just as much. He could tell she worried about being a burden. What if one of his less scrupulous neighbors decided to take advantage of her vulnerability? He'd given Scotty instructions about visitors to the ranch during his absence. Now that they were back, there wasn't much he could do to keep other men away. Her bakery business drew them like flies, as well as the appeal of her two unmarried sisters. It was an impossible situation.

As soon as the ranch house came into view, he knew something was wrong. Matty's cow stood by the barn door bawling to be milked. The garden, at which Bess toiled continuously, lay unattended. No laundry flapped on the clotheslines. The place looked deserted.

As if reading his thoughts, Jim pulled his horse alongside Luke's. "Doesn't look right, does it?"

Luke shook his head. Though every cell in his body screamed at him to gallop full speed to the house, one of the brothers had to stay with the ranch hands to help get the small band of sickly calves to the barn and the horses unloaded and brushed down. As Matty's husband, it was Jim's right to forgo the chores. "You go on in. I'll take care of things outside."

The speed with which Jim spurred his horse into a gallop told Luke they shared the same sick fear. Never before had emotion gripped him so tightly. Though he'd often been concerned about his parents or his sister, never had he felt the burden of responsibility that clung to him now. He realized as he slid from his horse and opened the corral gate that, no matter what happened with any of the sisters, each of them would always be a part of his heart. He took care of the animals, even milking the cow, which was obviously well past her usual milking time. His hands ached when he finished the job. Whoever had dubbed milking cows "women's work" had obviously never done it. He couldn't imagine how the sisters had managed the dairy alone after their parents' deaths. Of course, Ellis had been around; but after meeting the man, Luke strongly suspected he hadn't been of much practical assistance. With the cow once again released to her fenced pasture, he noticed the colt occupying the far stall, his leg neatly bandaged. Luke entered the stall, murmuring calming words to the colt just as Scotty came into the barn. "Howdy, boss."

"Hi, Scotty. What happened with this fellow?" Luke ran his hands down the colt's leg, noticing how neatly and firmly the bandage had been applied.

"I think he snagged his leg on some fencing wire. Miz Matty fixed him right up. Didn't even need me to hold him while she worked. As soon as she started talkin' to him, he settled right down."

"There's no fever in the leg. That's a good sign."

"Yessir. She cleaned the cut real well. Sent me to the cook shack for clean water three times. She don't do things by half measures."

Luke grinned briefly to himself as he left the stall. Scotty could give no higher praise. Conscientious and thorough, he strongly admired anyone who did a job as well as he would have done it.

"Ever'thing okay up at the house?" Scotty's inquiry told Luke what had brought the weathered cowboy to the barn.

"I don't know," Luke answered. "I figured Jim had more right than I did to skip out of chores."

"For now anyway," Scotty replied cryptically. "I haven't seen a-one of the ladies since last night, other than when I knocked this morning and Miss Bess told me they was okay."

The knot in Luke's middle tightened. If one of them had been injured or fallen ill, Bess likely would have told the cowboy. Only one thing he could think of would keep all of them indoors without explanation. Corrie's baby.

"Anything I can do for you, boss, so you can go on up to the house?"

Luke could have hugged the older man for his understanding, but it would have embarrassed them both. "Thanks, Scotty, but I think everything is done for the night. We'll need to check out the animals we brought back from the range with us, but that can wait until tomorrow."

"Okay then." Scotty turned toward the door then paused. "If there's anything wrong, let the ladies know that us at the bunkhouse will be sayin' a few prayers."

Luke nodded in acknowledgment. Scotty might not be the most refined of men, but he had a heart as big as the range and a faith as durable. When Scotty prayed, Luke knew God heard and responded.

The thought made him realize he hadn't yet turned to God with his worry. A pile of hay in a back corner of the barn had often been his place of prayer. He now dropped to his knees. "God, I'm sorry I didn't turn to You sooner. You know how Corrie is on my mind so much, to the point I'm not even thinking straight anymore. Please, Father, help me keep my mind on You and Your goodness. Whatever is wrong with the sisters, please provide us with all we need to meet their needs." He continued kneeling for several minutes in silence. He felt familiar peace slip into his soul. With the peace came the assurance that he needn't hide his feelings from his heavenly Father. Trying to hide from God, in fact, was a waste of time, since God knew his heart anyway. "Father, I want to be able to court Corrie and to win her heart, but both You and I know she's not ready for that. I couldn't bear to watch her marry another man for anything less than love, and yet I simply can't approach her with my feelings when she's so fragile. If she's the one You've designed for me, I trust You to bring us together in Your way and Your time. Until then, help me be patient and leave our hearts in Your care."

The burden of past weeks eased from his heart. He had no more assurance of the future than he'd had an hour ago, but now he felt able to leave the unknown with the only One who knew how it would turn out. With lighter steps, he strode toward the house. A lonely figure sat slumped on the steps.

"Hi, Bertie," he greeted her, playfully knocking askew the battered brown felt hat she so often wore. "Are you okay?"

A kidlike grin flitted across her face as she jammed the hat back in place. Then the somber look returned. "Corrie's sick, Luke. Matty won't let anyone else into Corrie's room, and Bess won't tell me anything. I know the baby is trying to come early, but they think I'm too young to talk about it. I'm not too young. I love her just as much as they do." She swiped at her eyes with a fist.

Luke lowered himself to the step beside her, holding back the urge that made him want to charge up the stairs. Even if he did get past Bess, Matty would bar his access to Corrie. He simply didn't have the right to be at her side. With a clarity that wouldn't have come to him a day ago, he realized the sister who needed him most at the moment wasn't the one who occupied his thoughts so frequently. He glanced sideways at Bertie, not wanting her to know he was studying her. Her reddish blond hair hung in braids always on the verge of coming loose. While the eyes of the other three sisters spoke of feminine understanding, Bertie's told of dreams of adventure, lively imagination, and a spirit that refused to be confined by convention. He rarely knew how to relate to her, with her mysterious combination of womanly appearance but childlike enthusiasm. At this moment, however, he felt an unexpected bond.

"I know how you feel, Bertie."

The girl's gaze snapped to his, disbelief, then disdain written across her face. "You can't know. She's not your sister. You're boss of your own ranch, not the youngest of five sisters."

"No, Corrie isn't my sister," Luke acknowledged slowly, hoping he didn't inadvertently reveal more than was appropriate. "But I've come to care a lot for the four of you. However, since I'm not a woman and not related to any of you, they won't tell me any more than they're telling you. That doesn't mean God won't let us talk to Him about her."

Bertie played with the end of a braid, seemingly thinking about what he'd said. Then with a defiant expression, she looked into his eyes. "I don't pray. Not since Mama and Papa died."

Luke's heart twisted with the hurt this child-woman couldn't express. "Well, Bertie, I think God knows exactly what you're feeling, and His heart hurts with you. When you're ready to talk with Him, He'll be ready to listen. In the meantime, you can be certain He understands what you can't say." After a few moments of silence between them, he rose and tiptoed through the front door.

Chapter 5

Luke's reception inside the house was pretty much what he expected. Jim sat at the table nursing a cup of coffee. If the look in his eyes hadn't warned Luke the situation was grim, the expression on Bess's face would have told him everything. Bess wasn't given to the abundance of smiles Matty usually displayed, but tonight her face looked pinched and tight. Luke knew she wouldn't tell him much, nor would she welcome any direct comments from him.

He didn't think she'd welcome a hug, either. He contented himself with pulling out a chair across from Jim and seating himself with the comment, "I've been praying, Bess."

He couldn't be sure, but it seemed tears might have shimmered in her eyes as she looked briefly at him. "Please don't stop," she said as she disappeared into the pantry.

It was just the opportunity Luke was waiting for. Having removed his boots at the door, he slipped soundlessly toward the stairs in his stocking feet. Jim's eyes both twinkled and warned Luke the ploy wouldn't work. Luke didn't expect to get far, but he had to attempt it. He had no intention of trying to see Corrie. Such a thing simply wouldn't be proper. But perhaps he could get a word with Matty. Just maybe she would tell him something—anything—to ease the knot in his gut. He sensed Bess's presence at the bottom of the stairs, but he refused to look back. If she wasn't going to say anything, he wasn't going to give her an opportunity. At the top of the stairs, he turned left down a hallway. At the end of the hallway stood the doorway to what had been his parents' room and had recently become Jim and Matty's. Corrie's smaller room lay just to the left. He wouldn't knock on the closed door. If Corrie was sleeping, he didn't want to disturb her. He just planned to wait around until Matty appeared.

He felt Bess's presence behind him even before her whispered admonition. "Luke, this isn't proper."

She wasn't saying anything he didn't already know. "I just want to hear Matty say she's okay."

Bess moved to stand between him and the door to Corrie's room. "I can't let you disturb—"

Before she finished the sentence, the door opened and a haggard Matty appeared. Locks of her normally tidy blond hair hung around her face. Worry lines radiated from her red-rimmed eyes. She shook her head. "Luke, I can't let you in."

"I'm not asking for that," he assured her though he wished with all his heart he had the right to ask. "I just want to know how she is."

Bess shook her head as though to indicate Matty should say nothing, but Matty just laid one hand on Bess's arm and another on Luke's. "We need a miracle," she said frankly. "The baby is still moving, which is a good sign, but the longer the labor continues, the more dangerous it is for both Corrie and the baby."

"How long has she been laboring?" Luke asked. He knew from working with animals how a long labor exhausted both mother and offspring.

Bess's mouth tightened, but Matty answered. "We don't know for sure. She hasn't been feeling well for a couple of days, but she didn't tell us how bad it was. Last night it got serious enough for her to tell me the details."

As long as she was willing to talk, he had one more question. "It's too early for the baby, isn't it?"

The shadows in Matty's eyes deepened as she nodded. "Yes, by at least a couple of weeks. That's why I'm worried. Pray, please, Luke. That's all you can do right now, but it's what we need more than anything."

"Ma-a-atty!"

The pained cry from the bedroom sent Matty scurrying back inside, and it made Luke's heart feel as if it were breaking. Bess steered him toward the stairs, though without reproof. He felt somewhat better for having heard directly from Matty, even though the information was not reassuring.

Jim looked up from the kitchen table when they returned. Luke explained, since Bess didn't seem ready to say anything. "Matty says things don't look good right now, but there's still time for a miracle."

"Maybe we should fetch Doc Mitchel." Jim looked from Luke to Bess and back again.

Bess's face brightened as soon as she heard the word "Doc." When Luke growled, "No," she whirled on him. "Why not? Corrie needs all the help we can get her."

"Doc Mitchel would be more trouble than help." Luke tried to keep his voice calm, even though he wanted to strangle his brother for opening the subject. "Jim, you know the doc is barely adequate for basic stitching and bandaging. I don't want his grubby soldier hands within a mile of Corrie." He stalked out of the kitchen and reached for his boots. Hanging around here would only get him in trouble.

Bertie still sat hunched on the steps. She turned at the sound of his steps, her hopeful eyes shining in the light that spilled from the doorway. "Is everything okay?"

"I wish I could say yes." Though every muscle in his body screamed for movement, some kind of action to distract him from the fear in his soul, he forced himself to sit once again on the step beside Bertie. "There's no way to know how things will work out."

Even in the dusk, fear shone vividly in the young woman's eyes. "Is Corrie dying?"

Luke draped his arm over her shoulders and drew her close. Propriety didn't matter nearly as much as giving what comfort he could. "I don't know as much as I'd like, Bertie. There are some things that just aren't appropriate for us to know." He felt her stiffen beside him. "I know it's not fair, but it's the way things are. Right now, what matters is Corrie. Even though we don't know details, we can be sure that God does. All we can do is trust Him to take care of her and ask Him to give Matty all the wisdom she needs."

"God didn't keep my parents alive."

Luke hadn't given much thought to the amount of loss Bertie had already experienced in her short life. How could Ellis have sent this child-woman away from the only home she'd ever known? On the other hand, getting away from him was probably the best thing to have happened to her. He knew of nothing he could say that would remove her fear or make up for the losses she'd already endured. He chose his words carefully. "Bertie, I can't explain why God let your parents die, just like I can't explain why He let my dad die. He's too big for us to understand all His ways. But no matter what heartache He allows, we do know for sure that He loves us with a love that's far beyond our ability to comprehend. No matter how big the heartache, His love is even bigger. He loves Corrie more than we do; I can promise you that."

Bertie sat in silence, appearing to ponder his words. Finally, she spoke. "Do you love Corrie, Luke?"

In all his thinking about Corrie, he'd carefully avoided that particular word. Hearing it spoken aloud gave him a jolt, even while it felt exactly right. Yet he didn't know how to answer the question. His feelings shouldn't be put into words until Corrie was ready to hear them. He sent up a quick prayer for guidance. Then before he could form a reply, Bertie spoke again.

"You don't have to say it. I can tell you love her. I hope she says yes when you ask her."

It surprised him how quickly her mind changed directions. At least she was no longer contemplating the possibility of Corrie's death. She apparently didn't realize the danger to the baby as well, and he had no intention of alerting her. "I need to ask you a favor, Bertie."

"Sure." The customary lilt was back in her voice.

"Corrie isn't ready to hear how I feel about her just yet. Can I trust you to keep it a secret?"

She studied him with an expression of womanly wisdom, which seemed to imply she knew more than he did. "She wouldn't believe me even if I did tell her."

"That doesn't matter." Luke made his tone firm. "Corrie trusts me right now, and that's very important to me. If she discovers my feelings too soon, it could destroy her trust. That would hurt more than if she never is able to love me back. I need your promise, Bertie."

"Okay, I promise."

He still didn't feel comfortable with her knowledge, but the matter had been wrested out of his control. In some ways, she might have not yet matured into womanhood, but her intuition was obviously full-grown. One of these days some besotted young man was going to take young Bertie for granted and end up with the surprise of his life. Luke grinned. Men liked to think of women as the weaker sex, but the more time he spent around women, the less he thought of that theory. They might be physically less strong, but in matters of the heart and soul, they had more going for them than most men could ever hope for. "Are you ready to go inside yet, little sister?"

"No."

"It's probably not a good idea for you to sit out here alone, and I need to go down to the barn."

"I'll come with you."

"I wish you could, but young ladies don't hang out with men in barns."

She giggled. "Now you sound like Bess."

Her lightning-swift changes between womanhood and girlhood made him smile. "Your sister is right more often than we'd like her to be." He mentally debated for a moment as to whether his next thoughts should be spoken, then he surrendered to the impulse. "I'll tell you what, Bertie. If you go up to your room, Bess will probably just be relieved you're inside where it's safe. Stay quiet, and you might hear Matty out in the hall. When you do, slip out and ask her about Corrie. She might be able to help you feel better."

Bertie grinned and disappeared indoors.

Luke trudged down to the barn. There wasn't much he could do in the dark, but he couldn't tolerate being in the house and unable to do anything to alleviate Corrie's suffering. In the corner by the workshop, he once again dropped to his knees. "Almighty God," he whispered into the hay-scented night, "Your Scripture tells us that You know the plans You have for us. While I want Your plan for me to include Corrie, at this hour what I want even more is for her to live and for You to spare the life of her little one. You know Matty is doing all that can be done humanly. With Your mercy, do more than we can do." His words ceased, but his heart remained focused on his heavenly Father. Peace enveloped him. He continued in wordless prayer, even as his legs cramped. The burden in his soul made his physical discomfort negligible by comparison. He couldn't have said how long he knelt before the burden eased, but when he stood, his legs shook. Lighting a lantern, he made his way into the workshop, where an idea began to take shape. Work on the ranch had kept him away from the woodworking he loved. He knew sleep wouldn't come readily tonight, so he might as well do something he enjoyed. The pile of fine-grained, smooth wood under the bench would make a fine cradle. Through the rest of the night, his hands shaped and smoothed the wood while his soul sent prayers heavenward.

Chapter 6

orrie woke to daylight streaming through the window. She felt sticky, achy, and still tired. She stretched, feeling the baby kick at the same time her leg cramped up so severely she let out a quiet cry. Instantly, Matty was by her side.

"Another contraction, Sweetie?"

Corrie could barely speak but managed to shake her head while straining to reach around her swollen belly to rub the cramped muscle. Matty read her body language and rubbed Corrie's leg with firm, experienced strokes.

"Ah, that's so much better." Corrie sighed as the pain abated. "I keep forgetting I can't tighten those muscles without penalty."

Matty massaged for a few more minutes then lightly stroked Corrie's belly. "How's the baby?"

Corrie grinned. "Busy as ever."

"That's a good sign. Any cramping?"

Corrie pondered. "I don't think so. I feel sore but not crampy."

Matty's eyes shone with delight. "That's good news. You fell asleep around midnight and seemed to sleep peacefully, which tells me the contractions may have stopped."

"When can I have a bath?"

"I'll have Bess bring up some warm water, and I'll give you a sponge bath."

"I can do it."

"No, you can't." Matty's voice rarely took such a firm note with Corrie. "Sweetie, you're not moving out of this bed except to use a chamber pot."

"Matty!" Corrie heard the whine in her own voice and hated it even while she felt powerless to get rid of it. "I'll die of boredom up here!"

"No, my dear one, you won't. You'll save your baby's life."

The bald statement jolted Corrie. She felt the shock widen her eyes.

"I'm not exaggerating, Corrie. If the contractions hadn't stopped, if your baby had been born today, he or she wouldn't have had a chance. You need to do everything you can to keep that little one happy inside you for at least another month. That means you need to stay relaxed and quiet. The slightest bit of exertion could start your labor again, and it might not stop."

Corrie felt despicable tears fill her eyes. She turned her head toward the wall so

Matty wouldn't see. If she lost this baby, her own life might as well end. But a month of being cooped up in this little room?

The first few days weren't as difficult as she'd expected. Her body seemed to crave sleep. Now there was no reason for her to resist the urge. Her naps frequently broke with the baby's activity or by her own bodily discomfort, but a change of position usually allowed her to drift back into slumber.

By the end of the week, however, her need for sleep became less acute. She had time to miss the rhythm of family life. Matty came in every morning with her breakfast and a sponge bath. Either Bess or Matty brought lunch and dinner. Matty usually stayed to chat while Corrie ate. Bess always inquired as to how Corrie felt, but she didn't linger.

In those hours of aloneness, Corrie couldn't help but contemplate the difference between her life as it was and the life she'd anticipated when she'd married Brian. He'd been a charming, jovial man. In fact, it had been Matty who had introduced him to the family. Corrie fully expected the two of them to make a match of it. But after only two visits, Brian started singling out Corrie. Thinking back, she shook her head at her own naïveté. She'd thought he was just being polite. Though she felt attracted to him, she'd kept her feelings out of sight, in deference to her sister. The night Brian had asked her permission to court her, she'd felt as though someone had tipped her world sideways. She'd refused to give him an answer until she'd talked with Matty.

Matty had assured her there was nothing romantic between her and Brian. "He views me like a sister," she'd said. "I can't think of anyone I'd rather see courting my other half."

Six months later, Corrie and Brian were married, Corrie wearing a gown stitched by Matty. Their marriage was better than anything Corrie could have dreamed. Occasionally, she wondered if she'd stolen happiness from Matty. She knew now that wasn't the case. Brian had never put the sparkle in Matty's eyes that Jim Collingswood had created almost from the first moment he and Matty met.

The only flaw in Brian and Corrie's marriage had been the lack of children. Corrie had so wanted to start a family right away, but month after month passed with no pregnancy. At long last, two years after their wedding day, Corrie knew her prayers had been answered. Three days after she'd told Brian their good news, an Atlantic storm swept him off the fishing boat and out of her life. A scant two months later, she was on the train with her sisters, history's most reluctant mail-order bride.

Tears flooded her eyes again and ran down her cheeks. She hadn't wept much over her loss. The pain had been too deep for tears, and the future too frightening. Now as she lay in a warm bed, surrounded by her sisters' tenderness and without the distraction of work, her pent-up grief began to flow freely. She couldn't lay facedown to weep into her pillow, so she pulled the blanket up to her face and stifled her sobs in the scratchy wool. She allowed herself to weep until it felt as if every drop of moisture had been wrung from her body. Matty would probably say she shouldn't cry so hard, for the baby's sake, but her sorrow refused to be denied its rightful release.

When the storm abated, she carefully eased herself out of bed. Matty had left the washbasin on the bureau. Corrie dipped a cloth in the now-tepid water, wrung it out, and then buried her face in the soothing coolness. The raw knot in the vicinity of her heart felt less tangled, less stabbing in its pain. Tears still ran but less intensely. It likely wasn't the last time she'd weep over the loss of her mate, but she felt a small measure of healing. Returning to bed lest Matty catch her upright, Corrie snuggled down into the covers and let a peaceful sleep claim her. She didn't wake until Matty brought her lunch.

The days passed, and Corrie came to relish her imposed solitude. She remembered, she wept, and she felt herself become stronger. One afternoon as she reminisced over her wedding, she recalled a private moment with Mama.

"I decided years ago I'd give this to whichever one of you girls married first," Mama had said, placing her big black Bible in Corrie's hands. "May it give you as much wisdom in raising your family as it's given me."

Corrie had treasured the link with her mother, especially after Mama's death a mere three months later. Still she'd spent little time reading the Book itself. Her life had been too full of Brian and new love. Yet, when gathering her meager belongings for the trip west, Mama's Bible had been the first thing she'd put in her trunk.

Devoutly hoping Matty wouldn't make a surprise visit, Corrie waddled to the trunk, which sat under the window. After just a few moments of digging, her fingers encountered the smooth, hard outlines of a book. She closed the trunk and carried the Bible back to her bed. She had no idea how long she lay there, tracing the edges of the Bible with her fingertips, remembering Mama. This had been one of her most treasured possessions. Though Mama had worked long hours every day, helping Papa in the dairy and raising her five daughters, each morning and each evening found her cradling the Book in her lap as she sat in her rocking chair. From an early age, her daughters knew not to disturb Mama when her Bible lay open before her.

Corrie had made her own profession of faith at ten years of age, mostly in response to Mama's strong, yet quiet, faith. Corrie wanted to be like Mama in every way, and faith was part of the package. But it had been an inherited faith, not her own. When her parents had been killed and then when news of Brian's death had come, faith wasn't where she turned first. It had been Matty who had bolstered them both, whose faith had kept them going.

Now Corrie felt a longing for a personal faith. She opened the Bible, not sure where she should start reading. One passage, then another, caught her attention, the words familiar from the many times Mama had read Scripture aloud. But nothing made her linger until some underlined words in John's Gospel beckoned. "Let not your heart be troubled: ye believe in God, believe also in me."

She couldn't remember a time when she hadn't had an abstract belief in God. But Jesus Himself was saying it wasn't enough. She scanned the surrounding verses and realized He was talking with His disciples, and yet it felt like a message designed for her personally. The verses that followed talked about keeping His commandments and then about Him sending the Comforter to be with them.

She gazed unseeingly at the wall across from her. A prayer formed deep within, though she didn't speak the words aloud. *Father God, I feel like I've known about You all my life, but now I want to know You personally, the way Jesus said we can. I need Your comfort, and I also need Your wisdom as I prepare to raise this child*—she paused; it was time to stop hiding from the truth—*these children alone. Please use these coming days of solitude and rest to help me learn to know You as my personal heavenly Father.*

Luke once again dismissed the urge to prop a ladder on the side of the house and crawl up to Corrie's window. It had been almost a month since he'd seen her, counting the week he and Jim had been out herding before the crisis. It was practically unbearable knowing she lay just up the stairs and around a corner but as remote from him as if she'd returned to Rhode Island. Matty had assured him Corrie and the baby were doing well, but she had been adamant that Corrie would not be getting out of bed for any reason anytime soon.

He tried to hide his loneliness in work. After putting in a full day on the ranch, he spent evenings in the barn and workshop mending tack, sharpening tools, and his favorite activity—painstakingly crafting the cradle. He couldn't recall why his dad had originally purchased the wood. It was fine-grained, smooth, and straight, so it must have cost a fair bit. Perhaps he'd been planning a storage chest for Mom or a hope chest for Annie. Whatever the original intent, Luke was sure Dad wouldn't mind the use he'd found for it.

Still, suppertime remained the worst part of the day. For some reason, it was then that he missed Corrie most intensely. Perhaps it was seeing the tender glances between Jim and Matty and knowing that an entire evening of togetherness stretched before them. Maybe it was just knowing that only a layer of wood and two strong-minded women separated him from the woman who'd unknowingly claimed his heart.

Whatever the cause, he'd even contemplated eating his supper at the bunkhouse. But that would stir up questions he preferred to leave unspoken. He pushed the beans around on his plate, knowing he'd better eat them or explain why he couldn't.

Jim's teasing tone interrupted Luke's mental dilemma. "Hey, little brother, if your lower lip were any longer, you could just use it to scoop your food into your mouth."

Luke looked up to see not only Jim but Matty and Bess grinning at him. Okay, so maybe he wasn't as inscrutable as he wished, but did Jim have to draw attention to it? "Speaking of big mouths," he tossed back, not sure whether his animosity was genuine or part of the sibling habit of communication he and Jim had developed.

"I'm just worried about you." The grin on Jim's face belied the serious tone he tried to maintain. "You look lonely, even though you're sharing a table with your favorite brother and three beautiful women."

Though repartee usually flowed freely between the two of them, on this occasion, Luke couldn't think of a single reply. Anything he wanted to say would only invite more teasing or, worse, solicitous inquiry from one of the women. He just wanted to be alone in his misery.

As Bess stood to serve slices from a cake that ordinarily would have had him licking his lips in anticipated enjoyment, he stood as well. "If you ladies would excuse me, I need to make a final check on a couple of ailing heifers."

The look in Matty's eyes could have rivaled the expression on Rhubarb's face as she stalked Ramon. "If you happen to be finished in an hour, Corrie has said she'd like some company for a few minutes."

Chapter 7

Since Luke's "chores" in the barn had been merely an excuse to get away from the table, he stayed outside only as long as he felt necessary to maintain his deception. As soon as he returned indoors, he stepped into the small wash-up room just off to the side of the entrance. Mom had insisted on the small room when they were building the house. "I want to make it easy for you guys to wash the barnyard grime off before coming to my kitchen table," she'd stated firmly.

Even when they were the only ones in the house, he and Jim still adhered to the standard she'd set. But tonight Luke took even more care with his cleanup. He shaved, praying he wouldn't nick himself in his haste. After changing the water, he washed his hands again, even scrubbing under his nails. In his room, he selected his "going to town" shirt and a clean pair of pants. Jim would likely tease him about "going courtin'," but Luke didn't care. He wasn't going to pay even a short visit to Corrie's domain while looking and smelling like a ranch hand. He paced as much as his tiny room would allow until enough time had elapsed that no one could tease him about being overeager.

Jim was seated at the kitchen table with a cup of coffee, apparently keeping Matty company while she washed dishes. Luke could hear the other two sisters discussing a difference of opinion in the parlor. Jim opened his mouth as if to say something, but a look from Matty quelled the comment.

She dried her hands then moved toward the stairs. "I'll just go up to make sure Corrie is ready for company."

Thankfully, Jim's silence held in his wife's absence. Only after Luke had been given permission to go upstairs did he whisper, "You've got it bad."

Jim's brotherly needling evaporated from Luke's mind as soon as he saw Corrie. Her hair hung loose and shining. She sat up in bed, leaning against the wall for support, clothed in some sort of dark blue, thick garment. Maybe it was what his mother would have called a dressing gown. She looked pale, but her eyes held more vibrancy than he remembered.

"Luke, you can sit here." Matty gestured toward a steamer trunk situated under the window and covered with a cloth. "I have a few things to do in our room, so you two enjoy your visit." She left the door wide open as she departed.

Luke didn't know what to say. He wanted to take Corrie's hand in his, enfold her in an embrace, any physical contact just to assure himself that she really was well.

"I won't break if you say something," she teased.

He chuckled to hide his surprise. The Corrie he remembered was too wounded and fragile to tease. What had happened up here in the past three weeks? "You're looking well," he managed to say.

She smiled in acknowledgment. "I am well, better than I've been in a long time. The rest has been good for me." Her hand lay on a large black Book by her side.

"You've been doing some reading?"

This time her smile glowed. "Yes. This was my mama's Bible, and I inherited it when I got married. I've finally been reading it."

Suddenly Luke understood the changes he detected in her face. Peace and healing had come to this fragile woman. Whatever had transpired between her and God had given her a strength he'd never guessed lay below the surface of her heartache.

"Isn't it amazing what God can tell us when we're finally able to listen?"

"Oh, it is!" The wonder in her voice caught at his heart. "Do you mind if I tell you what I've been reading today?"

"Not at all!" In fact, it would be a relief if she did most of the talking. He felt entranced by the changes he saw in her, his feelings intensified by the weeks of their separation. If he had to sit here just making conversation, he might say something that still needed to wait.

She opened her Bible to John's Gospel. Her gentle voice read a few verses, and then she went on to describe what the verses had come to mean to her. "I've never realized before how deep God's love for us is. I keep reading this one Gospel over and over. It seems every time I read it, I understand something new. Even the miracles Jesus did reflect His love for the people involved. Somehow, I'd always thought of Him as remote from human daily life. But He's not. He really cares!"

Luke couldn't help but grin in response. "I can't think of anything better to think about whether one is busy or confined to bed. I've been reminding myself often of how much He loves us. It helps to know He cares as much about my loved ones as I do."

Pink tinged her cheeks as she rubbed her huge belly. He could see in her eyes reflections of myriad thoughts chasing one another through her mind, but the blush gave him hope she'd heard, and maybe even accepted, the hint he'd just given her.

Before any more could be said, Matty bustled back into the room. "I hate to say it, but time's up. We need to get the little mama lying down again."

However, each night thereafter, Matty invited him upstairs again. The visits were always short, yet Luke felt a one-hour Bible study couldn't have encouraged his spirit more. Corrie obviously spent her hours alone not only reading Scripture but also in making its message practical. In his most private moments, Luke also hoped he wasn't imagining the development of an emotional bond between them.

The day before Thanksgiving, Matty pulled him aside. "Would you be willing to carry Corrie downstairs tomorrow so she can spend the day with us?"

He gaped at her while a multitude of disjointed thoughts tumbled through his mind. Delight at being given a reason to hold Corrie in his arms. Joy that her health was stable enough to allow her to participate in the holiday. Anticipation of having her around all day. Concern that the excitement might be too much for her. "Bringing her downstairs won't cause a relapse?"

Matty shrugged. "It's impossible to predict. At this point, though, if the baby does insist on coming, I think he or she would be big enough to make it. The benefit to Corrie of being part of the family celebration outweighs the risk."

"Have you talked with her about it?"

"Not yet. I thought I'd wait until after she eats breakfast in the morning. If there have been no complications in the night, then I'll tell her what we have planned. However," Matty looked sternly at him, though twinkles in her eyes softened the look, "I will count on you to help ensure that she doesn't overdo. I don't want her taking more than three steps by herself, and I don't want her sitting upright for more than half an hour."

Luke hadn't felt this elated since his dad had allowed him to drive the family buggy the first time. Of course, Jim had some observations to make as they did evening chores together. "I hear my wife has given you your assignment for tomorrow."

"Yup." Luke refused to say anything that would give Jim added ammunition.

"It seems significant to me that she didn't ask me, her husband, to help care for her sister. She asked a nonrelative, if you know what I mean. It's almost as if I smell romance in the air."

Luke focused on portioning just the right amount of hay for the horses they would keep corralled throughout the winter. "Perhaps she knows that you'll be so busy making moon eyes at her that you wouldn't be trustworthy for the job."

"Married men don't make moon eyes," Jim protested, as Luke had known he would.

Luke looked pointedly at the pitchfork Jim was aiming at the back corner of the stall in question. "They usually don't muck out stalls for milk cows, either."

❧

No major activities were ever planned for the Rough Cs for Thanksgiving Day, so Luke was able to finish his routine chores before breakfast. He even cajoled enough hot water away from the bunkhouse to take to the barn for a bath in an old laundry tub he set up in the workshop. He didn't want any scent of sweat or animal to be clinging to him when he held Corrie in his arms. A shave followed. Thankfully, the women had done laundry earlier in the week and ironing yesterday, so his best shirt and jeans were fresh.

Bess grinned at him as he entered the ranch house. He couldn't recall ever having seen that expression on her face before. She looked delighted with what she saw as she looked at him, as if he'd passed some test he hadn't known about. "Matty said you can go upstairs whenever you want."

Bertie stood at the counter stirring something and not looking happy about it. But as soon as she saw Luke, her countenance changed. "For true, you look fine, Luke. Corrie's sure to be impressed."

"Bertie!" Bess protested, though her eyes twinkled with laughter.

Luke felt heat creep up his neck, but he held Bertie's gaze. "Thank you for the compliment, but let's allow Corrie to make up her own mind, okay?"

Her eyes told him she understood his unspoken message. Bess looked back and forth from Luke to Bertie as though knowing there was more communication than she was privy to. But she didn't pry. "Go on then. I'm sure Corrie's impatient."

But impatience wasn't what Luke heard in Corrie's voice as he reached the top of the stairs.

"Matty, you can't ask Luke to carry me." She sounded embarrassed. "I'm sure I weigh more than one of his horses."

"No, dear one, you just feel like you do." Matty's voice was gentle. Luke could envision her stroking Corrie's hair as she did so often. "For your baby's sake, let him do this, okay?"

"I just hate being so helpless." Luke now heard tears in Corrie's tone. The sound twisted his heart. He paused, both to give Corrie time to collect herself and to give him time to think of a way to ease the situation for her.

Jim probably would have had a wisecrack to make her laugh. But Luke didn't want her to feel as if he were making light of her distress. Slowly he made his way toward her room, thumping his freshly cleaned boots on the floor slightly to ensure the women heard his approach. Before he reached her doorway, he called out, "Is the queen ready?"

The giggle from within reassured him, though it was Matty who answered. "I believe she is."

The view that greeted Luke as he stepped through the doorway almost made him trip over his own feet. Corrie sat on the edge of her bed, clad in a long, flowing dress of some soft gray material that brought out the blue of her eyes and gave her maternal figure the look of elegance and grace. Braids encircled her head, though tendrils of hair dangled around her face. He couldn't help the words that fell out of his mouth. "You're beautiful!"

Corrie's cheeks turned deep rose. "That's stretching a compliment, but thank you. Are you sure you're up to carrying me down the stairs? I'd never forgive myself if you injured yourself."

"Corrie." He spoke her name gently then waited for her to look into his face. "I promise you as your friend that if you're too heavy, I'll tell you. Can you trust me to be honest?"

She studied his eyes then sighed and nodded. "Okay."

"So if I don't complain, you promise not to give in to any sneaky feelings of guilt or embarrassment?"

"I'll try."

Before she could anticipate his actions, he slid one arm under her knees and the other around her waist. Instinctively, she curled one of her arms around his neck. "See? There's nothing to you. I've lifted feed bags that are heavier."

She giggled.

As he turned toward the door, he caught a glimpse of Matty's glistening eyes. What could he have said to make Matty cry? She was still smiling, though, so it must be all right.

Chapter 8

C orrie couldn't remember a more joyous Thanksgiving Day. She did feel awkward lounging in the parlor while her sisters did all the bustling and preparing, but the feeling didn't last long. Luke pulled a chair and a small table close to where she lay then set up a checkerboard.

"It's been ages since I played checkers," she informed him. "I probably won't be much of a challenge."

"It's been ages since I played, too," he replied with the gentle, just-for-her smile that sent shivers all the way down her spine.

"And even when we played every day, he still wasn't very good," Jim offered, setting a plate of fresh-baked rolls on the table beside the checkerboard. "Bess sent these in to tide us over until lunch."

Corrie played a game with Luke then watched the brothers compete against one another. The banter and affectionate insults didn't pause throughout the game. Bertie then joined them to play against Jim and then Corrie. Corrie felt as if her youngest sister spent more time studying her than the checkerboard, and she kept trying to reassure Bertie with smiles. Then she'd catch Bertie studying Luke, then seeming to try to study the two of them together. She'd never had the instinctive understanding of Bertie that Bess seemed to possess, but today's behavior was even more inexplicable than usual. Still, Corrie reached out to give Bertie a hug after the game was over. "Thanks for helping keep your useless big sister entertained."

The girl's gray-blue eyes flashed. "You're not useless!" With that, she left the room.

Corrie looked at Luke to see if he'd noticed the exchange. He nodded. "She's had a rough time of it while you've been laid up. She's been really worried about you, and Matty and Bess didn't explain much."

"It wouldn't be proper to tell her," Corrie explained in a rush of defensiveness.

"I know." Luke's tone became soothing. "That's what I told her, and I explained that I get told even less than she does. I'm not sure I helped though. She's lost a lot in the past few years."

Corrie instantly felt ashamed. "I've been so absorbed in my own troubles, I haven't given much thought to how she feels."

"She's doing fine," Luke assured her. "She just needs a bit of reassurance now and then, like we all do."

It took Corrie several seconds to realize she was staring at him. She simply couldn't imagine him in need of reassurance about anything. Before she could pursue the thought, though, Matty called them to lunch. Just that quickly, Luke scooped her up. He held her so lightly she could almost believe that he didn't notice her weight. It felt good to be supported by his strong arms, to have her arms around his shoulders. It felt as if they were pieces of a puzzle designed for each other. Before the thought could disturb her unduly, the rest of the family assembled around the table.

"Before I ask the blessing, I'd like to begin by stating what I'm thankful for," Jim said, reaching for Matty's hand. "I'm thankful that before I even realized I needed a wife, God sent a perfect helpmate to me. . .dropped her at my feet, so to speak."

Matty turned pink, and her three sisters laughed aloud at the memory of Matty's ungraceful introduction to Jim. When she could make herself heard, Matty spoke. "I'm thankful for Corrie's continued good health."

Corrie thought she heard a quiet, masculine-sounding "amen" from Luke's place beside her. "I'm grateful that God has given Matty the joy of marriage and the four of us a place to live," she said.

Bess spoke next. "I'm thankful the four of us are able to continue to be together and that we've come to a place where women's opinions matter."

There was a pause until Luke prompted gently, "Bertie?"

Bertie looked at her hands in confusion then at each of her sisters before speaking. "I'm glad, too, that we're together and that Corrie is okay."

"I think we're all in agreement on that, Bertie," Luke replied. "I'm also grateful God sent the four of you to share our home for as long as He leaves you with us. I know I'm stuck with Matty for the rest of her life, but I hope the other three of you never feel you have to be in a hurry to leave here. Our home is your home for as long as you like." His words addressed the three of them, but his gaze never left Corrie's.

"Thank you, Luke," Bess responded, saving Corrie the trouble of forming a reply that wouldn't embarrass her. "Now, Jim, if you wouldn't mind asking the blessing so we can eat before the food gets cold."

Corrie grinned to herself. Emotion would never get out of hand with Bess around to remind them all of practicalities. Jim's prayer was short, as usual, and then the serving dishes began to make their way around the table. Corrie felt she couldn't possibly do justice to all the wonderful food. She took just a dab of this and a bit of that, hoping to be able to sample everything. Still, she felt uncomfortably full by the time the meal ended. The babies had grown so big that her stomach didn't have room for much more than a snack. In a couple of hours, she'd be hungry again.

Luke carried her back to the parlor, and Matty followed them. "How are you feeling, Corrie? Not too tired?"

"I think I'm ready for a rest," Corrie admitted, "but, no, not too tired. It's been wonderful being back with the family."

"It's been wonderful having you back," Matty assured her with a hug. "Now just don't overdo so we can keep you here."

By the time Luke carried her upstairs that evening, Corrie felt ready for the quiet of her room. It had been a day full of fun, laughter, and family togetherness, but her very bones felt tired. Her back ached. Her stomach still felt overstretched from lunch. She let Matty help her into a sleeping gown; then she settled gratefully into bed. But sleep didn't come easily or linger long. She kept feeling Luke's arms around her. Had she ever felt such safety in Brian's embrace? She tried to recall a time Brian had carried her, but no such memory surfaced to banish the memory of Luke's arms. Was she falling in love with the gentle-eyed rancher? Had she loved Brian as truly as she ought if she could replace him so quickly?

It took Matty only a single glance the next morning to declare Corrie bedridden for another day. "We must have worn you out, dear one," she said. "Your eyes look like burnt holes in a blanket."

Corrie didn't object. While she doubted how much sleep she'd get, she needed time alone to get her emotional bearings again. After a restless nap, she turned once more to John's Gospel and to the verses that had first caught her attention. "Let not your heart be troubled. . .I will not leave you comfortless. . . ." The words brought peace, if not physical comfort.

It seemed no matter how she lay on the bed, her back ached. When Matty brought lunch, Corrie refused it. "I feel like if I eat anything, I'll throw up."

Matty's eyebrows knit with what Corrie termed her "doctor frown." "Any cramps?"

"No, but my back aches miserably."

Matty helped Corrie turn onto her side, facing the wall, then rubbed the lower part of her spine. "Right here?"

"Ahhh, yes," Corrie breathed. But the relief didn't last long. "Oooh, now that hurts worse."

Matty instantly stopped rubbing Corrie's back, moving her hands to Corrie's arm instead, where she stroked gently. "How about if I get a hot pack?"

❧

Luke was just finishing his second cinnamon roll after lunch when Matty came back downstairs from taking lunch to Corrie. A single look at her face put knots of tension in his shoulders. "She's having trouble again?"

Matty nodded. "Bess, we need some tea towels dipped in water as hot as you can stand, then wrung out. Luke and Jim, we need the water reservoir on the stove filled, as well as a large potful to heat on the stove." She studied Bertie for a moment, as if deep in thought. "Bertie, I need you to go through what's left of the flour sacks. We're going to need lots of cloths, so I'll need you to take the seams out. Choose patterns that we can't do much with. That purple one would be a good start."

Through the haze of his concern, Luke was glad to see Bertie's eyes brighten. Apparently, all she needed was to feel useful. He pushed back from the table, pocketing the remnant of his cinnamon bun. He'd lost interest in eating it, but Ramon usually enjoyed the table scraps he sneaked out of the house for him. On the way to the pump, he tossed the bun to the dog, who gobbled it. With energy brought on by worry, Luke had two buckets filled with water before Jim joined him. No words were exchanged as the brothers passed one another. Luke read in his brother's eyes the same concern he felt.

Once inside the kitchen, though, he found Matty waiting for him. "I need you upstairs."

Undeniable fear gripped him. "What's wrong?"

A skeleton of a smile crossed her face. "Corrie's asking for you. It may not be socially acceptable, but if your being there will help keep her calm, I won't stand in the way."

Luke stayed by Corrie's side throughout the afternoon and long after night fell. He lent his support when she insisted on pacing the hallway and helped Matty keep fresh hot packs against Corrie's back when she lay down. As the hours passed, Corrie's discomfort increased. It tore at his heart to hear her moans. When she squeezed his hand until it went numb, he willed the gesture to impart some of her pain to him.

Just as dawn was beginning to lighten the sky, he helped Corrie to her feet once more. She draped her arms over his shoulders and leaned against him as another spasm gripped her. Without warning, a gush of water poured over their feet. Matty instantly banished him from the room. "Go get Bess."

"Luke!" Corrie's voice was hoarse.

"He can't stay, dear one," Matty informed her tenderly. Though exhaustion ringed her eyes, not a trace of it showed in her tone.

Corrie looked up into Luke's face as she still clung to him. He marveled that she seemed to draw strength from his presence. He felt the bond between them, even though propriety didn't yet allow them to acknowledge it aloud. "Corrie," he whispered, "I'll stay right outside your room, okay? I won't stop praying until this is all over."

She nodded and allowed him to loosen her grip on his shoulders. He and Matty eased her onto the bed, and he left the room quickly before another spasm could take her. If he heard her pain-filled cry, not even his respect for Matty would keep him from fighting to stay by Corrie's side.

Bess responded instantly to his call. It seemed forever before she came out of the room again, her arms full of sodden-looking clothing. "Matty says it shouldn't be long now," she whispered. In moments, she reappeared, this time carrying a chair. Without comment, she positioned the chair outside Corrie's doorway then vanished back downstairs.

Luke couldn't have said whether minutes or hours passed. The chair stood watch as he paced the length of the hallway, sending wordless appeals from his heart to his heavenly Father. All at once, his absorption was broken by a small cry, hardly louder than Rhubarb's kittens. Then Matty appeared in the doorway, bearing a hastily wrapped bundle. "Take her, quick, and call Bess to come clean her up." She vanished back into the bedroom and closed the door.

He peered down at the squalling infant barely filling his two hands together. What could he possibly know about how to hold a baby? The thought had only a moment to register before the tiny eyes fluttered open. They gazed at him without recognition or focus, but Luke fell instantly in love. "So you're a girl, Matty said," he murmured, tucking the little one closer to his chest. "Welcome to the Rough Cs. You're most welcome here, little princess."

Before he reached the head of the stairs, Bess came barreling up, taking them two at a time. He wanted to grin at the uncharacteristic behavior, then at the joy of what he held in his hands, then at anything at all. "Matty say she's a girl and to get you to clean her up."

Bess reached for the baby. "Where's Matty? Is Corrie okay?"

Luke suddenly recalled Matty's haste in returning to the bedroom. Fear seared him once again. "I don't know. She seemed—"

The squalling of the infant Bess held suddenly became amplified. It took him a moment to realize a second cry had joined the first. Bess understood first. "Twins?" she asked, her voice cracking with amazement. "It's obviously a family thing." She headed down the stairs with her little bundle while Luke hurried to respond to Matty's second appearance in the doorway.

"Twin girls," she announced, surrendering the second bundle to Luke. "Ask Bess to get her cleaned up, too, then bring them back for Corrie to see right away."

"Is Corrie okay?" This time Luke's attention wasn't going to be stolen by feminine wiles, no matter how tiny or inexperienced.

Matty smiled broadly. "She is. She's tired but in good shape."

Relief flowed through him so strongly he felt his legs tremble. Matty placed her hands beneath his as he held the baby. "Careful, don't drop her. When you bring the babies back, I'll let you see Corrie for yourself."

It seemed to take forever for Bess to get the little ones cleaned up and wrapped in blankets. He held the first as she took care of the second. Then she placed the second little one in his other arm. He relished the armful. "Go ahead," Bess said, her eyes shining. "You deserve the honor of delivering them both to their mama."

He'd never taken the stairs so carefully yet so joyously. The longer he held these little ones, the more he felt his heart being overtaken by them. He'd witnessed birth many times in the barn, but nothing could compare to the wonder of the human life he held.

Matty held the door open for him as he approached. Then he was beside Corrie's bed, where somehow he managed to kneel in spite of his cherished burden. Her face was still lined with the agony and effort of the night, but she'd never looked more beautiful to him. "Corrie, I'd like you to meet your daughters," Matty said as she helped him lay first one, then the other, on Corrie's chest. She looked down at the babies, radiance replacing the night's imprint on her features. "They're beautiful," she whispered. "Twins, just like us, Tilde. Thank you." She looked first at her sister then held Luke's gaze for a long moment. "Thank you, too." Her attention returned to her daughters. Luke slipped out of the room and made his way quickly outside to the barn. He needed privacy before the tears of relief, joy, and love escaped.

Chapter 9

Corrie floated for days on the euphoria of love for her babies, whom she named Brianne and Madeline, after their father and their aunt. Though her body was sore and unbroken sleep seemed but a distant memory, she couldn't get enough of watching them, touching them, feeding them, caring for them. She had no idea how she would have managed without the ready assistance of her sisters. They kept the never-ending pile of laundry from taking over her room, brought her meals, and cuddled one fussy baby while she nursed the other.

In the evenings, she ventured downstairs. There she found both Jim and Luke eager to take their turns with the babies. She turned to mush inside every time she saw one of the big ranchers so tenderly cradling one of her daughters. One night she caught tears in Matty's eyes as Jim cooed to Madeline. Though Matty had a tender heart, she was rarely moved to tears. Was something amiss? Corrie studied her twin and decided the little ones had turned them all to mush.

Almost before she could catch a breath, Christmas arrived. The celebration wasn't the rollicking noisy time she remembered from her childhood, but the quietness of it suited her mood this year. She was surprised to find that each of her sisters had made gifts for her daughters as well as for her. Matty and Bess had sewn her loose, front-opening dresses. Each garment came with a belt, which would pull in some of the fullness as she regained her figure. They'd also sewn a pile of baby nightgowns, which they presented, wrapped in two soft blankets.

"Wherever did you get such soft fabric?" Corrie asked as she fingered the edges.

Matty and Bess exchanged smiles. "We bought it before we left Rhode Island," Matty explained, "knowing you'd need baby-type Christmas presents. There's enough fabric left for two larger blankets for when they're older."

Bertie had carved a lovely wooden plaque with the babies' names and birth dates. "That's all I had time to do," she explained. "I hope you don't mind having them share it."

Corrie embraced her younger sister, touched by the uncertainty in her eyes. "It's a perfect gift, Bertie. I'll treasure it always."

She hadn't noticed Luke leave the room, but now he appeared, lugging a large, burlap-wrapped object. "My present is mostly for the babies, but I hope you'll like it, too." He set it in front of her.

Corrie slowly pulled the burlap away. "Ohhhh," she breathed in wonder, running her fingers over an intricately carved wooden cradle. "It's even wide enough for both of them."

He grinned. "I did have to expand it after they arrived. Now that winter is here, I plan to make another so they can each have their own bed when they're too big to share this one. For now, though, I thought they'd be happier sleeping together."

Her eyes filled with the tears that never seemed far away. She'd noticed the girls did prefer to sleep not only together, but touching one another. That he'd so accurately perceived her children's needs touched her more deeply than his ever-present concern for her. As she blinked away the tears, she noticed a cutout carving at one end of the cradle. Four intertwined hearts. She counted them again to be sure the tears hadn't warped her vision. Four.

She looked into his eyes. His steady gaze held hers, and she knew. As always, he wouldn't press his suit. The cradle was his declaration just the same. If she wanted his heart, he was ready to give it. Not just to her, but to all three of them. She smiled her thanks then held out her arms for her babies, who were being cuddled by Bess and Bertie. "Time for mama and babies to have a rest." Her emotions had suddenly become too much for her, strangling her thoughts. She needed to get away to collect herself.

"May I bring the cradle up?" Luke asked softly.

She nodded and then made her way upstairs. It took a bit of shifting around to get the furniture arranged in such a way that she wouldn't bang her legs on something every time she moved, but eventually they found a solution. She settled the sleeping little ones in their new bed and nudged the rocker with her foot to set it in motion. "It's beautiful, Luke. Thank you."

"I enjoyed making it," he answered softly, one large finger tracing the hearts as the cradle rocked.

When the door thumped closed behind him, somehow his gentle presence lingered behind.

❦

As the New Year unfolded, the babies grew and Corrie regained her strength. She delighted in returning to the routine of the family life the six of them had established. Her life still centered around the babies, but there was always an extra pair of arms ready to cuddle them while she finished kneading a batch of bread or baking a panful of cookies.

Her connection with her twin didn't suffer either. Though no one else commented on it, she noticed Matty's pallor in the mornings. Sensing what might be the trouble, Corrie did her best to make sure coffee was ready before Matty came downstairs so she wouldn't have to smell it being prepared. If there were meats to fry or other strong-smelling foods to prepare, she did what she could to relieve Matty of the chore. She wondered when Matty would be ready to announce her happy news to the rest of the family.

In addition, there was always an undercurrent of awareness shimmering between her and Luke. Their gazes often locked over the supper table or across the room. She no longer wore her mourning brooch because it tended to get in the way while she was feeding the little ones. Somehow she didn't miss its weight.

One evening in early February, Corrie stood at the sink washing supper dishes. The chatter of the family swirled around her, and she reveled in it. She just was happy tonight, and it felt good after so many months of mourning and uncertainty. Bess sat at the end of the table with Brianne in her arms. Luke sat beside her, holding Madeline.

"Aren't you just the prettiest girls," Bess cooed. "You look just like your daddy, but you're still pretty, pretty, pretty. Your hair is curly like his, and you have his twinkly eyes."

Embarrassment and shame sliced into Corrie like twin knives. She hadn't noticed the resemblance, but now that Bess mentioned it, how could she have missed it? She hadn't been looking for their similarity to Brian. She'd been so caught up in the pink haze of her attraction to Luke, she'd not even considered her daughters' father, the one whose love had helped bring them into being. Hot tears filled her eyes as she rinsed the last few dishes and placed them on the counter to dry. Then, still blinking back the tears, she gathered Madeline and Brianne into her arms and carried them to her room. Tears dripped on their little heads as she nursed them and on their bellies as she changed their diapers. When she settled them into the cradle, she reached for her brooch on the bureau, and her weeping began in earnest.

She worked hard to keep her crying silent, both to avoid disturbing her daughters and to keep Matty from hearing her distress. There was no way she could discuss this with anyone. Yes, she cared deeply about Luke, but how could she do so if she'd truly cared about Brian? It hadn't been even a year since his death.

She forced herself to remember the awful day when she had become a widow. Her heart still ached over the loss, but she no longer felt emotionally crippled by it. Should she be able to recover so easily? She opened the brooch to stroke the lock of Brian's hair within. The hair could have belonged to anyone for all the comfort it brought her.

Sleep eluded her, even in the hours when her daughters slept. Every time she tried to slip into slumber, her thoughts chased one another in endless tangles, never creating a solution. Her love for Brian still caused her heart to ache. Yet her growing love for Luke demanded equal attention. What kind of woman could love two men?

The next morning, she didn't even try to go downstairs. As she expected, Matty came to check on her, looking no better than Corrie felt. "Are you okay, dear one?"

"Just a rough night." Corrie tried to manage a small smile. "You don't look so great yourself. When are you going to announce your news?"

Matty enfolded Corrie in a delighted, though shaky, embrace. "I should have known I couldn't hide it from you. Jim knows, but we're waiting another few weeks before we say anything. We like having our own secret."

Tears again pushed at Corrie's eyes, remembering hers and Brian's similar feelings not so long ago. "Don't push yourself too hard, okay? Remember what you told me—if something makes you sick, don't do it."

"Yes, Mother," Matty responded with mock resignation. "Would you like me to bring you some breakfast?"

"Only if it won't make you lose yours," Corrie answered, reaching for Madeline, who'd begun yelling for her own breakfast.

Just that easily a new routine established itself. Matty brought Corrie's meals and carried out the laundry. Corrie and her daughters remained ensconced in the bedroom, the one place where Corrie wouldn't have to face Luke or deal with her feelings. Without the distraction of his presence, her grief for Brian settled back into place, comforting in its familiarity and yet, if she were completely honest, feeling like a shoe that had its sole worn through.

Three days passed. Corrie's grief spent itself. The babies grew restless, having become accustomed to more company than just their mother. "You need to get used to this," Corrie told both herself and them. "The day will come soon when it will just be the three of us."

The conclusion had come to her slowly but settled in with certainty. As soon as the girls were eating solid food, she planned to move to town and resume her bakery business. She and her sisters had planned to make the jail habitable. Why couldn't she do it for herself and the babies? She knew it wouldn't be easy to meet their needs and support all of them financially, but it was what she needed to do. If, by the twins' first birthday, the attraction between her and Luke remained strong, then she would allow herself to put Brian's memory to rest.

A knock sounded on the door. "Come in," she said, expecting Matty.

Instead, Luke answered. "Are you decent?"

Panic coursed through her. She hadn't expected him to breach her hideaway. "No, I'm not. Just set my food out there, and I'll get it when I'm finished with the girls."

But the babies had heard his voice, and both started howling. She rocked the cradle, trying to settle them, but to no avail.

"Sounds like you need a hand."

At the repeated sound of his voice, the babies wailed even louder, and he had the nerve to laugh. "Sounds like they won't give you any peace until you let me in."

"Okay, come in, then." Corrie had to raise her voice to make herself heard.

Luke pushed the door open with his foot, carrying a plate in one hand and a tall glass of milk in the other. "Why don't I entertain the ladies while you eat?"

Corrie's stomach rumbled. One penalty of her self-imposed exile had been having to wait for food until Matty brought it rather than snacking whenever she felt hungry. Her appetite seemed insatiable these days. Gratefully, she accepted the plate.

Luke took a seat on the trunk and somehow lifted both babies into his lap. They stopped fussing, and both gazed at him intently. The shadow of Brian's memory threatened to fade in the bright light of the moment. Corrie forced herself to remember her grief.

Then she became aware of Luke talking. She focused on her food, but his words trickled into her consciousness. "What have you little girls been doing to make your mommy look so worn-out? You shouldn't work her so hard, you know. She's a wonderful lady." The babies cooed at him, and Corrie couldn't suppress a smile. "I'm glad you agree. You see, I need to tell you a secret. Your mommy loves a man whom I know must have been one of the best God ever created. She wouldn't have loved him if he weren't. He was your daddy. Then he had to go live in heaven and left your mommy all alone and very sad. I'm hoping one of these days, when she's less sad, she'll let me love her and you, too. I hope she'll tell me more about your daddy so I can help you get to know him at least a little. I wouldn't blame her if she didn't have room in her heart for more than one man, but I'm hoping that she will." He paused, leaned close to the girls, and whispered, "Someday."

Madeline let out a giggle and then Brianne did the same. Corrie looked at Luke in astonishment. "Do it again! See if they'll laugh."

He leaned close and whispered again, "Someday."

The girls grinned and then giggled again.

At that moment, Corrie gave up the struggle to keep her heart barricaded against Luke. There before her was the evidence. Her daughters needed a living man who could cuddle them, tell them stories, and, yes, make them laugh. She couldn't be everything to them, and with the bounty of Luke's love being offered to her, there was no need for her to try.

The passage from John's Gospel that had sustained her through the long days of her bed rest came to mind again. "Let not your heart be troubled."

She reached out to trace the hearts on the cradle's headboard. "Babies, tell Luke that someday is here."

Corrie's Cinnamon Buns

Prepare your favorite bread dough recipe. Let rise until double. Punch down, and separate out the equivalent of one loaf. Flatten this portion of bread dough to about ¼-inch thick. Spread thickly with butter then with enough sugar to cover well. Sprinkle with plenty of cinnamon. Roll dough together to form log shape.

Melt two tablespoons of butter in the bottom of a baking pan. Slice log into ½-inch slices and place slices cut-side down in the baking pan. When pan is full, let buns rise until doubled in size.

Bake in moderate heat in oven until buns are golden brown on top. Remove from oven and turn pan upside-down over cloth to let cool.

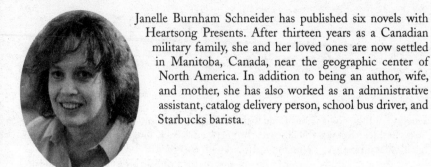

Janelle Burnham Schneider has published six novels with Heartsong Presents. After thirteen years as a Canadian military family, she and her loved ones are now settled in Manitoba, Canada, near the geographic center of North America. In addition to being an author, wife, and mother, she has also worked as an administrative assistant, catalog delivery person, school bus driver, and Starbucks barista.

FROM PRIDE
TO BRIDE

by JoAnn A. Grote

Dedication

To Linda Mitchell,
for telling me, "Of course you can write a book."
Thank you for your friendship and encouragement.

To Joe, Victoria and Joey—
Thank you for all the love, joy, laugher, craziness, and wonder.
You've made my life better and more beautiful in ways I
never dreamed possible.

Chapter 1

May 1869

From the hay-filled back of the Collingswood brothers' spring wagon, Bess Craig looked out at the crowd gathered in front of the Lickwind jailhouse for the Sunday service and bit back a groan.

Luke Collingswood looked back over his shoulder from the wagon seat and chuckled. "Looks like your usual admiration society is gathered, Bess."

"I'd be more impressed if I thought even one of those men came to worship the Lord instead of to ogle Bertie and me."

Beside her, Matty laughed softly. "Maybe the Lord's using you and Bertie to bring these men to hear His Word."

"Perhaps, but I doubt their ears are open."

The Craig sisters had been in Lickwind almost a year, and the bold attentions of the male population still amazed and unnerved Bess. A number of men had asked for her hand during that year, not even bothering to suggest the civilized tradition of courting. The winter months at the ranch had offered some, but not total, respite.

As Luke reined the horses to a stop, Bess glanced at the sky. Gray clouds rolled over each other. They'd been a mere shadow on the horizon when the group left the Rough Cs Ranch an hour earlier. No one had expected to encounter rain. Lickwind seldom saw more than a foot of rain in an entire year, as the area's sand and sagebrush testified.

"May I assist you, Miss Craig?" The portly banker extended his hand as Bess moved to climb down from the wagon.

"Thank you, Mr. Llewellyn."

As soon as her high-buttoned shoes touched the ground, she removed her hand from his and turned back to help her sisters. She didn't want to give Mr. Llewellyn any reason to believe she'd welcome his company at the service.

"I'll take the baby." Bess reached for Brianne bundled in Matty's arms then waited while Jim gently helped Matty from the wagon bed. Even such simple things as climbing down from a wagon were difficult for Matty with a babe expected to arrive in another month.

Luke rounded the back of the wagon. "Thanks, Bess. I'll take Brianne now."

Bess couldn't keep back a smile as she handed the baby to her father. He so obviously loved holding his children. She found it endearing.

She started toward the jail, her sisters and brothers-in-law close behind her. Immediately, the wind caught her gray cape and her dress's black-and-gray-striped skirt. In spite of her attempts to keep her skirt vertical, it danced about, revealing more of her ruffled petticoat than modesty allowed. Her face heated. The Wyoming wind waged a constant battle with the Craig sisters for their skirts and propriety.

The men who crowded the street between the jailhouse and the railroad tracks stepped back to make a path for Bess and her sisters. Men pulled their hats from their heads. Their greetings mixed into one. "Morning, Miss Craig."

"Good morning." Bess nodded at no one in particular, keeping her gaze on the open door.

When she reached it, she discovered more men filled the one-room building to capacity. Lean, dark-haired Parson Harris stood just within the doorway. "Good morning, Miss Craig. I believe I'll need to hold the service outside. Wonderful the Lord brought so many people." He smiled broadly.

"Certainly is, Parson," agreed Mr. Llewellyn, who had followed right behind Bess. "Afraid your congregation is going to get a mite wet though."

A rumble sounded overhead as if to confirm the statement. A moment later, a large raindrop splashed in the dirt at Bess's feet.

Bess stepped quickly aside to clear the doorway. "Corrie, Luke, you'd best get inside. We don't want those babes getting wet."

There was barely room for the four, even after Parson Harris stepped outside to allow more space.

The clouds opened and the rain filled the air with a *sh-sh-sh*. Men slapped their hats back on their heads. Bess and her sisters pulled their capes tighter and ducked their heads so their hat brims kept the worst of the rain from their eyes.

"Some of you gentlemen move outside," Parson Harris called into the building, "and make room for the ladies."

"We need someplace larger." Bess raised her voice to cover the sound of rain and restless men's shuffling feet.

"There isn't anywhere else," Luke reminded her.

Bess nodded briskly. "Yes, there is. Follow me."

The crowd parted again as she started through it. As soon as there was enough room, she broke into a run, one hand clasping her bonnet to her head, the other hand clasping her skirt to keep it from tangling with her legs. She knew from the sound of boots hitting the earth behind her that others followed.

"Where are we going?" Bertie asked from beside her.

Bess didn't answer. They'd already reached her destination. The heels of her shoes clunked against the saloon's boardwalk when she stepped onto it. The wooden awning offered welcome relief from the rain, which came down harder every minute.

"Bess?" Jim Collingswood's voice held a note of trepidation.

The saloon's large wooden doors were shut tight, hiding the batwing doors that offered customers easy access and tempted them with sounds of piano music and revelry during business hours. Bess pounded her fists against the door.

"Bess Craig, have you gone loco?" Jim grabbed one of her hands. "We can't hold church services in a saloon."

"We're closed," an angry voice announced from the other side of the door.

Bess continued beating with her free hand.

"Hold your horses," the voice demanded. The door swung open, revealing an unshaven man with wavy, golden brown hair that reached to his shoulders. A black patch covered his left eye. It took all Bess's courage not to step back at the sight of him.

Anger spit from Gideon Riker's unpatched eye. "Can't you see we're—?" Anger changed to confusion when he saw Bess then the crowd behind her.

"We need to use your saloon—that is, would you allow us to use your saloon for church services?" Bess amended.

Gideon's incredulous gaze met hers. "Church services?"

She lifted her chin and met his brown-eyed gaze unflinchingly. "Yes. It's raining, and yours is the only building large enough to accommodate everyone. Since you're not open for business, I was certain you'd wish to offer your premises."

Gideon hastily slid brown suspenders up over the shoulders of his gray Union Jack top, as if suddenly aware he stood before the entire town.

Behind Bess, Parson Harris cleared his throat. "We'll understand if you don't want us here, Mr. Riker."

Bess sidled past the saloon owner and into the building. "Of course he'll allow us to use his establishment."

The eyebrow above Gideon's patchless eye rose slightly as he watched Bess. She lifted her chin higher, silently challenging him to deny her statement. A drop of water fell from her hat brim and splashed onto her nose. She blinked in surprise.

Gideon's lips twitched into a smirk. He stepped back, opening the door wider. "I will not only allow it, Parson. I insist." He invited the crowd inside with a wave of one hand.

The matter decided to her satisfaction, Bess turned to survey the temporary chapel.

A boy of about ten, his long red hair falling over his forehead, stood beside the bar. He stared at her with wide eyes. Was that Gideon Riker's boy? She hadn't heard Gideon had a son, but then, there was no reason anyone should have mentioned the child to her. She flashed him a brief smile and continued to scan the building. She'd been inside for Ellis's trial, but she'd been too worried about the outcome to pay much attention to her surroundings. Besides, the room had been cleaned and rearranged before the trial.

The yeasty odor of beer filled her nostrils. The room was dark, even with the light through the windows and door. The walls were unpainted and the floor bare. Round tables surrounded by chairs stood about the room. A couple of chairs lay on their backs. Empty bottles and glasses stood on the tables and on the bar, which stretched across the opposite wall. A man appeared to be sleeping at one of the tables, but she couldn't be certain since he wasn't facing her direction.

"Amos, get Doc out of here," Gideon ordered the blacksmith. Bess caught her breath in surprise. The man sleeping off a drinking spree was Dr. Mitchel. Thank the Lord, Luke hadn't allowed that man near Corrie when she delivered her babies.

"Harry, where are you?" Gideon called, searching the crowd. The barkeep who'd played piano at the Craig sisters' weddings—a young man who looked about eighteen—stepped out. "Clean off these tables," Gideon ordered. The boy jumped to business.

The crowd trailed in. Some of the men seated themselves at the dirty tables. Some stood along the wall. A number of them chuckled and snickered at the situation.

Gideon, his hands full of bottles, waved toward the room. "Could use a little help here. You don't expect people to worship before the place is cleaned up, do you?"

Looking shamefaced, men stepped forward to help.

Bess noticed her sisters and brothers-in-law stood near the door. Jim gripped one of Bertie's arms, as though to make sure none of the town's rowdy men walked away with her. Probably wise.

Ever-helpful Matty reached for an empty glass on the table in front of her. Jim grabbed her elbow. "I don't want my wife's hands smelling like liquor."

Matty flushed and stepped back beside him.

Corrie, with daughter Madeline in her arms, slipped up to Bess's side to whisper, "Bess, are you sure this is a good idea?"

Bess started to respond, but something in the corner of her vision stopped her. She turned for a better look. "Oh, my."

"Oh, my," Corrie repeated.

Bess hurried across the room to where Gideon was noisily piling used bottles and glasses behind the bar. She leaned across the bar, not wanting the entire room to hear her. "Mr. Riker, shouldn't you do something about that. . .that. . .painting?"

His face grew dusky as he darted a look at the painting of a scantily clad woman. He muttered something she felt it just as well she couldn't make out. A moment later, chuckles from the crowd resounded as he removed the gild-framed painting and set it on the floor behind the bar.

Chairs scraped along the wooden floor as people found seats. There weren't enough chairs for everyone, so many of the men remained standing along the walls. Bess started toward her sisters.

Mr. Llewellyn stood, blocking her path, and indicated a chair he'd managed to keep anyone else from claiming. "Would you honor me with your company, Miss Craig?"

"Thank you, but I'll sit with my sisters." She hurried on, glad that thoughtful Corrie had kept a chair free beside her. Bess couldn't grow accustomed to attention from some of the area's most upstanding citizens. The banker back in Rhode Island wouldn't have given the daughter of a dairy farmer the time of day.

A piano stood along the wall at right angles to the bar. Parson Harris stood beside the piano and led the congregation in prayer. Then Harry sat down on the piano stool.

"Do you know 'Come, We That Love the Lord'?" the parson asked.

"No, sir."

" 'My God, How Wonderful Thou Art'?"

Harry's face brightened. "Yes, sir."

With a relieved smile, Parson Harris started the song. The congregation joined in. Bess and her sisters and the Collingswood brothers sang out strong against the background of male voices that stumbled over the words.

After the hymn, Parson Harris announced, "Mrs. Luke Collingswood has graciously agreed to sing for us."

Corrie stood and handed Madeline to Bess, who looked at her shy sister in surprise. Corrie had a lovely singing voice, but she'd never had the courage to sing alone in front of anyone but family. It seemed she was blossoming in all sorts of ways since marrying Luke in February in a quiet ceremony at the ranch. His face was bright with pride as he watched her move to the piano.

Corrie's voice rang out sweet and true. The men were so still, they seemed to have stopped breathing. As Corrie began the third verse, Bess realized the wisdom of her choice of song. Certainly, these men would relate to the words.

"All beauty speaks of Thee:
the mountains and the rivers,
the line of lifted sea,
where spreading moonlight quivers—"

"What's going on here?" A woman's harsh voice called out, halting Corrie's song.

Shocked and angry at the interruption, Bess turned. A pretty, black-haired woman of about thirty stood in the open doorway, fists planted on the hips of a garish red dress. Bess gulped. She'd never seen the woman before, but she knew instantly the woman was Margaret Manning, who flaunted her dancing girls before Lickwind's men—and the dancing girls flanked Margaret Manning now.

Chapter 2

Anger and disbelief fought for supremacy in Bess's emotions. Had these. . . women. . .no sense of propriety? Back in Rhode Island, such women knew their place, and that place was not in a church service or in the presence of decent women like the Craig sisters.

She pushed aside the thought that in Rhode Island church services weren't held in saloons, which were the usual territory of dancing girls.

"Well, well, well." Margaret Manning walked between the tables, grinning at the self-conscious men as she made her way toward the piano. "What would your wife think if she knew you were in a saloon, Parson?"

The color drained from Parson Harris's face.

Bess glanced about the room. Bess was sure the circuit rider was glad his wife hadn't accompanied him on the circuit this time. Why didn't one of the men do something?

Margaret stopped beside Corrie. Up close, Bess saw that Margaret looked older than her years beneath her powder and rouge. Margaret ran her glance over Corrie, who appeared too shocked to move. Corrie—with her blond coronet and gray and mauve gown—looked like an angel beside the dance hall woman.

Luke and Jim bolted to their feet. They were beside Corrie in an instant, glaring at Margaret. "Maybe you should leave, Miss Manning," Luke suggested in a threatening tone.

The woman laughed. "Don't worry. I'm not the big, bad wolf. I'm not going to hurt the little lady."

Gideon Riker clasped Margaret's elbow. "Why don't you let me see you home?"

Margaret tugged her arm, but Gideon kept his hold. "When did you turn your saloon into a church, Gideon? You didn't act so religious when me and the girls were in here last night."

His mouth tightened into a thin line. He started walking, and Margaret had no choice but to join him. "Let's go," he said to the other girls at the door.

The red-haired boy whom Bess noticed earlier stood beside one of the dance hall girls, a redhead who appeared to be about Bertie's age. Her green dress wasn't as flamboyant as Margaret's. "I'd like to stay, Gideon," the girl said in a low voice. "I haven't been to a church service in ever so long."

Gideon appeared to hesitate. He glanced back at Parson Harris, who shrugged as if to say he didn't know what to answer.

"I won't be no trouble, Gideon," she urged. She rested her hand on the boy's shoulder. "Walter and I will stand back here by the door, quietlike."

Margaret reached for the girl. "Come on, Regina. These people don't want sinners like us here." Her harsh laugh showed her contempt for the "good" townspeople.

The truth of her words shamed Bess. How could they turn aside a young woman who wanted to listen to the service? How could they know her heart? Bess shot to her feet, Madeline still in her arms. "Anyone is welcome to stay if they truly wish to hear God's Word."

A murmur ran through the room, but no one protested Bess's declaration. Gideon shrugged.

Margaret pointed her finger at Regina. "Don't you go turning religious on me." Laughing, Margaret walked through the batwing doors, followed by the two other dance hall girls.

Regina stayed, standing beside the door with Walter and looking young and frightened. Corrie, still trembling slightly from her experience, sat down beside Luke. Parson Harris cleared his throat and began his sermon. The crowd of men—most of whom Bess suspected would have enjoyed the dancing girls' presence under any other circumstances—breathed a collective sigh of relief.

When the final prayer was over, Bess looked for Regina. The young woman was slipping out between the batwing doors. "I'll be right back," Bess told Corrie, then started after the woman with the red hair and gentle expression.

Bess excused herself repeatedly as men tried to stop her to talk. If she didn't hurry, she'd lose sight of Regina.

The girl was in front of Amos Freeling's blacksmith shop when Bess reached the saloon's boardwalk. "Miss Regina, wait, please!"

The woman turned, a surprised expression on her pretty face. Men stared at Bess in shock. Bess's face heated, but she refused to allow her embarrassment to deter her. The rain had slowed to barely a drizzle and the wind had stopped, but Bess barely noticed as she left the protected saloon boardwalk and stepped onto the dirt road.

"I'm sorry, but I don't know your last name," Bess said when she reached Regina.

"Bently. Regina Bently. Thank you for speaking up for me back there, Miss Craig."

"You know who I am?"

Regina smiled. "Everyone around here knows who the Craig sisters are." Her smile died. "Same as everyone knows who I and the rest of Margaret's girls are. You shouldn't be talkin' with me, miss."

"I hope you'll attend our services again, Miss Bently."

Regina dropped her green-eyed gaze to the ground. "Most people won't take kindly to my presence at the meetings."

"I doubt there's one of them so perfect before God that they can refuse you the right to hear God's Word and worship Him. Besides, my sister and I noticed your voice during the last hymn. The congregation can use another beautiful singing voice."

A shy smile lit Regina's eyes. "Thank you. I'll think on your invitation." She glanced over Bess's shoulder. "Good day." She started toward the back of the blacksmith shop to the building where Bess knew the dance hall girls stayed.

As Bess turned around, a frowning quartet comprised of Jim, Matty, Luke, and Corrie joined her.

"I don't think you should be talking with her, Bess," Jim warned, looking uncomfortable. "Maybe you don't realize, but—"

"I know how she earns her living, Jim, but something or Someone made her want to stay at the service this morning." Bess looked from Matty to Corrie. "Perhaps the Lord brought us here for reasons other than we believed."

Her sisters exchanged startled looks. Then they smiled. Corrie nodded. "Perhaps He did at that."

"Now, Corrie," Luke started.

Bess glanced at the street, which was filled with men from the service. "Where's Bertie?"

Chapter 3

Gideon stood outside the batwing doors, wondering whether he was dreaming the unusual morning occurrences. Men still milled in the street, casting longing gazes at Bess Craig. The unpredictable woman was, of all things, talking with Regina in plain sight of the entire town. He couldn't recall ever seeing a lady speak to a dance hall girl. The men who'd been hankering after Miss Craig's hand in marriage were probably reconsidering about now.

Like all the rest of the men in the area, Gideon had made a trip to the Rough Cs to meet the Craig sisters. Jim Collingswood had snatched up friendly Matty right off. Then Luke married that sweet Corrie. Bertie was too young to interest Gideon.

But, Bess. . .well, he still remembered the sight of her getting off the train. He'd considered getting in line to ask to court her but changed his mind right fast. A lady deserved better than a saloon owner for a husband. And it was as certain as sagebrush in Wyoming that pious, proper Bess would agree. Besides, her face looked too stern to entertain a smile. And the way she dressed—severe, dark clothes like that gray outfit she wore today, her dark brown hair pulled back tight in a bun. Dressed more like a widow in mourning than a lady looking for a husband. No, sir, he didn't cotton much to being hitched for life to a woman as sober and proper as Elizabeth Craig.

Gideon yawned. He wasn't accustomed to seeing the light of day at this time of morning. He rubbed the palm of his hand over his face then grinned. He was the only man in town, besides Doc, who hadn't shaved this morning.

He heard a man clear his throat and realized Parson Harris stood beside him, Bible and hat in hand. "Thank you for allowing us to use your business establishment for the services, Mr. Riker. I hope we didn't cause you too much trouble."

"No trouble at all." Seemed more like entertainment to him, in fact. "Welcome to use it again any Sunday morning." He saw no harm in making the offer. It didn't rain often enough in Lickwind to expect Parson Harris to need the saloon again. Besides, once Bess and Bertie Craig married, church attendance would dwindle back to the normal handful of sincere faithful.

That was, assuming any man dared take Bess Craig on as a wife. Gideon chuckled, remembering the way she'd all but demanded the use of his saloon. He had to admit, he admired her gumption.

Gideon yawned again and pushed his way through the batwing doors. He should probably keep the saloon open with all those men in town. Some were sure to stop in for a drink. But all he wanted to do was get some shut-eye.

He stopped short. Bertie Craig stood behind the bar, her back to him. Beside her, Harry proudly listed off the different types of alcohol available, pointing at the appropriate bottles.

"Harry, what are you. . . ?"

Harry and Bertie turned to stare at Gideon as he stormed across the room, boots thunking against the wooden floor. "Get out from behind that bar, the both of you."

Bertie hurried out, fear on her freckled, tomboyish face. "For true, I didn't hurt a thing, sir. And I didn't even look at the picture."

"I should hope not." Gideon grabbed her arm just above the elbow. He started to escort her toward the door. She almost stumbled in her attempt to keep up with him. Her free hand pressed the brim of the hat to her strawberry blond hair to keep the hat from falling off.

A growl, accompanied by something yanking at his trousers, stopped him. The strangest-looking dog he'd ever seen glared up at him. He tried to shake it off.

"Don't hurt Ramon," the girl pleaded. "He's just being protective of me."

Gideon started toward the door again, his fingers still around the girl's arm and the dog dragging along.

Harry hurried alongside them. "Nothing happened, Gideon. I watched out for her."

"That's a comfort," Gideon said dryly.

"I know how to treat a lady." Harry's voice rose in indignation.

"Then you know a lady has no place in a saloon." He deserved this for being softhearted and taking Harry on as a barkeep. What he needed was someone with the brawn of Amos the blacksmith, who could squelch fights in the saloon. But he'd felt sorry for Harry. He was only a kid with no family to look out for him.

Bertie's smile beamed. "Bess says I'm not a lady yet, but almost."

Gideon groaned. *Miss Bess Craig must have her hands full with this one.*

"Besides, all us Craig sisters were here for church," Bertie protested. "We were here for Ellis Stack's trial, too, but I couldn't see much then."

"Unless we have another rainstorm on a Sabbath morning before your sister is hitched, you'll not see the inside of this saloon again."

"For true, that's why I took advantage of the opportunity."

Gideon stopped, his hand still gripping her arm, and stared at her. "Opportunity?"

Her face shone bright with innocence. "Yes, sir. The opportunity to see a den of iniquity up close." She squinted at him. "You don't look depraved."

He muttered under his breath and pushed open a batwing door, almost hitting Miss Bess Craig, who'd just stepped onto the saloon's boardwalk from the rain-soaked street. "There you are, Bertie. I was beginning to believe you'd headed back to the ranch on foot."

Gideon released his hold on Bertie.

"You can let go now, Ramon," the girl urged the dog.

To Gideon's amazement, the dog did as she said, though it continued growling.

Gideon nodded toward Bertie. "You'd best keep a close watch on this one, Miss Craig. If ever there was a girl named Trouble, this one is it."

Anger flashed from Bess's brown eyes. She reached for Bertie, drawing the girl into her embrace. "I'll thank you not to insult my sister, Mr. Riker."

Gideon felt his face heat from her reproof. His embarrassment fueled his anger. He'd been fifteen the last time a woman used that tone with him. He bit back the reply dangling on the tip of his tongue. "Sorry, miss."

Bess looked as though she'd like to refuse his apology, but she didn't. Instead, she said in a hard voice, "The Collingswoods, Bertie and I, and Parson Harris are planning to picnic in the jailhouse. We'd be pleasured if you'd join us, since you allowed us the use of your. . .premises for the service."

Pleasured? He'd bet his new house she wasn't a bit pleasured at the prospect of his company. "I'd be most honored, Miss Craig. Thank you kindly."

She nodded at him—a short, clipped sort of nod led by her pointed chin. "Come, Bertie."

He grinned, rubbing the palm of his hand across the stubble on his chin, as he watched them head next door to the jailhouse.

When Gideon started for the jailhouse twenty minutes later, he sported a clean-shaven face and smelled as good as the cheap aftershave from Jones's General Store allowed—just like all the other bachelors in the Lickwind vicinity. He even wore his best shirt. He chuckled as he walked along, amused that of all the bachelors at church that morning, he'd been the worst dressed and the only one not there voluntarily—but he was the one invited to picnic with Miss Bess Craig. Obviously not for romantic reasons, but that fact only added to the humor of the situation.

The sight that greeted him when he stepped inside the jailhouse knocked his pride down a peg. He evidently wasn't the only bachelor invited. He stood in the doorway and surveyed the men. If he'd prepared a list of the most eligible men in the area, these were the men whose names would be on that list: Jones, the owner of the general store; Squires, the feedstore owner; short and portly Oscar Hatch, the barber, with his cookie-duster mustache, and his lanky cousin Linus, the telegraph operator; Amos Freeling, the blacksmith; Mr. Llewellyn; the lawyer Donald Potter; and ranchers Josiah Temple and Clyde Kincaid.

Well, maybe Kincaid wouldn't make Gideon's list. Gideon hated to see the man enter the saloon. He cheated at cards as sure as wind whipped Wyoming.

"We're so glad you could join us, Mr. Riker." Mrs. Jim Collingswood smiled up at him. "The food is set out in the area that will be a cell once the bars arrive and are set in."

"Sure there's enough food, ma'am? You've quite a crowd here."

"Yes, isn't it nice? They all just showed up. This is such a friendly town."

"Yes, ma'am." *Friendly like a coyote after a chicken, and Bess Craig is the prey.* But Matty's comments restored his assurance that he was the only unmarried man here by invitation.

He made his way across the room, greeting people along the way, until he reached the barless cell. It was a mite crowded. Bess stood beside the mattressless wooden cot attached to the wall, where the food was set out. The banker, Llewellyn, and the lawyer, Potter, flanked her. Others stood about with silly grins on their faces, hoping for a handout of Miss Craig's attention.

Gideon smirked. Nice of Jim's wife to let it slip that none of the other men were invited. This could be fun. Gideon softened his voice to courting tones. "So nice of you to invite me, Miss Craig."

Unpleasant surprise flickered across the banker's and lawyer's faces—just the reaction Gideon hoped to see. With a sense of reluctance, the lawyer stepped back to allow Gideon beside Bess. The faint floral scent she wore nudged away the scent of Gideon's aftershave and set his heart to quick-stepping.

Bess Craig lifted her chin and gave him a cool glance. "You made it, Mr. Riker. Would you like some fried chicken and dried apple pie?"

"I surely would, miss."

She filled a plate and handed it to him.

"Thank you kindly." He winked at her.

She blinked, looking astonished, then blushed.

Llewellyn and Potter exchanged glances.

This is the most fun I've had since the Union Pacific gang moved on. Gideon took a bite of the drumstick.

Llewellyn hooked his thumbs on his vest pockets. "That house you're building is coming along well, Riker."

"That it is. Walls up, windows in, and roof on. Almost ready to move into." Gideon was right proud of that house. Doc Mitchel and Llewellyn owned the only other houses in town. Sleeping in the back room at the tavern was growing old. There was always someone coming around wanting to buy a drink when he was trying to get a little shut-eye. "I'm only waiting on the stove to arrive to move in."

Potter nudged Llewellyn. "Guess if we want to make a fortune, we should sell liquor."

Gideon thought the lawyer's grin held more spite-filled envy than amusement, but Gideon pretended not to notice and smiled amiably. "Business has been good for most in town since the Craig sisters arrived last June."

Oscar Hatch's cheeks jiggled as he chuckled. "That's the truth. Men in my place night and day wanting baths and their hair and whiskers trimmed."

"Can't keep shirts and Bay Rum Aftershave in stock at my place," Jones agreed.

"A businessman needs to take advantage of such things while he can," Gideon declared. "Once Miss Craig here and her little sister are married off, bachelors round here won't have any call to stay clean and smell passable good. Business will probably fall off so fierce you'll all be poor as church mice."

The men guffawed.

Gideon nudged Bess lightly and winked again, strangling his laugh at the lightning in her eyes.

"I'm so glad my and my sisters' presence has benefited you all." Her lips tightened into a thin line.

Gideon nodded. "Just like the parson said in the service this morning: 'It's good to be a blessing to others.' Right, Miss Craig?"

He almost choked on the furious look she darted his way.

Bess turned her back to him. "Mr. Llewellyn, who would I need to speak with concerning the possibility of renting this jailhouse?"

Llewellyn rocked back on the heels of his black boots—their shine showing even through the dust from Lickwind's only street. "Whatever would a little lady like you need with a jailhouse?"

"To live in it. There are no houses to rent in town. Not even a room."

"The Collingswood brothers aren't kicking you off the Rough Cs, are they?" Gideon asked. The Collingswood brothers weren't the kind of men to turn good women out on their own resources.

"Of course not. They haven't once intimated Bertie and I are an inconvenience, yet we most certainly are. Would any of you wish to support four women and two— or more—babies?"

Gideon followed her glance to Matty.

No one answered, but several of the men cringed. A few of them took a step back.

"I thought not," Bess continued. "In good weather, the ranch is still a long ride from Lickwind. How can Bertie and I support ourselves there? Even if we had goods to sell, the men haven't time to be driving us to town and back with any frequency. My brothers-in-law say they'll be starting roundup this week, so the men will have less time than ever to wait on us."

Llewellyn hooked his thumbs on his vest pockets again and gave Bess a down-right fatherly look. "Even saying that's true, how would living in town make a difference?"

"We'd start a bakery."

Llewellyn rocked back on his heels again. "Tempting as that sounds, I doubt you'd make enough to support yourselves on it."

"You might at least give us a chance. At best, the town benefits from our rent and our services. If we don't make it, what has the town lost?"

"I don't see how we can allow you to live here, Miss Craig," Potter intervened. "What if we need to lock up some criminal?"

Bess cast a withering look his way. "Not one man has been arrested since my sisters and I stepped off the train. Besides, there aren't even bars on the cells or windows."

"There will be soon." Potter exchanged a scowling glance with Llewellyn. Both shook their heads.

"I'm afraid our answer must remain no," Llewellyn said. "It wouldn't be seemly, two unmarried women living in the town jail."

"What else would you have us do?" Bess's voice did nothing to disguise her disgust. "Trek to South Pass to search for gold? Or support ourselves in the manner of Lickwind's other women?"

Gideon noted with satisfaction that the men had the grace to look embarrassed at her suggestion. Bess Craig wasn't his idea of perfect femininity, but he admired her grit. The sudden desire to fight for her cause rose up within him. He squelched it. He didn't mind letting the men believe she'd invited him to this makeshift picnic, but he didn't want her thinking he was interested in her. Besides, if ever a female didn't need a man defending her, it was Bess Craig—which is why it made no sense at all when he heard himself say, "You're welcome to rent my new house, Miss Craig."

Chapter 4

Three days later, Bess stood in the doorway between the kitchen and parlor, surveying Gideon Riker's house. It was May 10, 1869, her twenty-fourth birthday, and the first day of her life absolutely on her own. Of course, she and Bertie would share the house, but the responsibility for supporting them fell on Bess's shoulders. She'd thought she'd feel frightened. Instead, an excitement for the challenge ahead surged through her. She breathed in the scent of new lumber and sawdust.

Bertie, wearing the ever-present brown felt hat, stopped beside Bess. Bess slid her arm around Bertie's shoulders and gave her a squeeze. "Isn't it amazing how the Lord provided for us, Bertie? A new house, with a kitchen, parlor, and two bedrooms, when all we asked Him for was that one-room jailhouse. Oh, God is good to us."

Behind them, Gideon grunted. Ramon growled. Bess jumped in surprise. Turning, she saw her hope chest balanced on Gideon's shoulder. His defiant gaze met hers. "I'd think I might get some credit. Didn't see God out here hammering and squaring up walls and laying down a floor."

"For true, Bess believes God can work through the worst sinner." Bertie's eyes shone with sincerity.

Bess resisted the impulse to put her hand over her sister's mouth.

The look Gideon shot Bess showed full well he believed she thought God had found His worst sinner in Gideon Riker. "Well," he drawled, "I expect God works through good folk, too, though He might find it takes longer, their pride getting in the way and all."

"You've been most kind." Bess refused to address the sinner question or acknowledge that he was the last man in Lickwind she'd expected to befriend her and Bertie.

"Where do you want this chest?"

"Beneath the parlor window." Bess pointed to the window, which looked out on the back of the saloon some thirty feet away. "It will double for a chair until we can afford furnishings."

Gideon placed the chest below the window, straightened, and looked about the empty parlor. "I'll bring over a table and some chairs from the saloon."

Bess started to say it wasn't necessary but stopped herself. She sent a silent thank-you to the Lord for meeting yet another need. "That would be a pure blessing, Mr. Riker."

Bertie walked to the center of the room and whirled in a circle, her arms out. "Are you going to paint or paper the walls, too, Mr. Riker? And get a rug for the floor? And curtains and—"

"Shush, Roberta Suzanne. He's exceeded the bounds of generosity already, allowing us to stay here." Even unfinished, this house was a palace in Lickwind. She nodded toward the kitchen. "I see your stove came in, Mr. Riker."

"Arrived on yesterday's train," Gideon acknowledged. "Put it in right off. Figured you'd need it for those baked goods you're planning to sell. It'll be a lot easier to use the stove for that than the parlor fireplace. I haven't set aside a separate pile of fire-wood. Take what you need from the cord behind the saloon."

"We'll keep track of what we use and pay for it," Bess said.

He crossed to the stairway leading to the second floor. "You'll find two bed-rooms up there. I only had time to build one bed, though."

"A bed?" Surprise washed through Bess. She'd expected to sleep on the floor.

"Easy enough to do with leftover lumber. Sorry there's no mattress."

Same as sleeping on the floor. "Easy enough to buy a tick and fill it with straw." Bess matched his tone, mentally adding one more thing to her list of items to pur-chase at Jones's General Store: kerosene lamp, kerosene, candles, matches, broom, baking supplies, mattress tick.

They heard Jim Collingswood's boots cross the kitchen floor before he entered the parlor and set down two valises. "That's the last of it."

Not that there'd been much "it" to bring in from the ranch, Bess thought. Some kitchen items, her hope chest with its linens and blankets, her sewing basket, and the few clothes she and Bertie owned.

As though Jim's train of thought matched hers, he said, "Cow's tied to a porch post, and the crate with the chickens is on the back porch. Best keep a lookout against wolves until you get a shed and a chicken coop built."

Two more things Mr. Riker would need to supply, when he'd done so much for them already. Bess pushed down her guilt. He'd likely increase their rent for the out-buildings, but as Jim indicated, the buildings were necessary to protect their assets.

She raised her eyebrows in a look of question and expectation. "Mr. Riker?"

He scowled but acquiesced. "I think there's enough scraps of lumber left for something small. You can pay the rent for the outbuildings by sharing the milk and eggs with me."

Bess nodded briskly, relieved he'd agreed so quickly.

"If there's nothing more you need from me," Jim said, "I'll head over to the gen-eral store. Matty wants me to pick up some yarn for the baby clothes she's knitting. Meet you there, Bess."

"I'll only be a few minutes," she replied. He and Luke had agreed to arrange credit at the general store for the supplies she and Bertie needed. The women would repay them from their profits. Though a business arrangement, it implied the Collingswood brothers trusted her ability to make the bakery profitable, and that meant the world to her.

Bess, Bertie, and Gideon followed Jim through the kitchen and onto the porch.

The tan cow mooed a greeting, and the confined chickens fussed. Bess looked out over the land and smiled. It faced north, and there were no buildings in view for miles. "One can see forever from here."

"That's why I put the porch on the back of the house," Gideon said. "Didn't make any sense looking at the rear of the saloon when a body could sit out here and look at all of Wyoming. The purple sage makes a pretty sight later in the season."

Jim jabbed a finger in Gideon's direction. "I warned Bess this place is too close to the saloon for comfort, but she insisted on trying it. You let anything happen to these women, and I'm coming after you."

Gideon gave Jim a look Bess could only interpret as, "I'm their landlord, not their keeper," but he said, "I'll let my customers know the house is off-limits. And there's a bar inside the door that'll keep out undesirables."

"See you use that bar," Jim ordered the women before taking off around the cow and the corner of the house.

Gideon pointed toward a narrow building. "Had this built for you, too. Didn't think you'd want to be sharing the town's public necessary."

Bess's face warmed. "You've thought of everything."

"The well's this way." He took the same path as Jim. Bess and Bertie followed. They'd just reached the well when gunfire rang out, followed by the sounds of galloping horses and a cowboy's "Whoopee!"

The noise startled Bess. Then fear roared through her, rooting her feet to the ground. She grabbed Bertie and pulled her close.

"What on earth—?" Gideon's head swiveled as he looked for the source of the gunfire. "Get down," he barked. He pushed Bess to the ground behind the well. She dragged Bertie with her. Gideon all but fell on top of them.

"Oof!" *Now I know what's meant by the term "eat dust."* Bess choked off a chuckle. She wondered if she was becoming hysterical.

The sounds grew closer. Bess tried to see the source, but she could barely move beneath Gideon's weight. All she saw was Bertie's old brown felt hat lying in the dust two feet away.

A moment later the hat jumped as though alive as a bullet struck the ground beside it.

Chapter 5

My hat!" Bertie wailed.

"Quit that fool shooting!" Gideon roared. Fury and fear for Bess and Bertie burned like fire inside him. For the life of him, he couldn't figure out what was going on. Men usually weren't drunk enough to start shooting up the town this early in the day. If someone was robbing the bank, why were they riding behind the saloon?

Gideon recognized the cowboy's face. He'd seen it often enough in his saloon but didn't know the man's name. Gideon leaped up and grabbed the halter of the shooter's horse. The horse pulled him off the ground as it rose on its hind legs, frightened by the gunshots. Gideon fell to the ground, and the horse and rider raced between the saloon and jailhouse back to Lickwind's only street, where more gunfire and horses' hooves sounded.

By the time Gideon picked himself up, the women were standing. Bess brushed dust from her skirt, her eyes spitting fire, while Bertie examined her hat. "He almost hit my hat!"

"Be glad it wasn't on your head at the time." Gideon looked from one to the other. "You two okay?"

They nodded.

"Good. Get back in the house," he ordered. "You end up shot and the Collingswood brothers will have my hide. I'm going to find out what's going on."

He stayed close to the saloon wall as he headed toward the street, his heart pounding faster than train wheels chugging at full speed. Never knew where a stray bullet might land. He peered onto the street. Half a dozen men charged up and down the road on near-crazed steeds, raising a dust cloud like a thick, gritty fog and shooting off pistols—mostly into the air. Cautiously, he stepped onto the boardwalk in front of his saloon.

Jim was running toward him but looking beyond him. Gideon swung around, expecting trouble. He found it. "Bess!"

Jim halted beside them. "You all right, Bess?"

"Yes, but—"

Gideon pushed her against the wall, shielding her from possible stray bullets. "Where's Bertie?"

"In the house."

Gideon grabbed her arm and pulled her into the saloon. Jim followed on their heels. "You haven't the sense God gave grass," Gideon stormed. "You could have gotten yourself killed."

Bess jerked from his grasp and smoothed the dark blue calico of her dress's arm. "What's happening?"

"It's the Union Pacific," Jim answered. "Linus Hatch just received the telegraph. One word—'Done.' The railroad has reached the Pacific."

"They made it!" Gideon whooped. Grasping Bess around the waist, he swung her around in circles. "They did it!"

Her laughter rang in his ears. Even in the midst of his celebration, he was aware that her laughter was softer and sweeter than he'd expected. It warmed him right through to his bones.

That scared the daylights out of him. Scared him more than the shooting outside. He set her down and steadied her with his hands on her waist while she regained her balance.

Jim watched them with a strange expression.

Bess's eyes, which Gideon saw so often flash in anger or cynicism, danced with laughter. "Sorry, Miss Craig. Afraid I got carried away."

Bess dropped her gaze to the floor and smoothed back the strands of dark hair that had come loose from her bun. "No harm done, Mr. Riker. A little excitement is understandable under the circumstances."

He grinned. "Hard to believe the railroad reached here only eighteen months ago. Never truly believed it would make it all the way to the Pacific Ocean." If the railroad had run across the entire country five years ago, his life would be completely different today. He wouldn't live in Lickwind or own a saloon, and Stan. . . He pushed away the memories.

A loud clopping sounded against the floorboards. Bess looked over his shoulder toward the door, her mouth agape. He followed her gaze. A black horse stood between the batwing doors, half in and half out of the saloon. The cowboy who'd almost shot Bertie's hat sat astride the horse.

"Hey, get your horse out of my saloon." Gideon started toward him.

Bess moved quicker. She grasped the horse's halter and glared up at the man. "You could hurt someone, shooting up the town. Haven't you any sense?"

The man's face registered shock then amusement. "Let go of my horse, lady."

"I will not." She looked at Gideon. "Arrest him."

Gideon stared at her. "Arrest him? Me? I'm not a lawman."

She looked at her brother-in-law.

He shook his head. "Sorry, Bess. We could throw him in the jailhouse, but we couldn't keep him there."

"What is the matter with you two?" Bess demanded. "He's endangered people's lives. Get the sheriff."

Gideon snorted. "There is no sheriff. Besides, the men hereabouts have their own ideas of what is and isn't law-abiding behavior. You won't find twelve men in Wyoming who think a cowpoke celebrating the railroad's final spike is a crime."

" 'Fraid he's right," Jim agreed.

"Will you two get this woman off my horse?" the cowboy whined.

Gideon peeled Bess's fingerhold from the halter. "Back that horse up and keep it out of my saloon."

The cowboy gave a jaunty salute, smiled, and did as commanded.

Bess wheeled on Gideon. "No wonder the jail's stood empty all this time. Bertie and I could just as well be renting it."

"Couldn't agree with you more, but the banker and lawyer don't, and they've more say in the matter than I do. Now if you'll excuse me, men are wantin' to celebrate, and I intend to make some money off their plans."

Bess glanced about the saloon. Gideon was right. Men were entering, wanting to celebrate. She doubted their manner of celebrating was safer than that of the shooters in the streets. Likely gunfire would increase after the drink flowed freely.

And after everyone was done drinking and sobered up, they'd be hungry. She and Bertie could capitalize on that.

Jim squeezed her elbow. "We'll go out the back door. Safer that way."

"Wait a minute." She explained her plan to feed the celebrators. "Bertie and I will need supplies."

He frowned. "You can't be going to the general store in this fracas. Let's get you home safe. Then you can give me a list of what you need. I'll get it for you."

They headed toward the back door. Men watched her with curious expressions, but none made lewd remarks with Jim at her side.

She grabbed some firewood from the back of the saloon, much to Jim's exasperation. "The longer we're outside, the longer you're in danger."

"The hooligans are all on the main street right now. We need firewood to bake. It would be nice if we had a variety of wood to choose from, but it all heats, and I prefer it to buffalo chips. Here, you take some, too." She handed him a log.

"Women," he muttered, but he took the log and grabbed a couple more.

A few minutes later, Bess's list in hand, he stood in the doorway ready to leave for the general store. "You and Bertie stay inside and away from the windows. And use that bar to keep the lice away."

"Lice?" Bertie directed the question toward the door closing behind Jim.

"Unsavory men," Bess explained, lowering the bar. "Get a fire started in the stove. I'll write up a menu. We'll post copies at the saloon and telegraph office. Need to let men know we've got food to offer them."

Bess named their bakery the Back Porch and put the name in capital letters at the top of the menu. She allowed five hours before opening—time for Jim to return with supplies and for her and Bertie to mix and knead bread, heat the stove, mix eggless cookie dough, and bake.

"We'll put a rice pudding on the stove," she told Bertie while she wrote. "And a kettle of dried applesauce. The more we have to offer, the better."

Jim posted the menus and brought more firewood after he returned to the house with their supplies and before he headed back to the ranch. "I'll bring back some beef. Men are sure to gobble it up along with your baked goods. Round here men mostly eat what they hunt—buffalo, antelope, venison, rabbit. They'll appreciate a good beefsteak."

Bess welcomed his offer. They both knew there'd still be plenty of men looking for a meal when he returned. And later. "It's a sure bet the celebrating will go on all night," Jim said. "Men will pour into town as the news spreads. They'll be looking for meals tonight and tomorrow when they dry out from the liquor."

"I hope they've got money left after celebrating." Bess turned to Bertie while tying the sashes of an oversized apron. "Make sure you see their money up front before you take their orders."

Excitement, purpose, and hope bubbled up in Bess as she and Bertie baked. Their new enterprise was about to receive its first test. "It feels like Christmas," she confided to Bertie as she pulled the first brown, fragrant loaves of bread from the shiny cast-iron oven hours later.

"For true. Smells like it, too, from the baking."

"These loaves look good. I was a little worried. It's wise to season the stove by heating it a few times before baking in it the first time."

"Good thing you brought so much sourdough starter."

Bertie was right. Bess sent up a silent thank-you that she'd had the foresight to set the starter aside. She'd planned to begin baking the day after they arrived. God had known they would need it sooner. They also had the bread Corrie sent with them that morning, should they need something to sell before their own baking was ready.

All the while Bess worked in the kitchen, Gideon Riker slipped into her thoughts and had to be forcefully thrust from them. In the midst of kneading bread—her arms tired, her hands sticky with flour and dough, and her nostrils filled with the scents of sourdough and woodsmoke—she remembered the feel of his arms strong around her waist and his chest hard against her. Brushing at a stray lock of her hair, she remembered the feel of his long blond hair brushing her cheek as he spun her around. As the applesauce sputtered on the back of the stove, sending cinnamon scent into the air, she recalled the sound of his laughter, his breath brushing her ear. And she recalled how feminine she felt, held in his arms that way, sharing his joy and wonder at the world-changing event of the transcontinental railroad.

With each memory, it became more difficult to push the thoughts of Gideon Riker aside. *A saloon owner. Honestly, Elizabeth Craig. Have you no standards? Why did I ever agree to come to Lickwind as a mail-order bride? I haven't met a single man I'd trust past Tuesday, excepting the Collingswood brothers. At least Matty and Corrie married well.*

She was grateful her work helped to force her attentions from her daydreams. She put the dough into loaf pans to rise. Next she filled a kettle with water and set it on the stove then set out the new tin wash pan and scraped soap chips into it. They hadn't many plates or tableware. They'd need to wash dishes between customers.

The first customers trickled in before Jim returned—cowboys Jim had met on the way home who were hungry after their ride to town. The coins they exchanged gave a cheerful ring when dropped into the tin button box Bess and Bertie used to collect money.

Gideon slid back into Bess's thoughts, his laughter tickling her ear, as she set a huge galvanized coffeepot on the stove.

"Why isn't this door barred?"

Gideon's voice jarred her from the too-sweet memory. She spun around, as embarrassed as though he'd heard her thoughts. Her glance darted to the kitchen door through which he'd entered. "I guess we forgot it after the last customers."

"Don't forget again."

His obey-or-else tone angered her, but she knew the wisdom in his advice. "We won't."

Ramon stood beside her, growling at Gideon and the redheaded boy with him. "Shush, Ramon." The dog lay down but continued a low growl.

Bess's gaze fell on the rifle Gideon carried. "What's that for?"

"You." He held it toward her.

She put her hands behind her, shook her head, and stepped back until she bumped against the counter. "Oh, no."

"You might need it to protect yourself."

"I won't have a gun in this house. Besides, I don't know how to shoot one."

"I don't have time to teach you now. If someone threatens you or Bertie, just point it in their direction. If that doesn't stop them, cock the hammer and pull the trigger."

"I will not. Get it out of here."

He glanced at her sister. "Bertie?"

Bess reached her arm between him and Bertie, glaring at him. "Don't even consider asking it of her."

"If you won't use it to protect yourselves, at least promise you'll shoot it off if you have trouble. I'll hear it and come running."

"How will you distinguish the sound from the other gunfire in town?" Sporadic celebratory gunfire had sounded all day.

Gideon frowned without replying.

"That's what I thought. Are you and the boy hungry?" Bess recognized him as the boy who'd stood with Regina Bently during the church service.

"Yes, ma'am," the boy replied hastily.

Gideon rested a hand on the boy's shoulder. "This is Walter."

Bess nodded toward the boy. "Hello, Walter. I'm Miss Craig."

Gideon set the rifle stock gently against the floor. "Thought he might be a help to you. I'd appreciate it if you'd let him stay the night. Be safer here than at the saloon."

Bess refrained from asking in front of the lad why the boy should stay at the saloon at all. "Of course he may stay. Bertie, give him a bowl of rice pudding and a slice of bread."

"I'll be right back." Gideon left by the kitchen door; then he opened it and peered inside. "Don't forget the bar." Then he was gone again.

Five minutes later, he returned with a metal triangle and a small metal bar. Bess recognized it as the same kind of implement used to call the hands out on the Rough Cs. "Since you won't use the rifle, sound this if there's trouble. You can be sure I'll know its clang from any cowpoke's gunfire."

Bess accepted it solemnly. "Thank you."

"I best be going. There's a full house at the saloon."

"Then I doubly thank you for looking out for our welfare instead of your own business."

Bertie handed him a slice of bread spread thick with butter. "Don't worry, Mr. Riker. Ramon will protect us."

Gideon sidled past the still-growling dog. "Don't forget the bar."

༄

Gideon swallowed the desire to growl back at the gray excuse for a dog that lay in his path to the door. He usually liked dogs, but this one had hated him since he ushered Bertie out of the saloon last Sunday. He warily passed the dog, opened the door, and slid through it. "Don't forget the bar."

He almost collided with Linus and Oscar Hatch. He nodded at them and kept walking. The women wouldn't have time to bar the door, but he didn't fear for them with the Hatch cousins.

What had come over him that he'd offered his home to the Craig sisters? Someone must've slipped locoweed into the apple pie at the jailhouse Sunday. He'd spent most of the time between then and this morning finishing up the house and putting in the outhouse, with the help of grumbling Harry. Now he'd committed to putting up a chicken coop and a cow shed for the sisters, neither of which he needed for himself.

Worse, ever since that first gunshot earlier today, he'd spent his time worrying over those women. Twice he'd thrown himself between Bess and bullets. Never had he done a thing like that before in his life! The woman was downright dangerous. Wouldn't even take a gun to protect herself and her kid sister. Instead, he'd offered to answer that clanging call whenever they felt they needed protection. Pure foolishness, that's what it was.

He took a bite of the bread as he reached the saloon's back door. Mm. He hadn't had homemade sourdough bread in years. Mostly he just cooked up some biscuits on the little stove beside the bed in the back room.

The feel of Bess's soft cheek against his as he twirled her around that afternoon whispered into his memory along with the soft floral scent she wore. *Forget it. You don't need or want a woman like Bess Craig, even if she'd have anything to do with a saloonkeeper.*

But the picture of her brown eyes dancing with laughter as she stood in his arms persisted as he entered the bar with its yeasty smell of hops and the laughter of celebrating cowboys and dance hall girls.

Chapter 6

A t five the next morning, Bess sat on her hope chest in the otherwise empty parlor and slumped back against the window. On the floor beside the chest, her only lantern shed a flickering light. Laughter, piano music, and singing sounded loudly from the saloon. Harry wasn't playing hymns this morning.

Bess ran the palm of her hand lightly over Rhubarb's back. She lay curled on her lap, giving welcome added warmth. Bess and Bertie had brought Ramon to town with them to give Rhubarb a respite from Ramon, but the cat had other ideas. When Jim Collingswood arrived with the goods from the farm earlier that evening, the cat had jumped out of the wagon, surprising the rancher and the sisters. The cat made straight for Bertie and twined about the girl's booted legs with a purr that almost drowned out the noise of the celebrating cowboys.

Bess stretched, and her movement wakened the cat. Rhubarb jumped down and made her way across the floor and up the stairs. *Likely looking for Bertie,* Bess thought.

Was Bertie asleep? Bess had sent her to bed—with quilts since they had no mattress tick yet—three hours ago. Walter slept in the spare bedroom. She didn't know how anyone could sleep with this noise, but neither Bertie nor Walter had come back downstairs.

A knock on the door caused her to rise with a sigh. Another customer. She wasn't about to turn down the money. Perhaps she'd catch her second wind soon.

She set the lantern on the counter, lifted the bar, and opened the door. The redheaded dance hall girl stood on the porch, shivering beneath her shawl. "Miss Bently, this is a surprise. Won't you come in?"

"Miss Bently," Regina repeated with a touch of wonder in her voice. "Sounds nice. Ladylike." She stepped inside, and Bess closed the door behind her. "I'll only stay a minute. Gideon said my brother is staying with you. I just wanted to make sure he isn't a bother."

"Your brother?" Bess stared at her, startled.

"Yes, Walter."

"Of course. I don't know where my mind's gone. I guess I'm more tired than I thought." Bess wasn't about to admit she'd thought Walter was Gideon's son and maybe Regina's, too. A sense of relief slid through her. "Walter's no trouble at all. He's sleeping upstairs. Matter of fact, he was a help to us. Bertie and I had a hard time keeping up with all those hungry men."

"I hear your food is mighty good."

"Are you hungry?"

Regina hesitated, glancing at the kettle of oatmeal on the back of the stove. "I guess not."

"Why don't I slice you some bread? You can take it with you in case you get hungry later."

Regina hesitated again. "How much would it cost?"

"Consider it a thank-you for Walter's help."

"That's mighty kind. I was wonderin'. . ."

"Yes?" Bess encouraged as she pulled a flour-sack towel off a loaf of bread.

"Would you consider boardin' Walter? Gideon's been good about letting Walt sleep at his place, but—"

Bess turned around, bread knife in one hand. "At the saloon?"

"Yes. I know it's not the best place for a boy, but it's better than Margaret's place, where I live. And Gideon doesn't let the boy in the saloon durin' business hours."

Bess concentrated on cutting the bread, trying to hide her horror at a young child's only choices being a dance hall girls' home or a saloon. She swallowed hard. "Of course he can stay with us. There are two bedrooms upstairs. He can sleep in one."

Regina heaved a sigh of relief. "I'll find a way to pay you, I promise."

"If Walter is willing to help with chores, that'll be payment enough."

"You sure?"

"I'm sure." Bess handed Regina two slices of bread. She and Regina met each other's gazes for a long moment before Regina said softly, "You're a good woman, Miss Craig, and not just because you're a Sunday-go-to-meetin' kind of lady."

Bess couldn't remember when she'd felt so complimented and so humbled at the same time. What must life be like for Regina Bently that she thought it extraordinary another woman would treat her brother, a ten-year-old child, with kindness?

Regina played with the black fringe on her shawl. "Miss Craig, do you know how to read?"

"Yes."

"Might you consider teachin' Walter readin' and writin'? There ain't no teacher in Lickwind."

"Of course." She'd find time somehow. "I'm still working with Bertie on her schooling. One more student won't be a problem."

"Thank you kindly."

"Don't you know how to read?"

Regina looked at the floor. "No. My pappy didn't think it necessary for a girl."

"Would you like to learn?"

Regina raised her gaze. "Somethin' fierce."

"I'd gladly teach you."

"You'd do that?"

"Surely. We can start later this week."

Regina beamed. "Thank you kindly. I'd best get along. Margaret will be wonderin' where I am. She's a spitfire when she's mad."

When she opened the door, Gideon was walking up the porch steps. "Regina." He nodded to her as they passed on the porch. "May I come in, Miss Craig?" He didn't wait for Bess to answer. He slipped inside along with the raw Wyoming air, closed the door behind him, and cast a wary look around. "Where's the dog?"

"Ramon's upstairs with Bertie."

"I saw the light in the parlor window and thought I'd best check on you. Everything all right here?"

"Yes, wonderful. There's been a steady stream of men all night until the last twenty minutes or so. We've already made enough money to pay for the supplies we purchased at the general store and pay you our first week's rent. Bertie hates baking, but she pitched in with barely a murmur. We're so grateful the Lord brought us to town yesterday. I doubt there'll be many days we make this much money."

"You're right. News of your good cooking is traveling fast. Men at the saloon are talking your place up. Expect you'll see more of them soon as the sun's up. The ones who are still able to stand."

"From the music, I'd guess there are a few of those left. Time to think about breakfast soon. I'm keeping a fire going in the stove, as you can tell, so I won't need to build it up again. It's more comfortable in the parlor—not so hot." Bess led the way to the other room and set the lantern on the windowsill. When she turned around, Gideon looked distressed.

"I forgot all about bringing a table and chairs over."

Bess smiled. "You had a bit on your mind."

"Men at the saloon said you're selling beefsteak along with bread and baked goods."

"Jim brought the steak in from the Rough Cs, along with more bread and cake from Corrie and some extra eggs. Can hardly believe the way food flew out of this place."

"Hope young Walt didn't get in the way."

"No, he was a help." She grinned. "He even milked the cow for us."

"I didn't know he knew how."

"He didn't. Bertie taught him."

Gideon chuckled. "Well, Grandmother's bloomers."

Bess laughed at his imitation of one of Bertie's favorite sayings. "Miss Bently asked if Walter might stay with us. I said yes. I'm afraid I forgot it's your house and your decision."

He tilted his head and looked at her with a curious expression. "You'd be willing to take him in?"

"Yes. Weren't you?"

"That's different."

"Why?"

He appeared at a loss for an answer.

"You'll let him stay here?" she persisted.

"Yes. I'll bring his bed over tomorrow. It'll be much better for him staying here than at the saloon."

She wanted to ask why he ran a saloon since he thought it was a bad place for a boy. More than that, she wanted to ask if there was a reason he befriended Regina Bently in particular, taking her brother under his wing. Was Miss Bently special to him? Bess pushed away the questions. A part of her didn't want to know the answers.

"I will be needing that table and chairs," Bess said. "I'll be teaching Walter and Regina to read."

He gaped. "Here? In my. . .your. . .this house?"

"Yes. Where else?"

"I forbid it!"

Chapter 7

B ess stared at him. "You forbid it?"

"Yes. This is still my house. You and your sister may live in it, but I make the rules."

"You befriended Miss Bently. You took in her brother."

"I don't raise him. I just let him sleep in my back room and spend time there when. . .when he can't be with his sister."

"Why would you forbid my teaching them to read?"

"I'm not. I'm only saying that you can't teach her here."

Bess lifted her hands, perplexed. "Why?"

Gideon looked at the ceiling and back to her. "Have you thought what it will do to your reputation, having that woman in your home? What it will do to Bertie's reputation?"

She hadn't. It's true that back in Rhode Island, she wouldn't have considered inviting Regina into her home. But then, she'd never met a soiled dove in Rhode Island. She couldn't turn her back on Regina when she wanted to improve herself. "If not here, where? I certainly can't go to. . .to her home to teach her, and there's no school building."

"That's your problem. Find another place or tell her you rescind your offer."

Bess planted her fists on her hips. "You allow the woman to work in your saloon. Isn't it hypocritical to forbid her in your house, especially when her brother is staying here?"

"I won't change my mind."

And I won't rescind my offer. She'd find some way to keep her promise. For the moment, the best tactic appeared to be to divert his focus. "How did Miss Bently and Walter end up in Lickwind?"

"Same way a lot of us did. They were traveling to Oregon with their folks. Wagon broke down crossing a river. Their folks died. Lost everything. Not that there was much to lose, from the way Regina tells it. She and Walter made it as far as Lickwind before what little money she had ran out. They had no way to continue on to Oregon and no way to go back East. Some of Margaret's girls joined up with a traveling. . ." He cast Bess a sharp glance. "A service that trailed the Union Pacific crew back in '68. Regina thought that would be worse for Walter than living here, so—" He shrugged.

"But why did she choose. . .what she does. . .instead of something else?"

"What else?"

Bess lifted her hands again as she searched for possibilities. "Baking, like me and Bertie. Or sewing or doing laundry."

"Regina wasn't as fortunate as you and Bertie. She didn't have the Collingswood brothers or anyone else backing her credit while she laid in supplies and rented a place to live."

"Oh. I guess I didn't think it through."

"Seems decent folk usually don't when it comes to ladies like Regina."

"That's not fair."

"No?" He sighed. "Maybe not. I'd better head back to the saloon. I'll get that table and chairs over here. Don't forget what I said about Regina."

"How could I?" Bess retorted.

Gideon didn't answer. He just left saying, "Bar the door."

Bess swung the bar into place, venting her fury on the piece of wood. "Men. They're all impossible."

Three days later Gideon awoke from his first good night's sleep since the arrival of the telegraph announcing the driving of the final railroad spike. His saloon hadn't been that busy since the Union Pacific crew laying the track came through Lickwind. Those were good moneymaking days. . .or rather, nights. The railroad expected the crews to work during daylight hours.

He washed up, shaved, brushed his hair, and picked up the least-worn shirt he owned, trying to ignore the fact he attended to such things more regular now that Bess Craig lived thirty feet away. He wrinkled his nose as he buttoned the shirt. Time to wash clothes or buy new ones.

Gideon looked into his battered coffeepot. Some coffee still remained from yesterday. He stirred the coals in his stove and set the pot to heat. His stomach growled, and an image of hotcakes, fresh from the Craig sisters' stove, appeared large as life. That and fresh coffee sounded like heaven. Or temptation. He wasn't about to wind up outside their door every day like every other male in town.

He could hear chairs scraping in the saloon. Harry must be up and cleaning the place. Gideon never could make himself clean up the saloon before morning.

When he walked into the bar with a tin cup of thick coffee, he discovered Harry wasn't the only person there. At the sight of Bess and Regina sitting side by side at the table nearest the door, he stopped so fast the coffee sloshed over the edge of the cup. "Ow!" He winced and shook his hand.

The women looked at him.

He walked toward them, wanting to scold Bess Craig as if she were a child. He hoped Harry had wiped the table off for the women. "Morning, Miss Craig. Regina. What brings you two in here this time of day?" As if he couldn't tell from the slate between them with A-E-I-O-U printed on it in capital letters.

Regina's face positively glowed, in spite of the late night he knew she'd spent working. "Miss Craig is teaching me my letters. Ain't that something?"

Gideon forced a smile. "It surely is, Regina." He'd be glad for her if it weren't happening in his saloon. Or his house.

Miss Craig looked the part of the schoolmarm, dressed in gray as usual, with a prim black bow at her throat, a wool shawl wrapped about her against the cool May morning, and her dark brown hair prudishly pulled back in a bun. She contrasted sharply with Regina, whose red hair curled past her shoulders and whose green plaid dress, though more modest than most of Margaret's girls' clothes, was low cut and trimmed with lace.

He lifted his coffee cup and met Bess's defiant gaze over the cup's rim. "Not baking today, Miss Craig?"

"Fed breakfast to most of the men in town. Most don't sleep in as late as you do. There's more bread rising. Bertie's watching the oven to allow Miss Bently and me a little time together."

He ignored the jibe at his sleeping habits. "I've something on my own stove I'd like to ask you about. Would you mind?" He waved toward the back room.

Bess frowned. "Now?"

"Hate to interrupt the lesson, but the pot is on the stove right this minute."

As the door to the back room closed behind them, Bess looked around the area where Gideon stored inventory. "I don't see a stove."

"It's behind the curtain."

Bess took a step toward it.

"Where Harry and I sleep," Gideon expanded.

She stopped, her expression a mixture of curiosity and outrage.

"Don't bother going in," Gideon continued. "The only pot on my stove is filled with this awful stuff I call coffee." He took a drink. Grimaced. "I asked you back here—"

"It sounded more like a demand." Bess crossed her arms over her chest and stared at him, one toe bouncing against the floorboards in an irritated rhythm.

What right had she to be angry when she'd invaded his saloon? He pointed toward the door separating them from the bar and leaned forward, dropping his voice to a stage whisper. "What are you thinking, coming in here with that woman?"

"Do you normally object to that woman's presence here?"

He took a deep breath and counted to ten. It wasn't high enough, but he spoke anyway. "Didn't you understand a word I said the other night?"

"Yes. You forbade me to teach Regina in your house."

"So—"

"This isn't your house. It's your place of business. She's in here every night. How can you object to her presence here in the morning?"

He closed the space between them with two steps and brought his face close to hers. "You aren't in here every night. That's the point."

"You'll see me here every day from now on. I should think you'd be pleased."

"Pleased?"

She shrugged. "You claim it will hurt my reputation if I allow Miss Bently into your home. If I teach her here, everyone will know our relationship is that of teacher and student. You'll no longer need concern yourself for my reputation."

"You're determined to misunderstand me."

"I don't think I misunderstand at all. Now if you'll excuse me, Miss Bently and I only have an hour for the lesson, and you're using up precious minutes."

She brushed past him, entered the saloon, and closed the door firmly behind her.

Gideon stalked through the curtains to the stove and added more thick coffee to his cup. For a moment, he considered partaking of something stronger, but he'd given up drinking almost a year ago. An ornery woman like Bess Craig wasn't going to drive him back to it. He liked to keep his head about him, even if he did make a living helping others lose theirs.

It didn't do his temper a bit of good to find four doughnuts on the bar when he returned to the saloon. "Miss Craig brought them," Harry said, "for the use of the table. I said it wasn't necessary, but she insisted. I ate two already. They're mighty good."

Gideon grunted and walked to the other end of the bar, pretending to check the stock. He wouldn't be bribed by Bess Craig's baking. "Sweep the floor, Harry."

He kept his resolve for all of ten minutes before grabbing one of the doughnuts. Just one, he told himself. But that doughnut was the best thing he'd eaten since he went to Cheyenne almost a year ago to celebrate the Fourth of July, so he helped himself to another and almost considered it a blessing the day the Craig sisters moved into town.

Twenty minutes later Doc Mitchel strolled in.

"First customer of the day, just like normal," Harry whispered as he passed Gideon.

Only a few men came in before late afternoon, as a rule. "Least he didn't sleep here last night," Gideon whispered back.

Doc Mitchel didn't walk directly to the bar as usual. He swerved to the table where Bess and Regina sat. Standing across from them, he tipped his hat. "Morning, ladies. Miss Craig, what a delightful surprise."

Bess's neck and cheeks colored, but she met the doctor's gaze and nodded. "Doctor."

Gideon froze, watching the encounter, listening for every word and nuance. He didn't like the way Doc looked at Bess. A nasty expression had slipped over Doc's face. Some might call it a smile, but Gideon knew better. He could see Regina did, too, from the way she cringed.

"Is the good Miss Craig teaching you letters, Regina?" Exaggerated innocence turned Doc's tone syrupy.

Regina straightened her backbone but stared at her slate. "Yes, sir."

"And what would you be teaching the good Miss Craig?" Doc raised his eyebrows suggestively.

Gideon set the bottle he was holding down harder than necessary, walked around the bar, and headed for the table. He'd known something like this would happen sooner or later. Now he knew how Ramon felt protecting Bertie. Gideon felt like growling himself. Instead, he groaned as three more men walked in, all of them stopping to stare at Bess, Regina, and Doc.

Doc leaned on the table and grinned. "Why don't you show me, Regina? Or perhaps you'll show me yourself, Miss Craig? Or do you go by Bessie now?"

Bess surged to her feet. "Mr. Mitchel, I demand an apology. For myself and Miss Bently."

"Apology?" Doc laughed. It turned into a guffaw by the time Gideon reached him. Gideon grabbed Doc's jacket at the back of the neck.

Doc's laugh choked off. "What—? Gideon?"

" 'Fraid you're leaving here for the day, Doc."

"But—"

"Before you leave, how about that apology?"

The three male spectators snickered. Gideon glared at them. The snickers stopped.

"But, Gideon—" Doc wailed.

"You apologize, and I'll consider letting you come back tomorrow."

"Course I'll apologize. Meant to all along. Just teasing the ladies a mite."

"Uh-huh. Let's hear it."

Doc wiggled. "If you'd just loosen your hold a bit—"

Gideon let go.

Doc ran his fingers between his collar and his throat.

Gideon pulled Doc's felt hat from his head and slapped it against Doc's stomach. "The apology."

Doc clutched the hat with both hands. "Uh, ladies—"

"They have names," Gideon reminded.

"Uh, yes, Miss Craig. Regina."

"Miss Bently," Gideon suggested firmly.

"Uh, yes. Miss Bently. I'm sure you realize I was joking when I said…suggested… I realize my remarks were, um, tasteless. I'm sure two such fine ladies as yourselves will forgive me for my, um, breach of manners."

"Apology acceptable?" Gideon looked from Bess to Regina.

Bess glared at Doc. Regina stared, openmouthed, but nodded.

Gideon ushered Doc toward the door past the again-snickering cowboys. "Don't come back until tomorrow, Doc."

"Can't you send home a bottle with me? One little old bottle?"

"Try Cheyenne's saloons." He pushed Doc through the batwing doors and turned back to the saloon. He stopped, hands on his hips, in front of the three grinning cowboys. "You here for drinks, or will you be following Doc?"

"Drinks, just drinks." One of the men held up his hands as though Gideon was robbing him. All three back-stepped toward the bar, watching Gideon the entire way.

Gideon walked back to the table, his heart still pumping wildly from his anger.

"Thank you," Bess said, looking relieved.

Regina stood. "I'm sorry I caused trouble, Gideon."

Bess gave her a shocked look. "Dr. Mitchel caused trouble, not you."

Gideon exchanged glances with Regina. They understood each other. The saloon was their world, not Bess's. "It's all right, Reg. . .Miss Bently."

Her smile lit up the room.

All that for calling her Miss Bently? He never thought Margaret's girls cared that they were called by their given names. He hadn't even known Regina's last name until he heard Bess use it.

Bess rested her hand on Regina's sleeve. "Perhaps we should end the lesson for today. The hour's almost up anyway."

Regina nodded. "Thank you kindly, Miss Craig."

Bess handed her the slate. "We'll meet here tomorrow at the same time."

Regina glanced at Gideon.

Gideon clamped his lips together and looked away. Bess Craig would never forgive him if he told Regina not to come back tomorrow morning. But he couldn't clamp down his frustration at Bess Craig's foolishness.

"All right, Miss Craig," Regina agreed.

The doors swung behind her as she left. Gideon allowed himself to meet Bess's gaze.

She was smiling. "You were quite wonderful, Mr. Riker."

He snorted. "I told you this wasn't a good idea."

"But—"

"If you think this won't happen again with some other customer, you're wrong." Her smile died. Her face tightened into that rigid look he found so off-putting.

Gideon sighed. "All right, I apologize for insulting you. But the warning stands."

She glared at him and left.

He marched back to the bar where Harry was serving the three men in time to overhear, "Imagine one of Margaret's girls thinkin' she can learn to read."

Gideon glared at the cowboy. "You jealous 'cause you can't read?"

"Uh, no." The cowboy finished off his drink in one gulp and wiped the back of his hand across his mouth. "Let's go, boys."

Gideon watched them leave. Those women were costing him business. This wasn't good. This wasn't good at all.

Chapter 8

*T*he day hasn't improved one iota, Gideon thought, listening to a retelling of the morning's events by one of the men at the bar. Almost midnight and men were still laughing at Doc. Just so they didn't laugh at Bess.

A clatter broke through the laughter, music, and bottles clinking against glasses. It didn't register for a moment, but it went on and on and, suddenly, Gideon recognized the sound. The lunch triangle at the house! Fear shot through him.

He took off running. A crash resounded as the bottle he dropped hit the floor. He grabbed his rifle from behind the counter as he passed it and ran through the back room and out the back door. His chest ached with fright as he rounded the back porch of the house.

A lantern cast swinging shadows across the porch and yard. The cow stood on the porch, bawling. Bess was yelling and ringing the triangle.

Gideon heard a growl and slid to a stop so fast he fell down. He was up in a flash. His gaze searched for Ramon. He spotted the dog on the porch near the cow, growling, straining to get away from Bertie. "What's going on?"

Another growl, low and fierce and way too near, sent him onto the porch pronto. "What—?"

"It's wolves," Bess yelled over the clanging. "After the cow."

Something bumped into him from behind. He jumped and felt like his heart jumped higher than he did.

"What's going on, Gideon?" a voice behind him asked.

"Harry, what're you doing here? Never mind. Stay put. Bess, stop that banging." She didn't. "I thought the sound might frighten them away."

Gideon grabbed the metal bar from her. "It's going to frighten me away." He shot off the rifle. There were soft thudding sounds out in the night and then silence.

"They're gone." Bertie sounded surprised.

"They'll be back." Gideon motioned toward the open back door where Walter stood, wide-eyed. "Get that dog inside. He's no match for a pack of wolves. And bring me some lit kindling."

Bertie, Walter, and Harry together dragged Ramon inside.

In the lantern light, Gideon could see Bess's hair tumbling over her shoulders to her waist. He caught his breath at the sight.

"What are you going to do with the kindling?"

Her question brought him back to the present. "Wolves don't like fire. But they like cows staked out like a dinner invitation."

"We haven't a cow shed."

Business had kept him so busy, he'd forgotten his promise to build the shed. "We'll take her to the jailhouse."

"What will Mr. Llewellyn and Mr. Potter say to that?"

"I'm not planning to ask them. Where are the chickens? Did the wolves get them?"

"No. We put the chicken crate on the roof at night to keep them from the wolves."

"Good idea."

Bess insisted on going with him to the jailhouse. She led the terrified cow while he carried the torch and rifle. They stopped at the well for a pail of water for the cow.

"Are you sure the w–wolves will come back?" Bess asked on their way back to the house.

"I'm sure. Once they find the cow gone, they'll leave you alone. If it'll make you more comfortable, I'll stay at the house awhile."

"Don't be silly. You need to get back to your business." Her voice trembled in spite of her bravado.

The tremble gentled his own tone. "Harry can handle things."

"If you're sure—"

The relief in her voice made him very sure.

When they arrived back, Gideon sent Harry to the saloon, and Bess sent Walter and Bertie to bed. Then Bess and Gideon settled down in the parlor: Bess on the hope chest, Gideon leaning against the wall where he could see out the window, his rifle near at hand.

His gaze drifted to Bess's hair, where the lamplight played on it. "If you'd like to go to bed, I'll keep watch."

Bess shook her head and drew her wool shawl more closely about her. "I'll keep you company. How did you end up in Lickwind, Mr. Riker?"

Only the Craig sisters called him Mr. Riker. It sounded strange but nice, too. Like the respectful way people addressed each other back East where he'd grown up. "Came out after the war."

"Is that how your eye was injured? In the war?"

"Yes. After the war, my brother Stanley and I returned home to find our parents dead. Nothing to keep us in Virginia after that, so we headed to Oregon country." He paused, remembering the journey, the excitement with which he and Stan set out, the trials along the trail, the way it ended.

"Why did you stop here?"

He took a deep breath and let it out slowly. "Stan took sick. He's buried along the Platte River Trail, along with thousands of others."

"I'm sorry." Her fingers, soft and gentle like her voice, touched the back of his hand. He fought the desire to lift her fingers to his cheek, to bury his face in her neck, and comfort himself in her arms.

"When I lost Stan, I lost the last person who mattered in my life. I 'bout went loco. I turned away from the wagon trail with my prairie schooner, not caring where I was going, not caring it was still Indian territory, not caring about anything. Came across Lickwind. It was just a spit-in-the-wind place then. I took up residence at a table in the saloon and tried to drink myself out of this life." He gave a sharp laugh. "As you can see, I didn't succeed."

"I'm glad."

He shot her a curious glance but didn't pursue her statement. "As time passed, I pulled myself out of the bottle occasionally, but I never had a good reason to continue on to Oregon. People pretty much leave a man alone here, and that's the way I like it. In '67, someone discovered gold at South Pass. The saloon owner here traded the saloon to me for my prairie schooner and a note. I was mighty mad at God for takin' away my family. Sellin' liquor seemed a good way to pay Him back. Then the Union Pacific came through. They had their own traveling saloon to keep the crew happy, but the men liked seeing a different place for a change. Made enough money off the crew to pay off the note on the saloon and buy lumber for my house." He shrugged. "So that's my story. War and the trek west—those things are hard on families."

"Yes," Bess murmured.

"You lose anyone in the war?"

"No relatives. Friends." She smiled a little sadly.

"I'm sorry. Is that why you and your sisters didn't marry back East?" The war had killed off a lot of young men and made it difficult for those who returned home to establish themselves enough to support a wife and family.

"Perhaps to some extent." Bess sighed deeply; then she sat up straighter and squared her shoulders. "Are you still angry at God?"

He hadn't asked himself that question for a long time. He considered it for a minute. "Not so much anymore. Now it's more like I don't care."

"But you still run the saloon."

He shrugged. "It's the way I make my living. Man has to support himself. Besides, there's lots of men hurting inside out here. They need a way to forget that hurt for a while. It's the only way they can keep going. I listen to men's troubles and provide them something to take the pain away for a while."

"Wouldn't it be better to give them something to help them get through their troubles so they can stand up again after life's knocked them down?"

"Be glad to offer something like that, but if such a thing exists, I don't know what it is."

Bess stood up, her hair cascading down her back. Her gaze met his squarely. "God's love, Mr. Riker. God's unconditional love. Good night."

He watched her cross the parlor and climb the stairs. He wasn't sure he believed God loved anyone. He sure didn't know how God's love could help a person get through losing everyone they cared about. Bess Craig might believe in God's love, but to him, God's love was nothing but words.

Bess didn't fall asleep immediately upon slipping into bed beside Bertie. Her thoughts remained on her discussion with Gideon and on God's unconditional love. She recalled her conversation with Matty and Corrie after the church service in the saloon. She'd thought then God had brought them here to help change the hearts of Regina and the other women who worked for Margaret Manning. She still believed that. But she was beginning to believe God brought her to Lickwind to stretch her own soul as well.

She'd thought women like Regina crude and ungodly, not as wounded people who didn't know how to find God's love.

And Gideon Riker. She pictured his strong, lined face with a patch over one eye. She'd thought him rough and evil, tempting others with drink. Before tonight, she'd never considered he might be hurting and that, like Regina, he might not know how to reach out to God. But there was a tender spot in his heart. He'd taken in Walter; he looked out for her and Bertie; he had stood up for her and Regina against Doc Mitchel; and he wanted to help the men who came to his saloon to stop hurting inside.

Maybe God brought her here to see people as souls He loved, as hearts that needed healing.

"Help Gideon and Regina, Lord," she whispered into the night. "Help them find You, that Your love might heal their wounds and they might in turn be available to heal others. Amen."

When Gideon slid into bed hours later, after checking on the cow at the jailhouse one last time, he relived his conversation with Bess. He hadn't thought about God or His love for a long time. Now he was surprised to realize he'd told Bess the truth. He wasn't sure how he felt about God, but he wasn't mad at Him anymore.

He mentally kicked himself for getting involved with the Craig sisters. He'd rented them his house, protected them from bullets, attempted to protect Bess's reputation, even forced Doc to apologize to one of Margaret's girls, and now he was protecting a cow. Tomorrow—rather, later today—he'd build a shed he didn't need. Something had to change.

But later in his dreams, Bess Craig smiled up at him from the circle of his arms, her dark hair smelling sweetly of violets and framing her face in beauty; and before he woke, he promised to protect her forever.

Bess glanced up from polishing the stove as Bertie came inside. Walter and Bertie had spent most of the day outside helping Gideon with the shed. Keeping Bertie in a kitchen was impossible when there was such work as building to help with. Bess had noticed Gideon waited until after her morning lesson with Regina was over before beginning the building.

Bess shook her head in despair. Bertie's scuffed boots were dustier than ever, her skirt covered with sawdust, and the sleeves of her blouse snagged. "I declare, Roberta Suzanne. Mama would think me a failure indeed in the raising of you were she to see you now."

Bertie looked down at herself. "For true, I don't know why. They're only clothes. Besides, Harry says men here would marry anything that got off the railroad."

"Bertie!"

"Well, that's what he said. He doesn't understand why you haven't married up already. Harry says—"

Bess's backbone stiffened. "My marriage preferences are none of his business. Nor yours."

"Grandmother's bloomers, Bess, I'm only trying to be helpful."

"I've no intention of marrying at the moment."

"Then why did you come to Lickwind?"

"To watch over you and your sisters. I'll not marry until you're safely and well a wife, so you can quit contemplating possible suitors for me."

"Harry says you shouldn't be so off-putting. He says the men in town call you 'Bossy Bess.'"

Bess's mouth sagged open. She snapped it shut. "Do they indeed? I should think, in that case, they'd be glad I'm not interested in them as suitors."

"Harry says once you're married up, that's bound to change. The bossy part, I mean."

Bess raised her eyebrows and crossed her arms over her apron. "Indeed?"

Bertie nodded. "He says the right man will know how to tame you."

"Tame me?"

"I told him no man could do that."

"Well, thank you."

"Only love can do that, the love of a woman for a man."

Bess's anger turned to surprise. Perhaps little Bertie was becoming a woman after all beneath that unfeminine attire.

Bertie glanced over Bess's shoulder. The girl's face brightened in a smile. "Hello, Mr. Riker."

Bess wanted to sink through the floorboards. How long had Gideon been standing in the doorway? Had he heard the entire disgusting, embarrassing conversation? She bit back a groan. Likely, he'd already heard the town's feelings about her from liquor-loosened tongues in his establishment. Attempting to gather her shredded dignity, she pasted on a smile and turned to face him. "What can we do for you?"

"Just wanted to let you know the shed and chicken coop are finished."

"Already? My, that was quick." *If he heard our conversation, he's pretending he didn't.* Relief relaxed the muscles about her smile a bit.

"Had good help."

Bess walked outside with him to see the outbuildings and complimented him on them. He gathered up his tools while she stepped into the shed. He was ready to leave when she came out. "Let me know if there's anything else I can do for you," he said. He'd taken six steps before he turned around. "By the way, I agree."

"Agree?"

"No man will ever tame you, Elizabeth Craig." He winked, turned on his heel, and left the yard.

"O-o-o-oh!" Bess stamped her foot. It made only an unsatisfying soft thud. "It's time someone tamed you, Gideon Riker, and all of Lickwind."

꽃

Knowing the townsmen ridiculed Bess behind her back made it especially sweet when, within two weeks, two more of Margaret's girls joined Bess and Regina for lessons. All three ladies paid for the teaching—only a pittance, but Bess began the work without expectation of pay, so she accepted it as a gift from God.

Two more boys, Leonard and Jethro Smit, had joined Walter and Bertie in lessons at the house. Bess wasn't about to expose the children to the saloon. Besides, Mr. Smit understandably didn't want his boys near Margaret's girls. Mr. Smit also paid Bess a small fee. Every little bit helped. But it was exhausting trying to keep up with all the schooling, the housework, and the Back Porch.

Gideon kept close watch over the table where the women took their lessons. News had spread that he wouldn't tolerate harassment of the group. Men gave the table a wide berth, though Bess was well aware they watched from a distance.

Mr. Llewellyn, the banker, took up where Gideon left off, trying to convince Bess to give up teaching Margaret's girls. "Be reasonable, Miss Craig. How will it look for the wife of an upstanding citizen of Lickwind to associate with. . .women of their character?"

"I'm not the wife of any upstanding citizen."

"I'm hoping that will change." He gave her a you-know-what-I-mean smile.

Bess couldn't honestly say his statement surprised her. He came around the Back Porch three times a day and overstayed his welcome each time, but this was the closest he'd come to openly stating his intentions. "You think that should entice me to give up teaching Miss Bently and the others?"

"I should hope so." He folded his hands over his stomach and rocked back on his heels. "And after all, what good will learning to read and write do any of them?"

"What harm will it do them?"

"Now, Miss Craig—"

"Miss Bently wants to learn to read for a number of reasons—primarily so she can read the Bible one day. Does that sound like foolishness to you?"

He spread his hands. "I'm sure that's laudable, but—"

"But not laudable enough for a wife of yours to continue associating with her? Are you afraid she'll lead me into temptation?"

He looked shocked she would say such a thing. "Of course not. But your reputation, my dear—"

"I've not given you leave to address me by such an endearment. Do not do so again. Now, if you'll excuse me, I've baking to do."

She'd all but shoved him out of the house, her temper hotter than the perking coffee on the stove.

But when he'd left, she stood looking out the parlor window at the back of the saloon. Was she right in continuing her work and so quickly dismissing Mr. Llewellyn and his offer? She didn't like his attitude, but he was better able than most men to provide a home for her and Bertie. Was it unfair to Bertie to refuse the proposal at which he'd hinted, though she didn't care a smidgen for the man? "Guide me, Lord," she whispered.

Chapter 9

Gideon looked up from behind the bar on a hot June afternoon to see a contingent of surly-looking men enter the saloon. The group included most of the businesspeople in town plus a couple of ranchers: Llewellyn the banker, Potter the attorney, Amos the blacksmith, Jones from the general store, Squires the feedstore owner, the Hatch cousins, Josiah Temple, and weasely Clyde Kincaid. The only people not represented were Doc Mitchel, Margaret Manning, and Bess Craig.

This didn't bode well.

Might as well face it head-on—whatever it was. "Any of you gentlemen want a drink?"

They all did. He poured their drinks then said, "Now that you've drunk your courage, what're you here for?"

Llewellyn cleared his throat. "It's about the schooling going on in here."

More trouble for Bess. Gideon's blood began to boil. Whatever these men wanted, he wasn't going to make it easy for them. "You men want to join the class?"

Llewellyn uttered an oath. "We want you to put a stop to it."

Gideon nodded slowly. "You find women learning to read and write offensive to your morals, do you?"

Potter glared. "Women like that don't need to know how to read and write."

"Do they need a reason to want to learn?" Gideon put a dirty glass in the tin pan beneath the bar.

Oscar hitched at his trousers. "It don't seem proper, women like that knowing more than a man."

Gideon crossed his arms over his chest. "If that's what's bothering you, I expect Miss Craig would let you join her class."

"Aw, Gideon." Linus pushed his fingers through his hair. "We can't even come in here for a drink anymore for fear of running into Miss Craig. Decent men don't drink in front of God-fearin' women."

Come to think of it, Gideon hadn't seen much of this bunch in his saloon the last month. "She's only in here an hour or so each morning."

Llewellyn slammed his fancy gray hat down on the bar. "Tell the women they can't be holding their lesson here; that's all we're asking."

"You expect me to throw the women out forcibly? Any of you willing to do that?" Gideon looked from one face to another. "I thought not." He rested his elbows on the bar. "But there is a solution."

Every face on the other side of the bar brightened.

Gideon nodded. "Yup. We just need to build Lickwind a school."

"Build a school for Margaret's girls?" Llewellyn roared.

Potter glowered. "With our money?"

Gideon shook his head. "Not just for Margaret's girls. Miss Craig is teaching four of the town's youngsters at her house. You men considering marrying one of the Craig sisters might do well to remember—after marriage come babies. There'll be more youngsters needing schooling, and they might be yours."

He saw right off that was the wrong argument. These men obviously hadn't thought far enough to get to the cradle part of a marriage.

"Second," he continued before they had a chance to think on the first reason too long, "the building could be used for a church and a town meeting hall."

Potter snorted. "We don't need a church or meeting hall."

"I didn't see the parson holding any meetings in your office during the rainstorm last month," Gideon reminded.

Llewellyn carefully settled his hat back on his head. "I'm not aiming to pay for a school for nobody else's kids. If I wanted to spend my money on that sort of thing, I'd have stayed back East." He turned on his heel and headed for the door.

The rest of the men followed—all except Amos. When the others had left the building, Amos leaned against the bar. He smelled of metal and smoke, as always. His skin was almost as gray as his shirt from his work. He reached between his leather apron and shirt and pulled out a crumpled magazine. He smoothed the magazine out on the bar, refusing to meet Gideon's gaze. "I was wonderin' if you'd read somethin' for me."

"Sure, Amos." Gideon glanced down at the magazine and almost bit his tongue to keep from embarrassing the blacksmith. It was a mail-order bride magazine.

Amos opened it and pointed to a sketch. "Would you read 'bout her?"

Gideon read the glowing terms describing the prospective bride. He hadn't the heart to remind Amos the woman may not be as desirable as described.

"Would you write to her for me, Gideon? See if she'd consider comin' to Lickwind?"

"Why you looking to send for a wife, Amos? Don't you find Bess or Bertie Craig attractive?"

"Aw, Miss Bertie, she's not lookin' for a husband. And Miss Bess, she's too smart for a guy like me. Besides, it's plain as sand in Wyoming that you two are stuck on each other."

Gideon jerked up straight. "I'm not even in line to court her."

"I might not be able to read or write, but I know what it means when a man looks out for a woman the way you look out for her and when a woman looks at a man the way she looks at you."

"She doesn't look at me any particular way."

"If you say so." Amos tugged at his handlebar mustache. "Do you think Miss Craig would teach me to read and write?"

"Don't know why not." Sure seemed to Gideon this was one Lickwind man thinking about a wife, babies, and schooling. Gideon snapped his fingers. "Say, I just came up with a plan to get us a schoolhouse and church." He leaned closer to Amos and explained his plan in a rush. "You with me?"

Amos reached out one of his huge hands and shook with Gideon. "Count me in."

When Amos left, Gideon pulled out a chair, hiked his feet up on a table, and joined his fingers behind his head. Yep, a schoolhouse and church building would solve all his problems. He'd have his saloon back again. One of the men in town would marry Bess Craig then. After all, no one could expect a man to propose to a woman when she spent her days in a saloon with soiled doves, no matter how honorable her intentions. Once Bess Craig was married, he'd have his house back.

He allowed himself to daydream about life in his own house. His new house. No women to protect from drunken men or cows to protect from wolves. No men coming and going all hours of the day for meals or baked goods or to court women. No cats or dogs. Just him and his new house. That's all he wanted.

So why did the thought of it put him in such a foul mood?

❦

The hay-filled mattress ticking scrunched beneath the blanket when Bess sat on the edge of the bed. She pulled the pins from her hair, undid her bun, and started to brush her hair. The Wyoming wind filled it with sand, no matter how she wore it.

Bertie flopped down beside her. "Are you going to marry Mr. Riker?"

"What? Ouch!" The brush bristles caught on Bess's ear. "Why would you ask such a thing? You know I'm not courting him."

"Harry says anyone can see you and Mr. Riker are sweet on each other."

Bess's heart seemed to leap in her chest, but she only said, "Harry is as good as a newspaper—one that spreads nonsense."

"I like him."

"Harry?"

"No, Mr. Riker. Don't you think he'd make you a good husband? Better than that two-faced banker or too good-looking lawyer."

"Mr. Riker owns a saloon," Bess reminded. "If the Lord has a husband in mind for me, I'm certain he'll be a God-fearing man."

"Harry says he's seen you making calf eyes at Mr. Riker."

"I have not!" Bess swallowed hard. "Calf eyes, indeed. You must quit spending time with that young man. His language is frightful."

"He likes me. He wants to ask your permission to let him court me, but I said no."

Surprise washed through Bess. "He wants to court you?"

"For true."

Bess lowered the hairbrush and studied Bertie's face. The girl looked extremely pleased with herself, but she didn't look like a girl who'd lost her heart to a man. Bess breathed a sigh of relief. "Apparently, the young man has more sense than I believed."

Bertie sat up. "You think so? For true? Even if I don't dress like a lady?"

"You've a beautiful heart, Bertie. You'll be a blessing to a husband one day."

Bertie beamed. "I don't want to marry Harry, though. I don't want to marry anyone."

"Then the Lord must not think it's time for you to marry yet."

Bertie chewed her lower lip, a sure sign that she had more to say. Bess continued brushing her hair and waited.

"If I married Harry, you could get married, too. You wouldn't need to worry any more about ending up an old maid."

Bess dropped her brush. "An old. . ." She leaned forward to pick up the brush from the floor and hide her face.

"I'll stay with you always, Bess. I won't leave you to grow old alone."

Bess swallowed twice before she trusted her voice. "It's sweet you're willing to make such a sacrifice for me, but let's see what the next couple of years bring before we decide whether it's necessary."

Bertie flopped back, hands behind her head. "Do you think God truly cares about us?"

"Of course He does." But Bess's heart caught at the thought of the future spreading out before the two of them. She loved Bertie dearly and would never abandon her to live on her own, but she did want marriage for each of them. Corrie had Luke and the twins. Matty had Jim and their new son, Matthew.

Each day it grew more difficult to deny her attraction to Gideon Riker. Even if Gideon didn't own a saloon, Bess couldn't expect him or any man to take on the responsibility of Bertie along with a wife.

Sadness settled over Bess's spirit as she put out the lamp and laid down. She'd told Bertie the truth. She did want a God-fearing man for a husband. So why was Gideon Riker, saloon owner, the only man in the vicinity of Lickwind—or anywhere else in the country—who lit a candle in her heart?

Chapter 10

When Bess arrived at the saloon the next day, Gideon stood on the saloon's boardwalk. He grinned at her. "Morning. See my new shingle?" He pointed overhead.

She looked up at the sign that creaked in the wind that swept down the street. Large white letters advertised RIKER'S SALOON as they had since the day she stepped off the train, but this morning a large red X was painted through SALOON. Below it in red letters, someone had added SKOOL.

She burst into laughter.

Gideon joined her.

When they finally caught their breath, Gideon said, "It's intended as an insult, but the spelling shows how desperately the painter could use your lessons."

The mistake provided a fun example in her spelling lesson for Margaret's girls and brought many townspeople into the saloon to tease Gideon.

Bess noticed most of the men's humor changed to anger when they spoke to Gideon. The anger seemed to center on a large tin can on the bar. Curious, she approached Gideon when the lesson was over. "What is the can for?"

"It's the school and church fund."

"What?" Surely she hadn't heard right.

"Town needs a school and a church. No one wants to fund them, so Amos and I decided to do something about it."

She eyed him warily. "How?"

"Amos doesn't provide service to anyone unless they contribute money or labor to the school and church. We figure one building will suffice for both."

Bess shook the can. It rattled. She peeked inside. A handful of coins lay on the bottom. She raised her eyebrows and gave Gideon a skeptical look. "And Amos's customers come here to make their contribution?"

Gideon grinned. "Nope. That's my customers' contributions. I have the same rules as Amos. I serve no one who doesn't contribute."

Bess wondered whether God would want money raised from selling liquor to be used for a house of worship.

"Maybe the money from here will go for the school part of the building," Gideon suggested.

Obviously, he'd guessed her thoughts. "At this rate, it's going to be a long time to afford even a small building."

Bess's doubts were soon banished. The other businessmen, furious that they had to pay above and beyond the normal price for Amos's and Gideon's goods and services, began to demand the same of their customers. Soon all the businesspeople required donations as a prerequisite to providing services. As the fund grew, everyone stopped being mad and grew excited.

❧

One evening as dusk fell, Gideon slipped into a stiff new shirt, shaved for the second time that day, left the saloon in Harry's care, and headed over to the Back Porch. "Mighty nice sunset, Miss Craig. Could I convince you to go walking with me?"

Was it wishful thinking, or did she look pleased at the invitation? He knew it pleased him when she said yes.

He wasn't brave enough to jump right into his purpose in seeing her. "The school and church committee think we've enough money to begin plans," he told her. The banker, lawyer, and Linus Hatch made up the committee. Gideon had thought Bess should be on it, but the other men didn't agree. Bess suggested Gideon, but the other men didn't agree to him either. Both Bess and Gideon were grateful the rest of the town was finally behind the project, regardless of who staffed the committee.

"I'm so glad. Have they decided where to build it?"

"At the end of the street, by Doc Mitchel and Llewellyn's houses."

They walked on in silence a few minutes, Gideon working up his courage. "I'm making some changes in my life, Miss Craig. I wanted to tell you about them before you heard about them from someone else."

She stopped walking and turned to him, a question in her eyes and something that looked like fear in her face.

"Nothing awful," he hurried to reassure her. "I'm quitting the saloon."

"Quitting? Selling?"

He shook his head and laughed. "Can't sell. My conscience won't let me." He risked reaching for her hand. Hope flickered when she gently returned the pressure of his fingers. "My life changed the day you walked into my saloon, Bess Craig. I watched you and saw that unconditional love of God you talked about lived out in your life."

"Mine?" She looked stunned.

"Yours. You reached out to Walter and Regina and Margaret's other girls—people others thought beneath them. You've changed their lives. You changed my life. I couldn't deny God's love when I saw you living it."

Bess looked down at the ground. "You exaggerate my importance in God's work."

"I don't agree. I don't want to keep selling liquor. God's opened my eyes. I can't pretend anymore that liquor's going to help men who are cut up inside. I was angry with God for a long time. I'm not angry at Him anymore."

A beautiful smile brightened her face. "That's the best news you could give me, Gideon."

She didn't seem to realize she'd used his given name. The sound of it on her lips stepped up his heartbeat. Did her heart beat faster, too?

"What will you do with the saloon?"

"I have an idea about that, but it depends on you."

"Me?"

"Your Back Porch business has about outgrown the house. Do you think you'd like to expand it into a restaurant? We could build a kitchen in the saloon's back room. There are already tables and chairs and lots of glasses."

"It sounds perfect, but I'll need to go over the figures and see whether we can afford to rent it from you. And, oh, where will you live? Do you want your house back?"

"I have an idea about that, too."

He hesitated, rubbing his thumb across the back of her hand.

"Yes?" she encouraged.

"I thought if you're willing"—he swallowed hard—"we might court a bit. Until the church is built." He reached for her other hand. "Then, if you find me passable, we might start that church out right with a wedding."

Bess gasped.

He trembled. "Is that a no, Miss Craig?"

"No, but I can't be accepting unless you're willing to take in Bertie."

He swept her into his arms, laughing, and twirled her about, the way he'd done back in May. "Never crossed my mind not to, Bess. I love you. I'm plumb loco with love for you."

Her arms tightened about his neck, the sweet violet scent she wore filled his senses, and her soft laughter filled his ears. And then he heard the most beautiful words in the world. "I love you, too, Gideon Riker."

❦

Gideon stood before the simple altar at the front of the church completed only days earlier in a town church-raising. He held out his fist toward his best man. "Here," he whispered.

Jim Collingswood frowned. "What is it?" he whispered back.

"Reimbursement for the money paid Ellis Stack for Bess. A buck-fifty. Figure it's only fair I pay for it, seeing she's my bride."

Jim grinned. "Welcome to the family."

❦

Bess stood in the front of the new white church in Matty's wedding dress as Harry played the first strains of "The Wedding March." After one last hug from each of her sisters, Bess watched Matty start up the aisle, followed by Corrie. Bertie whispered, "I always knew you were sweet on Gideon." She grinned and followed her sisters.

Bess stepped inside the church. Her gaze sought out Gideon. He met it, smiling, and the warmth in it wrapped around her heart. Imagine this strong, compassionate man loving her!

She'd never expected anything as wonderful as Gideon's love to come from Ellis Stack's mistake. She should have known—God doesn't let mistakes happen. Ellis Stack's mistake was a miracle of love in disguise.

Bess's Eggless Cookies

½ teaspoon nutmeg
½ teaspoon baking soda
Flour to make thick enough to roll
2 cups sugar
1 cup butter
1 cup milk
Raisins or currants

Mix nutmeg and baking soda with 1 cup flour and set aside. Cream together sugar and butter. Mix in milk. Add flour mixture. Add more flour as needed to make the mixture thick enough to roll out.

Sprinkle with granulated sugar and roll over lightly with rolling pin. Then cut out and press a whole raisin in center of each; or when done very light brown, brush over while still hot with a soft bit of rag dipped in a thick syrup of sugar and water, sprinkle with currants, and return to oven for a moment. These require a quick oven if using a woodstove. For modern stoves, bake at 375 degrees for 6 to 8 minutes.

Recipe based on eggless cookie recipe from *Buckeye Cookery*, 1880.

JoAnn A. Grote enjoys combining her love of history and writing to create stories about characters who are sustained by reliance upon the God of Hope (Romans 15:13). JoAnn has had 40 books published since her first novel, *The Sure Promise*, was included in Barbour Publishing's Heartsong Presents line. In addition to being a novelist, JoAnn is a volunteer at her local historical society and a technical editor. She lives on the Minnesota prairie but has a special love for Wyoming, where *From Pride to Bride* is set in the fictional town of Lickwind.

FROM ALARMING
TO CHARMING

by Pamela Kaye Tracy

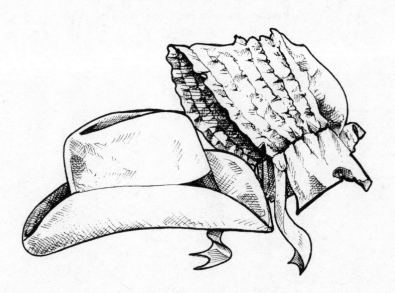

Dedication

In a book about sisters,
it only seems right to honor my own sisters.

To Roxanne Gould, the sister I recently found:
I look forward to creating memories that concrete a family.
I wish we'd met sooner.

To Patti Osback, my very first sister-in-law:
You were the perfect matchmaker.
I thank God every day for you.

To Cathy McDavid and Alison Hentges,
the sisters of my heart:
Words cannot express the meaning of our friendship.

Chapter 1

July 1869

The town of Lickwind greeted Thomas Hardin the younger much as it had bid him farewell all those years ago. Fistfuls of fine Wyoming dirt pelted his cheeks, this time flung by nature instead of from the hands of cowboys so angry at Thomas Hardin the elder they didn't care about the feelings of his impressionable fifteen-year-old son. Of course, in the last eight years, Thomas had seen more than his share of cowboy justice and knew sometimes it was called for, but just as often it wasn't.

Dust coated his throat, and he coughed as he turned sideways. He'd forgotten about the wicked western wind and how alive it often seemed. Today it whispered angrily as it swirled around him, pressing him to leave.

Leave? Not a chance. As soon as he cleared the grit from his throat, he wanted to meet the town head-on, let it know he'd returned and intended to stay.

Behind him, the pride of the Union Pacific hissed and growled like an angry tomcat, poised for flight but statue still. Heat from the iron horse blistered the air. Thomas blinked a few times, getting his bearings. Train travel might save time and energy, but he'd take a horse any day.

Horses meant freedom. When he'd turned sixteen, he'd jumped on the back of his father's best gelding and galloped away from his father and a memory that threatened to suck the very breath from his chest.

Horses also meant money.

Thomas took a coin from his pocket and danced it between his fingers. Spotting a young man lounging uselessly against what might be called an excuse for a depot, he called, "Hey, boy." Time to unload five prime mares, and Thomas could use some help. If bloodlines and spirit could be turned into a profit, he intended to make yet another fortune here in the mire of his childhood nightmares.

Horses also took a lot of time.

"Boy," Thomas called again, raising an eyebrow. Either times had changed or the young man sitting on the rickety depot step had a hearing problem. Money in Lickwind had never been so plentiful—except for the landowners—that a boy didn't keep an eye out for a way to make a little extra.

"Bo—"

"I ain't a boy."

No, she wasn't. Thomas could see that now that she glanced up. Freckles spotted high cheekbones. A hint of strawberry blond hair framed a face protected from the sun by an old, ugly, brown hat. A giant gray-and-black-striped cat indignantly climbed off the girl's lap; and belatedly, Thomas noted the brown skirt that graced the top of scuffed, brown leather boots.

"Roberta Suzanne Craig!" A brunette hurried across a dirt street. This one, from the tips of her high-top laced boots to the lacy bonnet covering her head, was not of the type to be mistaken for a boy.

Before he could move, the boy impersonator jumped up and hid behind him. Peeking over his shoulder, she asked, "How can I earn that money?"

Surprised, he answered, "I wanted help moving my horses."

"Sure, I can help, but you need to convince my sister."

He stepped aside as the pretty one skidded to a stop. She looked like a schoolmistress ready to dress down a truant pupil. He didn't want to get in her way. On the other hand, the tomboy one, Roberta, bobbed up and down like a cork in water. Truthfully, he didn't know which sister posed the bigger threat. He had the feeling that to side with the pretty one would earn him the ire of the other one.

Women.

He preferred horses.

"Bertie, you come around him now!"

To her credit, the girl—she looked like a Bertie—stepped to the side and met her sister's gaze head-on. Her lips pursed together, and Thomas decided that he'd like to see these two take on his two top hands, Rex and Mikey. Rex could shoot a mosquito at twenty paces. Mikey used a bullwhip to slice bread.

The pretty girl's words came out in a rush. "I've been looking for you all morning. You were supposed to make Butter Buds this morning. You know train days are always busy. Also, I checked your sewing basket, and there's enough dust on it to plant a garden. And you left dirty clothes on the floor again."

Before Thomas had an inkling what she was about to do, Bertie grabbed his arm and yanked him closer to the scolding sister.

"I'm helping with his horses. He's paying me. He's new to town. You always tell me we have to be neighborly."

Two pairs of eyes focused all their attention on him. He stammered, "Wh–wh–whoa, now. I j–ju–just. . ."

"Just what?" Hands went to her hips as Mrs. Bossy frowned at him.

"I th–thought she w–was a boy," Thomas admitted. He wished his tongue would return to normal size and that he'd never noticed the urchin sitting on the stoop.

Masculine laughter rang out behind him. At the sound, Thomas felt his teeth clamp together viselike. Mrs. Bossy smiled a halfhearted greeting. It was Bertie who caught Thomas's attention, and his opinion of her increased. She looked like a foul smell accosted her, and Thomas easily identified the source. Unless he was mistaken, Josiah Temple stood behind him.

This was not how Thomas wanted to face Temple.

Thomas wanted his wealth and power to counter Temple's local prestige. Instead, Temple not only heard Thomas stutter, but also witnessed him mistake a girl for a boy.

Lickwind may have grown, what with the railroad and all—and where had all these women come from?—but in other ways, it stayed small or at least small-minded. No one escaped the scrutiny of Josiah Temple. Thomas likened the man to a burr of a cholla cactus. He'd discovered the stubborn pricklies in the Arizona Territory. About the time he cleared a squatter from his right pant leg, three more settled on his left boot. They seemed to know when he wasn't looking, and here they came, clinging and pestering. Rex said he'd seen one jump more than a mile just to annoy a man.

"Mrs. Riker." Josiah took off his hat. "Good afternoon." With a smile that didn't reach his eyes, he turned to Bertie and said, "Boy."

Bertie stuck her tongue out.

Although it annoyed him to ape Temple, Thomas swept the hat from his head. He plain wasn't expecting womenfolk in Lickwind. Mrs. Riker didn't seem to notice, but the homely girl grinned and did the same. Thomas shook his head. Nothing about this day was turning out as he wanted. At least Bertie kept her tongue in her mouth as she smirked at him.

Mrs. Riker grasped Bertie by the arm. "Roberta Suzanne—"

"Bertie!" the urchin insisted.

"Roberta Suzanne, you are too old to be sticking out your tongue. Now march right—"

Bertie dug in her heels. "I'm helping him with the horses."

"That might mean you're assisting a horse thief." Temple's mustache barely moved, yet the words sounded as loud as thunder.

Thomas's fingers itched. Just one minute, no, two—that's all it would take to toss this depraved fool to the ground and pound his face to pulp.

But he couldn't. It looked like Lickwind had turned respectable. It had ladies, one who might swoon and another who might join the fight. Neither circumstance appealed to him. A lifetime of hate wouldn't let him walk away from Temple, but common sense warned that Thomas not act so rash as to find himself facing the end of a rope during his first day in town.

"You look just like your father," Temple said.

At age fifteen, Thomas had looked up to all the cowboys and few landowners. Not any longer. Now, he pretty much expected them to look up to him. "And you look like a man who'd pound a nail into the casket before the doctor filled out the death certificate."

"Tommy," Temple advised, "the best thing for you to do is hop back on that train and leave."

Thomas grinned. "Not a chance."

Temple said nothing.

"You got a problem with me?" Thomas didn't stutter now.

"That a threat?" Temple noted the gun and stepped in front of the ladies.

No doubt they—or at least the pretty one—thought he was being a gentleman. *Yellow-livered.* Just the thought made Thomas smile. "You're not worth my time." Thomas put his hat on and winked at Bertie before walking away.

❦

Bertie felt the hair at the back of her neck prickle. Usually Josiah Temple couldn't round a corner without her knowing. He'd snuck up on her today. She'd thought Rhubarb took off because of the man on the train, but now Bertie blamed Josiah for the cat's desertion. Cats were great judges of character, and Rhubarb never erred. The cat adored James, Luke, and Gideon. As for Josiah, Rhubarb wouldn't stay in the same room.

The man on the train obviously felt the same way. Bertie could almost forgive him for mistaking her for a boy.

"Nothing good ever came from a Hardin." Josiah looked bright, but Bertie didn't think it ran deep. Not if he didn't recognize the expression on Bess's face. Of course, Josiah wasn't even looking at Bess; he watched the man he called Hardin walk toward Donald Potter's law office.

Hardin. Bertie liked the sound of it. If Rhubarb had kittens again, Bertie would name the biggest, toughest one Hardin.

Bess's nose twitched just a bit. A true sign she'd been offended. "You know the man enough to judge?" she asked Josiah.

When Bess used her "teacher" voice, grown men cowered. Even Corrie's little girls, Brianne and Madeline, quieted. Bertie practiced the tone, but she never got it right. Matty said it had something to do with maturing.

Yup, Josiah was for true a fool. He rambled on, still watching Hardin. "I knew his father well enough to judge. We ran Tommy and his old man out of town when it barely rated as a town. Weren't but four or five settling families hereabouts. The Smits, when the boys were younger and before Rachel died." His voice dropped; and if Bertie hadn't known better, she'd think he was being reverent. "Then the Webbers moved on; they didn't squat but a few months and claimed it got too crowded. As I recall, I think the missus died right before they left. The Collingswoods, but I don't need to tell you about them." Josiah was too much the politician to leer, but Bertie wished she were a man so she could wipe that look off his face.

Josiah was a talker, always, but seldom did he concentrate on anything but himself. Tommy Hardin's arrival really must have shaken him. He barely took a breath before continuing, "The Kincaid brothers were among the first settlers. They beat me here. Cyrus, he was a smart one, not like his brother. Then, there was me. The cowboys were a lot rougher back then—'twasn't anything like it is today. Tommy Hardin's pa was the worst of them. Worked at the Kincaid spread."

Josiah finally turned to face Bess, and Bertie thought he took a step back. But he still wasn't smart enough to stop talking. "Caught Tommy Hardin's daddy rustling my cattle. I wanted to string him up."

Bertie waited to hear more, but Josiah stopped talking as the land office door closed behind Hardin.

Was Tommy Hardin a cowboy? He didn't dress like one or smell like one. Or was he a rustler like his father?

"It was just a surprise, seeing Tommy." Josiah had the good grace to look sheepish. "Excuse me, ladies, I said too much. Fact is, Scotty stuck up for the Hardins and so most of the men were willing to go easy on his dad."

It was a good thing Bess was just as mesmerized with today's events as Josiah, because it not only saved Josiah from the tongue-lashing he deserved, but it allowed Bertie to slink away unnoticed. Standing behind the railroad depot, she waited until Bess was safely inside their restaurant, The Back Porch, before hurrying in the opposite direction.

Oh, Grandmother's bloomers! Bertie couldn't remember anything so exciting as Thomas Hardin, unless you counted her sisters' weddings. And watching Josiah Temple puff up and then deflate just made Bertie's day.

Bertie peeked around the corner of the train. Any minute now Bess would realize she had neglected to retrieve her student. Escape now meant retribution later, but it would be worth it. Who could she get to accompany her to Matty's and Corrie's place so she could find Scotty? He'd saved Tommy Hardin's father from death. Scotty was a master storyteller. Bertie couldn't imagine why he hadn't already divulged this exciting tale.

Bertie pivoted but didn't manage even one step. In front of her stood the smallest man she'd ever seen. He smiled as Rhubarb wove between his ankles. The cat's tail stood straight up, a true sign of feline contentment. After a moment, Rhubarb deserted her bandy-legged quarry and investigated a cart so loaded with trunks that Bertie couldn't imagine this man pulling it. Bertie got the distinct impression he approved of her. Not a notion she gleaned from most of the adult population in Lickwind.

"Hello," Bertie said.

The man bowed, easily maneuvered the cart, and headed for the middle of the street. Not even the thought of Bess could keep Bertie from following.

Bertie figured that this day packed about as much excitement—at least for her—as had the day the sisters arrived in Lickwind.

The Chinaman positioned his cart out of the way in front of Donald Potter's office. He stood as still as Bertie had ever seen a man be and waited. A handful of people made it to town on Thursdays, but those who did were just as fascinated as Bertie. The Chinaman ignored the stares, and his stoic face didn't acknowledge the few rude words that were thrown his way.

Bertie grew uncomfortable. If Bess found out Bertie had spent an hour standing in the middle of town just staring at a stranger, there'd be a price. Most likely an essay on China's history!

A low whistle saved Bertie. Ramon barked and ran for Jones's store.

Scotty!

Bertie skidded to a stop before the cowboy had time to tie his horse to the post. "There's a man from China, and he's standing on the stoop in from of the land office. I think he came with a man named Tommy Hardin."

Ramon's head nudged Scotty's hand until the old cowboy chuckled. "If that dog herded cattle the way he herds you, he'd be worth something."

Bertie gave her favorite cowboy a quick hug.

Scotty's eyes lit up. "Little Tommy Hardin. Now there's a name I ain't heard in a while. I taught him to read from the Bible. Not sure it did him any good." Scotty grinned, his mouth cracking open in a toothless display of glee. "Spit and vinegar on two legs and some to spare."

"I'm taller than the Chinaman," Bertie announced.

"They do be skimpy fellas. The railroad employs scores of them."

"I followed him. He's definitely with Tommy Hardin, not the railroad."

Scotty cackled. "That boy could find trouble blindfolded."

"Mr. Temple said he was a thief."

"Well, now, there's some that think that and others who don't."

"What do you think, Scotty?"

Scotty frowned. "I think Tommy's father made some unfortunate choices, but that doesn't mean—"

"They call me Thomas now, and I see you're still sticking up for me." Thomas Hardin took the horse's reins from Scotty's hand and secured them to the post.

Bertie couldn't remember ever seeing a man so handsome.

"Hello, Miss Bertie, and good-bye, Miss Bertie." Thomas Hardin quickly dismissed her presence and slapped Scotty on the back.

Even as Scotty shooed her away, Bertie was wishing, for the first time, that she looked and acted like a woman.

Chapter 2

Bess Riker's kitchen floor shone like the bald spot on Amos Freeling's head. Bertie carried the water bucket out to the garden and emptied it. Her fingers were red and rough from the lye soap Bess favored. Scotty said the Indians lived on dirt floors; and when the floors got dirty, the Indians covered their trash with more dirt, thus creating a new, slightly higher floor.

For true, she loved July in Wyoming. Green as far as you could see and trees so tall they looked like climbing posts to heaven. The bucket banged against her leg as she headed back home, whistling for Rhubarb. The cat always managed to disappear. Today Bertie didn't have a hope for escape. Any minute now it would be time to head to school, and Bess remained thin-lipped from last week's spectacle.

Apparently the whole town had watched Roberta Suzanne Craig follow a Chinaman from one end of the street to the other. Albert Smit had even come to town special to warn Gideon and Bess that Chinamen were not to be trusted. Albert admitted he personally hadn't dealt with any, but he'd heard and thought that both Hardin and his friends should be run out of town.

Four hours later, with chores and schoolwork behind her, Bertie stood and headed for the door. Her first chance at escape in five days.

She'd barely made two steps before Bess asked, "Bertie, can you recite the nine rules for the use of capital letters?"

Bertie recited, and Regina Bently echoed the rules in a whisper.

"Bertie, you haven't done any piecework all week, and—"

"I need to look for Rhubarb. She hasn't been around all morning."

Bess looked up from the spelling words on Leonard Smit's slate. Her eyes surveyed the room where she held school five days a week. Usually the cat curled up on the floor near where Bertie sat.

Leonard always sat closest to Bess, not only because he needed the most help, but because he was smitten with her. His younger brother Jethro used to sit by the door, escape as much on his mind as Bertie's, but then Harry—Gideon's former barkeep—halfheartedly started attending, and Jethro lost his favorite perch. Walter, more family than student, liked to sit on the floor in front of the piano bench. His sister Regina usually sat next to him.

"Did you look in the shed?" Bess handed Leonard his slate to correct.

"During recess and before spelling."

"He wasn't at our house this morning," Walter offered.

"It's not our house," Regina reminded. They were staying in Frank Llewellyn's house while the banker was out of town.

"Do you want some help?" asked Bess.

A wave of longing washed over Bertie, and she almost said yes. The soft tone of her sister's voice reminded her of their mother—a memory fading faster than Bertie thought possible. Her sisters tried to make up for the loss. She went from having one mother to having four. Even Adele, for a brief time, tried to assume the role. In some ways, their smothering had obliterated any recollection she had of the sweet-voiced woman who called her Baby.

Baby.

The sisters had tried calling Bertie "Baby," but she'd put a stop to that. A neighbor boy back in Rhode Island taught her how to hold her breath until she turned blue. Matty scolded, Corrie cried, and Bess pounded her on the back until she hiccupped, but the sisters got the idea. For true, she hated being the baby of the family. It meant doing everything last, and it meant that the others could always do things better. Bertie didn't even want to try if it meant an older sister was going to judge. She learned to be a baby who didn't cry and who didn't come when called, except sometimes for Bess.

Bess, who sometimes had a soft voice so like Mama's.

Bertie closed her eyes. She intended to disobey her big sister, and the urge to follow the rules suddenly stalled her. "No, I'll find her."

As the door closed behind her, Bertie whistled for Ramon and pretended not to hear Bess's plea to stay out of trouble and not venture far. It wasn't that Bertie went looking for trouble; it was just that trouble always managed to find her.

The town of Lickwind didn't harbor a stray cat in its midst, neither near the smithy where Rhubarb liked to bat small discarded pieces of whatever Amos threw away nor behind the general store where Mr. Jones sometimes tossed the cat tidbits.

Mr. Jones saved the day. He might have been too busy loading up his wagon to entertain Rhubarb, but he wasn't too busy to close up shop and make some deliveries. The mention of Matty's and Corrie's names as a destination sent Bertie scampering back to Bess for permission to keep the grizzled storekeeper company.

Ramon jumped in back of the wagon and fell asleep. The sun beat down steadily as they traveled the hour it took to get to the Collingswood's ranch. Bertie suspected Mr. Jones wanted some advice from Jim about what supplies needed to be stocked now that the train was bringing more business.

At Matty's and Corrie's ranch, neither sister claimed a visit from the cat, but both enjoyed their enthusiastic greeting from Ramon. Bertie tickled the twins for a few minutes just to get them laughing. Baby Matthew slept; he was really too little to do much with. Ramon visited all his old haunts and pestered Scotty.

The sun dipped a bit closer to the west than Bertie wanted it to while Jones and Jim jawed about rising prices and populations. After good-byes were said, Mr. Jones headed the wagon in the direction of the Two Horse, the Kincaid spread. Bertie held on to the seat and tried not to bounce. Jones wouldn't like it. The only reason he allowed Bertie to tag along was, as he said, she "didn't act like most fool females." It was unlikely that Rhubarb had strayed so far as the Kincaid spread, but maybe the cat was as curious as the whole town of Lickwind.

Thomas Hardin had dominated the conversation at church last Sunday. Bertie listened to Parson Harris's sermon and tried to remember what the preacher looked like back in Rhode Island. He'd been shorter and talked louder. Bertie liked Harris better. He told more stories. Bertie wished he'd tell about Thomas Hardin.

Later, at the Riker home, Bess and Gideon tried to separate fact from fiction, but by all accounts no one considered it good news that the Hardin boy had returned to town. Even the news of a Chinaman took second place to a returning cattle rustler. Gideon had only raised a speculative eyebrow to Bertie's insistent "son of a cattle rustler" interjection.

In an ironic twist, Thomas—who once fled town with nothing more than the clothes on his back—rode into town followed by rumors of a healthy bank account and more cattle than even Josiah Temple owned. That Hardin had purchased Clyde Kincaid's ranch kept Bess and Gideon whispering well into the night. Bertie almost crawled out of her bed to lean against their door, so strong was the urge to eavesdrop.

The Kincaid ranch needed loving, tender care, Bertie thought, as she sat beside Mr. Jones and watched the world's ugliest ranch loom into sight. It looked exactly like what Clyde Kincaid deserved. The main house was a drab structure. Even from a distance, Bertie could see gaps between the chinks in the wood. There were two other buildings. One might be an outhouse. Who knew what the other was—maybe a henhouse?

Walking beside one of the smaller buildings was the Chinaman. Rhubarb meowed at his feet.

Rhubarb had the run of the town and its perimeters. She loved everyone and everyone loved her, but she only "talked" to Bertie.

Until today.

Bertie jumped from the wagon in time to watch Tommy Hardin exit the house. He joined the Chinaman and her cat. The man crouched in front of Rhubarb and looked to be offering the cat something.

Bertie sidled closer.

An egg? Yup, for true, Tommy was a cowboy. All the cowboys fed Rhubarb eggs. Someday Bertie half-expected Rhubarb to cluck.

❧

He'd purchased the Kincaid place almost sight unseen. Donald Potter, the attorney, tried to warn him, but Thomas had been waiting more than five years for prime property in Lickwind to become available. Maybe it was providence that Kincaid sold out.

Looking around, Thomas tried to associate Kincaid's spread today to the spread of yesteryear. When the Hardins worked here, Clyde's brother had run the show. Cyrus had been a tightfisted yet fair man, who worked his cowboys hard but provided for them. Thomas had no idea what had happened to the bunkhouse. If it had burned, surely there'd be charred remains. Instead, dying grass in varying shades of brown and yellow grew over his final remnants of a childhood memory. Clyde probably sold the lumber, anything for a buck. The barn was missing, too.

Donald Potter didn't recall the Kincaid place having many cattle, but when Thomas Hardin the elder put in his time, the spread had enough to make a young boy's eyes burn when the wind blew. Cyrus turned a profit, kept the money, left the ranch to Clyde, and headed for California and fool's gold.

Cyrus had been a fool to leave a working ranch to his younger brother.

Thomas often profited from the foolishness of others. What did it say in the Bible about fools? Something about being hotheaded and reckless.

"Look." Tien-Lu, the Chinaman, pointed.

Thomas glanced over his shoulder and almost moaned. Bertie Craig slid off the front seat of a wagon before the wheels ceased to turn. Any other girl might have inspired him to hurry over and assist, but not this one. She looked like she belonged to the land.

Donald said the Craig girls had a reputation for setting their sight on a man and turning his life upside-down until he married her. Seemed the town, up until a few months ago, had a thriving saloon and a well-visited bordello. Then the saloon manager faced off with one Bess Craig, and now there was a restaurant and church services instead of rowdy Saturday nights and hung-over Sunday mornings. The bordello remained, but business no longer boomed.

The other two sisters took the Collingswood brothers, perfectly good ranchers and horsemen, and turned them into homebodies. Thomas had neither known the touch of a mother nor the caress of a woman who loved only him, but he did know shrewd businessmen who sometimes put a gentle woman before a good business deal.

Thomas made more money than they did.

According to Donald, there remained one single filly in the Craig stable.

Thomas wanted her off his land before bad luck got a fingerhold.

"Hello, Jones. Glad to see you."

Jones jerked a thumb at Bertie. "I picked up a stray in town."

"You need something, Roberta Suzanne Craig?" Thomas ambled over.

She took off her hat and pointed toward Tien-Lu. "That's my cat."

Glancing behind him, this time Thomas did moan. The cat from the train depot, the one who'd lain on Bertie's lap so he'd thought she wore pants. It was partly the cat's fault he'd met up with Josiah in such a comical manner.

"Your cat's trespassing." Thomas frowned. The cat was as unpredictable as her owner. How had the feline gotten this far from town? To think he'd welcomed the critter to his spread and practically laid out the red carpet for a visit from this female.

He'd been amiss yesterday when he'd assessed the other sister as being the comely one. Bertie Craig had the prettiest hair he'd ever seen and more of it, too. It had been all bunched up under that hat yesterday. Today it reminded him of a horse's mane—shiny and blowing in the wind, long enough to stream behind her if the wind picked up. Or maybe if a man's fingers went exploring.

He shook his head, clearing it, then opened his mouth to suggest she take her cat and wait in the wagon for Jones's departure, but Bertie had somehow managed to cross the yard to the shed and was interfering with Tien-Lu as the man struggled to pull down a piece of lumber that far exceeded his reach. The silliest-looking dog jumped from the back of Jones's wagon and joined Rhubarb at Tien-Lu's feet, almost tripping the man. Thomas really should have pitched in and helped Jones unload the supplies; instead, he followed Bertie. He wanted to see what this slip of a female was up to.

"What are you doing?" Bertie asked.

"Making it into a house."

Thomas figured it was safe to assume that Tien-Lu answered in English because Bertie surprised him. Most white people, women especially, went out of their way to ignore Tien-Lu's existence. They certainly didn't talk to him. Tien-Lu had perfected the art of pretending he didn't speak or understand English.

Bertie made a face. "A house? It's too small."

"We don't need room."

"We?"

As if knowing they were being talked about, from inside the shed came Tien-Lu's wife and daughter, Trieu and Anna. Anna hid behind her mother, as always. The cat went straight for the little girl, arching her back to an impossible curve until her fur touched the tip of Anna's fingers, and the child had no choice but to reach down and pet the mewling feline.

Bertie's face transformed again. Thomas blinked. Yesterday she'd been a boy. Ten minutes ago, he'd recognized the hint of a woman. Now he saw the future and almost lost his breath at the possibility.

Bertie went to Anna and dropped to her knees.

"Her name is Rhubarb. She loves to be scratched right here." Bertie rubbed the cat's back until it collapsed, limp with contentment.

Anna hunched down and stroked Rhubarb's back.

"Rhubarb? Pretty cat." Anna spoke softly, in better English than her father. Her mother spoke no English, and no matter how Thomas prodded, Trieu refused to make an effort to learn.

"Rhubarb, what kind of name is that?" Thomas asked.

"My sister hates rhubarb," Bertie announced.

"Your sister hates this cat?"

"No, Matty loves the cat; she just hates the taste of rhubarb."

"What's that got to do with the cat's name?" Thomas wanted to get back to work, and he wanted this woman off his land.

"I named the cat Rhubarb to annoy my sister Matty."

It was the first time he'd laughed—at least a deep belly type of laugh—in months, maybe years. It felt good, and that scared him. He needed to get her off his ranch. He needed to stop conversing with her as if he enjoyed it. He needed to get back to work. Instead, he asked, "Don't you like your sister?"

"Oh, I love her, but I also like to annoy her." Bertie stood and brushed the grass off her knees. She looked at Trieu and said, "I'm Bertie Craig."

Trieu nodded but didn't speak. Bertie turned to Anna. "You really gonna live in this shed?"

Anna pointed at the dog. "What's its name?"

"Ramon."

"A nice, normal name," Thomas mused.

"I didn't name him," Bertie admitted.

"I want a dog," Anna announced.

The adults laughed. Then Bertie asked Anna again, "Are you going to live there?"

"For a little while," Anna said.

Bertie shot Thomas a dirty look. He raised his hands in helplessness. He'd offered the main house to Tien-Lu, but the man refused.

Tien-Lu wasn't great at taking orders, and neither was Bertie. Which is why instead of taking her cat and waiting in the wagon, like Thomas suggested, Bertie started offering advice not only about Anna attending school in town, but about rebuilding the shed. Soon she had Anna and Trieu slopping in the mud, making chinking.

Thomas frowned as he went to help Jones. Bertie Craig, quite frankly, was as much a nuisance as that cat.

Chapter 3

T homas opened his eyes in protest. Squinting, he tried to figure out what had awakened him. The walls were flickering, an orange and yellow inconsistent dance.

Grabbing his trousers, he jerked them on and stumbled from the house to face a small fire. For a moment, he stared in disbelief at the proof of a town that did not welcome him. Obviously the desire had been to frighten and not to harm. There'd be no saving the shed; and so it wouldn't spread to the dry grasses and weeds, Thomas headed for the well and shouted for Tien-Lu.

It took a moment as the small tent almost took on personality as Tien-Lu struggled from his bed. A lump to the left, a poke to the right, and one peg came loose before a pale face poked from the opening.

Thomas barked, "Get out here and help!"

Tien-Lu joined his boss and nodded. Anna and her mother soon crawled from the tent.

"I hear no noise," Tien-Lu muttered, stomping on burning embers. Together they put out the fire as Trieu put a fist in her mouth, biting back tears.

That didn't surprise Thomas. For the past week, Tien-Lu, Trieu, and Anna had worked tirelessly on the shed, turning it into what looked like a miniature cottage. Just that afternoon, Scotty and Bertie had shown up. They'd dismantled the old roof and started work on an arched contraption that Bertie insisted would prevent not only rain deposits but also allow better light. They were a team, that old cowboy and the young girl. Thomas had put off important work just to enjoy listening to Scotty fill Bertie, Anna, and Tien-Lu in on Lickwind's history. The man knew everybody and everything. He could find something good to say about just about everybody, including Josiah Temple.

The concept of five or six families founding Lickwind seemed to fascinate Bertie. Actually, there had been fewer. The Collingswoods were brothers. Amos Smit and Josiah were brothers-in-law. That left only the Webbers and Kincaids as stand-alone settlers.

Lickwind had certainly grown, and every day brought something new to be grateful for. Lost in thought, it took Thomas a moment to realize that a mass of snorting cattle stretched across the landscape.

"Impeccable timing," Thomas said.

"Thanks for the beacon." Mikey didn't dismount. The cattle, spooked by the fire, swerved in a direction opposite from the intentions of the cowboys.

Thomas, grateful to be diverted from the smoking remains of Tien-Lu's home, moved forward to offer guidance. "Rex on point?"

"Yup."

"Who's riding drag?"

"New guy called Jack."

For the next hour, while Tien-Lu diligently patrolled the area for errant sparks, Thomas, Mikey, Rex, and four new hands put the cattle to bed.

"Lose many?" Thomas asked.

Mikey bounced a coiled rope against his leg, exhaustion so tangible, it roiled off him like dust. "We lost some two-year-old heifers. They got spooked when the buffalo came too close."

Thomas nodded. "Any other trouble?"

"Buffalo made the grass a bit scarce. We sure were glad when we came close to Lickwind and saw the grazing land."

❧

Anna started school the next week. For the first time, Bertie looked forward to lessons. Anna, who'd never been to school before, was too excited to sit still. Bertie so enjoyed helping Anna that she forgot to pretend she didn't understand her own lessons. It took four days for Bess to catch on.

"I'm giving you the eighth-grade final examination next week," Bess declared.

Bertie had been playing at school way too long anyway. Ellis had kept her from attending, Bess had been determined that Bertie would finish, and Bertie had been content to drift along.

Bertie finished her math problems, hurried through her duties at the restaurant, neglected her household chores, and finally escaped out the front door. She was more than ready to move, and she knew exactly how she wanted to spend her afternoon. Not in the restaurant either. She wanted to be at the Two Horse, and just maybe Jones would be making a delivery. After all, Bess always said, "We're supposed to be neighborly."

But Jones only chuckled when Bertie skidded to a stop in front of his store. Pointing toward something behind her, he resumed sweeping the dirt from his front door. In front of The Back Porch, Gideon finished loading one of the restaurant's tables in the back of his wagon.

"You going somewhere?" Bertie asked, already guessing their destination.

"Thought we'd go visit Thomas Hardin and see what you and Scotty find so enticing." Gideon didn't look at her as he said the words.

Guilt painted red splotches across Bertie's cheeks. She'd never been able to keep things from Bess.

Gideon helped Bertie into the wagon and gave Bess one of those married looks that Bertie never could read.

"Gee up!" he shouted after settling in beside his wife.

Bess hugged Bertie, and because it felt right, Bertie didn't shrug away.

They were working on the main house now. Tien-Lu, Trieu, Anna, Bertie, and Scotty. Poor Thomas, Bertie thought. For a man who didn't want women on his ranch, every time he turned around, a new one appeared. Susan, the young wife of Jack, one of Thomas's newly hired cowboys, arrived by train just yesterday. She and Jack had taken a meal at the Back Porch. She was just Bertie's age, and she wore the contentment and awe of the newly married like a shawl around her shoulders. She never took it off, and it was a stunning example of joy, commitment, and love.

And now even more women would gather on the Two Horse soil. Bertie had no doubt but the Collingswoods were en route to this surprise picnic.

"I didn't realize Clyde left such a small house," Bess observed.

Bertie nodded, glad to leave her confusing thoughts for another time. "I'll bet Thomas lets Jack and Susan live in it."

"Bertie, you need to call him Mr. Hardin," Bess advised.

"I'll try to remember," Bertie promised.

Matty and Corrie were already pulling baskets and blankets and such from their wagons while their husbands carried chairs. Tien-Lu and Anna were busy spreading blankets on the ground. Thomas scowled from the doorway of the house.

Matty, jiggling baby Matthew, called, "Come help, Bertie. We've brought a feast."

Bertie had no choice but to pitch in. After a few moments, she asked softly, "Everyone knew that Scotty and I were coming out here?"

"Scotty's had Jim's permission since the beginning. At first, I was a bit concerned, but Scotty said this Thomas Hardin is a good man. Bertie, I've really been looking forward to today. I've been wanting to see this man that you've taken such a shine to. I've never seen you take such pains with your appearance." Matty reached over to push a stray piece of hair away from Bertie's eyes. "Except for Papa's hat." Matty's eyes softened as she gazed at the worn, brown felt hat on her sister's head. Matty said, "It might be time to put it away, Bertie."

Looking down, Bertie tried to figure how her sister noticed any difference. She mentally kicked herself. Certainly, she wanted Thomas to notice. How could she have been so dense as not to realize others—especially her sisters—might notice first!

"Oh, Grandmother's bloomers," Bertie muttered. Her sisters were joining forces. Any one of the sisters could have put a stop to Bertie's visits to the Two Horse, but all the sisters had had a hand in Bertie's upbringing. They wanted to see just what Bertie was up to. They wanted to see this Thomas Hardin who so had Bertie's head a-spinning.

Fried chicken, potatoes, corn bread, greens, and lemonade were soon unloaded; and the rumor of a meal brought forth the ranch hands hours before their usual suppertime.

Within minutes, a banquet was spread out and the prayer said. Bertie watched as Tien-Lu wrinkled his nose at the American fare. Anna hid behind her mother in a game of hide-and-seek with Bess. Susan and Matty discussed an upcoming baby.

Susan was in the family way? Bertie swallowed. Susan was two months younger than Bertie yet years more mature in actions and appearance. Unconsciously, Bertie touched the brim of her hat. Lately she'd been thinking more about her family and the loss of their dairy farm back in Rhode Island. All her girlish dreams, her memories of happiness, centered around dairy farms. Ever since arriving in Lickwind, she'd wanted one of the sisters to start a dairy farm. Her only hope had been Bess. But maybe instead of happiness being a place, maybe it was a person?

Where was Thomas anyway? She knew he hated a crowd, but he'd lost his scowl earlier after accepting a piece of Corrie's apple pie. Bertie headed for the remnants of the burnt shed. No doubt, Thomas was explaining his theory of the fire to some willing ear.

The ear turned out to be Corrie's husband, who deftly changed the subject from heat lightning to. . . "We hope Bertie's not bothering you."

"No, not a bit. She's been quite a help. I never figured I'd let loose a female architect on my land, but she's doing a great job. She and Scotty make quite a team."

Can a smile spread so big as to reach the ears? Bertie wondered. Thomas liked having her around!

"She's good with her hands," Luke agreed. "We, the family, are a bit concerned with her coming out here—"

"With someone of my reputation," Thomas finished.

"There is that," Luke agreed.

"Well, she never leaves Scotty's side. Trieu loves her. And little Anna's favorite saying is 'Grandmother's bloomers!'" Thomas laughed. "She's good for Anna."

The feeling of pleasure disappeared as the men laughed at her expense. Bertie almost backed away, torn by the guilt of eavesdropping and the pall of what she was hearing.

I'm good for Anna?

The baby, always treated like the baby.

"Sorry to hear you had a fire," Luke said. "Albert Smit was talking about it over at Jones's store. Guess you were lucky to only lose a shed."

"More than lucky," Thomas agreed.

"You think that fire started by accident?" Luke asked.

"Not sure."

The men were silent for a few moments; then Thomas spoke. "We do appreciate the chance of education for Anna. You sure your sister-in-law is ready for the backlash taking a Chinese into the schoolroom will bring?"

"You don't know Bess very well," Luke observed.

"Ah, but I know Bertie, and I guess if Bess is anything like Bertie, I'll be more than pleased with the outcome. That right, Bertie?"

It took a moment for Bertie to realize he was addressing her. Crouched behind the house, she'd been sure the men were unaware of her.

"Yes," she squeaked.

Luke had the audacity to pat her shoulder as he walked by in search of his wife. Thomas ambled by next. "Need something, Bertie?"

"Not exactly."

"What do you mean, 'Not exactly'?"

Bertie shook her head. "You think I come here because of Anna?"

"Mostly."

"I come here because it's where I feel at home."

"Where you feel at home?" Thomas echoed. "Here?"

"Yes, here."

He didn't know about dairy farms and security. He didn't know what she was trying to tell him because she wasn't exactly sure herself.

"How do you equate here with home?"

Bertie shrugged. She didn't quite understand her motives for wanting to spend so much time here at the Two Horse Ranch. For true, she felt needed, included; she felt as if these people somehow belonged to her. But even more, every time she caught a glimpse of Thomas, her whole body grew warm, and she suddenly had trouble breathing.

"Well, squirt, we like having you around." With a careless sweep of his hand, Thomas nudged her hat so it covered her eyes.

He walked away not noticing the scowl on Bertie's face. He liked having her around. She took off her hat and banged it against her leg.

Squirt?

She didn't want to be his squirt.

Chapter 4

Thomas knew that women had no place on his ranch, but now, watching his cowboys make a fuss over baby Matthew and Corrie's twins, he realized that children didn't belong either—at least not on his ranch. Maybe on some other ranch where fairy tales had happily-ever-after endings and the word *family* actually meant something. Family took too much time—time that could be spent growing the herd, making money.

One of the twins took a few steps, tumbled to the ground, and instead of crying—as Thomas thought most children would do—laughed.

Thomas figured Bertie must have been a child something like this.

"I see you cotton to my youngest daughter." Luke took the plate full of chicken bones out of Thomas's hand and passed it to Bertie. Before Thomas could step back, run, or grunt an "I don't think so," little Brianne nestled in his arms.

He immediately wanted to hand the child back to the proud father, but a quick glance around showed that he was the center of attention. At the Two Horse Ranch, he was supposed to be the center of attention. It suited him fine when giving orders about branding calves and split hooves. It didn't suit so well when, as the person in charge, he wanted nothing more than to admit he was scared to death of a little child. Brianne, who made a half-intrigued and half-irritated face.

Too close. Thomas gathered the girl under her armpits and held her away. Feet dangled in the air in way too trusting an attitude.

And that's when the little flirt smiled at him.

Bertie expertly adjusted Brianne's dress, reminding him that although Bertie often acted like a boy, he'd best remember her womanly side. And along with remembering that, he needed to remind himself that babies and women went hand in hand. When and if he decided it was time to take a wife, he'd go back East for one. He wanted a proper lady who would know her place, and that would be in the kitchen, not designing and rebuilding sheds into cottages, dividing houses, or riding astride horses.

He should have told Scotty to leave Bertie behind from the beginning, before he—and everybody else—started looking forward to the sunshine she brought.

Thomas started to pull the little girl closer, but she puckered up her lips, and her little hands fisted, twirling wildly in the air. Brianne turned a splotchy shade of red.

"You'd best give her to m—" Bertie started.

Brianne didn't exactly throw up. It was more a lumpy, white spit, and the aim was true. The stuff headed straight for Thomas's shirt.

Gut reaction transferred the child to Bertie's arms faster than Thomas thought possible.

"Something wrong, boss?" Rex asked.

"You step in worse than that all the time," Jack added, laughing.

Untucking his shirt, Thomas used the tail to dab at the wet spot. "Just surprised me, that's all."

Glancing at Bertie, he saw suppressed laughter in her eyes; but worse, she still held Brianne, who no longer wore a pained expression. Instead, with the same wide smile—one looking surprisingly similar to Bertie's—the baby held out her arms, clearly wanting him. He wouldn't have taken her, really, except she whimpered.

Hours later, Bertie's family gathered up the remnants of the feast, along with their children, and prepared to leave.

Thomas relinquished Brianne. He opened his mouth, every instinct urging him to say, "Come again, anytime." Instead, he said, "Thanks for the meal."

Luke said the words Thomas couldn't. "You're welcome to visit our spread anytime. It's been, what—a good seven years since you've been around?"

Thomas nodded. He'd spent a bit of time at the Collingswood's spread, probably unbeknownst to them. Scotty had been the pull. Thomas learned to read under the cowboy's direction. The Bible had been the only book Scotty owned. Thomas still carried it. Scotty and a few others saw past the rowdy father to the boy. But that all changed once the words "cattle rustler" became a well-versed whisper.

⁂

Fourteen-hour days did much in the way of helping Thomas push the thought of family to the back of his mind. He'd never had much luck with family—as any son of a cattle rustler could claim. He barely remembered his mother, and he didn't want to remember his father. It was best to acknowledge that the equation of Thomas Hardin plus family equaled heartache.

Still, it bothered him that Bertie no longer accompanied Scotty to the Two Horse. Scotty dropped by often, Bible in hand and preaching forgiveness on his agenda. He seemed convinced that Thomas should forgive his father. Forgive? Thomas had a hard time swallowing that notion, and Scotty offering up an address for Thomas the elder didn't make things easier. Still, Thomas put up with the visits because sometimes the old cowboy mentioned Bertie. Thomas also discreetly drew school-related Bertie tales from Anna. He was careful not to mention Bertie in front of Tien-Lu. It would only take the merest hint of interest, and Tien-Lu and Trieu would start sewing wedding garments.

Thomas spit out a nail and hammered it into a log. He should be glad Bertie had other things to occupy her time. No doubt, if she were here, she'd be organizing the rebuilding of the shed and stealing his precious nails.

He had plans for his nails.

Now that he had more cowboys to help with the cattle, he was putting his attention to his horses. He loved the cows because they helped line his pockets, but he loved his horses more. He loved being responsible for training them. He could take a wobbly colt and turn it into an outstanding piece of horseflesh. He loved bonding with the animal. And he loved the feeling of trust that he sometimes felt with his mount. It was a kind of trust he felt with few humans, and it bothered him that Lickwind—the place that had ostracized both him and his father—seemed to be filled with people who deserved trust. With that thought, he squinted at the sun and figured it was more than time to head for town.

He didn't trust banks, and Lickwind had a bank and a banker.

According to Donald Potter, Frank Llewellyn stuck out like a sore thumb. The banker wore bright colors and Eastern styles in a place where mud was the favorite color.

Frank had been East for more than a month due to some family emergency, but he'd returned to Lickwind on yesterday's train and would be opening the bank today. Thomas figured the dutiful ranchers—or any man with two pennies to rub together—would check their accounts first thing, so Thomas waited until well past noon before heading to town.

When Thomas finally took a seat in the banker's office, he saw judgment pass over the man's expression. Since the bank didn't rate a clerk, no one had announced Thomas. Frank figured he had an illiterate cowpoke in front of him. It worked in Thomas's favor. He often used a young, unkempt appearance to place his adversaries at a disadvantage. Today he used the cowboy persona through and through.

"Can I help you?" Frank, a chubby man shaped like a water barrel, rested his hands on his stomach and took on the look of a man used to giving advice.

Thomas took a wad of national bank notes from his pocket. "I'd like to make a deposit."

"You new around here? Maybe working on the Kincaid spread?"

"It's the Hardin spread now."

"Takes awhile for change to take root in Lickwind." Frank smiled condescendingly. "You get your first payday? It's a smart thing to start an account."

"I have an account."

Frank blinked, unable to mask his surprise. "You do?"

"Donald Potter opened it more than six months ago."

"Mr. Potter opened an account for Thomas Hard. . ." The banker's words tapered off as understanding dawned. "You're Thomas Hardin."

"In the flesh." Thomas couldn't—and didn't want to—hide the grin.

Frank sat up straight, took the notes from Thomas's hand, and opened the ledger on his desk. Dipping the pen in ink, he quickly made some notations, then fixed Thomas a receipt.

"This isn't correct," Thomas said after glancing at his balance.

"I assure you, I never err in my figures."

"Well, although it occurs to me to let the mistake remain, as it is in my favor, common courtesy demands otherwise."

Frank turned a bit red in the face. "I assure you, there is no error."

And there wasn't, at least not in addition and subtraction.

Thomas's finger didn't have far to trace. There should have been only three transactions listed: his original deposit, his withdrawal for the Kincaid ranch, and the deposit he'd just made. Instead there were four. "When was this twenty-dollar deposit made?"

"This morning. About noon I found a double eagle on top of a note asking me to credit it to your account. It was left on the front table. I assumed you were too busy to wait. I did wonder why you were so trusting."

"Let me see the note."

Frank pulled open the bottom drawer of his desk. Clamped together was a stack of paperwork that Thomas figured represented today's dealings. August 22nd had been a busy day, it looked like. The note—written on the back of what looked to be a handbill from some long-gone patent medicine man—about the twenty-dollar deposit was at the bottom.

Chicken scratch might be easier to read. Thomas's name and the amount were barely distinguishable scrawls.

※

"What do you mean, call you Roberta?" Bess's hands, buried deep in a mass of sourdough, stilled. "I'm not sure I can do that."

"Why not?" Bertie said, picking up a glass to dry. "It's my name." And while Bertie might be a name for a squirt, Roberta was a name for a woman.

At first Bertie had loved helping in the restaurant. Just standing on the wooden floors, looking at the gold trim, and admiring the sparkling chandelier made her feel like she was getting away with something decadent. After all, this used to be a place where spirits were sold. Somehow Bertie figured the ground should open up and swallow her whole just for being inside.

It was hard to believe that Gideon once ran a saloon. She gave the glass one last swipe. Drying dishes ruined the shady atmosphere somewhat. Her staid, one-eyed brother-in-law rated as the most serious of the three Craig girls' husbands. And God must still be smiling at the idea of a former saloon hosting Sunday morning sermons. Or at least it did before the new church was built and Gideon moved the piano over. Now that Luke took to preaching on Parson Harris's off-weeks, besides housing the school, the new church got plenty of use.

Bess took the glass from Bertie's hand. "Dry them smoothly, then set them upside-down. Why do you want to be called Roberta? Yes, it is your name, but you've always refused to answer when we use it."

"I was"—Bertie thought fast—"being unreasonable."

Bess started kneading again. "Anything else you want us to do differently?"

"I'm done with school. I passed the test, right?"

"Yes, you did."

"Can I work here at the restaurant for pay, maybe as a waitress?"

Bess bit the inside of her lip so severely that Bertie could see the indent. "I'll talk with Gideon. We are getting busier, and Regina could use some help. But. . ."

"But what?"

"What you can do," Bess said quietly, "is teach school."

Bertie made a lemonade face.

Bess laughed. "It's not that bad."

❧

But it was that bad, Bertie thought a few weeks later. The Smit boys weren't that impressed with the change, especially Leonard, who moaned every day for a week about the loss of his beloved Mrs. Riker. Just when Bertie thought she'd reached her limit and might need to knock the two boys' heads together, Jethro decided he'd reached the age to notice girls. Anna was too young to be a contender; the former soiled dove, Regina, was too old and, well, too worldly; and that left Bertie, who was only five years Jethro's senior.

Unfortunately, Bertie would rather find frogs in her lunch box than have Jethro's puppy-dog eyes follow her every movement. Some days it was all she could do not to stomp her feet and throw a tantrum in front of her students. Instead, she imitated Matty's patient voice and tried to stay calm. Still, she always felt relief when three o'clock rolled around.

Today was no exception. She waved good-bye to her pupils from the church's door. Jethro and Leonard disappeared down the street. For them, school meant freedom from the never-ending chores of a ranch. Mr. Smit did without them because he thought schooling might make them better ranchers in the long haul. He didn't even complain about sending them to school during the peak months of July and August. He claimed concern that they'd missed so much schooling. Bertie did admire that he wanted what was best for his boys. Gossip in Lickwind had Mr. Smit pegged as a wealthy man.

Anna rode behind her father on a horse so broad it could have carried Tien-Lu and five more men his size. Neither mentioned Bertie's absence from the Two Horse. Either they thought she was too busy to drop by or they didn't miss her. Tien-Lu just bowed and nodded his approval all the while appraising her with his shiny, black eyes as if she were supposed to say something, know something, do something.

To be honest, both the restaurant and school paled in comparison to the excitement of helping at the Two Horse. Helping at a place where she obviously wasn't missed. Thomas Hardin never even came to town. She'd never even had time to let him know that she wasn't his squirt.

Bertie stopped waving once Regina and Walter entered the restaurant. Besides Bess, Regina was the Back Porch's only waitress. She did a great job, and many of the patrons requested her. Bertie shook her head as she thought of the fancy banker, Frank Llewellyn, who often left the comfort of his home to eat at The Back Porch. And since Regina hired on as his housekeeper, the banker was almost bearable, although when Regina had time to clean was anybody's guess.

Still Regina's little brother, Walter, claimed Lewellyn was tolerable to live with. Though for a boy, living in Llewellyn's house was like living in a mansion, not that Walter had ever seen a mansion.

Watching Regina and Walter enter the restaurant made Bertie think about Harry, Gideon's old barkeep. She missed him. He'd been offered Regina's job, but he claimed it didn't pay enough. Odd jobs didn't suit him, schooling didn't inspire him, and Lickwind no longer seemed to have anything to offer him. One morning he'd not shown up for class, and that afternoon Bertie watched him board the Union Pacific for parts unknown.

The wind kicked up, sending Bertie's dress whipping around her legs. Maybe a storm was brewing. She closed the door and went to her desk. Actually, sometimes she liked the quiet of the church after all the students were gone. Growing up as the youngest Craig girl, she'd never spent much quiet, private time indoors. Seemed there was always a sister hanging around wanting to know what she was doing or wanting to tell her what to do. She'd escaped outdoors for solitude.

A few hours later, after she'd graded all the papers and outlined the next day's lesson, she blew out the lantern and headed down the steps.

Mr. Smit rode his horse straight for the church. Funny, it was much too early for a rancher to cease work. He took off his hat before he slid off his horse.

"Mr. Smit." Bertie hoped the man—who always looked like he had a stomachache—wasn't here to court. Since Bertie took on the role of schoolmarm, half the cowboys in Lickwind decided she was on the market.

"I need to be talking to you about my boys."

Oh, good. He was here to discuss Jethro's crush. She could deal with that. "Jethro will outgrow this, Mr. Smit, I'm sure."

"I'm disturbed that my boys have to be in a classroom with a dirty Chinese child."

"Dirty? The child is quite clean."

Mr. Smit's face reddened. "I shoulda came back when yer sister was a-teaching. She being older and all. But the truth is, I didn't have time. And now I'm here to tell ya that if the little Chinese girl continues in this school, my boys will stay home."

"Your boys are doing great. They've gone from being illiterate to reading from the second primer. That's extraordinary. You'd deny them an education because of your fear of a five-year-old girl?"

If anything, Mr. Smit's face reddened even more. "Not sure I want them in a classroom with a female got a tongue like yours."

"I'm not removing Anna from my classroom. Good day, Mr. Smit."

Mr. Smit got back on his horse, shaking his head. "You're young. I'll be talking to that brother-in-law of yours. He'll set things right. My boys have a right to an education. They're Americans."

Bertie closed the door behind her. Bess had already experienced outrage from Mr. Smit about Regina. Looked like it was Bertie's turn to deal with the man's prejudice. This time, however, Mr. Smit was picking on a defenseless child. Regina had been no stranger to the callousness of men.

If Bertie had her way, Anna would never witness it.

Chapter 5

J osiah Temple entered the restaurant as dusk spread out over the town. He strode
purposely for his favorite table by the front window. Bertie grimaced. Her table.
She'd already had a rotten day and now had to wait on the man who made her
skin crawl. He reminded her of Ellis.

"Coffee?" she asked.

"Yes, and I need to talk to Gideon."

"I'll tell him."

The men went through four cups of coffee before Josiah pushed away from the
table and left. Gideon looked ready to smash a window. Bertie and Bess peered from
the kitchen door and slowly came out. Gideon changed the front sign to CLOSED,
and brushing a hand across his eyes, he walked toward them.

"Bertie, something happen at school today that you want to share with me?"

"Mr. Smit came to visit."

"Mr. Smit!" Bess exclaimed. "Is Leonard sweet on you?"

"No, Jethro is, but that's not why Mr. Smit paid me a visit."

"Seems the school board's against the idea of a Chinese child attending public
school." Gideon leaned against the counter and shook his head. "According to them,
you either have to prohibit her from attending or stop using the church."

"What?" Bess gasped.

"Who makes up the school board?" Bertie asked.

"Llewellyn, Potter, Linus Hatch."

"Then why is Temple delivering the news?"

"Because he somehow swayed their opinions," Bess said grimly.

"I refuse to stop Anna from attending school," Bertie said.

"Fact is," Gideon said, "you can't refuse."

Bess's eyes sparked with challenge. "She can, and she w—"

"Josiah says he's already met with the school board members, and they're in
agreement."

"Those men attend church!" Bess exclaimed. "How could they? I expect this
type of prejudice from Temple but not from the others. I'll go talk to them."

"We'll both talk to them," Gideon said. "But for now, school's suspended for the
rest of the week. He's already spread the word. Bertie, he wants us to ride out and
tell Anna's family tomorrow."

"I won't. And I quit. I never wanted to be a schoolteacher anyhow."

Bess shook her head. "If you quit, then you're giving up. And we Craig girls are not quitters."

Gideon added, "Besides, you'll be punishing the innocent. I've no doubt the Smit boys wish they'd kept their mouths shut. Seems they were smart enough to keep her attendance a secret. Mr. Smit overheard them after school today. That's how he found out. You stop teaching school, and you'll be heaping a whole lot of guilt on those boys' consciences along with their losing out on schooling.

"And, fact is, if we don't ride out and tell Anna's family, Josiah says he will. Don't you think it would be kinder coming from you?"

"I'll do it," Bess offered. "But, then we're going to fight it."

"No," Bertie said. "I'll do it."

❦

Bertie woke early—not that she'd gotten much sleep, knowing that Gideon wanted to get this done early so he could return to the restaurant. Bess was staying behind to handle the few who might show up to order breakfast.

Bertie wasn't sure what words she'd use to crumble Anna's world. Bertie had been the first to suggest Anna attend school, and it just might have been Bertie's approach to teaching—so different from Bess's—that had the Smit boys so talkative. If Gideon and Bess came along, they'd take over. Bertie was the schoolteacher now. Not a baby, not a squirt. Sitting down, she tried to think of the words to say. In a way, she was like a student passing an invisible test. She just hated that she had to visit the Two Horse to expel Anna. Bertie wanted to return to the ranch because Thomas missed her.

Crawling from bed, she quietly opened her bureau, and instead of taking the old brown homespun she favored because it blended in, she took the blue-and-white-striped calico skirt that Matty had given her. She'd not worn it yet. Tucking in a white blouse, she briefly considered taking the time to iron out the wrinkles, but her stomach roiled, protesting against what she had to do today. Shoes were the easiest. No choice there. She wore boots, brown and made of leather, just like her father had. They looked funny and big, peeking out from under her skirt.

Ramon barked. Bertie took a breath. Any minute they'd be leaving for Thomas's farm. This morning she had to tell Anna not to come to school for a while. It almost seemed wrong to be wearing good clothes and doing something so ordinary as brushing her strawberry blond hair.

Her boots made loud *clop, clop* noises as she headed for the restaurant's kitchen. Funny, she'd never noticed before.

Bess stirred eggs into a big bowl. "You hungry, Bertie?"

"No."

For once, Bess didn't insist. "I did it again. Called you Bertie when you want to be called Roberta. Guess I can't get used to you growing up."

"You ready?" Gideon called from the front.

Bess offered a quick hug and ordered Ramon to stay behind. Before Bertie was really ready, it was time to go.

They weren't taking the wagon. Bertie half thought this was Gideon's way of trying to do something to please her. It had been awhile since she'd ridden. Funny, she hadn't really missed it, although at one time riding had been her favorite pastime.

She tossed saddlebags over one of Gideon's horses and plopped her father's hat on her head before climbing on the horse's back. Then she artistically arranged her new skirt and galloped after her brother-in-law toward the Two Horse.

A few miles out, she told Gideon, "I want to do the talking."

"You need any advice?" he offered.

"I'll look to you if I do."

"Fair enough." He left it at that, and she was grateful.

An hour later, Gideon was off his horse.

"What's wrong?" Bertie asked.

"He's taken a stone. It will just take me a minute to deal with it. You ride on ahead."

Freedom. She remembered it from when Papa and Mama were alive, and she experienced it now as she lived with Bess and Gideon.

Things were changing so quickly in her life that she almost felt like she was trying to catch a butterfly that always managed to fly just outside her grasp. She didn't like being a schoolteacher, but she could be good at it. She didn't enjoy being a waitress, although it was more fun than teaching, and she made money almost immediately. Why, a man from last Thursday's train left her a quarter. A quarter! He also proposed marriage.

She brought her horse to a walk, trying to give Gideon time to catch up. Lost in her thoughts, she saw the men before she heard them. At first she thought she'd stumbled across Thomas. She reined the horse and slid from his back. No, it was not Thomas, and there were two men. One sat on a fallen tree and laughed at something the other man said.

What was Josiah Temple doing on Thomas's land?

And who was the other man?

Josiah scared Bertie enough, and the other man looked meaner than a snake. She felt her legs start to wobble. She needed to get out of there before the horse snorted or before something else happened to alert the men of her proximity.

She quietly led the horse in the opposite direction and took off. She couldn't say which bothered her more: thinking about telling Tien-Lu and his family about Anna not being allowed to attend school or thinking about Josiah meeting up with what looked like an outlaw on Thomas's land.

❧

Thomas slowed his horse and squinted at a landmark. He wanted to mark his land's boundaries. He had an old map Cyrus had drawn and every reason to believe it was reliable, but it didn't look like he'd get much done today. A female—wearing a blue-and-white-striped skirt and an old, ugly hat—galloped toward him followed by Gideon Riker. Thomas couldn't help but smile. He'd have to be blind to miss the woman Bertie'd become.

The smile soon faded. As they neared him, he saw that something was wrong. He saw that not only was Bertie out of breath, but Gideon looked a bit concerned. His observations were confirmed as they slowed. Instead of a cheerful greeting, Bertie stammered, "Did you see the men?"

"What men?"

Gideon answered, "Bertie saw Josiah and some cowboy a few miles back. It spooked her."

"It wasn't a cowboy. He was an outlaw, and they were up to no good," she urged, wheeling her horse around. "I just know it. We need to find where they've gone."

Exchanging a quizzical look with Gideon, Thomas rode beside her as she galloped toward the east. He had to admire the way she handled a horse. Gideon followed a few paces behind. Finally, she stopped near a clump of fallen trees he'd been meaning to convert to firewood. Sweat glistened on her forehead, and her cheeks flushed a bright pink. "They were right here."

"Who was with Josiah?" asked Thomas.

"Some outlaw."

He almost laughed, but she didn't look in the mood for pranks. "An outlaw?"

"Yes, talking to Josiah."

"What were they talking about?"

"I didn't get close enough to hear."

"How do you know it was an outlaw?" Gideon asked.

"I've seen pictures of outlaws on the posters in Jones's store."

Bertie Craig was scared, and she looked up at Thomas with the same trust her niece had just a few weeks ago.

"Josiah is as free to roam it as you are. And, just because a man looks like an outlaw doesn't mean he is one."

Gideon added, "Bertie, I'm sure everything's all right."

She made a face and looked like she wanted to say more.

"Don't worry about us out here at the Two Horse. We'll be just fine. We can take care of ourselves. Besides, Josiah's a mosquito I'd just love to squash." Thomas rode next to her. "What brings you out to the Two Horse?"

"I'm here on school business."

He grinned. "Anna tells me you're her favorite teacher—never mind that you're her only teacher. She's pretending to read from the Bible each night. I think she mimics the stories you tell during the day. Most interesting. I've always thought Eve handed Adam an apple. Anna insists that the type of fruit is unknown. Is that your doing?"

To his surprise, Bertie didn't pick up on his teasing. If she'd been a different girl, maybe he'd think the glistening in her eyes was the beginning of tears.

"Bertie, what is it? Are you still afraid because you think you saw an outlaw?"

"I did see an outlaw."

"Phew, you are in a mood today. Why are you so grumpy?"

"Life isn't fair."

He wondered what brought this on. Life wasn't fair; she was right. He'd been dealt some bad luck early in life, but he'd dealt with it alone. According to Donald, the Craig girls had been dealt an equal amount of bad luck, only they'd had each other. He noticed the way the girls watched over each other, and the way they hovered over Bertie made him understand why she acted as outrageously as she did.

They rode toward the Two Horse. Bertie was silent, seemingly lost in thought. Gideon just shook his head. Thomas figured she'd open up soon enough. Something certainly had her vexed today.

But she didn't speak again. And when they got to his land and Anna's head peeked from a window, he heard Bertie take a deep breath.

Oh no. No wonder Josiah and the outlaw had Bertie so spooked. If Thomas had been any other rancher, he'd have blamed the calamities his ranch seemed to attract on the townspeople warning the Chinese away. But in Lickwind, it was the Hardin name that most people wanted to forget. It maybe just took the town a bit longer to target Tien-Lu.

"Teacher! You look so pretty." Anna burst from the house, a small tornado of energy with a smile that split her face.

And Bertie did look beautiful. Her hair, even topped by that ridiculous hat, cascaded down an elegant, curved back. She sat in the saddle poised and confident. The kind of woman any rancher would be proud to have by his side.

Whoa, those were thoughts Thomas didn't deserve to consider, especially not about this female who changed from a boy to a child to woman back to child on a whim.

"Anna, go get your father. I need to speak with him." Bertie's face looked pale under the freckles.

Thomas watched Anna turn around and fly toward the back of the house where Tien-Lu prepared the noon meal.

"You don't have the guts to tell that child she's not welcome in your school, so you'll tell her father and let him do the deed?"

"Slow down, Thomas," Gideon advised.

"I've got guts and plenty extra," said Bertie, pulling her horse to a halt in front of the house, dismounting, and tying Nugget to a post. "But if I didn't come out here, your friend Josiah volunteered. I figured I was the lesser of the two evils."

"Missy Bertie." Tien-Lu rounded the house, grinning and bowing. He handed her a pastry wrapped in a towel.

"Josiah's no friend of mine." Thomas felt like he was losing control of the conversation.

Anna held on to her father's knee. "I helpt to make that, Miss Craig." She cast a look Gideon's way. "Oh, I shoulda brought you one, too."

"That's all right, sweetie," Gideon said.

Bertie took a bite and closed her eyes in contentment. If only she were here to visit and sample Tien-Lu's cooking. Handing Gideon the pastry to finish, she knelt down so she was eye level with Anna. "What do you think, Anna, about me coming here to teach you on Saturdays so you won't have to travel all the way to town?"

"I like town. It's exciting. And Mama says I can't have a brown hat like yours, but I'm gonna keep asking."

"Town is exciting, but your papa has lots of chores, and town is a long way. Can we try it for a while and see how it works?"

Gideon cleared his throat, and Bertie looked at him, expecting some sort of rebuttal. "I'll bring the ladies out here; I'm sure Bess will want to pitch in. You think you can see them home, Thomas?"

Anna looked up at Tien-Lu.

He nodded, his eyes meeting Bertie's head-on.

It isn't fair, Thomas mentally agreed with Bertie's earlier statement.

"Okay," Anna whispered, looking unhappy.

"Great." Bertie took off her hat. "Oh, and Anna, this hat always helped me when I did my homework. Why don't you see if it helps you?"

Thomas swallowed, watching as a too-big hat enveloped Anna's face.

Chapter 6

homas frowned but didn't lose his temper. He'd arrived in town a few minutes ago to pick up the fringe-top surrey he'd ordered almost a month ago. Instead of parading through town with a first-class surrey, he surveyed the damage done by what must have been a madman wielding an ax.

Funny, he was more disappointed than mad. When he'd ordered the contraption, he'd been thinking about an Eastern bride, which Bertie Craig wasn't. Now he realized that when he pictured himself in the vehicle, Bertie's image was planted firmly by his side. No wonder her sister and brother-in-law worried. He'd been aware of Bertie's crush since she'd first tagged along with Scotty to pitch in with fixing up the Two Horse. What he hadn't been aware of was how much he really enjoyed having her around—the squirt.

Townspeople, gathered round as if viewing a social event, took it as a bad omen. With the exception of Saturday night fights involving cowboys letting off steam, this type of crime left Lickwind alone—at least since the rustling problem some years back. In Thomas's presence, no one mentioned that the Hardin name seemed synonymous with disaster. Since his arrival, the Kincaid place suffered a fire plus the theft of two saddles. Thomas and his men worked daily trying to build a barn, and often either work was destroyed or supplies went missing overnight. Thomas wasn't inclined to blame acts of nature for any of the calamities befalling him.

"Boss, what do you need me to do?" Rex asked. Along with the surrey, Thomas had arranged for the delivery of a stallion. Rex held Zeus steady. If anything, it was Rex who needed calming. He was not the sort of cowboy to stand around. All Thomas needed to do was point, and Rex would attack.

"Nothing," Thomas said, a strange sense of calm subduing him. He'd expected Lickwind to be unwelcoming—but he'd expected a frontal attack: bitter looks, refusal of services, and a sense of exile. Instead, looks were impassive or welcoming—thanks to the Craig sisters, especially that spitfire Bertie. His money guaranteed services even from those thoroughly committed to Josiah's camp. Instead of exile, his ranch was turning into a regular social community—complete with women and children.

And yet someone, stealthy as a shadow, struck when no one was looking. The surrey had been taken from the train and left beside the depot. It couldn't have been left alone more than an hour, but that was probably about how long it took.

Surprising to think that no one had heard anything. Thomas turned and marched down the street.

"You got an idea?" Rex asked, keeping up.

"A destination."

The bank was empty. Any customer it might have had now stood in the audience just outside the door. Thomas, more a main attraction than he ever wanted to be, headed for the bank's office.

Frank Llewellyn was not at his desk; when Thomas turned around to face the door, he met the guarded eyes of the banker. Sweat, courtesy of the August sun, dotted his forehead. Thomas knew in that instant that Frank had been in the crowd by the wrecked wagon—which meant he'd left the bank unmanned.

Their eyes met, the banker and the rancher, and almost in one accord they slowly turned and surveyed the lobby—both sensing what they would find.

Money, with a scrap of paper specifying Thomas's account.

"How much did you pay for the wagon?" Frank picked up the offering from the little table where customers often sat waiting their turn.

"Seventy-five dollars."

"Give me a minute. I'll count."

It didn't even take a minute. Frank might consider himself a contemporary of Josiah, but the continuous deposits made to Thomas's account by a person or persons unknown made Frank and Thomas partners of a sort.

"Seventy-five dollars," Frank verified. Neither man was surprised that the amount of the deposit matched what Thomas had paid for the wagon. In the past month, a deposit had been made each and every time something belonging to Thomas was stolen or destroyed. Two saddles meant another double eagle in Thomas's account. The bantam hen fetched a gold dollar.

Whoever made the deposits used quite a bit of patent medicine, because the scraps of paper were the only clues as to the benefactor. The store didn't sell this particular brand of medicine, which halted Thomas's momentary foray into detective work.

No one, save Rex, chanced entering the bank. It was as if the town thought an invisible line should keep them from getting too close to Thomas. Stepping out into the sunshine, Thomas looked across the town. Most of the townspeople had the dignity to pretend conversation. Albert Smit and Amos Freeling shook their heads in disgust. Thomas couldn't tell if their feelings were about him or about the situation. Even Doc Mitchel found the day's events more interesting than a bottle. Thomas didn't really care.

Across the street, he could see Bertie's look of sympathy. Rex tossed Walter a nickel, said a few words, and the boy headed toward Amos Freeling's blacksmith shop. Surely, something could be salvaged.

Thomas followed his heart to the restaurant. He hadn't taken the time to dine at the restaurant partly because he was too busy getting the ranch together and partly because he wanted to choose the time to rub his existence into the face of Lickwind.

He might need to rethink his strategy.

The kitchen was a lot smaller than he'd imagined. It had probably, at one time, housed liquor. An iron stove took up one whole wall. Hand-tooled tables were covered with an assortment of dishes and a row of still-steaming desserts. No one could bake like the Craig women. Bertie stood next to a small window. She was just finishing up the final twist of a very long braid.

"Bertie."

She took an apron from a drawer and turned to face him. He'd seen that face—in the flesh or in his thoughts—almost daily since coming to Lickwind. And always her eyes were snapping, eager, happy to see him. He'd never appreciated that particular "Bertie" trait.

He felt as if he were noticing her face for the first time.

Her eyes stared at him as impassive as the crowd outside. "That wasn't aimed at Tien-Lu; that was aimed at you."

A month ago, a week ago, maybe even yesterday, he'd have let anger roil over him like a rattlesnake ready to strike. But something he saw in Bertie's eyes warned him to take care with his words. "Not all men are good, Bertie."

"You think Josiah did that? You think that's why he was on your place with that outlaw?"

"Josiah's not in the crowd outside. I don't know who to blame."

"Were you going to take me riding in that surrey?"

"You would have been first."

They stood there, not touching, but both aware that something was changing. It would take more than a destroyed surrey and protective sisters to stop whatever it was.

❧

One week later, Bertie hung clothes on the line and took a deep breath of the flowers that dotted the fringe of Bess's garden. She loved Saturday, but since the dismissal of school, Saturday didn't feel quite so special.

In church last Sunday, Parson Harris spoke about laying your burdens at God's feet. It was past time for Bertie to hear that sermon. She'd been afraid to put anything at God's feet since her parents had died. None of her prayers about their safety had been answered. Later, while living with Adele and Ellis, Bertie had tried prayer again.

She'd always kind of thought God had forgotten about her, and that's when she'd stopped talking to Him. No wonder her sisters wanted to called her Baby. Bertie deserved it. She acted childish; she always had. But maybe bringing her to Lickwind had been the slow-coming answer to her prayer. Corrie always urged Bertie not to expect answer so fast. Corrie advised that Bertie should think of Abraham, who, after so patiently waiting, received what was promised.

Matty always claimed Bertie to be stubborn. Matty was right. It was time to pray again, and Bertie had something to pray about. Thomas had yet to step into church, although Scotty faithfully reminded him about services.

Scotty wasn't the only one either. Last Saturday morning, Gideon drove Bess and Bertie out to the Two Horse for their first tutoring session. Thomas drove them back, and Bess issued a standing invitation not only to church but to a meal afterward. Thomas didn't say yes, but he also didn't say no.

Bertie knew Bess was impressed with Thomas Hardin. As a team, the two women taught both Anna, Trieu, and even Susan lessons. Susan was an apt student and practically beamed at the thought that she might someday be able to read to the child she now carried. Maybe by that time the Lickwind school would be reopened. For the last week and a half, Walter and Regina took their lessons between meals at the restaurant. The Smit boys hadn't been allowed near Bertie and the family since school disbanded.

It was past time to make some changes. Her first one started weeks ago, when she'd ordered a hat from Mr. Jones. Serving food at the Back Porch gave her a little personal money. Ordering that hat had made giving her father's hat to Anna seem the right thing to do. And last Monday morning, she became the perfect sister. It did Bertie's heart good to watch Bess looking so mystified as Bertie willingly picked up not only her piecework but her clothes from the bedroom floor.

Whistling for Ramon, Bertie started back for the house. Two sharp barks greeted her. The dog burst from the back door of Bess's house and zoomed to Bertie's side. Rhubarb hissed, arched, and headed for a nearby tree.

"Why are you inside on such a beautiful day?" Bertie asked as she managed not to tumble over the excited poodle.

Inside Bess's kitchen, all the sisters gathered around the kitchen table. Matthew gurgled happily in an empty washtub on the floor at Matty's feet. The twins played with sock dolls and engaged in a nonsense conversation.

"We're finally bringing Parson Harris here full-time," Matty announced the moment Bertie came through the door.

"And since we already have a church," Corrie continued, finishing Matty's sentence, "all we need is a parsonage."

"So," Bess added, "we're trying to think of some kind of fund-raiser. Do you have any ideas?"

The sisters, pink-cheeked and excited, all looked at Bertie. She took a step back. It had to be a conspiracy. They wanted something, but advice about a fund-raiser probably wasn't it. They never came to Bertie for advice, although they went to each other for advice about Bertie. She narrowed her eyes and waited.

Bess grinned. "I'd love to do a box social, but with Bertie being the only respectable single female besides Regina, it might be terrifying."

The train's whistle saved Bertie from making the ultimate sacrifice. She'd been about to enter the kitchen and sit down with her sisters as an equal. Once she took that step, there'd be no turning back. She'd be expected to always sit in a buggy instead of astride a horse. She'd be expected to cook and sew willingly!

"Train's here," Bertie said by way of explanation as she bolted out the door. Only four hours overdue, the Union Pacific roared into a town no longer anticipating its arrival. It could not have chosen a better time to arrive.

"You expecting a package?" Linus Hatch winked.

Bertie smiled uncomfortably, although she knew it was too soon for the new hat's arrival.

Hmmm, Linus never used to wink.

She tugged her dress down so it covered the tips of her brown leather boots and pushed a strand of hair behind her ear before taking a deep breath of coal dust and heat. It was a warm September. Just over a year ago, she had disembarked from this very train. Her sisters had clutched clothes and determination and responsibility. Bertie had clutched a hatbox containing Rhubarb and the hope that she could recover what was left of her childhood. Her sisters had somehow known that Lickwind represented security and roots. Bertie knew nothing of the sort. All she wanted was a return to a way of life she barely remembered and to figure out why she never felt like she belonged.

Almost against her will, she thought of the Two Horse Ranch. Thomas's place—where she truly felt she belonged.

But why?

It wasn't like Thomas greeted her with open arms every time she showed up. No, he treated her much the same way he treated his new cowboys: half suspicious that she'd do something to muck things up and half boss telling her what to do.

Lately, he'd acted all stiff and uncomfortable. He almost tripped over himself before driving them back from Anna's tutoring to make sure Bess sat in front beside him.

Bertie grinned. Come to think of it, he was stuttering again, and she sure didn't think it had anything to do with Josiah. She liked to think it had something to do with her. "Yes, I'm expecting a package," she told Linus. "Did it arrive?"

"They've not unloaded the mail yet."

Bertie's first inclination was to take a seat on the step, but she didn't want to get her new pink-striped dress dirty. Matty had only finished sewing it last week. Bess said Bertie should save it for good, but lately every day felt good—just in case Thomas Hardin came to town.

Only one passenger disembarked—an older man with brown, rugged skin and the walk of one who was more at home in a saddle. He wore a hat pressed down over his eyes, as if he didn't want to be recognized.

"Can I help you, sir?" Linus asked.

The cowboy looked at Linus then noticed Bertie. He wearily removed his hat. He had startling blue eyes, familiar eyes, and Bertie thought she'd never seen anybody looking so lost.

Chapter 7

The preacher stood in the front of the room. He spoke the words to the sermon, but his eyes were not as bright as usual. Bertie liked and listened to Parson Harris. She knew him well because he was a friend of Scotty's. Bertie wondered what the man was thinking now that he stood before a crossroad in life. He'd been offered a church of his own, complete with a parsonage: roots, permanence.

It wouldn't be an easy decision. He was a circuit preacher through and through, and Bertie had spoken with him often enough to know how much he relished his time on the trail. Harris formulated his sermons on the back of his horse. He scratched down the words using his saddle as a desk. He rehearsed his sermons using the stars as his trial audience. And now Lickwind offered him—and his family—refuge. His wife accompanied him for the first time. Mrs. Harris wanted her man beside her every night. She worried when he roamed the open range for days on end. She wanted roots. She wanted their two sons to know their papa.

Harris really didn't have a choice, Bertie realized in that moment. The pull of family was a powerful magnet.

Bertie did not turn around to look, although she knew Thomas Hardin sat somewhere behind her. She wasn't surprised. Scotty had told her it would happen and to just wait. She hadn't seen Thomas arrive, but with the way everyone around her craned their necks at the commotion a short time ago, nothing else could have rated such rapt attention. Bertie didn't dare adjust her new hat, or Matty would notice and elbow her. The sisters were already atwitter at the idea of Bertie buying a bonnet at a store!

"Don't tell me what you paid." Matty had blanched.

"All you needed to do was ask," Corrie said, "and Matty would have made whatever you wanted."

Bess shook her head.

But Bertie didn't want a bonnet made out of everyday, already-been-seen material. She wanted one that was hers alone, and half the fun had been anticipating its arrival. It had taken three weeks and two trains for the color she wanted to arrive.

Lately Thomas was spending more time in town than on his ranch. Nightly he took his meals at the restaurant, always at one of Bertie's tables.

His stutter had finally stopped, but she'd welcome it back if it meant he said the words she wanted to hear. He didn't ask Gideon for permission to court. He didn't say I think I love you.

Think? Was there really any thinking involved? Bertie had considered it something of a lark when the men of Lickwind had flocked around her and her sisters. She'd retreated behind her papa's hat and old leather boots and been a spectator in a game that now held her firmly in its clutch.

The game of love. Her sisters had all been winners, and for once Bertie intended to follow their example.

She wanted to smile. She wanted the world to know that Thomas Hardin thought enough of her to come to the restaurant most every night and now, finally, to church.

The sermon looked to be nearing summation. Bertie had listened with one ear and agreed with Parson Harris's premise. It was easier to forgive a stranger than someone you loved. She'd always had trouble forgiving those she loved. She'd not forgiven her parents for dying. She'd not forgiven Adele for marrying a weak-kneed poor excuse for a man. She'd not forgiven herself.

Harris called for a prayer, and all around her heads bowed. Down the pew from her, Bertie noticed the man who'd arrived by train just two days ago. His head was bowed, and Bertie wondered if he knew etiquette called for the removal of his hat.

Bertie bowed her head.

After the amen, Harris called for any sinners to come forward and repent.

The church was a bit stuffy, but nobody was leaving. Even Corrie's babies and Matty's little one seemed to sense that now was not a good time to whimper. Parson Harris came from behind the podium and walked to meet the cowboy from the train, the one with the familiar blue eyes. He walked down the center aisle, reached the front of the church, shook the parson's hand, and turned to face the audience.

"Take off your hat," Bertie silently mouthed, and as if he'd heard her, the old man slowly removed his hat.

Even before she heard his name whispered, she figured out who the man was. This time Bertie did turn around and then stood up, pushing past Bess and Gideon, stepping over the twins and on Corrie in her hurry to get to Thomas.

To say that Thomas looked surprised to see his father at church was an understatement. Such a mixture of shock, denial, and anger crossed his features that Bertie momentarily paused and lost the opportunity to reach him. When she reached the church's exit, Thomas was already on his horse and galloping down the street.

A gentle hand rested on Bertie's shoulder, and Bess whispered, "Give him time."

Thomas Hardin the elder was no longer a typical cowboy. He sat at Bertie's table and passed his sheriff's badge around. Bertie poured him another cup of coffee and tried to imagine him stealing cattle.

The restaurant had no more room, and customers were eating while leaning against the wall. Josiah Temple was conspicuously absent. Even Albert Smit, looking pained, came to hear what Hardin had to say. Bertie didn't think Smit had ever put out money for a meal, not even for baked goods.

Jim and Luke frowned at the badge but listened to Hardin's story while Thomas's cowboys, Rex and Davey, flanked the sheriff as if worried he'd bolt.

Sheriff Hardin had no trouble talking. "I found the Lord, or should I say, He found me? I need to make sure my boy knows the truth. I didn't steal them cattle. I admit, I'm not proud of my behavior in those days. I was young and had more responsibility than I felt I could handle. I took to the liquor a bit more than I needed to. I did make mistakes, and I've laid my guilt at the foot of the cross. But I didn't steal them cattle. I had me a good job and good wages back then."

Jim spoke up, "Then why didn't you protest? Why didn't you say you weren't guilty? I remember the day you were run out of town. You acted guilty."

The sheriff had the grace to look at his feet. "Somebody paid me off. Just a few minutes before the posse arrived, I found a note in my saddlebag along with enough money to give me and my boy a new life—if we left and didn't say anything. I'm ashamed now to say I took it. That money meant the kind of life my late wife had always dreamed of for our son."

"Is that how Tommy got enough money to buy the Kincaid spread?" Amos Freeling asked.

Both Sheriff Hardin and Donald Potter shook their heads.

Rex said, "Tommy hasn't taken a cent from his old man. Not that it's anybody's business, but he's made his money from the railroad and more recently right here in southwest Wyoming, investing money in a very lucrative mine."

"That's right," Sheriff Hardin said. "It didn't take me but a few weeks to realize that in accepting that bribe, I'd paid the ultimate price—my son. He had no reason not to believe I'd become a rustler, and before I realized the importance of telling him the truth, he'd run away. If it weren't for Scotty tracking me down, I'd not know Thomas's whereabouts today. Looks like, in spite of me, my son has made something of himself."

"How many cattle were you accused of rustling, Mr. Hardin?" Frank Llewellyn stood up. He'd just finished a bowl of jackrabbit stew and clutched a spoon in his fist, swinging it like a judge's mallet.

Sheriff Hardin shrugged. "About twenty."

"And," Frank continued, "that was roughly eight years ago. Does anybody know about how much cattle would have been worth back then?"

Jim and Luke looked at each other.

"Depends on the weight of the animals," Jim said.

"And where they were sold," Luke added.

Frank gripped the spoon tightly, deep in thought. "Mr. Hardin, just how much money were you given?"

Sheriff Hardin took a piece of faded leather pouch from his belt. He unfolded it so that a small pile of bills spread across the table. "It's right here. Once Tommy left, I didn't spend no more, and I replaced what I had spent. It's a hundred and fifteen dollars."

"Cattle were fetching good prices back then," Luke remembered.

"Then we can figure you were given the cost of the cattle," Frank said.

"Makes sense now, but that sure didn't occur to me then."

"So, you were paid for stealing the cattle?" Luke asked.

"But I didn't steal the cattle."

"Whose cattle were stolen?" Linus Hatch wanted to know.

"A few head, here and there," Luke said.

"Josiah Temple's," Jim remembered.

Zeus had arrived with the broken surrey; and as of yet, none of the cowboys had been willing to climb on the beast's back. Over fifteen hands and high-strung, the stallion was purchased for breeding purposes, but every animal on the Two Horse needed to pull its load, and it was time for Zeus to be broken. The horse snorted and threw his head in a catch-me-if-you-dare attitude.

The horse's rebellion reminded Thomas of his father. Just how long had the man been in the area? Thomas shook his head. He wanted to blame his father for the mishaps on the ranch. But why? His father had nothing to gain by sabotaging his son. Why come back now?

Thomas stood, one foot perched on the bottom rung of the gate and the other planted firmly in the dirt. He'd been standing thus for over an hour trying to clear his mind, all the while debating the foolishness of breaking Zeus without the help of his men.

It was his fault. He had saddled up this morning bound for church. Rex, blinking away sleep and surprise, had followed, which inspired some of the other cowboys to see just what was going on. Susan and Jack always attended.

His cowboys were still in town with the church crowd. A crowd that hadn't blinked twice when he entered the door. Thomas actually felt welcomed as he took his place on a bench. At the moment, he couldn't figure what inspired him to saddle up this morning carrying the Bible Scotty had given him so many years ago. A Bible that hadn't entered a church since Scotty owned it.

Nothing had gone as planned from the moment Thomas stepped into Lickwind. He'd stuttered in front of Josiah. He'd bent the rules to allow Trieu on his place; and before he could blink an eye, along came Susan. Bad luck plagued the ranch, and the culprit eluded detection. His bank account reflected activity he had no control over. And now his father was in town and going forward in church.

The door to the main house burst open. A small figure in a brown hat came tumbling out and ran toward Thomas.

"Father says," Anna announced regally, "not to even think about climbing on Zeus's back. He says he has his gun, and he'll shoot you in the leg."

Thomas glanced at the house. He could see both Tien-Lu and Trieu staring at him from the window.

"Tell them I won't do anything foolish." Thomas plucked the hat from Anna's head. "Bertie said to wear this when you're doing homework. Why are you wearing it now?"

"I want to wear what Miss Roberta gave to me."

Roberta.

Thomas glanced at Zeus and plopped the hat back on Anna's head. "Go tell your family that I'll not be doing any riding today."

Roberta.

It was all her fault. It began the moment he climbed off the train, encountered Miss Craig, and stuttered in front of Josiah. He half blamed Bertie for the ease of Susan's entrance to his ranch. And, if Thomas were honest, part of the reason he'd not caught those responsible for stealing and destroying his property was because he spent more time thinking about and worrying about Bertie than he did thinking about and worrying about his ranch.

The only thing he couldn't blame on Bertie was the bank activities and his father's arrival. Zeus snorted one last time and pranced over to where Thomas stood. The horse cocked his head as if confused. Thomas stretched out his hand, wanting to touch the beast on the nose, but the horse backed up.

No, Thomas thought, *nothing has gone as planned from the moment I stepped into Lickwind.*

But he'd never been happier, and it all had to do with the presence of Miss Bertie Craig.

What was it Donald had said? The Craig girls had a reputation for setting their sights on a man and turning his life upside-down until he married her.

Married?

Chapter 8

Thomas had been feeling some camaraderie with Frank Llewellyn as they tried to figure out who was depositing money into his account, but he didn't expect that the banker felt the same. Monday morning dawned without interruption; and before Thomas could down his first cup of coffee, he saw the banker arriving at the ranch. Most bankers didn't make house calls, so Thomas figured something important had spurred the man into riding the hour plus it took to get to the Two Horse Ranch. They sat on Thomas's front porch. Tien-Lu poured coffee, and Frank shared the conversation that had taken place back in town at the restaurant. Thomas had heard it already from both Rex and Davey.

"I believe in your father's innocence," Frank said.

"Why? Because he's claiming to be a Christian or because he's now a sheriff?"

Frank took a deep breath. "Those are both sound reasons, but it's these money transactions. The money your father was given sounds close to what the cattle would have brought at market. Whoever is doing this to you did somewhat the same to him. It has to be an original settler. That narrows it down considerably. The Collingswoods, Kincaid, or Albert Smit."

His father had been given money? None of this made sense, not even the banker's interest. "Why are you so interested?"

"Funny how things work out." Frank fiddled with the top button of his coat. "When them Craig girls first arrived, I agreed with the Collingswood brothers. Lickwind was no place for women. But I admit I was wrong. Them women have turned the place into more than a mud street and a few lost souls. The whole town acts like a community now."

"What's on your mind, Llewellyn?"

"When you came to town, I was back East visiting my sister. She's sick. I went home, put things in order, and returned here."

"And?"

"I recently received a telegram. My sister's dying. I can either bring her three children here or I can go there."

"You're going there?"

"Yes. Watching the way those Craig girls stay together has made me realize that I'm all my nieces and nephews have. I'm putting my family first."

Thomas took a sip of coffee and waited.

"I'm thinking about asking Miss Regina to marry me. She's been taking care of me at the restaurant, always makes sure my coffee cup is full. And now that she's my housekeeper, I can see the riches having a woman's touch brings to a home. Lately I've been looking forward to seeing her smile. Plus, the way she always looks out for Walter, no matter the sacrifice, makes me think yesterday morning's service about forgiveness is truer than I ever imagined. If Miss Regina will have me, I'll take her away from here. Start a bank in my hometown and give us all a fresh start."

There was that word again: *forgiveness*. He kept hearing it from Scotty, and last week the preacher in town seemed quite taken with the notion of forgiveness. Thomas needed more time. He'd never admired men who made decisions without thinking them through.

"The way I figure it," Frank continued, "there are only two men in Lickwind who have enough money to purchase the bank."

"Me and Josiah Temple?" Thomas guessed.

"I'm not counting Josiah."

"Then who else?"

"Albert Smit."

"Smit has money? Now that's a surprise," Thomas could not help but muse aloud.

Frank agreed. "He doesn't look or act like he has much, but what that man can do with numbers is amazing. He knows when to sell and when to hold off. He's had money in the bank since it opened. Unfortunately, he's barely literate. Owning a bank wouldn't appeal to him in the least."

"You're friends with Josiah. He'd probably love to own the bank, so why are you sharing this news with me?"

"I've built that bank up from nothing. I'm proud of it. For a town with only one street, we have a bank to equal Philadelphia's. I don't want Josiah near it." Frank leaned forward. "The man owns Margaret's bordello, and it's about to go out of business. He'll run the bank into the ground for his own gain. And," Frank admitted, "truth is, Josiah has very little money. Right now he's land rich and money poor. But he'd find a way to purchase the bank, be it honest or not."

So Josiah owned the bordello. Thomas supposed he should be shocked, but he wasn't. "Fact is, as you well know, you can't stop Josiah from buying it if he can get the money. Law says you have to publicly announce that it's for sale."

"That's true, but—"

A horse and rider came over a nearby crest. Frank squinted, trying to make out the identity. Thomas stood. Donald Potter rode into view.

He reined in his horse, slid off in one fluid motion, and said, "I need to speak with you, Thomas."

"Whatever you have to say, you can say it in front of Llewellyn."

Donald didn't look inclined but went ahead. "You've got trouble, Thomas. Looks like the rustling problem has returned along with your father."

It didn't take long to set up a town meeting in Lickwind, especially when the price of cattle, the state of cattle, or the disappearance of cattle was in question. The town's leaders, except for Josiah Temple, wound up at the Back Porch. Bess, with a I'm-not-in-the-mood-for-nonsense look, told Bertie to stop making moon eyes at Thomas and to start peeling potatoes. All Bertie wanted to do was listen to the men like Bess got to. Distracted, she sliced her finger with the paring knife.

"Oh, Grandmother's bloomers." She stuck the offending digit in her mouth and looked around the kitchen, finally grabbing a clean dish towel and blotting at the blood.

Bess came back, more than a little annoyed. "They're done for tonight."

"I need to know. Is Thomas in trouble? Did his father do something? What's going on?"

"All I know is that some folks out near Cheyenne are missing cattle. Thomas is getting the blame, and now that his father's here, it's not looking good."

Bertie stood. "Thomas has nothing to do with that."

"I believe that. Oh, Bertie, whatever you're up to, I can't help but think it won't work. Thomas Hardin is not a churchgoing man. In all good conscience, I cannot permit you to consort with him."

Bertie moved the potatoes from the table into a pan of water. "I love him."

"You're too young to know about love."

"I'm the same age as Adele was when she married Ellis, and I'm the same age Corrie was when she married Brian."

"Adele was born old, and Corrie was born to be a wife and mother. Besides, Thomas Hardin is not a marrying sort of man."

Bertie closed her eyes, the urge to pray strong. "Bess, you know what this conversation reminds me of?"

"I'm almost afraid to ask."

"It reminds me of how you felt when you realized you were falling in love with Gideon. You had the same doubts about his character, about his walk with the Lord. But somehow you knew the true man—just the way I know my Thomas."

Bess's lips puckered, and tears shimmered in her eyes.

"I love him," Bertie repeated.

Bess stood still, so still that only the rise and fall of her chest proved life. "This is my fault. I should have curbed your actions. It's just," her voice broke, "you remind me so much of Papa, always dreaming, always moving, always so full of energy. I thought I was doing right by you."

"You did do right by me."

It didn't matter. Bess was sitting in a chair with her head in her hands. Bertie started to go to her, but Bess held up a hand. After a moment, Bertie quietly slipped out the back door.

The full moon did a good imitation of a lantern as Bertie walked the few feet to Gideon and Bess's home. She let herself in the front door and headed for her room.

How silly and young she'd been this morning.

She hung the green dress Matty had sewn for her on a peg and put on her nightgown. Huddled in bed, her stomach and mind flip-flopped with reaction to the day's events.

She loved Thomas Hardin.

She had to tell him.

Chapter 9

Thomas Hardin!" The cry, actually loud voices blended into one, sounded too close. Thomas let go of the post he was holding and stared at two frowning Collingswood brothers and one visibly irate Gideon Riker.

"Where's Bertie?" Gideon demanded.

Thomas walked to meet the men, giving a backward look at a barn that should have been finished long ago. He was missing about fifteen head of cattle and in no mood to hear about how he wasn't good enough for Roberta Suzanne Craig.

"She's at home with you," he growled.

"No, she left early this morning!"

Luke rubbed a hand across his face, worry lines running deep. "Bess thought you'd eloped."

"What!" Just when Thomas thought nothing else could surprise him, Bertie managed something.

"Bertie definitely insists that she's in love," Gideon said slowly. "Bess caught on yesterday that it wasn't just Bertie making moon eyes." His eyes narrowed. "I agree."

"W–we haven't t–talked m–marriage." Thomas's throat was closing again. Cattle were missing, his father was nearby, and now Bertie was nowhere to be found. He didn't like this. He didn't like it at all.

"Which way do we head now?" Luke asked.

Soon every man from both the Two Horse and the Rough Cs was out looking for Bertie.

❧

Bertie stood behind a cottonwood tree and watched as Josiah Temple and the outlaw moved Thomas's cattle south. She finally recognized the other man. Not an outlaw really, but he'd scared her and Bess a few months ago when he shot up the town after the railroad drove the last stake in.

One of the calves got his foot stuck between two huge rocks. Josiah got off his horse to dislodge the dogie.

Bertie bowed her head. Never before had she felt so sure that God wanted her to call upon Him. "Oh, Father. I need You beside me right now. I am so frightened. Father, I've acted shamefully, disobeying them, coming out here alone when nobody knows where I am. I need forgiveness. You've always taken care of me and blessed me with a family who loves me, yet I blamed You for my sorrows. Father, forgive me now, and help me know if I'm doing what is right. Please let Thomas find me."

The moment she said "amen," she felt better.

She'd come upon the men hours ago—she'd only wanted to go to Thomas, tell him she believed in him—but she'd never ridden so far out of town alone. She'd gotten lost, turned around, and instead of surprising Thomas, she'd stumbled across the real rustler. She'd started to hurry to the Two Horse but didn't want Josiah to get away.

Bad luck followed the men, otherwise Bertie never would have been able to keep up. First, Josiah's horse threw a shoe. And now one of the cows had its foot firmly wedged between two good-sized rocks.

She was about tuckered out from trying to keep up when another rider joined the men.

The men stopped beside a small stream to rest the horses and talk. Bertie sank gratefully to her knees. Grandmother's bloomers, she never expected anything like this.

Why was Josiah stealing Thomas's cattle? Josiah had tons of money, everyone said. Not that he was a good tipper when Bertie waited on him. He looked different this morning: a little wild and a whole lot scarier.

Bertie crawled to a closer tree so she could see the third man.

At first she didn't believe her eyes. Josiah patted the older man on the shoulder, laughing.

Albert Smit?

Bertie covered her mouth. Why was Mr. Smit with these men?

No, wait a minute.

Even from a distance, Bertie could hear the ominous sound of Josiah laughing as he knocked Albert to the ground.

Ramon chose that moment to find her. He trotted up, nudged her legs, looked toward the scattered cattle, and barked. Josiah's companion started in her direction.

Bertie took a breath. She was winded, but letting them catch her would not save Mr. Smit or Thomas's cattle.

Wishing she still wore her father's comfortable, worn boots instead of these new ankle boots, Bertie turned around and ran right into Thomas's arms.

※

Josiah Temple deserved to be the first man to call the Lickwind jail home. Donald Potter looked like he was enjoying himself as he filled out the paperwork that Sheriff Hardin promised to deliver along with the prisoner.

All last night and early this morning, the townspeople had gathered at the Back Porch and put together the pieces to a mystery that started before Thomas and his father had been run out of town. Albert Smit put his hand on the Bible and swore to tell the truth. "I knew all those years ago that Thomas Hardin wasn't responsible for rustling cattle."

Every resident of Lickwind leaned forward. Little Brianne nodded and banged her hand on the clean floor of the restaurant.

"Josiah gambled away the money his father left him. When we first moved out here, I gave him a sizable loan and tried to advise him, but things weren't moving fast enough for him. He started rustling so he could buy more land. At first I didn't know it was him; and by the time I figured it out, he'd already made it look like Hardin was not only guilty but also rustling from the real crook."

Jim paced the floor and asked, "And why didn't you step forward then?"

Albert hung his head. "He's my brother-in-law. My deceased wife's only brother. I promised her I'd watch out for him, only I've not done too good a job."

Thomas leaned over and whispered in Bertie's ear. "Jim and Luke might very well be the only two men who knew that Albert and Josiah were distantly related. They don't like each other much. Albert didn't even allow his boys to call Josiah their uncle. Yet every time Josiah messed up, Albert tried to fix it. He knew Scotty would keep the men from stringing up my father, and so Albert made sure we had enough money to start over. When I first got here, Albert made no secret of the fact he wanted me gone. He was doing more of the same when he made a fuss about Anna being in school. I figured he was cut out of Josiah's cloth. Turns out he knew I'd spur Josiah into thinking it was safe to rustle again now that there was somebody to blame. Albert's a good man in his own way. Every time Josiah destroyed something belonging to the Two Horse, Albert tried to make up for it by depositing his own money into my account."

"Poor Mr. Smit," Bertie whispered. "Imagine carrying all this on his conscience."

Thomas nodded and looked at his father seated next to him. The two men had started mending the broken fences of their past. Sheriff Hardin waited to escort Josiah on the next train. Rustling was often called a hanging offense, but not in a town where the Craig girls had any say. Plus, Scotty had already made his opinion known. Look at the good that had come from not hanging Sheriff Hardin.

Bertie looked around to see if Bess was looking. Bess and Gideon had not yet given Thomas permission to come calling. Yes, they acknowledged that Thomas had agreed to study the Bible with his father, but that didn't mean anything until he accepted the Lord.

Bertie grinned at the thought of Thomas studying the Bible with his father. After this trial, Sheriff Hardin intended to turn Josiah and his partner over to the proper authorities; then Sheriff Hardin would return to Lickwind. After all, the town already had a jail. It surely needed a sheriff. And a father needed a second chance with his son.

It took hours, but finally all the questions were answered. Bertie left the proceedings and hurried to the restaurant. Seemed a trial was good for business. She quietly tied on her apron. Gazing out the open window of the kitchen, she could see a section of the Union Pacific train track. How much her life had changed since that long-ago day when the Craig girls arrived in Lickwind.

Jim came through the kitchen door chuckling.

"What's so funny?" Bertie asked.

"Your young man," Jim announced.

Bertie couldn't help but smile. She liked the sound of that. Her young man. "Well, are you going to tell me what's so funny?"

"He just offered me a buck-fifty for you. Seemed to think that was necessary." Jim put a hand on her shoulder and said softly, "If that young man of yours ever gives his heart to the Lord, and if you're both ready, I just might take that money."

Before Bertie could respond, Jim disappeared through the door, and Thomas took his place.

A place he'd stay forever—in her heart.

For true.

Epilogue

June 1874

A milling crowd of youngsters slowly sorted itself out around the eight adults assembled in front of the photographer in the parlor of the Rough Cs.

Bertie tugged her renegade daughter closer to her, wiping at the dirt-smudged face. A full inch of lace hung from the four-year-old's hem. "Laura Hardin, look at you!"

Thomas watched the pair, an indulgent grin on his face. Not long after he made peace with his father, he'd also made peace with his heavenly Father. He'd carried that spiritual contentment into his marriage to Bertie. "I'm sure your mother never looked like that," he informed three-year-old Robert, standing proudly beside him.

"Oh, I couldn't count the times." Bess Riker sighed.

In front of her, three-year-old Kate Riker pulled on her four-year-old brother Stanley's arm. "Stand up stwaight," she ordered.

Bess and Gideon exchanged laughing glances. "Someone else is just like her mother," Gideon teased. Bess only smiled and looked content.

Her husband slipped his arm around her. "Quite an honor, having our pictures taken with Lickwind's next mayor."

"I haven't won the election yet," she reminded him.

"You will."

Seated on a nearby chair, Corrie Collingswood pulled squirmy one-year-old Daniel onto her lap to hide the bulge of her fifth child on the way. Beside her, Luke stood proudly with three-year-old Mark on his arm and the five-year-olds, Brianne and Madeline, in front of him. The growing family still lived in the ranch house, which had been expanded twice in the past five years to accommodate both Collingswood clans.

Matty waded through the knot of children as Jim called, "Kids, hurry."

Five-year-old Matthew stood on Matty's left; Bess arranged two-year-old Jamie on Matty's lap; and Jim grabbed almost-four-year-old Corliss away from Corrie's twins.

As soon as the photograph was done, Matty tugged urgently on Luke's sleeve. After a pause, during which she bit her lip as though holding back a cry, she said,

"Did you take care of things?"

Luke shot Jim a repentant grin. "Ahh, big brother, you might want to tote your wife upstairs. I sent Scotty for Doc Wilson."

"Why?" Realization dawned, and Jim's hazel eyes widened. "Today?"

"Now, sweetheart." Matty winced and rubbed her big tummy as Jim took the stairs two at a time with his wife in his arms.

Bess dashed past them, and Corrie followed as quickly as her girth would allow.

Matty had one more request before her husband deposited her on the bed and permitted her sisters to take over her care. "Tell Bertie to make the photographer stay. I won't be long, and I want pictures of these twins who are about to make their appearance."

Downstairs in the parlor, Madeline requested, "Auntie Bertie, tell us again about the big mistake that made you brides."

"It wasn't really a mistake, honey," Jim called as he returned downstairs to await the newest arrivals. "It was the beginning of countless blessings."

Butter Buds

1 cup butter
1 cup brown sugar
2 eggs, beaten
2 teaspoons vanilla
2½ cups flour
1 teaspoon baking powder
¼ teaspoon salt

Cream butter and brown sugar. Add eggs and vanilla. Sift in dry ingredients and mix until soft dough forms. Pinch off pieces. Roll in hands; then press down with form. Bake in 350–375 degree oven.

Pamela Kaye Tracy decided to be an author in second grade. When she grew up, God also put her in charge of a third-grade classroom (by day) and added a college reading class (by night). When not teaching, Pamela spends her time writing, sewing, reading, and staying active at her church. She makes her home in Arizona.

A VOW UNBROKEN

by Amy Rognlie

Prologue

Abby Cantrell stared at the date at the top of the letter, her eyes widening. April 29, 1881. Why hadn't Aunt Caroline told her it would be so soon? Dropping down into the chair, she smoothed the crisp paper, reading again the telltale words.

Dear Miss Peters,

I can't tell you how happy I was to receive your letter this past week. I trust that you, as do I, look forward to the approaching day when we shall meet here in Littleton. Enclosed is the train ticket, as well as a little extra money in case you have need of something. I will be waiting for you on the appointed day. Until then, I remain yours truly,

James Parrish

Abby jumped as footsteps sounded in the tiled hallway. Slipping the letter back into the Bible where she had found it, she stood and ambled over to the library window. The fading sunset cast shadows on the budding trees, holding her gaze until she heard the footsteps behind her, their sound muffled by the plush carpet.

"Beautiful evening."

The softly spoken words invaded the tumult in Abby's mind. She sighed, turning slightly to drape her arm over the shoulders of the small woman beside her. The comforting scent of roses embraced her. "What am I going to do, Mama?"

Hazel Peters smoothed her daughter's dark hair. "I don't know, dear. Surely God has a plan. . . ." She fell silent as Abby turned away to gaze out of the lace-framed window. The silence stretched, broken only by the sound of the mourning doves getting ready to roost. "But I do know this," Hazel whispered. "He said He would not give us more than we could bear."

Abby eyed the darkening sky. Her mind acknowledged the truth of her mother's words, but her heart felt the shadows of night moving slowly and surely, threatening to plunge her into a darkness unlike any she had ever known.

Chapter 1

James Parrish gripped his cap tightly at the sound of a distant train whistle. He scarcely noticed the porters checking the luggage or the scampering children. His concentration focused on the tiny, moving speck in the distance. Perspiration prickled at the nape of his neck.

Would she be on the train, as she had promised? He had waited so long, had pored over her letter, had dreamed of what she would look like. *Miss Caroline Peters.* He liked the sound of it as he rolled it around in his mind. He stared at the train, now close enough for him to read the letters on the side. The DENVER RIO GRAND RAILWAY. He peered anxiously at the windows, straining to see as the train squealed to a stop. Was she finally here?

He watched the passengers as they disembarked. Most were Denverites coming to Littleton for a day in the country. He kneaded his cap, his eyes locked on the straggling line of people. There. Was that her? His heart leaped as he spied a dark-haired woman coming toward him, a welcoming smile on her lovely face. She had almost reached him when an older gentleman brushed past him and grasped her arm.

James exhaled forcefully and turned his attention back to those still struggling down the narrow steps, their valises bumping their sides. He wished that he had a more detailed description, but the brief one she had sent him would have to do. He would find her if it was the last thing. . .wait. There. That had to be her. One of the last passengers to come down the steps, she paused at the platform as if unsure of herself. He watched her glance about, the fetching pink feather in her hat softly dancing, her arms full. He couldn't see her face very well until her gaze fell on him.

The woman smiled tentatively, and he started toward her as if in a dream, his gaze locked with hers. Finally, he stood in front of her. Her hazel eyes reminded him of the first greening of spring. She was beautiful. And so small. She barely came up to his shoulder. . . .

"Mr. Parrish?" At her softly spoken words, James realized that he had been staring.

"Yes, I'm Mr. Parrish." He winced at how stiff and formal he sounded. He had wanted to greet her warmly. Welcoming. But meeting this way was just so awkward.

"I'm glad to finally be here. And to make your acquaintance," she said.

Her voice sounded weary, and as James continued to study her face, he noted the purple shadows under those beautiful eyes. Her journey had been a long one, he realized. But did her eyes reflect more than weariness? Sorrow, perhaps?

He watched her out of the corner of his eye as he collected her trunk. She was so beautiful; he could scarcely believe it. Of course, he had made up his mind that he would love his new bride, no matter what she looked like. Yet the Lord had chosen to bless him with a beauty of a wife. He smiled at her tenderly then offered his hand to help her into the wagon. For the first time, he found himself wishing he had a nice carriage. Still, she knew he was a farmer. Surely she hadn't expected anything fancy.

He watched her gather her skirts to climb into the wagon. As she leaned into his grip to hoist herself up, her foot slipped. Instinctively, he caught her as she fell backward, catching a whiff of her perfume as well. He set her carefully on her feet, his heart pounding at her nearness. He wanted to hold her in his arms and never let her go.

She stammered out an apology, bending laboriously to retrieve her shawl from the dusty street. Straightening up, she met his shocked gaze. She was with child!

Dear God, what kind of cruel trick has this woman played on me? He gaped at her in silence. *How could she?*

Vulnerability briefly shimmered in her eyes before a glaze of weary resignation replaced it. "I suppose she didn't tell you."

"Who?" he croaked.

She raised her eyebrows.

"Who didn't tell me what?" He swallowed against the sudden dryness in his throat, trying to gather his thoughts and steel himself for whatever explanation she would offer.

"My. . .aunt. . .Caroline. . ." Her shoulders drooped and tears filled her eyes, threatening to spill over.

James reached out to her instinctively, as he would to a forlorn child. He put his hand under her chin, marveling at how soft her skin was against the roughness of his own. "It's all right," he whispered. "Can you just explain. . . ? I mean. . .I. . . don't understand."

She swallowed hard but didn't pull away from his touch. "My aunt Caroline. She didn't tell you that I was in the family way." Her words formed a statement rather than a question.

Silence settled between them as James struggled to comprehend her words. Why had Caroline's pregnant niece come, and not Caroline? Were they trying to trick him? If so, why? Was this all a big joke on him—the dumb farmer out in cow country? The heat began to rise in his face. How could he have been so idealistic— so hopefully stupid—to believe that he would finally have a wife?

He glanced back down at her, his mental tirade ceasing when he met the misery in her eyes.

"I'm so sorry," she whispered. "She said she didn't think you'd mind if I came in her place. She. . . I should have known she wouldn't have told you. But I can still work. I'll do anything you need me to do. I don't know how to do anything on a farm, but I can cook and clean, and. . ."

Her words trailed off as he scrutinized her. He couldn't believe someone so small could carry such a large child. He doubted she'd be doing much cooking and cleaning for quite a while. He shook his head in disbelief at this bewildering situation. "If you are not Miss Caroline, then I suppose I don't even know your name."

"Abigail Cantrell." She gave him a faint smile. "Most people call me Abby."

What else should he say? "Well, Abby. . ."

Her face clouded. "I guess I'm just not what you were expecting, Mr. Parrish. I'm so sorry. . . ."

He made an effort to grin but failed. "Can I ask you. . .why Caroline didn't come?" Did she decide that life on a farm would be too dull, so she sent her niece instead?

Abby looked pained. "It's a long story, Mr. Parrish. However, I assure your arrangement wouldn't have worked out anyway. Caroline is. . .would not be suited for the work."

Why does she keep talking about all the hard work? Sure, it is work to be a farmer's wife, but that's not the reason I searched for a wife. Only God knows how long I've yearned for a companion, someone to share life's sorrows and joys. James cleared his throat, hoping for some inspiration to seize him. What was he supposed to do with a pregnant woman? He couldn't very well marry her now, could he? But what else. . . ?

"Might there be somewhere I could get a drink of water?" she asked.

Abby's soft voice pulled his attention back to her. The look of utter exhaustion on her face smote his heart with regret. How long had he kept her standing outside in the blazing sun, and in her condition? "Forgive me," he said, giving her his hand.

She sighed with relief as she sank down onto the wagon seat, closing her eyes as if she would fall asleep right there. James clucked to the horses then glanced at her in concern. "Are you all right, ma'am?"

Guiltily, her eyes popped open. "I didn't sleep very well on the train, I guess." She gazed at him. "How far do you live from town?"

James swallowed hard, feeling slightly addled. *Surely she doesn't think I am going to marry her!* "Uh, not too far. I hadn't planned on us going home until tomorrow. . . but I guess. . ."

She bit her lip, obviously sensing his turmoil. "It's all right, Mr. Parrish. I should have known. . . ." She straightened her shoulders. "I don't want you to feel beholden to me. If you'll just let me off at a boardinghouse, I'm sure I can find some other work."

He gaped at her. What kind of man did she think he was? True, she didn't know a thing about him. But surely she didn't think that he would just dump her in a strange town. He was responsible for bringing her here, wasn't he? "I can't do that, ma'am," he said softly. "I'm sure we can work something out."

The relief in her eyes spoke volumes. After all, what kind of "work" could she find in her condition? The thought made him cringe.

"I'm a good cook," she offered timidly.

He smiled then, his first real smile since this peculiar situation began. "Well, I like to eat. So I guess we're off to a good start." *But what do I do now?* He glanced at her small, glove-covered hands clasped demurely in her lap. Or what was left of her lap.

"When is. . . ? I mean how long until. . . ?" He felt his face redden at his clumsy questioning.

"The child will be born in about six weeks, Mr. Parrish." She didn't smile, but he thought he detected a glint of humor in her large eyes.

"Ah, I see. Well. . .I. . . ." *Dear Lord, help me*, he pleaded silently. *I'm in over my head, and I don't know what to do.*

The voice in his heart replied, *Show her the way to Me.*

James swallowed hard then made up his mind. "Ma'am, I know that you're very tired. I'm going to take you to the boardinghouse, and we can talk more in the morning."

"Thank you," she said, giving him a small smile.

They drove the rest of the short distance in silence. James pulled up in front of his sister's house, jumping off the wagon seat as soon as the horses came to a halt. Abby was looking paler by the minute. Lifting her gingerly down from the wagon, he escorted her to Iris's door. "Hope you got a room ready, sis," he hollered in through the screen door.

Iris came running, her eyes widening as she took in the couple standing on her porch. Her gaze flew to James's face. He frowned slightly and shook his head, and she nodded, turning her attention to Abby. "You look worn-out, dear. Come in and let me fix you a cup of tea."

James silently blessed his sister for not questioning him. He released Abby into her care with a sigh of relief. "Miss. . .uh, ma'am, this is my sister Iris." He pasted a smile on his face. "I'll be back in the morning, ladies." Turning, he strode back to the wagon as fast as he could without actually running. What kind of a mess had he gotten himself into?

Chapter 2

A bby stared after him for a long moment, wondering what was going through his mind. He had seemed to be such a gentleman, although she was obviously not what he had expected. What in the world had Caroline told the poor man?

He was a lot younger than Abby had expected. *Yes, quite a bit younger,* she mused. *And handsome, too. With hair the color of sun-kissed wheat, eyes—*

"Come on in, dear," Iris repeated, breaking into Abby's wandering thoughts. "I guess James forgot to tell me your name."

Abby looked up to find Iris's brilliant eyes, eyes the same bright blue as her brother's, fastened on her face. "Abby Cantrell. I'm so sorry. . . ."

"Nonsense." Iris gave an unladylike snort, accompanied by a friendly grin. "You're tired from your long trip, and James brought you here so you could rest. That's no reason to be sorry."

Abby sighed as she slogged into the house after Iris, feeling as if she might collapse if she remained on her feet much longer.

"Now, you just sit down here and put your feet up on this stool," Iris commanded. "I'll bring you a cup of tea."

Abby obeyed, her heart warming at the genuine friendliness of the woman.

Iris reappeared with two steaming cups. Handing one to Abby, she settled herself comfortably on a floral tapestry settee. "Now, tell me all about yourself, Abby."

❧

James clenched his teeth against the jarring of the wagon as it bumped over the dirt road. How could the day's events have taken such an unexpected turn? He sighed as he pulled up in front of the farmhouse. He should have been bringing a bride home. But instead of a bride, he had a problem. A big one.

He did his chores mechanically then sank down in his favorite rocker in front of the hearth. Since she—no, since Caroline—answered his newspaper advertisement, he had dreamed of his bride sitting next to him in this very room, sharing treasured moments from the day, just being together. Now that's all it was—a dream.

God, I thought you were leading me. I thought I was doing Your will. He pictured Abby's face. She was all he had hoped for in a wife. Even in the short time he was with her, he could sense her gentle spirit. And she was beautiful, too, of course.

362

But what of the child? He wished he'd had the presence of mind to ask her more questions. How could she possibly even think that he would marry her? It wasn't just the fact that she was carrying a child, but that he felt somehow deceived. Had it been their plan all along? Was she running from some sort of trouble? *Maybe her family sent her away when they learned the shameful truth of what she had done—or had done to her*, he thought.

He felt his head begin to throb. What did she want from him? A sudden horrifying thought came to him. What if there really was no Aunt Caroline, and what if Abby was already married? Maybe she was running away from her husband. He had heard of such things happening. But then. . .he thought again of the wounded look in her expressive eyes, her shy smile, the way she carried herself with womanly dignity, and he couldn't believe anything sordid about her.

"Well, Lord, I guess You will have to show me what to do with this young lady," he said aloud. "All I know is, I prayed long and fervently for a wife. . .and Abby Cantrell is the one that arrived on the train." He picked up his well-worn Bible from the hearth. "If she's the one You sent me, I need to know."

"Lean not unto thine own understanding. In all thy ways acknowledge him, and he shall direct thy paths." The oft-read verse from Proverbs jumped out at him. He closed his eyes, remembering the still, small voice that had spoken earlier.

Show her the way to Me. Show her the way to Me.

After a long while, James rose and went to bed. Tomorrow should prove to be a day he would remember for years to come—his wedding day.

❧

His heart began a slow thump when he saw her sitting on Iris's porch steps, the morning sun glinting off her dark, shiny hair. She smiled at him, and he couldn't seem to remember anything he had planned to say.

He swiped his hat off as he neared the porch. "Good morning, ma'am. Did you sleep well?"

She nodded. "Yes, thank you."

He gestured to the step. "May I?" At her nod, he seated himself next to her, immediately assailed with her scent that he remembered vividly from yesterday, from that brief intoxicating moment he had held her in his arms. She smelled like a sun-drenched field of wildflowers. He scooted a little farther away, trying to regain his train of thought. "I, uh, thought we'd better discuss a few things," he said, feeling like an awkward schoolboy.

She darted an amused glance at him. "I'm not going to bite you, Mr. Parrish."

He grinned sheepishly, fascinated with the way her hazel eyes were smiling at him. "I've decided that we can still get married," he blurted.

Her mouth dropped open. "M—married?"

What is going on here? Surely she—

"Isn't that why you came here?" he asked cautiously.

She stared at him wordlessly for a long minute. "I. . .no. I did not come here to get married. Caroline told me. . ." Her voice trailed off, and her gaze turned compassionate. "That's why you were so disappointed when you saw me."

Disappointed? That wasn't the word I would have chosen.

"No, no," he said hastily. "Not disappointed. Just. . .surprised."

She didn't look convinced.

"I just never imagined—" He stopped as he noticed her lips beginning to twitch. Was she. . .laughing? He smiled into her eyes, a chuckle working its way up to his throat. "I guess it is kind of funny," he said.

She glanced back down at her protruding belly, but not before a soft giggle escaped. "Forgive me. It's just that—" She giggled again, and this time he laughed with her. Soon they were shaking with laughter, tears running down their faces.

He finally caught his breath. "Perhaps we should introduce ourselves all over again," he suggested.

She dabbed at her eyes with a lacy handkerchief. "All right." Her eyes still danced with laughter as she gave him her hand. "I'm Abigail Cantrell, your new housekeeper."

He bowed over her hand then captured her gaze with his. "Pleased to meet you, Abigail Cantrell. I am James Parrish, your future husband."

The light in her eyes dimmed, and he felt her small hand tremble beneath his. "I'm not so sure that's such a good idea, Mr. Parrish. You see, I'm not a free woman."

She felt him start. "I wasn't going to tell you all this, but I guess I owe it to you." She gently withdrew her hand from his. "I suppose you'll put me back on the train once you hear my story." It had taken all the courage she possessed just to leave home and all she had known to come west. And now—

He shook his head. "I don't think so."

She moved restlessly, feeling the weight of the babe in her womb and the still greater weight of her guilt bearing down on her. Why, oh why had she gone against Papa so willfully? Then none of this would have happened. She would still be enjoying the peaceful life she had always known.

She finally remembered the silent man sitting next to her, and she turned to gaze at him. Why couldn't she have met someone like James before—? She noticed the tiny laugh lines around his eyes and the gentle peace written there, drawing her like a magnet. Something deep within her reached out to him, as it had from the first moment they had met.

He watched her quietly as she studied him, and suddenly she knew that she could trust him with her life. "I'm not sure where to begin," she said, searching his blue eyes again just to make sure. "I guess I should tell you that I'm widowed."

He nodded, an unreadable expression on his face.

"My husband died six months ago." Her flat, emotionless voice matched her feelings. "We were just suspecting my condition at the time of his death." Shifting her weight, Abby tried unsuccessfully to find a comfortable position on the hard porch step.

"But if the truth be told, I don't regret the fact that Charles never knew about our child. You see, when my husband died, I learned that he wasn't the man I thought he was. . . ."

James frowned. "I'm afraid I don't understand."

She smiled ruefully. "I'm not sure I do, either, Mr. Parrish. And I'm not sure I'm up to explaining it all to you now. Perhaps some other day. But, suffice to say, my husband. . ." She stumbled over the word then began again. "My husband was involved in something. . .unlawful."

"And so?"

Abby raised her eyebrows, wondering why he hadn't made the obvious connection. How could she make it plainer? "My husband committed some crimes. Then he died. Someone has to pay for what he did."

He frowned again. "Pardon me for saying so, ma'am, but as much as I know about the law, I don't think that a widow is expected to be punished for her husband's crimes."

"Oh no. Not the law." She took a deep breath. "It's God that I'm concerned about."

"God? But God doesn't require—"

"I, too, did some things that I regret. And so I made a vow to God, Mr. Parrish, the day that Charles died. It cannot be broken." She could see the shock written on his face, but she plunged ahead, wanting to get it over with. "I will not allow someone else to be hurt because of my sins." It sounded so stark, so melodramatic. But it was the truth.

"And the vow was?" His voice was grave, his gaze unwavering.

The question reverberated in the quiet morning air, a cricket chirping under the porch the only sound for a long minute.

She closed her eyes briefly then opened them to look directly into his. "I have vowed that I will never love anyone again."

❦

James took in the earnestness of her sweet face, and his heart ached for her. How had she missed the fact that love is the very essence of God? How could she think that a loving God would want her to live life without love?

He gently reached for her hand, holding it firmly between both of his. "Abby, I would be honored if you would accept my hand in marriage."

She stared at him as if he had suddenly gone daft. "But I just told you—"

"You didn't promise God that you would never let anyone love you, did you?"

She dropped her gaze, but not before he saw the blush that colored her smooth cheeks. "No," she whispered.

"Then there's no problem. You need someone to love and care for you and your child." He smiled. "And I've been praying that God would send me a wife who I could love forever."

She met his gaze for an instant before staring down at her swollen belly again. "But I wouldn't be your wife. . .really."

He felt the back of his neck grow hot at the thought of it. He couldn't deny that he wanted her to be his wife in the fullest sense of the word, but until she was ready for that. . . "Look at me, Abby," he commanded gently.

He waited until she lifted uncertain eyes to his. "I promise you that I will take care of you and your baby to the best of my ability. I will honor you, and I promise you that I will never take advantage of you."

She swallowed hard. "Why?"

Why? Because I love you already, he thought, wishing he could take her in his arms and show her. "Because I asked God for a wife and He sent you, Abby."

"I don't deserve someone like you."

Her words were whispered, but the force of them nearly took his breath away.

God, please shine your grace on Abby, he prayed silently. *She's like a lost little girl.* "We all deserve to be loved, Abby."

"Are you sure?" A tiny spark of hope glinted in her eyes. "A lifetime is a long time, you know."

Long enough to convince you of my love. And long enough for you to return my love. He squeezed her hand. "I'm sure."

She gave him a small smile. "I hope you like my cooking."

❧

An hour later, they stood in front of the justice of the peace. Iris had picked a huge bouquet of wildflowers, and Abby held them tightly now in her shaking hands. James stood beside her, his hand warm on the small of her back. "Just a few more minutes, Abby. Then we can go home," he whispered in her ear. She looked like she was about ready to keel over in exhaustion. Yet to James, she was the most beautiful bride he had ever seen. A shaft of late afternoon sunlight found its way into the dim parlor, illuminating her delicate face. Though some might say he was getting a bad deal, he confidently believed that this woman would hold his heart for eternity.

Chapter 3

W ell, this is the old homestead," James said.

Abby allowed him to help her down from the wagon then gazed at the farmhouse appreciatively. It wasn't very big, but the place looked tidy and snug. Newly whitewashed and the wide front porch swept clean, her new home was a welcoming sight. She smiled up at him. "It's very nice, James." It still felt awkward to call him James instead of Mr. Parrish, but he was her husband, after all.

Could it have been only yesterday that she had arrived on the train from New York? Now, here she was—a newlywed. She still felt slightly stunned at the events of the last few hours. Yet somehow, she was at peace.

It wouldn't be hard to live with James, she decided, watching as he hefted her trunk out of the back of the wagon. She had never met a more caring, gentle man. Before she could pull her satchel from the wagon seat, James took the bag then led her down the well-worn path toward the house. In pleasant surprise, Abby stopped by the front porch. The sweet-spicy fragrance of a beautiful pink rose in full bloom enchanted her.

"Do you like roses?"

James's low voice broke into her thoughts as she bent slightly to sniff a large blossom.

"This is exquisite." She glanced up at him then swept the arid landscape with questioning eyes. "Wherever did you get a rosebush way out here?"

He shrugged. "I have friends who just made a trip back East. Had them bring it back for me." He smiled down at her. "I thought my new wife might like something pretty to welcome her."

Her eyes widened. What a thoughtful man! "How very kind. . . . I don't know what to—" Her sentence ended in a shriek as something cold and wet pressed into her hand. She whirled around, her heart pounding as she came nose to nose with the largest dog she had ever seen. She backed up a step, her legs shaking.

Where had the dreadful creature come from? She cast a pleading glance at James. "Can you get it away from me?"

He chuckled, reaching for the dog's collar. "Sit, Frank," he commanded.

Abby sighed in relief, sinking down onto the porch steps. "Is that yours?" she asked.

James grinned. "Now, that's no way to talk about a family member, Abby," he drawled. "This is Frank. He's quite a feller."

"I'll say." Abby eyed the panting animal distrustfully. "So, he's a male dog?"

"Yep."

She swallowed hard, almost afraid to ask. "Does it. . .live in the house?"

James appeared to be trying not to laugh. "No. Frank is a farm dog." He scratched the dog's floppy ears. "Though he does sneak in at night every once in a while when it's cold out."

"Oh." Abby peered at the dog again. Was he smirking at her? She didn't like the look in his eye. "I haven't been around dogs very much," she said.

"I kind of figured that." James plunked down next to her on the step. "But Frank won't hurt you. He likes you. See, just let him sniff your hand, like this." He reached out a hand, which Frank obligingly covered with dog kisses.

Be brave, Abby, she told herself. She reached her hand out toward the dog, stopping midway. "Why is it thumping its tail?" she whispered to James nervously. Maybe dogs thumped their tails right before they pounced on their prey.

James sighed, but she could still see the laughter in his eyes. "Frank is a he, not an it. And he's thumping his tail because he's happy."

"Oh." Abby folded her hands safely under her watermelon-sized stomach. "I'm very pleased to meet you, Frank," she said. "I'm sure we'll be friends," she added, fervently hoping that it would be so.

She glanced up at James, frowning. Why was the man making such strange noises?

The look on her face must have been the last straw, because his suppressed chuckles suddenly broke into hearty laughter.

"What is so funny?" she demanded. "All I said was—"

"I know!" James grinned. "I've just never heard such a polite speech to a dog!" He chuckled again. "I like you, Abby," he said, taking her hand.

She smiled back at him, her heart warming at his sincerity. "I like you, too, James," she said.

Frank gave a hearty woof, and Abby jumped. She would have to get used to the creature, she supposed.

James pulled her to her feet, keeping her hand in his. "Come on, Mrs. Parrish. I'll show you through your new home."

It didn't take long for Abby to get settled. She hadn't brought many things with her, since she had thought she was coming to be a hired housekeeper. A few dresses, her Bible, and a few items she had sewn for the baby.

James sat watching her one night as she hemmed yet another tiny garment. "Is it a boy or a girl?" he asked.

She glanced up at him. "Only the good Lord knows that," she said. "But I like to think that my baby is a girl." She studied his face in the flickering light of the fire. "Why do you ask?"

He shrugged. "Just curious, I guess."

She smiled then turned her attention back to the soft white material.

He settled back in his rocker, watching her. She seemed happy enough, he thought, noticing the adorable way she held her lips in a slight pucker while she worked. He had memorized every line of her lovely face in the past few weeks, often watching her when she was unaware.

They had fallen into a comfortable routine. He would spend the days out in the wheat fields, while she tended the house and garden. She hadn't been exaggerating when she said she was a good cook. It was comforting to know that when he finished with his chores, she would be waiting for him with a smile and a delicious meal.

Yet she had withdrawn from him since their wedding day. He had given her his bed, while he slept on a bedroll in front of the fire. She had seemed distressed that he had to sleep on the floor, he remembered with a smile. With such a kind and gentle spirit about her, how could anyone help but love her?

His eyes roamed to her stomach, and he watched in amusement as it moved with the baby's antics. He wondered if Abby was afraid. He had heard so many terrible stories about the travails of childbirth. Even his own mama. . . . He sighed. They would simply have to face any problems should they come and trust the Lord to protect Abby when her time of delivery arrived. Stewing about tomorrow's problems would do no good.

In the meantime, he wanted to get to know Abby a little better. She seemed so remote since that first day when they had talked and laughed so easily. Oh, she was friendly, but aloof. Distant. He had hoped that at least they could be friends, even if they couldn't be lovers. He sighed again. Maybe he had been dreaming to think that this marriage, a marriage in name only, could really work.

Father, I was so sure I heard Your voice that day, he prayed inwardly. *Please show me what to do. I want to love Abby and care for her, but I feel like she regrets marrying me.*

Show her the way to Me. The still small voice echoed in his heart, reminding him of the first day they had met. Wasn't that what God had told him that first day? But how could he accomplish the task?

He glanced over at her bowed head. Her dark hair glinted in the light of the oil lamp beside her.

"Abby."

She looked up, her hands resting on her stomach. "Did you need something?"

Yes, I need you, he thought, his heart suddenly pounding. What he wouldn't give right now to have the right to take her in his arms. However, he must be patient. "I was wondering if you would like to have a time of prayer together in the evenings."

She looked surprised, and his heart sank. "I'd like that very much, James," she said quietly.

"You would?"

She nodded. "My mama and my sisters and I used to pray together every night. I've missed that since Charles and I. . .since. . .for a long time," she finished quickly.

One of these days he would ask her to tell him the whole story, James decided. But not right now. Reaching for his Bible, he laid it on his knees. "Would you like me to read anything in particular?"

She thought for a moment, her head tilted to one side. "I guess my favorite has always been the psalms," she said. "Maybe Psalm 91?"

"That's one of my favorites, too," he said, smiling into her eyes. In fact, he could have recited it from memory, but he lowered his gaze to the page, deciding it would be safer to read than to lose himself in her large, hazel eyes.

" 'He that dwelleth in the secret place of the most High shall abide under the shadow of the Almighty. I will say of the Lord. . . .' " Before he was halfway through, he heard her reciting it softly with him. Closing the Bible with a soft thud, he laid it back down on the hearth then scooted his chair closer to hers. He reached for her hand, gently kissing her work-roughened fingertips before enfolding them in his grasp.

"Father God, Abby and I come before you tonight as your humble children. Lord, You have searched us and known us. You know our downsitting and our uprising and are acquainted with all our ways. There is not a word in our tongue, but Thou knowest it altogether. Thou hast beset us behind and before and laid Thine hand upon us. Such knowledge is too wonderful for us. It is high, and we cannot attain unto it. For where shall we go from Your presence? Where can we flee from Your Spirit? Even if we take the wings of the morning and dwell in the uttermost part of the sea, even there shall You be. When we awake, we are still with Thee. Thank You, Father God, that by Your Holy Spirit, You are present with us always. Please teach me how to be a good husband to Abby, Father. Bless her and the child abundantly. We thank You, Father. In Jesus' name, amen."

He raised his head, his heart too full for words, and saw the same written on his wife's face. And his soul rejoiced within him.

Chapter 4

A bby lay in bed, feeling her spirit moving within her as much as the child who kicked in her womb. She had never heard anyone pray like James had prayed tonight. Of course she recognized that he had borrowed a portion of his prayer from Psalm 139. Yet the way that he had prayed, with such assurance and fervor, amazed her. It had been so long since she had allowed herself to think of God as anything other than a tyrant. What used to be second nature now seemed unreal.

James was such a good person. She could tell from that very first day that she would face a constant battle to keep her vow. How easy it would be to love James and let him love her. She couldn't help but notice the way his eyes followed her around the kitchen. And he always remembered to thank her for the meals she prepared.

"Mmph!" The baby gave a hard kick, and Abby grimaced. It was getting harder and harder to find a comfortable sleeping position. She rolled over on her side, trying to concentrate on the soothing smell of lavender that wafted from the fat bouquets she had hung in the attic to dry.

The fire had died down, but in the moonlight she could see enough to make out the features of James's face as he lay asleep on his bedroll. How many times had she caught herself in the last few days, just before she reached up to caress his cheek or to smooth his fair hair off of his forehead?

He was becoming dear to her. But that must not be. She would not allow it. If she started to love him, he would be taken away. Just like Papa. Just like Charles. Just like—she wrapped her arms around her stomach, hugging the babe to her in the cold night. No, she wouldn't even think it. Not her child, too. Even God wouldn't be so cruel, would He?

She squeezed her eyes shut against the pain and fear that threatened to overwhelm her. But her efforts did no good. The fear was like a living thing, threatening to squeeze the very breath out of her body.

"Abby! What's wrong?"

Her eyes flew open to see James standing over her. She must have cried out. She shook her head, taking a couple of deep breaths.

He sank down on his knees next to the bed and laid a cool hand on her forehead. "What is it, love?" he whispered. "Are you in pain? Is it the child?"

She shook her head again, tears welling up into her eyes. Swallowing against the lump in her throat, she grasped his hand and clung to it. Slowly the bands of fear loosened from around her chest.

"I'm sorry," she whispered. "It's just that sometimes I'm so afraid."

She felt him nod.

"Do you want me to sit with you for a while?" he whispered.

No, she wanted him to take her in his arms and hold her until she felt safe again. She wanted him to lie next to her so she could feel protected. Loved. Secure. But that could never be. She was being weak to even let him sit near her and hold her hand.

She sighed. "I know you're tired. I'll be fine." She thought if he could have seen her face, he would have known she was lying.

He sat still for a few moments then brushed his lips across her forehead. "He will never leave you nor forsake you, Abby," he whispered.

The outdoorsy smell of his warm skin lingered in her senses as he returned to his makeshift bed to lie back down. She squeezed her eyes shut against the lonely tears that seemed determined to fall. Surely morning would come soon.

Morning did finally dawn, and with it a new resolve. She would gather the eggs today, no matter how the task frightened her.

James had shown her how to do it once or twice, but she still felt intimidated by the chore. The very idea of reaching under a squawking bird into its warm nest was unnerving, not to mention the possibility of roosters pecking at her shoes and fluttering in her face.

James had chuckled at her timidity and told her he'd take care of it. But egg gathering was really woman's work, she knew. Besides, he already had enough to do.

She timidly approached the front of the coop, basket in hand. She had first made certain that the hound, Frank, was nowhere in sight. She wasn't quite so afraid of the dog now, but her heart still skipped a beat when he came galloping up to her. She hoped he was as nice as James said he was, because he had awfully big teeth.

As the sun beat down on her head, Abby decided she had procrastinated long enough. "Well, little one, it's now or never," she said to her unborn child. Flinging open the door of the coop, she hollered, "Rise and shine!"

The startled birds flew everywhere, and Abby backed out of the coop, flailing her arms. "Shoo! Shoo!" she yelled, feeling ridiculous.

"I've never seen it done quite like that before," came an amused voice behind her.

Abby turned with a groan. "Hello, Iris."

James's sister grinned. "What are you doing, Abby?"

"Gathering eggs." She tried to keep a straight face then gave up. "I thought maybe if I made them all get out first, it might be easier."

"Hmmm." Iris made a comical face, and both women giggled. "Didn't your know-it-all husband show you how to do it?"

"Yes, but I can't stand reaching under those poor hens." Abby grimaced.

"Besides, the smell makes me feel ill."

"You do look a little green, dear," Iris said. "Why don't you go put the teakettle on the stove. I'll gather these eggs."

"You're an angel," Abby said.

Iris snorted. "Don't think I've ever been called that before," she replied. "Here, take this pie into your kitchen. I'll be in before you know it."

Abby headed toward the back door, feeling guilty for allowing her sister-in-law to do her work.

"Hello, girls," she heard Iris say soothingly, and she had to grin. She had never thought of chickens as girls before. She had a lot to learn about farming, that was for sure.

James had been pleased that the eggs were gathered, but Abby felt compelled to admit it was Iris who had done it.

"She's a sweet gal," he said. "She reminds me of my mama."

Abby knew his mother had died in childbirth years ago. "Mothers are very special people," she said softly.

He appeared to be very interested in the piece of pie on his fork, but she could see that his eyes had misted over. "You'll be a wonderful mother, Abby," he whispered.

She stared at him for a moment in silence. Why would he bring that up right now? She cleared her throat. "What kind of pie is this that Iris brought? It's very good."

He speared another bite and took her cue to change the subject. "You've never had rhubarb pie before?"

"Rhubarb?" She poked at the tart red and green chunks that swam in the sweet pink juice, the flaky crust crumbling under her fork. "I've never even heard of it. Perhaps rhubarb doesn't grow in New York."

"Come here and I'll show you." James pushed his chair away from the table and led Abby to a garden patch next to the well. He pointed to a leafy plant growing in the moist, black dirt. Abby had noticed it before, vaguely wondering at its enormous leaves.

"This is a rhubarb plant," he said. "You just reach down and twist on the stalk a little bit." He straightened back up with a slender stalk in his hand. "It's best in the spring."

She smiled up at him, conscious of his nearness as his arm brushed hers. "I think I'll do without the reaching down part for now."

He chuckled, reaching out to pat her stomach. Then apparently catching himself, he jerked his hand away. "Forgive me. I didn't mean—"

"It's all right, James," she said, touching his arm. "After all, you are going to be the child's father." *My goodness!* She hadn't really said that aloud, had she? She had thought of it before, of course, but wouldn't he think that she was being rather presumptuous?

The smile that lit his face was enough to reassure her that she hadn't said the wrong thing. He laid his hand gently on her stomach for a brief moment. "You're right, Abby," he said, his voice husky.

She froze, ensnared by the tenderness that glowed in his sea-blue eyes. What was he thinking?

She didn't have long to wonder. Somehow all of a sudden, she was enfolded in his strong arms. And in that moment, she couldn't think of anywhere else she'd rather be. Couldn't think at all, actually. She just knew that she had come home. She sighed, feeling safe and secure. Loved.

"Uhhh!" The baby kicked. Hard.

James backed away, his eyes wide. Abby had to laugh at the expression on his face, though she wished the moment had not ended so abruptly. "Guess this little one is getting impatient," she murmured, smiling up into James's face.

He grinned. "Me, too."

The look he gave her made her pulse pound, and she lowered her gaze to the rhubarb plant. Her commitment to keep her vow was becoming increasingly difficult.

Chapter 5

"Mmm! Something smells good in here!"

"James!" Abby whirled from the stove. "I didn't hear you come in."

He grinned at her, and her heart lurched. *He truly is a handsome man,* she thought. *What would it be like—?*

"Did you fall in?"

"What?" She blinked up at him, feeling flustered.

He chuckled. "Did you fall into the flour bin?"

"Oh." She brushed at her face with her apron then glanced up to find him directly in front of her. His blue gaze twinkled into hers as his hands gently cupped her face.

"I don't think you got it all off," he whispered, lowering his face to her.

Surely he wasn't going to. . . . Her arms slid around him of their own accord, it seemed. He kissed her slowly and tenderly then pressed her head to his chest. She stood in the circle of his arms, stunned at the feelings coursing through her mind and heart.

Even in her brief marriage to Charles, she had never felt such things. This man seemed to bring out her innate tenderness and vulnerability. Nevertheless, what was she thinking? She would be breaking her promise to God and sinning against Him if she allowed herself to love James Parrish, even if he were her husband.

She pushed her hands against his chest, her heart suddenly leaden. She could not break the vow she had made to God, not even if she wanted to. *And, oh how I want to,* she admitted to herself.

He released her slowly, searching her face as if he sensed the change in her demeanor. "You're precious to me, Abby," he whispered.

She gazed miserably at his beloved face. How could she have possibly thought she could live with such a man and yet not love him?

"Forgive me if I hurt you," he said.

She reached a hand up to his bearded cheek, loving the feel of the soft bristly whiskers—loving him. "No, I'm the one who's sorry, James." She bowed her head then, ashamed that she should be so weak.

"There's nothing to be sorry for," he told her, trying to draw her back into his arms.

However, she had turned away from him, fussing with the food on the stove.

He kicked at a hay bale that stood next to the barn door, watching as a cloud of dust rose and then settled in the still air. Why had she pulled away from him? She had felt so good in his arms. Just like God made her to fit there. He knew he probably shouldn't have kissed her, but after all, she was his wife!

Dear Lord, surely you haven't brought me this woman just to torture me! I love her, Father. I want her to love me. To want me for her husband. He sighed as he lit the lantern in the chill of the rapidly approaching dusk. What had she meant that day when she said she wasn't a free woman? Would her heart always belong to her first husband, Charles?

Would James have to go on loving her, with no love returned, for the rest of his life? His shoulders drooped at the thought. How many times had he longed to lay close beside her at night, sharing secrets and feeling their hearts beat as one? Didn't she know that he loved her?

He trudged through the evening chores at a snail's pace, his mind tormenting him with thoughts of what a true marriage could be.

Each passing day brought the birth of Abby's baby ever closer. Since the afternoon that he had kissed her, Abby had withdrawn even more from James. *She is holding up well,* he thought, yet he despaired every time he saw that wounded look in her lovely eyes.

"You look tired," he said one evening, watching as she sank into the rocking chair.

She sent him a weary smile. "It's been a busy day."

Indeed, it had been a busy week. Summer was in full swing, and it seemed every day when he came in for supper, there was another row of canned carrots or tomatoes in the pantry.

"You've been working too hard."

She shrugged. "I want to get as much done as I can before the birth."

She looked more than tired, he observed as he studied her. Almost haggard. His conscience pricked him. How could he have let her work so hard, especially with the birthing so close? She was probably used to having someone wait on her, he suddenly realized. "Tell me about your life in New York," he said. Maybe if she would at least talk to him, he could understand more of what she was thinking. After all, he really didn't know her.

She looked slightly startled. "What do you want to know?"

I want to know you, his heart cried. "Anything you want to tell me, love," he replied, moving his chair closer.

She stared into the fire. "I grew up there," she began, her voice soft, as if coming from a great distance. "Mama and Papa were so happy together. . . ." She stopped then, as if that was the end of the story.

"Were you happy?" he prompted.

She twisted her hands together then apparently noticed what she was doing and held them quietly in her lap. "Yes," she said. "I was happy. I had a wonderful family. I loved God. We went to church."

James nodded, feeling the "but" that must come next.

"Then I met Charles."

The statement dropped into the room like a cold, unexpected shower.

"He convinced me that we should get married." Here she stopped and almost smiled. "So we did. He was a master of persuasion." She glanced at James and shrugged. "Looking back on it now, I'm not sure I ever really loved him. But he convinced me into believing that I did."

James waited, alternating between fear and rejoicing. Fear at what she might say next, yet rejoicing that her heart was not bound to another man.

She shrugged again. "We had only known each other a month before we wed. Papa was livid." She gave James a sad smile. "I was with child soon afterwards. Then. . .a widow."

He grasped her cold hands in his. "What happened, Abby?"

"No one is exactly sure." She grimaced. "I had been over visiting Mama and Aunt Caroline while Papa went over to our house to talk with Charles about a business matter."

For long minutes the only sound in the room was the crackling of the fire and the squeak of the rocker blades on the smooth floor.

"There was a terrible fire, and Papa and Charles both died." Her voice was flat, devoid of emotion.

What could he say to her? "I'm s—"

"The constable said that Charles set it on purpose."

"What?" Was she saying what he thought she was?

"Only Charles didn't plan on dying in the blaze, too. He was supposed to live to 'share' in my inheritance."

James felt as if someone had punched him in the gut. No wonder she was reluctant to open her heart to someone again. *But I'm not like that,* he cried silently.

She took a deep breath and gently pulled her hands from his. "So, now you understand why I vowed to God that I would never love again. It was all my fault." She looked away. "I loved Papa, and he died. I thought I loved my husband, and he turned on me. Now, even Mama. . .she's dying."

How could she think such things were her fault? His heart felt like it was breaking. That phrase had always seemed like a figure of speech to him, until now. What could he possibly say or do to convince her?

Show her the way back to Me, the still, small voice said again.

He bowed his head, surrendering again to the One who is all-seeing, all-knowing, and never-changing. "Our lives are in Your hands, Father God," he whispered. "Take what we have and who we are, and use us for Your good. We are nothing without You. . . ."

He heard his wife softly weeping, and his heart rejoiced to hope that God's Spirit was at work in her life.

Hours later, James woke with a start. He could hear Abby thrashing around in the bed, her breaths coming in short gasps. Was it time?

He flew to her side, his own heart pounding. Abby's eyes were squeezed shut, her face contorted with silent terror. A chill traveled down his spine as he felt her fear.

"Jesus!" he prayed aloud, a near frantic urgency in his voice. "Oh, dear Lord, please help my wife. Release her from this consuming fright."

Abby's eyes flew open, and James held his breath, watching as the glazed look in her eyes cleared and her rigid body relaxed. Dropping to his knees, he pressed her limp hand to his face.

"What happened, Abby?" His voice trembled as he spoke.

Abby released a shuddering sigh. "Thank God," she whispered. "It was just another bad dream."

She closed her eyes. "I've had similar nightmares, but. . .but. . ." She opened her eyes to search his face. "This was the worst, by far. Oh, James, I thought I was surely going to die."

He stared at her, his thoughts racing. Apparently she had more to deal with than he had thought. This wasn't simply a woman going through grief. *Father God, please guide my every word*, he prayed. "What was the dream, Abby?"

She shook her head. "I can't. . . ."

"Yes, you can." He tenderly took her chin in his hand. "God doesn't want a child of His to be so tormented by fear."

"Maybe I'm not really God's child."

His heart broke at the bleak words. "Abby, you know God's Word. I've heard you quote the scriptures when I read at night." He smoothed a wispy dark tendril from her forehead. "The Bible says that if you believe in your heart and confess with your mouth that Jesus is Lord, that you are saved."

She nodded. "I've done that. But I don't feel His love, James!" Her voice was pleading. "Why would He make all those terrible things happen to me?"

He took her hand in his. "Abby—"

"I'm so afraid, James! I'm so afraid." Her hand tightened on his. "I just know that something is wrong with my baby. I just know—"

"Hush, now. You mustn't talk like that."

Pursing her lips together tightly, Abby turned her face toward the wall, but not before he caught the glint of betrayal in her eyes.

"Abby, please look at me," he pleaded gently. Minutes ticked by. The darkness in the large room slowly lightened by the break of dawn, yet she remained motionless.

James prayed silently, waiting.

Finally, she turned her eyes to meet his.

"Abby, as God's child, He says to you in Jeremiah 29:11 that He thinks thoughts of peace and not evil toward you. God does not do terrible things to us. Our enemy, Satan, is the one who does that."

She stared at him stonily. "Then why doesn't God stop him?"

"There will come a day when Satan will be bound and rendered helpless. You can be assured of that." He pressed her hand. "But in the meantime, despite life's most dire circumstances, if we saturate ourselves in the God's Word, we can experience His peace. Still, a part of the responsibility is ours, too, sweetheart."

She shook her head questioningly. "How is that?"

He smiled, patting Abby's bulging middle lightly. "When our baby is born, he will be hungry. And you will have milk to feed him, right?"

She raised her eyebrows.

"What if this little one chooses not to open his mouth? Will you be able to give him any milk?"

"Of course not. But—"

"You've been doing that to God, Abby. He's waiting for you to accept His peace and His mercy."

She turned her head away again, her long braid sliding over their joined hands. After a long time, her muffled words drew James's attention. "I think He's angry with me."

James gently drew her face toward his. "God is love, Abby. He *is* love."

"But I don't—"

"I know. You've thought and felt and said for so long that God is angry with you and that He doesn't love you—you don't feel or know the truth anymore." He smiled into her eyes, letting all of his love for her show in his face. "You need to start speaking truth and life instead of lies and death. The Word of God says in Proverbs that the power of life and death is in the tongue."

"Oomph!" Abby put a hand over her stomach, her eyes wide. "That was hard!"

James chuckled. "Nothing wrong with that little one."

Abby's dark eyes grew wistful. "I wish I could feel as sure as you do about it."

James ached to kiss away the cares of this woman the Lord had given him, but she needed more than his human love right now. He caressed her face with his eyes. Couldn't she see how much he had grown to love her? He picked up her small hands and placed them on her stomach, chuckling as the child within moved in response.

"My dear," he said, placing his hands on top of hers, "our Heavenly Father is the Creator of all life—including the life of this little one whom we are so anxious to meet. Don't you think that the God who breathes His life in us can be trusted to watch over us all?

"Listen, Abby. The next time you are tempted to allow fear to crowd your thoughts, why don't you pray and ask God to remind you of a Scripture that will replace your fear with His peace."

As the sun rose and the light seeped into the dim room, peace filled Abby's heart for the first time in a very long while.

Chapter 6

T he love of God has been shed abroad in my heart by the Holy Ghost, and His love abides in me richly." Abby hummed softly, the words of the scripture from Romans going over and over in her mind like the phonograph records that Mama played. Since James had taught her to use the scriptures to pray, a whole new spiritual world had unfolded for her.

Abby finished rolling out the piecrust to her satisfaction then she carefully transferred it to the pie tin. Wouldn't James be surprised to see that she had made him a rhubarb pie? She had gotten the recipe from Iris the last time they had gone to town.

Sinking into a kitchen chair to rest for a minute before cleaning up the floury mess, she patted the warm lump that rolled underneath her apron. Surely this child would come soon!

A familiar twinge of fear prickled in her heart. "Oh God, don't let—" She started, then stopped, shaking her head. "For God has not given me a spirit of fear, but of power, and love, and a sound mind," she said aloud. "Thank You God. I praise You for Your Word that gives me strength. Your word is a lamp unto my feet and a light unto my path."

She smiled as the child moved again. "I know, little one. I feel His peace, too." Funny how she had known all these scriptures since she was a small child and yet never realized the power that she possessed as a child of God. It was amazing, really.

She picked up the letters from Mama and Aunt Caroline. James had brought them home from town yesterday, presenting them to her with a smile. "You must be missed," he had said.

Her cheeks grew warm now as she recalled the tender way he had taken her into his arms. It seemed that he had begun to do that more and more often, she mused. Not that she minded, really, but he made it awfully hard to say aloof. Especially when he looked at her with such tender expression in his eyes. She dared not call this feeling "love," but then what else?

She turned back to the letters with a sigh, rereading each one. Apparently, that rascal Aunt Caroline wasn't the least bit repentant of her shenanigans. Abby thought of the elderly woman and smiled. It was so good to hear from her family. Yet she didn't yearn for home as she expected she would. Had she truly found a home of her own with James?

Her heart warmed as her gaze fell on the cradle. James had brought it home in the back of the wagon, covered carefully with an old quilt.

"I thought we might be needing this soon," he had said, presenting the gift to her almost shyly.

Abby ran her fingertips over the glossy oak. "It's beautiful," she whispered. There were even little heart cutouts in the headboard and a lovely white satin blanket. "You shouldn't have spent so much money," she said, fingering the coverlet.

He chuckled, the sound making her heart sing. "I'm not very good at working with wood, Abby. If I made the cradle, the poor child would probably have fallen through the bottom the first time you laid him in it!"

She laughed then succumbed to the impulse to run her fingers through his light hair. "I never heard of a farmer who wasn't handy with a hammer," she teased gently.

He smiled down at her, the merriment in his eyes fading into a different emotion. Pulling her to him, he wrapped his arms around her carefully. She leaned against him, reveling in his closeness.

"You must know that I love you, Abby," he whispered into her hair.

She stood still. Did she know that? She thought of him. Thought of all the little things that made up James Parrish. His attentiveness. His gentleness. The way he prayed for her and the baby, his handsome head bowed.

Yes, she knew that he loved her. Even more, she knew that she loved him. And yet, there was the problem. She couldn't love him, or anyone. She had promised.

She sighed now as she dumped the chopped rhubarb into the pastry-lined tin. *It won't help to keep going over and over it,* she told herself sternly. She had made a vow to God, and she intended to keep it.

Abby gathered up the large leaves she had cut off the tops of the rhubarb stalks. If she chopped them and fried them with a little bacon grease, she could serve the greens with the salt pork and boiled potatoes she was planning for supper. Feeling rather pleased with herself, she got out her sharpest knife.

※

"I'm as hungry as a bear," James said from outside the back door.

She could hear him scraping the mud off his boots, and smiled. She would have liked to have met his mama and thanked her for raising such a thoughtful son.

"I'm glad you're hungry, because supper is on the table." She couldn't help smiling at him as he clumped through the door and rewarded her with a kiss on the tip of her nose.

"You're a sight for sore eyes," he said, grinning at her. "When's that baby ever going to come? He should have been here two weeks ago!"

She blew out a good-natured sigh. "You weren't supposed to ask me again, remember?"

He poured water into the basin and plunged his hands into it, scrubbing vigorously. "A man can't help wondering, you know."

Abby smiled behind his back. "I heard my aunt Caroline tell many an anxious woman, 'The pear will fall when it's ripe.' "

He laughed aloud. "Sounds like your aunt Caroline's a pretty wise gal."

"She sent me to you, didn't she?" Abby could have bitten her tongue the minute the words were out of her mouth. Now he would think that she. . .oh dear. There he was looking at her like that again and. . .

The kiss was slow and sweet. Abby thought maybe she had gone to heaven. . . except that there wasn't any smoke in heaven, was there? Smoke? "Oh no! My pie!" She pulled out of his arms and rushed to yank open the oven door.

As she thumped the pie onto the sideboard, relieved to see it still intact, James peered over her shoulder.

"Some of the juice ran over," she mumbled, waving the smoke away with her apron.

James grinned at her sheepishly. "Seems I ought to be praising God for Aunt Caroline."

"What? Oh." She felt her face get red. Was he trying to torment her? She shouldn't have let him kiss her, and he knew it. "Supper's getting cold," she said tartly. She pulled out her own chair without waiting for him and sank into it.

James leaned back in his chair, trying in vain to hold back a snicker. He shouldn't tease Abby so much, he knew, but he couldn't help it. He loved the way she got all flustered and pink-cheeked.

She sent him a mock glare over the table, and he obediently closed his eyes to offer the blessing. He had scarcely said "amen" before she was up and bustling around again.

"Come sit down with me, woman!" he ordered playfully.

She ignored him, busily dipping lemonade into their stoneware mugs. James sighed and turned his attention to the meal. Everything smelled so good. He took an enormous helping of greens, wondering where she had gotten them this time of year. He thought that she had already harvested all the turnips and collard greens.

She dropped heavily into the chair across from him, wiping her forehead with her apron. "Sure is hot for September, isn't it?"

"Mm hmm," he said, his mouth full of potatoes. He took a sip of lemonade. "Fine supper you cooked, Mrs. Parrish."

She grinned at him, the weariness momentarily lifting from her brow. "My mama taught me right, I guess." She watched as he savored a mouthful of greens, her eyes widening when he grimaced.

Good grief! Where did she get these nasty things? It was all he could do not to spit them out on his plate.

"Is something wrong?" Her face was troubled.

He coughed into his napkin then hastily gulped some lemonade. "Just took a bite of something bitter," he said mildly.

She frowned, tasting a bit from her own plate. Her eyes watered. "You needn't have been so polite, James. They're downright inedible."

He tried not to laugh at the misery on her face. "It's not the end of the world, love. Where did you find these, anyway?"

She made a face. "Well, I wanted to surprise you, so I made a rhubarb pie and—what?"

He closed his eyes briefly then glanced at her. "Abby, rhubarb leaves are poisonous."

"What? Oh, no, James! I didn't know—"

He reached across the table to capture her shaking hands in his own. "It's all right. Neither one of us ate enough to have any effect."

"How could I have been so stupid?"

His thumbs stroked the backs of her hands soothingly. "I won't tell anyone if you won't."

She sniffed. "I hope you don't think I was trying to k–kill you." A giggle slipped out with the last word, as the humor of the situation struck her. "I can just see the *Denver Post* headlines now: NEW BRIDE KILLS HUSBAND WITH MESS OF GREENS."

James let loose with the guffaw he had been suppressing. Soon they were howling together, tears streaming down Abby's face. James took a drink, trying to regain a modicum of control but nearly choked on the liquid when Abby started giggling again.

Finally, they turned their attentions to the cold potatoes and pork, trying not to look at each other, lest they start again. Abby reached for the salt cellar, accidentally bumping James's hand. Their eyes met, which only started James off again with a snort. Abby got tickled all over again, her breath coming in short gasps.

"Stop laughing, James," she said between giggles. "I can't breathe!"

He raised his eyebrows. "Maybe you should take some of these greens to the next church social. Sure would liven things up a bit."

She made a face at him. "You said you wouldn't tell anyone about them."

"Who said I would tell anyone? We could just put them out on the table and let them speak for them— What's wrong?"

She giggled again. "Nothing. I just thought I felt—" Her eyes widened, and she grasped her middle.

James felt his mouth go dry. "Is it time?"

She nodded. "I think so. It must have been those greens."

How could she joke at a time like this? He scraped his chair back and rushed around the table to her. "Shouldn't you lie down?"

She smiled up at him, and his heart turned over. "I think it will be awhile yet, sweet—James." Her face flushed as she caught herself, yet she didn't break eye contact with him.

He stroked her smooth cheek with the back of his fingers. Had she really started to say what he thought she did? Could it be that she was beginning to feel for him even a small bit of what he felt for her? *God, please let it be so!*

"What can I do for you, love?" he whispered. He would never admit this to her, but he was scared stiff at the thought of losing her in childbirth. *God, please help me. . . .*

She leaned her head into his hand. "Just to know that you're here is enough, James."

❦

Abby's predictions proved true. Hours had passed since she felt her first labor pains. James had been almost frantic at first, but he regained his composure as he realized that the birth was not imminent. He had sat next to her throughout the long evening, marveling at the way her stomach would become rock-hard with each contraction. Easy and relatively pain-free at first, they were now becoming harder. More painful. Much more frequent.

"I think it's time to get Ada," Abby murmured.

James stirred from his dozing in the chair next to hers. "What, love?"

"I think you'd better get Ada now," she said, grimacing. *Whew. That one was the hardest yet.*

James clapped his hat on his head then bent to kiss her tenderly. "Shall I help you into the bed before I go?"

She nodded, fighting back the urge to pant. She didn't want to alarm James, but she was beginning to think that the baby would be here sooner than she had anticipated.

"Hurry, please," she whispered as the door slammed behind him. Why, oh why hadn't she let him fetch the midwife when he wanted an hour ago? Weeks before, Abby had decided that she'd rather have their neighbor, Ada McReady, as a midwife than a doctor from Denver City. Ada had assured Abby that she had delivered plenty of babies in her fifty years. And it was nice that she lived so close. Abby had met her a time or two in town, and Ada's husband, Andy, had dropped by with a loaf of her friendship bread when Abby and James had first wed. She was a sweet woman, and at this moment, Abby hoped she was also a speedy woman.

She lay back against the pillow, fighting back the tears. She hadn't realized it would hurt so badly. She tried to pray, but it seemed no words would form in her mind.

She felt like her insides were ripping, the pain and pressure increasing with each contraction. Where were James and Ada?

She felt the familiar blackness of fear beginning to creep at the edges of her mind. What if something was wrong? What if the baby was stuck? What if something happened to her child? All the fear that had been held at bay during the last few weeks of peace came flooding over her.

The pain tore at her, making her cry out. She squeezed her eyes shut tight, trying to think. She should pray. . . . She should quote some Scriptures. . . . "Jesus!" She screamed the name in prayer, unable to think of anything else.

Immediately the darkness vanished from her mind and calmness descended on her spirit. "Jesus," she whispered. He was there. She could feel the presence of God with her, as strongly as if another human being stood next to her holding her hand. He was God and He loved her. He would not abandon her.

Another wave of pain pulled downward on her body. She gritted her teeth. " 'The Lord is my light and my salvation. Whom. . .shall. . .I. . .fear. . . ?' "

" 'He that dwelleth in the secret place of the most High shall. . .abide. . .under the shadow. . .of the Almighty.'

" 'The Lord is. . .my. . .strength. . .' "

She opened her eyes to see James beside her, his strong voice repeating the words with her. He took her hands and held them tightly between his own. "I'm so proud of you," he whispered.

She smiled at him as Ada moved the quilts to check her. "He heard me, James," she whispered. "Jesus. . .He heard me."

James smiled at her through his tears. "I told you He would," he whispered.

"Well, Mrs. Parrish, I hardly think you needed me," Ada boomed. "You done almost had this babe without me."

Abby squeezed her eyes shut as the searing pain swept through again. "How much. . .longer?" she panted.

"Two or three more good pushes, honey. I can see 'is head already."

James gripped her hands tightly, his eyes never leaving her face. "You can do it, sweetheart," he whispered.

"The Lord. . .is. . .my strength. . .aaagh!" She gave one final push, and it was over.

Seconds later, she felt the hot, wet body of her daughter lying on her abdomen.

"Hello, little one," she said softly, reaching down to touch her with her fingertips. Her eyes filled with tears when she heard the baby's first quavering wail. "Is she all right, James? Is she truly all right?"

He watched while Ada severed the cord. Then he tenderly wrapped the baby in the soft blanket that awaited. He laid the baby in Abby's waiting arms. "See for yourself, love," he whispered.

And she did see. A beautiful, perfect baby girl. "Thank You, God," she breathed. "Thank You, thank You, thank You!"

She tore her eyes from the child to find James. He had moved across the room and was staring into the fire, his back to her. She frowned. Whatever was he doing way over there? She kissed the baby's soft forehead, and then she knew.

"James, come here please," she called softly. She watched him hesitate then turn to face her.

She studied his dear face as he came near. Oh, how she loved this man. He had married her, taken her in, provided for her, loved her—and what had she given in return? Was he so unsure of her feelings? Did he not know that she wanted him to be a father to her baby—their baby? Could she make him understand?

How she longed to tell him that she loved him—but that was not to be. She choked back the lump that arose in her throat. *God, why did I make such a vow?*

But if she wasn't allowed to give him her heart, at least she could give him this gift. She caressed his face with her eyes as he knelt down by the bed. "James, we need to choose a name for our daughter."

She watched as his eyes, focused on her face, filled with tears. He leaned over to place a tender kiss on her cheek then bent to kiss the baby's face as well.

"Isn't she beautiful?" Abby murmured.

James nodded, finally finding his voice. "Just like her mama," he whispered.

"Well, it don't look like you folks'll be needin' me anymore." Ada's loud voice made Abby jump. "I'll come check up on y'all tomorrow."

James jumped up to show the midwife out, and Abby turned her attention back to the baby. "Happy birthday, little one," she whispered. She smiled up at James as he neared her side again. "She wants her papa to hold her."

Chapter 7

O h, Abby. What a beautiful baby!" Iris held the baby close, her face radiant. "God has truly blessed you!"

Abby smiled. "It's hard to believe she's two weeks old already."

"And I love her name! Anna Joy." Iris kissed the baby's cheek gently. "I'm sorry I couldn't come earlier. I just wanted to make sure. . ."

"Oh, I'm glad you waited," Abby assured her. She would never admit to Iris that every day she had feared a visit from her sister-in-law. Of course, she loved Iris dearly. But since James had informed her of a smallpox outbreak in town, Abby had feared that little Anna would come down with the dreaded disease.

Even now she cringed inwardly as Iris bent her face near the baby's. What if she was carrying the disease? After all, people were in and out of her boardinghouse every day. She heaved an inward sigh of relief as Iris handed little Anna back to her. The baby gazed into her face, her blue eyes wide and innocent. Abby's arms tightened around her little daughter, her heart overflowing. She was still almost brought to tears each time she considered that this little human being had been entrusted to her care—hers and James's, that is. She glanced over to where he sat at the table, nursing a cup of tea. "Did you tell Iris that I have a new recipe for her to serve at the boardinghouse?"

James grinned at his sister. "Have any guests you'd like to see leave early, sis?"

"What are you talking about, James?" Iris demanded. "Abby is a wonderful cook!"

"Oh, I agree, Iris." He darted an amused glance at Abby. "She's very frugal, too. After she made a rhubarb pie, she cooked up the leaves for greens."

"Oh, no!" Iris gasped. "You didn't!"

Abby laughed. "I'm afraid so. I'm a city girl, remember?"

"Things are never dull around here anymore, that's for sure." James sauntered over to Abby, putting an arm around her shoulders. "God knew what he was doing when He sent me this lady."

Iris chuckled. "I can see that. So—do I get a nephew next time?"

Abby gulped, heat rising to the surface of her cheeks. Iris couldn't possibly know their situation. Undoubtedly James would be too embarrassed to tell his sister. "Well, I—"

"All in good time, sis. We don't want to rush things when we've only just started to get to know little Anna."

"Well, just don't wait too long." Iris jumped to her feet and smoothed down her skirt in one fluid motion. "Now, I'd best be gettin' back to town. A family's coming in from the Springs tonight." With a quick hug for Abby and a peck on the cheek for James, she was gone.

Abby sank down into the chair with a sigh. "Sometimes just watching Iris makes me tired."

James laughed aloud. "I know what you mean. She's always been a fireball." He crossed over to the cradle and leaned over to hear Anna's soft breathing. "Think we'll ever take her up on her suggestion?"

Abby wrinkled her forehead. *What was he talking. . .? Oh! How could he so casually mention that subject when he knows that I'm bound by my vow to God?* "I don't—"

He lifted his head to look at her then, and the look in his eyes took her breath away. "I want us to be a real family, Abby," he whispered.

"We are a real—"

"No, we aren't." He crossed over to her then, standing close enough that she could feel the heat radiating from his skin. "I want you for my wife—in every sense of the word."

She shivered as he ran his hands down her bare arms. Didn't he know how badly she wanted that, too? She closed her eyes against the pleading in his. "Don't you understand, James? I can't!"

He pulled her into his arms almost roughly. "Abby, you're my wife. I asked God for a wife and He sent you."

She pushed her face into the strength of his chest. Confusion flowed through her. If God had truly sent her to James, then He expected her to be the best wife she could be. Certainly God expected one's best. But then. . . She knew God also required obedience. And if she had made a vow to Him, she must not break it. Something terrible would surely happen to James or the baby.

The hopelessness of the dilemma swept over her. She was trapped. Trapped with a loving, desirable man who was her husband—and yet he wasn't. "I don't know what to do," she admitted finally.

His arms tightened around her, and he held her close for a long minute. Then he pulled away enough to look in her eyes. "I promised you that I would always love you and care for you, Abby."

She met his gaze miserably. "I know. And I'm thankful."

His grip tightened slightly. "But that's not enough for me."

She felt a burning shame well up. Was she taking advantage of him? Or was he saying that he now regretted marrying her since she couldn't—or wouldn't—meet his needs?

James watched the emotions play across her face and wondered at her thoughts. He was pretty sure by now that she felt at least a bit of love for him. Why couldn't she take that final step and admit it? Oh, he knew full well of her vow. But he had assumed that, by now, she would have realized her flawed logic. He had thought that, perhaps after the baby was born. . . He heaved a great sigh and dropped his hands from her shoulders. "Guess I'll tend to the chores."

The evenings were turning chilly now, he thought vaguely as he trudged toward the barn. He glanced back at the house, watching through the lighted window as Abby knelt to pick up little Anna. A lump rose in his throat, and he turned his eyes back to the well-worn path. "God, surely You don't require her to honor a vow that she made in ignorance," he cried aloud.

Only the lonely cooing of the doves answered him in the still night air.

૪๛

After several days of strained conversation between them, James longed to return to their easy camaraderie. Perhaps he had been too impatient. Maybe he had just pushed her too hard when she wasn't ready. They could use a good laugh together, he decided. He pushed open the back door, surprised to find the house dark and cold. Why hadn't she lit the lamps?

"Boy, I'm hungry for some greens tonight," he joked as he removed his hat.

Abby barely spared him a glance, her face anguished as she rocked Anna in the dim light.

James felt his heart contract. "What's wrong, Abby?" he whispered, coming to stand in front of her.

"I knew it. I just knew this would happen," she moaned.

He wasn't sure she was even aware of his presence. He stopped the monotonous motion of the rocker with his foot. "Abby!" he said, concern ringing in his voice. "What is it?"

She lifted her eyes to his, and his heart went cold. *Father God, please help me*, he prayed silently. He knelt down in front of her. "Abby. Tell me what's wrong."

She shook her head. "I knew it would happen. He doesn't love me, James. You said He did, but He doesn't."

"Abby." James took a deep breath. "Please stop talking nonsense. And tell me what has upset you."

Her body hunched over the baby. Her shoulders heaved with wrenching sobs. "Oh, James. She's sick, James. Our little Anna is sick. I just know she's going to die!"

He wrapped his arms around her. *God, help us,* he pleaded silently.

Tenderly, James lifted the infant from Abby's lap and into his arms. "Oh, dear God." The unchecked prayer slipped from his lips when he saw the blister-like spots that covered the soft, pale skin. "Dear God."

Hugging the baby to his chest, he let the tears fall. Yet, even as he held the child in his arms, his heart was filled with a sense of peace. He pressed a kiss onto the small forehead and drew a deep breath. "I can't put my feelings into words, Abby. But I feel confident that our baby won't die."

Abby shrugged her shoulders. "God allowed her to get sick. Why wouldn't He let her die?"

"I can't promise you that He won't, Abby, but I trust Him to do what is best for Anna and for us. He clutched the baby's feverish body closer to him. "We must trust Him with Anna. He loves her even more than you do."

"Don't you see? Tragedy just seems to follow me—"

"No," he said gently. "I don't see. Trials and tests and tribulations come to us all, Abby. Not just to you. He laid a comforting hand on her cheek. "God will give us the strength to face even this."

He handed the baby back to Abby then strode over toward the fireplace. He stirred up the fire and threw another log on. After lighting the lamps, he shrugged into his coat and jammed his hat on his head. "I'm going to fetch Ada. She's as good as any doctor in these parts. Besides, she's a woman of deep faith, and she can help us pray." James paused at the door, his hand gripping the knob. He turned to watch his wife. She sat in silence, blinking at the light. "I'll hurry back as quickly as I can, but don't just sit there and cry while I'm gone. Pray."

The door slammed behind him. Abby leaned her head back in the rocker and closed her eyes. *Pray? My prayers won't help. I've prayed and prayed in the past. Has God ever answered my prayers?*

Anna whimpered, and Abby automatically held her closer, adjusting her blankets. It had been hours since the babe had nursed. Abby's breasts felt achingly full, yet the baby refused to eat. "Come on, little one," she coaxed. "You need to eat." The child sucked weakly for a moment then turned her head away. Her little mouth clamped closed.

Abby sighed, and her tears threatened to overflow. The child wouldn't have enough strength to get well if she didn't eat soon. Abby slowly buttoned her bodice, suddenly recalling James's words of a few months ago. "Part of the responsibility is ours, love," he had said. "Just as you can't feed a baby who refuses to open its mouth, you limit God by refusing to accept His ways and His comfort."

Was she really doing that, she wondered? Could it be that God had really been there through her whole life, and she had refused to accept Him, the very One who would strengthen her?

It seemed that she had begun to learn His ways just before Anna was born, but somehow she had fallen and slipped back. She could see that clearly now as she looked back on the last few weeks.

She had slipped out of the habit of reading God's Word daily and had stopped praying so much when Anna arrived healthy and happy. How could she have done that? How could she have forgotten the way His presence comforted her during the birthing? "Oh God, forgive me," she cried inwardly. Was He angry with her? Was that why her baby was sick?

A few months ago she would have assumed this to be true, but now. . .she wrinkled her brow as she struggled to recall the verses James had shown her. Wasn't there one that said something about there being no condemnation for those who were in Christ Jesus? Yes, she was sure of it. James had explained that that verse meant that once she had confessed her sin and asked God to forgive her, He would. He wouldn't be angry with her. She sighed in relief.

" 'Why so downcast, oh my soul? Put your hope in God!' " The verse from Psalms popped into her mind with such clarity that she was startled. Could she really put her hope in God at a time like this?

She sat up straighter, feeling determination flood through her. "I will." She said the words aloud. "I choose to trust God this time."

Hoisting herself out of the rocking chair, she carried the whimpering baby over to the window. Gazing out into the star-filled night, she felt her heart stir within her. If God, who created all things, could love her, then she surely could trust Him.

Abby tenderly placed Anna into her cradle in hopes that the baby would rest. As she eased back into her rocking chair beside the cradle, the door flew open. James strode inside, followed by Ada. The neighbor scurried to the baby's cradle and began examining her with a physician's skill. James came up beside Abby and put his arm around her. "Don't be afraid," he whispered in her ear. She laid her head against his shoulder.

"I'm not," she whispered, marveling at the thought. "I'm not afraid."

As Ada worked over the child, rubbing a concoction of Croton Oil and Tartaremetic Ointment into the tiny chest, James began to sing a familiar hymn. Abby closed her eyes, joining her voice with his. The presence of God filled the room in a way that Abby had never experienced before. She opened her eyes, almost expecting to see Him standing beside her. When their song ended and Ada finished her nursing tasks, an expectant hush filled the room. James gently lifted the baby from the cradle, his hands trembling. The trio of adults huddled around the child, and Abby sensed God's presence encircling them as James began to pray.

"Father God, we bring little Anna to You." His voice broke. "God, we dedicated her to You when she was born. She belongs to You, not us. But God, we love her, and we know that You have the power to heal her." He dipped his finger into a jar of oil that Ada had retrieved from her bag of medicines and doctoring supplies.

"Father God, in Your Word, You teach us, if there are any sick among us, that we are to anoint them with oil and they will be healed."

Ada placed a gentle hand on the baby's chest and added her voice to James's prayer. "Dear Lord, on behalf of this precious little child, Anna, we pray that You will touch her body and spare her life."

Abby wanted to join James and Ada in their spoken prayers, but she was too choked with emotion to vocalize her petition. The words refused to leave her lips. She silently pleaded with the Lord, adding an emotional "Amen" to the others' prayers.

She felt her heart constrict as James rubbed a drop of oil onto Anna's forehead. Something gave way inside Abby at that moment. She couldn't hold back the tears as she realized, clearly and finally, that God loved Anna—and God loved her. He wanted them both to be well and whole. Although she couldn't fully fathom the thought, she suddenly understood that God loved her much more than she loved her own baby. She, Abby Parrish, was His child, just as Anna was her child. It was as if she had never understood that before.

She reached over and took the baby from James, her heart rejoicing in fresh revelation. God Almighty loved her!

Anna's sudden loud cry took Abby by surprise, and she smiled up at James when he chuckled. "I think she's hungry," she said in amazement.

He nodded, placing a large hand on the child's head. "I believe the fever's gone."

Abby pressed her cheek to Anna's face. It was smooth and cool. She felt fresh, happy tears streaming down her cheeks once more, but she let them fall freely. "Thank You, God," she whispered.

❧

The next few weeks were filled with wonder and joy, as Abby marveled constantly over God's love for her and His healing of Anna. Finally, she felt as if her heart was beginning to understand what God's Word said.

"It's like I see things so much clearer now," she said to Iris one day.

The older woman bounced Anna on her lap. "That's what happens when we open ourselves up to the Holy Spirit and let God teach us through His Word."

"For the first time, I feel like I really know God loves me."

"And your husband does, too."

Abby jumped. "James, I didn't hear you come in." Her face burning, she refused to look at Iris. Was he trying to embarrass her?

Iris handed the baby to him. "This little girl wants her daddy, and Aunt Iris needs to get back to town." She bent to hug Abby and whispered in her ear. "Don't deny yourself your husband's love, Abby."

Abby clenched her jaw. How could Iris know anything of her feelings? How could she know the many nights Abby had lain in bed, exhausted, yet sleep would not come? How could she know the anguish of love that could never be fulfilled?

Iris straightened up and patted her shoulder. "Bring that little one for a visit soon," she said, her bright tone belying the meaningful look in her eyes as Abby finally met her gaze.

Abby nodded shortly then blew out a sigh as the door swung shut behind her sister-in-law.

"What was that all about?" James's handsome face wore a frown.

Abby shrugged. What could she tell him? That she was ashamed because his sister had guessed the truth about their marriage? Or that even though she was now assured of God's love for her, she could never give her husband that same assurance of her love? Perhaps she should just go ahead and tell him of her love and disregard her vow to God. Yet the very thought made her shudder. Surely she owed God even more, now that He had healed little Anna.

"Abby?" *What is going on in her mind?*

"I. . .I'm sorry, James." She gave him a wan smile. "Guess I lost my train of thought."

He fought against a twinge of rising irritation. For days now, he had watched as she fluctuated between joy and despair. "Abby, if you're worried that I'm going to force myself on you now that you're no longer with child—"

"Oh no!" She looked shocked. "I never thought that."

Well, that's good, at least, he thought grimly. *Or is it?* Didn't she know how much he desired her as his wife? He had tried to be kind and very patient. But things didn't appear to be changing anytime soon. He had prayed the best he knew how. Quite frankly, his hope was waning. How long must his heart wait to hear her utter sweet words of love? His frustrated thoughts found their way into words before he had time to consider the consequences.

"Abby, I don't know what more I can do to win your love. Won't you ever love me—like I love you? Must you cling to that absurd vow of yours forever?"

Her face flushed, and he could have kicked himself for airing his regrets and disappointments so. Why had he so frankly exposed his feelings? Surely such bluntness would only hinder his cause, not help.

"I'm sorry," she said again. Her voice was quiet, filled with resignation.

So this was the way it was going to be. He placed the infant in her cradle then turned abruptly toward the door. "I'm sorry, too, Abby. More that you could know."

The door banged shut, punctuating his words with finality. Abby stared after him, despair threatening to overwhelm her. "God, what else can I do? I promised You. And I have to keep my vow, don't I? I promised that I would never give another man my heart. And now that I know how much You love me, how could I even think about breaking my vow?"

She buried her face in her hands. What had she done? *I never should have married you, James*, she thought in agony. *You're too good of a man to be stuck with me.*

The baby whimpered, and Abby tended to her automatically. "Mama loves you," she whispered through her tears. "Mama won't ever leave you, little one," she crooned.

God had saved her baby's life, and she owed Him a great debt, of that she was sure. Now she felt it was even more imperative that she keep her vow. Maybe she should do James a favor and leave. Then he would be free to find someone who could be the true wife he deserved.

❧

The following days were agony as a heavy silence settled between them. James spoke to her only when necessary, his mouth held in a grim line the rest of the time. He had moved out to the barn, for all practical purposes, even sleeping in one of the empty stalls.

Does he despise me so much that he can't even sleep in the same house? Abby wondered. She felt at an impasse, unable to find a solution. They couldn't go on like this much longer—and surely not for the rest of their lives.

"I should never have married you, James," she said softly one night.

He whirled around, his blue eyes filled with pain. "Please, don't utter such words ever again. I love you dearly, Abby. God answered my heart's prayer when He brought you into my life. No matter how you feel about me, I love you. You are my wife, and I am totally committed to you." His voice broke on the last words, and he turned away from her again.

She was powerless to resist the urge to wrap her arms around him. It was the first time she had dared touch him in days. With the gesture of affection, the floodgates of her soul opened. She laid her head against his strong back, feeling him stiffen at her touch. Then turning in her arms, he gathered her against him. He buried his face in her neck, and she felt his hot tears mingling with her own.

"I don't know what to do, James," she sobbed. "I don't know what to do."

He held her as if he would never let go. "Hush, now. We'll figure out the rest later." His arm tightened around her, protecting her, shielding her, giving her hope. Could there possibly be a way to have her husband's love and God's approval at the same time? She felt almost traitorous in thinking it.

She pulled away from him, searching his face as if she could will him to know how much she loved him.

He took a deep breath. "I'm sorry for my behavior of late, Abby." He cupped her cheek in his large, work-roughened hand. "I just love you so much, and I don't understand why we—"

"But you know why, James," she burst out in frustration. Why did he have to make it worse?

"No, I don't know why. If it's because you made some sort of promise to God out of ignorance—"

"It doesn't matter." She stepped back from him, as if putting physical distance between them would help her get ahold of her thoughts. "It doesn't matter. I made the vow, and I have to keep it."

"I don't believe that, Abby."

"What?" She stared at him as if he had lost his senses. "Doesn't God require obedience?"

He ran his fingers through his hair. "Yes. Yes, of course He does. But I don't think that's what we're talking about here."

She frowned. What was he getting at?

"I think that out of your pain and confusion, you tried to make a bargain with God."

She had never looked at it that way before. "But I still promised."

He sighed. "I know." He looked like he wanted to shake her. "But don't you understand? God brought us together, Abby. He has blessed you with a future and a hope."

She shook her head. It couldn't be that easy. She couldn't simply sit back and take what He had handed her, even if it was something good.

"God loves you," James said, as if reading her thoughts. "He sent Jesus to die, to forgive our sins, but also to give us life, and even abundant life, the Bible says."

Could that really be true? She pressed her hand to her forehead. "I'm just so confused."

"God is not a God of confusion, Abby." James reached for his Bible. "It says in here that God does not give us a spirit of fear, but of power and love and a sound mind."

"But—"

"Do you think being fearful and worried about this is what God wants for you?"

She shrugged. "But I don't deserve—"

"Deserve?" James interrupted. "Why, Abby, none of us deserves a single one of God's gracious gifts. We don't deserve them, nor can we earn them." He smiled. "I knew there was something that was keeping you from understanding this." He pulled his Bible from the table and intently flipped through the pages until he came to the verse he had been seeking. "Here, read it for yourself. The second chapter of Ephesians, verse eight. Do you see it?"

She looked where his finger jabbed the page. "For by grace are ye saved through faith; and that not of yourselves: it is the gift of God: not of works, lest any man should boast." She read it again, aloud this time. Before she could say anything, he was flipping pages again.

"Now, read this one," he pleaded.

"For. . .ye have been called unto liberty; only use not liberty for an occasion to the flesh, but by love serve one another." She squinted up at him. "What does this mean?" she whispered. Surely it didn't mean what she suspected.

James framed her face with his hands. "It means," he said, "that you are free. It means that we obey God out of love and gratefulness, not out of duty, debt. . .or fear."

She was speechless.

James put the Bible down and drew her into his arms gently. "Father God, please reveal Your love to Abby. Open her eyes of understanding. She is not to serve You out of anything but love and gratefulness. Nor for anything she needs to repay, and not because of anything she has done or not done. She is Your child because she accepted Your Son. And she is righteous in Him alone."

Abby lay in bed, her mind racing. Could it really be as simple as James made it sound? That she didn't have to work and strive to pay her debts to God?

She closed her eyes, hearing the chilly fall wind howling past her window. She shivered, pulling the quilt up tighter under her chin. In the faint light of the banked fire, she could see James sleeping in front of the hearth. *Dear James.* She smiled, glad that he had moved back in the house from the barn. She pictured him lying next to her, his arms holding her close.

Her cheeks burned guiltily at the thought. Surely God would be displeased with her if she broke her vow, and something bad would happen. It just couldn't be as easy as James had made it sound.

She heard Frank whimper outside the door, and she groaned. That dog never could stand to be outside when a storm was brewing. And from the sound of that wind, they were in for some snow tonight.

She crawled out of bed, shivering as her bare feet touched the icy wood floor. She must be crazy, getting up to let a dog in the house. Somehow the big creature had grown on her, she supposed. She'd better make sure the baby was warm enough, too. They were overdue for the first snowstorm of the season.

Frank scratched at the door again. "I'm coming," she murmured. Glancing out the window as she made her way to the cradle, her heart stopped.

Surely she was imagining it—no! There was another flicker—"James!"

He woke with a start.

"James! The barn is on fire!"

"What?" He pulled his trousers on over his long johns. "Get some water and prime the pump," he yelled over his shoulder as he flew out the door.

Her hands shaking, she grabbed the tin bucket, full of water, from its place beside the door. Closing the door softly behind her so she wouldn't awaken Anna, she stepped into the chill of the night. She ran toward the pump, refusing to think of what would happen if the fire reached the house.

Images of her home in New York, charred beyond recognition, flashed into her mind. She could imagine Papa's anguished cries for help, could smell the burning flesh—"Jesus!" she cried aloud. "Please help us!" She tripped over Frank and went sprawling, but somehow she managed to keep most of the water from spilling. She clambered back to her feet, hot tears streaming down her face. *Fear not, for I am with thee.* The bit of Scripture floated into her mind. *Fear not. Fear not.*

She reached the pump, feeling for the handle in the dark. Her breath came in short gasps, whether it was from exertion or fear she wasn't sure. The water began to flow, and as it did, she felt God's presence flow over her once again like the day He had healed Anna.

I will never leave you or forsake you, Abby. The Spirit's gentle voice broke into her consciousness.

James stumbled up with two buckets. "Keep pumping, Abby!" he shouted.

She obeyed, listening as the water gushed out to fill the pails. "I love you, James," she said suddenly.

For a long moment, James stood motionless. "What did you say?"

"I said I love you and I want to be your wife."

"Hallelujah!" He dropped the buckets and swung her into his arms.

"James, the barn!" she murmured against his lips.

He set her down reluctantly and grabbed the buckets. "God will see us through, Abby," he said.

※

And so He did. The fire somehow stayed contained in the tack room, destroying everything in there, but not moving beyond to the stalls. "It's a miracle," James said the next morning, as they stood gazing at the soot-covered room. Snow had fallen lightly, making the scene seem cold and unreal.

Abby nodded, her heart too full for words. The night had certainly been one to remember. After the fire was finally out, she and James had collapsed onto the rockers in front of the fireplace.

"Thank God you saw the sparks in time, Abby," James had said, his voice hoarse from the smoke.

She nodded. "I got up to let Frank in and glanced out the window."

He ran a hand through his hair, leaving it standing on end. "We didn't lose any of the animals. That's the most important thing." He stared at the fireplace, as if lost in thought.

Abby felt her stomach clench. Was he thinking the same thing she was? How could she have blurted that out, there by the pump? It wasn't as if anything had changed, really. . . .

A VOW UNBROKEN

"Did you mean what you said out there, Abby?"

She felt the blood rise to her face, but she couldn't ignore the look in his eyes as he turned to gaze at her. "I. . ." She saw the uncertainty flicker across his dear face. "Yes."

He slid down to his knees in front of her, laying his head in her lap. "You don't know how I've longed to hear you say those words."

She tangled her fingers in his blond hair. "I've wanted to say them for a long time," she confessed. "I do love you, James."

He raised his head. "What changed, my dear one?" he whispered.

How could she explain it? She shrugged. "I guess I. . . finally figured out that God is on my side. He is not hovering over me, just looking for ways to hurt me."

James nodded. "He is Love."

"Yes." She put a hand to his reddened cheek. "And so, last night, I felt that God wanted me to make another vow. A vow I am more committed than ever to keeping."

He looked stunned. "What do you mean, Abby?" His voice was strained and his eyes pleaded with her. "What are you saying? I thought you. . ."

"No, wait." She grasped his hands. "Let me tell you what I promised God. I vowed to love the Lord my God with all my strength, my soul, my mind, and my spirit. I intend to keep my vow and to never love another like I should love Him alone."

James gripped her shoulders. "Is there room in there somewhere for me?"

She moved into his embrace, her heart overflowing. "Always," she whispered. "I promise."

Epilogue

I t's a boy!" James's joyful shout was music to Abby's ears. Could it be possible that almost a year had gone by since the night of the barn fire? That night was forever imprinted on Abby's memory. It was a night of endings as well as sweet beginnings. The ending of fear and bondage. The beginning of life and love.

"I told you I wanted a nephew. Now, here he is," Iris sang out joyfully from beside the bed. "God has blessed you again, Abby."

Abby looked up to find her husband's tender gaze fixed on her face.

"Thank you," he whispered. "You've given us another beautiful child."

Her eyes filled with tears. How had God taken a bitter vow and turned it into an unending promise of joy? She held out her arms for her new little son then clasped James's hand. She kissed Anna's little forehead as she snuggled up close. "Mama and Papa will love you both forever," she vowed softly. And she smiled, knowing this was a vow that would remain forever unbroken.

Amy Rognlie is an author and teacher, who, like the characters in her books, has traveled many unfamiliar and unexpected paths in the course of her life. She has seen God's faithfulness every step of the way, and wants her readers to know that no matter what circumstances look like, God is good. Amy and her family live in Central Texas, where she teaches language arts and Latin, writes Bible study and Sunday school curriculum, and is involved with ministry in her local church and community.

FINISHING TOUCHES

by Kelly Eileen Hake

Dedication

To God, who gave me the desire to write;
the editorial team at Barbour that gave me the opportunity;
and my critique partners/readers,
Kathleen Y'Barbo, Julia Rich, and Cathy Hake,
who gave me their honest feedback!

Except the LORD build the house,
they labour in vain that build it:
except the LORD keep the city,
the watchman waketh but in vain.
PSALM 127:1

Chapter 1

Hannibal, Missouri, 1898

She's gone!" Pa rushed into Libby's room, his bellow waking her long before he roughly shook her shoulder.

"What?" Libby blinked the sleep from her eyes and pried her father's clenched fingers from her upper arm. Pa had been known to walk the halls in his sleep, but he seemed alert enough this time. . . .

"She's left on the eve of her wedding with Royce to elope with that Lyte chap." Sinking onto the edge of Libby's bed, he extended a piece of paper.

Fighting the sick fingers of dread snaking over her spine, Libby unfolded her sister's crooked creases.

Good-bye, the short note read. *I love Donald and have left to marry him. I know this wasn't the plan, but I have to follow my heart. Tabby*

No apology, no asking for forgiveness—the note of a girl who'd been loved by all, forgiven her faults, and who saw no reason to expect her charmed existence to change simply because she'd humiliated those who loved her best.

"She won't be harmed. Donald Lyte is besotted with her, and he's well enough off to provide for her. You needn't worry on Tabby's account." Libby traced the swirling loops of her sister's flamboyant writing, as delicate and lovely as the woman who wrote it.

So lovely, Captain Royce never spared a glance for her older sister. The man I've admired for so long. . . Tabby throws his love aside as though it were nothing. Libby's fist crushed the fragile paper before she caught herself doing so. She carefully smoothed the missive on her knee before passing it back to Pa.

"We must inform Captain Royce, Papa." Libby slid from beneath the warmth of her covers and slipped into a dressing gown. "The wedding must be canceled. The whole thing will be much the worse if the ceremony begins and Tabby doesn't show up."

"Yes," her father agreed dully, not stirring from his defeated slump. "No!" He stirred, his eyes filling with horror. "No, Libby, I can't cancel the wedding!"

"It cannot go on without Tabitha, Papa. We have no choice."

"No choice," he repeated. Suddenly, his hands clasped hers in a viselike grip. "I promised Gregory my daughter's hand, and so he shall have it!"

"Papa," Libby started slowly, fearing he might have slipped into the waking sleep, which had sometimes haunted his nights since Mama's death, "Tabitha has left. She will not marry Captain Royce. You cannot change that."

"I know; I know that." Papa's eyes gleamed in the light of her bedside candle. "I have more than one eligible daughter, after all. You will take her place tomorrow."

"I—? Papa, that's impossible!" Libby tried to pull away, but his grip tightened painfully. "He's in love with Tabitha! He asked to marry her, not me!"

"Nevertheless, you will marry him, Libby." He gentled his crushing grasp. "You will wed him, or we'll all be destroyed."

"Oh, Papa." Libby knelt beside him and patted his arm. "I already told you, Tabby will be fine. It's true, we'll have to deal with the backlash of her reckless and foolish decision, but the Collier name won't be *destroyed* by a bit of scandal. And Captain Royce. . .well, he did care for Tabitha, but I daresay he'll find another bride easily enough. So long as we don't make him a cliché—left standing at the altar—it will all come out fine in the end."

"No." Papa shook his head with such force, Libby heard the faint *pop-pop* of bones moving unnaturally. "It's not our reputations that will be destroyed, Libby—though surely that will come of it all, too. Our very livelihood is at stake. If one of my daughters doesn't marry Captain Royce tomorrow morning, my business is ruined."

"What are you saying?" She drew a deep breath and held it, bracing herself for the sharp, daggerlike thrust of his next words.

"I've accepted money from him, Libby. Large amounts of money to keep the business afloat—literally." A ghost of a smile chased across his face, leaving it even bleaker as it faded. "The shipping business would have failed without his investment. With this marriage, we were to merge more than our families—our businesses as well."

The breath whooshed out of her lungs as Libby realized the magnitude of the problem. They wouldn't just be dealing with a jilted groom, but a jilted groom to whom her father owed enough money to ruin them.

"Surely. . .surely Captain Royce wouldn't demand restitution to be vindictive. He's a good man." *A wonderful, handsome, honorable, hardworking man who has sat at our table, listened to our conversation, and all but become a member of our family. . .*

"We both know he would be within his rights to seek that. He'll be humiliated before the entire town of Hannibal—not to mention the fact that he genuinely cared for Tabitha." Papa buried his head in his hands, fingers viciously combing through his sparse hair. "He'll be furious."

Unable to refute the truth of his assessment, Libby held her tongue. But nothing could chain her mind or lock up the ache inside her heart. She should know. She'd been trying to do just that since the moment Captain Royce proposed to her younger sister.

"You'll have to take your sister's place. It's the only way to save face and still unite our families." Papa straightened and loomed over her. "I will send a messenger notifying Royce of the issue—and my proposed solution. I expect he will agree for the sake of his pride."

Libby winced at her father's statement.

Lord, I've prayed for You to take away my feelings for Captain Royce, to help me reconcile myself to his marriage to my sister. I prayed that if their plans were not Your plans, to make it so that Tabitha wouldn't be his bride. Anyone but my sister with the man I care for. . .I never dreamed You would make me that bride—or that I'd regret it so deeply. In my selfishness, have I spoiled things for everyone? Lord, please don't let it be so.

❧

"Come in." The low, melodious voice grated harshly in Gregory Royce's ears. This was not the soft, breathy voice of his beloved, but rather the tones of an imposter. He pushed open the door to find the room empty, save the lone figure seated at the dressing table. He could see no evidence of Tabitha, no indication that this was a cruel trick designed to make him all the more grateful when she glided down the aisle into his waiting arms. His last spark of hope flickered and sputtered.

"So it's true." The words came out clipped, his displeasure evident. He shut his eyes for a moment, reminding himself this was no more Elizabeth's fault than his own, and doubtless she was as wary as he. *Is honor worth such a price? Ah, but if not, what does a man have? I certainly have no love, not with my bride eloping with another man. What do I say to this woman whom I never saw as more than a friend. . .a sister? How do I ensure she's willing when I know that I, for one, am not?*

"It is bad luck to see the bride on her wedding day." Elizabeth's bowed head reflected only brown curls, the pose concealing her face. "I'm sorry, Captain Royce." The apology was for more than her downcast visage, and he knew it instantly.

"I believe we are past that now." The words came out sounding gruff, his consonants razor sharp and cutting.

"True." She raised her head, presenting her face in the mirror. No thick fall of straight blond locks, green eyes tilted slightly at the corner, patrician nose, and rosebud mouth reflected back to him. Instead, he saw a softly rounded face, pert nose, hazel eyes fringed with thick lashes, lips turned down at the corners. Elizabeth couldn't compare with Tabby—and it seemed to Gregory that she knew it well. "We're far past the point where silly customs can ward off bad luck, aren't we?" She gave a brave, if tremulous, smile. It never reached her gaze.

"No." He cleared his throat and tried again. "I meant we're past the point where you call me Captain Royce. A bride should call her husband by his Christian name. I'm Gregory."

"I know." She turned so she faced him completely, rather than conversing through the flat plane of the mirror. "And you should call me by mine. Elizabeth to most but Libby to family."

"Thank you, Libby." Gregory cast about for the right words to say when everything tumbled around as though intangible. "I wanted to see. . .I need to know. . .are you willing to go through with this? Commit yourself to a marriage of convenience only?"

He saw her wince and mentally kicked himself for being such a brute. "Are you quite sure you're not being forced into anything?" Stupid question. For one reason or another, they had both been forced into this situation.

"Yes." She met his gaze more steadily. "Quite sure. I will see you in the chapel, Gregory." She inclined her head toward the door, only slightly, but with a clear message.

"Until then." He gave a bow and left her to her preparations. What more could he possibly say? They'd be exchanging solemn vows in mere moments. Gregory walked about the grounds until the time of the ceremony, standing through it as though no more than a block of wood until it was his turn to speak.

Looking into her hazel eyes glistening with unshed tears, Captain Gregory Alan Royce had the distinct sensation of someone slugging him in the gut. A man could be forgiven for such a thought when he was marrying the sister of the woman he loved.

"I, Gregory Alan Royce," he gritted from behind a forced smile on what should have been the happiest day of his life, "take thee," *Tabitha Bethany Collier*, he mentally vowed even as he substituted, "Elizabeth Anne Collier, to be my lawful wedded wife. . ."

The knot in his stomach clenched more tightly with every word he spoke until he got to "for better or for worse," when an irreverent thought offered some relief.

It can't possibly get any worse. Not when my bright little Tabby ran away with another man to avoid wedding me. Not when I've been publicly rejected and saddled with the spinster of the family. Not when the house I've labored to construct for my beloved bride will never feel Tabitha's soft footsteps, hear her tinkling laugh, or see her sparkling eyes.

"As long as we both shall live." The final words throbbed in his temples as he sealed his own fate. Elizabeth was now his wife, and Tabitha lost to him. Forever.

Chapter 2

Libby did not sit beside her husband as she imagined most newlyweds did. Rather, she rode into their future across from Captain Gregory on the seat that made her face backward.

The seat that made her stomach churn.

Oh, well. It's been roiling all day, anyway. When I really think about it, it is fitting—this marriage is as backwards as this seat. All the same, I wish I wasn't stuck looking back at what I left behind. It seems I can't look forward no matter how hard I try. How do I face the uncertainties before me when my thoughts are troubled by the past? Tabitha couldn't have known the havoc she'd wreak.

She sneaked a peek at her husband—*her husband!*—to find him staring bleakly out the window, resignation dulling his gaze, tension tightening his strong jaw and forcing his posture to be rigid. He had the look of a man on his way to the gallows. And the same noose he faced threatened to strangle her as well.

"Cap—Gregory?" she ventured, her voice sounding small and hesitant to her own ears. "I was wondering. . ." Her boldness abandoned her and left the question unspoken. Would he elect to have a wedding night, after all? And how could she tell him she'd had no motherly advice. . .that their aunt had passed down marital wisdom solely to Tabitha. Libby had no idea what she was supposed to say to her husband, and her heart broke at the thought he might bed her while wishing for her sister instead—as he'd done during their wedding that day. Would she ever be more than a weak shadow of her sister to the man she loved?

"Yes?" He turned to her, inclining his head as though encouraging her to speak. As though grateful she was making an attempt to ease the horrible weight of their mutual silence.

"I wondered if"—her courage fled immediately, leaving a spineless heap on the carriage seat—"if there was anything you wanted to tell me about the house. Servants' names, the way you want things run, your favorite dishes, and so on." She finished her question too brightly, striving to push aside her discomfort.

Of all the things. . .I know his favorite dishes. I ask Cook to make at least one of them whenever I know Captain Royce is coming to dinner. After all this time, it was a foolish question. Just look at that gleam in his eye. . .the faraway glint that says more clearly than words that he's drawing away. The regret painting his features as he sees the bride he's bought.

407

"Jenson is the butler, Mrs. Farley the housekeeper, Mrs. Rowins the cook. There are three maids—Daisy, Rachel, and Grace." He rattled off the names by rote, obviously uninterested, while Libby struggled to remember them. It might not be important to him, but it was imperative she, as new mistress of the house, get on well with the staff. "Larken is the stable master, and Mr. Barnett is overseeing the construction of the additions. That should be about all you need to know."

"The additions?" She closed her eyes, suddenly remembering Gregory's long, enthusiastic descriptions of the house he was building for Tabitha. She'd forgotten in the press of the wedding and the prospect of marriage itself that she'd be living not only with a man who loved her sister, but also in the house he'd designed and built for her. She'd stepped into Tabitha's life.

"The house is not finished, yet." If his terse answer hadn't conveyed the message clearly enough, his pointed return to staring out the window of the carriage certainly did. The conversation was closed. . .and so, Libby imagined, was his heart.

Stop it, stop it, stop it! She chastened herself. *You decided to marry him so you could make his life as good as possible—to make up for Tabitha's desertion, to show your own love of him. You can't go thinking maudlin thoughts and being selfish. Someone has to be strong enough to work at this marriage, and it's only fair that that someone be you!*

Having given herself that encouraging, albeit silent, speech, Libby straightened her spine and resolved to make Gregory's house. . .no, *their* house—a showplace of her love. She would give it her time, her attention, and her focus, and as she worked to make his life comfortable, he'd become comfortable with her. He'd come to appreciate her efforts, and in time, maybe he'd look on her with something more. . . .

Please, God, she prayed. *I know I've no reason to expect it, perhaps no right to ask that he return my feelings in some small measure as time passes, but I have to try. After my selfishness, my envy of my sister's fiancé, and the way it's all turned out, it's the least I can do.*

❧

Gregory sucked in a breath as Cranberry Hill came into view, his chest tightening—not with pride, but regret. Tonight he brought his bride home. . .but it wasn't the bride he'd planned on, and without Tabitha, Cranberry Hill would never be the home he'd envisioned either.

As they ascended the hill, Gregory's heart sank. There, its Greek Revival architecture silhouetted by the pale moon, Cranberry Hill waited. What had seemed full of promise—a foundation for the future—now seemed stark and bare, cold and forbidding. The glassless windows he'd planned to fill with stained glass chosen with Tabitha now gaped as blind eyes. The sharp corners of the house, which he'd hoped to soften with wraparound porches where he and his bride could sit together in the evening, now gleamed with warning. The house seemed exposed as no more than dangerous angles and barren edges by the lack of trees and flowers, hedges and garden paths he'd thought Tabitha would love to create.

Gregory turned away from the sight of the house he'd loved, seeking solace from the crowding thoughts of loss. He looked up only to be confronted once again with the visage of his bride. No matter where he looked, all he could see was what he was missing. Everything had become a dark reminder of Tabitha's betrayal and the mockery she'd made of Cranberry Hill—of him.

❧

Libby barely had time to nod at the servants assembled in the great hall before the housekeeper whisked her up to her suite of rooms. As she passed through the corridors, Libby managed to register how, though the house stood empty for the most part, its construction had been seen to with loving detail. Every glance showed luxurious spaces, large windows that would allow daylight to pour into the house. It was a house waiting for its mistress to fill it with warmth and family—waiting for her to make it a home.

And I will, she promised herself. *Carpets, furnishings, draperies, windows, trees outside. . . . There's much to be done. And every project I accomplish, every little thing I add, will proclaim that this house belongs to Gregory and me. I will make my mark on this house as I will make my mark in his life. With God's help and a little determination, I can make this marriage work.*

"This is the master bedroom," Mrs. Farley declared proudly, making a sweeping motion to encompass the impressive sight.

"Oh," Libby breathed. This room was a dream sprung to vivid life, and she was careful to take in only portions of it at once lest she be overwhelmed. Gregory had seen to every detail, from the silk wall hangings in rich cream to the plush carpeting in deep blue and the heavy oak armoire claiming the corner near a cozy stone fireplace. Before the fireplace sat two wingback chairs, turned toward one another as though inviting the master and lady of the house to relax beside the fire. Libby's gaze followed the graceful lines of the tall chairs and beyond. . .and she caught her breath. There, against the back wall, protruding into the middle of the room, stood the bed. Mammoth, hewn of the same beautiful oak as the armoire and sporting a carved headboard and four posts, it seemed to fill the entire room, though Libby could see a settee in the rounded corner beyond. The blue silk canopy matched the cream-and-blue patterned coverlet and plump pillows. Without a doubt, the bed was the focus of the room. . .and it rapidly became the focus of her thoughts as well.

The master bedroom—his bedroom. The room I'm to share with him. Tonight. Libby closed her eyes against a surge of apprehension. When she opened them, she realized that Mrs. Farley had begun speaking once more.

"The master bath is through the door beside the armoire, here." She pushed open the door to give Libby a glimpse inside.

She caught the impression of sparkling white tiles and gold-finished fixtures as Mrs. Farley turned a knob and added fresh water to the already steaming clawfoot tub.

"We thought you might like a bath." The housekeeper's ears turned red. "A nice, warm soak to relax you and make you comfortable-like. Master Royce went to the study, so you'll have some time to yourself. . . ."

"Thank you." Libby gave a short nod, and the woman bustled out of the bathroom.

"Daisy put your things in the armoire and dresser when they was sent over, so you should have all you need. And if you want anything, just use the bellpull and one of us will come straightaway." The woman folded her hands in front of her apron. "And when you and the master ring for breakfast in the morning, we'll bring in a tray of fruit and muffins and eggs and such. Master Royce prefers coffee, but do you have a liking for chocolate instead?"

"Yes, please." And with that, the woman left Libby to prepare for the night ahead.

Chapter 3

With nothing better to do, Libby gave in to the lure of the hot bath, luxuriating in the water until it finally began to cool. She pulled the drain, wrapped herself in a fluffy blue towel, and peeked around the door to see whether or not Gregory had come to her. What she'd do if he had, she couldn't say. He hadn't, so she tiptoed to the dresser, searching through the drawers until she came to one filled with familiar, soft flannel nightdresses. She donned one, dismayed to find it was not loose or comfortable, as a nightdress should be, but close-fitting, stretched across her chest and hips in a way that left her feeling exposed. Libby drew it off, quickly grabbing another only to encounter the same problem. The truth of the situation hit her.

These aren't mine. Everything in the room belonged to Tabby. When Mrs. Farley said the maids had put away the clothes she'd sent over, she assumed her things had been brought. Instead, she found the garments she'd lovingly packed and sent for her sister two days ago—before everything changed.

Libby carefully folded the first nightgown and laid it back in the drawer before wandering toward the fire and collapsing into one of the overstuffed wingback chairs. *Here I am, in Tabby's nightdress, in the room Gregory decorated for my sister, in the home he built for her, and all I can do is wait.* And so, she sat and tried to distract her thoughts from why Gregory wasn't with her yet.

And she waited.

⁂

Gregory glowered at the ledger spread before him on the desk in his study. He stared, unseeing, but knowing what it said by memory alone. Neat columns listed dates, prices paid, and shipping arrangements for lumber, tile, railing, cement, windowpanes, shutters, columns, cornices, bricks, and stone—everything required to build the house in which he now sat. A record of how he'd spent his time and money for the past year, preparing for what would never be.

Lord, rage burns in my belly, the weight of betrayal presses upon my chest.

How could Tabitha have done this to him?

Worse still, how did he not see that she had not returned his regard? Had he been so blinded by her beauty that he missed her selfish nature? She had made a

411

fool of him! A mockery of all he offered her—everything she accepted. Now Libby waited in his chamber—no, *their* chamber—where he should be on his wedding night. But he could not go to her. Not when he'd thought so long about marrying her sister! So here he sat, a prisoner in the jail he'd constructed for himself, bit by bit. Never had an architect constructed such a fine goal. Never had Gregory dreamed his dreams would fail.

What am I to do with this bride who should be no wife of mine? Father, I seek Your peace but find it obscured by the cloud of my new marriage. Help me know what to do, Lord.

No matter how hard he tried to find an avenue of escape, he found nothing. Tabitha had eloped with Donald Lyte, leaving Gregory to wed her sister or be made a laughingstock.

Maybe, he mused as he thought of the strange woman upstairs, *it would have been better to be a laughingstock.*

Gregory fisted his hands in the hair at his temples and groaned. *No.* More was at stake than just his pride. That would have ruined his business, too. Clients needed to know he was a man who delivered on his promises, who had everything under control. If they lost their belief in his ability to do that, it would all be over. And after the money he'd paid to help William Collier and to build Cranberry Hill. . .he couldn't afford that. None of them could.

That's it! Abruptly, Gregory knew what he'd do to avoid this sham of a marriage without losing face. Dipping his pen in an uncapped bottle of ink, he began to scratch out a message.

❧

Libby awoke the next morning to find herself inside the enormous canopied bed, snuggled under the covers. Alone, she could find no memory of having left the chair before the fire.

I must have fallen asleep, she deduced. But she must have drifted off while sitting before the fire. There wasn't a chance Libby would have climbed into his bed to wait for him! She knew she hadn't.

Gregory wasn't in the room now—he must have come in and found her sleeping then carried her to the bed. Why must she be such a sound sleeper? Had he even tried to awaken her? She sat bolt upright at her next thought.

Did he think I was trying to avoid him? Did he spend the night beside me? She could feel the heat of her blush creep up her neck and into her cheeks.

Desperate to know, she looked at the pillow beside her, intending to search for anything that would show he'd slept there. An indentation in the pillow, something. . . but all she found was a folded sheet of paper with her name written on it, resting on a pristine and undisturbed pillowslip.

"Libby," it read. Not "Dear Libby" or "My Darling Bride," but simply her nickname. She bit back a sigh at the stark beginning and tried to focus on the few lines scrawled across the page. Maybe he'd tell her what he planned for the day or how he hoped to make the marriage work. . .

Libby,

    I've been called away on business and will leave early this morning to oversee a paddleboat run. I should be able to return in a fortnight.

    I've already made arrangements with the bank, so you may furnish the place as you see fit. Mrs. Farley should be of great assistance.

Gregory Alan Royce

She flipped the paper over to make sure nothing more was written on the back. Blank. A few curt words, a handful of sentences, and no apology or endearment whatsoever. Libby felt her shoulders slump, and she drew her knees to her chest, scanning the lines once more to be sure. It was the letter of a man happy to get away.

From me. She pressed the back of her hand against her lips to suppress the powerful swell of emotion. Gregory had never wanted her before, and she'd been a fool to hope that a ceremony would change his feelings. How could she have ever thought he'd soften toward her so soon? Her husband was a strong man who had known what he wanted, but he had been cheated out of it. Expecting Tabitha and ending up with herself instead—it wasn't too difficult to imagine his bitter disappointment.

When Tabitha became engaged, I feared I'd never be wed, that I'd be the lonely spinster for the rest of my days. All my prayers, all my dreams of having a love of my own, a home and family outside of my father's. . .and I inherit Tabitha's castoffs. Tears slid down her cheeks as she shut her eyes. *How was I to know that marriage to the man I wanted would leave me more alone than ever? At home I had Papa and the servants I've known my entire life. Here I have nothing.*

Wrong. A small but powerful voice shook her from her self-pity with its conviction. She considered for a moment, dropping her head in shame and relief.

Lord, how could I have thought for a moment I had nothing when I have You? You will neither leave me nor forsake me, and with the power of Your love and the force of Your will, anything is possible. Thank You. Her tears were of gratitude now.

How foolish of her to wallow in pity when she'd been given so much for which to be thankful. Papa's business was saved, Tabitha was safely wed to the man she loved, and although it wasn't the way Libby had dreamed it, so was she. Of course, Gregory was struggling with the situation. Who could blame him?

It was up to Libby to be the best wife she could be, make his house a home and this marriage a family. She, for one, had meant every word of her marriage vows. Now was the time to live them out.

She pushed aside the covers and sank into the thick cushion of carpet beneath her bare feet. Libby rifled through the delicate dresses made for her petite sister until she found a shapeless brown piece that accommodated her more generous frame. One of the first things she needed to do was have her own things sent over. She cast another glance at the bursting wardrobe and reminded herself to have the maids pack up Tabitha's things and return them. They had no place here, and Tabitha, no doubt, needed them.

Fully dressed, her hair pulled back in a loose chignon, Libby threw open the door.

"Oh!" A startled maid, her hand raised as though to rap on the door, quickly recovered and bobbed a curtsy. "Mrs. Royce is waiting in the parlor, ma'am. We tried to say you wasn't at home, but she insisted I fetch you immediately."

"Ah. I'll see her straightaway." Libby pushed her thoughts of exploring the house to the back of her mind and made her way to the parlor with a quick prayer for strength. Surely Gregory's mother would have questions about...everything.

Chapter 4

"Mrs. Royce." Libby stepped into the room and politely acknowledged her new mother-in-law.

"Elizabeth," the woman returned. As she perused Libby unabashedly, Libby did the same.

Mrs. Royce's black hair, so like her son's, bore streaks of white. Age had stolen none of her handsome looks, for hers was no soft prettiness but rather the attraction of lively intelligence and inner strength.

"Daisy will bring us some refreshments shortly." Libby made small talk as she sat on the settee opposite the other woman. "I'd imagine it's a good time for us to get better acquainted. Gregory should be pleased to return and find us. . .companionable." She finished with a slight smile, hoping Mrs. Royce would feel the same way rather than blame Libby for the unfortunate situation they had to deal with.

"So he has left, then?" Mrs. Royce huffed in disbelief. "I could scarce credit it when I read his short note. Inexcusable behavior." Her gaze warmed as it rested on Libby. "I assure you I did raise him with manners, my dear." The warmth in her eyes fled as she set her jaw. "Though he's every right to his anger after the cruel trick your sister played upon him. My son deserves better than that type of treatment."

"Absolutely." Libby nodded. "Gregory has been coming to my father's house for many months and has always been a perfect gentleman. And no gentleman deserves to be thrown over on his wedding day." She leaned forward, encouraged by her mother-in-law's comments. "I don't blame him for needing a bit of time to himself after the. . .upset."

"You're a wise woman, Elizabeth." Mrs. Royce settled back as though ready for a long chat. "And, though I know Gregory fancied himself in love with Tabitha, I warned him she was a flighty chit who wouldn't be a match for him."

"I am fully aware of the repercussions of my sister's actions," Libby spoke more stiffly now, "but she is my sister and will make a fine wife."

"I didn't say she wouldn't, m'dear." Mrs. Royce patted her knee consolingly. "Simply that she wouldn't have made Gregory happy. Now, now, don't say anything at all. It's good that you're loyal to your sister, but Gregory needs more from a wife than a pretty smile and girlish charm."

Libby sat in silence, unsure how to respond to this pronouncement. It didn't seem to matter, as Gregory's mother plunged ahead.

"You see, Elizabeth, I'm of the opinion that this will be a much better marriage than the other would have been. After Gregory gets over his wounded pride and realizes it, you'll do well together."

At this, Libby was so shocked—and pleased—she couldn't do more than gape at her new mother-in-law.

"Do close your mouth, Elizabeth." Mrs. Royce smiled and removed her gloves. "I've come to help you."

Gregory stood at the helm of his largest paddleboat the day after his wedding, looking out across the mighty Mississippi River. Usually the majestic sight soothed his nerves, reaffirmed his faith, and made him give thanks for the wonders God created. Today, glutted with the water from plentiful spring rain, the glorious river showed her less favorable side as the current did its best to push his vessel off course.

Bits of flotsam dotted the water, proving to be much larger and more threatening than they initially seemed, lurking beneath the hidden depths of the river's face. The mighty Mississippi, long his friend, had turned her power against him on this voyage. She, like his mother's hastily scribbled response to his notice, urged him to return to his unwanted bride.

"Women," Gregory growled to the breeze, "always contrary." *And formidable,* he added silently as the *Riverrider* narrowly avoided a large, mostly submerged patch of jagged rocks.

All the same. The river, with her smooth-flowing surface, turns to a churning threat at a moment's notice. *Tabitha fits the pattern, with her guileless gaze, showing only at the last moment her ruthless determination to leave. Ma, with her calm demeanor and steely resolve, hides her true strength until it is absolutely necessary to unleash it.*

Leaving charge of the boat to his first mate, Gregory made his way to his cabin. The more he thought about it, the more he knew he'd made the right decision. Better to have time to sort out the way he wanted to handle things than be blindsided by Elizabeth. There was no telling what she'd want to do.

As he sat at his desk to overlook the cargo log, Gregory couldn't concentrate as he pondered the mystery that was Woman.

No wonder Adam was undone by Eve—women always have the element of surprise!

"Help me with what, exactly?" Libby chose the words carefully, uncertain how this woman could help her make her marriage work but somehow believing something wonderful lay ahead.

"Adjust to your new life, of course." Mrs. Royce beamed and gave a tiny wink before adding, "And show you how to make the adjustment easier for Gregory, too."

"Thank you, Mrs. Royce—"

"Sarah, please call me Sarah."

"Thank you, Sarah," Libby started again only to realize she'd forgotten what, precisely, she'd meant to say. "And friends and family call me Libby."

"Libby." The older woman tested it out and nodded. "That suits you far better. Fits your warmth and sparkle."

"Sparkle?" she echoed faintly. Tabitha was the one who sparkled.

"No one ever told you that?" Mrs. Roy—*Sarah* harrumphed. "That's what comes from losing your mother at such a young age. Men, my dear, tend to have difficulty looking beyond the superficial. However"—she pondered for a moment—"I think you'll find Gregory to be an exception, when given time enough. He always was a thinker—like his father."

"Oh." Libby had the feeling the conversation had moved along without her, since she was still marveling over being told she had sparkle.

"Yes. Now," Sarah squinted at her and questioned, "I suppose you've always heard that Tabitha was the pretty one? Heard more comments than you cared to about her loveliness, swiftly followed by some statement about what a good girl you were or some such thing?" She waited for Libby's nod then kept on. "Well, Tabitha *is* pretty—"

Libby fought to keep the smile on her face. Would there be no end of comparisons between her and Tabby?

"In an *obvious* sort of way." Sarah's tone caught Libby's attention once more. "But I think that makes it rather. . . commonplace. You have a loveliness that is far more than what meets the eye. I've been watching you girls for a while, you see. I know that you're the heart of your family, always putting your sister first, seeing to your father's comfort—it's easy to tell when one pays a moment's attention."

"We're a family," Libby protested. "We watch out for each other."

"And so you should. But you do the lion's share." Sarah sat back, satisfied with her point. "And that, dear Libby, is how you sparkle." She seemed to catch Libby's disbelief because she shook her head. "Let me put it this way, m'dear. Tabitha is like crystal—full of color to catch the eye. You, on the other hand, are like a window. You let the light of love shine through you and onto others. It's the best kind of sparkle there is!"

"I—" Libby blinked furiously to hold back what seemed a flood of tears. "No one's ever said anything half so wonderful to me." She took the handkerchief the other woman held out to her and soaked it through before regaining a semblance of dignity. "Thank you."

"It's nothing more than the truth." Sarah moved to kneel before her. "And I thought now, at a time when so much seems to have happened to throw you off-kilter, you might need to hear it from someone who's been around long enough to know."

"I'll never forget it."

"See that you don't, Libby. Now that you realize what it is you contribute to a household, let's get started."

"Yes!" Libby exclaimed. As Sarah rose to her feet, Libby stood to join her, determined to lavish love on this woman, her son, and their house. "Let's make this house into a home Gregory will be glad to come back to!"

Chapter 5

Telegram, Cap'n!" Mr. Bates thrust the paper toward him as Gregory oversaw the unloading of the cargo hold.

"Thank you." He took the message, absently tapping it against the side of his leg as two men almost dropped a crate. The telegram would wait, but it seemed his men might not be able to keep a grip on things.

"Cap'n?" His voice now hesitant, Mr. Bates wouldn't meet Gregory's gaze.

"Yes?" Gregory raised a brow, wondering what could be keeping the man from assisting his mates with the work at hand.

"Not that it's any of my concern," he hedged, "but the telegraph operator made particular mention of the.... Wait, how did he put it? Said he'd never seen the likes of it before, and that..."

A growing sense of unease unfurled in Gregory's stomach. Suddenly, the innocuous sheet of paper in his hand became a forbidding trap. Only one person would have sent such a remarkable telegram.

"Your mam sounds a lot like his," Mr. Bates finished. "So...I thought you might like fair warning before you read the thing." With one look at Gregory's expression, the man scuttled away like a crab trying to outrun a vicious seagull.

Resigned to finding a lecture from his mother, Gregory unsealed the message and groaned at his first glimpse. The telegraph operator hadn't lied—who but his mother would send such a personal message through Morse code? He straightened his shoulders. Yes, he respected his mother, honored her as well he should, but he was a grown man. He'd make his own decisions, and that would be the end of it. But to decide how to respond, he'd have to read the thing.

GREGORY ALAN ROYCE–*STOP*–YOUR HASTY DEPARTURE HAS REDUCED ME TO SENDING THIS TELEGRAM–*STOP*–YOU DIDN'T RESPOND TO MY NOTE–*STOP*–THINGS WENT AWRY, BUT I HAVE FAITH THAT GOD HAS PLANS FOR THIS MARRIAGE–*STOP*–I'VE BEEN GETTING TO KNOW YOUR NEW BRIDE–*STOP*–SHE IS A WONDERFUL GIRL, AND I THINK YOU'RE FAR LUCKIER THAN YOU KNOW–*STOP*–I UNDERSTAND YOU HAVE A BUSINESS TO MAINTAIN, BUT DON'T FORGET THE IMPORTANT BUSINESS LEFT UNFINISHED AT CRANBERRY HILL–*STOP*–THERE IS MUCH TO DO

HERE, AND WE EAGERLY AWAIT YOUR RETURN, WHICH I'M CERTAIN WILL
BE AS SOON AS YOU CAN MANAGE–*STOP*–GOD BLESS YOU, SON–*STOP*–
SARAH ROYCE–*STOP*

Gregory let out a snort of laughter. The message—so proper but underlined with steel—was so typical of his mother that a smile crept across his face. *She should teach politicians just what to say to make their comments unassailable but crystal clear.*

Here, again, was the proof of feminine trickery. Sweet words designed to elicit the desired response. Any man would have kept it short and simple: *Get back here, NOW.* But that wasn't his mother's style. Gregory shook his head ruefully.

Lord, I know You speak through Your Word, pastors, and the wise counsel of church elders. I just wonder how often the subtler influence of our mothers is directly traced back to Your will.

Summons or no, he already intended to return. Leaving his bride—albeit the wrong one—with no more than a note on the morning after their wedding was a knee-jerk reaction to the death of his carefully laid plans.

"Mr. Bates!" Gregory strode toward his first mate. "I'll be in my cabin. As soon as the cargo is exchanged, we return to Hannibal." *And Cranberry Hill.*

❧

"Isn't it perfect?" Libby breathed, surveying the newly renovated parlor. *Her* newly renovated parlor.

"To tell the truth, I can scarce believe the difference," her mother-in-law agreed. "Has it only been twelve days since we first sat in an empty room with bare floors and no more than a pair of settees thrown in the center?"

"I'm certain of it." Libby grinned. "Between this room and overseeing the main entry, I've needed every single minute!"

"And you've done a lovely job. When you showed me the color for those wall hangings, I had my doubts, but the primrose seems just right in here."

"Yellow was a bold choice, but with the circular windows, the light pours in to make it bright and airy. The eggshell upholstery on the settees and new chairs softens it a little bit."

"Where on earth did you find this rug?" Sarah sank into the plush carpet, its muted tones of rose, gold, and cream centering the room.

"At the emporium, tucked away in a corner. When I saw it, I just knew I had to bring it home. And as soon as it was here, I realized the throw cushions and drapes needed gold trimming to match." Libby stepped around the room, eyeing the crystal-based lamp on an elegant end table, the porcelain mantel clock next to a vase of yellow roses. Not a thing stood out of place, all blended into a sense of inviting harmony she hoped would soon be the tone of her marriage, as well.

"The gold trimming really ties the cream and yellow together. You've a wonderful eye for color, Libby!" Sarah's approval widened Libby's grin.

"I thought the new marble tile in the entryway blended well." She cast a glance through the double parlor doors, thrown proudly open, to glimpse the entry beyond.

"Indeed. The sandy slate tiles from before were a poor choice," Sarah mused. "The white of the marble brightens the place, turns the attention to the grand stairway, as well it should. The slight golden veins through the tiles are what make it truly blend with the parlor. You have outdone yourself, my dear!"

"You helped pick out most of these things," Libby reminded her new friend. "It wouldn't have come together so quickly without the benefit of your expertise!"

"Pfft." Sarah waved away her gratitude. "I love shopping—any excuse will do. Though I must say"—she cast an admiring glance at her surroundings before continuing—"it's even more of a pleasure with results such as these. Gregory will be very surprised when he returns from his business trip."

"I hope he likes it," Libby fretted. "His note said I could put the house in order, and surely you would have mentioned it to me if he abhorred yellow, but it is a rather dramatic change." She stopped, considering how to phrase her next thought without abandoning diplomacy. "And he's had enough dramatic changes recently to last him a good long while."

"Ah." Sarah drew closer and reached for Libby's hands, giving them a reassuring squeeze. "But sometimes a dramatic change is precisely what's needed to show a man what's right in front of his nose. Speaking of which. . ." Her words trailed off.

"What?" Now Libby squeezed Sarah's hands, prodding her.

"I hope you take this in the spirit it is intended, my dear, but the house isn't the only beautiful thing here that could benefit from some attention and color." Her mother-in-law withdrew her hands from Libby's grasp and cupped her cheek. "It's time we showcased your loveliness. I daresay you'll be surprised by what you see when you put yourself in my hands."

"I've more than enough serviceable clothing," Libby hedged. "Though I could do with a few more aprons—getting this house into shape is surprisingly messy with all the construction!"

"Serviceable doesn't mean feminine," the older woman continued ruthlessly, "or flattering. Don't you think some lovely things, perhaps a new hairstyle, would put a spring into your step? Every woman should make the most of herself."

"Agreed. And I'm making the most out of my talents by making this house into the home where Gregory will want to spend his time." *I may not be able to make him want to share his life with me, but Cranberry Hill could prove an irresistible lure.* Libby left the thought unspoken but was certain Sarah knew, anyway.

"You're doing a wonderful job, that's true." The other woman's eyes gleamed with determination. "But I've a gift for knowing what will flatter the figure and bring a bloom to the cheeks of a young woman who never spent the time to experiment with such things before. Surely you wouldn't deny my gift?" Her eyes were widely incredulous now. "Not your mother-in-law!"

"It's not that I'm denying your gift, I'm just asking that you use it to help me with Cranberry Hill." Libby pasted on a smile.

"I'm already doing that, Libby." She strode—no, stalked—up to where Libby had retreated. "Behind your modesty there is a surprise waiting to be discovered. Let's make the most of it!"

"Now, Sarah," Libby admonished. "You can't turn a sow's ear into a silk purse." *And I'll never be the beauty Tabby is.* She forced cheer into her tone. "Let's just keep our focus on Cranberry Hill for now. Have I told you what I'm planning for the music room? With a little added elegance, it will do well as a ballroom, should we ever have need of one. Come with me."

Though Sarah frowned at Libby's obvious evasion, she followed her new daughter-in-law farther into the house. Libby was simply grateful Gregory's mother hadn't pressed the issue of her admittedly plain appearance. Lovely dresses couldn't conceal the fact that she wasn't the bride Gregory had wanted.

Chapter 6

"**G**ood to have you home, Captain Royce." Jenson gave an angled bow at the waist before taking Gregory's coat.

"Mm? Oh, yes." Gregory looked up long enough to dismiss the butler before returning his attention to the floor beneath his feet.

The slate-gray tile he'd ordered and overseen as it was installed was no more. And he couldn't say he mourned the loss, not when its replacement was fit for a palace. In place of the gray lay the finest marble tile, golden streaks threading gracefully throughout the main entry. His footsteps clicked sharply as he moved toward the grand staircase, intent on a good bath and shave before he greeted his wife. *My wife.* He shook his head and kept moving.

Out of the corner of his eye, he caught a glimpse of the parlor to his left. He halted, making a measured turn to verify his first impression. It was correct—she'd decorated the room in a soft butter yellow turned sweetly vibrant by the afternoon sun. He detoured into the parlor to explore farther. Gregory moved toward the center of the room, halting as a feminine voice spoke from the doorway behind him.

"Welcome home, husband." Libby sounded warm but hesitant.

"Thank you." Gregory moved to face her. "It's good to be home." The platitude escaped him before he had the chance to examine it. Was it good to be in the home where he'd brought the wrong bride? More importantly, was this even his home anymore?

He cast another glance around the room, taking in cream drapes with gold braid and fringe, settees and chairs furnished in the same eggshell, softening the yellow silk wall hangings. Even the rug beneath his feet, tempering the hardwood floors with luxurious depth, matched the décor.

"What do you think?" His wife sounded downright nervous now, and Gregory mentally kicked himself for his long silence. She'd obviously been hard at work.

"I like it." He made the decision aloud, surprised to find it true. "Yellow wouldn't have been something I would have chosen, but it's just right in here."

At his nod and words of praise, she beamed. Gregory stood stock-still for a moment, transfixed by his bride's sudden transformation. Libby's smile lit her face, brought a sparkle to her eyes, and almost seemed to make her taller.

I'll have to make her smile more often. The thought caught him off guard, and

Gregory wondered why he'd never noticed Libby's smile before. He'd known her for months, shared countless meals with her. It was hard to believe she'd never smiled in front of him even once in all that time. He must have been distracted by Tabitha.

The thought brought him crashing back to the reality of his disappointment. Clearing his throat, Gregory excused himself from the room.

"I'll freshen up and see you at supper." The question came out sounding more like an order than a polite request.

"I look forward to it." Libby had raised her chin as though answering a challenge. "Though it will be served in the breakfast room tonight, as we began renovating the dining room yesterday afternoon."

"Very well." He strode past her, boots clicking smartly on the new marble tile as he made his way to the staircase. The sound almost seemed to echo in the large space of the house.

When he reached the second floor he turned left by habit, only to be brought up short. The master bedroom was where Libby slept now. If he went there, it would be tantamount to announcing his intent to share the room—and its bed—with her. He made a sharp turn to the right, unwilling to make such a weighty decision before spending more time with his unexpected bride.

❧

Libby stood in the parlor, trying, as she had many times before, to see it as Gregory would. As Gregory had.

When the housekeeper informed her the master of the house had returned, Libby hastily made her way downstairs to greet him. He'd already left the entryway, robbing her of his reaction to the new floor. She'd headed for the library, since that's where he'd disappeared on their wedding night, only to see him standing in the doorway of the parlor.

The light from the windows shone on his dark hair and illuminated the breadth of his shoulders beneath his jacket. His hands clasped behind him, legs spread for balance, he could easily have been on board one of his ships, surveying his domain. Which seemed to be precisely what he was doing here.

Libby opened her mouth but found herself reluctant to speak as her husband moved farther into the room as though drawn to its warmth. She bit her lip as his gaze swept the room, taking in the drapes, the newly refurbished settees, and even the carpet now beneath one of his black boots.

Still silent, Libby took in his every motion—the inquisitive tilt of his head, the measuring way he swept a hand along the back of the settee, and the way he compared the time displayed on the porcelain mantel clock to his own watch, nodding as he returned it to his pocket. When it seemed he'd fully assessed the room and would turn to find her gauging his reaction, Libby hurriedly said the first thing she could think of before he caught her watching him.

"Welcome home," she'd told him, as though it were her place to do so. And, strange though it felt, it was.

"Thank you. It's good to be home." His words sounded sincere, if awkward, before heavy silence fell between them. Gregory glanced around the room once more as though weighing his words before he gave his opinion. Still he remained quiet.

He hates it. Suddenly, she questioned her choices. Soft primrose and eggshell? What had possessed her? *I should have chosen what Tabitha would have—deep jewel tones vibrant enough to enhance her own beauty.* The bitter tang of failure clawed its way up Libby's stomach while she awaited his verdict, spilling out in a rush of blurted, desperate words.

"What do you think?" She winced as she heard herself demand that he share his thoughts with her. But she had to know.

When he praised her efforts, Libby locked her suddenly shaky knees, putting a hand to the door frame to steady herself. She could feel herself smile, practically from ear to ear, knowing that ladies gave tiny, polite, demure smiles, but unable to reign in her joy at the first hint of approval from her husband.

When he told her he'd go freshen up and see her later, at supper, she saw another opportunity to win his admiration. As he headed up the steps of the grand staircase, Libby rushed to the large kitchen hidden behind. She bypassed the cook for the moment, flinging open the door to the pantry and eyeing its contents. What would Gregory enjoy the most?

"I'd like to change tonight's menu," she informed Mrs. Rowins, who merely nodded. "As the captain is home now, we'll have more than a simple supper. Instead, we'll need to serve multiple courses. Not seven," she hastily amended as the cook blanched, "but certainly a soup course and a main course and dessert."

"Oh, yes." The cook nodded, obviously relieved not to be called upon to prepare a feast at the eleventh hour.

Libby had taken to a bit of soup and some cold cuts with biscuits on a tray for her supper. Since the dining room wasn't useable and the master wasn't home, it had been a sensible arrangement. Now that Gregory was back, meal plans needed to change. She and the cook put their heads together, planning a simple but robust meal of his favorites.

When all was settled, Libby headed to the breakfast room with one of the maids, issuing last-minute instructions that it be dusted, scrubbed, polished, and set for supper. As she left another room in a flurry of activity, she smiled. She would pull off this mistress-of-a-grand-house thing yet. Gregory would have no cause to complain of her ability to manage Cranberry Hill.

Libby turned to the master suite, coming up short when she realized Gregory might well be using the water closet. After all, he was the master of the house, and this was his room. He didn't forfeit his rights because he had elected not to share it with her on their wedding night. Now that the shock of it all was further behind them, would he come to her?

Libby tentatively stepped into the room, both relieved and crestfallen to find the door to the restroom wide open, the room beyond completely empty. He'd chosen to use a different room for now, perhaps out of consideration for her. Perhaps out of his own discomfort. Libby firmly pushed the troubling thoughts away. Now was her time to prepare, not wallow in doubt.

She freshened up, repinned her hair into her customary chignon, and stood before the enormous armoire. She flicked through her dresses, suddenly wishing she had taken Sarah up on her offer to "make Libby over" or had, at least, ordered a few more stylish items.

No. I'll not become a pale imitation of Tabitha. When Gregory comes to accept me, it will be for who I am without any furbelows or gewgaws to mask me. Her decision made, Libby changed into her best dress, a pale mauve with lace edging, and slid her feet into delicate leather slippers in a slightly darker shade. She may not look as though she'd stepped from the pages of *Peterson's Magazine*, but it was a vast improvement over the dowdy gray dress and walking boots she'd worn earlier.

So Libby went downstairs to meet her husband, a prayer on her lips and hope in her heart.

Gregory came back to find the feminine touches that would make Cranberry Hill a home—furnishings and decorations and whatnot. Even better, he'd discovered a delightful supper companion for what might just be the best meal he'd eaten in the past year.

Beef and barley soup was made warmer still by Libby's earnest inquiries about the *Riverrider* and her crew. No idle conversation here. He got the impression she really wanted to know about his day-to-day life.

Thick-cut pork chops and buttered baked potatoes served alongside her generous smile went down a treat. Amazing the way her smile transformed her face from somewhat ordinary to riveting. Gregory almost found himself regretting his much-prized electricity as he imagined what the soft flicker of candlelight would bring to their table.

Just when he was sure he couldn't swallow another bite, the maids brought out his favorite dessert—rhubarb pie.

"This is my favorite!" He accepted a large slice and tucked it in with relish.

"I know." Libby's soft whisper had him putting down his fork to concentrate on her words. "I remembered from when you ate at my family home."

"It's wonderful." He realized he didn't just mean the delicious sweet—there was something touching about having a wife who remembered his favorite dish and arranged to serve it to him on his first night home. He savored the dark coffee as she shyly mentioned plans for Cranberry Hill, seeking his opinions about what he wanted their home to be. Incredible how her ideas so nearly matched his own.

For the first time, he'd felt the faint stirring of hope that this marriage could work. Despite Tabitha's betrayal and the destruction of his carefully laid plans, Gregory saw that his mother might be right—he was fortunate in his bride. A new confidence replaced his earlier misgiving, and it seemed only natural to take the next step when darkness fell.

❦

Gregory awoke the next morning with a navy blue canopy over his head and his wife by his side. Her head cushioned in the nook between his arm and chest, her glorious hair brushing over both their pillows.

He looked down to see the dark sweep of her lashes against the rosy bloom of her cheek, a faint smile toying at the corner of her mouth. The warmth of her breath fanned against his side while he remained still, loath to waken her. In sleep, Libby was all sweet vulnerability and softness.

My bride. Strange how the thought no longer shot arrows of remorse through the center of his chest.

Now he cautiously slid his arm from beneath her neck, fingering the silken strands of her hair as he withdrew. Angling himself on one elbow, Gregory pressed a gentle kiss on Libby's brow before leaving the warmth of their bed.

Lord, he prayed as he dressed quietly and slipped out the door and down the staircase, *thank You for watching over me. It could easily have been the end of everything when I chose my bride rather than listening to Your will. Libby may never be the bride I wanted, but I begin to wonder whether she's the bride You knew I needed. Bless us as we seek to make this marriage work, Lord. Amen.*

Gregory strode into the library, which doubled as his study, intent on getting to work. There was business to be done, after all. He banged his knees as he sat at the too-short desk, setting it to a dangerous wobble. Gregory had to move fast to keep the day's mail from sliding to the floor in an undignified heap.

He began to go through the pile, divvying the letters into categories as he went. *Bill, invitation, invoice, bill, shipment request, accounting information for last quarter, invitation...* He stopped as he came across a thick vellum envelope, which bore only the Cranberry Hill address. No return address, no name of sender, nothing to indicate whether the message was for him or Libby. Something about the looping curls of the writing tickled the edges of his memory....

Tabitha. His throat seemed to close at the realization. What could she possibly say to him after she'd left him standing at the altar, humiliated and betrayed before the entire city? How dare she write now! But it must be important or, at the very least, the heartfelt apology she owed him.

Gregory slashed open the missive with such force the letter opener jabbed him in the thumb. A drop of blood welled on the pad of the injured finger, smearing onto the envelope as he withdrew the paper inside.

I'm so sorry, the first line read. No introduction, no use of his name whatsoever. Gregory crushed his hand into a fist, ignoring the sharp pain from his thumb. He unfolded the rest of the paper to read the note in its entirety.

> *I'm so sorry. Please believe that I never intended things to happen as they did. I truly love Donald and know he adores me just the same. We're wed now, on a trip to Boston to meet some of his old friends from university. It will be weeks before I come back to see you. I've heard the news...how the wedding went on without me. Such a thing was beyond my imagination. Please, please, please forgive me, Libby.*

Libby? The name pulled Gregory's attention away from the remainder of the letter. Tabitha's letter was to *Libby*? And she was asking her sister to forgive her for forcing *Libby* to marry *him*? Had she really thought he'd be such an awful husband? *Where's my apology? Where does she seek my forgiveness for forcing me into marriage with her sister? Surely it must be further in...*

> *But I know you'll make the best of the situation—you always were the strong one. Besides, I've always secretly thought you might have feelings for Gregory. Don't worry. You've hidden it well, but a sister knows...perhaps this marriage will turn out to be the best thing for you both. You'll make him happier than I ever could, I'm sure of that much, at least.*
>
> *All my love, Tabitha*

Gregory read the letter three more times, turning the paper over and staring at the blank back side of it as though expecting a secret message to appear. None did. That being the case, he pawed through the other mail on his desk, seeking a twin letter meant for him. He found no such thing. Burying his head in his hands, he groaned aloud.

Libby has feelings for me? The notion knocked him off-kilter. *Is it better to have the sister I do not love but who cares for me than the one I do love but who cares not for me? And now that I've consummated our marriage, will Libby come downstairs with stars in her eyes and the expectation of storybook romance?*

The thoughts swirled around his brain, pounding in his temples, until Gregory could take no more. Stalking into the entryway, he shouted for Jenson to fetch his coat. With that, he strode through the door and headed for the docks.

※

Libby snuggled in the warmth of the bed, unwilling to open her eyes and lose the memory of Gregory's tenderness to the challenge of a new day. Taking a deep breath, she peeked through her lashes to find an empty space on her husband's side of the bed.

He had awoken and been careful not to wake her as well. Libby smiled as she pressed her hand into the indentation of her husband's pillow. Today they'd truly begin their life together as man and wife. In the eyes of God, they were joined forever.

Filled with sudden energy, Libby hopped from the bed, wincing only slightly at the soreness in her muscles as she made her way to the restroom. She hummed as she washed and readied herself for the day, eager to spend time with Gregory and seek his opinion on all the plans she had for Cranberry Hill.

She glided down the stairs, peeking into the study to see whether her husband had begun work for the day. Seeing only a stack of opened mail, she headed for the breakfast room. How wonderful it would be if they could start the day with a meal together.

But he wasn't in the breakfast room. Or the parlor, the music room, the dining room, any of the spare bedrooms, or the widow's walk atop the house. Libby felt the tension in her brow as she sought the housekeeper, thinking perhaps Gregory had left a message with Mrs. Farley.

She found the housekeeper enjoying some toast in the kitchen. "Excuse me, but did my husband go out this morning?"

"Yes, he did." The woman swiftly rose to her feet and dusted crumbs from her apron. "Left less than a quarter hour ago."

"And did he leave notice of where he was going?" At the woman's silent head-shake, Libby tried again. "Did he say when he'd be returning? If there was anything in particular he'd like for dinner this afternoon?"

"Not to my knowledge, ma'am." The woman pulled a folded piece of paper from an apron pocket. "He did direct Jenson to see that you received this."

Libby turned away from the woman's curious gaze and unfolded the note to find a single line.

Gone on business. Will return.

Gregory Alan Royce

"Very well." Libby straightened her shoulders, determined not to show her discomfort. She addressed the cook. "We'll have ham sandwiches with egg salad and fresh fruit for dinner this afternoon. Please have things ready at twelve thirty sharp. We will, of course, be dining in the breakfast room again."

With that, Libby swept out of the kitchen and made her way into the dining room. Today the workers would begin installing the chestnut wall paneling she'd selected for the lower half of the walls. She'd also selected a decorative chair rail in matching wood to add polish and ease the transition from paneling to paint.

The workers had already painted the walls a deep shade of burgundy. The color would have been too dark, save for the electric lights unique to Cranberry Hill. Until Gregory returned, she would throw herself into remodeling the house. That should occupy her mind and make the time pass quickly.

The morning flew by in a whirl of hammering and noise. Dinner came and went—Gregory had yet to return. Libby oversaw the installment of the furniture she'd purchased. The china cupboard stood at one end of the room, the buffet at the other, and the matching table with seating for twenty stretched between. The hours plodded more ominously as suppertime arrived but her husband had not.

As Libby sat at one end of her new dining room, her only companion an empty place serving, her appetite fled. After an entire day had passed, she could no longer deny the truth. Their night together hadn't meant to him what it had to her.

Gregory had left her. Again.

Chapter 8

A week passed, then another. Libby found constant reminders of her husband's desertion in almost every corner of Cranberry Hill. His half of the bed obviously had not been slept in, his clothing untouched in the armoire. No scratching of pens came from his study, no shared meals in the breakfast room or conversations enjoyed in the newly refurbished parlor.

Libby directed the cook to make simple trays once again. The dining room sat in darkness, never showcasing its new luxuries. Her footsteps echoed on the marble tile of the main entry. The staircases stretched to reach empty rooms, not the least of which was the nursery.

Lord, her heart cried as she stood in the doorway of the barren room, *I thought Gregory realized we could build a marriage together. He came to my bed, filled my heart with hope, and snatched away the dream once again with scarcely a word. I don't know where he is now or when he'll return. Even after he left, I prayed that You would bless me as You blessed Leah. But she bore her husband a son, and I carry no child beneath my heart. Will I have no family to love—no husband, no daughters, no sons—no laughter and joy?*

Tears slipped down her cheeks, dripping onto the collar of her serviceable brown dress. Drawing a shaky breath, she swiped at them with the back of her hand before heading downstairs. The workmen had finished the conservatory yesterday, and it was time she decide what she wanted to fill it with. Libby would be visiting another type of nursery later in the day.

She wouldn't go until that afternoon, which left her the entire morning to fill. Libby wandered around the floor level of the house, absently taking in the changes she'd already made and more determinedly taking note of what else she wanted. The dining room, parlor, and breakfast room were completed. The conservatory simply needed to be filled. She made her way to the music room.

Large and wide, with two sets of double doors leading outside, the room should have been welcoming. As it was, it simply seemed hollow. The floors lay rough and unfinished, snagging at her slippers. The walls bore nothing but bare paint, the only furniture a lonely pianoforte in the corner. Even the electric lights cast no warmth.

Libby walked the full length of the room, planning her changes. It wasn't long before she could practically see the room as it would be, newly laid parquet floors gleaming, a raised dais gracing one end of the room, large enough to hold a string quartet. Silk wall hangings in light green contrasted with heavier drapes in a darker shade, all highlighted by electric wall sconces.

Wanting to make a note reminding herself to consult the electrician, Libby realized she'd left her notepad in her room. It didn't take long to fetch it and quickly map out the décor for the music room. Done up as she planned, it would serve as a ballroom, too. They'd need whitewashed chairs with green cushions to line the walls. Libby wanted one more look at the dimensions of the room before she went to the shops.

As she descended the steps, the doorbell summoned Jenson from the pantry. She reached the main entry as he opened the door to reveal—

"Tabitha?"

"Libby!" Her sister rushed across the hall to envelop her in a crushing hug. "Oh, Libby, you have to forgive me!"

"We'll adjourn to the parlor, Jenson." Libby interrupted Tabitha before she could pour out the whole story in front of the butler, who couldn't quite hide his interest at the tableau.

Libby ushered Tabby into the parlor, closing the double doors behind them. The moment they sat down, Tabitha was off and bursting out with apologies once more.

"I had no idea Papa's finances were dependent upon my marrying Captain Royce," she babbled, her hands fluttering in distress. "That you'd have to take my place... I never thought..."

"Neither had I," Libby agreed. *Nor Gregory, for that matter.* "But what is done is done."

"If you're not happy, you can come live with Donald and me. We have that lovely little house on Charter Street now—his father gave it to us as our wedding gift." Tabitha fairly beamed with pride. "It's not half so grand as this." She gestured to encompass the surroundings Libby had put so much time and thought into.

"No, I can't." Libby shook her head. "We'll make the best of what we have. Gregory, so far, is rarely home. . . ." She winced at the dull throbbing in the back of her throat, refusing to add that he stayed away because he didn't want her. "And it doesn't matter what the size of your house is." *More rooms mean more to be left empty and alone.*

"All the same, it's our home, and we'd be glad to have you." Tabitha tripped blithely along as one of the doors swung inward. "No one should be trapped in a loveless marriage, Libby. I wouldn't have fled my own if I knew I'd be condemning you to the same fate."

"Condemning?" Gregory's voice thundered from the doorway, his face folded in a forbidding scowl as he strode into the room.

❦

He came to a halt at the side of Tabitha's settee, not allowing himself to look at her. Instead, he focused on Libby. She'd gone pale then red as he made his way over, raising her chin.

"Is that the way you feel, Libby?" He lowered his voice and raised a brow. "Condemned?"

"No, of course not." Libby met his gaze, but he saw a shadow of doubt flicker in her darkening hazel eyes. "Tabitha was just being"—she glanced at her sister before finishing—"dramatic."

"She does have a flair for the dramatic," he agreed, rounding on the woman who'd jilted him. He refused to be distracted by the light blond of her hair, the wide blue eyes so filled with dismay at the sight of him. When she didn't respond, he prodded further.

"Leaving a man at the altar certainly qualifies as dramatic, wouldn't you say?" He loomed over her, turning his gaze back to Libby. *Did Tabitha really think I'd be so awful to her that marriage to me is a type of doom?* He felt the muscle in his jaw twitch, and he gritted his teeth.

"Oh, Gregory—" Tabitha began, but he wouldn't let her speak.

"No. I believe we've had enough drama in the past month." He held up a hand in dismissal. "Now, *my wife* and I have things to discuss. I trust you'll see yourself out." Gregory walked over to hold the door wide, refusing her the option of dawdling. Once she'd left the house, he slammed the parlor door shut, covering the distance between himself and Libby at a rapid pace.

"Gregory, that was rude," she chided as she faced him.

"My apologies." He sat for a brief moment before bolting up again, his steps eating the length and breadth of the room as he paced. "I suppose I should have been more polite to my fiancée who eloped on the eve of our wedding."

"You've every right to be angry with Tabitha," Libby soothed, putting out a hand and laying it on his arm in an attempt to stop him. She closed her eyes for a moment when he shook her off.

"Good to know." He loosened his collar. "It's always nice to have permission to be mad at the lying woman who betrayed you."

"She is my sister." Libby's voice hardened. "That hasn't changed."

"Everything else has." He strode toward her, drawing just short of standing on her toes. "You know that as well as I do."

"Yes." Instead of shrinking back into the settee, she tilted her chin to look up at him. "And with change must come compromise if things are to work out."

"Compromise? What am I to compromise on with Tabitha?" He raked his fingers through his hair and thumped onto a nearby chair. "If you'll recall, she dishonored the last deal we made."

"This is no longer about Tabitha." Libby leaned forward. "This is about the two of us reaching a compromise. She just happened to be visiting at the same time you came home."

"It's my house." He glowered. "I've every right to be here. She doesn't." *Not anymore.*

"She's my sister," Libby repeated slowly. "She'll always be welcome in my home. We have to find a way to reconcile that."

"No." Gregory got to his feet. "Tabitha will never be welcome here."

Chapter 9

"You're not thinking about leaving?" Libby stood up, hands clenched at her sides. "Because in a month of marriage, I've seen you for no more than three days—less, if you want to be particular." At her words, he'd stopped midstride. She pushed ahead. "So you can see why I'm certain you wouldn't walk out on our first disagreement after forbidding me to see my own sister. Such a thing would be. . ."

"Would be what?" He turned and stalked toward her, his voice low and deceptively soft. "My right as master of this house? Your duty to carry through with my wishes?"

"Unconscionable." Libby met his gaze, refusing to give an inch. "Walking out on your wife now would be unconscionable."

"Libby—" He drew a deep breath. "I'm not trying to punish you."

"What would you punish me for?" She furiously blinked back the tears that sprang to her eyes. *For not being the bride you wanted? For not reviling my own flesh and blood?*

"Nothing. But as my wife you must support my decisions."

"Not when your decision cuts me off from my family." She shook her head sadly. "I know Tabitha hurt you, Gregory—"

"She didn't hurt me!" The words exploded with incredible force. "Tabitha came close to humiliating me, it's true. But she made me furious—it's a mistake to confuse the two." His eyes sparked with a barely banked fire.

Recognizing her error, Libby sought to regain ground. "Of course she's provoked your ire."

"See that you don't forget it." With that, her husband headed toward the door once again.

"I'm the one who's hurt." Her whisper sighed in the deserted room as Gregory didn't even look back.

❦

"I've decided to take you up on your kind offer," Libby announced as she walked into Sarah's modest home.

"Excellent!" Sarah tugged on the bellpull, summoning a maid. "I'll need my cloak, Betsy. And please have the carriage pulled 'round. We'll have need of it today!"

Libby kept a smile on her face as the maid scurried away, but it didn't fool her friend.

"But why do you look as though you're preparing to do battle?" Gregory's mother narrowed her eyes. "What has my son done?"

"I've not come to bear tales, Sarah." Libby rubbed the back of her neck to ease the tension. "Suffice it to say that I'm not doing this for Gregory. I want new dresses and so forth to please myself."

"Very well." The older woman didn't probe. "I couldn't believe he came home for a single morning before going off on his third trip since your marriage. I'm beginning to think he needs a business partner."

Libby refrained from offering her opinion as to what, precisely, Gregory needed. She was, after all, a lady. Instead, she made an announcement.

"The study will be finished within a few days. I'll be sending out invitations for my first dinner party at Cranberry Hill."

"It's about time you entertain guests!" Sarah looked Libby over, a shrewd gleam in her eye. "I take it this means you know when Gregory will be back. What is the date to be?"

"A week from tomorrow." Libby couldn't help but add, "Though I do not know whether or not my husband will be in attendance."

"You're hosting a dinner party without Gregory?" Sarah's tone was flat, disapproving.

"Yes. I've scarce seen my husband for three days out of the past thirty-seven." Libby pleaded with Sarah to understand her unconventional decision. "I can't spend all my time alone in Cranberry Hill. Why am I working to make it beautiful if no one will ever see it?"

"Agreed." Her mother-in-law drew her brows together. "Gregory has always been one to go his own way, so let it be on his head that you're left to your own devices."

"Then I can count on your assistance?"

"Absolutely. I know the most charming soloist who should provide your guests with after-dinner entertainment in that lovely music room of yours. . . ." And with that, they began planning the evening.

They ironed out the particulars during the carriage ride to Madame Celeste's shop, who, Sarah informed Libby, was the most talented hairdresser in these parts.

"Such lovely hair," Madame Celeste mused, combing through Libby's heavy locks. "Ze curl must be freed, no?"

"I keep it so long because the curls spring wild, otherwise," Libby explained. "It ends up looking like a dandelion when it's shorter."

"*Non, non,*" Madame protested. "You use ze pomade to tame ze pouff and is lovely."

"Exactly my thoughts," Sarah interrupted. "And a few locks cut shorter around the face to frame her eyes."

"*Exactamente.*" Madame nodded her approval and, at Libby's hesitant nod, rinsed her hair with a shampoo smelling of lemons. "Zis will lighten ze color," she promised. Then the woman set to her task with comb, shears, and an almost frightening enthusiasm.

Libby closed her eyes as, with the snip of the scissors, locks of her hair littered the floor. *It's time I took better care of myself, took more care with my appearance.* She cracked an eye open to see Madame's gleeful smile and snapped it shut once more. *This will be worth it. It has to be!*

&

As the *Riverrider* pulled into the dock, Gregory argued with himself.

Should he spend the night in his cabin, as he'd done so often over the past six weeks, or go back to Cranberry Hill? Ah, but going back to Cranberry Hill would be perilous enough in the light of day.

Loath though he was to admit it, through much prayer and thought, Gregory had to face the truth. He'd treated Libby horribly. She had every right to flay him with her words the moment he stepped over the threshold. After all, what kind of man deserts his bride directly after their wedding night—twice—before throwing her sister from their parlor?

Granted, Tabitha deserved far worse from him, but Libby did not. When it came right down to the bare bones of the matter, she'd had even less choice about this marriage than he had. He had faced humiliation and a heavy toll on his business image. She'd faced the betrayal of her sister and the financial destruction of her father should she refuse. And, to boot, she was saddled with a negligent, angry groom who disappeared when he should have been seeing to their marriage.

Father, I've made a mess of things. Part of me says I should go home immediately and apologize, try to compromise with Libby. The other part of me argues that it would be unfair to arrive at night, expecting her to welcome me when it would shortly be time to go to bed. I cannot expect that of her.

Ah, but I could sleep in one of the spare bedrooms so as not to pressure her. And it would be so good to be home. . . .

No matter what difficulties lay between them, he knew Libby had made Cranberry Hill the warm, welcoming home he'd always intended it to be. His desire to be home, to begin patching things up with Libby, immediately won over.

A short carriage ride later, he pulled up to a house blazing with lights. He let himself in, drawn up short at the sight of a magnificent chandelier, crystal drops of all different sizes capturing the light over the grand staircase. The sight was breathtaking so as almost to distract him from the sweet notes coming from the music room. Almost.

He followed the sound of the pianoforte and a woman's breathy soprano to find the music room completely transformed—and filled with guests. He stood in the doorway, staring blankly for a moment as he struggled to process what was going on. Surely Libby wouldn't entertain without his presence? What wife would open her husband's home in his absence?

His wife. There was no denying the truth of what lay before him. Where was she? Libby had some explaining to do. He silently surveyed the crowd of no fewer than twenty people, scanning for the long, honey-brown locks of his wife.

Gregory recognized his mother first, his gaze slipping past the attractive woman seated beside her until a niggle of recognition made him focus more intently on. . . *Libby?*

Chapter 10

Libby's hair, much shorter now, tumbled from a loose knot in riotous curls. A few soft tendrils framed her lovely eyes, drew attention to the generous curve of her smile as she tapped her gloved fingers in time with the music. She easily outshone every other woman in the room—all save her sister. Tabitha reclined only a few seats away.

His good intentions forgotten, Gregory strode down the side of the room until he was level with his wife. He touched her bare shoulder, scarcely registering the softness of her skin as he jerked his head toward the door in silent command. Her eyes wide, she followed him into the hall.

"Just what do you think you're doing?" His hissed question garnered attention from a few of the guests, and Libby ushered him into the study.

For a brief moment, Gregory was nonplussed by his surroundings. A massive mahogany desk stood in one corner of the room, easily large enough for him to draw up a chair. Floor-to-ceiling bookshelves adorned two entire walls, filled with rich, leather-bound sets of volumes and folios. Electric lamps sat on thoughtfully placed tables to cast light in every corner.

Squashy chairs and a leather sofa curled near the cozy warmth of the gas fireplace, cushioned by a rug in shades of deep blue and crimson. The room bespoke a woman's thoughtfulness to meet her man's needs, evidence of the type of harmony their marriage should enjoy.

Harmony that didn't exist. Remembering the reason she stood before him now, Gregory nearly choked on his anger. How could the same woman who made Cranberry Hill the home he'd always wanted stand there so blithely after denying him the pleasure of seeing people's reactions to it? How could she cheat him of his role as master of the house? *How dare she announce to the world that she doesn't need me?*

"Well?" Gregory thundered this time, grinding his teeth. "What do you have to say for yourself?"

❧

"It's good to see you, too, Gregory." Libby closed the door behind them, shutting out the strains of a lilting melody and ensuring their discussion would remain private.

"Good to—" His mouth opened and shut again, giving him an uncanny resemblance to a fish out of water. "What are you playing at?"

"I'm *playing* at nothing." She said no more. Let it rest on him to dredge up reasons to argue. Libby was tired of it.

"Then what do you call that"—he gestured toward the music room while searching for the word—"spectacle?"

"A dinner party, of course." Libby watched as her husband pulled a thick cigar from his pocket. "I'll have to ask you not to light that in here."

"Excuse me?" As he shook out the flame of his match, the sparks in his eyes glowed. "Last I checked this was my house."

"And it still is," Libby agreed pleasantly. "But since last you checked, I did stock and refurbish this library. I won't allow Papa to smoke in here—it ruins the books, you see. Makes them musty." She watched as he looked at the room once more, unable to hide his admiration for the luxurious furnishing.

"Very well." He still managed to sound disgruntled even as he tucked the cigar back into his pocket then returned to the more pressing matter. His eyes narrowed. "A dinner party?"

"Precisely." She inclined her head. "Albeit one you interrupted. It's rude to leave one's guests, you know."

"It's rude to throw a party in a man's house without informing him, much less inviting him." His rich baritone was silky smooth, a signal of danger she'd come to recognize. "Isn't it customary for the man of the house to be present at such proceedings?"

"Traditionally." Libby fought to keep her temper but lost the fight when Gregory's chest puffed up in triumph, his gaze scornful and dismissive as he began to speak once more. She swiftly cut him off. "Though it is also customary for the man of the house to spend time at said house. With you absent almost continuously for the past two months, it would have been nigh impossible to coordinate a gathering according to your timetable."

"That would almost prove an acceptable explanation—a worthy argument, even, but for one fact." He moved forward, effectively trapping her against the end of the sofa. "You disobeyed my wishes. Tabitha is here."

"Yes." Libby raised her brows. "*My sister* kindly agreed to support me by attending my first party, even though she'd been unceremoniously ordered away when last she stepped foot in our home."

"A good wife obeys her husband's edicts," he countered.

"Marriage is supposed to be a partnership." Libby laid a hand on his arm. "We'll both be stronger when we stand together."

"Tonight you chose to stand beside your sister." He pinned her with his gaze. "Will you choose to stand beside me instead?"

"I want to, Gregory." The tears worked past her defenses at last as she whispered, "You're my family, but I can't stand beside you when you're not here."

"Do you want me by your side, Libby?" His voice rumbled with doubt.

"Yes." Her heart hammering in her chest, Libby broached the subject that could well tear apart their newfound trust. "Gregory, I understand if you don't want

Tabitha at Cranberry Hill—it was wrong of me to disregard your wishes and have her here—but I still love my sister."

"I see." He stiffened and pulled away his hand.

"I won't have her here again," she vowed, snatching his hand with both of hers, willing him to listen. "But I need to be able to see her other places."

"We'll see." His frown softened, and he laid his hand over hers, covering her with warmth. "It's not right for me to expect your support when I've withheld mine for so long." He cupped her cheek with his other hand. "We'll do better from now on, yes?"

"I hope so, but I need an answer about Tabitha. I don't ask you to spend time with her, but I do ask that you let me do so." She held her breath as she waited.

"I respect that." He finally agreed. A faint smile replaced his frown now. "But I'm going to have to exact a price, I'm afraid."

"Oh?" Libby sensed he was being more lighthearted. *Anything you want, Gregory.*

"You're going to have to follow this one final edict." His expression turned serious once again, making Libby's heart plummet.

"What edict?" She somehow dredged up the courage to ask.

"You will never"—he closed the distance between them, taking her into his arms—"under any circumstances, cut your hair without my permission again."

And as he smoothed his large hand over her curls, gently tugging them to watch as they sprang back into place, Libby could speak again.

"You don't like it?" She squeaked, full of remorse.

"No." He threaded his fingers through more of her curls and lowered his mouth to hers. "I love it." His whisper fanned across her lips as he kissed her. It was a good while before he drew back and touched his forehead to hers. "Do you agree to my terms?"

"Oh." Libby smiled at him, sliding her arms around his neck. "I think that can be arranged."

Chapter 11

The days and weeks slipped by, fluid as river water, while Gregory worked to improve his marriage—and Cranberry Hill. He fell into a comfortable pattern with Libby. For the first time, the captain who set up his own business, set out on capitalist voyages, and never rested long enough for life to become mundane had fallen into a rut. And he liked it.

He'd wake up to find the sun shining and Libby's head pillowed against his side. Together they shared a hearty meal in the breakfast room before separating until dinner. He spoke with the architects, raising a low stone wall around the property and seeing the roof of the carriage house installed. Libby, for her part, saw to the running of the tiny details that made Cranberry Hill run smoothly.

At dinner they discussed their plans for the rest of the day. After he took care of business and paperwork, they fell into the habit of meeting for a short ride or walk in the afternoon, discussing possible landscaping projects to best showcase Cranberry Hill. Typically they would attend a dinner given at a friend's house. Occasionally they hosted one at Cranberry Hill, but not since they had begun construction on the wraparound porches.

The days may have melded into one another, but each was full of partnership, encouragement, and progress. Their excitements were minor but made richer by their shared joy. Slowly, the relationship grew and prospered, colored by the nuances they lavished on Cranberry Hill and each other.

Only one thing troubled Gregory's thoughts, marring the happiness he'd found. Libby had been forced into this marriage. Granted, she'd made the best of things, and her sister's letter hinted that his wife might bear deeper feelings for him, but had he made up to her his horrible neglect during the first months of their marriage?

Libby loved their home, lavished attention upon it, and shone with satisfaction as she surveyed the house. No doubt about it, Libby was happy at Cranberry Hill. The question was, was she equally happy with him?

He could think of one way to find out. Gregory left the accounts in his study and stopped by the parlor, looking for Libby. He finally tracked her down in the sewing room upstairs, hemming some sheets.

"There you are," he greeted her as he crossed the room to drop into the chair beside her.

"Here I am," she agreed, teasing him with the soft smile he'd come to crave. "What did you need?"

"I've an important question to ask you." He leaned toward her as he spoke. "Think about it before you answer. I don't want to push you into anything, mind."

"Go on." She pushed on his arm to accompany her demand. "You're making me nervous with all the suspense!"

"I've another business trip to take." He paused, pleased by the way her eyes widened and smile faded. *She'll miss me*, a voice in his heart crowed. "I'd put it off so as to spend more time with you, but it can't be postponed any longer."

"Don't worry, dear." She set aside her sewing. "It's been wonderful having you here, but I understand you must run your business." A twinkle came to her eyes, made green by the rich shade of her dress that day. "So long as you come back and stay awhile without rushing away again."

"I wouldn't do that—" he vowed. "Again," he added, being completely honest. "We both know I already pushed my good fortune to have such a patient wife."

"If I recall, she pushed back when she had to." Libby gave him a peck on the cheek.

"She's an amazing woman," he confided. "In fact, I was hoping that amazing woman might consider going along with me on this trip. What do you say, Libby?"

"Absolutely!" She sprang out of her chair. "When are we leaving? Where are we going? What types of things will I need to pack?" She scooped the rest of the sewing into a basket in the corner and tapped her foot impatiently as she waited by the door. "Why are you sitting there when there's so much to do?"

"I'm just taking a moment to appreciate my beautiful wife," he assured her. A few steps, and he had her in his arms. *She wants to spend her time with me. Me.* "We'll leave tomorrow, if you like. You pack a few dresses and such. I'll take care of everything else you need."

※

Thank You, Jesus! Gregory asked me to go with him on his next business trip! Things have been going so well since the night of that first dinner party, and I've been truly grateful. . .but You know my heart, Lord. You know I wondered whether it was the idea of having a home, the pastime of putting the finishing touches on Cranberry Hill that really captured his heart. Now I know his affection is for more than the house, lovely though it may be.

Libby practically skipped down the hall to the master bedroom, already planning what dresses to take. She would pack underskirts, chemises, pantaloons, silk stockings, and garters, of course. The dresses were more difficult. She threw open the doors of the great wardrobe and began flipping through her outfits, thinking aloud.

"I won't need a riding habit for a trip on a paddleboat," she decided easily. "And I suppose we won't be dressing for dinner. . . though perhaps once we've reached the city? I'll bring along the sapphire evening gown then. . ." She plucked the dress out of the wardrobe and laid it on the bed, along with the undergarments she'd chosen. A day dress in light green followed, accompanied by a similar frock in rich rose. She'd wear the cream-and-gold at the departure.

A few other dresses made the pile on the bed grow ever higher, until Libby judged the selection complete. "Now. . .where did I put the trunks I'd brought over from Papa's house?" She thought for a moment before vaguely recalling the storage in the attic. She made her way to the small stairwell behind the master bath.

The stairs brought her up to the attic beside the access to the widow's walk. She rummaged around the boxes until she found her trunks, carrying them one at a time back to her room. When she came back for the second, she spied a small door next to the maids' quarters. Curiosity getting the better of her, she put down the trunk and walked over, trying to open it.

The door wouldn't budge, though it appeared to have no lock. She grasped the knob more tightly and pushed, hearing the rattle of a lock on the other side. *Intriguing.* Libby went through the maids' quarters, searching for an entrance through the wall shared with the small chamber. Nothing.

Must be a construction mistake of some sort. Brow wrinkled at the mystery, she retrieved the other trunk and made her way back to her bedroom. She'd be sure to mention it to Gregory. After all, he'd been involved in designing the house and drawing the blueprints. He'd want to know about the mysterious sealed room with no access. Of course, it could be like the basement, an area taken up by the steam heater and electric wiring. It could have been sealed for safety.

Half an hour later, she'd packed everything into the trunks. Fighting the feeling she'd forgotten something important, Libby searched through her dresser drawers and bathroom cabinets. In a last-ditch effort to pin down what she'd forgotten, she opened the wardrobe once again. Pushing aside coats and dresses, she spotted her old black hooded cloak wedged in the back corner of the armoire. She tugged but couldn't pull it out.

Determined, she pushed her upper body between two dresses and tried again, pressing one hand against the back wall for better leverage. Libby swiftly found herself flat on her face, half sprawled in the wardrobe as the back wall of the armoire sprang back to reveal a secret staircase.

Chapter 12

Pressing her palms against the wardrobe bottom, Libby levered herself to her feet. She spent several moments staring in disbelief, unable to believe the sight before her.

What is a hidden staircase doing behind my wardrobe? More importantly, where did it go? Libby stepped through the clothing and into the small passage. Her hands encountered a light switch as she groped at the walls to gain a sense of her dark surroundings.

Instantly, the yellow glow of electric lights illuminated the way, almost beckoning her forward. Unable to resist, she followed the narrow passageway, up into a dark space. Squinting, Libby could see that she was in a small room. She groped about the walls, hoping for and finding another light switch.

She blinked for a moment before seeing that the room stood empty, not so much as a picture, rug, or old rickety chair gracing the barren space. *Why?* She moved farther into the room, searching for some clue as to why it even existed. Her eyes fell on the doorknob—and the lock beneath it.

The room in the attic that locks from inside. Elated that she'd made the connection, Libby unlocked the door and opened it, still not quite understanding why Gregory would have commissioned a third stairway to the attic. There was already one leading here from the second floor, which she'd used not long ago, and one that connected the attic to the pantry.

The second was to give the maids ease of movement as they bustled between the kitchen and their chambers—Libby's elated excitement died a swift death as she turned to see the maids' rooms just beside her.

It was suddenly so clear. There was only one reason why a man would construct a secret stairway from his bedroom to the attic, which held no more than the maids' quarters. And how brilliant of him to have hidden the passage at both ends— a spring-loaded wardrobe in the master suite below, a mysterious door above, locked from within. All to conceal the sordid truth from a wife's prying eyes.

Gregory thought of everything, Libby admitted even as she relocked the small chamber and returned to the bedroom she shared with him. Almost tripping over her just-packed trunks, she stopped for a moment before mechanically unpacking them. Her chest ached from the simple act of breathing, the daylight streaming in through the windows as sharp as daggers to her eyes.

Now what am I to do? Footsteps shook her from her reverie.

"Libby?" Gregory's excited voice floated up the stairs.

She looked around, wild for a way to avoid him. *Not now. I can't face him now!* Inspiration struck with an ironic blow, as Libby opened the back of the wardrobe and darted inside the stairway she shouldn't have even known existed. Sinking onto the bottom step, cradling her knees against her chest, Libby listened as Gregory stomped into the room and back out.

She could have sneaked away, but what was the point unless she was ready to confront her husband? So Libby sat in the secret stairwell in the dark and prayed.

ᘏᕬ

"Where are you?" The playful question lost its humor as Gregory checked room after room without finding Libby. Perhaps she'd been freshening up when he'd gone to their bedroom and hadn't wanted to draw attention to it? He loped back up the stairs.

No such luck. The room was empty save two trunks near the open wardrobe. He smiled at the evidence his wife had been packing for their trip together. The smile faded as he realized Libby was still missing. Gregory mentally ran through all the rooms of the house—parlor, dining room, breakfast room, kitchen, music room, spare bedrooms, sewing room, nursery. He'd checked them all.

She wouldn't have left without telling him, so where could she be? He circled their bedchamber, more restless than he should have been at his wife's sudden disappearance. Try as he might, he couldn't shake the feeling that something was wrong.

Think, Gregory. Where would she be? He rejected the basement. The only things down there were the steam heater and electrical wires. Libby would have no reason to venture there. *The attic?* He couldn't imagine why. Besides, she still should have heard him calling. *The widow's walk!* That had to be it. Libby was on the flat, railed walkway set atop the house.

He'd had it built following the sailor's tradition. During troubled times, a sea-man's wife could stand atop her home, looking out over the water, and wait for her husband's safe return. Libby had never mentioned it to him, but the housekeeper had said Libby liked to venture up there on fine days.

This will be a good chance to try out the hidden stairwell. I've not seen it since its installation. Smiling broadly at the thought of showing Libby his secret staircase when they returned to their room, he pushed on the back panel of the wardrobe, feeling along the revealed wall for the light switch.

As light flooded the stairway, Gregory saw his wife huddled on the bottom step. He sank to his knees immediately, grasping her cold hands and chafing them between his own.

"Libby? Libby, what's wrong?"

"Don't." Her voice sounded dull as she jerked her hands from his grasp and scuttled away from him.

"Don't what?" He tried to catch her eye, but she'd turned her face from him.

A sudden image of her falling down the dark staircase made his stomach roil. "Libby, are you hurt? Let me see."

"Can't you already see?" She gave a hollow bark of laughter. "It's obvious to me."

"What is?" He crooked a finger beneath her chin and turned her face toward his. He breathed a silent prayer of thanks when he saw no purple bruises or angry bumps. "What happened since we spoke in the sewing room?"

"This." She waved her arms to indicate the stairwell, knocking his hand away in the process. "I discovered your secret, Gregory. Stop acting as though it's nothing."

"You're upset because I hadn't shown you the staircase?" He tried to clarify things, but they seemed more muddied than ever.

"Oh, yes, I'm upset about the staircase." She drew a shaky breath before glaring at him. "How could you design such a thing in the house you built for your bride? I know I'm not the bride you had in mind, but that makes it no better! The *maids*, Gregory?"

"What are you—?" In an instant, he understood. "You're talking about how the stairway leads to the attic, near the maid's room. You think…" He couldn't even bring himself to the words, instead recoiling from the very thought. *Is that what she thinks? After all the time we've spent together in the past weeks, she can believe such a thing of me?*

"Why else," she demanded fiercely, "would you construct a hidden passageway from your room—*our* room—to the attic?"

"I built it so my wife would have easy access to the widow's walk during bad weather." He spoke through stiff lips. "I didn't want you climbing the outside stairs when they were slippery with rain or ice. Forgive me for thinking my wife would be concerned and want to keep a lookout for my ship at such times."

"Why lock it from the inside at the attic door?" she questioned, her eyes showing the first faint gleam of hope.

"So no one could enter our room," he explained. *She was devastated at the thought I'd carry on with one of the maids—not because her pride was hurt, but because she cares for me.* The realization softened his outrage that she had believed the worst.

"Oh." The tiny sound melted the rest of his wounded pride.

"I'd never do something like that—no matter who my wife was." He scooted up to crowd beside her, nestling her in the crook of his arm.

"You're a better man than that." Libby wiped her eyes and gave a tremulous smile. "And I've always known it. I don't know why I jumped to such an awful conclusion…."

"It made sense at the time." He squeezed her shoulder. "The important thing is you believe the truth, so we're ready to move on."

"I do." She nodded vehemently. "I overreacted, Gregory. I'm so sorry for that. You see"—she drew a deep breath before continuing—"I've always admired you, from the first night we met. And even now, when things are going so well, it's easy for me to believe that I'm not the wife you wanted."

"You weren't." At her gasp, he smiled. "You're far more than I ever wanted in a wife, and I know I'm blessed to have you, Libby. We may have started out on shaky ground, but I like to think we've found a solid path together."

"Me, too." Her hair tickled his cheek as she nodded.

"But even more than that"—he knew the time had come to speak the thoughts he'd hidden for too long now—"I love you, Elizabeth Anne Royce."

"I love you, too." Her words came out garbled as she wept all over his surcoat.

"Now then, that's enough." Gregory rubbed soft circles on her back as she composed herself.

"I'll never get enough of our life together," she murmured, looking up at him with love shining in her eyes. "It makes tears of joy keep springing up."

"I can think of a better way to celebrate." He smiled as he lowered his lips to hers. Neither one of them spoke for a long moment. When he caught his breath again, Gregory added the finishing touch. "Let's fill our nursery with beautiful babies."

"Mmm." She nestled closer. "I'd say that is a wonderful idea."

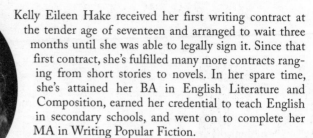

Kelly Eileen Hake received her first writing contract at the tender age of seventeen and arranged to wait three months until she was able to legally sign it. Since that first contract, she's fulfilled many more contracts ranging from short stories to novels. In her spare time, she's attained her BA in English Literature and Composition, earned her credential to teach English in secondary schools, and went on to complete her MA in Writing Popular Fiction.

Writing for Barbour combines two of Kelly's great loves—history and reading. A CBA bestselling author and member of American Christian Fiction Writers, she's been privileged to earn numerous Heartsong Presents Reader's Choice Awards and is known for her witty, heartwarming historical romances.

She and her gourmet-chef husband live in Southern California with their golden lab mix, Midas!

If You Liked This Book, You'll Also Like...

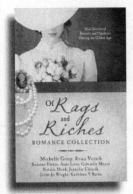

Of Rags and Riches Romance Collection

Nine couples meet during the transforming era of America's Gilded Age and work to build a future together through fighting for social reform, celebrating new opportunities for leisure activities, taking advantage of economic growth and new inventions, and more. Soon romances develop and legacies of faith and love are formed.

Paperback / 978-1-68322-263-7 / $14.99

Seven Brides for Seven Mail-Order Husbands Romance Collection

A small Kansas town is dying after the War Between the States took its best men. Seven single women are determined to see their town revived and devise a plan to advertise for husbands. But how can each make the best practical choice when her heart cries out to be loved?

Paperback / 978-1-68322-132-6 / $14.99

JOIN
US
ONLINE!

Christian Fiction for Women

*Christian Fiction for Women is your online home
for the latest in Christian fiction.*

Check us out online for:

- Giveaways
- Recipes
- Info about Upcoming Releases
- Book Trailers
- News and More!

Find Christian Fiction for Women at Your Favorite Social Media Site:

 Search "Christian Fiction for Women"

 @fictionforwomen